The Devil You Know

Other Books by

Wayne Johnson

Don't Think Twice

Six Crooked Highways

The Devil You Know

A Novel

Wayne Johnson

THREE RIVERS PRESS
NEW YORK

The author wishes to acknowledge his debt to Kenneth Grahame's
well-loved children's classic, *The Wind in the Willows.*

Copyright © 2004 by Wayne Johnson

Published in the United States by Three Rivers Press, an imprint of the Crown
Publishing Group, a division of Random House, Inc., New York.
www.crownpublishing.com

Three Rivers Press and the Tugboat design are registered trademarks of
Random House, Inc.

Originally published in hardcover in the Unites States by Shaye Areheart Books,
New York, in 2004.

Library of Congress Cataloging-in-Publication Data
Johnson, Wayne.
The devil you know : a novel / by Wayne Johnson.—1st ed.
1. Boundary Waters Canoe Area (Minn.)—Fiction.   2. Children of divorced
parents—Fiction.   3. Wilderness survival—Fiction.   4. Canoes and
canoeing—Fiction.   5. Fathers and sons—Fiction.   6. Teenage boys—Fiction.
7. Criminals—Fiction.   I. Title.
PS3560.O3866D48   2004
813'.54—dc21   2003011616

ISBN 1-4000-8227-7

Printed in the United States

Design by Lynne Amft

10 9 8 7 6 5 4 3 2 1

First Paperback Edition

For Karen

Acknowledgments

I owe a debt of gratitude to many people for this book. First, I am especially grateful to my wife, Karen, for helping to make this work possible. Her humor, encouragement, and sharp critical commentary (as well as her twirling dances and the occasional cup of coffee) were invaluable to me. *Très magnifique!*

I would also like to thank my many friends for their support: Mike and Mary, Richard and Kathryn, Thom and Meredith, Tom and Elaine, Vik and Raj, Margaret and Jan, Frank and Susan, Sam C., Chris T., Chris N., Leola, Kevin, Clay, Jerry D., Darrell, Amy M., Nath, Heather, and Kim, and Shirley and Kim and the Dyersville Library group.

I owe a debt of gratitude to my wonderful editor, Shaye Areheart, who responded to the vision of the book from the first and helped me bring out the best in it through her superb editorial assistance.

Thanks to Madison, Robert S., Patsy and Martin, and Wendy.

And finally, I thank my real life Gaiwins, both the ones I know—Richard, John Buck, and Jane—and the ones I don't. Thank you, with all my heart.

The devil you know is better than the devil you don't.
—FOLK PROVERB

Something is always with us, in the darkness as well as the light. And if this is true, then one must walk through the world, even in darkness, by the same light one saw when all was light.
—JAMES ALAN McPHERSON
A Region Not Home

The Devil You Know

WITNESS HOW IT BEGINS ONE SEPTEMBER MORNING IN Edina, Minnesota, a well-to-do suburb of Minneapolis, on a field behind a school like a thousand other schools. David Geist inches toward a chalk line in the grass where, one by one, the sophomore boys in second-hour PE throw a softball, their gym teacher, Mr. McCoy, over at the hurdles now, while here, Coach Hedberg records their distances on a clipboard.

It is a lovely morning, the temperature seventy-two, the air dry and with a hint of apples in it, and leaf smoke, and this . . . chill, autumn coming on, and the oaks not yet beginning to turn.

David, fifteen boys back from the front of the line, kicks at the grass with the toe of his tennis shoe, disinterested for the most part, but slightly anxious.

The softball throw is kid stuff. Of not much consequence. Just a little competition, throwing this softball. But here, today, Coach Hedberg has his football team out with David's class, and some of Hedberg's kids are in the line with David and his classmates, like senior Rick Buddy, who, weighing in at two-forty, dwarfs most of the younger boys—Buddy, who is rumored to be a terror, something David has heard already, not yet at the school a week.

But David, waiting, is paying him no attention, not yet. His mind wanders; he's hungry, he thinks, since he missed breakfast, but he did get his sister's, Janie's, into her, that was good. And now, pumping his legs, he imagines running the Highland cross-country course, tells himself he won't mess up on the hill again, which brings on all the things he's messed up. You're a fuck-up! his father's told him. And it is as he's telling himself not to listen to any of that—You're ugly, Don't stand there with your hands in your pockets, You're a goldbricker (it's just Max, his father, at his worst, talking, he tells himself)—that he hears a rough shout, in a garbled, almost unintelligible voice:

"GUF OFFA ME, *YOU!*"

And when David glances up from his shoes, he sees Buddy is punching a spindly kid toward the front of the line, Greg Becker, nicknamed Bucky for his protruding front teeth and his awkward, palsied way of moving. Greg has CP, and when he runs, he trips all over himself. All the sophomores know this, they've known Greg for years, know that he is not retarded, even though his face, when he smiles, telling a joke, always self-deprecating, to amuse others, twists grotesquely, and laugh they all do, at Greg, tease him about his spidery arms and legs, his enormous feet.

Yet they also know that they will try not to do it cruelly.

But Buddy does now, lays into him, jabbing him so hard that he tries not to cry, and when McCoy, across the field, has his back turned and is looking away, blowing his whistle to start a line of sprinters, Buddy swings Greg around his middle, hand over hand, around, and around, and around, until Greg begins to retch, but stays on his feet, and is crying finally, "Stawp, stawp please, PLEASE STAWP!" but Buddy doesn't stop, and when he can't stand watching it anymore, David breaks from the back of the line, heading for Buddy.

What happens now will eventually culminate in the death of one of David's family; and, in his thinking when it is all over, perhaps worse.

What happens now will change David's life forever, but then, one could always argue that this thing here, what will happen in the next few moments, is insignificant, is just boyhood fooling around. And for all anyone could see, were he standing back of the cyclone fence that encompasses the Hornets' field watching, it would appear to be just that: just some minor scuffle in a line of boys throwing a softball, Coach Hedberg, ignoring Buddy's fooling around, sizing up candidates for his football team. He needs players, a quarterback, kids he can groom.

So. Just boys, on a green field, and one coming up the line now, this boy, David, ropey-limbed, all sinew and bone, a runner, passing the others to stand in back of Buddy, who has finally released Greg, who, holding his hands out for balance, stumbles toward the line like a blind man, blinking and weaving.

"What do you want?" Buddy says, setting his hands on his hips, eyeing David.

Is it *this* moment, now, when David's fate changes?

Buddy reaching out to grab Greg again, and David knocking his thick hand away, and stepping behind Greg to hold him upright, until he can do it himself?

Or does this just lead up to it? Does it make what will come possible?

Moments later, blinking, and still weaving side to side, Greg hurls the ball, though far more palsied than he would have had he not had his balance tampered with.

Across the field, a boy shouts back a distance. "One hundred twenty feet!"

Coach Hedberg marks this down, *NC*, No Consideration, and the line moves forward, bumping into Greg, who, shaking his head, hasn't quite got his balance back.

All Hedberg says is, "You want to try again?"

And when Greg declines, glaring, then jogging off with the others, who play at running hurdles on the section of green track behind them, David turns to Buddy, who has gotten into line behind him.

He wants to say, The kid's got CP. You know that, don't you? But of course Buddy knows. Anyone can see it, the way Greg's knees knock together and his head doesn't sit right on his neck, how it kind of wobbles around.

"Next up," Coach Hedberg says. "Name?"

And rather than explain why he's out of alphabetical order— why would he, anyway, since Coach Hedberg obviously saw the whole thing and said nothing—David just gives it.

"Geist."

Coach Hedberg glances up from his clipboard, aware of some insubordination here.

"F'in' retard doesn't know alphabetical!" Buddy says, so loudly everyone can hear, and Roach and Groenig, Buddy's friends down the line, guffaw loudly.

David fixes his eyes on the fence separating the field from a park where, years before, he'd played with his father, his father happy then, his mother some seeming sprite, all before the hard times.

Don't, this voice inside him says. Because he just feels it there, this danger in what he's considering doing. And he struggles against it.

The morning is beautiful in that way of autumn mornings. It doesn't matter, it's just kid stuff, not worth getting worked up over. There's dew on the grass, gemlike, and the smell of burning leaves in the air, and birds calling. Everything in the moment has a feeling of suspended time.

As is David's thinking suspended—caught between a deeply buried rage and an intelligence that tells him not to let it out. He could step free of this here, and the danger he intuits in it.

But how could he know? How could anyone know what will come of this morning?

So when Coach Hedberg says, with obvious irritation, "Just take your turn," and glances at the sheet on his clipboard, and Buddy sharply jabs David in his side, the knuckled pain almost blinding, David's heart jacking a fistful of blood into his head, David says, as if in some voice not his own, "Hey, Buddy. Million bucks says you're not big enough to throw the ball over that fence."

Buddy can't resist the challenge, the opportunity to show the others what a tough guy he is, so he steps up to the line, all the while mouthing quietly, meanly, "Fucking faggot like you, couldn't get close to it, jackoff pansy shitheel, like I should listen to you, ya little fucking—" Posturing, and lumbering, and making a big deal of himself. And like that, he hurls the softball, and it goes a good distance all right, but falls well short of the fence.

David steps up to the line. "What did you say I was?"

"Faggot—" But he doesn't say the rest of it. Hedberg giving him a cross look.

David can feel his heartbeat in his neck. He's gotten that far-away feeling he knows too well, all that a gift from his father, a legacy he will not speak so much as one word of, for years, but which has brought him here.

Or so he thinks. This thought his weakness, and what will nearly kill him.

"What did you say?" David says, just to make sure the others have heard it, and to make clear what he will do now, hopes he can do.

And when Buddy repeats what he said earlier, but now, under his breath, mouths a racial epithet as well, David charges the line. But it is with a pitcher's windup, to the surprise of them all—eight years gone into making David's arm what it is, and all his father did to him behind it now, this the real thing, the only thing, and he releases the ball high, and with a snap, like a punch, all he has in him in it, and the ball rises higher, then higher yet, Buddy even then realizing the extent of his error, already guffaws in the line of boys, "Who's a faggot, Buddy?" coming from Roach, as the ball not only clears the fence, but drops out of sight into the creek a distance behind it.

"Where'd you learn to throw like that?" Coach Hedberg says.

David shrugs. "Nowhere."

It is his final stab at Buddy, but even better is Coach Hedberg's following behind him with his clipboard, and David saying he'll think about football, sure, he's thrown a football, but it's all for Buddy, because David has no intention of playing for Coach Hedberg—even after Coach Hedberg sees how he can run, and wants him for a receiver—and two weeks later, when he and Buddy meet on the field again, it is only because their practice times overlap—David on the cross-country team, Buddy playing football. But it is there, that night, David realizes the extent of *his* error, Buddy's eyes on him, cold, penetrating, calculating.

Not a boy's eyes at all—a man's. Buddy bearded, enormous, and wishing him harm.

But there's an everydayness to it all, this morning, the field, the light, the autumn leaves, his thoughts, and having taken his swing at Buddy, he dismisses it, what he's done, and even later in the day, turning to a girl in calculus, who he can hardly bear to look at she is so lovely, feels only a whisper of it, uncoiling, prescient, waiting.

And here, now, in the autumn glow, David runs by Buddy, elated.

And in running, he empties his mind of one thing after another, as if casting off physical baggage, the mess at home with his mother, who is so distracted she can't seem to remember anything, Jarvis, who's been pressuring her to move them all in with him, pressing for marriage, Janie disappearing in her clown act, the house a mess and needing repairs they can't afford, and Buddy's eyes, sullen, burning, following him.

All that he jettisons, running, running lighter, running into his stride, until the time he is only breath, and motion, free, in his dream of life nothing sticking to him, even himself—no, *especially* himself.

Greenstone

1

ALL GOOD THINGS COME TO THOSE WHO WAIT, GOES THE old saying, and David had been waiting now nearly thirty minutes under the entryway roof of Edina Morningside, the rain coming down in cold, rapid bursts, and that some*thing* he'd been waiting for, his mother in her beat-up Ford, hadn't come. His teammates had been shunted away long before, one after another, by parents in new Cadillacs, and brothers with hopped-up GTOs and 'Cudas, and sisters in new Toyotas and Volvos, and now it was only David under the roof, and it was with a certain freedom, and irony, that he stepped out into the rain, his books slung over his back in a canvas bag and the rain cool on his face.

He glanced down at his wristwatch, that old saw coming to him again, his mother was always saying it, *All good things*—and he did feel that, that something big was coming, life changing and, he assumed, wrongly, it had to do with what he'd nearly done today—and he checked for traffic and crossed at the light, happy to be outside and moving, to be able to collect his thoughts.

His mother had forgotten to pick him up again. Which was always a minor embarrassment anyway, her pulling up to the school in their old station wagon, and here he'd been given the opportunity to take a four-mile hike in the rain instead. Too stupid to get out of the rain. Well, he was in it, and it wasn't so bad, he thought, and he quickened his step, and for a time he was, even walking along the rain-glossy street, deep in a reverie. Saw himself running, pulling ahead of Terry McGovern, he would do it, beat him, had almost done it at the meet today, he should have pulled ahead of McGovern before that last hill, sprinted by him, even if the ground had been uneven there, and anyway, he was two years younger than Terry, just fifteen, and Coach had said his time was incredible, and it had been.

Push it, Coach said. Don't wait for anything. Push it now. You push it, you could take State next year, or at the worst, two years from now. You gotta push it, Davey, he'd said.

David shuddered in the cold. Still, thinking about it, he very nearly broke into a run, for the joy of it, but he was wearing his hard-soled boots, and that stopped him. He came to another light and, taking a long step from the curb, further distanced himself from school and what was really troubling him there.

And just then he decided to tell no one about that, or about what he'd done today in track.

Striding toward the highway fence he had to climb to cross the highway, he thought of his father, and what he'd said the last time they'd talked.

What do you have to go out for a pansy sport like that for? Running. That's for losers who can't take football. You can throw the ball. I taught you. You should be bucking for quarterback.

Even thinking of his father now put a frown on David's face. Because what he always seemed to be implying but never said was: David was small. Which he wasn't. He was just under five-eleven, and one fifty-five, which for his age wasn't small at all, but his father made him *feel* small.

Small. When he could run ten miles across uneven ground faster than almost anyone in the state.

You're fucking rawhide, kid, his coach had said. What is it that gets into you?

David never told Coach that when he ran he thought of all the slights his father had tossed at him, thought of the beatings that had gone on before his mother had forced his father out, all in well-to-do Edina. Things like that didn't happen in Edina, and God knows, if they did, you didn't talk about them.

And it occurred to him that Max made *all* of them feel small— even now when he'd been out of the house almost three years.

David was thinking that when he crossed the service road bordering Highway 62, went down the grassy slope in the rain toward the fence that ran along it. He traversed the slope, the grass slick under his feet, and the smell of exhaust ashy in the wet air, his thoughts going now from his father to another bully, Rick Buddy, who, since he'd thrown the ball that morning, seemed determined to break him, even though David would never give in, didn't cower, or sidle away from him. He had no idea why he didn't—though he hadn't with his father, either. But it was going to come to something bad, this Buddy thing. Because now the other Hornets were teasing Buddy that David had gotten the best of him.

That's really what was waiting for him. Buddy. What troubled him now.

David tossed his book bag over the cyclone fence, then climbed over it, careful to avoid the barbs on top.

The traffic on the highway was moving at a good seventy or so, and it was dark, and raining, and he knew he'd have to be careful.

It was a little after evening rush, and he stood on the shoulder, his stomach rumbling. A car sped past in a hissing rush and David bolted across the north 100 exit ramp, the pavement slick under his feet, a car that must have been doing ninety honking and barely missing him, and David felt himself kick, and he was flat out running across the westbound lanes, a second car coming on, the driver laying on his horn, a smeary, harsh, red sound, and then David was standing in the grassy median.

Cars passed behind him, and in front of him, most of them with their lights on.

He wasn't so much worried about being hit as he was about Officer Diehl showing up. He caught his breath, then felt his bag on his back, which seemed lighter, and he got a sick feeling, didn't even want to look to see if he'd lost something.

From the median he could make out the house alongside the highway, just up the rise from the entrance ramp and in back of the cyclone fence, the lights on, and the car in the drive, that old Ford.

She'd forgotten him big time, and he wondered what he'd say to her when he got in.

Then he bolted across the two eastbound lanes and entrance ramp, went up the hill and fast—Officer Diehl had stopped him right *here* a few weeks ago, and even though David had explained he'd have to walk an extra two miles if he went south, to the crossover, Diehl hadn't been sympathetic.

I see you out here again, he'd said, I'll take you into the station. No ifs, ands, or buts. Got it?

As he bolted up the hill to the fence, it occurred to David that he didn't care.

2

DAVID CAME THROUGH THE DOOR INTO THE WARM HOUSE expecting to smell something to eat—he'd imagined roast beef, he supposed because his mother's, Rachel's, as he thought of her, birthday was coming up, and he'd been thinking about that, what to get her, and that she'd always liked to have roast beef for her birthday, but there was nothing, nothing but the patter of Janie's feet. She came running barefoot up the long hallway and scooted behind the washer/dryer alcove, peered impishly out at him. This made David's eyes glass up, and he had to turn his head aside, was too embarrassed to let her see.

"David?" his mother called from her room down the hall. "David, is that you?"

Janie stepped out into the hallway and gave David a stern look, mimicking their mother. Janie was just seven, and very pretty, but it was this . . . pixie something in her that David loved. He loved Janie.

They were in this together, had been for years.

"She's all mad because you promised you'd call if you were going to be late again."

David swung his bag onto the table by the door and shucked off his wet jacket.

"David?" Rachel called again.

"No, it's the boogeyman!" he called back.

Janie saw the mud on his boots and knew he'd climbed the fence and run across the highway. She pointed, and David shook his head and put his finger to his lips. Now Rachel came up the hallway, her reading glasses on, pressing a strand of her hair back behind her ear. She'd been doing her office work at home again. Janie smiled at her.

"I thought you said you were going to call?"

David shrugged. He wasn't about to tell her she'd forgotten to pick him up after practice, because that would be another cause for Rachel to go on one of her crying jags. Or to get depressed and lock herself in her room, or maybe even worse, she'd hug him, and apologize, and tell him what a rotten mother she'd been.

She'd done that once, and it had just about killed him. Anything but that. So he said, "I'm sorry. I got caught up in that nerdo High Q thing after practice and just forgot."

Rachel gave him a stern, sideways glance. She knew David didn't spend much time with the High Q group now that he had cross-country; she'd gotten him into the group, and he'd made friends there, ones he went to a movie with now and then, but only that.

Years earlier, this had made her nervous, how he never stuck with one group, until she'd realized it was just David's way: He was, in large part, solitary. Liked most to read, science books usually, and make things, rockets, and flying model airplanes, kept odd pets, like salamanders, or newts, loved anything alive, or with fur, and to be outside.

And now, too, he was crazy about running—and Janie, *always* Janie. The two of them were always kidding around, Janie making David laugh.

"You weren't out with Vern or Cleve Ellis, were you?"

David wasn't going to go near that one. Vern and Cleve were brothers David used to hang out with; both had been sent up to Shattuck, a military academy, for messing around with drugs.

"He was playing chess," Janie said.

Chess was the catchword for whatever he'd been doing when he came home late. Rachel never checked his story out. Chess. Or bowling. David smiled at that, his mother across from him giving him that dubious look again. David ruffled Janie's hair.

"Come on, Sport, do you have to give all my secrets away?" he said.

Janie beamed from ear to ear, and David felt some darkness in him lift.

"What's for dinner?" he said, even as he moved off toward his room at the back of the house.

"What do you want?" Rachel said, behind him.

David looked over his shoulder. They were back into their usual ritual, and he felt safe. She would ask, and he would offer to make dinner. It had been that way since his father had left, and that's just what they did.

Later that night, he was hunched over his desk, working on differential equations. He had to be up early, for zero-hour German, which he hated, another of his father's great ideas, one that reached down into his life and messed things up. The best research in ophthalmology is being done in Germany right now, his father had said. David did not know why, exactly, he couldn't say no to his father, but he couldn't, and so he'd signed up for it, and he hated it, but then he didn't care much for high school, with the pep rallies, and nonsense about *our team,* and the school colors.

It all bored him. Like these differential equations, he thought. What was the point? Who cared what the volume of this bookmaker's irregular object was? Jesus.

David lit another cigarette and was careful to blow the smoke out the window so his mother wouldn't smell it. He was sure she did anyway, but she didn't say anything, and maybe she was just resigned to it.

David was taking a deep tug on the cigarette when he saw something move in the doorway. He fixed his eyes on his calculus text, waiting—here would be another lecture from his mother, but no heart in it.

That's what killed David now. And this sense of suffocation in the house.

"David?" Janie said.

She put her head through the door, her eyes porcelain blue and with that kid-something there that just grabbed him. He felt bigger around Janie, stronger, not in a boastful way, but almost as if he were his sister's father, and not her brother.

"What, Sport?" he said.

"Can I come in?"

"Of course you can."

She pattered on bare feet to his bed beside the desk and leapt in and pulled the covers over her head, then slowly lowered them to peek out at him, giggling.

"Okay, what is it?"

Janie laughed, then got a serious look. "She's crying. I can hear it through the wall again."

David let go a long sigh. He knew Rachel wasn't crying, and that Janie had resorted to this lie in order to talk to him made him feel tired—Rachel did cry some nights, but it was David who'd told Janie about it.

Janie said now, "You're not supposed to smoke."

"Don't you go smoking," David teased.

"I won't," Janie said.

"Well, don't."

"Then why do you?"

David shrugged. He closed his calculus text and spun his chair around. He got up and sat on the end of the bed, his back to the cool wall.

"Pull your feet in, Sport," he said.

She did that and he yanked one of the pillows from the headboard and wedged it behind his back.

"So what is it, really? Mom's sleeping by now, kiddo."

Janie considered this, averting her eyes. She smiled at him, and he saw she was holding something in and he rumpled up her hair.

"Come on, Sport, you can tell me."

"Tell you what?"

"Did you have another dream?"

For a second Janie turned away, pulled the blanket over her head again. David pulled it down.

"You did, didn't you."

David didn't ask her to recount it. She'd done that one time, and it had upset her—the dream had been so dark and violent, it had surprised even David—Max had been cutting David into pieces and putting him in a bag—so now, as he had in the past, he reached for a book on his shelf, and he read to her.

"'The mole had been working very hard all the morning, spring-cleaning his little home. First with brooms, then with dusters; then on ladders and steps and chairs . . .'"

David read on, glancing over at Janie. As in the past, Janie didn't make it much past the first page before she was fast asleep, and David reached to the foot of the bed and covered her with the quilt. Janie was a cold sleeper, sensitive to temperature; even when it was in the fifties outside, she always had to be bundled up against the weather.

David carefully went back to his desk. Janie liked to sleep with the light on, so it was no problem to open his calculus text and work now, and he lit another cigarette, and for a second, glancing at Janie's elfin, smooth-skinned face, felt settled. He worked a problem with enjoyment, Janie sleeping to his left.

But then he remembered Rick Buddy. After practice tomorrow, he'd run into him.

Always, on Fridays, the cross-country team used the track behind the school, and recently, to the amusement of all, Rick Buddy waited there to get his jabs in. It made David feel leaden, and then he recalled what his father had said years ago. Some bully goes after you, you gotta just hit first and hit hard. You hit any bully *hard enough* and he'll back off, and no one'll be calling you a sissy. I don't ever want to hear any whining from you about bullies, because bullies you take care of yourself. Got it?

Well, he had Buddy to himself, all right. Buddy, who'd promised to get him. And get him good.

I'm gonna cripple you, kid, he'd said that first afternoon when the football and cross-country teams had shared the field. I'm gonna cripple you, and right when it'll hurt you the worst. Right in front of everybody.

All right, David decided. No matter that Rick Buddy weighed two-forty. He'd move, and move fast.

There at the desk, the light on, his heart raced imagining it, knocking Buddy down, but in his heart of hearts he wasn't convinced. Yet here was his father speaking to him again.

It's all willpower. You decide to do things, then you get the job done.

David had known, always, when his father said these things, that it was some drill sergeant of years past talking to him, somebody in the army. Not Max. Somebody who had formed his father, who'd had no father.

Shipshape, Soldier, Max had said when David was barely tall enough to reach Max's knees.

David snapped out the light and sat in the near dark.

Was the thing he'd sensed coming all this time *this* thing? Not having to break through in track, but having to stand up to someone like stupid, dog-eyed Rick Buddy? And if he did, would he have put off all Rick Buddys, like his father had said he would?

Or was Rick Buddy just part of it?

Moonlight spilled through the window on Janie's face.

But was life really all just climbing on top of each other, or knocking down Rick Buddys, as Max had told him it was? Because if that was true, when did you stop? And who could possess anything of real value then, if it only made you a target for those who'd try to take it away?

David smoked in the dark, all this melancholy in him.

His father had always criticized him for siding with the so-called underdogs, the losers. Cross-country, what a loser sport, son. Who cares? You don't get the girls, you don't get the respect.

But even in his chair, David felt that rush of motion, the trees falling back, and that beautiful moving into his stride, and passing John Pretorius, today, and then the others, and running side by side with Terry McGovern, he'd hit his stride, and he just knew, just knew he could have beaten him, goddammit! if he'd had another half mile. But he hadn't bet on that length of hill, and he'd run stride for stride with McGovern, with more on tap, but McGovern, on the hill, had more lift, more strength, though only on the hill, and back on even ground he could have taken him if he'd just put back more pain, because that's what it was, eating pain, pushing through pain, and staying focused, and pushing through that feeling that your lungs and heart would burst, if you could push through that burning, until you reached that clear, clean rush, and staying quiet, could use the ground under you, and like Coach said, take the fastest in front of you, and fucking run his goddamn back down, and when you can see the end, spend it all, every goddamn thing in you, and that's where David saw he'd failed.

If he'd had time to look at the track before, if he'd have known that hill was there . . .

If he hadn't missed the bus that morning, or had eaten breakfast, or if his mother, Rachel, hadn't told him his father had called . . .

Fuck it, he said to himself. Stop making excuses.

If he stopped smoking . . .

He crushed the cigarette out in the ashtray, then bending over the bed, tucked the quilt around Janie's face, and went off into the living room, where he covered himself with the afghan on the couch and slept.

3

THE FOLLOWING DAY WENT BY IN A WASH AS ALWAYS, BUT this one even more so, the halls a pasty gray, and his teachers irritated with him, even Mr. Oberstar, who really was terrific—taking his test now with the others and running it through the mechanized grader, and there being one snapping noise, just one, when his went through, and David angry with himself, thought, What had he missed? and Mr. Oberstar watching David, studying him, so that David had smiled a big All-American Boy smile.

He knew all that cellular stuff backward and forward, so maybe it was something he'd missed the days he was out of school, in court over this thing his father had dragged them into, some hearing over new visitation rights, the thought of which put him in a clammy sweat. He'd tried not to think about it all morning; Max hadn't even shown up at the hearing, but it had turned out he'd been in surgery, doing a hip replacement. This time, his absence not just an excuse, the hospital calling, and the judge rescheduling the hearing, now not to take place until December.

Thinking about the hearing made his heart skip beats and his eyes feel dry, and the morning passed slowly.

And then there was lunch, and after it Miss Schwartz's class, Track 1 English, and her precious crap with "Shakespeare the Immortal Bard"; and Mr. Seeman's Chinese History, which was okay, but through it all ran this thread of anticipation, something more upsetting than the visitation hearing, David pinned to the wheel of time, or fate, or circumstance, willing himself not to even consider what was most on his mind . . .

Buddy. Buddy would be waiting for him after class.

And lacing his Adidas up after school, in the locker room, in his shorts, Dean Simonson, his "cross-country friend," as David thought of him, clapped him on the back.

"Way to go, Geist!" he said. "Man, that was really something yesterday!"

There were more than a few kids who congratulated him, and David was surprised. In fact, he was almost grinning at it, would have, if it hadn't been for Buddy.

Maybe Buddy'd just give it up, now that David had placed in the meet?

David went outside with Simonson, the day warm yellow, and the light soft, and the smell of burning leaves in the air, all of which he loved, and back of the track he pumped his legs, then stretched in the grass, his hamstrings burning.

He tried to focus on running some fast 440s, saw himself burst off the blocks, had his chin on his right knee, his leg extended, his left leg bent behind him when he heard the rattle of plastic behind him and felt two thick hands on his shoulders, pressing him down, so the burning in his legs was searing.

He couldn't find his voice for fear that Buddy might really injure him.

"Hey, cut it out, Buddy!" Simonson shouted. "You could mess up his back."

"Yeah, cut it out," another teammate, Pretorius, said.

Buddy gave out a low guffaw and let go.

"Get up, faggot," he said.

David jumped to his feet. Behind him, his teammates stood watching. Long hair, wild looking, thin in running gear.

Dean Simonson said, tossing his head, "Come on, Davey, let's take a fast one around the track."

Right there, David could have moved. Simonson had given him an out. But he didn't. If he had, maybe Buddy wouldn't have said what he did, "You're just a runner 'cause you're afraid, ass-hole. You think you're hot shit because of what you did throwin' that ball, you and your faggoty ass baseball bullshit. You are never gonna amount to shit, because you're made of faggotty shit, and you *are* shit. But most of all, you're *scared shit,* Geist."

David stood an arm's length from Buddy, his hands twitching, his head a bright burn. He couldn't think, caught out like that. All of David's silence, his dogged persistence, his focus came out of a generalized fear, one that he hated in himself. He was terrified of something, and it came to him in dreams, in moments when he wasn't prepared for it, this whooshing, swooping dark something, and only his being strong around Janie made it go away.

Making it go away for Janie was his only refuge.

Only, now it faced him in the person of Rick Buddy, who looked around to make sure the coaches weren't out, then lunged at David, said, "Boo!"

David jumped back, but not much.

"You're such a pissant you're even afraid of your own shadow, aren't cha," Buddy said.

There in his shoulder pads and cleats, Buddy was smirking.

"Afraid to so much as breathe, that's you, asshole."

Then, before David had even a second to think of moving, to swing on Buddy, Buddy had him by the hair on the back of his head, and ran his face into the cyclone fence in front of the bleach-ers, so his nose hit the thick wire and he tasted blood. Buddy jerked his knee into David's stomach, clapped him over his ears, and when David swung hard, struck Buddy dully in the mouth, Buddy caught David's hand and bent his thumb back until David felt something there give with a dull, painful tearing.

"Say 'I give.'"

David did not say it, and Buddy kicked him with his big knee again, knocking the air out of him, so that David sunk to his knees, here the smell of blood and newly mown grass and dirt.

But he wouldn't say it, there was no way, but something in him told him to just give in, say "I give," and he was arguing with himself about saying it, that he should say it, but then there was a sharp whistle, and there was that rattle and clatter of plastic that is football gear, and the whole team moved off onto the field, and Buddy with them, and when Simonson came over to see how he was, David shrugged his hand off his shoulder and headed inside, was crossing the field to the locker room, even as Coach was shouting, "Now, where the hell is Geist? Did that goddamn goober Buddy run him off? If he did, so help me—"

But no one said anything.

———

He made it up Xerxes, to the podiatrist's. He'd had to have a cast put on his left foot when he'd broken two bones in it running the year before, and when he came in, Dr. Parker looked up over his receptionist's elaborately done hair, an Afro with a green ribbon seeming to hold that balloon of dark hair down.

Dr. Parker, unlike their family physician, was black, and David thought here he could pass off his messed-up thumb as a sports injury.

"I'm gonna— Hey, David," Dr. Parker said, and he bent over his receptionist and motioned David into the back, and David wondered, from the look Dr. Parker gave him, if his nose had begun to bleed again.

He went to the room at the back of the hall where Dr. Parker had worked on his foot, and minutes later Dr. Parker came in with an ice pack, and said nothing, just handed it to David, nodded a kind of you-know-what-to-do-with-it nod, and while David held the pack to his face, Dr. Parker fixed an aluminum splint on the thumb of his right hand.

When he'd finished with that, he said, "I want there to be an understanding between you and me, David. I know what this is, and you know what this is. You have anybody to go to?"

When David didn't answer, Dr. Parker got him on his feet, then turned him toward the table and had him lie on his back on it.

"You hold that against your nose, and I'm going to get more ice for your hand. You don't do anything for either, so it's not that kind of situation. All you've got is a sprain and contusions. I don't have to so much as make a record that you were here. But if it's going to come to this again, you're going to call me. You're going to promise me that, or I'll call your mother right now, and we'll get to the bottom of this. Do you understand me?"

David nodded.

He lay back with the ice on his nose, and there was Dr. Parker's reassuring voice in the clinic outside, and then he was in with more ice and had David hold it over his hand, which he lay across David's stomach.

After a time David watched the ceiling, and at first he imagined dramas in which he pummeled Rick Buddy to within an inch of his life, crunching blows to those dull eyes of his, a devastating kick to the testicles, ten knee jabs to the breadbasket for every one Buddy'd given him, and after some time had gone by, those thoughts faded, stupid kid thinking, he told himself, and the throbbing in his hand and face took over, hot, itchy throbbing, and he held the ice there, and the buzzing of the lights became louder, and there was the opening and closing of doors, and cars starting out in the lot and driving away, and finally it was just Dr. Parker who came in to look down at him, his eyes sad, and his movements deliberate and slow, as if something weighty were pressing on him.

4

HE GOT THE DOOR OPEN WITHOUT MAKING ANY NOISE, AND was halfway to his room when he heard Janie come bolting up from the basement den, her bare feet sharp on the runners. She nearly ran headlong into him, and when she saw his face, she skidded to a stop and put her hands over her mouth, turned one way and then the other, stomping her feet she was so upset. David caught her arm and spun her around, pinned her against him.

"Shhhhhh."

"She's not home!" Janie nearly shouted. "And you're late! Mrs. Toreman's here because of you!"

"Okay, Sport. Okay. All right?!"

He let go of her, and she wouldn't look at him, as it upset her so badly.

"Tell Mrs. Toreman she can go now, okay, Sport?" David said, and with a push, sent her for her sitter.

He went down the hallway to the bathroom, and as he was studying his face in the mirror, bruised blue already, he heard Mrs. Toreman go out. For years, Mrs. Toreman had watched Janie in pinches like this.

When he stood in the hallway again, Janie stared.

"It's the overhead lights. They're making it look worse than it is."

"Is not!" Janie shouted.

"Well, it's not like I'm gonna go blind or anything."

Janie looked up at him, in her face this incredulity, and he realized his left eye had nearly closed up.

"You're not?"

"I'm sure it looks worse than it is, Sport."

Janie wrinkled up her face, then peered at him over her elbow. David stooped and nodded her over. She sidled toward him. Although his nose was throbbing something awful, he raised his arms comically and made a growling noise, and Janie let go a girlish squealing and ran from him, giggling, and he chased her through the living room and caught her from behind, and thinking, oh, Jesus, does that smart, swung her around in circles, until she begged him to stop.

He set her down and she bent toward him.

"Can I touch it?"

"Sure."

Janie leaned forward, this almost—David thought—clinical interest in his face, this intrigue, while she was concerned, too. She touched what must have been the darkest part of his swollen eye.

"Does that hurt?"

"Sure does."

"Why didn't you say so?"

She really wanted to know.

"You wanted to touch it, kiddo. That was the deal. Didn't say anything about whether it hurt or not."

"It's hot," Janie said. "Looks like an eggplant."

David had to laugh at that. He stood and put his hands on his hips.

"What about dinner?" he asked.

"Mom made that old hotdish again, it's in the kitchen."

David glanced at his watch, then got his hand around Janie's shoulders and propelled her toward the kitchen with a light push.

Janie set the table while David, at the stove, adjusted the burner under the pot of hotdish. There was a note on the lid. It read:

> *Heat this on the stove and make sure*
> *Janie eats. I might not be back until*
> *late, so don't wait up.*
>
> > *Love,*
> > *Mom*

Don't wait up. David, his stomach clenching, dropped the note in the trash; he'd hoped this *problem* of his and Janie's had gone away, but he could see now it hadn't, and he knew he'd have to think how to fix it.

He did that while he was readying their plates, then brought their dinner to the table and sat.

"She's seeing that Mr. Filibuster again, isn't she," Janie said, seeing the look on his face.

"Don't go repeating things that I say without—"

"I think he's a dinkle-pooper."

David smiled at that. "That's a new one," he said.

"I'll bet they're over at Bridgeman's."

Bridgeman's was Janie's favorite restaurant. They were most

likely not at Bridgeman's, an ice cream and shrimp basket kind of place.

"Sure, that's it," David said, then added, "And don't tell Mom I said that about Jarvis, all right?"

"What, that he talks too much?"

David reached out to ruffle Janie's hair, but she dodged and he missed her altogether, and they ate in silence.

It wasn't just that Jarvis, this guy his mother had been seeing, talked too much. No, it was that he was like Max in a way, his mother getting back into something with a blowhard, only this guy was even more so, a real-estate agent and developer who knew everything and everyone in the Twin Cities, or so it would seem, if you believed half of what he said.

By comparison, Max, his father, an orthopedic surgeon, was quiet.

Eating, David was almost sick thinking about Rachel getting hooked up with Jarvis. Here it would be, all over again, some version of the same thing—Jarvis and the calls to the office, the important business meetings that ran until early in the morning, the lies and the posturing.

Only he couldn't imagine Jarvis at this table, or any other table, with them. He'd been out with Jarvis and Rachel a few times himself, once skeet shooting, Jarvis trying to pal up to him then, and dispensing endless pointers, which, David knew, were all aimed at proving to Rachel what a fatherly guy he was, and what an expert, all over again, Rachel always within earshot when he did it. It had so aggravated David that he'd cleaned Jarvis's clock shooting handguns later, which, eating now, he had cause to consider.

Jarvis's behavior that night was the best ammunition he had against him—if he could only think how to use it.

Shooting handguns, he'd thought he'd force Jarvis to show his true colors so Rachel could see what she was in for, what Janie and he'd be in for. But maybe, he thought now, glancing up at Janie, who grinned, bravely, so that he bent to his plate again, maybe he'd only driven them together instead.

In the car that night, after David had taken Jarvis down, Jarvis had ranted about his pistol, about how the barrel was off, had been messed up by the machinist who'd worked on it, fixed the trigger (Jarvis had boasted *before* shooting with David about the gun's something-or-another grams of draw), but then, in the car, the gun having failed him, he'd given David a look that he'd gotten too many times from Max, when Max had come home drunk and beaten him when he was in bed, and trying to rise out of sleep.

Something twisted in Max, something gone wrong, and he, David, the target.

It upset David, and he thought now, bent over the hotdish, Janie across from him, that it was up to him to put the brakes on Jarvis, steer his mother from this guy—for Janie's and his sake, and for Rachel's—because, even that night, she hadn't *seen* Jarvis, hadn't gotten it.

She couldn't have, or why would she be out—David shook his head at the thought—why would she be out late with the guy? Again?

But she was, no doubt, even after that ugly time at the range.

That night, when they'd gone target shooting, had plugged bowling pins at a range in Hopkins, Rachel had seemed amused by it all, Jarvis putting a lot of stock in his handgun, an enormous Colt Python with a six-inch barrel. He'd given David and Rachel .38 Specials. David hadn't told Jarvis that his uncle, from the time he'd been little, had taken him to a sandpit nearby, and he'd had exactly this gun, the SW .38, and they'd plugged the *frickin'*, as his uncle had said, daylights out of tin cans, tossing them in the air and plugging them, and he'd loved his uncle Bobby, and they'd just had fun for the hell of it, whole afternoons of plugging cans, and then targets, and moving targets, and when they were disgruntled, bottles, which made a satisfying shattering sound.

So, at the underground range in Hopkins, David had suppressed a smile when Jarvis had taken the Python out of the purple-velvet-lined case, his big fucking dick of a gun—David read that loud and clear—and then got out the two smaller guns, the .38s.

That he was some gun collector, all handguns, David didn't like, either.

"I never held one of these before," David said.

Jarvis knew Max, David's father, had been a pheasant and duck hunter, and that he'd brought David along, so when they'd been out earlier skeet shooting, there'd been no surprise that David knew how to handle a shotgun. But no one, not even Rachel, knew about Bobby's and David's afternoons at the sand-pits plugging away with those .38s.

"Have *you* ever shot one of these?" David asked Rachel, giving her a warning look.

There are things boys, of any age, don't think about their mothers, and David wasn't thinking them about Rachel that night, either. But he saw them all the same, how she'd worn the black turtleneck that showed off her figure, and she had some figure, had done up her face and had a kind of hot glitter in her eyes.

"No," she said sharply. "Your father wouldn't have one in the house."

This shut David right up. Shocked him, really: And it made him do what he did later. He knew why Max hadn't let Rachel have a gun, even when he'd moved out—having a gun in the house wasn't safe for *her*, Rachel—and it made David feel all the more desperate about driving this prick Jarvis off, and so he only smiled for Rachel, broadly, here this grim little spectacle he had to orchestrate now for the sake of both of them.

"Okay," David said, giving Jarvis a confused look. "Where's the . . . safety on this thing?"

Jarvis gave him a big lecture right there, that chrome-plated Python hanging suggestively from his hand, explained the "sport of pin competition," as he called it, shooting bowling pins stacked in rows.

They got loaded up, took their positions, and had at the first set. Even with the ear protectors on, the sound was loud, an irregular thumping, *Whump! Whump-whump-whump!* Jarvis knocked down all of his pins but had gone well over the allotted time. Rachel knocked down two and splintered the neck of two more.

David only nicked one—or that's what it looked like, Jarvis there grinning at him.

"Give up?" Jarvis said. "Or are you ready for a real lesson? I mean," he said, "you don't got a clue with that little pea shooter."

"I'll get the hang of it," David said, and Rachel looked at him askance, knew he was lying, but about what she couldn't tell.

They went through three rounds of pins like that, and David let himself knock down a few.

He had the feel of the gun now. His uncle's .38s had had hair triggers, and he made a triangle of his arms now, the way his uncle had shown him, his uncle the war hero, the rifle corps marksman, who got all long-faced if anyone asked him about Omaha Beach, and even longer if his Purple Heart was mentioned.

Get your body steady, and let the gun do the walking, he'd said. Squeeze off the shots, even if you're moving. Bobby'd toss up a can, the can spinning end over end, or rising in a high, looping arc, or underhand, and he'd yell, Lead it! Lead it! and David would knock them—each and every one—down. Even the high ones, which nearly disappeared overhead. Bobby'd been one terrific pitcher, until the war, and he'd come back himself, but something—kind of, David thought—*broken* in him. Something . . . gone away, which was part of what scared David.

Bobby dying, sort of, the way people seemed to, but going on anyway.

And his mother had almost been there, just like Bobby, two years ago, unable to divorce Max but unable to let him move back in again, all this time gone by now since they'd separated, and then she'd started *dating*, as she'd called it, to make their separation final, or so she'd told David, which had led them to Jarvis, and this range.

Jarvis now nearly gloating, there with the big Python. Red Sansabelt slacks, red-and-blue-plaid Munsingwear sports shirt, the little alligator over the pocket, thick wrists and fingers, a clunky gold watch there.

David had run him clay pigeon for clay pigeon out skeet shooting, and Jarvis meant to pay him back.

"How about a gentlemen's bet?" he said.

"Me?" Rachel asked.

"No, Billy the Kid there," Jarvis said. "Mr. Hotshot, Bat Masterson. Our whiz kid there with the fuck-up friends. What do you say?" Jarvis knew how he'd been kicked out of the school for smoking pot at a dance, with his friends Vern and Cleve, and how he'd been caught, later, driving his then-girlfriend's car, an open bottle of whiskey with them. All that last spring, after he'd gotten his driver's permit, and had gone . . . haywire, sort of. And Jarvis'd had to bring it up.

But now, here it was. They'd gotten to it, this open antagonism.

Rachel had already discussed with David that Jarvis was getting serious, and she'd asked David what he'd think of behaving around Jarvis.

Why? David had asked.

Jarvis thinks you need some—discipline was how he put it, she'd said.

He'd known right there he was in real trouble, so bad he'd felt a bubble of almost hysterical laughter rising up in him, discipline, you bet. And from Jarvis?

But here, now, at the range was his opportunity. He could make Rachel see what she was getting into without having to tell her.

"Okay," David said.

Jarvis grinned. He had a slot for a mouth, teeth that were short, artificially white. "Or should we make it for something?"

"What?" David said.

Jarvis scratched his face, as if he'd just thought of something.

"How about you put a new face on that attitude of yours?"

David recoiled as if he'd been slapped. Rachel wouldn't look at him.

"What about you?" David asked.

"Me?"

"Yeah, you," David said.

"Name it."

This so threw David off he didn't know what to say. He didn't want to insinuate Jarvis on them any more than he had to, and anything he'd ask for would do just that. If he won something from him.

He had to hand it to Jarvis, David was thinking, he was one smart son of a bitch. Calculating. Sure of himself. But then, he'd had to go head-to-head with Max all those years, and Jarvis was no match for Max.

"A vacation, just my mother, Janie, and me." He nodded to Rachel. "She's always wanted to see Niagara Falls," he said, which made Rachel's eyes dart. She'd never said any such thing.

Rachel laughed, cutting her eyes at David, then smiled at Jarvis.

"Worst happened, I'd meet you there," Jarvis said, winking at Rachel. "How'd that be?"

"Wonderful," Rachel said, and gave David a sharp, disapproving look.

Okay, he'd screwed up, David thought. But he couldn't let Jarvis win now, either. He'd have to push Jarvis, see if he could throw him off.

"Ready?" Jarvis said.

David nodded yes, and Jarvis pressed the timer.

The buzzer went off, and David passed into that calm he went into when he ran, nothing but what was in front of him, just the pins, and he squeezed off all six shots, taking down six pins, then used the quick loader and had six more in, took down the remainder and, in the zone, as he called it, and while Jarvis was still hammering away with that big dick of a gun of his, David took down the last of Jarvis's pins, too.

Jarvis had only set his gun on the range counter, his mouth working. It took everything in him not to say what he had on his mind. But his eyes said it anyway, even when he smiled, then kissed Rachel.

Still, all that following week, Rachel would hardly speak to David. And Jarvis, at the range, had only laughed, finally.

"Jesus, kid," he'd said, and clapped David on the back, "you really showed yourself, didn't cha?"

"Why are you just sitting there?" Janie asked, and David shook himself out of it.

"You look like Halloween," she said.

David laughed. "You mean my face or—"

"You could just tell her to make Jarvis go away," Janie said.

David set his hands on his forehead, bent over his plate. When he glanced up, he said, "It isn't that simple, Sport."

"Why not?"

David let go an exasperated breath. "Someday you'll know," he said, but in his heart he hoped not, and later, when he tucked Janie in for the night, he pressed her, tenderly, to him.

"Pleasant dreams, Sport," he said. "Only pleasant dreams."

———

The remainder of that week passed without event, only David's contusions, rather than lightening, darkened at first. Rachel asked about them, and David told her there'd been a pileup in cross-country, which was sort of true, and that he'd gotten an elbow in the face, and had fallen hard and sprained his thumb.

But the bruises now were like some mark of shame, and he wore them that way. There'd been a dance coming up, and he'd intended to ask Sarah Houdak, a quiet, long-legged, lovely girl who struck him dumb, who'd look back at him when he'd look in her direction, her books held over her chest, to hide what she couldn't, but now David didn't want to get near her. Not looking the way he did.

And, what Buddy's done had gotten around school, and at times when people looked at him now, he got this creeping sense of their studying his face, proof there of the rumors they'd heard, and he turned away.

David, in helping Greg Becker, a Morningside pariah, had taken on Buddy. His classmates, it seemed, were only interested in what would come of it.

How this thing would be worked out.

5

FRIDAY MORNING OF THE FOLLOWING WEEK, WHEN THE bruises were their blackest, Janie came into his room and sat on his bed, kicking her feet as he jammed his books into his book bag.

"I gotta go, Sport," David said. "I miss the bus again and it'll be a big mess."

Janie's bus came twenty minutes after David's, at which time Rachel left the house, too.

"I'm worried . . ." Janie said. But she just fidgeted and couldn't say what she wanted to, and David stooped down.

That Rachel had been out late again the night before, very late, led David to believe she was going to dump some bomb on them about Jarvis, and he was thinking it was what Janie had on her mind, too.

"Okay, Sport," he said. "Spill it."

"You remember Julie Invisible?" she asked.

David said he did.

Julie Invisible had been Janie's constant friend the year Max and Rachel had adopted her as a last-ditch effort to save their marriage. She'd come from some bad-off family, had suffered things neither Max nor Rachel would name, but David hadn't needed them named. After all, why, otherwise, would a four-year-old girl believe in some invisible protector—unless she'd really *needed* one?

Just minutes into the house, the day Rachel and Max had brought her home, she'd come down the hallway and sat beside David on the living-room couch.

Ill-fitting pink dress, secondhand patent-leather shoes, facing forward, her eyes large, and intelligent, and saying nothing, and when the silence had become awkward, David asked, leaning low,

"Should I call you Janie?" and the girl had shaken her head, so certainly, she'd surprised him.

He'd had to think of something, right then, and somehow the most inappropriate name had come to him, for this small, bony girl with the big eyes and slender, tiny hands.

"How about if, just between you and me, I call you . . . *Sport*? How about that?"

And she'd looked up at him, and it seemed, for the first time in he couldn't remember how long, someone really smiled at him.

"Yeah, Sport," David said now. "Sure, I remember old Julie."

"I wish I could go like that."

"Where?"

He was concerned that he'd miss the bus, but he wouldn't cut her off.

"With you. If, like Julie did, I could get real, real big, and—"

David felt his eyes burning, and reached for her, gave her a squeeze.

"It's gonna be fine, Sport. *I'll* make everything fine," he said, and he would remember it, some short while later, and it would keep both of them alive.

6

SATURDAY OF THAT WEEK, RACHEL MADE A BIG DINNER. SHE was home early from work, a dental practice she managed, five dentists on rotation, and for once she wasn't so tired that she barely just got through it, her eyes vacant.

No. Today she had the kitchen windows open—it was unseasonably warm—and she was baking something when David came in from his day of painting for his uncle. Something chocolate, and with nuts.

"How was your day?" she said, standing in the door of the kitchen.

She had the apron on, the one Max had given her years ago

for Valentine's Day, on it overlapping red hearts on a white-and-black background. It was almost painfully cheerful, and so was she.

"Okay," David said, suspicious.

He stepped closer and Rachel gave him a peck on his cheek.

"How's your uncle Bobby?"

"He's fine," David said. He didn't say that Bobby was drinking again, he could smell it—not the vodka, but the tomato smell was a giveaway.

"You get a lot done?"

David tossed his bag in the hallway. "How'd you get off so early?" he asked. It didn't sound right, sounded almost like an accusation, and so he said, "I mean, it'll be nice to have dinner together. Whatever you're making smells great."

Rachel said he'd see, it was something *special*.

David smiled, but he could only think that *somewhere* in this, Jarvis, that asshole, would have to fit in, and turned and went out of the kitchen, reached for his bag in the hallway, and Rachel said, "Don't smoke in your room, David," and he stopped there, just out of sight of her.

He thought, *Now* would be the time to say what he had to about Jarvis. But he couldn't. Not with her making such an effort.

"I'm *not* smoking," he said.

"Well, all the same," she said, "please don't smoke in your room. You could catch things on fire—"

He put his head around the doorjamb to look at her, and she grinned.

"Janie hasn't said a thing, so don't get that into your head."

"*Mom*," David said. It sounded strange, he hadn't said it in some time. "I don't—"

"Yes, I know," Rachel said. "I know *you don't smoke,* but all the same, don't do it in your room, and don't in the garage. Promise?"

David said he wouldn't, and he turned up the hallway, mumbling to himself.

Janie was home a short while later, jumping from a silver Mercedes and running to the stoop outside, where David was smoking.

"So, how was the party, Sport?" he asked.

Janie shrugged. "It was okay, but kinda dumb."

She put out her hand. The nail on her index finger was black underneath, and the whole finger swollen.

"I did *just like you*," she said, proudly. "I didn't tell *anyone*, and I *didn't* even cry."

It made David nauseous, looking at her finger, and he held her hand as if it were a small bird.

"Listen, Janie," he said, and as he was telling her how this wasn't right for her not to cry, or have someone help her, and how she should tell Rachel, Rachel called them inside.

At the table, Rachel got a dish of ice for Janie's finger and made her keep her hand in it.

She lit the candle in the center of the table, and David relaxed: Rachel wasn't going to tell them she was marrying Jarvis or anything like that, after all, he could see that now, and Janie's blue eyes sparkled in the candlelight, Janie joking, and David laughing, and he saw that his mother looked a little like that actress in *It's a Wonderful Life*, across from him, tossing her head back, laughing, too, just now *happy*, all three of them, and he thought, I will remember this night always, and he did.

7

HE REMEMBERED THAT NIGHT OVER THE FOLLOWING AFTER-noons at practice, when, time and again, Rick Buddy sidled up to him, and before anyone could see, kicked his knee into David's thigh so sharply David saw black, and felt this void in his head, and David getting a good punch in once, splitting Buddy's lip, only Buddy, rather than backing off, had made it clear *here* was just more cause to do David real harm.

And he remembered that good night back at the house, too,

because, even though things were shaping up, had since their dinner, Rachel home evenings now, and cleaning, even painting the living room and kitchen, he just knew Jarvis was out there, waiting to swoop down into their lives.

And whether Janie would show it or not, she knew, too. *Something* was up.

"What if he comes here?" Janie asked one night she'd wanted David to tuck her in. "If he does, will you look out for me?"

"Listen," David said, pressing her quilt up under her chin. "No matter what happens, I'll watch out for you, it's a promise. For all time. Okay?"

And he read to her, perched there beside her, until her breathing got deeper, and when he was certain she was asleep, he carefully lifted himself from the bed and went into his room, and under the light, smoked, and worked, and tried not to think about Jarvis, or Buddy, or whatever else was out there waiting.

And remembered that earlier, wonderful night, and cherished it.

8

BY THE END OF THAT MONTH, DAVID HAD SWUNG BACK AT Buddy enough that Buddy didn't casually sidle up to him anymore, give him charley horses that turned the sides of his thighs marbled black and blue, but that was little comfort, since Buddy'd gotten more serious about the whole thing, smirking and making guns with his hands, and pointing them at David and making shooting noises, and then grinning, and winking at him.

It got so it bothered David so much he couldn't concentrate nights, and he sat at his desk, smoking whole packs of Camels, drawing on a pad, sometimes anatomical sketches from *Gray's*, taking great care to render the smallest details in alveoli, or epiphyses and joints, or muscles.

One night, when he couldn't sit to study, he got up, right at two, and he crushed out his cigarette, and dressed in his sweats and shoes and went out, ran ten miles around Lake Cornelia, and to the old drive-in theater near 494. When he charged quietly into the yard again, he checked his watch, six-minute miles for the whole ten. He kicked at the ground.

It wasn't fast enough, *goddammit,* he thought, then saw his mother there on the stoop, dressed in slacks and a green blouse, but her feet bare.

She patted the stoop, and he sat beside her, trying to catch his breath. The moon, waxing and huge, seemed to smile out of the poplars in the Kleinmeyers' yard adjacent to theirs.

In the past it had always been Max who'd done this, waited for him when he'd snuck out, but then he'd been drinking, and that stopped. Rachel snapped a pack of Salems against her palm, lit one, offered the pack to David. Rachel, blowing a plume of smoke in the direction of the moon, cleared her throat.

"How are things at school?"

"Fine," David said.

He had decided, two years ago, when things had been at their worst, to keep his mouth shut around Rachel. One evening, after he'd been told by his trumpet teacher at Schmidt Music not to come back, not to waste either of their time if he wasn't going to practice, he'd gotten a shouting-at in the car from Max.

Max had still, back then, taken him to practices and things, and he'd done so that evening. Disgusted with David, he'd clapped him alongside the head when they'd gotten back to the house. David, traumatized by it, had sat at the table after dinner, Rachel washing dishes behind him. When he'd said he wanted to kill himself, Rachel had run to the kitchen drawers and yanked out a sharp, serrated steak knife, and had screamed at him, "Let's both kill ourselves right now!" at the end of her ability to endure, too, and he'd bolted for her, had wrestled the knife from her, and it was this that had come between them these last two years, because David, in his thinking, was not about to utter a word about his difficulties.

Not one word that might hurt her, or get her going like that again. Never.

"You're sure now," Rachel said, and when he gave a curt nod, she sighed, then said, "I'm a little worried about your sister."

"What about her?"

"She's not sleeping."

"She isn't?"

"No."

"But I read to her and she—"

"She's faking," Rachel insisted. "Believe me."

"She is?"

"She does it all the time."

Now the two of them had something to talk about. It was a relief.

"Why?"

Rachel shrugged. "They were pretty hard on her, where she came from."

David swallowed at that. He tried not to think about any of it, because it only got his heart clocking in his neck. Those fantasies were *seriously* violent. Were anyone to hurt Janie, he didn't know what he'd do. But there was little he'd stop at.

They sat on the stoop, minutes longer, the night sounds around them, crickets, a car with a bad muffler going by on the highway, a night bird calling, and when Rachel rose to go in, David looked up at her.

"Can you just help me out here, just a little?" she said. "Because things are going to change around here soon, and a lot."

David's heart sank. He waited for her to go on. He was sure it would be about Jarvis now, how she'd accepted some proposal, and he sucked in a very deep breath, and when Rachel only stood, looking out into the night, he said, "I know already, anyway."

And Rachel glanced down at him, more than surprised. "You do? He talked to you?"

David nodded. He didn't trust himself to say one word about Jarvis. Not now, not here. He'd have to do it in the morning. He didn't trust the dark, the simplest arguments seeming to go crazy then.

Rachel stood in the doorway a moment, and then she said, "All right, then," and she went into the house.

———

When he woke the following morning, he stood from his bed with a kind of wooden willfulness, then made scrambled eggs for Janie, who came into the kitchen sleepy-eyed, her hair ratted, so he had to run a comb through it, Rachel already gone, an hour early, a note there on the refrigerator door.

> *David, forgot to ask you to*
> *be back at the house by six.*
> *Janie, don't eat cereal. We're going*
> *out to dinner!*
>> *Love,*
>> *Mom*

No doubt she and Jarvis would announce their plans over dinner now, and David was angry with himself, having missed his opportunity to halt things.

9

HE WOULD LATER THINK OF THAT DAY AS THE ONE THAT LED to the others, those days following that shaped his life as he could never have anticipated. That day passing in some seeming slow motion, in school, David waiting to get to it, this Jarvis thing, each hour passing like an eternity, until, with a sense of relief, seventh hour was over, and he headed for the locker rooms, and track, in the main hallway, Sarah Houdak passing him, holding her eyes on his as he went by, until he looked away, abashed, but he was thinking of her, so much so, entering the locker room he did not see Buddy behind the towel dispenser, grinning, and he let go a great relieved breath.

Outside, he stretched, then took a slow lap around the track to warm up.

Outside and moving, he felt some dynamo in himself taking over—all that he'd been thinking was nothing, nothing at all, just chaff, and here, now, he came alive. Running 880s.

He pushed himself, hard, through practice, and now made one last fast lap, and turning to go inside, Coach gave him the thumbs-up. He'd asked David if he needed help with Buddy, but David had told him no, since Buddy no longer bothered him on the field.

And like that, he descended the steps to the locker room, and where the hallway T'd, on either side were Steve Halloran and Todd Wickstrom, in green-and-white football gear.

"Hey," David said.

He pushed at the locker-room doors, but they wouldn't open, and he thought, for a second, he just hadn't pushed hard enough, but when he gave a second, very hard push, even using his shoulder, he broke out in a cold, awful sweat, his legs leaden under him and, the yellow light from outside blocked off suddenly, he glanced over his shoulder, and there in the hallway behind him was Buddy, Buddy whose thighs were so thick he seemed to waddle, rather than walk, and he swung on Halloran, hit him squarely in the face, tried to go by, but Wickstrom caught his shirt from behind, spun him around, and the two of them, Halloran and Wickstrom, held him by his arms, David kicking for all he was worth, but Buddy pummeling his ribs anyway, Halloran and Wickstrom getting their shots in, too, so hard he was sure they'd break something, all of it lasting only seconds, the blows heavy, hard-knuckled speed punches, and then they went hulking off in opposite directions, and he was kneeling, and vomiting, when Simonson came on him, and Simonson said, "Hey! Buddy do this?"

David nodded, holding it all in, choking with rage, and humiliation. With his head down, he put his hand around his back and waved Simonson on.

"I'm going for Coach."

"*Don't!*" David said.

"Why not?"

"Because I said so."

"Somebody's gotta—"

"I said *don't,* and I meant it! Now, go on!" he said, and when Simonson instead came closer, he nearly cried, "*Get outta here! Leave me alone,* all right?!"

———

They were walking east on Sixty-sixth, David and Janie dressed in their yakkety-yakkety clothes, as Janie called them, because, she said, people always sat around talking when they got dressed up, like they were talking now, she said, sagely, and while they walked, the traffic whooshing by, Janie told a story about Bobby Halvorsen, and how he'd been gluing a noodle to some paper for their art project, and had somehow stuck it up his nose, and sneezing, had gotten it way up in there and had to be taken to the hospital.

"I'll bet that was exciting," David said. He was amused at the thought of it. It was a good distraction from the pain of trying to walk. And thoughts of Jarvis.

At the house, Mrs. Toreman had told him they were to walk the three blocks to the Galleria, where Rachel was having her hair done, and where they were to meet her at the Angus. Meet *them*.

"The best part—" Janie said.

"The best part?" David asked. He wasn't thinking too straight, having taken two of Rachel's Darvons and chased them with wine.

Janie smiled. Not meanly, but the way any kid would. "The best part was when Mrs. Meyer tried to get him to just kind of . . . *sneeze* it back out, and he just sucked it in there even farther. He looked like this."

Janie made one of her faces, and David laughed. He couldn't help it. His whole life was stupid, not unlike that kid with his damn nose. Try to do one thing, and something else happened.

But he was sure he'd tell Rachel about Buddy now.

He'd just have to do it, he told himself, whether it made him look . . . *small* or not.

———

As they were passing through the heavy, swinging wooden doors of the Angus, Rachel rose from a table in back, and they stopped there for a second, stunned at her. She was wearing some low-cut blouse, and her hair was done up in rich, dark curls that tumbled over her shoulders. She'd done her eyes, and they seemed enormous, and she spun in front of the table, and David glanced away when she dipped, her breasts embarrassing him, but something in him, at the same time, saying, Oh my God.

"You look like a actress," Janie said as Rachel scooped her into her arms.

David almost grimaced at that, hoping it didn't ruin his mother's moment: Rachel *had* been an actress.

"*An* actress," Rachel corrected, and laughed, Rachel now very nervous, and they settled around the table.

They ordered hors d'oeuvres and made small talk, eating the hors d'oeuvres, and after a time, Janie joking, and David and Rachel laughing, Rachel glanced at her watch, the diamonds in it sparkling, and David thought, No way was he going to talk with Rachel about Buddy now, not here, and there wouldn't be a time later tonight and, grimacing, he thought he could stick tight with Simonson, take care of it that way.

He was thinking about all of that, and about Jarvis, and worrying that the Darvon and wine were too much—there seemed to be a kind of high hum in his head—and as he turned to tell Janie to put her napkin on her lap, he registered someone coming in the door.

He was backlit, in silhouette, a solidly built man with a squarish head, broad shouldered, but just then hesitant, even awkward somehow, and as he was striding toward the table, David was thinking, This isn't Jarvis, and then he was rising to shake hands with whoever it was, and he saw who it was, and something just broke in him, even though he tried to hammer the thing silent, it just hurt like hell, and he was trying not to let it get to him, but his eyes had—goddammit—glassed up anyway—it was the goddamn Darvon and wine—and here was his father, Max, reaching for Rachel, and then Janie, who'd come out from behind the table, and David was thinking, So nothing's changed, when Max, smelling of lime aftershave, had gathered just his mother and Janie to him, but then Max had his thick, heavy-wristed hand around David's waist, very nearly lifted him out from behind the table.

"Hey, hey, my babies!" he said, and David, torn in ten ways, hugged back with that part of himself that still could. And when all the fluster was over, and his mother had cleaned up her mascara, and she sat, Jesus, breathing heavily, and that blouse tight, so she bulged out, looking like, like Rita Hayworth or something, and Janie was looking between David and Max, she knew David too well, David nodded *yes* to Janie, and she let herself sit grinning, enjoying herself, and a waitress in a red dress, taking a cue from Max, nodded to someone in the kitchen, and platters of sizzling food were brought in, and David thought he wouldn't be able to breathe.

10

THROUGHOUT THE DINNER DAVID SMILED, REPLIED WHEN spoken to, and gave the appearance of enjoying himself. But he was watching. Taking it all in.

He'd seen Max's smile long enough to know he was genuinely happy now, laughing, and telling about his and Rachel's secret "dating" this last month.

He let other people talk now, though, which was different.

Still, David, even with Max holding back, could just sense it, how he was diminished by this man. David loved Max—he was, after all, his father. And Max *was* something, all right. Socially charming (he'd got the waitress eyeing him), successful, outgoing. He laughed loudly, expressed his enthusiasms, from Viking football to why Nixon was the one, again, with a conviction that naysayed all other opinions.

You couldn't breathe to think around the man, he was so certain of his world.

But now, after this fall, and the beaten-down feeling he'd gotten all September, David let himself be drawn into it, Max's world. Even allowed himself to remember better times, which came to him now, like strains of sad but lovely music.

"David, Max is asking you something," Rachel said.

"What?"

"I'm already going," Janie said, grinning with genuine enthusiasm.

"Where?"

"I got tickets to a Vikings game this weekend," Max said. "Right up near the press box." He winked. "Just used a little palm grease and . . . voilà!" He brandished the tickets over the table.

"We're all going," Rachel said. "I mean, if you want to go."

David said he'd like that, and Max flung his arm around David's shoulders and squeezed him, caught Janie in his other arm and did the same.

"Four Musketeers!" Janie said.

David laughed. But then he saw Max's mouth twitch—he didn't get it, her joke, he was going to correct her, David just knew he would, but now he didn't, he waited, and thought not to.

"Who are they playing?" David asked, before Max could let it out. It surprised David. Why had he done it? Saved Max from himself?

"Green Bay, at Memorial. Remember how we went to those games there?"

David did. Those were the happier years, which, with time, had become not so happy.

"You always wanted a Coke with ice, even when it was so damn cold," Max teased.

Janie was looking up with big eyes, left out, and David said, tousling her hair, "You'll like it—" and he almost said *Sport,* but he caught it in his mouth, and Janie blushed that he had caught it, and he said, "It's kind of like a circus."

Here, again, Max's mouth twitched, that touchy disapproval there. To him, football players were gods, the stats just proof of it. David felt no such thing, nor did Rachel, or Janie, but it seemed a good outing anyway. Safe. Outside. Away from the house and around people, where he could see if Max still had in him that *other* Max, the one who'd hit him in his bed nights.

And even as he was thinking that, the lights dimmed slightly, there was the thumping of a door opened from in back, and three waitresses strode to the table with a cake held high, singing

"Happy Birthday," candles blazing, setting it in front of Rachel, and David, shocked at himself, realized he'd forgotten entirely.

That Max only winked when he saw David's surprise, didn't twist something out of it, or jab, made David think maybe, maybe Max had changed.

"Make a wish," he said.

"A big wish!" Janie said.

"One for every one of your twenty-five years," Max said.

Rachel laughed—she hadn't been twenty-five for ten years—smiled at them all, then squeezed her eyes shut, this look of . . . *hope* on her face, and blew the candles out.

11

THE VIKINGS GAME FELL ON A DAY DRY AND WARM, ONE seemingly alive with some preternatural light. Max picked them up at the house in his new car, a Jaguar sedan, and they parked in back of the stadium, leaves rattling across the lot as they walked toward it, bundled in wool blankets and here the smell of tobacco, and barbecue, and the sound of an announcer echoing out into the lot, and all the color, the home-team fans in purple and white, and the Packer fans in green, and there was something beautiful in the moment, Rachel and Max up ahead, approaching the ticket taker at the fence, Max and Rachel laughing at something, and David behind with Janie, buying her a big, salt-dotted pretzel when he was sure Rachel wasn't looking. Janie liked salty things, and David rolled his eyes when she'd finished it before they even reached the gate, where David got a sick feeling for a moment, that this was all bullshit, the tickets—Max had had tickets to a North Stars hockey game one night, and there'd been this big argument at the gate, and they'd been sent away—but here they were inside now, and the stadium opening before them, enormous, all color and light, purples and whites on one side, greens and golds on the other, a dirigible going by overhead, a banner flapping behind, on it: *Wally McCarthy Oldsmobile*. In the air was the smell of brats and charcoal, perfumes and cologne. The announcer's voice echoed, so that it seemed to come from all directions, "And number eight-one, Carl Eller!" and there was a stamping of feet that shook the stadium, a cheer going up.

"You want to find our seats?" Max said, and with that familiar gesture, he cocked the ticket stubs at David, so that David did not reach for them, because, in the past, the joke had always been that Max, even as David did reach, had jerked things away.

But Max didn't do that now. He pressed them, almost a little sadly, into David's hand, and then he clapped David on the back and said, "Take 'em up. I'll be right back."

David looked at the tickets. They were prime center seats, better than Max had intimated they were, and David said, "Come on," and Rachel followed, Janie in hand behind her.

They got situated, put down the wool blankets, and Rachel took out field glasses.

"Want to look?" she said.

"Let me see!" Janie said, and David handed the field glasses over.

"What are you seein' there, Sport?"

"Nothin'," she said, but with a certain defensive something in it, so David nodded and took the glasses. He looked where Janie had been looking.

Max was arguing with a guy in a peaked cap at the concessions stand. David put the glasses down.

Money. It was always money that got Max started. He'd never known what all had gotten crossed up between Max and Rachel, who was looking off in the other direction, but there'd been arguments about money. Lots of them, and bitter. Though even David had known that it hadn't been about the money really, but something . . . *some*thing even Bobby, his uncle, couldn't tell him.

A punter was on the field, practicing kicks. Then a girl squeezed by, in the aisle ahead, and David's heart clenched, pretty girls always did that, and this one was very, very pretty, and as she moved away, this green-eyed, auburn-haired girl in her navy pea-coat, she shot a glance back at him, and he smiled like a complete idiot, his face instantly hot, and this shrinking, and compulsion at the same time, to stand, even to say something as stupid as, Has anyone told you how beautiful you are?

"Boy, she sure gave you a look, didn't she?" Rachel said, and poked him. "She was really something, wasn't she?"

David felt his face do this stupid thing it always seemed to do. It was like some idiot pushed out of him, contorting his face, everything that was silly and embarrassing in it.

Even being out with Max couldn't suppress it.

"Your face is all red," Janie said, as if stating some arcane fact. "You look all googly."

"Googly?" Rachel said. "I think he looks handsome. Don't you?"

"Googly," David said.

"Right," Janie said, confirming this as fact. "Goofy and wiggly."

David and Rachel laughed, Max coming toward them now with an armload of concession stuff.

"The stinker down there tried to tell me I gave him a ten when I—"

Rachel gave Max a bland look. He almost shook himself, then let go a deep breath, and smiled.

"Hey, Team," he said, and handed Janie a cardboard carrier of hot chocolate, which she passed to David, and so on, until they were all sitting, cups of steaming cocoa in hand, and there was all that ballyhoo on the field, cheerleaders in red sequined outfits sparkling in the light, high-kicking on that saturated green AstroTurf, and Max, while Rachel was watching with the field glasses, gave David a wink, and with a quick dip of his hand, poured liquor into his hot cocoa, not much at all, and David grinned there, not sure what to do, but not wanting to ruin things, and then the game went on, and when they got more cocoa, to ward off the cold, Max gave David another shot, and he felt all dopey, and loved Max, in some bizarre way, and Janie and Rachel, he wasn't drunk or anything, just a little loopy, after all, and he'd taken toots out duck hunting with his uncle Bobby, just last year, and in the sun he felt he should be frightened, because Max had always been a kind of demon when he drank in the past, drank too much, that's when the punching and hitting had happened in the middle of the night, but it didn't matter now, because Max was laughing, and—*fun*, and Rachel was laughing, and Janie, too, and now and then the girl looked up at him, and his heart turned over slowly, and when the game was over, and they were filing out, the Vikings having won—which was something in itself, Fran Tarkenton had tossed some beauties—the girl passed right by him, she had the most beautiful eyes, and he looked right at her, and she turned her head over her shoulder to look back, and then she was gone in the crowd, and David out in the sun felt he wasn't sure what all, but he was feeling it all evening, through dinner at a pizza place, and even when Max was dropping them off at the house in Edina.

Maybe Max was okay now? he thought.

Still, Rachel didn't ask him that evening, though David felt it was in the works, and it wasn't until the schnapps buzz had completely worn off, later, that he was left with this anxious, almost panicked feeling, though he felt, too, a bit the part of a coconspirator, but wasn't sure exactly how. The liquor was part of it, but wasn't it exactly.

And, after tossing in his bed for hours, he went down the hall to Janie's room and sat on the floor beside her, and staring into the dark, let his mind run, and what it ran to had happened in dark just like this, Max's fists hard as stones.

He'd promised himself never to forget, and he hadn't.

12

MAX WAS COURTING THEM NOW, NOT JUST RACHEL, BUT Janie and David, too. There was a picnic at Highland Park, just Janie and David and Max, and they'd thrown green Bank of America Frisbees after they'd eaten thick submarine sandwiches from Janie's favorite haunt, Mario's. They'd gone putt-putt golfing

at Cirell's one afternoon, too, just the three of them, Janie thrilled
at putting an eagle on the thirteenth hole, where you had to aim
through the spinning vanes of a windmill, and to the Science
Museum in St. Paul, where Max lectured almost incessantly at
each exhibit, first the reptiles, and then a demonstration of optics,
followed by a Van de Graaff generator, which had made Janie's
corn-silk hair stand up on her head like dandelion seed, and
finally, one day, all four of them, Max, Rachel, Janie, and David,
went down to Lake Calhoun, just off Highway 7 and Hennepin,
the day beautiful and warm, and they'd sat onshore and watched
the sailboats and a number of canoeists skim over the lake until
rose-colored dusk called those canoeists in, gliding on the glassy,
still water, and Max reclined on the quilt with them onshore,
telling how he'd almost been AWOL once in the army, because
he'd gotten on the wrong bus in Manila—"I took the Portola bus,
instead of Ruell, just wasn't paying attention," he said, making a
dumb-guy face—and Janie and Rachel laughed, and Max poked
David, who laughed, too, but was mulling over how, years ago,
this was the kind of story Max never would have told about himself, and sat back, the low sun in his eyes.

And in that spirit, Rachel had looked at David, and then at
Janie, something suddenly serious in it, something Max was not to
see, and didn't, and in her look was a world of things: Is this all
right? Will you forgive me if I'm wrong? Is there anything here I'm
not seeing? That you've seen? And she turned slowly to David,
and they shared a very somber, flat look, and David almost imper-
ceptibly nodded, it's up to you, and Rachel tossed her head back,
and spun around, laughing again, and said to Max, "Come over
to the house, come over for dinner."

"I'd love to," he said, and David felt for the man, could really
see how Max felt, Max clearing his throat, and coughing, what he
felt right there. Choking him.

Come over to the house.

———

But if coming over to the house was a good thing for Max, it gave
David nightmares. He woke time and again in a sweat, reliving the

pummelings he'd suffered those nights Max had stumbled in late, when Rachel hadn't come home, and suffered all over again those things he'd said. *You'll never amount to anything. You're good for nothing, you lazy goldbricker. You're ugly. Anyone ever tell you that? What the hell are you always standing there with your hands in your goddamn pockets for?* Max had shouted, and even though David balled up in his bed, and faced the wall, Max had turned him over and hit him in the stomach.

This was the Max that haunted David. And in school, he was falling into himself, as though he were looking out of a cave, a feeling that scared the hell out of him, because he worried, with an icy fear, he might fall into himself entirely.

Which made it worse. This fear of himself. Of feeling like he was watching himself. Which he did now. Over lunch, with the Chess Club, discussing opening strategies, picking at his plate, tasting nothing, all the while his mind on Max, feeling again those jabs to his ribs, and hearing what he'd said.

Through all of it, watching himself, as was Buddy now, too. Buddy, who winked at him in the hallways, and made cryptic, suggestive threats, the worst of which had been, "You're gonna have a crowd to see it, Geist. Count on it."

13

THE EVENING MAX WAS TO COME TO DINNER, DAVID CUT practice to be home early, where he found Janie in the kitchen, near hysteria. She'd gotten it into her head to bake a cake, because Rachel had meant to and hadn't had time, and even as David came through the door, he could smell an almost nauseating sweet something burning, and could hear Janie jabbering to herself in the kitchen, "Oh, *why* did it do that? *What* was it that was *too* much?" and when he rounded the door into the kitchen he saw the mess, cream-colored cake batter all over the wall behind the stove, the mixer upended, and the oven covered with Janie's prints in yellow batter, and the cake, in the oven, rising over the side of the pan she'd put it in, the batter smoking and burning, and Janie turned to David, her face bunching up, and said, "I was just *trying*—"

And there she began to sob, and David swept her into his arms and held her.

"Come on, Sport," he said, but something caught in him, and he was sobbing, and couldn't stop, even though it really hurt, until he realized he was scaring Janie, and he held her away, and they looked at each other.

"I think he's a . . . *fuckhead*," Janie said, shocking David with it.

"You don't know that," David said. "And besides, I'm the one who said it, and you don't know him. Not really." He wanted to say to her, Don't *ever* say that, not even around me, but this wasn't the time to get into it.

"I see the way you look at him."

David had to turn away. "It'll be all right."

"But it's *not* all right."

"Janie, he's not like he was."

"He did something to you, I know it," Janie said.

David set his hand on the table. "We'll clean this mess up. We've got an hour until Mom gets home. She'll never see it."

Janie's face got long, and David's heart ached to see her smile.

"Come here," he said.

"No! I won't," Janie said.

"Why?"

"Because I'm scared."

"Come here, Sport," David said. Then he nearly whispered. "Come on."

She didn't move, only stood looking off toward the oven, and David went over to her and got down on one knee, and he pulled her into his arms, Janie resisting him at first, then laying her head on his shoulder.

"I told you once, and I'll tell you again. I'm gonna watch out for you."

"How?" she said.

And something came to David unbidden, something he was to

recall many times, not long from then. I will protect you with my very life, he thought, but what he said was, so as not to frighten her, "Whatever it takes, Sport."

And *that* he remembered later, too.

14

THEY MADE QUICK WORK OF THE KITCHEN, OPENED THE windows and aired out the burned smell, and David got another cake together, from scratch, a one-bowl deal, and in the pans and baking before Rachel had even gotten home, Rachel coming through the door in something new, something David immediately recognized as silk, when she took off her coat, silk the color of water, and Rachel smelling of something wonderful, something like distilled violets in it, and the smell made him think of spring, and Janie was yakking up the cake, all she and David had to do was take it out and frost it.

Which they did, while Rachel got freshened up in the bathroom.

She set the table with china they hadn't used in years, and when that was done, Rachel did something with David's hair.

"You need to get it cut," she said, but then smiled. "I'm just nervous," she said.

In the past, Max had always been late, and they sat at the table, seven o'clock now.

"Well," Rachel said.

David drummed his fingers on the tabletop. Here was this last moment, before Max came into the house, and Rachel was smiling bravely, it seemed to David, or was it hopefully? And what about her life before Max, David wondered, did she want that still? Was something of that other life still there, or had it died altogether?

And now they interrupted each other, as if they had some pressing unfinished business between them, Janie saying, "Hey, Mom, when is the long weekend?" and David replying, "NEA, that teachers' thing?"

"No," Rachel said, "Thanksgiving."

"No, before that," Janie said.

But it was all just nerves.

15

THE DOORBELL RANG, AND THEY SAT FOR A SECOND, AS IF stunned still—what faces should they wear? What roles should they play? And David saw that his mother had, maybe, more than anything, wanted to stop acting, at least at home, and when he saw her stand, knowing what was in it, some of it, and not wanting to know the rest, saw the dignity in her, he stood also, but then the moment changed when Max began to bang on the door and alternately ring the bell.

"Hey, come on, open up," he was nearly shouting through the door.

Rachel's eyes narrowed, disapproving.

"Hey, open up!" Max shouted.

Rachel, with David and Janie behind her, bent to swing the door open.

What they saw there was not Max, but boxes in fancy green-and-blue foil wrapping paper, Max's fingers gripping the largest two on the bottom, both white.

"Pizza Man!" Max said, his voice coming muffled through the boxes.

Rachel and David and Janie laughed. David got the storm door swung open and Max wobbled through with the boxes, balancing them, and Rachel took one box after another off the stack.

"What is all this?" she said.

"David and I like pepperoni, you don't," Max said. "Janie likes Canadian bacon and pineapple." Max kissed Rachel and then added, "And chopped garlic on yours, extra black olives, and let's see . . ."

"Mushrooms," Rachel said.

"Lot's of 'em," Max said, and slipped off his raincoat, under it a new suit, pin-striped and blue, and he pulled at his tie, removing it, and tossed his coat over a chair, and they all went into the small, warm kitchen.

Max cut the pizzas with a circular cutter, his fingers thick, and hair on his knuckles, and his shirtsleeves rolled up, and some sauce squirted on his shirt, and he looked down at it, at his obviously very expensive shirt, and he grinned, and said, "That's one for the dry cleaner!"

This, David thought, was *not* the old Max. Nor was the pizza. And even a torte, some fancy French thing, and two bottles of imported beer, which, when Max pulled them from the last box, had Rachel frowning, and Max popped the caps, handed one to David.

"Come on," he said, "Buddy here wants one. And anyway, he's gotta take the edge off his war wound. What'd you do there that you're limpin' like that?"

David turned the cold bottle of beer in his hands. He laughed to himself. *Buddy.*

"You know, cross-country. The ground's uneven."

"You fast?"

"I'm okay," David said.

Rachel was going to say something, something specific about exactly how *okay* he was, but David smiled a warning smile at her, which she understood. She was not to let Max into that part of his life. He wouldn't forgive her if she did.

"Is there something I don't know?" Max said.

There was, around the table, an uneasy silence, which, in seconds, grew into a whole world of unsaid things, so that it became a veritable white-hot hum.

"I got a part in the school play," Janie said, smiling, and David was shocked at it.

It was a lie, and he felt himself sweating, even as Janie went on about her part, and what surprised him was this: She was a pretty good little liar, using all the details from the part she'd lost, and cried over, to make it real. Still, David felt something warm but uneasy in his middle, and he was about to stop it all, when Rachel asked, "Was that the one you needed the costume for?"

"Nope."

"That's great," Max said. "Can I come?"

Again, a strained silence fell over the table.

"It's just for people in the class," Janie said.

Now Max caught on to the lie, but thought that the lie was—they hadn't thought he'd *want* to see the play, so hadn't bothered to tell him about it. He almost bitterly bit on his piece of pizza.

"Hey," he said. "I've got a—"

He was going to say *surprise*. Rachel smiled at Max. Not now, whatever it was, that look said, and David's heart banged up against his ribs, thinking they were going to spring it on them, right here, that Max would be moving back in, or whatever.

Why otherwise the boxes with who knew what was in them?

"Okay," Max said, and passed a wrapped package to Janie, then one to David.

"What is it?" Janie said, and Max replied, "Well, open it and find out. I mean, this is just-for-fun stuff, okay?"

Janie tore the wrapping off the package. She loved tearing into things, and even forgot herself now, forgot her reservations around Max.

She lifted up what, it wasn't obvious at first. It was a plastic bag filled with what looked to be hairy marbles, green and blue, and red and yellow, some a nondescript tan. Janie did not look up from the table, but her face went through a transformation—surprise, disappointment, then hurt—and even as this was happening, and David was thinking, Goddammit, Max got up and went to the sink and was back at the table with a glass of water.

He winked at Janie. David almost wondered if there might be something sadistic in his father—he'd always done this, shocked people, his humor was like that. In a restaurant, when a waiter would say, And how was your meal, he'd put on a serious face and say, Awful, just awful, and just when the waiter, or waitress, was about to deal with the problem, Max would flash that All-American Boy smile, and laugh, ha-ha! and the waiter, or waitress, would smile uneasily and laugh, too. And Max would say, all cheer and goodwill, Just kidding!

"Janie, here, look," Max said. "Open the package."

"I'll just put them in my room," she said, certain now he'd given her turds of some kind as a joke.

"Go ahead—" David said, and again, caught himself before it came out of his mouth—*Sport*. "Open it, Janie."

Janie reluctantly tore the top of the bag off, holding it away from her face.

"They smell funny."

"Take one out, that blue-and-green one," Max said.

"*You* take it out."

David raised an eyebrow at her, and Janie dipped her hand into the bag and took one of the blue-and-green balls out, uneasy.

Max slid the big glass of water over in front of her plate, and Janie looked up at him.

"Plop, kiddo!" he said. "Drop it right in there."

Again, Janie looked over at David and he nodded.

"What is it, Max?" Rachel asked. She'd been quiet all this time. "It won't explode, will it?"

"Nah," he said. "Come on, drop it in."

Janie dutifully dropped the ball into the glass, averting her head suddenly, holding her hands over her face, and when there was no explosion, she peeked through her fingers.

Then removed her hands from her face entirely.

The ball had settled to the bottom of the glass, and now some transformation was taking place, green strands springing from it, which became palm trees, and then the ball flattened into a disk, part of it yellow, a beach, and on the beach was a sea turtle, and Janie's eyes now were wide, and staring, and David just then forgave his father all kinds of things, because he had brought something wonderful back to them. Magic.

Max, at his best, did that: Look at this leaf, he might say. See the veins in it? How they branch out? Now, an older leaf, like this gingko here, this is central venate. There's sexes to these trees, too, did you know that?

Rachel bent closer, to look into the glass. "Where'd you get them, Max?"

"That Chinese place," David answered, glancing over at Max, "where they had the magic tricks and swords and beads and all that. Over on Portland. Right?"

"You remember that?" Max said. "You couldn't've been more than three or so the last—"

"I remember," David said. And then, even shocking himself, he said, "I remember *everything*," sounding so ominous, he had to joke, "You gonna ride that turtle there, Janie?"

"And they're all different?" Janie asked.

"Well, of course, kiddo," Max shot back, "they're all different colors. Can't you see that?"

David felt a flare of anger in himself. His father could bring it out in him, just like this; still, he gave in to it now, his voice sharp.

"It was a rhetorical question, Max," David said. "She was asking for confirmation, that's all, and you didn't understand her."

Max let out a short, angry exhalation, then smiled affably.

"Sure, Janie," he said, and winked at her. "Each one's something different. Go ahead, guess. Wait, the three of you guess. Think *color*."

And they did that, laughing, and dropping the balls in water. And just then, it was all—once more—

Magic.

16

"OKAY, HOW ABOUT YOUR BOX THERE," MAX SAID, AFTER A time had passed.

David still wasn't sure he wanted to open it. He sat looking into the window, at their reflection there, even as Rachel reached over to squeeze his shoulder.

"All right, all right," he said, and he tore at the butcher paper Max had used to wrap whatever it was, and Janie and Rachel were leaning in as David tore off the last layer of it, another joke of Max's, and here some fancy shiny blue paper, under the butcher paper, and David tore that away, and in his hands was a dark green box, eight or ten inches long, a logo on the top, a man in a canoe, drawing back a paddle.

David took off the lid. Inside the box, against a blue velvet lining, lay a knife, double-edged, in an elaborate leather sheath, one that could be hung from a belt, or strapped to a calf, the knife jewel-like. Set in the end of the handle was a thick glass bubble, a compass.

David lifted the knife out of the case. It was a fillet knife, but it was so shiny, and so sharp, there was something dangerous in it.

It was a Svea, a Swedish knife, the best, and David knew exactly what it had cost—a small fortune. He'd seen them more than a few times in sports shops. His uncle Bobby had carried one of them overseas, claimed it had saved his life.

David was shocked at the gift. Always, his father had bought them the cheapest things, and he'd dreaded shopping with his father, because when he did, he came home in off-brand shoes, off-color clothes, the bottom rack, always, even though Max, doing the kind of work he did, made what David could only guess at.

David didn't know what to say. But Rachel did.

"You've got to give him a coin, David," she said, "or a knife as a gift is bad luck."

David reached into his pocket and felt a hot swelling in his face. He had nothing in his pockets.

"How about a dollar?"

Max laughed. He was a walks-under-ladders kind of guy. No superstition for Max.

"No, really," Rachel said.

"Come on, honey," Max said, "you don't honestly believe in all that nonsense, do you?"

Rachel reached behind her, opened the junk drawer in the phone nook, and got out pennies from the tin mint container there. She handed the pennies to David.

"Give one to Max," she said, and Max put out his hand, grimacing in humor, and David handed a penny across the table, and then held a couple out to Janie, and to Rachel, and put the last penny in his pocket.

Something in the back of his mind told him, though, the coins had to be his, so the luck was bad on the knife, and he feared it a little, and then he thought, What a load of superstitious bullshit, yet when a gust of wind pummeled the kitchen window, rattling it, he startled.

"Can I do another *beach ball*?" Janie said.

David and Rachel laughed, but not Max. The three balls Janie'd dropped in had each had some kind of water, some tiny beach area.

"Sweetie," Max said, "I told you, they're all *different*."

"It was a *joke*," David said.

"What's funny about that?"

"It's a pun, hon," Rachel said, and lifting her eyebrows, made a *Get it?* face.

She stood now, brought over the cake David and Janie had made.

"Max insisted," she said. "When I told him you two had gone to the trouble to make it."

"That's right," Max said. "I wanted to see what the *two sisters* could bake up," he said, his joke a slap in David's face, Max retaliating for David's having pointed out that what Janie'd said was a joke, though even as he said it, Max was reaching across the table to tousle David's hair the way David did Janie's, saying, "I'm just pulling your leg! You're gonna be bachin' it pretty soon, and hell, anybody'd rather eat stuff that tastes good. Right? Hey, the cake looks like a million bucks."

"It's beautiful, David," Rachel said.

The cake was not beautiful. The icing was slightly lumpy, because there had been lumps in the powdered sugar they'd used. And lumps in the cocoa. The icing had pulled the cake surface up, and so it had gotten bits in it, and it all looked badly homemade, David thought, with the glossy torte Max had brought at the end of the table to compare it to.

"Hey, pretty good for a box cake," Max said.

Rachel smiled, but it was strained. She didn't think Max's jab at David was funny at all, and Max saw this, or, rather, that she was irritated with him. He realized he'd made yet another faux pas and, meaning to extricate himself from it, smiled and told them about this new and clueless receptionist at work. A *guy*, of all things, he said, making a swishy gesture with his hand, who'd put one of those weird little cactuses on his desk, the kind with the fleshy-colored top part that they grafted on, as if the goddamn thing were a flower because it was orange.

"What's a guy messing with flowers for, anyway?" he said, and no one at the table answered.

It took Max a second to realize that he had dug himself in still further, by saying what he had. "I mean, seriously," Max said, "plastic flowers look more real than that thing."

"But they're *not* real," David said.

"What's the difference? They *look* more real, and you don't have to water the dumb things."

Rachel set her hand on Max's forearm, and he caught himself there. He'd been about to give one of his lectures. Make things even worse.

This, right here, David thought, was the old Max. Force equals mass times acceleration, P-V equals N-R-T. Max's world worked according to physical laws, the laws of entropy, and conservation of energy and mass, and mechanical and biomechanical laws, all of them infinitely complex, but this man was clueless, sort of, to the human equation. *People* Max just didn't get most of the time.

Dumb as dog shit, David thought. Asshole.

He was thinking this, realizing his anger polarized his thinking, put him in a snit, which was nothing compared to the rage he felt, if he let himself feel it, which he began to, and he began to think, for Janie, and for Rachel, he'd do it right here, tell them who Max really was, and what he'd done, take the goddamn knife Max had just given him, and give Max some of it back, if that's what he wanted, when Janie jumped up, ran her fork into her cake frosting, and made a mustache with it over her lip. A chocolate-frosting mustache.

Janie smiled, her teeth looking all the more white for the frosting.

She looked ridiculous.

David and Rachel and Max all looked at her glumly, and then they began to laugh, and laugh so hard, they could barely stand it, and Rachel grabbed a hunk of the cake and mashed it into Max's face, so his eyes were white in the brown frosting, and he mashed frosting back in her face, and Janie in David's, all of them digging into the cake, tossing it, and they all reared back, laughing, and Janie jabbed her hand into the expensive torte, and there was this stunned silence, and then a roar of laughter, and they were throwing the torte at one another, and eating it at the same time, David jumping up from the table and throwing a chunk at Max, and Max, laughing, hurling a chunk back, and Rachel, swallowing the wrong way, began to choke, laughing so hard she couldn't stop, and there was this little circus, Max getting behind her and whacking her once, and that fixed it, but since he couldn't see her face, he struck her again, which got a whoop out of her, and they all burst out laughing again, until they sat, dumbly at the table, breathing deeply, and Max's eyes got glassy in all that frosting on his face, and he said, "God, I've missed you all," and Rachel pointed at him, and they all laughed again, hysterical, pointing at one another, and the mess in the kitchen, and laughed, and laughed.

17

THERE WERE TWO MORE DINNERS, THESE OUT AT RESTAU-rants, and they somehow or other navigated a Max abyss now and then, but the man, it seemed, had learned to laugh at himself, and that made a difference. Max still did not stay at the house, not so much as one night, and Rachel did not stay out, either.

Not all night, anyway. She was back at twelve, or one, but no later.

Rachel hummed to herself when she cooked now, and she had more time, and they sat nights at the dinner table, the dark coming on, and it was warm and light in the house, and they ate, joking, and Max entered their conversations, and they laughed at some of the things he said, but not meanly now, but as if the man were some clown suitor, but not really, this man who said the wrong things *and* the right things, both, and David didn't think much of those years earlier, though they were very much still there.

As was Buddy, who was not about to leave well-enough alone.

No. There was something really *wrong* with Buddy. He wasn't, after all, just a bully, though, being who he was, a Hornet lineman, made what was wrong with him somehow acceptable.

Buddy, David had discovered when he'd asked his older teammates about him, was the stuff of entertaining legend. All his older teammates, if asked, could tell some story about him.

That Buddy, who worked at the Edina Country Club, had one night, for a joke, jacked off in the cole slaw, and got a laugh out of seeing people eat the stuff, all the football guys there to see it. And another night, Buddy had caught a cat, put it in a burlap bag, and beaten it to death on a post. This at some party down by the Mississippi River.

More than a few people had seen him do it.

So, knowing this, David didn't take walking home lightly, since Buddy was lurking out there, and on days he knew he'd miss the late bus now, he had Rachel pick him up.

Today, though, she'd forgotten, again—he worried about why she might do that—and he tried to walk home calmly, but then, even with his hard-soled shoes, he ran, the entire four miles to the house, thinking he'd have to tell not just Rachel about Buddy now, but the police, too, which would brand him as spineless for the duration of his years at Morningside.

Small. A *small* person.

And he resisted that, thinking maybe Simonson and his teammates could help him. Or Coach. But in the house, and over dinner, Rachel was silent again, which put all those thoughts out of his head.

Here it had to be something about Max, something—

But neither David nor Janie could make sense of it, Rachel's mood, this sad, happy, excited, worried something in her. And she surprised them when she asked now, "What would you say to a vacation?"

David sat back, surprised. "Where?"

"The Boundary Waters."

"You mean this summer," David said.

"No, next week."

David shook his head, in him this shocked confusion. But—still. The Boundary Waters!

They had talked about making the trip for years, the three of them, the trip being a kind of dream thing they embroidered on. The Boundary Waters were a place Rachel had spent summers in her teens, when her father, Ben, had owned a cabin there. David had been up many times with his uncle Bobby since Rachel and Max had separated, and each had been a kind of resurrection for him, so much so he rarely talked about it, preferring to keep it to himself.

So it was a place *inside* him, as much as a geographical place, and whatever was alive in the world, and in him, was there, something of that quiet when he ran, but in the Boundary Waters it was a place. A *real* place. Just quiet, and water, and island after island, moss and lichen covered, and bald eagles in the pines, or soaring, one so closely David had heard the wind in its wings.

He had a big meet on Wednesday, but after that?

"Okay, what's the deal?" David asked.

"Ten days," Rachel said. "Leave on Thursday, back on Saturday or Sunday the following week."

Janie was all excitement—she'd never been, and wanted to go now after all David had told her about it. Her eyes were glassy with excitement, but David felt some awful turning in his stomach, sensing what was coming.

"It'd be with Max," Rachel said. "I can't get off work, but he's arranged the whole thing. He got you out of school, Janie, and you too, David. There'd just be a little make-up work when you get home. All you'd have to do is be ready Thursday."

"What about gear?" David said.

"Max said he'd take care of everything."

Max, David thought to himself, hadn't so much as slept in the backyard in the tent David had had, when he'd done that in his boyhood. Why go somewhere else, Max had said, when everything's here, in the Cities? And besides, he'd said, *people like us don't camp*. The way he'd said it had prevented David from asking why.

At the table now, David felt, more than thought, ten reasons not to go, but with Janie giving him that please-please-please-*please* look, he kept his mouth shut.

"Just think about it," Rachel said. "Okay?"

David nodded, Janie glancing shyly between them, and then, thinking to say something pathetic, or manipulative, or outright whiny, Janie bent over her plate, but said not word one.

For David. And it touched him.

18

HOURS LATER AT HIS DESK, READING ABOUT MITOCHONDRIA and vacuoles in paramecium, but distracted, wondering whether he and Janie should go or not, he closed his book, then went outside and sat on the stoop.

He knocked a cigarette from his pack, and when he heard the door open behind him, he knocked a second out, and Rachel sat beside him, dressed in her black slacks and green shirt with the orchids on it. The clouds had thinned and the moon came out.

"David," Rachel said. "I want to explain something."

"He's already asked you, hasn't he?" David said.

Rachel let go a plume of smoke in the damp, chill air, the moon riding in the trees across from them.

"Yes," she said.

"And this is like a test or something, some—"

"No."

"No? How?"

Rachel lifted her head, looking off into the dark and thinking what David couldn't tell.

"I'm not asking you to do it for *me*," Rachel said. "I want to hear it from *you*—and Janie."

"That almost makes it worse," David said.

"You love it up there."

"That's true."

There was a long silence, and they smoked, each thinking what the other didn't know.

"I'm sorry it was hard back then," Rachel said. "I really am."

David felt something in himself get colder, distance himself from it, as if he were at the scene of some accident.

"Max is good with Janie," Rachel said.

That David gave assent to. They *were* good together. Janie could jerk Max's chain, bring out the Max David did love. There was the asshole Max, and then there was the Max who went out of his way to help people, had traveled all over, told funny stories, and had been some football hero in high school, a tight end, a runner like David.

David could never, honestly, go all one direction or the other with Max. But he couldn't forgive him, either. And he couldn't speak it: *Max beat the fucking shit out of me years ago.*

He wouldn't say it. And the strange thing was, even now, if Max were to say just two words, and mean them, David would let it go. Just two words. *I'm . . . sorry.*

But Max had had a hundred opportunities this last month, and he hadn't.

And there sprung up in David this . . . childish hope, he thought. Maybe, out alone—up there, in the Boundary Waters— he could *talk* to Max. Maybe that's what the man meant to do, was asking for. A chance. Just that. Maybe there never had been the right time to talk. And then he thought of Janie.

He wanted Janie to see it up there, when it was still magic. Just be in it, not think about it. He wanted to give it to her, as a gift.

And suddenly he felt happier. Decided.

"All right," he said, standing and brushing down his pants, and Rachel set her forehead against her palm, the cigarette cocked at a dejected angle, and it occurred to David that she thought he had refused.

"I mean," he said, "all right, I'll do it, okay?"

Rachel smiled up at him, and he reached for her hand and gave her a lift up, and suddenly she was . . . girlish, nervous.

"You will?"

David told her, yes, he'd said he would, she could call Max. And inside, even as he got ready for bed, he could hear her on the phone, and there was this feeling in the house as if he'd done the right thing—he thought he'd done the right thing—and he went in to see if Janie was asleep, and she looked up at him out of the dark, her eyes big and glassy, and disappointed.

"We're goin', Sport," David said, and even in the dark he could make out her smile.

It was the kind of smile some people'd give their lives to have flashed at them, the whole world in it, and a love, and joy, that lit him from inside.

"See ya in the morning, Sport."

"Davey?"

"What, kiddo?"

He waited a moment, but she just stared out of the dark at him, and he shut off the hall light behind him and went into his room, and there slept, caught in dreams of great light and darkness.

Mettle

19

EVERYTHING THE WEEK THEY WERE TO LEAVE FOR THE Boundary Waters bode well for a spectacular trip. There was high pressure holding, and the air was dry, and sharp, and chill. Rachel was in great spirits, but as the day approached for David and Janie to leave, she was, for moments, quietly apprehensive, even struck dumb and immobile, and then her face would change, and she might smile and laugh, like she did now, at the table, eating dinner early so she could take David over to Hoigaard's, a sporting goods store, on Highway 100, where he could pick up some last things.

Rachel craned her head around the window frame to glance outside, as if the weather alone was assurance of all that weighed on them.

"You couldn't ask for better weather," she said, nodding at Janie, who smiled bravely, David winking at her and poking her under the table, so that she kicked him, and hard, but then they bent over their plates again, and there was something, David thought, *bittersweet* in the moment, Max most likely moving back in after the trip, and maybe this chapter of their lives over, and not one of them saying it, that they'd stood by one another, Rachel working longer hours to keep the house, and David cooking, and Janie cleaning up and joking, and joking, and joking, dear Janie, and they still would, after Max moved back in, look after one another, but it would be different.

So it was with some reluctance that David stood and took the dishes to the sink, and setting them in the stainless-steel basin, he wiped his hands dry.

"You ready to go, Janie? Mom?" he said, and in moments they were out of the house.

In his room again that night, and Janie and Rachel asleep, he went over the things he'd bought at Hoigaard's. Lay them on his bed, one at a time, making sure he hadn't forgotten anything.

Checked off the list he'd made.

"Cold-weather survival you want fat," his uncle Bobby had taught him. "Fat and protein. Ounce for ounce you get five times the cals and slow burn. It'll save your hide. Don't go for the lean jerky if you buy it as survival food."

So, ten packs of greasy jerky. Check.

And a space blanket, in case something went wrong with the tent. Check. Iodine tablets for the water. Check. A Marbles water-proof match container and self-striking matches. He screwed the lid off, looked inside. Fifteen matches, all with white-sulfur heads. Check.

Flint and steel in a thin plastic container. Duofold long-sleeved undershirt, and a second for Janie, who tended to get cold. The cotton on the inside, he knew, worked as a wick, and the wool outer layer kept you warm even when the suit was wet. First-aid kit, with Betadine and yards of flat pressed gauze. Powdered sucrose in packets of grape HI/HO drink mix.

"You lose ninety percent of your body heat through your hands and feet and head, but most of all your head," Bobby'd taught him, "so always bring a hat and gloves."

So David had bought a nylon shell with a hood for himself, and one for Janie. They were orange, nearly glowed there on the bed, cheap hunting rigs—Janie would hate wearing hers—but they would do the job in a pinch. Compass? It was in the knife. Maps? Max had them. Ground pad? Closed cell, so he could kneel on it, paddling, and a shorty, only forty inches, for Janie.

He went over all of it, touching each piece of survival gear.

20

JUST AFTER ONE, WHEN HE WAS SURE THERE WAS NOTHING he'd forgotten, he slipped on his jacket and went outside and sat on the stoop. It was chilly out, and he lit a cigarette, eyeing the moon.

Then he heard the door open behind him and Rachel was sitting beside him. He motioned with the pack.

They smoked there, the moon rising over the trees.

"I'm not *making* you do this?" Rachel asked.

David didn't say anything at first, because he couldn't.

"It's different," he said. "And anyway, he's different."

Rachel set her chin in her palms, her elbows on her knees.

"Will you do something for me?"

"Yes," David said. "I'll look after Janie."

"No," Rachel said. "That's not it. I know you will." She paused, letting go a tired breath. "Just *give him a chance,* all right? Could you do that? For me? *Promise* to?"

David blew off a plume of smoke in the chill air, and nodded. "All right," he said. "Promise."

And Rachel crushed her cigarette on the stoop, and got up, and cupping David's head, David feeling himself go tense at her touch, she kissed him, on his cheek, as she hadn't since he was a boy and none of it had happened.

"Good night, David," she said, and went inside.

He heard the door shut behind him, and then Janie and Rachel's muffled voices moved away into the back of the house, Janie unable to sleep again. Somewhere up the block, in one of the neighbors' yards, a dog barked.

That small, frightened person inside him was watching again, and a voice said in him, You could still say something, call the whole thing off, not go, and he said to himself, alone there on the stoop, "Ah, go to hell."

And like that, he lit another cigarette, and sat in the dark, thinking nothing really, just this important moment here, this juncture in his life *waiting* for him. Again.

Out there.

21

THAT NIGHT, *OUT THERE*, INNUMERABLE THINGS WERE HAPpening. Invisible lines of fate, and time, and circumstance were being drawn. A President was ordering surveillance that would later bring about his demise and public humiliation. At a then unnoteworthy university, student protesters were planning a march that would claim that institution's place in history.

Approaching an intersection, the light long gone yellow, a boy named Chip, double dating, his tougher buddy in back with his girl, would decide to push the yellow—while the speeding drunk approaching the light ninety degrees from him wouldn't see the light at all, or even know he'd hit something, until moments after.

In downtown Minneapolis, an older woman, having seen the look on the girl living in the apartment across from her as the girl walked up Nicollet hours earlier, decided that night to bring over a cup of tea, just worthless Lipton's, in a blue willow cup, and the girl, seeing the woman there, in her door, and the cup, asked her in, and all that she'd planned, writing the note, and using the gas oven, she dismissed, and the day following, thinking about it, she decided that wasn't what she wanted after all.

And, too, that evening, a canary, escaping its cage, darted out a second-story window, free, but into Minnesota October air, and was seen flying by children miles distant, near a laundry vent, where it tried to stay warm, and the children caught the canary in a wooden apple basket and brought it into the house, and the children's mother, seeing how the canary was shaking, put it in a shoe box under a light, and the oldest of the children, a girl, so entranced with caring for the bird that evening, holding it, the feathers so dry, and light, and the bird so gemlike to her, so golden, that *somewhere* in her, there was this deciding that her life would be about birds, and so it was.

In a tavern on Highway 61, at the south end of the Twin

Cities, two men, out drinking for the evening, laughed about their troubled relations with their exes, and the younger joked about an easy solution to alimony, and the older of the two put on a serious face, said, Don't even think it, you're way bigger than that, and for just a moment, the younger man, looking away, closed his eyes so tightly he saw stars, and his friend said, Don't even think about goin' down that road, drunk or sober.

I'll help you, all right?

And that night in Austin, Minnesota, just a hundred miles south of Minneapolis and David's well-to-do suburb of Edina, a whole cast of characters were caught up in a howling, dark wind, one that would soon become a killing storm.

Here, in Austin, this *other world*—with which David's was about to collide.

And tonight, at the heart of it, was a man named Jack Carpenter, who sat with his sister, Carol, in her double-wide at the dining-room table, while her boys watched television in their bedroom. Here, the trouble, as Jack understood it, was his sister's husband, Stacey Lawton, who was at the Mower County Jail, held these last few days on charges of assault and battery.

"He really needs your help on this one," Carol said, "more than I can say."

Now Jack lit a cigarette and turned to the living room to avoid Carol's penetrating eyes and what she was asking him to do: save her husband's job at Dysart, the meat-packing plant just five blocks east, to float their life in Austin.

But turning from her was little consolation.

Because in this *other* world it was everywhere, even in the living room, in the green plaid sofa, and La-Z-Boy recliner, the brown Naugahyde torn and the yellow foam bulging out, in the grimy path on the carpet leading into the kitchen:

Dysart.

Austin, a town of about twenty-one thousand, seemed all about Dysart, and butchering cattle, and all that went on there, and this Jack Carpenter gave it some thought, at the table with his sister, how he'd become snared in it.

Jack, who'd wanted to go up to the Twin Cities to study at

Dunwoody, a trade school, to be an electrician. Or, he'd dreamed, maybe college. Maybe.

Only he'd met his wife, Lena, at the end of high school, and she'd been expecting by April, and like his father before him, he'd taken on summer part-time work, and that way had held out against Dysart as long as he could, his high-school football buddies, one by one, succumbing to Dysart, and his pay so poor doing grounds work at the golf course he'd finally gone over to Dysart himself, and the overtime had paid so well, and he was young, and ignorant, and then they'd put him, since he was so "gol' darn smart," in some lower-management position, and they'd let him in on some of the secrets of the place, and he, not knowing this was all manipulation, he'd come to feel somewhat responsible for his old buddies, half the damned Austin High football team, it seemed.

And then there had come a second, and then third child, and there had been incremental wage increases, and bonuses, and then there'd come the influx of Mexicans from down south, and all his old buddies who were slackers, and had been pushing for the easier jobs, had begun asking Jack to *get* those jobs for them, begged him for them, and for job security, even with the bottle flu days they took off, and since these men, these former friends, had families, too, Jack had tried to help them, though at times they seemed beyond help, most of them like his idiot brother-in-law, Stacey, taking out twenty-five percent loans on fancy Camaros and Firebirds, the cars never paid off, and the cars repossessed, and these men buying even yet more expensive cars, now Corvettes, always "cherry," they said, but under their fiberglass skins the cars rattle buckets, and the loans for them taken out against the wishes of their now, for the most part, unattractive and overweight wives.

They worked as secretaries for the car companies in town, or insurance, and what all else, the women bored to tears, and bringing in nine-by-thirteen sheetcakes of Betty Crocker and Duncan Hines, and eating them, and looking like two-hundred-plus-pound bears, and their husbands chasing teenagers in the nearby college towns, Mankato, or Winona, claiming to be on overtime shifts, and asking Jack to cover for them, cover their jobs, extend a hand when they were drowning in debt and what all else he didn't want to think about, and in that way Jack, without having wanted to, had become invaluable to his once friends and teammates, especially now since the Mexicans were eating them alive, the Mexicans working like machines.

The Mexicans, they were the problem, weren't they? Jack thought. But no, he knew that wasn't so.

Jack, at first, had hated the fucking wetbacks because they made his life hell. They came up from California, or Texas, and they had families, too, some of them aliens, which made those men easier to deal with, but those who were not aliens were a real threat. They wanted a life here in the United States, even if it was in fucking Austin, and they wanted it bad. And they kept everyone's wages down. Shit wages were riches to them.

So he'd started to hate them, for the trouble they made for him, but then he'd started to hate his so-called friends, too.

Now, just this month, someone had threatened on the phone, his voice disguised, to kill him if he didn't keep certain people on shift, fire certain wetbacks.

When he hadn't, his car had been vandalized, and the kids at school began making things tough for his son and daughters. Still, Sundays this month, Jack had taken them with him to St. John's, where the majority of his Dysart coworkers sat in the pews around him, nursing hangovers, one of them having made the threat on the phone, he was sure, and their children eyeing John Jr., twelve, Lisa, ten, and Sally, six, meanly and with narrowed, angry eyes.

And even though at St. John's, perhaps, he felt his wife's absence the most, and got these suck-uppy looks from the other parishoners that reminded him all over again about his job at Dysart and how much he hated it, he attended weekly without fail.

Because in this place, for some reason, for Jack, God was here, more than any other place, and he prayed. He prayed for strength, and to be patient, and to have compassion. *Dear God,* he prayed—

As he did now, in his sister's, Carol's, double-wide. *Dear God, help me.*

Even knowing, for all his prayers, he'd received not many

answers, if any at all, and Lena still threatening to take the children, and making some progress now at Hazelton, in the Twin Cities, Dysart paying for it, and there was this awful irony in it: If she got clean and sober, he thought, she'd take the kids, he just knew it, if he didn't leave Dysart. And, well, if she tried to do that, he still loved her, you don't stop loving people because they got desperate and crazy with stress.

In some ways, it was worse that she didn't just hate his guts, so they could both get on with it. She'd written him a note last week, and it had hurt him.

> *Jack,*
> *I love you now as I always have. But*
> *what's happening I can't live with. It's*
> *not the drinking, but our lives. Can't*
> *you see it's just taking everything?*
> *And can't you see what it's done to*
> *you? You were such a kind boy, and*
> *what are you now? I don't blame you,*
> *who could? But when I'm done here,*
> *everything must change.*
>
> > *Lena*

Not *Love, Lena,* just *Lena. Such a kind boy,* he'd thought.

But if he wasn't kind, which God knew he'd almost been destroyed trying to be, what was he?

And now, here at his sister's table, turned so as not to have to look at her, he thought, for the umpteenth time, *I could leave. I could leave and just go anywhere.*

Take Lena and the kids.

He was thirty now, knew Dysart inside and out, but what else did he know? He could repair cars. That wasn't so bad. Or repair anything, and what about Dunwoody? It was still up there, in the Twin Cities, but then his head, always good with figures, calculated what he had looking at him: college for John Jr. in a few years, the kid was smart and Jack wouldn't let it get by John Jr., and where in God's name was *that* money going to come from?

And how to work it all out? A more expensive rental in the Twin Cities? A house he'd be tossing good money after bad into? And throw away his pension with Dysart? And what about all the dopes he was keeping on there, they'd all go down the toilet.

And moving? Just that? Finding a new school for the kids in some shitty part of the Twin Cities they could afford to rent in? And when was he going to figure all of it out? He was so god-damned tired after shift, he collapsed, night after night, in the living room, sleeping in his clothes on the davenport, and getting up like that mornings, to make coffee and see the kids were dressed and make sure they were on the bus, brushing the girls' hair, and making sure they had lunch, only then to mess with hotdish for them to eat for dinner, later, and then off to Dysart, and there was always overtime, which he was never paid for on salary, and now after all these years, it was beginning to wear worse than thin.

Could you come in, Jack? I know it's after eleven, but Carmody has some family business to attend to, Carmody's boy is in trouble again.

Not a kind man? What was he then?

"Violent," Lena had said. "Violent *isn't* strong, Jack. You were strong when I met you, kind and strong, but look at you now."

In the last year, he'd begun to act out at a nearby tavern. One night, someone told him with a sneering look that he was in Dysart's pocket.

This had struck Jack silent.

"Don't got nothin' to say?" this fattish lout who'd been Jack's star linebacker taunted. Tibbits. Jack had saved Tibbits his job earlier that year and had not told him, so as not to humiliate him.

"You got something to say to me," Jack replied, "you'd better say it so I can understand it."

And Jack's once-linebacker had obliged him, hit him, and Jack had broken the man's jaw, nose, and three ribs, and might have even killed him if he hadn't been pulled off by Carol's husband, Stacey, and two other once-teammates.

But even then it had been a turning point. After Jack had been released, and his name was in the paper, along with Tibbits's injuries, Lena had run.

Run right to Hazelton, where all kinds of shrinks were telling her what a bad man he was.

Or so he thought.

So when Carol called him up, alarmed that her husband, Stacey, had gotten into a brawl with some wetbacks and had nearly killed one, and would be charged with manslaughter if this Jesus Garcia died, he'd listened, he owed Stacey that much for Stacey's having helped pull him off Tibbits, and Carol weeping that, after all these years, they'd lose everything, and Jack had driven over, a sense of doom in him—his whole life at Dysart, and in Austin, laid bare before him, in all its killing difficulty.

———

"We weren't raised like this," Carol said to Jack now, and Jack, crushing out his cigarette in the black tray there, said, "No, we weren't. But Stacey was."

It shocked Carol that Jack would say it, but it needed saying.

"What if you got him out on bail?"

"What if I did?"

Carol knotted her hands in front of her. She'd been pretty once, still was, sort of, but there was that ashen something that got into people who worked for Dysart, and both she and Stacey did, Stacey, even after all these years, still down on the killing floor.

"Carol," Jack said, "*what* are we talking about here?"

And Carol only stared into her hands, silent, Jack waiting for her to ask what she really wanted, which was for him to put himself out for Stacey somehow. Which wouldn't have been too bad, but for Stacey's friend Penry being caught up in this mess.

Penry, who, with Stacey, and a third former teammate, had pulled Jack from Tibbits that night.

No, Stacey wasn't the real problem at all.

Jack had no doubt that Stacey himself hadn't done much damage to the wetback. Stacey'd always been a follower, going all the way back to grade school, a guy who waited until long after the first punch was thrown to jump in. Stacey, with his limp hair, and pasty skin, and sort-of smile, and hands that hung at his sides, or were jammed into his pockets, his parents, too, Dysart employees.

Even playing football, Stacey'd never been a starter.

Yet what no one was saying now, and what the police knew, and so did Jack, was that Penry, Stacey's pal, had most likely been the one who'd done the hard hitting, and Stacey was taking the rap for him since he had no priors, had a clean sheet, even some pull with the local police, who'd played on the team.

No, the problem wasn't Stacey, it was his sidekick Penry—or was it the other way around?—and he had to think here before he'd let himself get mixed up in something involving Penry.

Penry was a borderline character some said was retarded, who was everybody's clown, though a mean one. Penry'd dropped out of high school and gone right to Dysart, on the floor, working second shift, but kept on drinking with the football team anyway, even stinking of blood after his shift, Penry, later, taking on back-to-back shifts so he could buy a brand-spanking-new Firebird with a big screaming eagle decal on the hood, and even aftermarket tires and wheels, Cragers, that must have cost him a small fortune.

Penry, who, when the car's newness had worn off, had let Stacey drive it on dates, and Stacey in major debt to Penry for it.

Penry, who *seemed* stupid. Dufus Penry, *The Goat.*

Even now it amused Jack, in a dark way, to remember how Penry'd gotten the nickname, out drinking with Jack, and Stacey, and Jack's once-running back, Larry Munson—the third man who'd helped pull him from Tibbits.

The four of them crammed into a booth at The Tap, Munson had been waxing loquacious about Paige Lowe, the daughter of Lowe's Auto, beautiful Paige, and they'd all gone silent, the others at the table, in that silence their tacit expression of what they thought Munson's chances were with Paige, and into that silence, Penry, in a voice he must have considered sage, given his experience, having been out of high school a year already, said, "Give up the goat, Munson."

Which at first all of them at the table had thought a joke, which got a guffaw, but when they realized Penry had no idea what he'd said, they whooped and hollered, and laughed, so much so, later, when Penry wasn't around they referred to him as The Goat.

But then Penry had been the first to get laid, and with him mealy Stacey Lawton, Penry dragging Stacey to a local whorehouse, where, it was rumored, Penry had a steady date. Penry'd dragged them all over there later, the four of them, only Jack, when he'd been paired with a Mexican girl who looked not a day over thirteen, had suddenly felt sick, and had gone right back outside, suffering taunts of *Pussy* from Penry and Lawton for weeks after, but then he'd met Lena, with her ash-blond hair, and long legs, and that way of smiling that just slayed him, he just couldn't get away from this one, he didn't want to, no matter what, and that had been that.

And in the years since, Stacey had changed very little, and Penry, The Goat, not at all. Penry, behind the veneer of dumbness, Jack suspected, a pretty skilled manipulator.

Look, he thought, even now he's gotten Stacey taking the fall for him.

And what about Larry Munson, his once-running back? Was he caught somewhere in this mess?

All this Jack, at the table, Carol, his sister, desperate across from him, had to consider. All this in the space of a minute.

If he'd let himself get involved here. Because if he helped Stacey, who was surely covering for Penry—and he wasn't sure why he would be—what was to say Penry wouldn't involve Stacey in something worse?

Something ruinous, even—and the word that came to Jack's mind was *fatal*.

Which Jack thought was possible, because he'd begun to suspect, especially where Penry was concerned, there was some larger plan.

And then, too, none of the guys seemed to really know him anymore, but things got back to them.

Penry lived over the garage at his parents' place and spent most of what he earned at Dysart drinking, and playing pool, and gambling on sports events—which he did very badly at but never wised up to. And he disappeared when he got his time off, and if you believed what people said, he was up in Minneapolis on Lake Street, this rumor proven true when he was charged with rape and aggravated sodomy, this with a girl underage.

But in a *whorehouse*—the girl looking eighteen, but three years younger. There'd been some confusion about what she'd been doing there, and the fake ID she'd had in her purse. Which had turned the focus of police interest from Penry. And then the charges against Penry were dropped, for reasons no one ever knew.

Innocent until proven guilty, Penry said when they'd asked him about it.

He didn't say he *hadn't* done anything. Because by this time, even Penry had wised up to the fact that he should keep his mouth shut. It got him in trouble. And got people around him in trouble. But this time, Stacey, his sister's husband.

"Why doesn't Stacey just *give Penry up?*" Jack said. "That's what this is all about, isn't it? What *Stacey* owes Penry? And Penry's gotten caught in his own shit, finally, right? Stacey's clean, so it's unlikely they'd come down hard on him—is that what it's about?"

Carol said nothing, only made a big production of getting another cigarette lit, her hands shaking. It bored Jack a little, and made him angry. He wanted to be home with the kids, he had so little time with them, and here it was late already and his night shot. And for what? For something Stacey should have figured out before, and if not, if Stacey got caught up in these messes with Penry of his own volition? Well, Stacey could sit in jail for Penry then. To hell with it. Both of them could go for all he cared.

Carol, seeing the look on his face, said, "You're in no place to pass judgment here, Jack."

He had to think about that. She was referring to what had happened with Tibbits. How Stacey had done right by him that night, stopping the fight.

"What's Stacey hanging around with Penry for, anyway? I mean, you don't—"

"No, I *don't* like him. But you don't just turn your back on friends."

"Penry is *Stacey's* friend, Carol, not yours."

When Carol didn't answer, Jack got a worse-than-sinking feeling. Okay, so the worst was true. Penry had done some serious damage to the Mexican, more than had been reported in the paper. He was a powerful, squat man, his forearms thick and heavily muscled, his fists like thick, hardened bone. Penry, Jack knew, was certifiably dangerous—he'd seen Penry defend himself on the cutting floor. He supposed it was *that*, more than anything, that flabby old Stacey saw in Penry, what Stacey admired there, or needed. Penry, for better or worse, could seriously kick ass.

Jack glanced up from his scarred hands.

"So, if it's gotten rough now, why not have Stacey tell the truth? What's to prevent him from doing that?"

"Stacey already made a formal statement to the police—that he did it."

Jack slapped his hand against his forehead. "Now, *why* in the world did he do that? Why didn't he *wait* until you brought a lawyer in?"

"The wet—the *Mexican* was all right then. He was just . . . roughed up."

"So what is it now?"

"His kidneys are bleeding."

"His kidneys are bleeding," Jack echoed.

From the bedroom came the sound of police sirens, and then gunshots.

"Turn that down!" Carol shouted, and the sound of the sirens diminished, but their significance wasn't diminished at the table. No, the quiet heightened that.

"This is just too much," Jack said.

"I'm asking you to help me," Carol said. "And help my boys. I mean, what if they *convict* Stacey?"

"If that happens, he'll tell the truth, and if the Mexican comes to, all the better—*he'll* testify to who did the shitkicking—and if it comes down to Stacey's word or Penry's, who's gonna believe Penry over Stacey?"

Carol winced, sucked down the last of her cigarette, and

before it was even out, lit another. It was then Jack really saw what it was about.

"Okay. What's Penry got on you?" Jack asked.

"Nothing."

"He doesn't?"

Carol's face colored. Here was something he hadn't anticipated. Complicity. Scratch the surface and don't be surprised what's under, he thought, but he was always surprised anyway. Always, he wanted to believe people were better than they were, himself included.

Carol's eyes slid away from his. He could still hear the TV back in the boys' room. Okay, he thought, this is *really* bad. She and Stacey've really gotten messed up with Penry somehow.

"You want my help, you'd better tell me, and now," Jack said.

Carol sighed. She smoked some minutes, then tapped the cigarette over the ashtray near her, on it bright sunflowers, and a logo, in bright white letters, *Alive with Pleasure!*

Jack got a sour feeling looking at it, and at his sister's hand, which was too thin.

"Well, you know how we weren't making it, just a couple years back, what with Darien's ear infections and my trouble?"

"Didn't your insurance cover that?"

Carol laughed. "Hardly."

Jack nodded. He thought he'd gotten it now. For a time there, two years ago, he'd seen higher-than-average waste counts, but then that had stopped.

"Where'd they do it?" he said. "Steal the meat?"

"They worked it out at the lot in Kansas City, where they loaded the cattle."

"So they underweighed on the trucks at the shipping yards, then cut on the floor here at Dysart, and weighed the meat, and passed the surplus out. Right?"

Carol nodded. "A lot."

"You mean a lot of people were in it?"

"No, just Stacey and Penry, and the drivers. And a couple guys in Kansas City." Carol tapped her cigarette over the ashtray, then glanced quickly up at Jack. He could tell she was lying, but about what part of it he couldn't tell.

"All right," she said, sensing he'd caught her out. "And a couple management people on our end. Don't go giving me that *shitty* look. You've got no right. You're making management money, so don't you look the fuck down at us." Her voice broke there. "Do you think I want to be living in a fucking trailer when I'm forty? And stuck here, and Stacey off with that—" She didn't say *Penry*. "And what about my boys, what about them?"

It was here that Jack began to feel himself lift away from the kitchen.

There seemed to be some dark, almost astronomical force working on him, this dark electricity, the current some horrible low buzz.

He'd only felt like this once before, when his mother had died.

He thought, Jesus . . . Fucking . . . Christ. If he got messed up in this the wrong way, *he* could get killed. Management was in on it. All the way back to Kansas City. There were organization people out there, the Cirricionis, and who all else he could only guess.

"So what's the charge against Stacey right now, aside from assault?"

Carol shook her head. There wasn't anything else yet, but neither of them had to say what would happen if the Mexican died.

Jack asked, "What's his bail?"

"Ten thousand."

"Carol," Jack said, and was about to say, Even *I* don't have that kind of money, when Carol stopped him, holding up her hand. He thought she was going to ask him to re-mortgage his place, which he wasn't going to do.

Jack, with the house.

If he had to fight Lena for custody of the kids, he didn't stand a chance of a snowball in hell unless he had the house free and clear.

"I'm not asking you to do anything with the house," Carol said.

"So what *are* you asking?"

"If *I* can come up with the bail money—"

"And where would you get—" But he understood now. So, what were they sitting on then? How much had they stolen from Dysart?

"They don't pay us a wage we can live on, so don't give me that goddamn judgmental look of yours. It's the last time I'm going to say it."

"I wasn't."

"Fuck you, Jack."

Jack stood up, angry enough to go, but she took hold of his sleeve. He would have cause later to wish he'd gone then, but family had called, and he'd had no choice in the matter, he told himself, but that was a lie, too.

"I'm not asking you to do anything you wouldn't normally do."

"Right," Jack said, and he sat again.

"You go hunting this time of year, right?"

"Just get to it," Jack said.

"I'll put up bail for Stacey, and you go hunting up north. Take Stacey. If the Mexican dies, Stacey'll go over the border."

"That's insane!"

"Is it? Penry's getting some people to lie for him, that somebody other than Stacey did it. And there was this *rumor* going around already that'll help."

"*Rumor?*" In Jack's experience, rumors usually had in them, somewhere, an element of truth. "What *rumor?*"

"That *killing*—no, *in*juring—the wet—" Carol paused to think how to put it. "This rumor's been going around that it's all *political*. That somebody from outside did it. That they framed Penry, to make it look like some bar brawl, only the wetback got hurt worse than—"

"*Political.*"

"Don't act stupid, Jack!" Carol nearly shouted. "People are saying this was . . . 'preventative,' that the wetbacks are trying to—"

"Organize, right? When what the Mexicans are *really* trying to do is cut into the stealing? Is that it?"

Carol tapped her cigarette over the ashtray.

"Just a couple," she said, glancing up at Jack, this sorrow on her face. "But the rumor is that somebody in *higher* management set the whole thing up. Maybe even one of the owners."

Jack kicked back from the table.

"Remember?" Carol said. "Years ago, before the wetbacks, there was all that talk on the floor about organizing?" Her face puckered. "Well, they're fucking *never* gonna let it happen, Jack."

"Who's the Mexicans' inside guy? Who's messing with everybody, trying to cut in? Do you know?"

Carol laughed, bitterly.

"It *was* this . . . Jesus Garcia, but we didn't know who else was with him. . . ." She took a tug on her cigarette. "So, you see?"

"No, I don't." Jack ran his hand through his hair. "And why can't Stacey just go up *himself*? *Hunting*? If he wants to be near the border so he can run? What do you need *me* to go for?"

Jack cupped his chin in his palm, thinking, his eyes narrowingly suddenly.

"Penry was the one who suggested the whole hunting thing, to post bail and have Stacey go up—cross the border if the Mexican dies. Didn't he?" he said.

Carol wouldn't look at Jack, only nodded.

"And Stacey went for it? Even Penry's insisting he go along, just to make it look right? That they were just going up hunting?"

"All of it," Carol said. "It's all Stacey'll talk about now."

Jack set his hands on the table, eyeing her. Hunting accidents up north were common, and Penry, going alone with Stacey? What was to say that Penry wouldn't just take Stacey out, because Stacey *would* talk, sooner or later—tell who'd really beaten the Mexican—if it came down to saving his own skin.

And even if the Mexican *did* pull through? If the Mexican kept his mouth shut to avoid more of the same, or just disappeared along with his family?

Penry wouldn't want someone like Stacey with that kind of leverage on him. A witness. So—

"The whole thing is . . . *fucking crazy*, Carol. Just *go to the police*."

"Right. I'm going to beg some . . . *cop* for protection, because

I *think* Penry might be setting Stacey up. And *then* what? If it comes out what we've done? *We'd* lose our shitty little pension, this . . . *fucking* trailer, and what I've saved for the boys' education'll end up in some lawyer's pocket keeping me out of jail. And if Stacey stays put in jail, and the wetback does die and Stacey's convicted? He'll get five-to-ten, minimum."

But in all that, Jack had heard it. *We.* Carol, culpable here. She'd do time, too.

"What was your part in it?"

"I knew about it, all along. And when we started taking more meat than they underweighed in Kansas City, I changed the weight lists in the office."

Jack rapped the table with his knuckles, stunned. "If the Mexican does die, and Stacey does go over the border, Penry's gotta know he'll talk. If not right away, then when they catch up to him. How's it gonna go down then?"

"That's up to you."

"What do you mean 'that's up to *me*'?"

"Penry said if Stacey had to run, he'd just go back to work. And he'd fix the problem with the witnesses—they're illegals—*if* he could get something in lower management, on the floor."

"Like hell," Jack said.

"You *didn't* listen. On . . . the . . . floor."

"On the floor! *Shit!* There *isn't* any such job there!"

"Then *fucking make one*! You're in management! Make up some job, for me, for the boys," Carol said. She was looking at him now, big eyed, terrified, all hope nearly gone. "All you'd have to do, after, is keep an eye on Penry—just give him . . . *look* at him, so he *gets it.* That he better follow through or else. That you've got things, from *me.* And I'd have to deal with what I had to deal with."

"Which is what?"

"*Things.* I'll tell Penry, and he'll know."

Jack stared across the table at his sister. It was all too much.

"I didn't mean *that*," she said. "I wouldn't be a part of anything like that, taking Penry out."

"Then what the hell *did* you mean?"

"If Stacey goes, I'm leaving, too. I got things on Penry'll keep his mouth shut. I'll take the kids up to the cabin, use my sick days, I've got almost three weeks, and we'll see if Penry can fix the problem with the witnesses—run them off. He's working on it already."

Jack shook his head. That Carol was considering running with Stacey seemed—

"I suppose you've taken your savings out of the—"

"They *weren't in the bank,* Jack. Just *think* for a minute, will you? Just our salaries from Dysart went in, which barely paid the bills."

"And you *really* think Penry can make those witnesses disappear with—*what*? Money? He say he was going to pay some cops to run them off? And even if you did give Penry that kind of cash, and even *if* I *could* promise Penry some management thing on the floor, what have you got on Penry to make sure he'll follow through? What's to say he wouldn't just pocket your money? I mean—you *don't* know him the way I do."

Carol smiled and crushed her cigarette out. "Don't I?" she said. "See, if we go, and Penry does anything . . . *funny*? That girl he got into it with, up in the Cities? I looked into all that, and Penry messes with us, she'd tell just what he did."

"Why not *now*?"

Carol gave Jack one of those looks she reserved for the stupid, or slow. Jack was neither, but he was a man, after all.

"She's a *girl,* Jack. Just a girl. She was never turning tricks. She was waiting for her mother to get off shift. See? It would cost her, she's in high school now, has a boyfriend, lives with her father, some asshole lawyer in Moundsview. Getting into it would cost her big time, and then some."

They sat at the table, smoking. Around them the double-wide now had about it an almost suffocating blandness, the Kmart lamps, and the beige carpet, and the kitschy mirror in back of the front door oppressive.

The cop show was ending with some crescendo of noise in the boys' bedroom.

"You'd take the boys?"

Carol nodded.

"This is crazy, you know that, don't you? Especially counting on Penry."

Carol didn't answer him, she tapped her ash over the ashtray. *Alive with Pleasure!*

"So what'll it be, Jack?" she said. "You going to help us out here, provide a little protection, for me, and the boys, and Stacey, or what?"

Jack, setting his steepled hands over the table, set his chin on them, his eyes vacant, and shook his head at it all.

"And *why* would you need protection if, like you say, Penry's on your side? If you've got this all figured out?" he asked. "Just so we've got this clear."

Carol turned to Jack, tapped her cigarette over the ashtray again.

"Because," she said, "I could be dead wrong about all of it."

22

THURSDAY, THE DAY THEY WERE TO LEAVE, DAVID WAS whistling when he came out the doors of Morningside, moved toward the row of yellow-and-black buses waiting alongside the curb, his classmates, already boarded and chattering in them, so loudly they sounded not unlike a flock of unruly birds.

David threaded through his classmates remaining on the walk, his mind elsewhere, and a spring in his step.

Excited.

The whole day had passed, as if in slow motion, David waiting for this moment, all the usual ritual, up after six, breakfast for Janie, but Rachel off to work early, and David seeing Janie onto the bus, and David missing his and clambering over the cyclone fence and bolting across the lanes of traffic to get to school again, and all that suffocating dry air in the classrooms, and the bell ringing at the end of each interminable hour, and all of it going by him in a daze, until the last bell had rung and he'd been set free.

He was going up north! In just an hour now, he was really going, and Janie with him!

And thinking about the trees, and water, he did not notice the sudden rise in the voices coming from the buses, lost in his thoughts, and he felt the hand on his shoulder like a steel clamp, and his heart leapt, and Buddy said in his ear, *"Hey!"*

And he kicked David with his knee, so sharply David saw black, felt his knees buckle under him, and even then he jabbed with his elbows, the kids on the buses yelling, "Fight! Fight!" "Kill him, Buddy," and "Get that fucker, Geist! Hit back!"

And even as he felt his left arm caught, and twisted sharply up behind his back, so he was sure it would break, he punched for all he was worth with his right, frenzied, this terror in him, Buddy was going to do it, injure him, ruin his season, or worse, as he'd promised, was going to cripple him, this crazy panic making it impossible for Buddy to hold David, so he spun away, low over his feet, but Buddy grinning and coming on, and just then, his biology teacher's voice, Mr. Oberstar's, rang out—

"Hey! What do you think you're doing there?!"

And Buddy turned to face Mr. Oberstar, who stood glaring, a clipboard at his side.

"You want a suspension? Huh?" he said. He looked between David and Buddy. "Either of you?"

They both stood, arms hanging at their sides, breathing hard. David's bus driver honked his horn, motioned for David to get on.

"Get out of here!" Mr. Oberstar said, and he gave both of them, Buddy and David, a push toward their buses, and as they were moving toward them, Mr. Oberstar called out, *"I'm watching you, Buddy!"* and Buddy turned to David and, grinning, said, "Next time, you won't be so lucky, little buddy."

David climbed the stairs onto his bus, his right leg cramping, and for the first time in how long he couldn't recall, he humped toward the back—past the girls in their striped shirts and blond hair and boys with their wispy mustaches and bangs over their foreheads, all of them excited, and trying not to look at him, but glancing up anyway as he went by, until David, sitting, looked out the window in a hot silence.

Then closed his eyes. The variegated autumn light cast down

through the leaves on the trees played over his eyelids like friendly fire, and he sat back in his seat and breathed deeply, knowing he had now, for certain, to do something about Buddy, only he'd wait until he got back from up north, which was a relief, and when the bus lurched to a stop some time later, he got off, limping, and trying to correct it, walked to his driveway and went up its curving length and into the house, where Janie was all packed up and alternately anxious, and happy, and silly.

"I'm-going-to-your-favorite-place," she chanted at David, in the way kids would chant *I know a secret that you don't,* and he swooped down and, grasping her under her arms, swung her up and around, whooping, and laughing, and they went outside, David hefting the gear, which made him give in to the limp, his leg hurt so badly, and waiting there in the sun, David did not smoke, and Janie told him he could, she wouldn't tell, and he said, "No, Sport, I don't even want you to think about doing things like that. You don't have to cover for me, ever. Okay?"

"So what happened to you?" she shot back. She'd noticed his limp.

When David didn't answer, Janie made a face, looking up the length of the driveway.

"You don't say things," she said.

"That's not lying, that's just not saying things, Sport. There're times not to say things, or even to think about them," and here he tousled her hair, to get her off it, then tickled her, until she fell over her bag and was laughing so hard she couldn't breathe.

"Stop it!" she shouted.

"This is gonna be fun, kiddo," he said.

Janie made a big, toothy I'll-try-for-you smile. David smiled in return, and Janie laughed.

"Countdown," David said. "Door locked?"

"Locked and bolted!"

"Got the right gear?

"Got everything!"

And at that moment, Max's winter car, the Cadillac, a bright red canoe on the top, crested Sherwood Avenue and came silently down the hill, Max in the windshield looking happier than David had ever seen him, and he thought, This is what Rachel's seeing, did see—what I never saw.

Max swung around in front of them and stopped. He nearly jumped from the car, suddenly some pitchman, dressed in a yellow shirt and off-manufacture designer jeans, which David saw at a glance were too tight for canoeing, he'd bust the knees out in no time, and tennis shoes—green with grass stains, he must have been mowing his lawn. But there was something familiar in it all, and David had to laugh, this memory of his father coming to him from someplace so old it had about it a feeling of otherworldliness, as if it were cloaked in perpetual morning light.

It came at him with the near shock of revelation: Max, for all his posturing, was authentically excited about this trip. It wasn't just for show. But what it was for, otherwise, David could not let himself think. That was too dangerous—that Max had felt so deeply, and hidden it, was a terrible revelation to David. That Max could lose so much yet show so little made David soften, and he didn't dare do that just yet. Couldn't. Not around Max.

So, just this now was enough. Letting himself be lifted by Max's enthusiasm. Max, who had put on an orange life preserver and was flapping the two sections behind him as if they were wings, running in circles around Janie.

While Janie keened to it, ran to Max and he swung her out and onto the lawn, David stepped over to the car, to look at the canoe.

Max and Janie came over, and Max slapped the canoe's bow. It was set upside down on the roof of the Cadillac, the gunnels on ridged blocks of hard green rubber, the bow and stern tied to the bumpers of the car, the ropes knotted fastidiously—cinch knots and half hitches. That was reassuring, but the rest of it?

"Cedar," Max said, thumping the canoe, and David forced himself to smile. "It's smoother in the water, lighter—a hell of a lot lighter—and its profile makes for easier paddling. What do you think?"

What Rachel had said the night before came to David, causing him to pause. *Give him a chance.*

"You bought it?"

Max nodded. "Figured it'd be good on the lakes in town later. Got it for a song. A *song*."

David grinned. There were a chain of lakes that ran through the west side of Minneapolis, Calhoun, Harriet, Lake of the Isles, and Brownie Lake, all interconnected, they'd been on one of them together that night, earlier, and Max was right, on flat, calm water, and with shore a small distance away, this would be the canoe. Light off and on the car, slick on still water.

Or racing.

For all that, the canoe was a beauty, and he wondered what Max must have spent. A canoe like this cost two, three times what an aluminum canoe would. In town, it would be a real trophy—here, down south, the lakes and shoreline all soft.

But up north, the lakes were granite and basalt bottomed, and only fools, or racers, used cedar canoes there, and never on white water.

Only people who wanted the best for speed used cedar canoes, paper thin and extremely fragile.

Like this one.

"How long is it?" David asked. If it was what it should be, it'd be too short, anyway. They could get something else. Rent something.

"Eighteen feet."

"Great," David said. Great. Well, Max had gotten that right. He smiled, for Max.

But why had it been so cheap? Something was wrong with the canoe. It was too long for a racer, by a foot or more; even a two-man racer was never over sixteen feet, but here he'd bought an eighteen-footer, probably built as a showpiece, to sell other, shorter canoes. Max was always buying things at discount places, never the best, even though he had the money for the best, but this time he'd gone to one of the better places, and gotten hooked on the sucker display model. David was trying to cheer himself up, to give Max a break, and here was this canoe.

Up north, the damn thing could kill them.

Whereas aluminum or fiberglass canoes could take colossal

battering without punctures, or cutting, one good smack would open up a cedar canoe. This canoe. And the draft, the distance from the gunnel to the water, was only three quarters of what it should be—it *was* what it should be for a weekender or a racer, but not for a canoe you'd travel in, making this canoe easier to capsize, even with a third person, Janie, sitting in the middle. So it was the very sleekness of the canoe that made it all wrong, but boy, oh, boy, did it look nice.

"Let's see the paddles," David said.

Max took one from the back of the car. It was solid spruce, the shaft of the paddle of relatively good diameter, the blade thick enough to bear striking something—rocks, up north—without breaking. Not a racing paddle, something right for the job here.

"Did you get a third paddle?"

"In the trunk," Max said.

The warm autumn sun beating down, David lifted his face, his thoughts a dark tangle. Should he say something? Get off to a bad start? Because nothing would bring out the Max he'd lived with like this would. Sorry, wrong canoe, Max.

But then David thought he was being too hard himself. With Janie along, they were just going to bob around anyway, so what was the big deal?

"Great weather, isn't it?" Max said, mistaking David's turning his face to the sun as just that.

"Beautiful," David said.

There was a hint of chill in the air, dampness, but according to the weather service, which David had called that morning at Flying Cloud Airport, the high pressure was holding, and the two-week forecast was for cool and dry weather, lows in the forties, highs pushing sixty.

"I got extra food," Max said, "just in case."

Janie bumped up against David. Grinned at him and poked him in the back. She knew him well enough to see there was something he wasn't saying.

"Cut it out," he said. He meant Janie. "So what'd you get?"

"All in the trunk."

David shrugged at that. He was tempted to ask to see it, but he decided that would be hostile, and he didn't want that now, he had the canoe to think about, and anyway, when they got up in Ely tomorrow morning, he could push things if he had to, after breakfast. There were no end of outfitters in Ely, where they could rent a canoe if he still had this bad feeling.

Give him a chance, David. Right, he thought.

"Well?" Max said. "Should we get going?"

They tossed Janie's sleeping bag in the back, where Max said she could use it as a pillow if she wanted to sleep on the way up, jammed her pack between the seats, and swung David's bag around, a Korean-issue mummy bag, cotton outer and inner, and thick with down, which Max mentioned, how big it was, which it wasn't at all, it packed to a diameter of nine inches, weighed only three pounds, but was good to fifteen below zero.

"You'll sweat in this," Max cautioned, as if Max knew what he was talking about.

"That's why it's cotton," David said evenly, "not nylon. And its high range is almost fifty degrees, because it breathes."

"Breathes," Max said, and he grunted at David's bag, the weight of it, swinging it around into the car, and closing off the far side of the backseat, so Janie was in a kind of cave, which she thought was neat, sitting there in the middle and excited, and Max said, "Got everything?"

David said he had. He turned to look at the house, white with black trim, the enormous elm in the front yard casting the front yard in shade. A breeze blew from the north and he shuddered, a chill running up his spine. Was it just the breeze, or was it something else?

Nothing would be the same when they returned, he thought. But how that would be so, he had no idea, and he shrugged at the thought.

"You leave some lights on for your mother?" Max asked.

"Front and rear, and the kitchen."

Max slapped him on the back and handed him the keys, and said, "You drive. I . . . am . . . bushed."

23

THEY HEADED OUT OF THE CITIES, THE HEAVY CAR EATING up the miles, the plains rolling out under them, hardscrabble towns on the horizon, usually first a silver water tower looming up, with *Go Falcons* or *Spartans State Champs* spray-painted on it in red or black letters, and the town then, a main street, a grocery, and a bank, and houses built out and away into the furrowed farmland that rolled, and pitched, once pressed under the glacier that had receded, in geological terms, not long ago at all, just ten thousand years, to the north. And here, still, remnants of that glacier around farmers' fields, the erratics, anything from stones the size of pumpkins to boulders the size of cars, turned out of the soil and made into rough borders of stone teeth around farms, the stones becoming fences, and here and there antiquated green threshers or red bailers sinking into the soil and rusting into oblivion, and a line of smoke across the horizon from a chimney, and everywhere this almost golden autumn light, and deciduous trees following the creeks, most of them poplar, or birch, or sometimes scrub elm, gone to winding lines of gold and red and brown, and in the air, the smell of manure, but to David not a bad smell, because he associated it with his trips up north with his uncle and, at the wheel, he wanted a smoke, Max listening to WCCO, which struck David as the biggest bunch of bullshit he could think of, these false, chuckling, cajoling voices of Boone and Erickson, but which, he admitted to himself now, he envied—just a little. Such optimism! Such team spirit! What about those Vikes, hey? And there followed football talk, all that "Well, if the team continues to work hard, and we have more of the luck we had last month, and our quarterback holds out, why, there's no telling how far we'll go this year, maybe to the Super Bowl. Don't you think?" The Vikes? David thought. They stink, what else was new.

All of it stunk. The ads for Wally McCarthy Olds—Come on

down, get a free hot dog and popcorn—the offers and come ons, the shuck and hustle of it, and David told himself to stop it. Just stop it.

So he didn't listen to the radio, opened his window so the air whistled, pleasurably ruffling the hair on the left side of his head, and the land, loping, and wider and more open by the mile north, rose and fell under them, here in this immense car, and ten days from now, he thought, this would be over, and how would they remember it?

He tugged at his collar. Max now settled against the window. Janie was asleep in the back.

He carefully turned the radio down, and then off.

Put his nose into the air, and slowed outside a small town, glancing at the gas gauge, plenty and then some, and bringing the car down to thirty, passed by grain silos, towering cement fingers, and the gas station, and a small restaurant, with a sign on it that said, *You Are Entering the North Woods—EAT,* and going out of town, he did not speed up, for the land was bathed in gold, and the trees down along a tributary of the Mississippi shimmered in the light, molten, and he felt all over again, leaving the plains to the south, a kind of homecoming, and thrilled to the first sharp, resinous hint of pine, and the sky overhead aboil in lavender and purple washes of stratus, and a V of ducks winging out of a slew heavy with cattails, so the rim of the world was suddenly alive with birds, and they rose over the car, in an undulating geometric pattern, David putting his face into the windshield to watch them go over, geese now he saw, and their far-off cries not unlike a distant barking, and the geese swung south and east, and there remained one lone hawk, circling, and it took David's breath away, this lone bird, wings carefully feeling the air and rising on the last of the day's invisible currents, he could even see the bird's wing-tip feathers, cutting the air precisely, and exactly, the bird turning its head, there, over a field of undulating grasses that danced and swayed in the slow end of the day's breezes coming down from the cold and jeweled north, and like that, the bird, riding those breezes, tucked its wings back, a black dart now, the car even there across the field and looking into the last of the sun, the sun there on the horizon a goblet of orange fire, and the bird bisected the sun, exactly, and then the bird, a rabbit in its claws, lifted out over the field and swung north and into the line of purple darkness there, which David drove into.

Everything new and alien we experience molds us, changes us, in some internal dimension. So it was as if in a dream, David finally stopped the car at a gas station, and they all got out to stretch, and Janie used the restroom, the station lit unnaturally bright in all that cavernous darkness of the last of the plains.

It was a kind of bubble of consciousness in a vast sea of nothingness.

But not if you looked, stepped out from the lights, into it. Then the trees came clear, and a raccoon that had been foraging through a garbage can in back loped away, and David breathed deeply, the raw smell of gasoline behind him, which also had its associations of engines and motorcycles, his boy's dreams caught up in it, but he was happy to leave that behind now, the scent of pine drawing him north.

"David, come on," Max called.

David got in on the passenger side.

"See anything?"

David said it had been a nice drive, pretty really. And it had been.

24

HE WAS SLEEPING WHEN HE WAS AWAKENED BY THE SMELL of water. They were topping a rise now, and off to their right, miles distant, were buildings the size of aircraft hangars, alight with blue lights, and just beyond them the dark of Lake Superior, and here the plains fell away entirely, and the undercrust of earth, the first of the greenstone, ran jagged and magisterial along the coast, pine covered, and they climbed again, the highway leading right into it, this other world, as if they were passing through some gateway, through the neck of some bottle and into a world old, and pure, and uncompromising, a land of fierce life, where pines, somehow, grew right out of cracks in stone, thousands of them, and the animals came out in the open, here, now, up ahead, in their headlights, a white-tailed deer crossing the highway, and Max cursing and the car tossing them forward as it slowed, and the deer loped to the far side, and a snow fence there, fully six, eight feet high, and as if on wings, the deer leapt, to clear the fence, and there was that moment when it seemed to hang over the fence, something magical there, eternal, because in it was some grace of motion, exquisite, not human, yet remembered from some time before memory, and was gone again.

"Would've hit the damn thing if I hadn't been watching," Max said.

"What?" Janie said, waking.

"Just a deer," David said.

Janie put her face to the window in back.

"I missed it."

"You didn't miss anything, honey," Max said.

———

They reached Ely a little after midnight, the town not much in the off-season, just so many pole barns, and low, two-story buildings with the names of outfitters emblazoned across them, *Beland's Wilderness Canoe Trips, Canadian Border Outfitters, Pipestone Outfitting, Rom's Canoe Country Outfitters,* and the streets for the most part broad, and here and there a car parked up to one motel or another, always the blue or amber sign there, *Vacancy,* and they pulled up in front of the last on Main, and Max said, Wait a minute, and went inside, and was back moments later, and when they got out of the car, now the night around them was not plains darkness, but woodlands darkness, something different, which you could feel, almost as if with your hands, the air rich with the scent of pine, and cool, pure water, and wood smoke.

In their unit were two beds, and without any discussion, David lugged out his Korean bag, and Janie, in some half-sleep, crawled into one bed, and Max in his clothes lay on the other and pulled the spread over him, and even as David was passing into that other world of sleep, Max said, "Good night, kiddos," and David pulled the bag up under his head, just then, somehow, in his half-sleep, just a boy all over again, and all hope and brightness of the world ahead of him, untarnished.

And loved, yet.

And like that he slept, and slept deeply.

25

HE WOKE ABRUPTLY, THE ROOM DARK, AND ALIEN TO HIM. For seconds he did not know where he was, and then it came to him, and why he'd wakened, and he dressed, and taking the room key on the table in back of the door, slipped out, locking the door behind him.

Outside, he went up Main, the air bitter chill, and the stars overhead like chips of ice, and this pitch-pine smell, sharp and clean, and the world just suggestions of itself in shadow. He needed to find a phone. He'd promised to call Rachel. He would have waited until morning—it was just after one now—but he just knew she was awake, there on the couch waiting for his call, and was worrying that it had all gone wrong.

She wouldn't say it, when he got her on the phone, but he knew it anyway.

So, knowing that, he'd awakened, and he went up the dark street, the road gritty under his feet, and quiet, and on Third, he was about to come up the last of the boardwalk and dodge around the Coke machine there, to the phone, the one he'd used when he'd come up with his uncle, when he saw someone jog across the street.

David was too close to back away, and there was a streetlight behind him, so he stood behind the Coke machine. There was the hinged creak of the booth door shutting, and a flash of light, and David looked around the Coke machine, the man in the booth, lit suddenly, heavyset and bent over a sheet of paper—was he especially short? Or was it that he was leaning over the paper like that?—but the light went out.

That he heard nothing but night sounds and the hum of the refrigeration unit in the Coke machine, he would remember later.

Lives would depend on it, would change because of it.

And he would remember that the man was arguing with someone in a low, harsh voice, almost a whisper; he hadn't heard David, and David hung back, leaned against the wall beside the big Coke machine, in white letters, *Enjoy Refreshing Coca-Cola*.

"He won't?" the man said, through what must have been gritted teeth. "Well, then, you tell him again who it is that's calling." A night bird warbled off in the dark. "Yeah. I know what you said. I got him up here, and I'll flush him out. I used his own sister, stupid cunt." There was a pause. "If he won't come in with us, of course they'll go along."

Now another man, enormous, his hands in his pockets, came up the street. He glanced at the figure in the booth, and seeming to recognize him, bent nearly double, coming crabwise at him.

David shrank into the dark, his hands suddenly slick with sweat.

"You're management, Throgmorton," the man in the booth

said. "You take care of the witnesses, or this whole thing is fucked. Yeah, *you, too. Get it?* I'll take care of Hank here." There was another pause. "Yeah, right. You fucking better."

David heard the booth door slam back, and the plastic *ca-chunk* of the receiver being put down, and the man in the street lunged into the booth, and the two men were fighting, the wall behind David's back shuddering with it, David's heart kicking up, they were really pounding each other, but then they were laughing, and were out in the street, the bigger man feigning throwing a pass, and the thickish man who'd been in the booth, in moon-shadow, running for it, his hands up.

"How's the hose monster?" the bigger man said, a little meanly, in a hoarse, low voice, a loud whisper.

"Ah, bite me," hissed the other. "And her name's Judy, if that means anything."

"I think Judy came in a brown paper package, C.O.D."

The smaller man kicked at the larger, and then they passed under elms, into the dark.

———

David waited until he was sure the men were gone, then swung into the booth and fed quarters into the machine. It made a mechanical clattering so loud he pulled the door shut behind him, the hairs on his neck standing up, but then the light came on, and he banged the door back open again, trying to see into the dark.

Even with the door open, the booth smelled of sour beer, and piss, and he shifted his feet in the dark, trying to move out of the booth with the receiver, but the steel-wrapped cord was too short, and he stepped on something paper, which he swept up, absent-mindedly smacking it flat against his hip, just as Rachel was picking up on the other end.

"Hey, it's me," David said.

He had lifted the piece of paper and was trying to read it by moonlight. It was covered with phone numbers, and what all else he couldn't see.

"Why are you whispering?" Rachel asked.

She was trying to sound sleepy, but David knew better. The

phone had only rung once. He could imagine her there on the living-room sofa, the phone on the end table beside her.

"We're here. Everything's fine."

"It's after one, David."

He didn't want to say he'd forgotten her, so told a lie.

"Janie got carsick on the way up, you know the way she does, so we stopped a few times."

"Oh," Rachel said.

David was still peering at the sheet of paper in his hand. He looked up the street but didn't dare close the door for the light. He thought to leave the piece of paper in the booth; it seemed hot, dangerous somehow.

In the back of his mind, he knew it was like that baseball he'd thrown, pissing Buddy off.

"You're sure you're all right? I mean, you could always— Is Janie really all right? Is that why you're whispering?"

"I'm not in the motel," David said.

"Where are you, then?"

"Outside."

"Where outside?"

"All I said was—"

"I don't *care* what you said," Rachel said, and she rambled on about his safety, that he shouldn't be wandering around in the dark in a strange town after one in the morning, and while David listened, nodded, not paying attention, saying Yes and Uh-huh at the right moments, he jammed the sheet of paper into his pocket, wishing now he hadn't lied about Janie.

"Listen. It's *wonderful* up here. Everything's just . . . *beautiful*," he said finally. "Really."

———

He thought to head back, but he had his cigarettes in his pocket, and so walked in the opposite direction of the motel, smoking and looking up at the cold, sharp stars. He smoked three cigarettes, identified Mars, low on the horizon, and here was Orion, and Andromeda, and Perseus, and the North Star.

Perseus, what had it been about Perseus? Right, son of Zeus, slew Medusa and saved Andromeda, that's why he'd been thinking of the two constellations together.

He bent his head farther back, the whole dark sky overhead lit with diamonds.

His nervousness back at the booth seemed nothing now, and he stubbed out the last cigarette, and in the dark walked briskly, but approaching the motel, again, something jangling his nerves. This time, though, it turned out to be Max, who was waiting for him on the steps leading up to the motel porch.

"I was looking all over for you," he said, that tone of accusation in his voice David so hated.

David stood a few yards back, his eyes fixed up the street. He didn't want to get into it, and anyway, night had always been the bad time between them.

"She wanted me to call, and I forgot," he said. He knew that would put Max off, and it did. This complicity between him and his mother. Or just the mention of Rachel, as if she were some weapon, against Max. "I told her everything was great," David said, this a gift, after hitting Max with Rachel.

After all, Max himself had called Rachel after they'd arrived, from the room, but he understood why Rachel would have David call.

"All right," Max said, and he stood, setting his hands on his hips, and there was a certain sadness in his stooped shoulders David felt. "Don't go out like that again, all right? There're people out you might not want to run into." He shook his head. "I damn near bumped into someone who was—I don't know—running to that phone booth over by Herter's. Son of a bitch saw me coming from there—I figured that's where you'd gone and . . ."

"What?" David said.

When Max only shrugged, and turned toward the motel, David mounted the stairs, and passing Max, David pressed his shoulder.

"Come on, let's go in," David said, but he felt, just in that moment, some betrayal.

He could have told Max, after all, about the man he'd seen in the booth, and the conversation he'd overheard, and the piece of paper in his pocket.

But they hadn't ever shared confidences, and so he didn't.

And anyway, it wasn't anything, he told himself, and they went inside.

26

"Up! Up!" Max called out. He was throwing the shades back from the windows, and the light was sharp, and bright, and beautiful.

He cranked one of the windows open, and there was the distant drone of logging trucks passing through town, and pine-scented, lake-chilled air poured into the room, and David rose, skin puckered, grabbed his fresh clothes, and dodged into the bathroom and stood under the showerhead, the hot water pouring over him, this like some baptism, his life in the Twin Cities washed from him, and he stepped out of the shower, the room over-warm now, orange-red lines of filament in the heater set in the wall, and Janie was knocking at the door, and he dressed and stepped out with his belt still in his hand, and the cold in the bedroom now was wonderful, clearing his head, and while Janie was showering, he tugged on his canvas tennis shoes, which Max glanced at, disapproving, but Max didn't know, you didn't wear heavy-soled boots like he was wearing in a canoe, but David was so taken by the morning, and the light, and here all this possibility that he said nothing, none of it mattered, that the canoe was too round-bottomed and the freeboard not what it should be for touring, and here Janie stepped from the bathroom, her hair up in a turquoise towel, which made both David and Max laugh, she looked like Rachel, what she'd done to her hair too womanly for her, like some borrowed gesture.

"What's funny?" she said.

"Nothing," David replied, and he nodded for her to get her

things, which she did, and when they were all dressed they went outside, the light just now, here, coming as if the world itself were being born, and in that light, none of the night things mattered, and they went up the quiet street and by the outfitters, jays calling from the pines, now a few cars parked here and there with canoes tied to roof racks, and the canoes, without exception, all a dull gray aluminum, all Grummans, or Alumacrafts, which shot some hesitation through David again, but he thought, with Janie along, they'd be taking it easy, anyway.

———————

Which he told Janie to do, when she was ordering inside.

Max had gone back to the men's room, and David leaned over his menu, at the top, *The Pines* in purple mimeo, and said, "Sport. You won't be able to eat all that."

Janie made a face. "Yes, I will," she said.

David shook his head. The waitress, a rough-looking woman in her late forties, dressed in a starched white shirt, cocked a thick stack of menus against her hip.

"You want me to come back?" she said.

David said no, and gave Janie that big-brother look he gave her from time to time, then thought of Max, and how he'd felt, Max pinching pennies all the time, and for what reason? And he suddenly said, smiling, "She'll have the Fisherman's Special."

He told the waitress he'd have the same, and at that moment, Max strode to the table, and sat, and ordered two eggs over easy and toast, "Don't break the yolks," and the waitress gave them a grin and was gone.

When she returned, Max's plate in her left hand, and David's and Janie's balanced on her right forearm, heaped with sizzling steak, David caught Max frowning.

Then Max pasted a smile on his face, and made, glancing at his watch, what he thought was a joke, which embarrassed David, but David could tell it irked Max that they'd gotten something— what was it? Expensive? Because it wasn't, really. So was it they'd ordered things unnecessary? Or was it indulgent? But then Max laughed, dismissing the waitress.

"Last big meal before bread and water, right?"

David must have frowned at Max, because Max let out an even bigger laugh.

"Look at your brother," he said, poking Janie.

She glanced over at David, and seeing the concern on his face, she seemed frightened suddenly, her fork held up like an exclamation, and David smiled for her.

"He's kidding. We're not having just bread and water," David said. "Come on, don't scare her like that, Max."

Janie looked between David and Max, then went back to eating.

David, for a few minutes, though, wouldn't look at his father.

Always his jokes were undercutting, had something else in them, which David was all too well aware of. Now this bread-and-water business, which was a jab at them being along at all, their mother's prisoners on the trip, which was some guilt thing.

But why would Max say it? Did he expect David to counter him so he, Max, would be reassured? Was he supposed to say, No, it's not like that at all, we love you, Dad? Or some such shit?

And there were the other things Max said that David always seemed to get caught up in—like he already had this morning.

"Look at that," Max had said, walking over, and David had looked, a whole world out around them, trees, houses, the road, and when it became obvious he didn't see what it was Max meant, he asked, "What?" and Max said, "What do you mean, 'what'? Do you have eyes in your head, or are those turnips? The *bird*, the *goddamned bluejay there*, didn't you see it?"

Give him a chance, Rachel had said.

So he'd said, "Yes," just that, trying to be ambiguous, meaning, either, Yes, I did see it, or, Yes, tell me about it, but Max had taken it as Yes, he had seen the bird, and jumped right on him.

"Okay, smartie, why'd I even point it out?" he said.

And like that, he'd been caught in the lie, which he'd told only to try to please Max, even though he'd learned fibs like that around Max usually got him into even worse trouble—You know what I think about liars, David, he'd said, long ago, back when, if he caught David out like this, he might not speak to him for the better part of a week.

So he'd learned to say No, he didn't see, which then branded him as stupid, which he knew he was not, but which necessitated his wearing the dunce cap anyway, and then he'd get the lecture, like he had this morning:

"That bluejay had another bird in its beak. Jays'll do that, did you know that?"

David said nothing, he wouldn't get into it.

"Jays are nest robbers," Max said, to him this some great woodlore. Or had it been another jab at Rachel, at how things had turned out?

David had nodded.

It was about the only thing Max knew about birds, and his knowing it made him an expert. Max was an expert about every and anything. If he'd read about it, he was an expert. Read about it in the *Reader's Digest,* he'd say. Did you know the average man eats seventy pounds of processed sugar a year?

No, David would say, thinking such a figure was bullshit, another *Reader's Digest* "I Am Dan's Hangnail" article detail. Still, Max thrived on such details. Like his joke when the waitress brought the food.

"Let's see how long it took to get the food here," he said, pressing a button on his watch.

"Sixteen minutes and forty-five seconds."

"What?" the waitress said, nonplussed.

"Took you sixteen minutes and forty-five seconds to get the food to the table. Start to finish."

This, Max thought, was funny.

Thinking about it now, about any of it, though, put David in a funk.

"How's your meal, kiddo?" he said to Janie.

"It's delicious," she said, "and good, too."

David laughed. Max across the table frowned—again, he didn't quite get it.

———

But outside, none of it mattered—not that David had doubled the tip Max had left on the table, just to make it fifteen percent. Or that Max was, now that they were nearly back to the motel, irritable.

It was beautiful out, jays calling in the pines, and an inland pelican gliding sharply overhead, gulls, thirty or so, circling out over the trees, a phosphorus white against the gray scrim of clouds on the horizon.

Max parked the car in the lot and strode over to their unit.

Janie was skipping circles around David, then moved her legs in some complex approximation of playing hopscotch. The kid was a natural, and David told her so, then swung her by her arms, calling, "Monkey! Monkey!" which Janie loved.

In their motel room they set their bags on the blue-and-green paisley bedspread near the window overlooking the road headed north out of town.

It was awkward for David, because at this point, usually, he and his uncle Bobby had a ritual worked out: They'd read the maps, study the topography, and settle on the best route, taking into consideration how many portages they'd have to make, and how to avoid the steep ones. The long portages never mattered that much, but steep could require a rope, and climbing, and hauling the canoe up a rock face, and they'd never gone for that.

He sat at the table just in back of the window opposite Max and Max got out the maps, which were black and white, and on thin, shiny paper. David was surprised, too, to see there were no topographical markings on them, and the portages only measured in rods, a rod, David knew, equaling a little over five yards.

He wanted to ask where Max had gotten these maps—they weren't detailed at all, and he worried about the paper they were on, if the ink was water-fast.

"You got a map case?" he said.

Max glanced at his watch. "We can pick one up, all right?"

David said that would be fine. Everything that was screwy, he was thinking, was all right because this wasn't a serious trip, anyway.

What the hell. This was a float in the tub—albeit out in the woods—so it didn't matter.

Sitting across the table from Max, David thought he loved

and hated the man both. He smelled of aftershave and soap. Anything with perfume you didn't wear in areas with bears. The Boundary Waters Canoe Area was that. And these maps were hardly more than outlines of lakes and islands on white sheets of paper. Yet here was Max, this forge-ahead optimism to his planning—even though Max had never been up to the border lakes.

So his practical approach was ignorant, didn't take into consideration the obvious, like portages, or the prevailing northwest wind.

"I thought we'd go in here—Gunflint, Knife, Kekekabic," Max said, pointing to the east side of the map.

"That's good," David said. And it was—he knew the area. "That's the Voyageur's Highway."

Max said nothing, he didn't know what David was talking about, but he wasn't one to ask when he didn't. It was another of Max's irritating habits. If he didn't know something, he'd nod, giving the appearance he was in agreement. That he understood, not unlike what David had learned to do from him.

"We go in here, at Bearskin," he said, and tapped his finger along a chain of lakes.

Bearskin, Duncan, Rose; Little Gunflint, Gunflint, Magnetic; and then a river, Pine River, and more lakes, the names magic, but this undercurrent of threat here, a darkness in Max's ignorance, and in his persistence in appearing as though he knew what he was doing.

Gneiss Lake, Devil's Elbow; then Maraboef, and portages—how long or how challenging, they could only guess at, given the poor maps—another river, Granite River, to Saganaga, Swamp, and more portages, portages everywhere, to Otterrack, Little Knife, and Knife Lake.

David had cut through Knife Lake once, with his uncle Bobby, and it was rough country, here the greenstone rising in two, to four-hundred-foot escarpments, and the lakes zigzagging.

There were more lakes in the route, Anit, Panhandle, Makwa, Mora, the route ending at Round Lake.

Max traced the route with a red felt-tipped pen.

David looked for the scale on the map. There wasn't one. He

knew Knife Lake, though, and judged the scale on the others by that. He was beyond being surprised now, was more concerned about how he could change Max's mind about things if he had to.

"That's between a hundred- and a hundred-twenty-mile trip," he said, as neutrally as possible.

"That's perfect then," Max said.

David didn't know what to say, he was so stunned. The route was anything but perfect. About the third day in, they'd have a hundred-ten-rod portage. David pointed this out, and that the lake following the portage ran at an angle toward the west, so if the prevailing westerlies were blowing, crossing that distance after what could be a difficult portage—could be grueling.

"We'll take the western shore, be sheltered," Max said, and scooted his chair back, finished.

David bent over the map, his elbows on the table. It was possible you couldn't take the western shore there, if the water was deep and agitated—wavey, with sheer bluffs—but there was no way to tell from the map.

"There a problem?" Max said.

Later, David would have cause to remember that moment, because he would realize how much he was goaded into doing what he did.

But his hestitation gave Max the opening he needed.

"You really want to see some country or not?" Max said.

This, of course, was not the question. The question was, How tough are you? Are you a sissy, or what? and worst of all, What, don't you trust me?

All of it made David's head swim, but then the old adrenaline kicked in. He was suddenly . . . *pissed,* really pissed about it, all of it. Pissed at Max and his doctor know-it-all bullshit.

"All right, to hell with it," David said, which was about as much protest as he could muster against Max just then.

Max did not ask what he meant by that.

They sat at the table a moment longer. Max slapped David on the shoulder, then grasping him there, shook him good-naturedly.

"What do you say, Davey—this'll be fun, huh?"

David was thinking, If it didn't work out, this itinerary, if

Max had trouble paddling, or Janie just got tired, or whatever, they could bail at any time. Turn back, cut the trip short. And that thought was what decided the matter.

He'd wait and see.

"A real trip," Max said.

"Right," David said. "A real trip," that's exactly what his father was going to get.

27

WHAT HAPPENED AFTER THAT, DAVID HAD CAUSE TO THINK about, and to blame himself for, later—though he didn't understand that assigning such blame, and to oneself alone, is grandiose, much in the manner of Max's overconfident way in the world. David's version of his father's hubris had just taken a different form. You're responsible, David, for what happens in your life, Max had always told him, and whether he consciously believed it or not, that belief had taken root in him, perhaps too much. Was not tempered by consideration of chance, or fate, or circumstance. So that *If I had onlys* stemmed and blossomed and multiplied tenfold from actions he could only guess the outcome of, some of them seeming inconsequential at the time, like throwing the ball farther than Buddy, or here, giving in to his father to keep the peace.

Later, David would wake in drenching cold sweats, night after night, to ask himself, Why hadn't he seen things for what they were? Or *had* he, he asked himself, as he had helping Greg Becker that morning, and done the wrong thing, anyway? After all, helping Greg had been one thing, but throwing that ball had been another.

Why, really, had he done it?

Like this moment now, and what followed.

David stood at the table, and Max stood with him, and they went out to the car.

Janie, out front of the motel, was playing with the motel cat, black, heavy bodied with white boots and face, and Max avoided Janie, knowing that this would be the next thing she'd be asking for, the kid just loved cats, she'd be asking him for a cat, it was obvious, and the strange thing was, cats just loved her.

David saw how Max hardened against it, watching Janie draw the fishing line in the sand path, and the cat darting after it, and David felt that warmth again when Max shrugged.

Max could be a hard-ass with him, but not with Janie.

If she asked, if Janie asked just now, David knew, Max would get her a cat, later. David could just see it in him, how he even wanted her to ask him. Here, now, when the cat was rubbing up against Janie's legs, and when she dodged out into the empty morning street, and the cat came with her, stretching, then butting its head up against Janie's hand, which she held, as David had taught her, the back of her hand out toward the cat, the cat's bell tinkling brassily and small.

"Don't play in the street there," Max said, but with this affection in his voice, a voice he had for Janie, and she came back toward the motel, and there picked up the piece of string again, and had the cat chasing it.

This, David thought, was beautiful—girl and cat, this symbiosis, more dance than anything.

David followed Max around to the trunk of the car, and Max had his key out and opened the trunk and David looked in—this he'd been dreading since they'd left Minneapolis, and his fears about Max and the food did not go unrewarded. Here were two brown shopping bags, and he went through them, cans of Dinty Moore beef stew, two five-pound blocks of individually wrapped slices of Velveeta cheese, four loaves of Wonder Bread, half-crushed bags of noodles—now, that was right, the noodles—and presweetened drink mix. Instant coffee, that was good, too. A pint of whiskey for a drink if he wanted one, Max said.

Max had brought a cooler, a red Coleman.

"What's in it?" David asked, realizing he'd gotten an edge in his voice. With his father, it seemed they were always on the edge of something.

"Frozen steaks, hamburger."

"What do you want to do with the cooler?"

"What about it?"

"We can't bring it," David said.

"Why not?"

David set his hands on his hips, kept his eyes on the trunk.

"It's too wide," he said.

"Not if we put it in lengthwise . . ."

"Believe me," David said, "with that center thwart, you can't put it in lengthwise. How's Janie going to have any room?"

This pleased Max not at all. He somehow hadn't thought of that.

David slid the cooler to the side. They had food for, maybe, six days, tops. Less if the burger or steaks spoiled before they could eat them. But it was cold nights now, so maybe not. David felt the whole weight of it coming down on his shoulders. It was his call here, but he didn't want to get into it with Max.

Max had made all the typical weekender's assumptions, so what was the big deal?

David supposed it was that Max hadn't so much as asked somebody what he'd need. Max had never been out, and he'd been too proud, or too stubborn, or just too full of shit to spend an hour or two looking into it all. But even that wouldn't wash. If he'd been too proud, too full of himself, for that matter, he could have just called Hoigaard's, and they'd have given him an earful right over the phone, nameless, faceless, told him what was what.

But a goddamn Coleman cooler? David laughed to himself and Max bristled.

"What about the tent?" David said.

"A Timberline," Max said, the wings of his nose flaring. "That all right?"

David told him it was. That was good. But then Janie was calling to the cat behind him, "Kittie kittie kittie, here, kittie, come here, kittie," and he knew he'd have to do something about the food. For Janie.

But what David was aware of now was this: He had ten dollars on him, the last of his savings from painting apartments with his uncle Bobby. It made him almost sick to have to ask for money, worst of all from his father, but he was going to have to do it and, like usual, Max was going to humiliate him when he did.

This was the little ritual they'd gotten into, when the beatings had started at night, when he'd asked for his allowance all those years ago, and suddenly it was all right there, even in daylight, and David was sorry he'd ever thought he could do this, come out here with Max, but then he thought of Rachel.

Of course, she'd asked him, so it was different, so he didn't blame himself entirely, but he cursed himself anyway, here at the trunk, and now Janie, who'd worked as some salve between him and Max, gone with the cat.

But it was thinking of Janie that stopped all that hesitation.

"We need a Duluth pack," David said. "We need a dining fly, twelve by fifteen, ripstop nylon. We need some dehydrated potatoes, maybe some vegetables, and powdered soup. We need a map case . . . a spare paddle. I don't see any paddle here."

"All right," Max said. "So what the—" He was going to say *fuck*, but said, "What don't we need?"

"All I'm saying is—"

"I understand what you're saying just fine. So why don't you just say it?"

"Just . . . give me some money, and I'll go get the things. I know Herter's up the street, I've been there."

Max had his wallet out. "What do you want, fifty? That do it?" He held the money out at David as if he were holding out his blood, or his life. "Here," he said, shaking the two twenties and ten. "Take it."

"I've got ten," David said.

"You don't have *any*thing."

This shocked David. He wanted to say, What do you mean I don't have *any*thing? But he'd already retreated inside himself.

Never come out, he told himself. Never.

For Janie, then, he thought.

He struggled with thoughts of striking Max in the face; it occurred to him, the reason Buddy'd gotten to him the way he had was this, right here. He was used to taking it, had been since he'd been little, and then his father so huge, as he seemed even now, like some psychological trick, because Max wasn't, really, much larger than David. Max had twenty-five, thirty pounds over him, most of it fat.

"I'll get the things we need," David said, and took the bills. "Shouldn't take more than minutes."

"I'll drive you."

"No, don't," David said, turning away, and, moving up the street, he said over his shoulder, "Gotta be able to carry the stuff to portage it, anyway."

———

Inside Herter's he moved around the back of the store still in such a rage he couldn't see for it. It was a black mood he was in, the kind only Max could put him into, and he thought to go outside again, and just walk, walk it off, and he tried to decide what to do, leaning against a table stacked with portable stoves, some white gas, some Sterno, some propane. He idly handled a can of propane, his mind still tripping over itself, all that old crap coming up, and in it he got this sense of unreality.

And now, here he was talking to this guy, a badge on his shirt, *Herter's/Brian,* and he was very matter-of-factly telling him what he needed, and in minutes they were at the register, and David paid him, and they exchanged some pleasantries about the weather, and the clerk asked had he heard about the dump they'd gotten in Anchorage, a record breaker, which could be on its way south, and he helped David arrange the gear in the Duluth pack, which he'd rented, and so put the receipt in his wallet and then he was outside, and he smoked a cigarette, there beside a snarling wooden bear, half again his height, and David, looking at it, thought, Wrong species, this was *Ursus horribilis,* a grizzly, and there were no grizzlies in northern Minnesota. All black bears, *Ursus americanus,* though, since they'd habituated to having people around, and eating garbage, they could be dangerous, too.

Still, in his present mood, it calmed him somewhat, looking at the bear, and he crushed out his cigarette and moved up the street, the Duluth pack's straps digging painfully into his shoulders. But that was normal. And the pack was only partially full, and of no consequence. He told himself he'd done the right thing, and there was some satisfaction in that.

Yet the moment he was later to painfully remember was nearly upon him.

He was still sweating slightly at the humiliation of his father giving him the money—at *how* Max had given it to him. And at his, David's, having—even given that situation—taken it.

*You don't have any*thing.

He'd done it for Janie, he told himself, but that was a lie, because he'd been afraid for himself, too.

And like that, he approached the motel, and from a block back he heard voices. Something coiled and vicious there. And among those voices, but outnumbered, and so outpowered, was Max's. And David rushed then, the pack on his back nothing now, but then coming around a station wagon, two flat-bottomed Alumacraft canoes on the top, a sticker on the rusted rear bumper that read *Meat Cutters Unionize!*, he saw them, around the trees there, Max and Janie, at the car, and in front of them, at the motel, the men, hunkered in chairs on the porch, Janie yards back from the argument.

David slowed down, and then stopped.

He listened, from where he was standing, could see the four men behind the rail, his father at the Cadillac, leaning combatively toward them.

One man, who seemed almost ashamed to be sitting with the three others, looked off up the street and saw David, and knew he was the son, right off, which stopped David in his tracks. And that, for David, was another cause for regret later.

Regret and shame.

If he'd come out right then, maybe this man, who'd had some kindness in his eyes, maybe he would have stopped it. Because this bigger man, eyeing David, shook his head, and David, understanding, nodded in return, staying to the rear of the car, out of sight.

Don't put your old man in a position of having to be tougher than he is, the big man had signaled. And David had hung back.

But later, when it was all over, he asked himself, Had he done so to prevent things from getting out of hand, from escalating? Or out of cowardice?

And what could he have done, anyway?

Because by then their charges had gotten far beyond them, David's, and the big man's—who David would not know as "Jack Carpenter" until all of what came with the investigation later, though, even here, David sensed some dark complicity in the three with him. Yet most disturbing was this:

The shortest of the men with this "Jack," as if in some déjà vu moment, David seemed to know. But from where he could not recall.

But then, all three of the men with this Jack seemed somewhat familiar, only David just then couldn't have said how. Wouldn't know until long after it was all over who these men were:

To Jack's left, Larry Munson, just "Munson" here, Jack's former co-captain on the Austin Chargers football team, who, unbeknownst to Jack, had for some time been part of the theft going on at Dysart, and so had been asked to throw in his oar with the others, Munson rawboned and unshaven in his cutter's khakis, and wearing a pair of Red Wing boots, this sharp pleasure in his eyes, which David saw, and inwardly recoiled from.

And to Munson's left, Stacey Lawton, a man David recognized on sight as a coward, and a bully, the one to jump in *after*, Lawton's near-hyperthyroid eyes bulging, and his upper arms and back thick, fattish, and around his middle a sizable beer gut, and even, in this subtle morning light, wearing a baseball cap, *I'm With Stupid* emblazoned across the crown, an arrow pointing to his left, a kind of willful, and small, meanness in him, Lawton wearing green twill pants, and thick-soled work boots.

But it was the one on the far end that sent a shudder up David's back, this shortish familiar man, Dennis Penry, whom Munson and Lawton called The Goat, when he wasn't around to hear it—this man who would inhabit David's nightmares all his remaining life. He was the kind of person one avoided.

David knew that at a glance.

Penry couldn't have been more than five-four, but he was bulletlike, his features squashed together, his nose upturned and piggish, his forehead low. He wore aviator glasses with bottle-bottom-thick lenses, on his hands on the porch rail, like gaudy brass knuckles, those ugly Jostens rings, the kind no one wore, really—if they bought them at all. But Penry did, one a class ring, and another football—they'd been football buddies, David saw, and he assumed, wrongly, and with a kind of relief, *here* was what he'd thought familiar, Penry reminding him, in some vague way, of Buddy.

But Penry, he was retarded, or looked it, was a mechanic, or something, they all were, but then he put them together with the car—no, meat cutters, David thought, recalling the bumper sticker, and he thought, Max had no business getting near them, but here Max was, arguing with them.

David saw all that at a glance, and that Jack, on the end, was of a different order from the others. As if he were some chaperone, or what he couldn't say.

But Penry—"The Goat"—there was something wrong with him, in the way he was smirking, and in his milky-white skin, and flat, reddish brown oily hair, and in his thick hands on the porch railing.

He was ignoring the argument and was watching Janie and the cat. It was as if this short man were rubbing shit all over Janie, just by looking at her, David thought, but here was Max, out in front of the car, taking in none of it, and then Penry turned to Max.

"Like I told you, a canoe like that, you oughta be on a pond," Penry said. "You got taken, and then some."

"What do you call those cattle boats you got on top of your jalopy there?"

"Those Alumacrafts'll take a *poundin'* and keep on goin', unlike yours."

Max shook his head, glaring—he understood the insinuation. The threat. I could whup you, pussy boy. Watching, David felt—deep inside him—a kind of twisted pleasure, and at the same time felt shame at it. A very deep pleasure, and worse shame.

Max, before he'd beaten David, had always poked David in his chest with his index finger, his finger like an iron rod, which was maybe the worst of all.

Who do you think you are? Max had said. *You just can't take criticism, can you? What are you sniveling about? Can't you take it?*

You've always got that ugly look on your face.

Now Max was fussing with the canoe ropes on the front bumper of the Cadillac. From the way Max was muttering to himself, David thought it was all over, but then he saw the color rise in Max's forehead, and he got a sick feeling in his stomach.

"You got as big a mouth alone as you got with your pals there?" Max said, turning to look at Penry.

Penry, Munson, and Lawton laughed. Jack, beside them, took a deep breath and set his hands on his knees.

David felt something in his mouth, but whatever it was, it didn't come out.

Maybe just, *Dad,* which he didn't use around Max. Come on, Dad, let's get out of here. But he didn't say it, only stood, as if transfixed by the awfulness of it, behind the cars.

"You best watch your mouth," Penry said. "You got a girl there to be lookin' out for."

There was a second when David didn't know what to think, but he was oddly surprised at Max, how he swelled, became something he'd never seen.

It was frightening, what this meaningless argument was becoming, and all the while, he, David, was aware that all he had to do to end it was step out, out from behind the cars here. He set the pack down now, intending to.

But here was Max, shaking his head at the stupidity of it all, turning to the car again.

Max made a point of testing the ropes on the canoe, making sure they were taut, but when there came a snickering from up on the porch, he spun around.

"You got something to say?"

"I already said it," Penry said.

"What'd you say, just so we're clear on this?" There was a new edge in Max's voice, and it positively electrified the air.

Penry, though, knew where to jab now.

"Best watch out for that girl, you hear? There's bears out on those islands."

Max turned to face all four. He set his hands on his hips, and he soberly regarded Penry again.

"I see you out on the lake, coming into our camp, I won't warn you first."

David felt his brows knot at that—after all, what was Max implying here?

"What's to say I don't do just that?" Penry asked.

"Do what?"

"Come for a little chat?"

He seemed to be implying that there was something between them, himself and Max. But now the big man on the end, Jack, spoke up.

"Shut up," he said.

"Shut yourself up. The doc and me were just havin' a little . . . *understandin'*, weren't we?"

"You," Max said to Penry, "couldn't understand the sole of my fucking shoe."

This sent Munson and Lawton kicking back in their chairs and laughing.

"He got you there!" Lawton said, jabbing Penry with his elbow. "Jesus, did he get you! Dumber than the sole of his shoe, that's—"

Jack Carpenter bent forward and glanced down at Penry to see how he was taking it. There was no sign of humor on Penry's face, his skin taking on an even more ashen pallor. Then Penry smiled as if he hadn't smiled in years, dentures, his teeth bone white. Fake.

"All right," the big man on the end, Jack Carpenter, said, standing. "Let's move on and get some breakfast here. It's time, isn't it?"

Munson and Lawton stood, too.

There was a path through trees, a shortcut, and Jack Carpenter took it, and Munson and Lawton followed, Penry sitting there, glaring at Max, until Jack shouted, "Penry!"

Which name stuck in David's head like a hot poker.

And at the mention of his name, some door closed, or at least came closed a distance, so that Penry stood, smiled that smile again, and said to Max, "I'll be seeing you," and went off in the direction of the other men, their voices cajoling, and Lawton saying, loudly, "—sole of his shoe—now, that's a new low, Stupid!" And Penry laughed, David recognizing his voice, he was sure of it, it was the kind of laugh you'd hear in a nightmare, full of menace and dark possibility. More a bark than laughter.

But still, he couldn't *place* it.

David came around the back of the Cadillac, uneasily, as if he'd only arrived now. Janie was blinking in the bright sun, pulling at her hair the way she did when she was upset. Max was jerking at the ropes holding the canoe down, his gestures full of a rage that David had only seen directed at him.

"What was that all about?" David asked, his eyes on the men up the path.

"I was just talking to somebody."

"Who?"

Max spun around, and in that way David was too familiar with, he said, "I said it was *nothing*. All right?"

"All right," David said, but it was not all right, and when Janie came over, hugging the cat to her chest, her eyes were big and she was shaking.

She knew David had been standing there. She looked from David to Max and back again, gulping a little, as if she might cry. David stepped over beside her, and throwing his arm around her shoulder, and squeezing her, whispered in her ear, "Promise."

And Janie, clutching the cat, nodded.

———

They had the car loaded and were off to the ranger station before the men returned.

Max asked David and Janie to wait in the car while he went up to the ranger station, Max going up the steep hill purposefully, and David and Janie saying nothing in the car, Janie with her chin propped on the front seat, near David, but there between them this awkward quiet, neither knowing what to say, and David, to be busy with something, taking the map case he'd bought at Herter's, and folding the now-critical midsection maps he bought there, into Ziploc bags, and reaching into his pocket for the sheet of paper he'd found in the telephone booth, he did likewise with it, sealed the folded sheet in a baggie, and slid it into the case under the maps, all the while turned to his right and hunched over so Janie wouldn't see the sheet with the numbers and names scrawled on it and ask what it was—David himself didn't know, but again, as it had last night, it felt hot, dirty, awful somehow, even hidden as it was—and he rummaged around in the top flap of the Duluth pack, beside Janie, fitting the map case in the pack pocket under the heavy plastic window, yellowed and scratched and sewed into the heavy green canvas, eager to be rid of the maps and sheet of paper, and sat back, his thoughts tangled, anxious, and in light of the rest of it, the sheet with the numbers on it was forgotten, it was their itinerary he'd have to get Max to change, but they had topographical and relief maps now, and he was thinking of this other route to the west, and Janie said, "What's taking him so long?"

"I don't know," David said.

He was anxious to be gone, but then, anxious, too, about going out onto the lake, those men out there, somewhere. Maybe. He knew Max was submitting their travel plan, a day-by-day version of it, and these men would be doing the same, and that made David doubly wary.

It was possible, just possible, those men could find out where they were going.

Unlikely, but possible.

He was thinking, maybe, when Max returned he'd say something about changing their itinerary, and then Max's feet, then legs, were visible through the blue tinting in the windshield, Max coming down the slope from the ranger station, and the sun bright, and the car warm, even with the windows open.

Max thumped down behind the wheel.

"Okay!" he said loudly, and with so much assurance, David felt disinclined to say anything. Max started the car, then craning his head over his shoulder, backed out, and driving east, got his sunglasses on and wrapped the bows around his ears.

He smiled at David and slugged him, jovially.

"What?" David said.

"Yeah, what?" Janie said.

Max glanced over at David. He was going to say something, then changed his mind.

"What say we drive up to Grand Marais, and go in there."

"You got maps?"

"Sure do!"

David felt himself smile at that. He kicked back in the seat, into the heavy vinyl, craned his head around to look at Janie, and all that darkness went right out the window.

David knew what Max had done: He'd given the ranger their old itinerary. It was a bit dangerous, but not really, and they'd come out on the same day, in roughly the same place, and they'd never see the four men who'd been at the motel.

It was impossible. There were thousands of lakes out there.

They'd be fifty miles from them, to the east, and the lakes were all theirs again.

28

AT THE MOTEL THAT NIGHT, JACK CARPENTER WAS TIRING OF the waiting game. He didn't want to be implicated in some criminal mess with Stacey, or Penry, but he saw, sitting out on the porch in the dark, while the other three, just down from him, laughing, and farting, and telling jokes too old and stupid to be entertaining, drank themselves blind on Old Turkey, that he'd gotten himself into a worse-than-dangerous spot.

All that was sickeningly clear to him.

Why, after all, should he believe what Carol had told him was true? Or that Stacey wasn't involved in some way she might not be aware of? For all he knew, the whole thing, aside from Stacey's charge of assault, might have been engineered to guard their job security. Jack had promoted a Mexican, just the week before, to co-supervise the cutting floor, a man named Joseph Martinez, who was honest, hardworking, and something of a leader. Jack had told everyone under Joseph, especially Stacey, who'd been passed up for the promotion, that he'd had to do it, promote Martinez, because over half the workers on the cutting floor were Mex now, and he needed someone down there to manage them, or there'd be terrible trouble.

But what Jack hadn't said was this: He'd have hired Martinez anyway.

He worked blazingly fast, almost too fast, really, for safety, but was determined to make life work in the plant, for him and the others there, and *not* just the Mexicans, and Jack *liked* the man. Which no way could he say to anyone—nor could Joseph say it of Jack.

But it was true. He liked Joseph, with his deep-set dark eyes, intelligent eyes, and the picture of Mary and Jesus he kept in his pocket. His slow, considered way of breaking up fights. His low mutter at trouble, Haysus, Maree-ah, Yosepha!

And now what? Even if Stacey did run—and was that why they were really up here anyway, given it seemed an almost impossible plan?—he was shouldered with the burden of this theft business. Or was he?

Jack glanced down the porch at Munson, Lawton, and Penry.

Penry had stuck straws up his nose and was braying like a donkey, while Munson and Lawton, laughing, slapped at him.

Jack gave Munson a level look. Munson he'd asked to go with them so he'd have somebody to back him up if it came to that. Munson sobered for a moment, but when Stacey said, "Fuckin' jackass! Get it?" Munson let go a mouthful of compressed air through his lips, Penry braying again, and making a farting sound, and all three broke out in laughter, nearly falling from their chairs.

"Hey," Jack said, sharply, "keep it down! There's other people staying here!"

"Yeah, well, who the fuck are you, our chaperone or something?"

This from Penry, and then the three of them were laughing themselves breathless.

Maybe it was the pot that was making them so stupid, Jack thought. He'd smoked the stuff when he was a teenager, but had laid off after he'd taken management at Dysart. It was some education, not getting loaded, and spending time around people who did, an education and then some.

"We need some pussy," Penry said.

"Where you gonna get pussy around here, Stupid," Stacey said.

"Ah, fuck you!" Penry said.

"Let's get fucked up," Munson said, and handed the brass pipe down.

"Want some, Hank?" Munson said. It was his one effort at reestablishing his tie to Jack, but the nickname put Jack off.

All the full-timers on the cutting floor at Dysart who hadn't made management called him Hank, he was never sure why, but he didn't like it.

"I say we go find the doctor and fuck his little girl, and then fuck him," Penry said.

There was a shocked silence, even from Lawton and Munson, and then they hit Penry, all the harder, around the head, Penry snorting like a donkey again, but when Penry stopped braying, he turned to look down the porch at Jack, who was glaring at him.

"I don't want to hear shit coming out of your mouth like that again, you hear me, Penry?"

"Aww, fuck off," he said.

"Yeah, fuck off," Stacey said. "You and your fucking management horseshit. I mean, just who the fuck do you think you are?"

Jack, when he'd been captain of the football team, had had to deal with this before. Had dealt with it for years at the plant.

"You think about what you just said," he told Penry.

"Ah, fuck you all over again. What would you know, anyway, you fuckin' spick lover."

This struck Jack with the force of a blow.

"What did you say, Penry?" he said. He was standing now.

"He didn't mean nothin'," Munson said, and Stacey shot out, indignant, "The fuck he didn't."

"So what is it?" Jack said. "I wanna hear it."

"Fuckin' gasbag," Penry said.

"You want to talk to me, Penry?" Jack said.

"Fuckin' blown-up fuckin' Dysart gasbag!"

Now it had gone too far. There was a heavy silence and Munson said, "Ah, Jesus, Hank. Fuck, I mean *Jack*. It's just drink talkin', what him and Stacey's sayin'."

"The fuck it is, Munson," Stacey said.

Munson put a restraining hand on Stacey's shoulder, pushed him back down when he tried to stand. Stacey caught Munson in the face with his elbow, and then Stacey was up, only a yard or two between him and Jack.

"I'll tell you something, you . . . fuckin' *asshole*. We stood behind you when you said not to strike, and you promised better wages, and better this and fuckin' that, and ten years down the line, what do we got?"

"I *got* you better wages," Jack said, something stentorian in his voice. "You *got* better working—"

"Sure," Stacey said, throwing out his arm and pointing his finger at Jack. "Sure, you're a fine one to fucking talk, dressed up in a monkey suit and tie and in your office, and then after all this goddamn time, some management job comes up, and who do you give it to? The *fuckin' spick*—not me, not Munson, not—"

Jack didn't have to say, Penry? You think Penry could work management?

Stacey was leaning, weaving a bit, toward Jack.

"Siddown," Munson said. "You said your piece."

"No, I ain't," Stacey said. "I know about you giving Carol those bonuses, and she's gotta do everything but suck your god-damn dick for 'em, and be nice, and all that shit, and you playing hangdog and sorry Hank with your wife gone and maybe takin' your kids, and needin' that huge fuckin' house for just you, just you in that big ol' house, and me and Carol in a double-wide, like everybody else here, and every fuckin' time there's a management position, it goes to somebody else, and you fuckin'—"

Jack cleared his throat, he was going to say, You forget why we're up here?

But it occurred to him, he was almost sure now he didn't know himself. He knew not to say word one about what Carol had told him about the stealing, though.

"You pull it together, show you got leadership ability, you'd get promoted just like anybody else. Cut back on all your bottle flu days."

But it was a lie. Management had told Jack he was never to promote Stacey Lawton, or Larry Munson. Penry wasn't even a consideration.

"That all the fuck you got to say?"

They were still standing, but now were just an arm's length apart.

"What do you want me to say, Stacey?" Jack said, but his heart was racing.

Even Munson, he saw now, was ready to take him down if he so much as moved. All three of them would.

"Hell, even *I* could tell those *spicks* just how to get off," Penry said.

And Munson tossed his head back and laughed, and Stacey with him, Penry, again, not understanding the humor in what he'd said, and Jack uncomfortably moved back, to grip the railing that Penry had gripped earlier, when he'd been looking at the little girl.

"What would you do in management, anyway?" Munson said, and shook Penry.

And Stacey Lawton did the same. Shook Penry.

It had always been like this, and Penry, not quite getting it, glowered, and then made a face, and Munson slapped Jack's arm. "We were just messin' with ya, Jack, can't you take a joke?" he said, and the three of them sat again, and were joking, but when Jack turned his back to them, and stood there with the railing under his hands, he knew what was at stake.

He took a deep breath, the *schook! schook! schook!* of the three of them opening beers behind him.

Now Munson prodded him with a bottle.

"Jack, ol' boy, have a beer."

Jack turned and smiled for the three of them. He took the beer and drank from it, but all the while, as he was forcing a look of calm on his face, something inside him was crawling, and he was thankful he hadn't suggested they move off into the woods so as not to bother the other people staying at the motel.

And it was time now. Stacey for the last two days had phoned Carol, just after ten, to see if the Mexican had died. They'd taken him off critical, but they still weren't sure, and then, too, the witnesses to the thing were proving to be unreliable, or so she'd told Stacey.

"You gonna call Carol, Stacey?" Jack asked.

Stacey rocked up out of his chair, then stumbled back into it.

"Ah, shit," he said.

He tried to get out of the chair again, and Jack said, "Listen, I can make the phone call easy as you. I'll do it. Anything you want me to say?"

The three of them looked at one another, between them some private joke, Penry trying not to spit it out, and Stacey said, "*Don't*, Stupid! *Don't now!*"

Jack tried to smile for them, then went down the stairs and off into the dark, and Stacey called to him, trying to suppress his laughter, "Ask about the kids, all right?"

In the dark, Jack tossed his hand high over his head, a will-do wave, and then he was moving up the street, by parked cars shiny in the moonlight, and he was not smiling, and he was moving quickly.

———

"Joseph?" he said, calling from the phone booth just outside Herter's.

"Jack?"

There was an awkward silence. Jack had never called him at home. Even his name felt a little strange in Jack's mouth, or he felt as if he weren't pronouncing it quite correctly, and felt like a fake if he tried.

"Listen," Jack said. "I want you to check the weights on the trucks independently, have somebody spot-check up the road."

"Only the police can do that."

"I know," Jack said. "You're friends with Barrera, aren't you?"

Barrera was the officer doing the investigation on the beating, the one Mexican officer in town.

"When?" Joseph said.

"On shift tonight."

"Tonight?"

There was another awkward silence.

"You aren't gonna tell me what this is all about?"

"I can't."

"Does it have something to do with Lawton, or is it Penry?"

"It might," Jack said, intentionally being ambiguous. He didn't want to implicate anyone just yet.

Joseph swore on the other end of the line.

"You know something I don't?" Jack said.

"I don't have to tell you how it is down on the floor, you were there years back."

This struck Jack as something new now, though.

"You think this wasn't just some bar brawl?"

"The witnesses have all gone off, Jack. Without them, what's Jesus's wife got?"

"Gone off? What do you mean?"

"You know *exactly* what I mean. Each and every one's disappeared."

"He gonna make it?"

"Maybe, but even then . . ."

Jack heard steps on the wooden planking down from Herter's.

"Don't forget what I said," he spoke sharply into the phone, and pressed the lever down with his finger, still holding the phone to his ear, then fed more coins into the slot, his back turned, punching out the number, and had Carol on the line, and, in a loud voice, was blathering about the weather, and what they'd done, even as Munson came up behind him, his eyes glassy and hard.

"Wanna talk to Carol?" Jack said, and Munson smiled, as if relieved at something.

"Stacey sent me down, forgot something," Munson said, and when Jack lifted the phone to Munson's outstretched hand, he worried Munson would feel he was shaking.

Jack stepped back into the dark.

"Carol?" Munson said. "Yeah, sure. Great weather. Sure. You didn't?"

Munson looked at Jack, then nodded.

"No, Jack *didn't* say. They really think he's gonna make it? Surgery? Uh-huh. But that's goddamn great news. Sure. Yeah." Munson was about to put the phone down, when he said, abruptly, "Oh, Carol, Stacey said— No, he's not here, he and Penry went off to get some stuff. Right. Anyway, he wanted me to ask you to have Stan over at Conoco check the radiator, make sure there's enough antifreeze in it, he plumb forgot." Munson pressed the phone tighter to his ear, his eyes narrowing. "What?" There was another pause. "All right. I'll tell him," Munson said, and he hung the phone up, but even as he did, Jack could hear Carol talking on the other end. "Jack? Jack, are you there?"

"What'd she say?" Jack asked.

"She wanted me to tell you your insurance agent called at her place, looking for you, he wants you to call when you get back. A Dick Lutz," Munson said, and Jack shrugged, but his heart was kicking something awful.

"Dick Lutz" was a code he and Carol had used when there was something to say between them and someone was within earshot, or sometimes at the table, over dinner. They'd done it since they'd been kids. Dick Lutz had been a neighbor who'd put out poison in his yard for cats. I do feed the birds, he'd warned. Still, when Jack and Carol's cat, Tiger, a tom that liked to roam, disappeared, they'd blamed Lutz, and hadn't forgotten.

So it was all at once a warning, and a finger pointed in some direction, and now, a forgiveness.

Jack didn't want to move from the phone, and his head tangled with excuses to go into town so he could find some way to call Carol again.

He had to get to another phone, but here Munson had his elbow, was steering him back toward the motel.

"What were you waitin' on there, Jack?" Munson said, in his voice something sharp. "You should've told me the good news right off!"

Jack, for a second longer, resisted moving from the phone, feeling the rush of blood in his neck, and his eyes thick with it, and his mind a hot nothing, and then, shrugging, he moved up the road with Munson, and just when Jack's breath began to come evenly, Munson slapping him on the back, they were met on the road by Penry.

"Stacey's off!" Munson said, and added, "Who you got to call now?"

"Girlfriend," Penry joked, his teeth white in the dark.

"You're lookin' a little hangdog," Penry said, slapping Jack's shoulder as he went by. "We gotta celebrate! Ol' Stacey's off the hook! Soon's I get this call over, okay? We'll make a night of it, hey?"

"Right," Jack said.

29

THEY WERE IN IT TOGETHER NOW, DAVID THOUGHT, AND SO when Max made a big deal of passing up yet another place to park the Cadillac, David didn't ask what Max was doing. Now they'd drive up a spur off the main road from Highway 12, or what had been the old Gunflint Trail, and then, where the road met a lake, Max would look this way and that, the water tantalizingly close, and beautiful, blue and mirror smooth, and he'd shake his head, and turn around and drive out again, and it all seemed like nonsense, but Janie, sitting in the back, her head perched between the seats, didn't ask why they tried one launching sight after another, here in white pine, and birch in full autumn gold along shore, and the gravel crackling under the car and spitting musically off the hubcaps, and here, just now, Max not seeming to give a shit if the paint got chipped, which he always had made noise about before, or the windshield broken, or something dented, which had always made David feel worthless, that his father cared more about his shiny cars, or his gear or whatever, and not one of them mentioned the men at the motel, though Max, David suspected, knew David had not only seen them but had maybe even heard all of it, and not come to his aid, but that was forgiven for his silence here, for not bringing up how Max had brought out the worst in those men, and finally, now, turning left once again, they drove due north, the sun brilliant on their right, and here was a huge erratic, a boulder the glacier had left, many millennia ago, and when Max approached it, the road turning in a hairpin around it, Max smiled broadly, and there was an authentic, happy moment, when Max saw that others had parked their cars behind the erratic, three cedars growing off it, one on each side and one at the top, and Max threw the car in park, and they got out and stretched, having been hours in the car.

Max walked back up the road, in the direction they'd come, and David knew what Max saw, that the erratic, some ten, fifteen feet high and thirty feet wide, blocked the view of the car from the road, and Max walked farther out, and when he came back this time, he scuffed over their fresh tracks, all the way up to the car, and then rubbing his hands together, and taking a cheerful swing at David to muss up his hair, said, "We're here!" Janie understanding this as a signal that she could run down to the water, while David and Max lifted the canoe off the top of the car.

"See, it's light!" Max said, almost as if an apology, and David said, "That's great, it *is* light."

It wasn't exactly, but David was so caught up in being away from all that ugliness that it *felt* light, and he swung it expertly off the top of the car, Max watching, he'd been ready to help with it, but here David had it himself, and Max, also, given the circumstances, wasn't going to do his usual, run things. Bark out commands as he had in the past.

"Sixty-six pounds," he said. "A Grumman eighteen-footer'd weigh about eighty-five, ninety."

David carefully navigated the path down toward the lake, Max behind him.

"Sure you got it?"

"I got it," David said.

Janie stood to the side when David stepped over the rocks, all granite onshore, and more, smaller erratics, and here some columnar basalt.

He swung the canoe around so he was holding it with both gunnels against his chest; then, leaning forward, he set it on his upraised knee, his right foot fixed on a stone, and with his leg braced like that, David turned the canoe right side up, eased the stern down to the water, and sliding the glossy length of it over his jeans-covered knee, worked the gunnels through his hands until he set the bow down, lightly, on the rocks.

Janie was going to step into the canoe when David tossed his arm out, stopping her.

"Best way to learn how to use these things is on the water, but I'll tell you, okay?"

Janie nodded. Max was walking toward them, the Duluth pack on his back, and other gear hung off his arms awkwardly.

There was something in the light that was reassuring, even a new start, and they all felt it, and that the bad thing had happened already, the dark energy that had been there all along was spent on someone else, was spent somewhere else, and they were almost giddy with it.

"You look like a hat rack," Janie said to Max.

All three of them laughed. David just loved Janie then. All over again.

Where'd the kid think of this stuff?

"I feel like a . . . hat rack," Max said, laughing and shrugging the gear off.

All three of them went back up to the car, the light coming on brighter, and they made trips down to the canoe, and packed what they didn't take in the trunk, and the wind blew in off the lake, but had in it the quality of the sunlight.

And for just this time they were happy. Max suggested they dump the itinerary altogether and just head out north, northwest, they could handle whatever came up, and they'd just wing it, do exactly what they wanted to.

They'd push through just as much country as they wanted to, how was that?

David said that was fine, and since it was almost eleven, they ate, and David didn't mind the Velveeta; in fact, out in the bright, sharp air, it tasted wonderful, the day itself like that, here, though none of them could have named it then, this moment of grace, for the mind registers it as something unearned, and so one doesn't speak of it, because to do so is to start all over again that balancing, and weighing, Is this enough, Am I happy, Why am I here, Why am I doing this, because in this moment, especially one like this, there is something of eternity, and in Max's dumping the itinerary there was something unformed, but having infinite potential.

A promise of something new, a gift.

They could, from this spot, go in any of ten directions, and from those directions, over living water, cross pine-backed islands, or peninsulas, and they knew that if time permitted, they could take this water all the way to Hudson's Bay, an unfathomable distance, and all now in near readiness, the canoe, almost like some magical transport, and in their bodies, the knowledge that here, now, they would carry themselves out, and as far as they knew, all that existed out there other, but was already becoming them, and this moment the physical form of what was already becoming myth, their trip, this moving out into, not the ordered geometries of cities, and all that one did in them, but something close to the skin, something that would write itself on their bodies, though only David knew about the blisters, the aching knees, the sunburn, windburn, and the rhythm that the canoe brought to it all, or how the islands were more than that, were, strangely, oases, were like markers in cities, like time, like minds, like life itself.

And there was this in the moment: perfection.

That was what held them there, sitting on the rocks onshore, after they'd eaten, the sun in the trees, and a red-tailed hawk circling like some lost soul over the broad, untrammeled vastness.

Alone, here, one could be anything.

And together? They had an identity the father was not about to speak, for fear it would be rejected. Family, again. And, too, speaking it would bring out the cajoling, and criticizing, which was his concern, masked by fear, bring out his own warped self, created in the forge of yet another family, which in turn had formed his.

And the boy, maybe, for a time, would not have to be older than he was, would not have to, moment by moment, manufacture a personality to show to the world. But here, since he knew this life better than his father, or sister, he felt awkward. He knew far more than his father did, was the expert here.

Yet even given that, he should not be the one to start it, perhaps only to help it work.

And did he really want that? For things to work out? Something in him had said absolutely not, but here, in this moment, he really did ask himself, What if? (What *if* he let Max in, if he were like this? As Max was *now*.)

And the girl, she could stop clowning. Stop working so hard, stop humiliating herself to save the others, she was so tired from it, it was killing her, she had dark circles under her eyes, a girl of seven, going on eight, but with a very sharp mind, but loved for the clown she'd made herself out to be, the act becoming so ingrained it had become indistinguishable from herself.

So they sat, the cool, sharp wind on their faces, and the lake shucked up wave after wave against the red canoe, and they did not want to start it, any one of them, because they all knew, with the first word, the first gesture, their postlapsarian life would begin again, that life of opposites, and of friction, of disappointments, yet of moments of joy, and even, at times, moments like this.

Coming with stillness, and a sense that just now, just here, of all places, and of all times, *here* was everything, was perfection, just now.

David, wanting the moment to last, just . . . so much as seconds longer, without speaking, pointed to the silver-green backs of sunfish, golden bellied and dappled green, that schooled offshore.

Janie tossed them a piece of bread, and the water was broken with the feeding fish.

"All right," Max said, and just like that, they were back in the everyday world.

But it was right that Max had done it; had gotten them moving, had spoken first.

"You got the stern, right?" David said to Max. "You want me to show you a few strokes?"

"Hey, you put the paddle into the water and pull it back. It's a no-brainer. I mean—"

"Fine," David said.

He'd known, even down in Minneapolis, it would be like this. But Max would see soon enough. He, David, wouldn't be the one to spoil the spell here.

"So you're in first," David said.

He could see that this made no sense to Max, but Max wasn't going to show himself to be ignorant, and so he stepped into the canoe, and as all beginners do, when the canoe rocked, he stretched up, hands over his shoulders, and David had to shout, "Hands on the gunnels, low over your feet! Stay low when you spin around! Okay?"

Max nodded, but David could tell he was irritated.

But he'd had to raise his voice. He had Janie sit on the bow, to pin the canoe in place, and David hefted the Duluth pack in, a terrible weight with the canned stew and frozen steaks and gear, and Max's kit. Lifting the pack over the gunnel, a good seventy pounds, his back burned, and he spun the pack over the center thwart and into the bottom of the canoe with a loud, hollow clunking.

He set a cushion down in front of the pack and over the thwart, then slid the extra paddle against the hull. Then came his day pack, stuffed full, behind the bow seat, and the tent and overfly and bags.

"Now what?" Janie said.

David stood at the bow and handed Janie in. She grabbed the gunnels, smiling to herself at how easy it was, and how she'd gotten it. Balancing if she stayed low.

"Am I gonna get to paddle?" she said.

David could see Max, behind her, was thinking not.

"Of course," David said.

Janie sat on the cushion, her back up against the Duluth pack.

"Hey, this is nice," she said.

David looked over her head at Max.

"Anything else?"

They had already discussed how they'd find the car. The spur they'd taken was numbered: 85 S. They could canoe south later, however they wanted, leave the canoe, and take 12 east, and get the car that way. Drive back to pick up the canoe whenever.

The canoe, weighted so heavy in the rear, lifted at the bow.

The canoe had floatation compartments fore and aft, and Max had said you could remove them, to really cut the weight, but they'd want them now.

His hands on his hips, David stood looking north.

He was thinking they'd forgotten something, that was for sure, you just never knew what, until you were three days out on the water, and by that time it usually didn't matter, anyway.

Rain gear, cold gear, food, matches, extra paddle, tent and dining fly, first-aid stuff, emergency gear, soap, iodine tablets. Sleeping bags.

Location of the car.

Gloves, unlined leather, but . . . hey, it was almost sixty out, and it would be above freezing at night.

Warm hat—a stocking hat, he'd forgotten that.

His new knife with the compass in the handle he had strapped to his calf, under his jeans. Wearing it, he felt both some actor in a silly drama and like the real thing.

"Okay," he said. "Ready?"

Janie nodded apprehensively, while Max, in back, tried hard to look like he knew what he was doing.

David grunted lifting the bow, then giving a hard shove, the cedar hull grating on the coarse sand, heaved the canoe out, swiveling expertly over the bow deck, braced on his forearms and bringing his legs in just in front of the bow seat, while the canoe drifted out onto the lake backward, into deep water.

David, sitting, picked up his paddle.

"Hard on your left," he called back over his shoulder to Max, who gave an almost herculean stroke, digging in with his paddle so deeply he went down over the gunnel, the canoe listing on its side—*Goddammit fuck all!* David thought to himself—the goddamn canoe, even with as much weight as they had in it, was tipsy, due to the hull—and he threw his weight opposite to counter, shouting at the same time, "Hey! *Stop! Get down!*"

The canoe settled, and David craned his head over his shoulder, Max glowering at him.

"Let's see what you did," he said.

Max started to dig in again, and David said, "Stop!"

Max obliged. The canoe was drifting slightly, a northwesterly carrying it by a point of land. David turned to face across the lake a moment. He knew today would be the hardest, the potential ruin of the whole trip.

He had to keep his feelings out of his voice, because here he was angry with Max.

"Listen," and then he said the magic word, or the word that cost him almost everything.

"Dad," he said.

Max turned away suddenly, and then David did, too.

Hey, David thought to himself, this awful burning in his throat. *My God.*

And Max said, "Okay, Davey"—which diminutive he hadn't used in years—"you tell me how to do it."

And like that, David did.

"If you're going to sit, put one leg out, cock the other under you, and pull against the center of the canoe—up the leg that's stuck out. Okay?"

Max did that, and David—carefully, and kneeling—made long, slow strokes on the opposite side, and in the opposite direction, backstroking, until they came around one hundred eighty degrees.

David switched sides then, and calling over his shoulder for Max to as well, gave his first real pull, up the canoe's centerline, to port, his right hand on the grip of the paddle, and drawing with his left, then again, the water gurgling alongside the canoe, and like that, they eased away from shore, and David put off telling Max about the strokes, and kneeling instead of sitting, and instead paddled quickly, two strokes for each of Max's, to keep the canoe on point, which was at first exhausting, but then there came that silence he found in running, and with the light on the water, a million blue diamonds in all that green, and an island, their first, miles up the lake, he labored, something close to song in him.

30

WHAT DAVID HAD MEANT TO DO FOR AN HOUR OR TWO, HE did all that afternoon, and into the early evening, until they came alongshore of an island, one with old iron mooring pins set in the lichen-covered granite shoreline.

David helped Janie out, then walked the canoe around the shore to a cleft in the granite, where other canoeists had tied down—you could tell by the gray smudges of aluminum on the granite—and there David gave Max a hand out, and they, silently, and with near exhaustion, packed the gear over a rise to a flat spot that overlooked the length of the lake.

There was almost no wind now, and with the air still, bird cries seemed to carry forever. Just the gulls, and at one point, what they thought might be the clunking of paddles against a canoe, but they saw no one, and so set up the tent, and David had a fire going, and discovered Max had sprung for tin cups, which burned your lips if you had anything warm in them—cups were one thing you wanted to be plastic—and they only had one pot, an aluminum one, and a half-assed fry pan and Teflon spatula, which would melt, but to hell with it, David thought.

He had the steaks out, and he cut birch sticks, and skewered the steaks, and opened a tin of corn and set it over the grate the Forest Service provided, and Max all the while worked on the tent with Janie, and David turned to see Max was trenching around it, and he had to go back and tell him, "Nobody trenches anymore— it's illegal, for one thing, and second, it causes erosion, you'll ruin this whole site if you do that," and Max was going to go ahead and do it anyway, but David told him the overfly on the tent was the reason you didn't need to trench.

"See?" he said. "You pull the overfly cables as far out from the tent as possible. Then the water drains off. And you have the tent in a declivity."

"Declivity?" Max said.

"It's low here. Move it back up there." David pointed. And Max began to disassemble the tent, and David laughed.

"Hey, Dad," he said, and Max grinned, then shrugged.

"What?"

"Just take the stuff out, and pick the whole thing up by the frame."

"You can do that?" Janie said.

When they had the gear out, David showed them. He lifted the tent by the thin, segmented aluminum poles.

"It looks like a kite," Janie said.

Max and David laughed, and Max and Janie moved the tent back, and David went down to the fire. There were two logs at an angle to the fire, to sit on, and David sat, stirring the can of corn, and the steaks sizzling, the juice dropping onto the coals and David's mouth watering.

He itched for a cigarette but wasn't about to light one.

Then here came Max and Janie behind him, and he handed them the aluminum plates, and steel knife and forks, and David cut a corner off one of the steaks, pronounced them done—even though it was obvious they weren't—though squeamish Janie shoved hers right into the coals so that David had to lift it up.

And they ate as the darkness came on, the moon lifting buoyant and bone white out of the pines.

When they'd finished, Max sat back, looking at the ring around the moon.

Janie had slid down the log until she was sitting on the stone, under it, the log behind her back, her head slumped forward, and like that she was asleep, and David nodded at her, and Max said, "Just let her sleep," but David didn't, he got his hands under her, and she threw her arms around his neck, and like that he carried her up to the tent and slid her, clothes and all, into the nylon bag, and he went down and sat beside Max, thinking this would be awkward now, but it wasn't.

They cleaned out the pot the corn had been in, and brushed their teeth, and went back and sat by the fire. On the lake, a breeze stirring up chop, the moon was reflected like scoops of quicksilver a million times over.

"You want to take the bow in the morning?" David said, and Max said that would be fine.

There was all that between them, and especially what had taken place in the dark years ago, so David felt oddly defensive again, especially now, but Max kept his distance, and they didn't speak, it being too soon.

And when Max, finally, blinking, and near sleep, rose, David said good night.

———

He bolted to his feet when he felt a hand on his shoulder, something holding his arms down in his dream, David, for a moment, still in that other world, even with his eyes open, but it was only morning, and it wasn't someone pinning his arms at his sides, it was his sleeping bag. Max had pulled it up over him, in back of the fire, even wadding his jacket there for a pillow, and David, sheepishly, shook himself, then slid from the bag and snatched up the big pot and trod down over the rough stone to the water, and resting on his heels, took a hard look over the trees and islands as far as he could see in all directions.

Not one line of smoke, he thought, and smiling to himself, he went back up to the fire Max had started and got the coffee going and then woke Janie.

"Sport," he said, shaking her shoulder. "Hey, Sportnik, wake up," he said.

31

BACK IN ELY, JACK CARPENTER, HIS FEET PROPPED ON THE porch railing, the sun boiling bright orange out of the trees so he had to squint against it, was waking, too, though he'd been up for some time.

He'd assumed they'd be heading for home, now that Stacey had called Carol, and it had turned out the Mexican hadn't made it through surgery, was dead, but the witnesses were gone, had run off somewhere, and others were coming forward to say that Stacey hadn't done the beating, had been across town.

All of it made Jack uneasy, the too-convenient disappearance of the witnesses, and the others coming forward to provide an alibi for Stacey after the Mexican had died.

Now he crossed and recrossed his boots on the porch rail, trying to calm himself.

Earlier this morning, he'd seen Stacey returning from behind the motel where he'd been airing his sleeping bag, and Stacey had not seemed jubilant, his head down, and muttering what to himself Jack couldn't tell. Yet out on the porch, a short while later, Stacey had given a big whoop when Munson and Penry had shuffled out, rumpled, and hungover, in this big show of relief.

"Stacey's off!" Munson—he was thinking of him that way now, rather than Larry—had nearly shouted, slapping Jack on the shoulder. "Let's all have breakfast!"

Jack had declined, and they'd driven off up Main, laughing, and poking at each other.

With his feet up, and the sun in his eyes, he was thinking he should have gone with them. For his own safety, if nothing else. Stacey getting off so easily seemed rigged. Fixed. And their elation seemed much the same. An act. But he was sure Carol wouldn't have told anyone she'd let Jack in on their stealing.

But then, why *Dick Lutz*? Why had she warned him? And about what? He'd thought to call Carol, first thing this morning when the others went out for breakfast, but when he'd picked up the receiver in their unit, a recorded message informed him that long-distance calls had to be arranged with the manager. And the manager's office was closed.

Open at Nine, said the card in the office window. *We Take American Express*.

Even now—having waited what seemed an eternity—it was only an hour or so after daylight.

He thought to try the pay phone again, but the last time, when he'd walked over to it, up the street, Stacey'd been there, and Penry and Munson in the restaurant window across the street had waved to him, so he'd come back to the motel and aired his bag.

Now, on the porch, rocking on the rear legs of his chair, he felt a near panic, about calling Carol, but if he walked to the opposite end of town, he'd pass the restaurant, and the others, and anyway, wasn't he being just a little paranoid?

Still, it had been like that since Munson had given him Carol's message—*Dick Lutz*. They hadn't let him out of their sight, and when he'd finally insisted he take a walk last night, and alone, and he'd left, seconds later, there had been Munson at his side, yammering away, all good-old-times bullshit and weren't they still great pals.

It was all a mess.

He couldn't just go on at Dysart. If he stayed, he would have to expose not only Munson, Stacey, and Penry, but his sister, too. And who all else he couldn't even guess. He felt caught in some daylight nightmare, one he couldn't think himself out of. But then, maybe part of him had needed just this to cut himself free? It was what Lena had been telling him for years, that it would take a disaster to cut him free of Dysart.

That was one bright thought in all that seemed so dark now.

Lena.

On their way back down to Austin, he wanted to swing by Hazelton, in Minneapolis, and talk with her. He figured Pen and Stacey and Munson could wait an hour or two while he did that, could occupy themselves downtown, and after, they could get back to Dysart, and their lives.

And he would cut himself free—the thought of which was both terrifying and exhilarating.

He was thinking this on the porch, and that he should, right now, call Carol, no matter what, when Munson pulled in front of the motel with the station wagon, the canoes on the roof, and got jauntily out, tossing the door shut behind him with a *ca-chunk!* He'd assumed Munson was having breakfast with Penry and Lawton, but now Munson made a point of calling cheerfully up to Jack, "Hankster!" and the manager of the motel came out, in a red plaid shirt, a man in his seventies, sweeping, and he looked Munson over, and Munson said to him, "How far a drive is it over to Grand Marais?"

"An hour," the manager said. He was looking, with narrowed eyes, at the beer bottles they'd left on the porch, a case and then some. The green bottles were strewn from one end of the porch to the other.

"You boys tied one on, did you?"

"We got some vacation time, Pops," Munson said. "Gotta blow off some steam."

Jack was watching Munson now, much in the way the manager was.

"We'll clean it up," Jack said, an apology in his voice.

"I'd appreciate it," the manager replied, then added, "You plan to make that much noise again, I'd appreciate you move on tonight."

Jack gave Munson a hard look; when the manager turned his back, Munson made a stroking gesture from his groin.

"What's up at Grand Marais?" Jack asked.

"Are you blind, or what?" Munson said, pointing to the canoes.

"I'm not going up there."

"Come on, for Christ's sake," Munson jabbed. "I'm *not* gonna have that—" He shook his head and rolled his eyes and said, "Fuckin' Penry in my canoe. And . . . shit, when was the last time you went anywhere? Huh?"

Jack let go an exasperated breath; he didn't want any part of this, hadn't from the first.

"Come on, Cap, just for old times. We're footloose and fancy-free here. When's the next that'll ever happen again? Whaddaya say?"

"Where are Lawton and Penry?"

"I left 'em on the third load of pancakes."

Jack snorted. Stacey was working on one first-class gut, but Munson and Penry still lifted together a couple times a week, spotted each other, had stayed hard.

"I don't know . . ." Jack said.

"We don't gotta be with 'em all the time, we can take off and get a half-hour lead or something."

"Yeah, that's true," Jack said, and giving the impression of deciding something, pursing his mouth, said, "But nah. I've got things to do."

"Hey, sir?" Munson said, addressing the manager, suddenly almost greasily obsequious, the old man sweeping up leaves, standing with his broom.

The old man didn't say anything, just looked at the two of them, but mostly at Munson.

"If I give you one of our bottles of Seagram's, could you tell us where to go in on the Gunflint?"

Jack felt embarrassed at it, Munson's inclusive *us,* and stood, brushed his pants down. The manager was shaking his head, disgusted, because it appeared Munson was drunk, and it being barely after eight.

"I'm taking a Greyhound," Jack said, tossing his coffee over the rail, then crossing the porch. He meant to get his sleeping bag in back.

Munson shook himself, and as Jack passed him on the stairs, Munson took hold of Jack's shirt and pulled him closer, and Jack smelled it then, the bourbon on Munson's breath, and Munson said, in a low voice, "I helped you all that time ago. Now it's *your* turn."

"Like how?" Jack said.

Jack meant, How had Munson helped him? It had always been Jack bailing Munson out, Munson with his pregnant girl-friend, driving her down to the Twin Cities to get it "fixed," as Munson had put it, or picking him up from the Austin jail the time he'd gotten the DWI.

"You aren't gonna leave me here with those two assholes, are you?"

Jack turned his back to Munson. If he hadn't, maybe he wouldn't have gone for Munson's ruse, because Munson was grin-ning, and he was not drunk, not even a little.

This the manager saw, and clearly. Which, much later, he would tell the police.

"A day trip, then," Munson said. "We'll just get out on the water, and that'll be it."

Jack was still facing away, but the old man gave him a look now he couldn't understand, eyes sharp, one eyebrow raised, a look Jack finally took as condemnation.

The old man was giving both of them disgusted looks, Jack thought, and Munson said, behind him, "Jack, I sprung for the gas coming up, I got your breakfast, and your dinner last night. Now you can play along for a few hours until Dopey and Dippy are drunk enough we can stuff 'em back in the car and go home. You can do that much. And, anyway, Carol's gonna have your head on a platter if Stacey doesn't make it back, now things have turned his way."

But the mention of Carol only hardened Jack's resolve. *Dick Lutz.*

"Just drive up with us, we'll float around, and we'll head on south around dinner."

At that, Jack nodded, got the bag from the line behind the motel, and went inside and packed, all the while cursing himself, cursing Carol, and Stacey, and his whole goddamn life, and thinking, still, to just walk through the door of the motel, and down the road—he knew Greyhound stopped here, he'd taken it up from Austin himself, when he was just sixteen—but then he didn't want to get them thinking the wrong things.

What Carol had told him was nothing if Joseph didn't get the proof on paper. And, later, he'd need that for protection, for sure. He was certain Carol's telling him about the stealing hadn't been part of the plan, she'd done it out of desperation, but sooner or later, she'd tell Stacey, and there'd be consequences, ones he'd have to live with, most of them a lot worse then spending a few hours with two assholes and an old friend gone distant and strange.

But he was lying to himself—it was the dead Mexican that weighed most heavily on him now. He was all too well aware of how that had been worked out, and it didn't sit right with him.

The dead Mexican was a warning, to the other Mexicans, and to the management, and they'd gotten away with it. Now, in all good conscience, he couldn't leave Dysart. Not until he did what he could about it.

That he couldn't just walk put him in a cold sweat. But he couldn't give any of it away, not here, he thought, not with things the way they were.

So, for the time being he'd just go along, he thought, shutting the suitcase and pushing the latches home, something final in it.

32

JACK WAS AT THE WHEEL, THE CANOES CASTING SHADOWS ON the hood as they drove east on Highway 116 and through Burntside State Forest toward Big Lake, all pines here, and a breeze coming through the crack in the window sobering him, even as the assholes, as he was thinking of all three of them now, even Munson, cut up in the station wagon. It wasn't even ten, and the three of them had worked through most of a case.

Buckhorn. Which they were calling Reindeer Beer, because of the stag on the label, this as if it were the funniest thing they'd ever heard, not something they'd come up with when they were sixteen, and playing JV football, and even then, the joke was borrowed, Jack was sure, in the way most kids' scatological playground jokes were passed from one group to another, and that made him think of his kids, his daughters, Lisa and Sally, lovely, like their mother, but in that giggling phase, blond, and in pigtails, and amused by toilet humor, and John Jr. coming home with this quirky song from camp, which he'd sung, the girls in stitches for it.

> *Going down the highway, goin' sixty-six*
> *Lisa let a gasser and put us in a fix*
> *The wheels wouldn't turn*
> *the motor wouldn't run*
> *Lisa let another one and—*
> *Blew us to the sun!*

The odd thing was, Jack, at the wheel, could remember singing it with his sister, Carol, in the back of their parents' big Oldsmobile station wagon, and how it had amused them, and how it lent itself, back then, to repetition, which seemed to drive their parents crazy, and the truth was, even now Jack had no idea where *he'd* first heard it, yet even as low and coarse a thing as it was, it tied the two generations together, separated by years and God knew how much struggle, and with a big ache in him, he thought of John Jr., Lisa, and Sally, with their grandmother in Austin while he was away, and Lena, at Hazelton—he wanted so badly to see her.

How would he explain his not leaving Dysart now? That it had to do with the dead Mexican?

"I have to get out of here or I'll die, Jack," Lena'd told him, just before she'd left for her parents' place in Minneapolis.

But it hadn't been just this year. Every year there was this argument; he knew enough about management to get a better job up in the Twin Cities, she'd told him, in one of the suburbs, and she'd claimed he had no friends down in Austin, he just wouldn't admit it to himself, and that had hurt him, because, he'd told her, he had more friends than he'd ever wanted, since getting the management job.

"I don't mean *those* kinds of friends," she'd replied.

And always there'd been Munson, who, thinking back now, had helped out, helped put a new roof on after the twister nearly took the house that time. Munson, who'd taken Lena over to the hospital when her contractions started with Sally, since Jack was on shift and it was a rush, near Christmas.

But they never did anything socially, he and Munson, and in fact, with the raucous voices of the three in the car, he realized ten years had gone by, and he'd done nothing socially with any of them, didn't know them at all anymore. Just as Lena had told him he didn't. And he thought now, he didn't like them, anything about them. Their politics, or lack of them, their attitudes, or prejudices, or—what embarrassed Jack to think it—their mean, futureless lives, and here he was in the car with them, one of them.

"Have a beer," Stacey said, and reached over the backseat to poke Jack in the shoulder with a bottle.

"I'm fine," Jack said.

"I didn't fuckin' ask you how you were, dumbshit, I said, 'Have a goddamn beer!' "

Jack glanced at his watch. He took the beer, gave it a tilt, and took the smallest sip, then set the beer between his legs.

Penry, to his right, said, laughing, "I always said you were a big prick!"

Stacey put his head over the seat to see what Penry was talking about and then let out a belly laugh, and Jack moved the bottle, jammed it between the armrest and the seat.

"Lighten the fuck up, Jack," Munson said.

Jack steered the car up the road. They were coming into a clearing, to their left a resort, Big Lake Lodge—now, there was a clever name, Jack thought.

"Pull in there," Penry said.

Jack asked what for, and the three of them belted out, "BEER!"

Jack swung around front, and they got out and stretched. It was a beautiful, bright day, and Jack just wanted it to be over with, and so he stood leaning against the car, and Penry made a big deal of forcing that beer Stacey'd given Jack before into his hand again, and the three went inside, quietly enough, but then there came some kind of ruckus, and the owner, that was clear from his bearing, decisive, angry, followed Stacey and Penry and Munson out, who were damn near staggering, which they hadn't been, each with a six-pack, and the owner, in his dun-colored duck-hunting jacket, *Big Lake Lodge* embroidered on the pocket, gave Jack a harsh look, Jack, even now, obviously in charge, and Munson said under his breath, "Get in the car," and the manager was still coming on, and for one second, Jack shared a look with a girl there in the front window of the office, a pretty girl, who'd been watching him, on her face this look of longing, to be away from here, and Jack was struck by it, seeing Lena's face there, and as Penry and Lawton and Munson had known he would, Jack, shamed at this public display of drunkenness and bad behavior on the part of his friends, got into the car and pulled out, the tires crackling on the gravel, back onto the main road, and a short time later, Penry said, "Fuck it, pull up here."

They were no distance from the lodge, and there was something skewed about it all, how the three of them had made for the car, seemingly drunken, though now, in the car, they were laughing again. Just silly. Not drunk.

"What did you do?"

"Just what we said," Penry told him.

"No," Jack said. "What'd you do to the owner back there?"

What Jack was not seeing at that moment was Munson, behind him, crushing caplets of Percodan and Valium in a beer cap with his ridged thumbnail.

While Penry told how he'd popped a cap in the office, and sprayed the manager, Munson tipped the white powder into an open bottle and got it sealed again.

Jack, pulling up a wooded side road, could feel the change in their laughter, something really dark in it, and he got a galloping feeling in his chest, but then they were all laughing, and Munson slapped him on the back of the head while they cleared the distance to the lake, and then they had the canoes down and in the lake, and they were paddling right by Big Lake Lodge, the manager standing there onshore, glaring at them, his hands on his hips, and Penry and Lawton flipping him the bird, and finally, Penry, nearly falling backward out of his canoe, so that Stacey had to hold his hand to keep him from going over, dropped his pants and mooned the owner, and Munson paddled back east, and they went up a stretch of beautiful shoreline in the two canoes, gulls calling and circling, and Jack, just then, thought, This was the end, he was happy for all of this, he would walk away from it all.

He'd rub the filth from his hands, be done with it, with Munson, Lawton, and Penry, be done with his whole life in Austin, and with Dysart. He'd give the authorities what he knew, and just walk, with Lena and the kids, and then they went around an island, and he dug in with his paddle, and they cleared some distance, and went up a channel, the trees so high it was like being alongside some green-hulled ocean liner, but the pines and water feeling like some resurrection, brilliantly green and blue, and the channel a mile or so long, no one on it, but a stiff breeze blowing from the northwest, slowing them, and Munson handed him a beer, which he didn't want, he didn't need a buzz here, he loved this place, but hated the present company, but as if it were all over already, and this history, something he'd think about later and say to himself—*lucky*. Lucky he'd seen his life that weekend of the mess with Stacey for what it was, what Lena had been trying to get him to see for so long, and he figured he might just make it with Lena now, his life in Austin over, all of it, with Dysart over, and when they all ribbed him about what a fucking teetotaler he was, he downed the bottle.

"Chugalug, chugalug," Stacey and Penry and Munson chanted.

Even then in Jack's mind, how he would think of this day, and with the promise of new life, he felt, immediately, this inky something in him that wasn't right, and felt alarm, but didn't know what it was, and was afraid to say anything, paddling, and heading farther up the lake now, about feeling ill, and then, as if from a distance, he heard Munson say, "Let's take a picture," and Jack bent around to see Munson's smiling face.

Munson had a camera there, and he said, "Stand up, Jack," and for some reason he did, felt himself standing, holding the bottle just for show, and there was the snap of the camera's shutter, and then two more, and just when he was about to sit again, he had to he was so dizzy, the canoe shifted under his feet, and he felt himself going over the side. He hit the bitter-cold water and reached, instinctively, for his boots, going under, and got one off, he'd done it before, falling in duck hunting, but when he struggled for the surface, there were three faces there, and then hands, an infinite number of hands it seemed, that held him under, pushing down on his head, his shoulders, his hands, and when he thought his lungs would burst, and he tore at the surface, got his hand on the gunnel of one of the canoes, something struck his hand, and he went under again, and he whooped, then again, this strange, strange sensation in his lungs, and the hands were there, hard as iron, and holding him under, and he thought, even as his vision seemed to narrow to the smallest line of watery light, and he kicked one last time, that he'd made some kind of terrible misjudgment.

33

Driving the big station wagon, the morning after, Stacey Lawton shuddered.

What he'd set in motion, through Carol, had worked, and he felt both stunned at it and darkly elated, even through his hangover. He very nearly wanted to whoop, after all the years of Jack's comments about his, Stacey's, saving for a house, and with what? And passing him over at Dysart, goddammit, for that Mexican. After all those slights, going back to junior-high football, when Jack had cut him off second string, for being too fat, he'd said. Or had it been for running too slow? But now he'd given Jack a length of rope and he'd hung himself with it, shown himself, the way Stacey'd been trying to show Jack to everybody else all this time.

Jack had done just what Stacey'd said he'd do—but Stacey hadn't, yesterday, had to say so. Penry'd done all that for him.

When Penry'd called down to Dysart, to check with their man in management, Jack's guy Martinez was already snooping around. So Penry'd called the phone company, to see what numbers had gone out from the pay phone, there in Ely, and bingo, Jack had called Martinez at home.

Bad as he was with numbers, Penry'd remembered at least that one, and saved them all. Penry'd known the number, he'd said, for having had to call there on bottle flu days since Jack had given Martinez the floor manager job.

No, Stacey hadn't had to say a thing.

"It's his life or ours," Penry'd said, Munson standing beside him in the dark, not quite believing what Penry was telling them, about the phone, and Martinez, Jack ratting them out.

Penry, who, Stacey was relieved to see, was talking in the car like this whole thing was *his* idea now, even that they were up here "hunting."

But it had been Stacey, not Penry, who'd made sure that in their plans, each of them had a hand, literally, in pushing Jack under the water.

So they were *all* in it, and there was no way out, for any one of them.

But even now this dark elation Stacey had been feeling in the quiet car was becoming something else. Driving up 7, and then 3, to connect with the Gunflint Trail, Stacey was humoring Penry again, and it seemed Munson, gone silent in back, was, too.

"You had him in your canoe," Penry said, turning to Munson. "You're the one's gotta play this thing the most. How you just turned and he went in. How you tried to go after him, even dove for him."

"All right," Munson said. "But you two are witnesses. That's the deal."

"That's the deal," Penry said.

"Fucking *right* it's the deal," Stacey said, but his voice never carried weight, so he felt he had to add, "We stick together on this one."

They had left Jack's body in deep water, in the channel, but weighted down with large stones. They would have to dive for it later—and it would have to be Munson, since his story'd be that he went in after Jack.

The Big Lake lodge was only a mile away, and they'd come in fast, with Jack, and Munson shivering, and near hypothermia.

It would be another distraction.

"The cold water'll completely throw off anyone knowing when Jack died," Stacey said. He glanced over at Munson, who didn't seem altogether convinced—or was it something else now? Stacey'd seen it on television one night, how some coroner had misjudged the time of some guy's death in a lake a lot like this one up in Alaska, because the cold water kept the body perfect. What they had to do now was stay out of sight, for two days, or even until Sunday.

"Maybe coming in Sunday would be better," Stacey said, and added it'd be better because they'd all have to mess with work the following day, down at Dysart, and everything would get confused, how long they'd been away and where they'd been, and they'd have the funeral and look sad and all that.

Munson had been for going right in with Jack's body, just another drunken accident, but Penry had said that'd look suspicious. The story would be that they lost Jack in the dark, miles out on the lake, and looked for him in the morning, thinking he'd made it to shore, that Jack had played some dumbass joke on them.

"We should stay off the lakes. I mean, what if somebody sees us out there? Without Jack?" Stacey said now, turning from the road to look at the others.

"Fuck it," Penry said. "It'd be worse if they see us just camping onshore. How would *that* look?"

Munson shook his head. "Shit," he said. He wanted to say, *Should have listened to me, there were other ways to deal with it,* but he didn't, because now, this morning, the whole mess felt different.

Not like last night, when they'd come off the lake in the dark and got the canoes on the roof, and Penry'd jumped in and steered them in the direction of Grand Marais on these back roads. Anytime they could have pulled off into the woods, but Penry had kept them moving, until finally they'd gone up a side road, and back of the campfire they'd built, they'd gotten drunk, and toasted ol' Jack, fucking asshole, but Lawton and Munson sensed, already, Penry had something else in mind.

Penry *knew* something, and they'd moved east again early this morning, Stacey driving, and Penry making some big shit-stink about not going in here, and not here, they couldn't understand why, even now, they were still moving east, taking side roads, and turning out to the highway again, but now with what they'd done with Jack, they had these days to burn off and then they'd be back down to Dysart and they'd forget, on the cutting floor—or, maybe, with a better man in place, who'd promote them all now, come fuckall whatever they did, somebody they could bring into their deal, they'd be making big bucks, all thanks to that straight-fucking-arrow Jack being gone.

"Nothing you can do with somebody got a head swollen the size of a goddamn watermelon," Stacey said.

Munson grunted assent, but it was something Penry'd said the night before.

Penry'd got them all talking like that, how they'd all wanted to kick the ever-loving motherfucking goddamn fuck out of Jack all these years for screwing them over, and in the middle of their frenzied jabber, boastful, and loud, to cover their sense of having been betrayed, and humiliated, and worse, having lost so much time, time that amounted to their very lives, Penry'd pointed out how Jack had let that asshole doctor fuck them right up the ass there at the motel, hadn't said word one for them, hadn't stood up for them, not so much as a word.

"'You couldn't understand my fucking shoe,'" Penry, riding shotgun, said, recalling it.

"'*Sole* of my fucking shoe,'" Munson corrected.

Stacey was about to say, He meant you, Penry, not us, but didn't let it out. He glanced up at a road sign, then at the gas gauge. Half empty.

"Asshole," he said.

Penry, riding shotgun, grimaced, "I still say we oughta go scare the shit out of that doctor, let him know who's who. Run him out of his camp," he said. Penry, in the silence that followed, shot looks back over the seat at Munson, then over at Stacey.

Stacey shrugged, then glanced back at Munson in the rearview mirror.

"Let's just scare the bejesus outta that asshole, what do you say, Munson?"

Munson had his eyes fixed on the trees flashing by the windows. Talking about it last night had been one thing, but now, in daylight? But what of it?

They'd get out there, he thought, and they wouldn't find them. They'd curse their heads off, and Stacey and Penry would blow off all the steam they needed to, and when the time came, they'd pack up and head west and get their bit of theater over.

And besides, he hadn't liked that prick of a doctor, either.

"What about Jack not bein' with us?" Munson said. "What about that?"

Penry opened his window a crack. "We'll draw straws, see

who goes. If anything, we'll tell him we split up, that Jack's over on the west side, with whoever's left out. Drank too much. Okay?"

And like that, they drove a distance farther, went up yet another spur, still not good, and another, until Penry found one that suited his purposes, or so he said, and they hid the station wagon in a ravine where no one would ever see it, covered the top with branches, and when Munson and Stacey shouldered the canoes, Penry came on behind them with the Duluth pack, taking one last, hard look through the trees to the road east and below them—where, in the red and gold maple leaves, something shone, black paint and chrome and glass, the doctor's car, Penry was sure of it—and considered the work he'd done better than good.

34

DAVID WAS EATING THE LAST OF A BURNED PANCAKE, perched on a shelf of mossy granite, Janie below him, humming to herself.

"What's that you're humming, kiddo?" David said.

"I don't know."

Max got a camera out, a big thirty-five-millimeter Nikon with a telephoto lens, and both David and Janie grinned slightly, and Max said, "Come on, we're having a great time, you can smile better than that."

David and Janie gave him their for-photos smiles, and after the click of the shutter, went back to eating, Max, a bit peeved, going down the rise of granite to stand with his back to them at the water's edge.

David reached down to muss Janie's hair; he knew he did it too often, but— He glanced down at his plate, a burned pancake there.

"You can have my last pancake," Janie said. "It's not burned."

"I like burned pancakes."

"No, you don't."

"Yes, I do."

David doused the pancake in syrup, then, with his fork, jammed it into his mouth, so his cheeks got round, pulled his upper lip back, making chipmunk teeth. Janie laughed at him and he took a big sip of coffee, forgetting about the tin cups, and burning his lips a little, and saying, "Youch!"

"What's that bird?" Janie said.

A small black-and-white bird had scooted up to them, cocking its head expectantly.

"Camp robber," David replied. "A chickadee."

Max, from the water's edge, glanced over his shoulder at them and smiled.

"Why's he got to get so mad about things?" Janie said.

David shrugged. "I don't know."

They'd had some tiff about packing things up, and David had shown Max how to fold the tent, when it became obvious it wouldn't fit in the tent sack for being too thick.

Thirds, David had told him, and this had set Max off, and when David had explained that the company designed the tent that way on purpose, so you didn't fold it on the seams, so it would last longer, this only appeared to make Max even more irritable.

He'd burned the pancakes, too, which neither David nor Janie cared about—and had tried to reorganize the Duluth pack to "make it more efficient" but had only made it more bulky, so that David had had to repack it.

That David thought it was funny, the bulging pack, had put Max in a pure snit.

But now, out here in the cool air, he knew what would do the trick.

"Hey, Dad, come on. Eat this last pancake here," he said, still, something in him cringing at it, something saying to him . . . what was it? Traitor? Or was it something worse? But then, it didn't matter now.

He kissed the top of Janie's head as Max came toward them, and Janie understood and got the pancake on Max's plate, and he almost looked . . . abashed.

"Okay, Cap'n Ahab, where we off to today?" David said.

Max mimicked talking to a parrot on his shoulder.

"That's Treasure Island," Janie said proudly, and David did not correct either of them. It wasn't in him to do it. Ahab was Melville's creation, not Stevenson's, a world of difference, and no parrot on Ahab's shoulder. But what was the use?

"You read that yourself, Janie?" Max asked.

Janie picked at her shoelaces and said nothing, and David said, "We read *Treasure Island* together, didn't we?" Which they had.

Janie glanced up, giving David a smile that was worth the world, and then some, he thought.

There was that awkward silence again, which Max had a way of bringing on, and so David turned to the lake and said to Max, "Well?"

"You pick."

In all directions there were bodies of water, and islands.

There was a beautiful narrow lake to the north, and at the end of it, ten, fifteen miles distant, a large butte of gray granite, one variegated rise of stone heaped on another, the whole of it magisterial, pine-sided, and flat on the face, and up from a steep climb, perhaps of three, four hundred feet, there was a meadow, and even from this distance, David could make out the roan deer grazing in all that green.

But due west, up this lake they were on now, were jagged lengths of cliffs rising sheer out of the water, here and there on them a lone cedar, growing out of seeming nothing, and there was something intriguing in the play of the light on the water, and David knew there might be eagles nesting here, or hawks, and then a bird burst from a rock face, a bald eagle, and with powerful beats of its wings, it rose over the cliff face and circled.

"Let's go there," David said, pointing west, and so it was.

———

They broke camp and moved off over the mirror-smooth blue water, and Max, as they'd agreed the day before, took the bow, and David overpowered him, intentionally not J-stroking, and

Max grunting with the effort of trying to pull what he thought was his portion in the bow, but David knew it was not physically possible for him to do so.

Hercules couldn't have done it, and he was playing the oldest canoeist's joke on Max, and Max was mystified at himself, no matter how hard he paddled, the canoe veering yet again.

And David in the back was watching, at first amused, and then at some distance, and now and then he used the J-stroke to bring the canoe around a bit, and then Max bent into it, encouraged, thinking now he was doing it right, and even though he knew not the first thing about canoes, or what he might be doing wrong, and had no idea why he might be failing here, he would not turn and ask David how he might do it better.

At first it was funny, and Janie was oblivious to it all, sitting and watching the three hawks that soared over the rock face a mile west of them. And high over them the bald eagle.

David bore down again, pulling strongly on his right, as his father had done the day before, and the canoe turning to the left, south yet again, and Max, a V of sweat down his canvas-covered back, and where his hair was thinning a glistening of sweat, and David took one stroke for each of Max's two, and still David could bring the canoe around to the south, and he thought, surely, Max had to be aware that David was barely paddling at all, yet, David realized, with this very light and somewhat round-bottomed canoe, they were still making fine progress, and he was surprised to be enjoying it, the canoe, what he'd taken for a dangerous thing at first, just this very thin skin of cedar between them and the water, and the somewhat undersized thwarts, and the ribs in the hull thin—to reduce weight—and even the seats not solid, but cane mesh, expensive, no doubt, but they'd have to be replaced every other season, and who'd want to pay for that?

But here, all three of them, in this place of stone and water, trees and birds and deer in the highlands, and everywhere now ducks migrating, winging sharply out of sloughs and turning south.

David took two long strokes, not flaring the paddle in a J, and Max, almost doubling the speed of his strokes to try to correct the direction of the bow, shaking his head, and tiring, but still, he was not going to ask.

And David saw in it, suddenly, the depth of the man's entrapment in himself, and what, David couldn't understand, wouldn't allow him to so much as ask what he might be doing wrong, even here, where he knew next to nothing. Moment by moment, he saw that Max's world had to be exhausting, yet, even then, in the stern, part of David took pleasure in testing him, so easily overpowering his father, a kind of pleasure that was not unlike picking at a scab on an abrasion, one that hadn't entirely healed, though David also felt a tired and terribly won stalemate—here the man was beaten, but he wouldn't say so.

He wouldn't even acknowledge that he wasn't doing his job.

He was going to go on paddling like crazy, until David got tired of it. But that wasn't going to happen, because, given the advantage David had at the stern, he could bring the canoe around anytime he wanted, exactly as Max had all yesterday, by clumsily, easily, side-stroking.

All this David knew in his body without thinking, because of all the miles he'd covered in canoes with his uncle Bobby—Bobby playing brutal games with him, until he'd learned all the tricks of the canoe, even how to swamp it and use it for flotation.

Max could use a bow pry, even, David knew, if he wanted to straighten out the direction, and get back at David, and in the way the man had held things over David's head, all those years ago— *my* car, he'd said, I don't want grape pop spilled on the seats of *my* car; *my* house, this is the way we do things in *my* house; and there was his work, which, when David had had boys over one night, had been the reason they couldn't stay up late and joking, because Max had to get to *his* work in the morning, and *his* work made their money—so David held this canoeing over Max's head now. He couldn't stop himself.

In the stern of the canoe he remembered it all, Max, all those years, asking David at the slightest provocation why he was such a goldbricker, so lazy, and in all of that the man was a kind of machine, David had thought, he was like a tank, a tank just running over them, he and Rachel and Janie. And all the while, he'd be grinning, boyish, always boyish, and there was always this impenetrable something about Max, so that David felt, at times, this *Max* wasn't a person, but some exterior, some version of a person he had created to present to the world.

Which David knew everyone did, but there were moments, with other people, when all that fell away, and the real person emerged.

Not so with Max.

And here, in the canoe, even when Max was really struggling to pull his weight, in a veritable lather, his back sweat-soaked, and the muscles on his bared arms shaking, he was not going to ask.

Just wasn't.

And David once again, giving two powerful strokes, sent the canoe veering, and Max tried to compensate, again, but now a small island, only a half block long, was nearly due south, and David stroked powerfully, saying nothing, and overpowering Max completely, now that the joke of it had more than worn off, and there was no pleasure in it anymore, fooling with Max like this, because he had to do something about it.

"I'll take the stern," Max said. "After lunch, all right?"

"No," David said.

"What do you mean, no?"

The way Max had said it brought all the bad times back in a second, all the man's rigidity, his impenetrability, his sometimes cruel willfulness.

Right there, David knew he was capable of striking his father.

There was enough anger in him to do it, just below the surface, all those years of it, packed up, and he was bigger now, though, still, not as big as Max.

"What do you mean, no?" Max said again.

"Not until you learn how to do the strokes."

David felt breathless saying it. He couldn't believe he'd done it. The canoe drifted, and Max looked at David over his shoulder.

"*What* did you say?"

"You heard me."

"You got *something to say*?"

"I said it."

"No, I said—"

Janie, between them, seemed to shrink down. It occurred to David that Max might just bend back and strike him, but he'd get a big surprise if he did.

The canoe drifted a distance, Max glaring, and in David, plenty of things to be said: rigid asshole, fucker, son of a bitch, selfish asshole. He'd always been afraid he'd say it all, if he said so much as one word of it, even *hinted* at what he felt. And he felt he might just do it now.

"Ah, baloney," Max said, and ran his hand over his head, bowing slightly, so that David saw Max was not just thinning, he was balding.

And again there was that awful quiet, and then, just then, just for this one moment in the man's life, he looked back over his shoulder at David and, grinning, said, "Hey, I just thought it was *me,* that I was gettin' old, Davey. You know? It was so . . . damn hard up here in front. You put up with that yesterday?"

And all the anger David had been feeling became, just then, a kind of grief. And he felt his eyes glassing up, yet here there was the distance, still, and Janie watching, not so afraid for them now. She'd seen it, too.

"Ah, hell," Max said, "I suppose I could get a rug like your uncle Bob, pretend I was one of the mop tops."

David laughed. "Who?"

"The Beatles."

"Mop tops?"

"Sure. They called 'em the Fab Four, too." Max laughed. "Shees. Time passes." And then, with a look of melancholy, just a nanosecond of it, he was somebody else, a dispossessed father, a man aging into a life alone, and he drew himself up sharply and smiled that smile David had so come to hate, the Jack Armstrong All-American Boy smile, that Horatio Alger smile, that shit-eating, fly-the-flag-we'll-get-it-done-boys smile, which now David knew was something manufactured.

He got something from it, especially among all those men in his generation. But David had to ask himself, It saved them, during the war, but what about after?

What cost after? Did it ever occur to these men what this cost their sons and daughters?

But then the smile vanished, and Max grinned, himself: "All right, Woodsmaster David, show the old dog how it's done."

And, on the small island, David did exactly that, and with a warmth that was a surprise to him.

35

RESURRECTION COMES IN SMALL MOMENTS WE DO NOT sometimes recognize. And it is so much that way, one philosopher noted that we lives our lives forward but understand them backward.

So it wasn't until later that a small, reciprocal gesture on Max's part healed something in David. When David was in the bow again, and Max in the stern, Max took great care to keep the canoe on course, and David paddled almost effortlessly, always aware Max was making it so.

They'd passed the cliff face, late, since on the small island it had taken Max so long to get the feel for the strokes, and since Janie had gotten right in there alongside Max, and David had taught her the strokes as well, bow and stern strokes, assuming she'd forget them, but she'd learned the strokes faster than Max had, though she'd had trouble with coordination:

Ojibway J, pull, C stroke; draw, crossover-stern-draw, pry, and brake.

Janie had been excited, but she'd gotten into the canoe when it was over with something like disappointment. She didn't really believe they'd let her paddle, so she resigned herself to sitting low in the canoe.

Now they stopped on another small island. There were no end to them, and after they'd stretched, and walked off their stiffness, they got back into the canoe. Max, while David held the bow for him, bent low to say something to Janie. Janie, with surprising agility, stepped into the canoe, low over her feet, hands on the gunnels, all the way to the stern, where she swung around. David wanted to laugh, but she looked like promise itself there, smiling, and then Max took the middle, and David shoved off; Janie was frozen there a second, the canoe drifting backward from the small island aimlessly, and David said, over his shoulder, "Draw on your left," and David braked on his right, and they spun the canoe around one hundred eighty degrees, and Janie said, "Where to?"

And David turned to look at her and said, "It's all yours, Janie."

And the look she gave them, both David and Max, was something—eyes bright, and there this pride in her—and Max bent over the gunnel suddenly, brushing at his face with the back of his hand, his eyes having glassed up, and a line of muscle tight across his jaw, and David said, "You all right there?" and Max's muffled voice came back to David: "I'm fine, I'm fine—just needed a bit of water," he said, cupping up a handful.

———

They changed places at a number of islands, and Janie took the middle again, exhausted, but she didn't say that, and she was pleased with herself, and this was a pleasure, and the sun was high overhead, and the day still young, and they stopped again, at an island not more than a block long, meaning to be off quickly, but Max found a deep area of dried moss and lay down in it, and was asleep in the sun in minutes, and David and Janie went around the backside of the island, where there were bulrushes and a length of sand down near the water, and they skipped stones there, David teaching Janie how to find the flat stones to skip, and how to angle herself and lay the stone flat-side to the water, and toss it with a flick of the wrist, and David counted twenty skips on one toss, and Janie was frustrated, plunking one stone after another into the water, until he stood behind her and took her hand, and gently bent with her, showing her how to keep her forearm parallel to the water, and she snapped a stone off, and got seven skips, and then he couldn't stop her, she was amassing a pile of stones to skip, and David took stones from her pile, tossing them, intentionally not so well or so hard, so

Janie was bragging she'd beat him, and he let her beat him, even though she knew she hadn't, and the clouds scudded by overhead, cumulus, billowing, and caught in the sun, the clouds illuminated as if from inside, and all the while, David wanted to ask Janie what she thought.

If living with Max was going to be all right.

But it wasn't Janie who had the problem with Max anyway, and he, David, would be gone in a couple years, and there'd be just Rachel and Max and Janie.

And maybe it was just a son Max had a problem with, one like himself?

So he only sat, waiting to see if Janie would come and sit by him for a minute, and then she did. She turned her face to the sun and let it warm her, and she smiled, not able to see David, since her eyes were closed.

"What do you think Mom's doing?" she said.

David glanced at his watch. "She's off lunch break and is back to work." David whistled a bit of "Whistle While You Work."

"She doesn't like what she does, does she?" Janie said.

This surprised David. "What makes you think that?"

"I just know."

David said nothing, picked up one of Janie's stones and threw it into the lake, the stone going in sideways with a loud, dulcet *plunk!*

"If Max comes back," he said, "she can do something else."

Janie considered this. And it so bothered David, that she'd taken what he'd said the wrong way, as if David were asking her, Janie, to save Rachel, that he added, "I mean, if it's all right and everything."

"I didn't like Jarvis," she said.

David laughed. "Jarvis was an asshole."

"You're not supposed to talk like that," Janie said. "You told *me* not to."

"Well," David said, "it's true."

"Asshole," Janie said.

"Yup," David said. "Sometimes it feels good to just say it,

what you think. Like about Jarvis. What would you say about Jarvis?"

Janie glanced over her shoulder. "I thought he was a camel poot."

"*Camel poot?*" David couldn't help laughing. The kid was always surprising him.

"He was always doing that thing with his neck. And he smelled funny."

"That was his cologne, kiddo."

"I didn't like it. It smelled like . . . toilet cleaner."

"What else didn't you like?"

"His hands were all hairy. And he talked funny, all loud and everything, like you were deaf or something."

"What about Max?" David said. He got a nervous feeling in his stomach saying it. If Janie said something bad, he'd have to get into it with Rachel, and just the thought of that was painful.

"He's nice—to me. And he's funny."

"Funny?"

"He's like you sometimes."

This really took David aback. He was surprised at how hurt he felt. But then, Janie didn't know the Max that he knew, and maybe she'd never know—and he wouldn't tell her, ever.

"It's okay, then?"

"I like it out here," Janie said.

"I didn't ask you that, Sport."

Janie frowned, then lifted her head suddenly and smiled, her juvenile teeth new, and oversized for her face, and David saw, really, for the first time, that she was going to be pretty. Maybe beautiful.

"If you stay—at home, I mean—everything will be fine," she said.

David, unable to say a word, put his arm around Janie.

"I promise," he said, and Janie smiled again, and they were up, and chased each other through the trees, and back of Max stopped, quiet, and they threw pine cones at him, until he sat up abruptly, looking one way and then the other, not sure where he was for a moment, and then he threw pine cones back, heavy, sap-sticky cones, and David and Janie marched into camp, and David got water boiling, and Max and he had coffee, and they shoved off again, pulling hard for a ridgeline, one beyond a number of others, each, in succession, more faded than the last, until they reached the one they'd decided on, which was higher than all the others.

It had been visible the entire length of the lake, seven or so miles, but hazy, like a suggestion of a place, a dream place, and the now-late-afternoon light played off the poplars on the broad lake-facing slope so that it appeared as if a river of molten gold flowed there, but alive, rippling.

A place enchanted, but what enchantment? And a place neither David nor Janie would ever forget.

By the time they reached the shore of the ridgeline, it was late afternoon, between day and evening. They made camp, and it was all easy, since the site had been used often, given the view and the beauty of its location. The last campers had even left a stack of wood, cut in equal lengths, a courtesy, which Max set out to duplicate, working quickly with the hatchet while David and Janie got the tent up, and the fire started, and David had the cans out, and left Janie at the fire, getting out the bags, and opening the portable kitchen, and he went down to the lake, fitted the sections of his rod together, and cast out from shore with a treble-hooked Dare Devil, which flashed red and white in the last of the sun, and the wind blowing down and over the site from the northwest, but the site sheltered, and the water dimpled, so that the pike here did not disperse at the drop of the lure in the water, and David caught three pike, and filleted them and tossed the offal to the gulls that tucked and dove out of seeming nowhere to fight over the offal, then lurched out of the water, trailing intestines, and skin, and rose to drop over a ridge adjacent to them, all the while those gulls that had not arrived earlier fighting for the remaining scraps.

David got the fillets in the pan, sizzling in butter, and Max came down with a load of wood, and he turned to David, not happy.

"You got a license?"

"No," David said. But then the obvious occurred to him, that maybe Max had gotten one when he picked up the gear. "Do you?"

"That's beside the point," Max replied.

David looked up from the pike fillets. They smelled wonderful, and he was hungry.

"So you want me to dump this out or—"

"Don't be ridiculous."

"I wasn't."

They were tired, and here was the old Max, and David was not happy to see him.

"Laws are made for a reason, David."

"Is it any difference if I catch them? If we're going to both eat them, anyway?"

"Don't ask questions like that," Max said. "I'll lose respect for you. You weren't raised like that."

David wanted to say he wouldn't have been fishing if Max had made the proper arrangements for food, but it would have been a lie, but then, almost perversely, he did say it, and it shamed him.

"Everything's wrong, then," Max said.

"I didn't say that."

"Well, what are you saying, then?"

There was so much between them that no place to air even the least of it existed.

Show the man one card in your hand, you'd be showing him all of it. And what then? It was depressing, because no matter what he said, Max would glower, and snap at him, and all the good that had come before would descend into this . . . morass of little antagonisms.

And all of it was humiliating, too, because David couldn't seem to stop himself from doing it, getting mean and small, any more than Max could.

But Max was such a goddamn oaf about disagreements, David thought. Once, when Max and David had been out having dinner with a real-estate friend of Max's, Max had gotten into an argument right there at the table over Vietnam, and he'd let go the whole domino theory, and the Red Scare, all like some taped propaganda, and the scary thing was, Max seemed to believe every word of it.

Like this fishing thing now.

"Okay, so let's say *I* went up and cut the wood, and *you* went down by the lake—"

"I told you, don't insult yourself."

"Laws like this are there to protect the resources—"

"You *don't* bend the law just to suit yourself."

David thought to say they were here without a permit, had registered at the wrong inlet, and had left a bogus itinerary—what about that? But he didn't. Janie came down from the tent, bits of down in her hair. She pointed to the pan.

"What's that?" she said.

David and Max exchanged glances, and then Max said, handing Janie a tin plate, "Walleye," which it wasn't, and David put a fillet on her plate, and one for Max, and told Janie how to get the bones out—northern pike were full of bones, he told her—and they ate in that awkward silence yet again, but the pike was extraordinary, and then Max lunged at Janie when she began to choke, but it was nothing, and they all laughed, relieved, and it was good again, until Max and David went down to the shoreline and scrubbed out the pan with sand there, and Max said, "Just *ask* first in the future, can you?"

"What?" David said, surprised at this. "Ask what?"

"If you're going to do something like that."

Max reached sharply at David, but he didn't poke David in the chest as he had in the past, he slipped a small plastic packet into his breast pocket, and squeezed his shoulder.

As Max turned to walk back up to camp, David took the package from his pocket.

It was a fishing license, his name on it.

He was at first angry, very angry, and then before Max had gone too far, he said, "Why do you have to do things like that?"

And Max turned, and there was this look on his face, a heaviness in him, that looked like years of failure, and sadness at it.

"Because I'm your father, David," he said, "and I'm trying to do my best by you."

Which struck David dumb, so that when something occurred to him, something to say, the moment was long, long gone, and he was just there by the lake, with the wind in his ears.

———————

What is love, that it can so readily become hate or a desire to wound the loved one who has failed us? And how do we bear what we do to each other at all? And even then, this creaky, rickety thing, under constant attack, and leaking blood from countless injuries, limps on, and again, and again, surprises us with moments of pure transcendence, some lasting only seconds, that we remember lifetimes, moments that somehow (almost) mitigate those seconds, and hours, and days, and weeks, and months, sometimes years, of bitterness and struggle, and here and there, even in all that, is the punctuation of laughter, and moments of real love, connection so pure it is unspeakable.

That's what their last night together was like.

It had those moments. Which, in turn, made it possible for David to do what he did, later.

Grace, received, has power ineffable.

Love, even greater.

36

THAT NIGHT, AFTER THEY'D FINISHED EATING, AND SAT BY the fire, in the dark, the loons began to warble. It had been an unseasonably warm autumn, but now there was a chill in the air that hadn't been there before, a double ring around the moon, rainbowlike in its brilliance, even seen through the trees over them.

David said they should definitely head south, that the loons got crazy before bad weather.

He'd expected Max to argue that he'd checked with the National Weather Service before they'd left, but Max agreed it would be a good idea.

"If we go back in and we don't get hit by it," he said, "we can paddle around close to shore, camp out in the woods just off the highway. How's that?"

David nodded, drew his jacket over his shoulders, and Janie said she was cold, so they built up the fire and it snapped and crackled, and when the moon lifted out of the trees, Max sang, in a surprisingly fine voice, that of a crooner,

> *Oh Mr. Moon, Moon*
> *Bright and shiny Moon*
> *Won't you please shine down on me*

"Sing it," Max said to David and Janie, "and I'll sing counter."

"What's that?" Janie said.

"Just start," Max said, and David and Janie did, and when they hit the end, Max signaled them to repeat it, and then Max harmonized over them, and it was so good they stopped for a second, amused.

"You got a great voice, Davey," Max said.

"I do not," he said.

"You do, though, really. So does your mother. That's how we met, you know?"

Janie interrupted Max to ask how she sounded.

"Great," David told her, and Max nodded, but she'd worked herself up to it now.

"This one's funny," she said, and she sang in a high, reedy voice,

> In the boarding house where I lived
> everything is getting old
> There are gray hairs on the but-ter
> and the bread is green with mold

Janie paused, then grinning, sang again,

> When the dog died it was hot dogs
> When the cat died, catnip tea
> When the landlord died I left there
> Spare ribs were too much for me.

Max laughed, and David did, too. David was thinking about Jarvis, and what she'd said about him, that he was a camel poot.

"Where'd you come up with this stuff?" he asked.

"I don't know," she said.

It was so warm there by the fire, they lay back and watched the stars. There was a ribbon of magenta, emerald, and indigo northern lights over the back of the ridge, the night heavy with the feel of time, as if time itself here were palpable, substantial, all times one time, and this whole world here an illusion, and only that echoing thing inside real, this indefinable something, and the three of them together, and yet all three not, so that there was both this wanting to be carried along in the flow of it, this beautifully happy yet melancholy time, this reminder that all things came into being and disappeared again, and that even this place here was nothing but some physical manifestation of a dynamic that was, really, in motion, and their sense of being here, now, and the northern lights playing over them, and the loons warbling, far off to the north, so that the wind carried their voices like lost souls to them, was timeless, and pure, just itself, almost, and only Max knowing how much you lost, because youth cannot know loss like this, it knows potential, the future, and lives in the present, looking to the promise of the future, for to truly know loss early removes us from life, so that we forever stand at a distance, and even living, know already *this* is gone, will be history, this, too, shall pass, not only what is difficult, but even all that we love. Even joy.

But to all, these realizations come in moments of stillness, oftentimes in autumn. Realizations that sit Buddha-like in anyone, once they come.

Everything *does* come of nothing, and returns to the same. But what beauty between!

And that true beauty only to be experienced by those who look, even for a moment, the length of a breath, into the face of that truth.

For it is the fear of this realization that lights cities, fuels the great diversions, and for most, even a taste of it is too much, and those who run fastest and farthest from it are talkers, and fabricators, and inventors, running, always running from this realization, while a small few, oftentimes hated, or ignored, run into it, this moment of stillness, and hold it up to the light, not horrified, but seeing the beauty instead, all of it, though those who can't bear this moment break it, always, fill it with neon, with noise, so many saying nothing, or polarizing what is real in some makeshift battle, which is diversion again, all bright lights, and funhouse mirrors, and propaganda, yet in the quietest moments, when all this stops, we tell our stories.

All we have are our stories, and embedded in them are ourselves, what bits or pieces remain, that we carry, or are carried in us, what of ourselves we can grasp, even as we, too, are passing away. Knowing it or not.

All this, in the space of a breath. A feeling, an intimation, a pause.

And David was feeling all of this, in the dark, out with Janie and Max, back of the fire.

Had a minute passed, or an hour?

"I remember," Max said, breaking the silence, "when I was a kid, your uncle Leonard and I sold the *Saturday Evening Post*. Got to this time of year people weren't wandering around downtown so much when it came out, and we'd stand there and freeze, and it got so bad we got a *Star* route. Up at four, had one hundred thirty Sundays apiece, each must've weighed four pounds, and we didn't have a cart, so we got a bicycle, with a rack on the handlebars, but couldn't afford inner tubes for the tires, we were in the Depression then, and no one had money for anything, so we stuffed the tires with grass, and we'd ride that thing around like that." Max laughed. "When it snowed it was hard to find grass for the wheels and we'd stuff them with wadded-up newspaper."

David had heard these stories before, but here, he was not bored, or disinterested. Just now, he felt this proprietary . . . something. And he was surprised at how much of his father's old story he'd forgotten.

"Tell me that old one about how Herman destroyed that Packard."

And Max obliged him, Janie sinking down the log again, until her head pitched forward, her chin on her chest.

"She asleep?" Max said.

And quiet again, the spine of the island rising up under them, it seemed, they were pushed up into that dome of stars and infinite darkness, broken by ribbons of northern lights.

Beautiful, and awful.

David nodded, then lifted her into his arms, and carried her to the tent, and zipped her into her sleeping bag, in her face, even now, not really innocence, because Janie understood a great deal, but a newness, a blush, he, David, needed so badly, needed to protect, so that he could re-create that in himself.

Could recall it.

And walking back to the fire, he felt a certain dull irritation at Max there. He shouldn't have let her lie on the cold ground, but had. David had felt Janie shuddering, even in her sleep, as he lay her in the sleeping bag.

"You get her tucked in?" Max said.

David said he had, and he sat and watched the fire, almost bored, but at the same time, hypnotized by the flames. It would die down soon enough, yet if he tossed on more wood, it would be an invitation to sit here longer, and talk, and not knowing what he wanted, but needing to do something, he dropped more wood on the fire, and the flames leapt up, and at that moment his destiny was changed, this small act, a deciding one. Among others.

But here, feeding the fire.

37

ALL THIS DAVID WOULD CONSIDER LATER, SOME OF IT WITH deep remorse.

But then, how could he have known what fruit his actions would bear, as with the fire?

Had he and Janie and Max left on Wednesday of that week, instead of Thursday, most likely they would never have crossed paths with Jack Carpenter and the others at the motel. Or if Max hadn't had to work overtime to take the days off, he might not have been so irritable when they had. Or if David had not argued with Max after breakfast, or if he hadn't had Buddy riding him that fall, he wouldn't have gone off alone to Herter's, or if he and Max had worked out the supplies earlier, it wouldn't have been an issue in the first place, and then Max wouldn't have said what he had to Penry, wouldn't have drawn Penry's attention, or David, not in a snit, would have stepped into it, and could, maybe, have cut things short there.

Or maybe if David hadn't picked up the piece of paper in the phone booth, Penry wouldn't have had the motivation to come after them.

Just a piece of paper that, as far as David knew then, meant nothing.

But even given all that, there was, when David examined it later, a web of imponderables, other *if-thens*, and *if-onlys*. Some seemingly buried fate in the workings of the world itself. And things he would never know, even after, or could never have so much as guessed at.

That Penry, had he not been the butt of jokes, the clown, the fool, might not have acted at all on what Max had said. And had Stacey Lawton done his job at Dysart, and not followed in his drunken father's footsteps, he might have won for himself one of those lower-management positions, but in Lawton, the imprint of the lost life was there from his father. And Munson, who'd had no father, had been looking for one all his life without knowing it, each raggedy day on the floor, and out drinking after, always finding someone like Jack Carpenter, who had some substance, was substance itself, tall, and quiet, and long-suffering, though, too, Jack was just a man. As was Joseph Martinez, whom Munson, Lawton, and Penry had despised all the more because he was like Jack, and was driven to carry his people with him, as was Jack.

Joseph, round-shouldered, and heavy, and this amused sadness in his eyes.

And had the management at Dysart not so badly abused its workers, or relied on illegal immigrants for cheap labor, had Dysart management not pitted cheap labor against local labor, and had not these local men been forced—by lack of vision, or lack of opportunity, or by proximity to Dysart—to work for the meat-packing giant, Dysart might have been forced to change, offer a living wage.

Value its workers.

But no. It remained, like some monumental vortex, even here, on the border of Canada, exerting its influence, and labor, each day, fighting for its diminishing life, so that life became cheap, and someone, like Penry, when that last shred of what remained of him was insulted, had to lash out against it to remain alive at all.

To feel alive.

Because there was almost nothing left of Penry, but this wild and costly dream.

Fool, idiot, clown, dumbshit, failure—and much worse—he

had become the physical personification of all that his so-called friends feared in themselves, and because he brought it out, where they could see it, and make light of it, he was precious to them.

Had been, to what was left of Stacey Lawton and Larry Munson; but not to Jack Carpenter, because Jack had never once joined them in quitting.

But Jack was gone now, and some strange alchemy worked without him present. And the one who had united them in shame now became the spokesman, and anyway, Penry had the most energy.

The most rage.

So was it ill fortune? Fate? Destiny? that it was Penry, at the east end of the lake, who urged the others to push on, just a little more.

They had planned to rise early and return to the channel, where they would play out their story of drunken revelry, and of how Jack had fallen into the lake, and it being dark, and their not being able to find him after, all of them thinking, he'd swam off. With a buzz on, and dope clouding their thoughts, and fueled by Penry's rage at Jack's betrayal, they had acted quickly, and together. Had even left themselves what had seemed the perfect out.

But now Stacey and Munson were sitting back of the fire, just beginning to be afraid for themselves, and this awful energy had crept into them, this darkness they'd called forth in themselves, and wasn't to be put back, and as they were sitting under that dome of accusing stars, trying to be themselves, they knew that they as a group were done for. When they got back to Austin, they would meet another time or two, drink and act silly, and Penry would shove straws up his nose and laugh, and they'd talk about the whores they were screwing at the brothel in town, and what they'd do when they got that bonus, or the hot submanagement job with Jack gone, how they'd put the Holley 750 CFM double pumper on the 'Vette, and maybe put in a high-rise cam and new, lower differential gears, and it would all be show, because it was over already, and they were afraid of one another, and loathed one another somewhat, because now each owed the other his life, and being in debt this way is untenable, and so they would go their own ways, and not being social, not any of these men—it had been asshole Jack Carpenter with his smile and easy ways who'd drawn them together—they could almost sense the endless hours of television, and uninspired Hamburger Helper dinners, and the endless hours on shift, hacking, and cutting, and rendering, and it made them even more rageful, this new vision of their lives. So when Penry said, It was all because what that fuckin' doctor'd done, *he'd* brought on how things had gone down with Jack, they jumped to it, giving the doctor a show of their power, because their frustrated lives had just now become unbearable, their impotence all too clear to them, and their inheritance, the future—if they were even so lucky as to have one—rose before them a wasteland, and so they moved into the coming darkness, as if into a light that would save them.

38

"YOUR MOTHER TELLS ME YOU SMOKE," MAX SAID.

This, coming out of nowhere, surprised David. He shrugged and poked uncomfortably at the fire with a stick.

"Sometimes," he said.

"You're a runner. I'd think you wouldn't want to do that."

David had no idea how to respond. But this had been the way Max had been years ago, too. Still, he'd give him a chance.

"What do you mean?"

"Just what I said. You want to get serious about running, you'll have to cut it out."

David wanted to tell him he *was* serious, he'd already set a state record, for sophomores, for Christ's sake.

"Your uncle Bobby smoke?"

David nodded, and Max grinned to himself, a so-that's-it sort of grin, and David said, "It wasn't Uncle Bobby. I've never smoked around him."

"You don't."

"No," David said. He felt exasperated at all of this. Why were they talking about smoking?

And then Max said, "Hey, I'm sorry." He tossed a piece of wood into the fire and a burst of sparks climbed into the night over them. "I went through hell giving it up."

"You smoked?"

"Sure, everybody in the army did." Max turned, stretched on the ground, his head braced on his palm, his face turned into the firelight. "Remember that place down near the Mississippi we used to hike with Len?" David had loved Leonard, but then they'd moved away.

Max laughed, but it was a melancholy laugh. "We called it the secret place."

Just those words evoked another world altogether, as if the boy, five or six, were still alive in David somewhere, and that world, even here, had that magical look of possibility.

"You liked to swing on the fox-grape vines, play at Tarzan."

"Did I?"

"You don't remember?"

But he did, and he remembered, back then, too, there'd been the trips out to construction sites, where Max was having homes built, and there was the smell of greenwood, and that heavy, earthy smell of freshly poured cement, and they'd have dinner after, and David always got the hot roast beef sandwich, and apple pie, and he cautiously eyed these real-estate people his father was doing business with, always sensing Max's disappointment in him—he had sometimes had trouble talking with one or another of these men, who were, to David, all very loud, and false, and forward, pumped his small hand in theirs, just because it was the thing to do. But with Leonard it had been different.

Len with a voice loud with some infectious enthusiasm, overweight, always eating pastries, drinking "highballs," driving recklessly in his big Cadillacs.

And there'd been others, friends of Max's, more calm, and affable. Men he'd liked. Eddie Green, Ray Shelton, Don Lavender.

"Do you remember?"

"Yeah, I do," he said. "I just hadn't thought of that for . . . I don't know how long."

He wanted, then, to tell Max about Rick Buddy, or about how hard things had been, about, even, how Rachel had been and how he worried about her. He wanted to tell Max about what she'd done with the knife that night, but Max wasn't altogether invited in yet. Or back, or whatever it was.

"How would you like to go up to Alaska sometime?" Max asked.

When David didn't answer right away, Max jumped back in, something almost hurt in his voice: "I mean, we'd have a guide and all that, maybe fly in, something like that. Go with somebody who really knew the area around Denali, something like that."

David was smiling, a wry, odd kind of smile. Yes, he liked the idea of Alaska. And even with Max, well, fuck it, they could tough it out.

"Really?" he said.

Max laughed. "Remember when you went off on that Jack London kick?"

David wasn't so sure. "Did I?"

"I read all that to you when you were sick."

This was a memory so old, it brought with it the smell of Vicks VapoRub, and damp air from the steamer, and that room upstairs, and the lamp on.

"You were crazy for all that," Max said.

"I was, wasn't I."

Max winked. "Bet it never occurred to you that reading all of that to you got *me* thinking about it. And I have been, sort of, all these years."

David had to look away. Yes. That was what he said to himself, just then. Okay then, *yes*. But he wouldn't say it, Yes, let's go, because he realized that saying it would be saying much more.

He'd be saying, Yes, come back, and maybe even he'd be saying, Yes, I forgive you, which he certainly wasn't.

But he *wanted* to, which surprised him. Oh, how he wanted to.

He wanted to say yes, but he only prodded the fire with a

stick, and wanted, almost desperately, to smoke, for some strange reason. And all the while he waited for Max to prod, as he always had in the past, waited for Max to tell him, You're not feeling what you're feeling, or to say, Why not, when Max knew, David was sure, why he, David, couldn't answer why not, why not go to Alaska, not without saying the things he needed to say but couldn't.

And so they sat watching the fire, and Max turned away, there, out on the lake nothing at all but darkness, and here the fire between them, and warm, but the two terribly uncomfortable, and the silence went on so long, Max finally cleared his throat, and David nearly startled at it, afraid of what Max might say.

"You know," Max said, "if I had a chance to do it all over, I'd do things differently."

David did not answer.

"Things aren't always what they seem, David."

Lifting the stick out of the fire, David held it up to his face, the flame on the end of it flickering.

"I thought you said not to make excuses," David said.

Max scratched the back of his head, pursed his mouth.

"You can't live like that, David," Max said. "Sometimes you can only do the best you can."

David jabbed the stick back into the fire. Was this Max's idea of an apology? And that he seemed to be excusing himself, for all those nights, made David suddenly angry again. No, furious.

But he was heartsick, too. He stood to make some gesture, to march off, or to say something harsh, but it wasn't in him to do it. Instead he let his head drop back, the wash of cold stars overhead, and torn like that, felt the fire on his legs, one moment his mouth working with all he could say, and had said to his father in moments of quiet all these years, those things that rose hot in him, all indignation, and outrage, and there, too, in it a kind of help-lessness, or loss, that kept his mouth shut, because, after all, why ask for what wasn't there, or wouldn't be there?

But what was all this, then? This trip, and talking like this now, and what Max had just said? What about his having asked him to go up to Alaska?

How long would he hold on to all that, what happened in those bad years?

And just when he was about to say . . . *something*, it had been there, taking shape in his mind, some offering, anyway, of forgiveness, which was going to cost him terribly, Max said, bitterly, "You know, you were always *difficult*."

"Difficult," David said.

The word came out of David's mouth as though he were spitting out something bitter, it almost had a flavor.

"You didn't listen to anything," Max said.

He wanted to say, Maybe it was the way you said things, or asked for them. But then, who was he to say this when, now, he couldn't say what *he*, David, needed to?

And so he was struck dumb there, as he so often was around Max, and had been, but a feeling of futility in him now, which brought with it a feeling of being trapped. Yet even then something would not let him leave the fire, let him leave Max. Some hope, or was it just disbelief at the turn their conversation had taken.

"Maybe there was a reason I didn't listen," he said.

"Sit down," Max said.

"No."

"See?"

David shook his head. There was that burning at the back of his throat that signaled what he thought of as weakness. None of this felt good.

"So you're saying I was always like that," he said, but what he meant was, even before he could remember, there was antagonism between them, and Max had caused it.

"Remember the time I tried to show you how to tie your shoelaces?" Max asked.

David did remember.

"You wouldn't do it."

"No," David said. "I wouldn't do it for *you*."

He said it loudly enough that he turned to look up the rise of stone and mottled lichen to the tent, in the dark the tent more gray than green, the mouth of it open, Janie inside, and he wished she hadn't gone in already, that she were here, and that he and Max were not having this conversation, because he felt just then the rage he'd felt so often, now recalling his father's thick, muscular hands over his, on the shoelaces, and how, when he'd forced his father's hands away, he'd tied his laces with a one-looped knot, and how Rachel had come over to see what he'd done, and laughed, and said how clever he was, coming up with his own knot, and how Max had said, It isn't right, in that way he had, passing judgment too often, and how, with those thick-fingered hands, he'd torn the knots apart and said, Do it. Do it right. And Rachel had said, If he wants to tie them that way, and it works, why shouldn't he? And Max had looked up at her.

Because it isn't right, he'd said.

And Rachel had done nothing, but her silence was damning, and when David wouldn't do it Max's way, Max had taken his arm and yanked him to his feet and swung him around, and meaning to spank him, had smacked him in the small of his back, knocking him over, then lifting him off the floor and nearly throwing him into one of the chairs at the table.

"You can eat when you do it right," he said.

By then Rachel was at the stove, and when she brought the eggs to the table, they were burned, and she said nothing, only shoveled them onto Max's plate, though even worse was her silence, and all David could do was sit and try not to be there.

"You had to do things your own way, even when they weren't right," Max said.

"What is *right*?"

"You know what's right."

"No, I don't."

He could see this upset Max, because he, too, was holding back all the dark things he could say. And that he had anything to say, after those nights he'd beaten David in the dark, and after all the humiliations he'd heaped on him, made David wonder, with a kind of deep awe, at the wrongness of this man, at how such a person could be in the world, but he knew men such as his father were everywhere, and many of them were successful, in the world's terms, but he saw his father as some caricature of a person, with his sentiments, his aphorisms, his clear-cut rights and wrongs.

He almost envied his father and his generation of men their rectitude; what power, to think your world was the world itself.

In his mouth were the words, You are so blind, so deaf—he even thought *stupid*, but no, Max was not stupid—but then, how does a man get to be in his forties and think like his father did?

"You don't think *you* had anything to do with all that?" David said now.

"With what?"

"My being"—and he could hardly say it, for the hurt, disgust, and awful wonder he felt at it—"with my being *difficult*."

"You were willful."

"And what's *that* supposed to mean?"

There was in Max now his clinical detachment. At his clinic Max was a god. Do this, move here, put this there. All people rushed to his commands. And David could see it rankled him not to have this dynamic work between them. Didn't he realize, David thought, you couldn't order people around? Not family.

And he certainly didn't his peers, or his friends.

Still, he never, never asked for anything, he ordered, always had.

"Let's not go into this now," Max said, standing and brushing down his pants. Here, another order.

He was slightly taller than David, and David saw immediately his father had done it to intimidate him, shut him up, and David wasn't going to tolerate it. Without thinking, he'd lifted the stick out of the fire and stood there with it, a hot poker.

I could jab this through his chest, he thought—which he would recall later, with such pain, he would feel himself shrink at it.

"What if *I* want to?" David said. "Go into it now?"

"Fine," Max said. "But I don't have to if I don't want to. I say, I'm quits on this. You're just getting into one of the moods you get into."

"*Moods?*" David said.

He glanced up at the tent again; now he didn't care if he woke Janie. He could feel his heart in his neck, jacking blood into his head, where it made his eyes swell.

"And what was it all about those nights when you beat me, huh, when you hit me, when I was sleeping, right out of my—"

"I *don't* want to hear about it, David," Max said.

"You just don't *get it,* do you?" David said.

"Get what?"

"You push, and you push, and you push, you and your—" But David's voice was cracking now, and what he'd meant to be strong, and forceful, an accusation, came out almost as if he were begging, and he couldn't stop himself.

"If I *ever* had to ask you for something, sure, maybe you'd do something about it," David said, "but it was always as if you were cutting your arm off to do it."

David felt his eyes glassing up, and he was furious at himself—how odd, he could hate himself enough almost to wish himself dead, but when he turned on Max, all he could feel was this . . . abyss, like some hole he fell into, pulling him in all directions, and him feeling his throat swell, and his body betraying him.

It had always been like this, and he'd felt it when Buddy had come after him, this paralyzing something.

"All you do is *take,*" he nearly cried. "*Every . . . fucking . . . thing . . .* is about *you.*"

"Stop. Stop it!" Max said.

"No. *You* listen," David said, holding the burning stick out.

"Are you threatening me?" Max said.

David felt a burst of rage lift his arm. He needed to move. He felt he would explode, and he reared back and hurled the stick out into the lake.

"That make you feel better?" Max said.

David turned to him. "Fuck—you," he said.

"What?"

"I said, 'Fuck—you,'" David said, and stepping closer to Max, his fists at his sides, said, "Fuck you—fuck you—fuck you—fuck you.

"You get it? *FUCK—YOU!*"

He knew he would hit Max if he stayed, Max standing there, for once struck dumb, and he charged up the path, going by Max, drove his shoulder into Max's, Max's shoulder substantial, but he went by anyway, and even as he was walking up and by the tent, Janie stirring inside, he felt this phantom weight in his shoulder, the mass of his father, and he was cheering for himself, was in a way ecstatic, and at the same time felt a kind of fuck-everything feeling, fuck school and his precious future, fuck the house, and fuck that asshole Jarvis, fuck them all and fuck everything, and as he was thinking it, he felt a kind of wild freedom—he could leave, leave it all, leave the house in Edina, and Morningside, could leave Rachel, and leave Simonson and the team, why bother with running, stupid sport, no one cared, leave his books, and everything in the house, but then he thought of Janie.

When he thought of Janie his eyes burned and his throat swelled up, and he was pushing the limbs of trees aside, but was still moving toward the end of the island.

But already his mood was changing, some phantasm, something inside, attacking him.

He would be close to no one, love no one, but already he knew he loved Janie.

Stupid kid. If Max hit Janie, he knew he'd cut him apart, there'd be no stopping him. He would hurt Max so bad—

And he heard Janie's voice now, like some song, she'd gotten up, was talking to Max, and he moved farther down the island, away from them (from Max, whom he loved, too), he had to think, had to think, because he was kidding himself. And what was he going to tell Rachel?

Sure, have Max come back. Why not? He'd leave, that was the solution, live with . . . where would he live? And trying to think of some solution, and tearing at the brush, he went farther down shore, and into the dark, now blocks away, and over the ridge, and the blackness of the night sky was like a cauldron, and he punched at the dark, until he'd spent himself, and he sat, the stone ledge under him cold, and hard, and he forced himself to slow his breathing, to think, which he still couldn't until, he didn't know how much later, the dark underwent a subtle transformation, now pouring out emptiness, and loss, and the stars overhead shone like beacons from another world, peaceful, and cold, and dead.

Calmer now, he fought an impulse to return, to apologize, but thought, Why do that since Max felt nothing, though worried every moment about Janie, worried that Max might take it out on her, and he hated himself for not going back, for Janie, but he knew Max wouldn't say so much as a cross word to her, because if there was need for something, or someone, for Max to pour out his darker self on, it would be David.

So he indulged himself, took his time here, alone in the dark, sitting on the cold stone, the stars overhead, and trying to get control of his feelings. He was caught somewhere between a rage to make it all right again, or at least what it had been, and a desire to just dive into the mess entirely, to just get to the end of it, and have it over. But he knew, too, that would never happen, because it was always there, this darkness, the trick was learning to carry it somehow, without letting it cripple you, like it had his uncle Bobby, and so many others, and thinking this, he drew his knees to his chest, and he told himself he would carry what was alive in him, no matter what, this wonder at the world, what he felt about it, but what he could not then name.

He'd carry it for Janie. He could do that, he thought. Just that.

Whether it killed him or not.

39

FROM THE EAST, ON ANOTHER ISLAND, PENRY SAW AN ARC of orange drop from some height into the darkness that had to be the lake.

He'd given up trying to find the doctor for the night and had set up the tent and begun that slide into what would be sleep, but now here was something.

He'd just taken a hit from the beer can they'd perforated with holes and made a pipe out of, sucking the smoke in through the pop-top hole, and the daze the alcohol and marijuana had put him in had taken on a dreamlike quality rich with the possibility of a kind of dark pleasure.

He had been imagining, all day, how he would humiliate the doctor by running him off, his girl there to see it, though he had been telling himself it was about the sheet of paper. He was sure the doctor had it, the sheet with Throgmorton's and the others' numbers on it. He'd seen the doctor near the phone booth that night—it had to have been the doctor who'd taken the list from where he'd dropped it. He needed that sheet, he thought, for all he'd planned to work out at Dysart. He had to get it.

But what had driven him onto the lake wasn't about that at all, really, the sheet only gave him a reason to persist. To pursue the doctor. For the truth was something much darker. He wanted to humiliate the doctor, in the way he perceived the doctor as having humiliated him.

It would have to be something painful, and thinking on it, he was jazzed up. Psyched. Pumped.

Penry wouldn't have said he enjoyed inflicting pain on others, but it was true. It was some kind of twisted, hidden pleasure, and he was drawn to it as if it were some craving, some itch he had to scratch, though afterward he felt this darkness for days, after the good feeling was gone, sometimes even a week, but he didn't think any further than that. Always, these feelings found another object.

Yesterday they'd found Jack.

It had been a long way around, from hurting the Mexican and getting Stacey to say he'd done it, to bringing Jack down, but it had worked, even his idea to lie about calling the phone company, to say Jack had called Martinez. Penry'd felt pretty clever having thought to do that, but he didn't feel good about it now, he felt devastated, and couldn't think why.

Jack *had* screwed them, after all.

And he'd just suggested that they drown Jack that way, and now they'd gone and done it, and everything was ruined and they weren't saying it, and something buzzed in his head, this heavy, dark amperage, stoned now. The buzz was worse than harsh, and he needed a way out of it, and he knew how.

He would kick that doctor around if he could get to him.

And he'd have Stacey and Munson with him to see it, they'd do it together.

That's what he was thinking when he saw the arc of orange that fell, what must have been down a sheer face, to the lake, and went out.

"Did you see that?" he said to Stacey.

"What about it?" He was sitting back of the fire, his eyes big with dope.

Munson was sitting like some statue with a beer can in his hand beside Stacey. He hadn't taken a sip from it, or moved, in what seemed an eternity.

"Munson," Penry said, this urgency in him.

Munson didn't so much as turn to look at Penry. He sat, glowering, facing the fire. Munson's not so much as saying boo to him now scared Penry. He needed both Stacey and Munson on the floor back at Dysart, to send out the meat, or the whole deal would fall through.

Usually, Munson would have shot something back at him, like, What do you want to go out there for, numbnuts? Or, You're three cans short of a six-pack, Pen, what makes you think going out there'll getcha the other three?

But Munson wasn't saying anything at all now, and Penry felt that old, humiliating aspect of himself rising up, this clown, this buffoon, this beloved pied-piper doofus, this somebody he'd created to fit in, which always became, in the end, himself, but it seemed awful now, a caricature of a caricature.

Doofus Penry doing doofus Penry.

And anyway, there was no way he could tell them about what he knew the doctor had. Just the thought of them knowing about what he'd been up to made his face go hot.

So it was fear, first, he told himself, that got him moving. He had to get that damn sheet of paper.

"I say we go over and see who it is," he said, harshly, "and if it's the doc, we dance on his nuts." Penry did a little jig there. "See how he likes that."

Grim as Stacey looked, his eyes bruised-looking and tired, his hands shaking, he laughed at Penry, which encouraged him. Penry felt a rush in it, a kind of control. He danced a little more, shadowboxing.

"Pow! Pow! Take that, and that," he said.

Munson kicked Stacey, as if to wake him.

"*Sole* of his fuckin' shoe," Munson said, for the first time raising his eyes to glare at Penry. "You couldn't understand the *sole* of his *fuckin' shoe*."

Penry felt his face knot at that, he'd almost forgotten, and something thick as a fist drove up in his head; his eyes felt bulgy.

"Right," Penry said, eyeing Stacey. He was trying to control his voice, keep a lid on it. "You gonna take shit like that, Stacey?"

Stacey lifted his can of beer and drained it.

"I could use some fun," he said, and laughed.

He was eyeing Munson, who, with a look of disgust on his face, jammed a stick into the fire.

"What do *you* say, Munson?" Stacey said.

Munson glanced up at Stacey, then Penry. "Why go over there?" he said. "It's after eleven and we've gotta be out of here by six to get back."

"What if they've *already seen us*?" Penry said. "*Without* Jack?"

Munson stared into the fire. "They're up the lake, and if it was dark when they came in, they *couldn't've* seen us." Munson paused, then added, "No way."

"Don't you want to know if it's them?"

Munson's eyes widened slightly. He hadn't thought they might have been seen. If they had been seen from the lake by strangers, nobody'd know them from Adam. But if it *were* that doctor and the girl . . .

But what if it were? Then what? But if it weren't, they'd be home free again.

Saying nothing, all three of them back of the fire felt that abyss widen again, threaten to swallow them. They were all near crazy with it.

Penry had nobody, Munson thought, but he and Stacey had families to protect. Had houses and mortgages and all the rest of it. Penry had his beat-up Firebird and what was in his two-bedroom apartment over his parents' garage. Aluminum pots from yard sales, and those Budweiser girl posters on his walls.

"All right," Munson said. "*I'll* go."

Penry and Stacey exchanged looks. Neither liked what Munson was implying.

"Who told you *you'd* go?" Penry said, sharply, and Stacey added, "Yeah, who decided that?"

Right there, Penry saw Munson going south, and taking the highway, and he could say and do anything. Penry, after all, *had* started it. In his thinking, Munson or Stacey could blame Jack on him.

Premeditated—that got you capital 1, the death penalty if they caught you.

"Listen," Penry said, now playing the voice of reason, "two of us go out, take two canoes. One stays here, waits. We see who's there and head back, and that's that. It's a no-brainer."

The three of them considered this, weighed it out. It made sense. No one person could split, leave the others to take the rap.

"So who's gonna go?" Stacey asked.

Munson didn't like it, but there seemed nothing he could say.

"Let's flip for it."

"Fuck that," Penry said.

"What do you mean, fuck that?" Munson turned to Stacey, as if to get some backup here, and Stacey turned away.

"You were the runner all those years back," Penry said, eyeing Munson.

"What do you mean by that?"

"Just what I said," Penry replied.

Munson didn't like it at all. What if they meant to just leave him on the island, blame Jack on him? Plus, this was establishing some precedent, and he couldn't have that, Stacey and Penry calling the shots.

He suggested pulling straws, but they didn't trust one another enough to do it. Still, Munson was determined not to just let them go. Because deep in him was this desire to just leave himself. Pull out and come up with some kind of story, leave these two assholes here.

He could see himself doing it, if the opportunity presented itself.

"All right," he finally said, digging into his pocket and pulling out a quarter. "First to call it gets first call."

The other two nodded. Munson tossed the coin and let it fall on the granite, the coin ringing sharply, and Munson snapping his boot down over it.

"Heads," Penry said, over Stacey's and Munson's "Tails."

Munson lifted his boot and the three stooped low in the dark. Heads.

Munson reached for the coin.

"Give it," Penry said, and Munson slapped it into his palm.

Penry tossed the coin up, the coin lifting, flashing now silver and sharp in the firelight, and he said, "Tails," and again the three stooped over the coin after it had fallen.

"Tails. Stacey goes with me," Penry said.

Munson nodded and stepped from the fire, but he did not once turn his back to them, even as they lifted the canoes and set them in the water, and moved off.

The significance of their having taken both canoes was not lost on Munson.

Munson watched until they'd been swallowed in all that immensity and silence of the lake, and he kicked the fire down, and sat with his back to a rock wall, and listened, listened for his life, but both Penry and Lawton were experienced with canoes, and their strokes did not break the silence that settled heavily over him like some falsely comforting, velvet doom.

40

STACEY CAME ON FROM BEHIND, STOPPING AND STARTING, wary and bent down low. There was no moon now, and Stacey was thankful for that. There was a slight breeze blowing from the northwest, and it carried the scent of the fire to them, but from this distance he still couldn't make anything out but Penry, nearly a city block—or it could have been more—ahead of him.

He felt something larger than upset, disgusted with all of it, and with his goddamned life, and he jabbed at the water, bringing the canoe in.

They'd take a look and go back and tell Munson it was nobody, and they'd leave in the morning, and they'd get their story airtight, he wouldn't think any further past that.

But part of him, a part he didn't recognize in himself, but that was buddy to Penry, thrilled at their approach, felt now alert, and hard, and even powerful, hoped it was the doctor.

———

Penry forced the canoe off to the right. Behind him now, Stacey hissed, trying to get him to turn around, but Penry paid him no attention. The water was calm, and lucky for him, there was a rise on the east side of the island so that those at the fire couldn't see them coming, not even if they were in the tent on the ridgeline. But when he got closer he saw that the whole upper end of the east shore was a rock face, rising from the beach, where there was a canoe now, until there was a drop of a hundred feet or more to the water, and there only a few dark cedars growing out of the fissures that broke up that stretch of stone.

But he would wait to pass judgment here, and he drew closer, and finally saw the face was unscalable, but he was too close now to go around, and so he cut left, just yards offshore, still staying out of the line of sight, and Stacey, he knew, seeing him do it, would think he was only doing what they'd planned, cutting in to get a look, and so he stayed well back but followed left again, coming under the ridge, so as not to be seen.

————

There was a beach, a rim of sand, that wrapped around the east and south side of the island. Stacey watched as Penry took one last stroke, the bow of the canoe sliding up onto the sand nearest the ridge, and stopping, and Penry getting out, and Stacey, from a distance, watched Penry, down low, run his hands up the gunnels, walking the canoe up to where it was on the sand and then drawing it up farther so it wouldn't drift off.

Penry stayed low, and crouching like that, climbed along the path that bordered the ridgeline, passing the fire, until he was even with the tent, but fifty yards or so back in the dark. Someone came out. From where Stacey was on the lake, the tent just a luminous rectangle of green, whoever it was, stretched, taller, long-limbed, and Stacey recognized him, his heart pounding so violently it hurt.

It *was* the doctor, after all, and his girl came out after him, and Stacey was thinking, He's seen him, Penry's seen him, and now *why doesn't he go?*

The doctor and the girl went down to the fire and sat on the logs behind it, and they were talking, just talking, and Stacey tried to swallow, his mouth suddenly dry. It all meant nothing, he told himself, just like Munson had said. That the doctor and his girl were farther west on the lake meant that they'd come in earlier, since not one of them, not Stacey himself, or Penry, or Munson, had seen or heard them go by, and all that talk about roughing up the doctor he'd thought had been just that, talk.

But Penry was back in the trees by the tent doing something now, Stacey couldn't see what. So that Stacey broke out in a cold sweat, his whole back chilled, and a prickle running up his spine, because he knew this was going to be bad, and he was thinking about canoeing over to Munson, staying clear of the whole thing, so that when Penry came out into the light, just enough to wave him over, he said to himself, Not this time. He wasn't up for it, for Penry. Not really.

Stacey, rocking on the water in the canoe, did not move.

What? What could Penry want?

He felt as though he were pinned down on the water, something fused in his head. Right there, his thoughts in a hot tangle, he told himself he knew what Penry was going to do, and recoiled from it. But the part of him that was buddy to Penry was thrilled.

Penry was going to do better than just scare the fucking bejesus out of the doctor.

Still, Stacey, gritting his teeth, tried to wave Penry back, but Penry was already moving.

———

Penry crouched behind one of the erratics on the slope down from the tent. His heart was jackrabbiting, as he thought of it before he did these things, that *something* in him bursting to get out. Now, in a moment, Stacey would beach his canoe and they'd get to it.

Penry fixed his eyes on the dark there. His hands were sweaty and he felt this white-hot buzz in his head, and he stoked it, getting ready, remembering insults, the cap Munson and Carpenter and Stacey had put on his head, the dunce cap, and all those things they'd said to him, and that others had said, *No, Stupid,* and *Jesus, you idiot, Penry,* and *Our idiot brother, Penry,* and *We love you, old Pen, but boy, are you dense, bud.* And his coach, *What do you got in that head of yours, boy, rocks?* And the first girl he'd done it with, Judy Leach, for twenty dollars, and how after, she'd said, when he asked her about himself, she'd joked, *That's why girls can't count, since a two is a six, around guys like you,* and he'd been so insulted, he'd joked about it when he was out drinking with Stacey and Munson and Carpenter later, and they'd all just sat back and laughed until tears came to their eyes, and when he'd said, What? What? I mean, Jesus! I know a two from a six! Stacey had slapped him on the back, and the others had kicked back laughing again, in hysterics, saying, What a bitch, Pen, or Aren't girls just like that? and slapping the table, breathless with laughter, and he realized Judy had gotten him but good, only then Penry realizing there was no way to take back what he'd said about himself, through recounting to the others what Judy had said.

Which had, even that night, gotten him ten varieties of pencil-dick jokes, which had left him protesting, It isn't like that and you know it, the others bellowing then, drunken, Show us, Pen. Show us!

Which he did the night after, at Donna Lee's on Lake, in Minneapolis, and in the room, the door locked, he'd swung the girl around and taken her from behind, no fooling, and he'd been doing it like that since, and most of the girls wouldn't go near him, and so he had to pay all the more for it, for being like that, and always someone seeming to laugh at him, or there to humiliate him, but here there was no one but the doctor, and Stacey, whom Penry was going to use now.

Ninny Stacey, who never knew what he was thinking or what he wanted, or was whining about one thing or another. But who was . . . *excitable*.

Who knew the drill.

They'd driven off more than a few of the Mexicans this way, would drive off more. It was all drill now, but he was excited, with something deep down and dark in him, something that wanted out. Really out this time.

You couldn't understand the sole of my fucking shoe.

The doctor'd pay for saying that. He would. Penry'd make him understand, and after, after he sent Stacey away, he'd get what the doctor had taken in the phone booth.

He could see things at Dysart all working out, but he had this here, now, to finish first.

———

Stacey came around the east shore, beached the canoe, and climbed the hump of granite, but stayed low behind the white pine and erratics. The fire lit the trees, and Stacey came on, his legs trembling.

He couldn't put Penry off now, he thought, because he had to get Penry back with him, or it would all be over, their plan for dealing with Jack, and it was this goddamn doctor's fault, and so when Penry nodded, *Do it,* he came out of the trees as Penry strode down from the tent, and the doctor stood to ward off Penry, reached for the hatchet at his feet, and Stacey stepped up behind him and hit him hard across the back of the head, and the hatchet flew from his hand, and Stacey punched his hands up and under the doctor's arms and got him in a headlock, and held him.

Just as he'd held the Mexicans, waiting for Penry to start punching. Like with the wetback who had started this whole mess. When they had them, Penry usually telling them what he thought, You piece of wetback shit, You fuck, You filth! You take my job or go to somebody about this, I'll kill your kids!

And it was always the mention of the girl, or boy, that broke them.

And sometimes, later, Penry would look them up, or tail people, threaten to kill a close relative, and when all the hitting and shouting was over, Penry, with the bloodshot eyes, saying, You think you and your Mex pals can come after us? Ten to one, asshole. Get out of town! And they'd walk whoever it was up some dark alley, kicking him in the breadbasket and kidneys, in the testicles, and heave him into some dark yard.

But this huge something blossomed in Stacey's head now, like an explosion. No, he thought, thinking to turn Penry away, to run off to the canoes, but the doctor was stronger than Stacey thought he'd be, and Penry was swinging around, running after the girl, who was bolting for the trees, Stacey thinking Penry just meant to stop her screaming, her scream so sharp, he grit his teeth against it.

Then Penry caught her, in her purple down jacket and flowered pants, clapped his hand over her mouth, and she bit him, and he dragged her by the back of her jacket to the doctor, and Penry forced her down on the ground.

And here Stacey felt himself draw back, this was *not* part of the drill, and the doctor, in that moment, drove an elbow into Stacey's ribs, and he felt a fierce heat there, and terrible pain, but hung on, his head whipped side to side, and just when the doctor had broken his grip, Penry swung on him, a roundhouse, smacking him across the side of his head, and Penry shouted, "Kick him! Kick his feet down, goddammit! Kick his feet out!"

Stacey kicked at the doctor's feet, but he wasn't going down. He was a powerful man, and Penry hit him again, and Stacey hung on for all he was worth, then got his legs kicked out in front of him, Stacey barely able to keep him down, his ribs burning something awful, so that every time the doctor struggled, he nearly lost him, the doctor jabbing with his elbows and not staying put at all, as Penry, time and again, caught the girl and dragged her back, and pressed her down in the dirt, the girl kicking, and Stacey shouting, when he saw what Penry meant to do, *"Pen! Pen! What the fuck are you—"*

Penry swung around with a block of firewood, hitting the doctor alongside his head, but the doctor just kicked all the harder for it, and Stacey bore down on his neck, the doctor had almost gotten his hand on the hatchet, down on the ground the way he was, and he jabbed at Stacey's ribs again, something broken there, so all Stacey could do was hang on, in his head this bloodred haze of pain.

"Pen! Goddammit!" he shouted. "Stop it! Stop it, Goddammit, Pen!"

Pen had the girl pinned down, and in one vicious move he yanked the girl's pajama bottoms off.

"See this, asshole?" Penry said, glaring at the doctor.

The doctor tore at Stacey's arms, the hatchet was right there on the ground.

Penry had a thick, short penis, had his pants down.

Stacey said through his teeth, "Penry—*no!*"

The doctor gave one last desperate kick, nearly sending Stacey over backwards, and Stacey wrenched at his neck, Stacey breathless, and fading, forcing the doctor down, who shouted now, "So help me God, I'll kill you! Every last one of you, I'll kill you, you touch her!"

Penry spit in his face, roughly spreading the legs of the girl with his knee, the girl crying, and thrashing under him.

Stacey, seeing Penry was going to do it, reared back, wide-eyed, dragging the doctor with him, away from the hatchet.

"Goddammit, Penry!" he bellowed. *"Don't you do it, don't you—DON'T YOU DO IT—"*

41

DAVID, SITTING AT THE WEST END OF THE ISLAND IN THE COOL dark, heard what seemed to be a shout, then Janie's voice, a kind of ululating cry becoming a scream cut short, and he stood, his heart racing.

He listened, a breeze rustling the pines.

But there wasn't anything, just the night sounds again, and the breeze whooshed in the trees, and he was thinking he'd move anyway, go back, he was trying not to let himself get carried away, yet he was wound up all over again, he'd have to just go back and try to make the best of it, and then he did hear a shout, *"Don't you do it, don't you—"* and a piercing scream, Janie's, and he moved, first with long strides, telling himself it had been his father's voice he'd heard, altered by distance, but there'd been something about it not like his father's voice at all, and his breath came shallow and he was moving up the backside of the island, up through the trees, and in the absolute dark, careful with his feet. There was a third path up the middle of the island, he'd been on it earlier, and he moved quickly, nearly running but not running, because he was trying to listen, and when he was off the path, and feeling for the middle, the woods path, he was still trying to listen, and this panic in him he was trying to suppress, but his mind grasping after some explanation.

He couldn't believe Max was shouting at Janie. They just weren't like that.

He hit the path and went over it, then found it again, ran up a slope so steep, at one point he had to use his hands to pull himself over the brush and erratics, the stones cold and sharp under his hands, until he could see the light of the fire up ahead, and when he came over the rise his heart gave one enormous kick before he even knew what it was about, because what he saw made no sense at all.

He saw something tangled and dark a distance back from the fire, and in the firelight, something there on the ground, and somehow knew it, for what it was, but could not believe it, and he wanted to bolt down, and knock it all away, a kind of shock in it.

He reached for his leg, just above his boot, the knife there, and he was still on the middle path, and he saw in his mind a way to do it, take the two men there, but even thinking it, believing it, a part of him did not believe that he would do it, it was impossible, but he was breathing, here, right in front of him Janie on the ground, and that man bobbing over her, and now the knife in his hand, he moved down the path behind the tent, saw now the hatchet on the ground, just in front of Max's feet, he could get the man who had his father from behind, sweep up the hatchet—

And even moving, he felt in himself a stillness, he would surely die, or must die, but he could not watch this, in the light, Janie, her eyes reflecting the firelight, glazed, and this—

And he suddenly recognized them, the men from the motel, who'd been sitting on the porch, and he was filled with even greater fear, because they were bigger, and the short one had those thick arms, but he was closer yet, even moving as he thought all this, the tent coming up now, and in seconds he'd be in the open, a hundred yards downhill, there was no turning back, and with each step, preparing to move, he thought, He was going to do it, going to do it, going to do it, he'd take out the man behind his father and he'd sweep up the hatchet, and if he could, he'd cut the man over Janie in half, he'd—

And as he came astride the tent, all that he'd lived for and practiced for came into play, and he bolted, his legs powerful and elastic on the ground, arms pumping, and where there were erratics he leapt over them or bounded from them, driving as he had in practice over rough ground, his eyes on one spot.

———

Stacey heard the footfalls and turned, shocked, to see someone in dark clothes, teeth bared, coming at him, legs pumping, and thinking the boulders and scree on the slope would slow him, he struck the doctor again, but when he looked up, he knew, then, he'd misjudged the boy, his shocked mind registering it, just a boy, but he came on through the erratics as if he were flying, something almost inhuman in it, and he lifted away from the doctor, as if in slow motion, but the boy already on top of him, and there was the flash of steel in firelight—

———

Penry reared up to see the boy catch Stacey in the neck back-handed, a roundhouse punch, at the worst, he thought, and even as he thought it, Stacey's head cocked over to the side, as if it weren't connected to his body, and the doctor jerked him down and over his back, hot blood jetting across Penry's forehead and in his eyes, blinding him, and he jerked out of the girl, rolling and yanking up his pants, caught the hatchet there, and had it up just in time to counter the boy's swing at him, but still blinded, and kicking the boy hard, so the boy was knocked back, he ran, trying to wipe the blood out of his eyes, he couldn't see to kill the boy, and he ran, blinking and cursing, trying to clear his eyes of the blood, but couldn't, and then the boy was behind him, breathing hard, faster, slashing at him, the kid could run like nobody Penry'd ever known, and he went up the ridge, he had short, powerful legs, knew to bolt up the steep path, he had only yards on the kid, he could climb better than anyone, but the boy still came on, came on, came on, breathing right down his goddamn back, and Penry spun, just back of the ledge, took a swipe at the boy with the hatchet, the hatchet, slick with blood, flying from his hand, and knowing it was the only way, when the boy came on again, the knife flashing, he pitched himself over the rock face.

———

David slid to a stop just back of the ledge. He heard the man falling in a rush of air, then a powerful wet slap in all that darkness.

He wanted to go down, but he couldn't see a way to do it, and then thought to try to spot him in the water, desperate to know if he'd survived the fall, but he knew to find the hatchet first, and began to rake his hands over the rough stone and lichen, all the while the knife bunched in his now-shaking hand, he'd need both the knife and hatchet, because there were two others out there, besides this one, and he was shaking in the dark, on his hands and knees, then had it, the hatchet, heavy, cold steel, but knowing that this was not over now, it had only started.

There was a splash down on the lake, then another, and his heart rushed with the thought that he was swimming up shore and would come in again, and he had to get to his father, and Janie, he had to, and he was staring in the dark, blue spots in his eyes, he couldn't decide what to do, but he knew if he got to this one, the others would not come so soon, and he'd have—a half hour, maybe, and he was west of where they must have beached their canoes, and so, muttering to himself with rage, he charged down the ridge, the hatchet in his left hand, the knife in his right, and it was at that moment he heard something cracking, and he bolted the remainder of the slope, was in time to see the thick-armed man paddling off in the darkness, Penry, a canoe in tow, and he was tempted to shout in rage at him, but he was as terrified now as he was angry.

He'd gotten off the island. Now they'd all be coming.

And then he saw what the man had done, he'd broken their canoe, punched a hole in that thin cedar hull, and David felt in himself a swelling, his whole body hot and his heart tripping and running.

For sure now, they were coming back.

They were coming back, all three of them, and this one, here, dead.

———

He ran back into camp, his father still slumped over the man he'd cut, the man's neck severed to the vertebra, and the cut clean and a dark pool of sticky blood matting the pine needles and stone.

He didn't want to move Max just yet.

He didn't dare speak. Janie lay there, dirt and needles on her thighs.

He stood, and could not get his breath. Then he was crying,

suddenly, at Janie, crying and hiccuping, and couldn't stop, and when he bent down over her, terrified to do it, because—because of her eyes, he thought she might be dead, but she was breathing, and he looked down into her lovely girl's face and he thought, If they don't come back I will go out and kill them.

But he had to stop that, and he bent down now, and looking at Janie, these words came to him, *pudenda,* and *labia,* and *vagina,* and there was blood there, and still he couldn't speak.

He could not open his mouth, and began to cry again when he did.

"Goddammit," he said. Finally. But it just got him going again, and then he saw how she'd been torn, and rocked on his heels and thought he had to do something, and he went over to the dead man and ran his knife up his shirt, cutting off the buttons, and spat in the man's face, and then was laughing, he couldn't control it, and he cut the chambray shirt into a large square, and when he went back over to Janie, he got down between her legs again, and he touched her, where she was torn, and his whole face bunched up and he couldn't see for crying, and Max saw him and only shook his head, not me, her, and he couldn't hold his hands still for weeping and he tried to put her back together down there, and he knew he had to get the dirt off, and he had to—to use what, to—antiseptic, that was it, and if he could dry the labia off, and he saw her there like that and couldn't help himself again, and he was laughing, and crying, and when he touched her, there was this thing that reached down and lifted his whole body, as if he were some puppet, and then, even as it had come, he felt some calm, and then he bent down, and he was dead calm, and he stood and went up to the tent and got the whiskey, and when he poured it on her, he thought, *Genitals,* but she didn't flinch, and he felt all that rise up in him again, the crazy, warbling laughter, and he thought, Stop it.

Stop it. And he bent between Janie's legs and cleaned her off the best he could, but now this cold fear in him, the word coming at him, *catatonic.*

He knew, somehow, he would have to try to bring her out of it.

David finished cleaning Janie, then dried her as best he could, and used the tape and gauze he had to hold the torn flesh together.

He thought, doing it, I will kill that son of a bitch and cut off what he did this with. I'll cut it off and . . . *shove it in his mouth.*

But he had to move. He had to move and then some.

He tied the piece of cloth around her, tightly, and got her pants on, then carefully lay her down again.

He couldn't speak yet. And when Max looked up at him, his eyes turning as if not in a face, or a head, but in a skull, David knew it was bad.

"Leave me," he said.

And right there David was in the throes of it again. He could not do this, he thought. He could not do it, could not do it.

"No."

"You have to."

"Can't," he said. And he thought up an excuse to shut him up. He couldn't take it.

"Why?"

"Just won't."

David spun around. He had . . . how much time? No time. There was a hole in the canoe.

"You have to go," Max said.

"Shut up," he said. It surprised him.

David turned his back to Max; he had to think but he had no time for it.

But then he knew what he would do. He marched up to the tent, yanked off the overfly, and digging in his gear, got out the glue that had come with the tent to proof the seams. It was really just airplane glue, but they sold Max an extra tube, and David, walking down to the canoe with the green overfly in his hand, was talking to himself, or was it some kind of prayer?

He knew he had maybe as little as a half hour, or forty minutes. And they had to be off the island, earlier, because he had to paddle the whole weight himself.

He set the overfly back of the fire and went down to shore. The two holes in the cedar hull were nearly exactly the shape of the stone used to make them, lying there beside the canoe.

That was the saving grace of the thin hull—it was so thin, the stone had punched nearly splinterless holes in it, and David swung the canoe around and up.

He set the canoe back of the fire, and in minutes had cut two patches of ripstop from the tent overfly, and abraded and cleaned around the holes in the hull, leaving no splinters—one bad splinter and that would be the end of it. He got out the tube of seam sealer and set down a thick bead of it around the first hole, then lay over it a square of the nylon. He pressed the material along the bead of glue but didn't flatten it. Then he fixed the other hole, set down the material, and dragged the canoe closer to the fire, on which he'd tossed more wood, to make the glue dry faster.

It'd make no difference now, more light here. Whoever it was out there knew they were here.

David cut two more squares of cloth and glued them down inside the hull, then reached around to press the sheets together, the sealer permeating the nylon and the beads of sealer setting up where he'd abraded the varnished wood of the hull.

He jumped to his feet and brought the hull closer to the fire, all the while thinking he had to be careful—if the nylon got too hot, it would pucker and melt, so he had to brace the hull with rocks a safe distance back, had to be careful that the breeze didn't change, didn't blow the flame into the nylon patches.

He strode up the hill to the tent, and swinging the Duluth pack out, dumped everything from it, the canned goods first, which scared him, dumping food, but he had his pack and the jerky in it, which he'd never thought he'd have to use, any of it, the space blanket, or freeze-dried packets, and he thought, Thirty hours, they could be out in thirty hours, and he left the cans there, and the other heavy things Max had brought, left his Nikon and lenses, left the tent and poles and took the plastic ground cloth and yellow nylon dining fly; if they needed a tent, the ground cloth or dining fly would to have to do, and he had the space blanket, and carefully forced the down bags in the pack, just one pack, he had to be able to carry the canoe and gear at the same time, and only brought two bags, because he was going to hold Janie, he knew it, he'd hold her, like . . . he was going to . . .

But he couldn't think about it.

He threw the big Duluth bag over his shoulders, cinched the straps tighter, went down to the fire, and there checked the canoe.

The material was tight, and he cut a yards-long piece of rip-stop from the overfly, and like an enormous green bandage, pulled it tightly over the outside of the hull and down on the gunnels, and with a spare pair of shoelaces he'd brought, tied the ends secure.

He thumped the nylon over the holes, and it made a sound like a drum would make, and he lifted the canoe again and carried it to the water, and got the Duluth bag over the two holes, another good thing, that they were near the middle, and the pack pressing like that, it was a pretty good fix, though he wouldn't kid himself, it was temporary—until he could find a cabin, with some Grummans, or an Alumacraft, put away for winter, everybody had them, they weren't worth taking down to the Cities when the season was over.

When David had the canoe set up, he glanced at his watch. His hand, blood-covered and dirty, looked as though it were someone else's, was oddly distant, a flesh-colored glove held under his eyes.

Fuck it, he thought, climbing back to the fire. Twenty fucking minutes. It took his breath away. He had no time at all.

He bent down and lifted Janie, and when her arms just hung at his sides, lumpen, he felt a hot and terrible loss in him, but he wouldn't accept it.

He got her in the canoe, in the middle, and had to leave her, the canoe holding water, bobbing there—and if she came to and went into the water?

"Max," David said, "I'm gonna lift you, but you gotta help."

"Won't go," he said.

David tried to get his arms around Max, lying there on the ground, and Max pushed him away.

"Go away. Get the hell out of here. Davey—"

But Max's saying it only made David all the more determined.

He tried again and Max punched at him, and David, who'd been on the edge of tears again, felt suddenly furious, and he lifted him over his shoulder and, Max's feet dragging, carried him toward the canoe.

"You never did listen to your old man, did you," he said, and it made David angry again, until it struck him, his father, even now, here, was joking.

And David staggered into the water, up to his knees, freezing, frigid water, but he couldn't turn to get Max into the bow, his legs suddenly threatening to collapse under him, and Max said, "Can't do it, can ya."

And David thought, Fuck you, and with the last thing in him heaved Max over and into the canoe, and right then his father looked up at him and said, "Gotcha. You didn't know you could. But I always, *always* did. Never figured that out, did you?"

42

HE BEGAN TO SHAKE LEAVING THE ISLAND. HE WAS SHAKING so badly his teeth were chattering, upset again, at Janie, her eyes vacant, her head lolling back as he paddled, thinking, Dammit, dammit, which way?

He could go south, but that was obvious, and there were three massive islands ahead, to the west, but how to make the move that would throw them off?

And he had to be lucky. Or he could get out the map, just seconds would make the difference, and he did that, got the map out, and his Bic lighter, and held the flame over the page, and couldn't find them anywhere, couldn't find the name of the lake Max had told them they were on.

Max bent his head around and saw what David was doing, and said, in a voice David had never heard coming from Max, "I'm sorry."

And David felt the night split open with dark possibility.

He understood, just then, what Max had done. The new maps David had gotten hadn't, after all, gone this far east, and to get them moving, Max had taken them in and just trusted to luck, the lake they'd come in on as good as the next, any lake, and it wouldn't have been a problem, not really, to head out north for a few days, and to canoe south after, and hit the highway and get to the car like that.

It was the way people had used the waters before the maps and regulations.

In a second, David saw many of the decisions he'd made about their gear were the wrong ones. About the tent, about the canned food.

He turned to face the direction they'd come, the moon not visible but lighting the lake. Labyrinthine, the water barely distinguishable from the islands.

Where *wouldn't* he go?

Or where, up one of these things, might there be a short portage?

He could carry Janie, but what about Max?

Where would somebody build a cabin?

The canoe rocked in the lake; the patch was holding, but he wanted to run into a cabin, or a lodge. Could be anywhere, but he surely didn't want to run out of water, hit land just yet.

No long portages, he just couldn't.

He looked behind them, due east. They'd be coming from that direction. South was too obvious, and the water there too broad and open. And west, into the heart of the complex of lakes, would be safe at first, but a terrible gamble, trying to get out after.

So he took the channel northeast, which would cross over them, he hoped.

They had to be lucky, stay quiet and low on the water, hope the island there didn't open somewhere to the south, so they could be seen. The men coming now would never think he'd cross over, not at first, and anyway, from here it was just a two-day shot south down to the car.

He could do that, just that, he thought, and took long, powerful strokes, but he was beginning to shake again, and he reached into his bag and tore off a piece of the salty jerky, then reached over the hull and cupped a hand of water to his mouth, shoved the jerky in and chewed quickly, and taking up the paddle again, quietly sent the canoe up the channel.

———

Penry burst up shore, moving to the fire and kicking away Munson's coffeepot.

"What the hell is—"

"Goddamn fucker cut Lawton!" Penry shouted.

Munson was already on his feet, towering over Penry.

"*What?*"

"I was just gonna rough the asshole up a bit, and he swings on me with a fuckin' "—Penry motioned to his face, the spray of blood—"a *fuckin' knife,* and nearly takes Lawton's head off."

"Now *wait a minute!*" Munson said. It was all coming at him too fast. "Wait-one-minute!" he said. "*What* happened?"

"He said he called somebody, down in Ely, before they left. Let 'em know he'd run into some people he thought—" Penry held up his hands, as if in frustration.

"You *asshole,* Penry!" Munson said. "Some people he thought *what?*"

"'Might be *up to something.*' That's what he said."

"Up to fuckin' *what?*"

"He came around the backside of the island," Penry said, taking the opportunity, hoping for luck now. He was still trying to catch his breath. "When he saw it was gonna get rough, he asked where Jack was. Laid all that shit about talkin' to the rangers on us."

Munson's eyes widened at this. It took his breath away. It hadn't occurred to him, yet, to question some or all of what Penry was saying. Penry seemed too authentically panicked.

And besides, it was what Munson had feared. This was just confirmation of it.

"Why didn't he ask where *I* was?" That was the limit of Munson's canniness. "And how the fuck would he know Jack's name?"

But Penry, the liar, had had more practice over the years, and besides, he'd had time to think, paddling back, and even did now, could play slow—being thought stupid gave him leeway. No one thought he could put two and two together, and Munson thought the same.

"I *didn't* say he did."

"Didn't you?" Munson said.

"I said he saw just the three of us go by."

"And *when* was that?"

"Fuck if I know! They must have stopped earlier for shore lunch, and we went right by."

"Fucking great!"

"I *told* you," Penry said, feigning an almost frenzied exasperation at how Munson just wasn't seeing what had happened, the new situation they were in. "They *went by here,* later, and he thought something was wrong, and so he looked. And there wasn't any Jack, and you know how he stuck out with us."

"God-*dammit!*" Munson said.

"You can say that again. I mean, he can say what he did to Stacey was self-defense, see, since we came up there on the island."

Munson heaved his leg back and gave the Duluth pack there a furious kick.

"He's dead." Munson glanced up at Penry. "Stacey's dead, that's what you're saying."

"Stacey doesn't mean shit now. That doctor's out there, and he's going to head down to Ely."

"Shit-shit-shit!"

"What are we gonna do?" Penry said.

It was his problem now, Penry's, to make Munson say it. Or at least think it. All Penry had to do was get close enough, and he could take care of the doctor and his girl. They couldn't let them go, not now.

"They'll be gone if we wait," Penry said.

Munson gave Penry the disbelieving look he'd wanted to see. It would all work out yet.

"What are you saying?" Munson said.

"I'm saying," Penry said, pointing out into the dark, as if

something were coming after them, "they get away now, we're lookin' at premeditated, and that can get you the fucking chair, asshole, that's what I'm sayin'."

"I thought you said he—"

"For *Jack*!" Penry shouted.

Munson put his fists at his sides. "Fuck!" he said, and kicked the ground with his boot.

"Well, you can cry about it," Penry said. "Or"—and here he pointed out onto the lake—"we can get the fuck out there and save ourselves. It *doesn't matter* what you or I do alone now, we're gonna go down, and in the *worst-fucking-humiliating* way, if we don't get out there."

Penry was thrilled with himself. He still hadn't said it, and he could see Munson was moved.

"What if we just—"

"If we just *what*?" Penry said. "Just *make something up*? Tell the cops that we just, what, ran? You know what kind of people they are, the doctor and his kind, and what kind of people *we* are. *Think*—think of all those fuckin' years at Dysart, and what the management did to us. I mean, shit, we're lucky to be alive, the way they treat people like us."

Munson was looking out onto the lake. Penry knew to push it.

"Why's *anyone* gonna think some campers going missing thirty, maybe forty miles apart have to do anything with each other? I mean, we've got to get back over to Jack still."

"I don't like it," Munson said.

Penry almost had to turn away. He'd think of this, he thought, later, as something near magic, how he'd saved himself, and anyway, that old life was dead.

He just had to get out now, and he knew how he had to disappear. And anyway, he had nothing. Even the Firebird was worthless.

He still had his back turned to Munson, was facing the lake.

He knew not to mention the girl.

"He gets down to Ely, it's gonna be over for us. Don't you get it?"

"You just shut the fuck up, Penry!" Munson said. "I don't want to hear it!"

But he knew Munson was on the outside now. He hadn't been there, couldn't know what had really happened, and Penry could say anything, how would Munson know? And that's when Penry thought to say it:

"He's got Stacey's wallet."

This struck Munson almost bodily. He got that zipper-mouthed, wide-eyed look again. Pissed at everything, and the situation so bad, it was no use blaming anybody.

Penry let his head drop back, then shook himself, playing stupefied. The wallet was sharp. So sharp. He let the quiet go, not knowing what Munson was thinking.

When it had gone on too long, he said, in a tone of revulsion, "He *hurt* that girl."

"No, it was you, wasn't it," Munson said, coming on strong, glaring.

So strong, and so fast, shaking Penry by the shoulder, that Penry was thinking to himself, Shit, too much, he'd gone too far, but he was stuck in it.

"If *I* did something," he nearly shouted, his voice a hot accusation, "then why did he cut *Stacey*? I mean, why do I have a spray of blood across *my* forehead and . . . I mean, Jesus—Stacey's my friend, but shit, he shouldn't have done that, but now that he has, they will fucking hunt us down and they will put us right in the fucking chair."

He did not use his name. Larry. They had never been like that, and Munson would have taken the whole thing apart.

"All right, I'm going," Penry said. "Time's up."

"Going *where*?"

"If they're gone, what Stacey's done is gonna get us fuckin' fried."

Munson held his hand to his mouth, stricken. He was big, and his free hand hung at his side. Something was turning there in his head, but Penry couldn't think what. For a second, Munson moved over by the axe they'd brought to chop wood, and Penry, with a flush of blood to his head thought, *Mistake*.

But when he didn't reach for it, Penry said, "It's *us*, Munson, don't you see? No one's gonna save our asses. No one ever did."

Penry threw his pack over his shoulder and went down to the canoe.

"You got both canoes back," Munson said, as if it had nothing to do with anything.

"That was the deal," Penry replied. "Remember?"

Penry tossed his pack into the closest one and pushed off. Munson, still onshore, said, "You're gonna freeze going without a tent."

Penry was moving away from shore, paddling. If Munson didn't come on now, he would double around in the dark and take him from behind. Use the axe.

But then he heard a racket, and a clatter, and cursing, and in minutes there was the splash of Munson's paddle behind him, and not until they got to the island where it had all happened did they stop.

––––––––––

Penry got out first, shocked to find the doctor and his son and daughter, he had to assume, had made it out in their damaged canoe. He went up the ridge, and with a fear in him, almost total, and blocking the path, turned Stacey over in the now-thick, coagulated blood. He reached into Stacey's pants pocket, and something like dark joy in him, palmed his wallet even as Munson came on, dropping the wallet down his shirtfront so it stopped at his belt. He made a big point of staying low, he couldn't stand with the wallet there, making a production out of his grief over Stacey, when all he could think was he had to find the boy and his father and the girl. And he would run, later.

After Munson.

But he needed Munson now, he thought, and when Munson stooped to touch Stacey's face, Penry got the wallet into his back pocket, his wallet already in his pack. He did this calmly, stealthily, as if he were rendering on the killing floor at Dysart, careful not to cut himself with a saw, and blood everywhere.

He did everything calmly now. Everything that had happened outside him had driven him to this moment, and he could face it if he thought about it that way, about himself that way, and he moved now with no remorse, like a man going about important business, even asking Munson to go down to shore to see if they'd left any sign of what direction they'd gone, while he went up to the tent site to see if, somehow, he could find the sheet of paper he'd lost in the phone booth, tore through everything, his hands quick, and powerful, scrabbling through the gear, the rods and reels, bait case, but there was no sign of it, and then he bundled the rest of it, a girl's day pack, purple with flowers on it, and cans of stew, a shaving kit, toothbrushes, detritus, and with Munson's help, they cleared the entire campsite, bundled Stacey and the rest of it in the tent, and weighted it with rocks, and sunk it far off-shore, and were back, quickly, clearing away all the remaining signs that anyone had been there and, likewise, sunk that, and moved out past the island, and were stunned to see the three channels to the north, and the larger, wider channel to the south, the maze of lakes to the west.

"I say we split up," Munson said.

He'd moved a fair distance from Penry, far enough out so that Penry, with his short, thick arms, could never catch him if they had a falling-out.

"What time is it?" Penry said.

"What difference does it make, if you don't know when they left the island?"

Penry shook his head. "Daylight. How many hours do they have before daylight?"

Now Munson checked his watch. "It's five after twelve. So they have six, almost seven hours of dark."

They floated there, each in his canoe.

"Listen, you take the furthest west, I'll take the middle," Munson said.

"What about south?"

"Look at it. You think they'd go down there?"

Even in the dark, they could see the lake stretching south was nearly a mile wide, and who knew how long like that it went south. Too exposed, too open.

"But what if they did?"

"You saying you want to go down there?" There was that note of suspicion in Munson's voice again.

"I could check it out," Penry replied, "take an hour or two, and either I run into them or I come back up, say, like you said, and I take the middle. Couldn't have taken the east, because that would have been the closest to us, and they'd have wanted to pick up some distance."

This, to Munson, was inarguable. Penry was right. It was the way to do it, and they'd find them, and wait until dark again, and finish it.

It made him sick all over to think like that, but everything was wrong now.

"That's it, then?" Munson said.

"No," Penry said. "We get separated, we try to get back together. We need the two canoes, so we can tell the cops later that Jack and Stacey were in the same canoe. Went into the drink together and drowned."

Munson wanted to say, Who are you kidding? But he was buying time. And it was possible. It did happen, men drowned like that all the time. And, anyway, this wasn't a bad thing, separating from Penry. He couldn't think around him. He suspected Penry now, he just felt something.

"Listen, we have till tomorrow night, that gives us almost forty hours," said Penry.

"What of it?"

"We take this"—Penry pointed with his paddle to the lake going south—"down to the highway, and we can hitch a ride to the road and go in for the car."

"You really think this'll work?" It was as if Penry knew something he didn't.

"It has to."

Munson turned his back to Penry, trying to make himself believe it.

"What?" Penry said.

Munson only shook his head.

"Listen," Penry said, "he *killed* Stacey. You saw it. And he's out there now. I mean, *what* are you thinking, sitting there like that?"

"I'm not thinking shit," he said.

What he was thinking was, How did this happen? How did he come to be here, like this, with Penry, whom he'd never liked? And he saw his mistake, now, had been shunting that first cart of porterhouse to Door 26.

Taking the envelope the following day, left in his glove compartment.

Opening it. Two hundred dollars, free and clear, he'd thought, but had known otherwise.

But no, it had all been about Jack.

Jack had screwed them all, and he felt maybe the worst about that. About what Jack had done, hiring those Mexicans, and then even going to the phone to call Martinez on them, who, thanks to Penry, was in for a surprise.

"Remember what that asshole doctor said to you," Penry said. "About being too dumb to—"

"He didn't say anything to *me*. He said it to *you*, Penry, for being such a loudmouth."

But he wondered. Who *had* he been talking to?

And with that, Munson turned and began to paddle toward the mouth of the channel to the west.

"I'll see you," Penry called from behind him, "after I check it out to the south. And if we get separated, we'll meet at the car, right?"

Munson waved the paddle over his head, a signal, yes, the paddle glistening in the dark, and the water coursing down its length onto Munson's hand, and he stared for a second, oddly experiencing the water as if it were blood, blood on his hand, on his forearm, dripping down the length of his arm, and coldly by his armpit, and down his side, and he shuddered at the thought, and quickly dipped the paddle into the lake again, and drew himself further into the darkness that was the lake.

43

THE TEMPERATURE HAD DROPPED, AND DOWN ON THE water it was damp and cold and chill. David reached into the lake with the paddle, and drawing back as powerfully as he could, he tried to J, to keep a straight line, but found he was having difficulty doing it, he was shaking so badly, exhausted, and what had been hot sweat on his back now bitterly icy.

At the three channels north, he'd gone up the farthest east, knowing if he could keep moving in that direction, he could break south when they were safe, and take a straight shot back down to the highway. It was the only thing he could think, and that, closer to the eastern gateway to the whole area, there might be others out. But he placed little hope in that, and he was right not to. It was very late in the season, and no one was out, and his only hope was to keep moving.

The dark, now, he thought, was the only thing he had on his side.

In the stern, he shuddered, drew the paddle back again, propelling them up a channel, high and pine-sided, and Max tossing in the bow, rocking the canoe, so that David had to reach for him with his paddle and poke him, until he settled, though David worried he should tie Max down so he didn't hurt himself, but then if they capsized, Max would drown, no doubt about it, and so he would have to try, as best he could, he thought, to just keep Max quiet, to save him, and Janie, and all the while, the canoe had been gliding closer to shore, and David paddled sharply away from it, sculling to pull the canoe to the right, but the shore cut into the water, in the dark, closer, closer yet, until he heard a terrible rasping under the hull, a stone on wood scraping, and he cursed himself for blindness, and almost panicked, swung the paddle over to his left, poking inches above the water with it, and struck gravel, and bent into the paddle, pressing against it to move them from whatever it was, and the rear half of the canoe rattled up the length of it anyway, scraping loudly, an esker, a ridge of gravel that had been formed by a subglacial stream millennia ago, not so dangerous in itself, but for the deadwood that had probably collected along its length, there were always branches, or deadheads—old stumps with roots jutting in all directions from them like knives—along eskers, any of which could puncture the ripstop nylon covering the holes in the hull, and he levered the paddle around on his left, against the esker, so as to turn the canoe out onto the dark, calm water, and there felt, even as he was trying to release the paddle, the paddle flex, then break with a crack down near the blade, and he was sick at it, wanted to curse, but didn't, instead remembered he'd set by the extra paddle, tied along the gunnel.

David tossed the shaft of the broken paddle into the canoe, then dipped his hand into the bitter-cold water, his fingers immediately numb, desperate to find the blade, but terrified they'd hit deadwood, Max and Janie there in front of him, dark silhouettes, which made him think, just then, they're both dead, and he ran his hand desperately through the water, and he still did not find the blade, but he had to find it, he just had to, and now his left arm was numb up to his elbow, and with the spare paddle, he sent the canoe backwards, and when the stern struck the esker again, he leaned out of the canoe, and cocking his right leg under the rear seat, he bent over the gunnel, putting his head down near the black water, sighted down the length of the esker. There was just enough starlight so that, where the deadwood lay, the stars did not shimmer on the surface, there in the dark the deadheads bristling, broken roots and branches all angled out from the esker, and straining, his head down near the water, he managed to make out something roundish in it all, and he drew himself back into the canoe and moved forward through the sharp roots and branches, one of the branches catching the hull below the waterline and making a loud, sharp scritching. Using the other paddle, but only on the right side, so he wouldn't break it, he moved farther up the esker, through the deadwood, and the blade of the broken paddle bumped up against the hull, and he reached for it and pulled it into the canoe, then back-paddled, so the stern swung out into the open water, and in the starlight, he saw the esker in its entirety, hooked out into the lake farther up, all deadwood there, a barrage of sharp-pointed roots and sticks rising right out of the water, and he shuddered at that, how he'd nearly paddled right into it, and he backed off onto the lake, and he moved as quickly as he could, out and around the esker and farther east, shoving another piece of jerky into his mouth, tasting nothing but salt, and cupping handfuls of the flat, bitter-cold lake water into his mouth.

———

Move, he thought. Move. Just keep moving. Just keep moving.

He was singing it to himself, it was a kind of mantra in the dark. Because he assumed, wrongly, the three men could trade places, and always there would be a fresh paddler, someone to haul from the stern, or there could be, anyway, in at least one canoe, and set up like that, he thought, he had no chance at all against them, unless he got lucky, unless he kept moving, unless he could continue to move east, ahead of them, then south, then east again, and south, until he'd done it so many times that the likelihood of their making the same moves in the dark was astronomically small. And there was the problem of not having the tent, if it got colder, and if he had to make a fire, he would have to be very careful about the smoke.

And now Max was saying, "Stop."

He was not going to stop, this queasy feeling in his middle over what might be wrong with Max—brain damage, he thought—and there was Janie, what could he do with Janie? He wanted to stop, get hold of himself, but kept moving, because if he wasn't moving, then what?

Still, he'd begun to shudder, his whole body convulsing, and he got a Snickers bar out of his day pack and shoved it into his mouth, chewing again, and not feeling, or tasting, a thing, until he tasted blood, he'd bit into his cheeks, but it didn't matter, and he dipped into the lake for more water, and Max said, again, "You have to leave me."

David didn't listen. Max was starting to say strange things. He'd been doing it for some time. David listened to none of it, his mumbling, and talking to himself. But David moved back on the seat, as if away from it.

"You know why I left Rachel?" he said, but he said it as if to someone other than David, as if to one of his friends.

David had heard Max on the phone sound like this, back when Max had made calls from his den, in that bad time.

He told himself he was not going to listen. He wouldn't. Janie had curled up in a fetal ball, just in front of him. She had her thumb in her mouth, and for a second he turned to look behind him, nothing there but darkness and water and more darkness, and part of him wanted to stop, he'd stop, and when they came by, he'd lure them onto one of the islands, and he'd kill them.

But there were three of them, and they were big, rough men, except the one, he'd been different, it was hard to imagine him out here at all, but that was wishful thinking, it was all stupid thinking, angry thinking, that he'd go after them, and he tried to let that anger work to keep him moving, but it wasn't working, not as it had, because he was exhausted, and he was beginning to sleep, eyes open, paddling, and now this fear, it was fear he was moving away from in the dark, and not even of the men now, though that was there, but of Max, of Max's injury.

"You know what?" Max said.

David didn't answer. Reach, pull, J, he thought, pulling the canoe through the water, then reached for the water yet again.

Reach, pulllll, J.

"Lipschitz did it, you know. Did you know that?"

Max had sat up in the dark, was glaring at David. He tried to ignore him, but Max lunged at him, and without thinking, David swung the paddle around and jabbed him, so he went down in the bow, his head thunking against the bow plate, but he got right up again.

"You," he said.

David had his heart right up in his throat.

"Shut up, Max!" he said.

"Not gonna shut up. Not this time. No, you can shut up!" Max said, then added, "You know why Lipschitz was gone those afternoons?"

David reached for the water again. Drew the paddle back. Max sat up, turned to his left, the canoe shifting so badly, it went up on its gunnel, and David got the paddle under Max's arm and broke his grip, so that he thumped down again.

"You," he said.

"Right," David said.

"You listening?"

But it wasn't David Max was talking to, though David saw, if he answered, Max stopped trying to climb out of the canoe.

"You listening? You hearing me?"

Reach, pulllll, J. "Right here," David said. "You're coming in just fine."

Anything to keep Max down. He'd seen something like it one time before, a brain-injured boy—motorcycle accident—in Max's unit. Max had put the boy's right leg back together, but the brain injury. . . . The boy had been calling to people who weren't there, had to be tied down with nylon webbing.

The brain swelling goes down, Max had said, we'll see where he's at.

"It's Lipschitz's been taking the Lidocaine," Max said.

Lidocaine?

"He injects it between his toes. That's how he does it. High as a kite all day. He's doping the vials. What do you think? I think he's gonna get us screwed."

David brought the paddle in too close to the gunnel, and it made a drumming sound, which echoed off the lake. His heart clenched like a fist.

He froze there when he tried to listen; he could hear something behind them. Another wood-on-gunnel sound . . .

But was that just the echo, or was it the men behind them?

Max was climbing again and David poked his arm out.

"You know what bothers me the most about Lipschitz?"

"No," David said.

"She slept with him, at the clinic. Now, what do you think

about that? Huh? Not some stranger, not just anybody, but that fucking Lipschitz. Of all people, Lipschitz!"

She slept with him, at the clinic.

David, at that, stopped paddling. He bent over, did not want to hear it, in it that old and paralyzing pain that was so familiar. He did not want to know what had been between Rachel and Max, but he couldn't *not* want to know, and so when Max said, again, "You listening?" David said to himself, Move. Move. Lift your arm, that's it, over the gunnel, draw back. I'm not listening, but part of him did.

"Yes," David said.

"I mean, Charlie," he said, "it was Lipschitz. After all I did for him. I helped that asshole get through clinical—he wouldn't've made it if I hadn't. I mean, I think of the two of them, and it just kills me. It kills me, and . . . and I get so goddamned mad, and I'm waiting, and waiting, I'm not going to ask her, because if I do, then it's over, I know it is. And I know Lipschitz is stealing the Lidocaine, and I mean, why should I have cared anyway, why not let the board deal with it, after what he's done? And then I go home, and the house is quiet, and . . . and I *hit* my boy, I *hit* him, and I don't know why."

Max was sobbing, there just in front of David, and David kept the canoe moving.

Max swung his hand up, but there was something almost palsied in the motion, fevered, that caused David to feel all that dread again, which kept him moving.

He was hot again, and sweating terribly, but it was not from exertion, and he knew that when they stopped, he would have to start a fire to dry his clothes or he would suffer hypothermia, and, too, he saw the stars seem to glitter, really glitter and throw down prisms of light, and David knew what that was, and while Max was shouting in the bow, he closed his mind to it, but some part of him listened still.

Ice crystals at high altitude, which meant a cold front, and moisture.

Moon dogs would mean snow. The geese were all moving and there'd been that dump in Anchorage—

"She said she didn't know if she felt anything for me, she couldn't tell. That it was probably too late. And there I was, with Lipschitz grinning in my goddamn face all day, and after what I'd done—"

Rain would be bad. But he was not going to get rain. If it came down, it'd be snow. They could use the down bags, like jackets, if they had to—

"I couldn't do anything about it. It was all just . . . too much, and then Rachel's brother lost his house and she'd bailed him out, didn't tell me—"

But they'd have to get off the water, though the men could track them then. He didn't want to get caught up some box canyon, or a ravine, but they needed to be out of sight.

Max lurched up in the canoe, almost high-siding it, and David reaching over the gunnel on his left to counterbalance.

"Don't do that," David said.

"Don't do what?"

"You're high-siding us, stop moving!"

"Who are you to tell me anything?" Max craned his head around, his eyes crazed. He didn't seem to recognize David at all.

"I'm going to have to—" David said.

"Ah, shut up."

"Just don't move."

"I'll move whenever I want to."

"I'm warning you," David said, alarmed.

Max began to get up, turn around over the seat, and David reached with his paddle, the paddle dripping all over Janie, and struck Max, so hard he surprised himself, Max's head hitting the gunnel and the canoe making a fleshy drum sound.

And when Max tried again, David feeling as if he were in some nightmare, Max's motions spidery, and confused, David poked his hands off whatever he braced them on, and when his father's head came down yet again, with that fleshy clunking, David nearly shouted, Stop it! but couldn't, because his voice would carry, and so they kept this up until Max sat, and when he so much as tried to turn, David poked at him, hit him with the wet blade of the paddle, and Max swore in long strings of profanity, You fucking goddamn— and David waited for him to rise again. And when he didn't, David began to draw the canoe through the water again, tried to bring back some rhythm—reach, pull, J; reach, pull, J—but Max was shouting again, working his head in circles.

"Yeah? It went right down the goddamn toilet, four hundred thousand dollars. Right. All of it. It's gone. But you know what"—and here Max was quiet again, even still, and then he let go something like a gasp, and was crying—"I don't care about the money, it's all the rest of it.

"It's *all* gone—"

And then he was saying what, David couldn't understand, and he was running his hands through his hair, only his right hand came up glossy in the starlight, but not with water, and David realized it was blood, and knew he would have to cut into one of the islands.

———

He checked his watch. It was after five, he'd been on the water over five hours, and the patch had held, and he'd tried to see, in the dark, anything on the islands they'd passed, a place to stop, and had seen nothing—had been looking for starlight in glass, for so much as a block of darkness on a ridgeline, or back of a point, cabins, but he'd seen nothing, though that didn't mean the cabins weren't there. In fact, he'd seen them when he'd come up with his uncle, had seen the canoes in front of them, and had envied those who owned the cabins, some even with float planes down at the docks. DeHavillands, or Pipers, or Cessnas. All float planes.

But none of that meant anything now.

He brought the canoe up one more length of water, perhaps a quarter mile, his clothes wet with oily, rank sweat, and a fan of the lightest blue rising in the sky ahead of them.

He looked hard north, there a gently sloped island, what he did not want, and then south, and there saw an irregular spine, and he swept his paddle wide on the left and brought the canoe around, and began to look for the remnant of bulrushes, there a soft bottom where he could beach the canoe, and he saw bulrushes then, just out from a hook of dark trees, and he moved toward them, until he felt the bulrushes rustling under the hull.

David backpaddled, swung the canoe around one hundred eighty degrees and brought the stern in, until it shucked up on the sand, and when he got out, his legs gave way completely under him. He sat, stunned at himself, stunned that his legs would do this, then pulled them under himself and slowly stood, only then realizing he'd been on his knees all this time, and his legs had not been comfortable, they had gone numb with cold, in the hull inches of ice-cold water, the patches were leaking after all, but his father had been heavier, and in the bow, and so the bulk of the water had collected there under him. David kicked his legs, trying to get the feeling back in them, then reached into his pack and ate two more Snickers bars. He would eat all of what he had in the pack if he had to, and would kill something to eat, or catch it.

He just would, because the moment he'd been hoping for, but had been inwardly dreading, had come.

He would have to find an enclosed area—that's why he'd looked for the irregular spine, because he wanted erratics, wanted to see if he could find an enclosure, where he could build a fire, and they could hide if need be.

The rangers would come looking for them in how many days? Almost a week. It was too long. And even then they'd be looking on the wrong side of the border lakes basin, fifty miles west. And what about the cold?

But he wouldn't think about that. He had to get Max out of the bow, and by a fire, he'd been sitting in that icy water, and Janie had to be wet, too, and God knew what else, maybe their sleeping bags were wet, and it was all too much to think about, so David didn't. He drew the canoe up, tied the bowline to a pine there, went up a yards-wide, rocky path. Campers had used this island, and that was both good and bad—it meant the island was not only accessible, but on some map, and he climbed, the blood and warmth returning to his legs, and he passed knee-high erratics, then shoulder-high, forcing himself up a steep section of path through the high, dark pines, the stone rough with lichen, and all the while knowing he couldn't carry Max here, so doubled back, and instead of following the steep path, followed the shore to the left, and found another, narrower path, and his heart leapt at it, and he paced in his head, thirty, thirty-one, thirty-two, thirty-three paces, up a smooth stone rise, broken by scrub, red willow and pinchberry, and saw them there, a jumble of erratics, and the face of one luminous as skin in near dark, and David strode the remaining distance to it, and there found an enormous sink where water, under the glacier that had receded here thousands of years ago, had carved out a space going back tens of feet into the green-stone rock face, the ceiling soot blackened, and under the rock ledge, wood off to one side, left there for a fire.

44

DAVID NEARLY BOLTED DOWN TO THE CANOE, THEN LUGGED the Duluth pack out, shouldered it, then got Janie in his arms and, his legs trembling, forced himself up the slope. Under the ledge, he threw down the one dry bag and lay Janie on it, at which point she curled up again, her thumb in her mouth, her face to the back wall of stone.

David carried up the remainder, the wet bag and his day pack, and after checking on Janie, went out again, and using the hatchet, cut two birch saplings and chopped branches from a tamarack, because he knew he could bend them.

He worked quickly, skinned the branches and set them over the two poles, both about ten feet long, then took the remainder of the overfly, which he'd used to make the patches, and tore strips off it. He bent the tamarack branches, five of them, over the poles, and bound them tight with the overfly strips, the longer branches at one end, so the poles formed a long, approximate V, and David got under the travois and set the poles, at the wide end, on his shoulders, and the fit was not right, was too broad, and he had to adjust it, but only a little.

When he tried it again, and the poles fit squarely over his shoulders, he went down to the lake with it, stumbling, and picking himself up again, and got to the canoe.

He could not stop now, even though his legs were threatening to collapse under him. He had to do this, and the canoe only came up so far, out of the water, Max so heavy the canoe bottomed out.

"Goddammit!" David said, and he reached into the canoe for one of the paddles.

He tested the lake bottom here, smooth, solid stone, and slick. He pushed the canoe out again, Max trying to rise now, but his head lolling to the side.

David stepped into the bitter-cold water, his boots filling with it, and drew the canoe parallel to shore. He got hold of Max's vest, and Max punched at him, and struck him in the face, so that he stumbled back and nearly lost his footing, almost overturning the canoe with Max in it, and had to crouch suddenly to prevent himself from going in, striking Max in the face with his elbow.

"Go to hell," Max said.

And, at that, David hauled Max up by his vest, Max's knees catching on the gunnels and his feet flopping down in the water, and David dragged him roughly to the travois he'd built, and set him in it, then went to the front and took the poles over his shoulders, and bending to it, tried to drag the travois up the slight incline, and found he couldn't.

He stood there in the traces, numb with cold.

He set the poles down, and with them Max, a great, leaden weight, and went and looked, and there, at the feet of the travois, was a ridge, just inches of stone the feet of the travois had caught on, and he could either get Max off the travois, and—

But getting him back on would be . . .

Roll him, he thought, and he rolled Max over, Max mumbling something, and he drew the travois up a few feet, and took Max under his armpits, and knew he could never carry him up to Janie and the gear this way, but got him even with the travois, and rolled him back onto it, Max suddenly grabbing his shirt, so that David, in a sudden panic, had to hit him.

Max's head lolled away, he was still finally, and David took up the travois.

Now the feet slid on the rough stone path, then caught again, and David stooped, his thighs burning, and he gave a fierce lurch, and the travois budged again, and then gave away so quickly David burst forward, and caught himself with his hand, on the greenstone.

"Fuck," he said, and he lifted the travois slightly. And, like that—a yard at a time—he hauled Max up the incline, the travois stopping over and again, and David nearly lowering it to the ground, and yanking on it, and cursing, and pulling, so he felt it down the length of his spine, until he got Max up the hill and under the rock outcropping, where he wrapped Max in the remaining bag.

Daylight was on them, and he knew he had one more thing to do.

He had to either hide the canoe onshore, which was iffy, or he could carry it up here.

But it occurred to him he'd have to work on the patch, and so he carried the canoe up, fitting it in front of the open area of the sink, and chopped tamarack branches and tossed them over the canoe until it couldn't be seen from shore, much less from the lake.

Done, David crawled on his hands and knees into the sink, and drawing Janie in her bag onto his lap, sat with his back to the wall, listening, watchful, or so he thought—but in seconds he was dead asleep.

45

It was Penry who saw it first.

Penry, who had headed north again. There'd been nothing on the wide, south route, which he'd followed for miles and then some, and paddling north now, had had to fight the northwesterly that swept down on him, blew bitter cold in his face and chest, making a sail of him, so he had to crouch and paddle, which made his back burn, and here he was, right where he'd started, where he and Munson had agreed to meet, the water cobalt blue with the coming light, and he saw, on the shore where they were to meet, no canoe.

No red anywhere that he could see, he was looking for just a line of it, their Alumacrafts had it around the gunnels on both sides.

And he was angered by this, since, most likely, Munson had done what he'd done, gone the distance, and farther, only he'd, Penry'd, gotten here first. And he couldn't believe Munson had found them.

And thinking that, he moved toward the distant shore, shuddering at the chill air, and compensating for the northwest wind, he swung his paddle wide, the light coming on to the east, this robin's-egg blue tinting the sky alive, and he took a deep breath, and wanted to go on, and even as he was thinking it, he saw dark clouds coming in from the west, and enormous snowflakes came whirling ahead of them, like schools of fish, whirling and turning, and turning again, to strike the water, and were gone, yet above the water, this endless whirling of snowflakes, and that ashy, snow smell in the air, which, before, he thought beautiful, but now experienced as some judgment, the wind, and the snow, against his odds of survival, and he cursed it all, cursed everyone who'd made him who he was, paddling to shore, where even now the sudden snow caught on the needles of the pines, and in the red willow, and on the birch and tamarack, and he was suddenly almost panicked to get out of the canoe, to get off the black water, which he felt just then might swallow him, not leaving a trace.

But onshore all that thinking stopped.

Penry got out Stacey's wallet. He dumped out his ID, BPOE card, receipts, but kept the Standard Oil card and cash.

And then he waited, anxious.

———

Munson, down shore, was watching as Penry dumped the wallet. He knew at a glance what it was all about, and, too, he'd had time to think, paddling like an insane person up that west-and-northern-reaching channel. He'd gone quickly, even having to paddle into the wind, and had used the breeze to his advantage returning.

But now, snow.

It was coming down in fits and bursts. Munson pulled up his collar against it, zipped the collar open, and unrolled his hood.

As he watched Penry come in, it had occurred to him that he should wait, since he was early, and see what Penry would do, pulling into shore. But he'd never figured on Penry getting out the wallet.

Penry'd lied to him—the doctor didn't have it; so what else had Penry lied about? It occurred to Munson, just then, that he was not dealing with someone as simple as Penry made himself out to be, and he was struck by a cold, calculating fear, and he thought, I could just take him out.

After all, the doctor and the girl hadn't seen him, Munson, on the island. He could go to the authorities himself, he thought, but there was all that with Jack, the thought of which filled Munson with such self-loathing that he felt his mouth twist at it.

Still, Jack had betrayed them. Or, he thought, something sick in his stomach, had he?

Or had Penry just put them up to it?

But he was in it now, this mess, and there was no going halfway. He wanted his life back, and desperately—the trailer, and his wife and kids, and his job on the Dysart floor. All that seemed something other than a burden to him now, that former life—it seemed suffused in a warm glow, unattainable, lost—and Penry could help him get it.

If they could just stick to the plan, he could deal with Penry later.

And anyway, it was just the way the world worked.

When the going gets tough, the tough get going, Coach Walters had always said. And, too, he'd always said, *Nice guys finish last.*

Well, it wasn't going to be nice.

————

Penry was holding his hands under his armpits to warm them when Munson came around the point in his canoe. He waved to Munson, in the falling snow, and Munson came nearer, and finally drew the canoe up and was out.

"Anything?" Penry said.

"No."

"Snow'll work for us."

"Makes it harder to move," Munson said, "wind like that, and they'll be farther east now. Got a head wind. Had to go that way."

"They'll have to make a fire—left their tent behind. We see smoke and that'll do it."

With a shake of his head, Munson nixed that.

"He wouldn't be so stupid as to do that. Not now, not today."

"The fucking hell he—" But Penry cut himself off. He'd been about to say, The kid isn't gonna be as smart as that, but Munson didn't know about the kid.

He'd come right out of nowhere, and so fast that Stacey hadn't reacted quickly enough, or he just didn't have it in him. The kid had been fucking unreal, though—no two ways about it. He was goddamned dangerous.

But the snow, a burst came down now.

"You know," said Munson, "we're not exactly set up for the cold, either."

"We get up high, find some ridge, maybe we could see tracks."

"Maybe."

The two would not look at each other, and it occurred to them that they should, just then, each for his own reasons, and they glanced over, each grinning disingenuously at the other, neither any good at faces, or concealing their feelings, and it would have been funny last week, or all the years before, but here it was sobering.

Munson took in this new Penry, a chill shooting up his back— maybe it wasn't just that Penry wasn't so stupid after all; maybe he just flat out wasn't who they'd thought he was, period.

Munson brushed away the snowflakes that had caught in his

eyelashes. "We'd cover more distance if we stay in two canoes," he said, looking away.

"I say we give it more time."

"How much time?"

"We can change our story, if we have to."

"Why talk about a new plan until we need one?" Munson said. "We still have the better part of a day."

But they both knew that their chances of finding them now— in Munson's thinking, it was the doctor, and in Penry's, it was the doctor and the boy they were gunning against—were not good.

Unless the doctor started a fire, Munson thought. If it got cold enough that he'd need one, out like that without a tent.

Both men looked to the east, up a channel bristling with dead-wood, an esker swooping around to the right, all sharp shale, out front of it, the blue-black water swallowing the snow, and second by second, more heavy snowflakes, an infinite number, swirling out of the now-heavy gray sky.

In his plaid cap with the earflaps down, Penry turned to face east. He seemed to know something, but Munson couldn't tell what. And, anyway, they had to have gone in that direction, he thought. The doctor'd gambled they wouldn't figure him for that kind of risk taker, going north and right over them, and, here, he'd beaten them—

So far.

But neither he nor Penry was about to admit it, and so Munson said nothing, but instead went to his canoe and pushed off from shore, and headed east, and Penry came on behind him, and crossing the lake there was between them a somber quiet, the snow coming down and blanketing the trees, both of them looking for signs of the doctor, on the shorelines of the islands they passed, where, in the bulrushes, red-winged blackbirds clung miserably to the occasional cattail.

And they passed each island like that, looking for the stray broken branch, a line of overturned pine needles, any sign at all, even the sounds of their paddles striking the hulls when they did, swallowed up, and so their passing seemed like that of nothing more than ghosts, and in each man this registered as some judgment of his place in the world, a zero, a blemish on a world they'd never entered, really, and inwardly, in their purpose, they fought against it, this feeling of being completely annihilated, and so moved with a rage that only the threat of final and complete exposure of that truth could bring out in them.

46

DAVID STARTLED AWAKE, IN THE DARK, THIS WEIGHT ON him, pressing him down, which he threw off, and stood, or tried to, and hit his head, on what he didn't know, and was knocked on all fours, his hands on rough, cold stone, and it all came back to him, and breathing deeply, to quell his panic, he tried to see by the rim of daylight coming around the canoe and the tamarack and cedar boughs he'd set over the canoe, and his thoughts came at him like blows, each seemingly impossible, but true, and he fought against an impulse to just do nothing, huddle back in the dark, but got Janie, not so much as even whimpering, which filled him with dread, back against the wall in the bag, and forced himself out the side of the stone enclosure, and stood in the falling snow.

He raised his hand to his forehead, trying to think.

He was out of things to think right now, and he knew what this was, this not thinking, it was shock, and exhaustion, and he reached back into the sink and drew out his pack, not into the near light, because the day pack was red, and got out the jerky, and he took his plastic cup and went down to the lake, the snow falling heavily, and beautifully, and he was reminded of how he'd loved to ski, when Max had last lived with them, Janie, four then, not much more than a toddler, and how jaunty Max had looked, always stylishly dressed with his long red scraf, and his mother's laughter, like light, and he forced that thinking away, brushing the snow from the shoulders of his jacket, because the snow was of a heavy sort, and though it collected in the tamarack and cedars and pines, it was not cold enough for it to stay, this wet snow, and he dipped his cup into the lake and sucked a mouthful of water from it, and forced in a stick of the jerky and chewed, and let go a great sigh, and then came a paroxysm of rage, and pain, and he had to breathe through his nose so as not to choke.

When he'd gotten control of himself, pushed that other person down, and away, so that he felt as if he were in some husk of a body only, but still here, he put himself to it again.

What did he have to do to keep them alive?

And he got caught all over again in choking, and said to himself, Fuck it all, fuck them, and even said, Fuck me, fuck what I feel.

Fuck—

And a calm, almost like grace, settled in him, but he felt an anger burning in him, too. He'd get them out. That's what he had to do. *All* he had to do.

He'd get down to Ely, and what happened to them out here, that would be somebody else's job, tracking down who'd done it, and ending all that, but he knew he was lying to himself.

He would have to do it *himself*. He just knew it.

All right. There was the leak in the canoe to fix, and he had to find another, a Grumman or Alumacraft, any canoe, or maybe he'd find a boat and motor, but he'd have to find the cabin first, and if he did, maybe there'd be a shotgun, or something. Maybe. But he shouldn't count on it.

And he cut off the fantasy he had of using such a gun, and told himself he had to be *here, now,* because that's what his *mind* was doing.

No, *he* was doing it. *He* was running away.

He slapped his face, and hard. It surprised him that he didn't really feel it.

But when he touched his head, where he'd bumped the stone ceiling of the sink, it hurt plenty, and he poked himself there with three fingers, and that jolted something awake in him.

Should he move in the daylight or not? Was it worth the risk? Was it?

He kicked at the stone under him. How should he know? But he did know this: They were out there, the three men, and they were looking for him.

They were even now moving toward them—somehow. He could just feel it.

And the snow. It could be terrible for him if he moved in daylight and had to portage. That would leave tracks you could see for miles. Still, he'd have to do it sooner or later. He could carry the canoe, and Janie, and use the travois for Max. But how much light would they get today? He checked his watch. It was half past eight. He'd slept three hours.

And he had to get back in and check on Janie and Max.

Even the thought of Max made him sick. And thinking it, he looked at himself for the first time, and his heart kicked up, because he didn't remember stashing his knife again, and he whacked his calf with his palm, and breathed deeply, because the knife was there, and he had a compass, but the knife had come to mean more, so much more, because Max had given it to him, and it recalled that night, their last night, which seemed a lifetime ago, and he had to go back up to the sink, he was in his head again, dammit, and he forced himself up the incline of stone, and pulled the canoe away to the side, and there saw Janie, lying in that fetal position on the cold stone, and he knew if he didn't get her off it and back into the bag, she wouldn't make it, and so he did that, got her back into the bag, and she stirred, but only to pull herself in tighter, and David thought he would wait, move at night, or even, tomorrow, and he could—

But he had to look at Max now.

Max had rolled in his bag so that his head was lower than his feet. There was a crust of blood around his head and on the bag. The bag was almost muddy with the blood crust, but Max was breathing, and David thought not to move him, not to wake him, but he was cold, badly cold, hypothermic cold—and therein lay the next problem. Which was making a fire, but one that would not give off much, if any, smoke.

Deadwood. But with the snow, everything out there was wet. Wet wood smoked. Even birch bark, which made a good starter, did, too.

But if he could find partially burned wood, that would be best, and there was the wood the last campers had left, but it was so old, it had been maybe years since the last campers had been here, and when he grasped the end of one of the sticks, bracing the other end on the stone floor, and gave it a kick in the middle, it broke not with a crack but with a dull, rubbery give. Worthless.

So he would have to go out. He yanked the space blanket out of his day pack, blue on one side, and silver, like aluminum foil, on the other, placing the foil side down over Janie and Max in their bags.

He got out the ground cloth, which was really not a cloth at all but a sheet of plastic, happy it was army green, and wrapped it around himself, stooping low all the while so as not to hit his head again.

Then he went out, taking the hatchet, cursed the slow-falling, wet snow, the smell of pine sharp and pleasant, though bad for indicating how wet everything was and, if he listened, there was even a sibilant dripping hush.

Everything was wet. Sopped. It was warm enough that the snow was melting, but the temperature was dropping, and more snow might accumulate overnight, which made him, as he went up a path, wonder if he should move. If there wasn't enough wind, an ice crust would form on the lake, and the ice would cut the patch he'd put on the canoe like sharp scissors through thin silk.

He saw that in his mind, *zippppp*. And in the cold water, how long could they last? Ten minutes, before they went under, dopey with shock.

He ached to leave the island, but he could see, even with the low cloud cover, there would be too much light. But the low clouds would help with the fire.

Now, when he looked to the west, in what breeze there was blowing down the length of the lake, gray vapor rose from the backs of the still-warm islands and lake almost like smoke, and seeing it, he decided to stay put, and clambered up a fault on the back of the island, then crossed over it, where, in the shade of it, rightly, he'd thought cedars would grow.

Tens of them here, scrubby, sheltered and dry, and he kicked down to them, the hatchet in hand, the ridge in back looming overhead, and then higher, and he went to the third tree in, which had lost out to the others outside it, and died, and he carefully chopped at the base, making sure he didn't strike the rock face with the hatchet, which necessitated his striking downward as well, and he worked up a sweat, and when the tree toppled over, David was surprised to see behind the cedar, petroglyphs, and he marveled at them, in the gray light, the nearly bloodred markings, here some kind of creature that looked to be a snake with horns, and above it, a stylized figure of an eagle, it, too, in that color of dried blood and nearly grown over by the green lichen, and he felt some chill run through him, because just by looking he understood the relation of the figures, this thunderbird, and serpent, and he pressed his palm flat over the eagle, and felt his throat swell.

Just that.

But then the moment was gone, and when he brought the hatchet down again, he cursed himself, because he had, in his haste, neglected to think about blisters, and on his right palm now, the top layer of skin had separated from the one below it, and he would have to be careful not to tear it. So he wrapped a piece of the ground cloth around his hand, then dragged the first of the small cedars over the path to the sink, and even as he paused there, before going in, he looked back up the distance of stone he had descended and his heart fell.

The snow was heavy enough on the ground that there was a thick, brushed line leading, sure as an arrow, to where they were hiding.

Anyone seeing it would know it for what it was. The mark as good as a neon sign.

And so David dragged the other trees down, careful not to tear the skin in his palm, but having to take the time to brush the snow from the stone so it looked to have melted, a sheer slope of greenstone, and he was shaking with cold and wet when he finally ducked down and went in.

47

HE GOT THE WATER BOILING AND POURED INTO IT ONE OF the food packs he'd bought at Hoigaard's. His mouth watered at the smell, and he stirred the noodles with a stick, having left all the utensils at the camp. But he had the cups, metal cups, but for his plastic one, and minutes later, when the dehydrated muck that was Chicken Divine—that's what had been printed on the package—was done, David was struck by what he had to do.

This would be the hard part.

Janie first, because he knew what she was suffering was not physical, not in the way it might be with Max. But he was afraid for her, and dealing with either of them now was almost more than he could bear.

And he knew, absolutely knew, that he must not communicate this fear. Not to Janie, anyway. But it would be hard not to.

And so he skidded back on his rear, the space under the overhang even warm, and just coals burning in what had been his fire, and he got behind Janie and drew her in her bag up to him, between his legs so that he cradled her, and said, "Janie, it's David."

She was still curled in a ball. He did not try to take her hands from her face—she'd cupped her face in her hands—but only held her, and he felt sick, all over again, and wouldn't think about it, and said, again, "Sportnik. It's me. I'm going to take care of you. But you have to listen to me now."

He still didn't move, only held her, and in his mind, so as not to weep, he imagined stabbing the short, thick one, and when it got really sick, what he thought to do, he started over again, just stabbing, and he had to relax his arms, because he'd begun to shake, and then he was crying and couldn't help it, that shitty hysteria getting the better of him, and he couldn't manage it, it was really coming at him, rushing, like a train, like some black mass inside him, his heart kicking up with it, and he thought, It's not about you now, David.

Stop it. For Janie.

And he did. He took a deep breath. Okay, that was better, he thought. He would think nothing, nothing at all, but that he was going to get them out.

(Kill them, a thought said, kill them, all three, and by God, something in him swore, he'd do it, too. But there came with the thought the realization that he had killed one of them already. It shocked him.)

He imagined moving again, and the three of them in the canoe following, and the highway, getting to it, and someone there to help them, and he held that image in his mind like some koan, and worked it, that thought, as he supposed Catholics did prayers on a rosary, and fixing his mind on each step, thought hard on making it happen, until he was calm again.

All right, he thought.

"Janie," he said. "You have to eat now. Will you eat this for me?"

He sat like that for what seemed an hour, and then began to stroke her hair as he had when she was really little, when she'd come to live with them, and she'd cried, and said those silly things that had made him love her, this peculiar girl.

"Ratty was down by the bank one sunny morning," he began, and even as he did, he knew she was listening.

And he went on, making it all up, and he knew she was aware of it, that he was making it up, and he went on like that for some time, now and then this catch in his voice, so he had to stop, and when he got stuck at one point, and he thought it was all useless, that he'd failed, and he was spiraling into a despair that did not mind death, saw it as nothing, she reached out and put her arm around him, pulling her face to his side, and she began to cry, and he cried with her, and when there was nothing left in her, she slept, her head against his side, and it was all taking too long, and it occurred to him that it was a very bad sign that Max had not stirred, the worst, which made him want to check on him, the thought of which terrified him.

And the food had gotten cold, but what matter, only he was freezing from underneath, the stone cold under him, and he slid over to Max's bag, Janie still cradled on him, and he, with great reluctance, reached out and touched Max's neck, and was relieved to feel his pulse there.

What time was it? he wondered. Eleven. It seemed he'd been doing this forever.

Time had assumed some new and other proportion.

In the space under the ledge, each minute seemed endless, because he could not force any of this, couldn't force Janie to eat, or Max to wake, yet time passed too quickly.

He had to move, he thought, but he couldn't set Janie down, move her aside, because if he did, could he bring her out later?

He'd heard about someone going catatonic, and when people hadn't acted fast enough, the damage, for some reason, had been permanent.

And there was the possibility of infection. She was torn.

But he would have to deal with that later.

So he sat and held her, and hummed, songs he'd forgotten he even knew, "Old Paint," and "Yellow Rose of Texas," and campfire songs, and then, while she still lay with her head against his chest, averted, so she wouldn't have to look at him, she said, "I'm hungry," and David set the pot on the coals again, and in minutes had his plastic cup full of hot soup, and held it to Janie's mouth, the Chicken Divine, this stew, not much more than warm, and she ate it, spilling some on the bag, but David nearly ecstatic, and Janie, her voice full of false bravery, said, "That tasted like chicken wallpaper paste."

David gave a laugh, but then he was afraid he was going to lose it again. He stroked her hair, fine silken hair, pressed her shoulders.

What could he say, or should he say now? Anything? Nothing? Should he act as if it hadn't happened?

And then he struck on the only true thing he could say.

"There's no use saying what happened didn't happen"—and here Janie hardened against him—"but we're still us, right, Sport? You're still my Sport, right?" he said.

Janie only clung to him.

"Listen," David whispered, leaning over her. "I'm going to get us out of here, but I need your help. Do you think you could help me?"

And that she hesitated not one second to nod made him swallow hard.

"Okay, then," he said. "Do you want more?"

Janie nodded and he poured the cup full again and gave it to her.

And in him was this: He was almost desperate to say, I'm sorry.

But would things have been different if he'd been there with Max and Janie? They might have just killed all three of them then, surprised them at the fire.

And so he said nothing.

He waited until Janie'd gotten the soup down, and then bent over her and, squeezing her harder, said, "The first thing you can do to help is to promise me, whatever happens, you'll listen to me. Because—" He wanted to say, Because it is going to be hard, harder than you can imagine getting out, but he couldn't say that. "Because I need your help to get us out. Even more than I needed your helping me out at the house. Okay?"

David squeezed her again.

"Sport, I knew you were."

And she nodded. Okay. So she had, too, and it touched him. Truly.

"So whatever happens, if you feel like crying, or if it gets . . . if it gets *really* hard, I'm going to say to stop it, and you're going to have to. Can you try?"

"I can do it," she said.

"All right," he said, and then told her he had to check on Max, and Janie said nothing, and he told her he wanted her to go and fill the smaller aluminum pot with water, but to be absolutely careful, she had to go down in the direction the snow was coming from.

"Snow? It's snowing?"

"It'll melt," David said, this tone of false reassurance in his voice he disliked. So he added, "And if it doesn't, we'll be okay anyway. Okay, Sportnik?"

He pulled her hood over her head and handed her the pot, and she moved awkwardly, hesitating at the opening of the sink, terrified, the sort of diaper he'd put on her chafing at her legs, but worse, reminding her.

She held there, like a would-be parachutist in the door of an airplane.

And then she was gone, and David carefully took the lower end of the sleeping bag Max was on and slowly turned it around, so Max's head was higher, his feet lower, and he was nearer the fire, or the coals really, and since there wasn't enough light, David had to draw the canoe back farther, and now, with the brighter light outside, he saw that one of the patches in the hull had torn almost completely, and that the Duluth pack's holding the patch down was the only thing that had saved them.

Had the patch gone there at the esker, where he'd broken the paddle . . .

The thought made him shudder.

Maybe, he thought, if they just stayed here until the rangers knew they hadn't made it out on time, they'd have a better chance?

But no—how long, in this kind of weather, and burning wood, and making smoke, could they put those men off? Not days, that was for sure.

No, they'd have to move.

David slid back, and with the new light, was afraid to look at Max. He bunched up the Duluth pack, thinking to press it behind Max's back so he could get him sitting. It was a hopeful thing to do, assuming at all that Max would be able to sit. And if he couldn't?

This was going to be the worst, David told himself, reaching for Max.

He turned Max onto his back and immediately saw the blood. He thought he might vomit, seeing it, he'd been bleeding from his left temple, and when he looked vaguely up at David, David saw the sclera of his left eye was red and his pupils unequally dilated—

the left eye a pinprick, and the right now wide, appropriate to the relative dark.

"Max," David said.

This, he told himself, again, was going to be the worst.

"*Max,*" he said, louder, and having to nearly shout, he knew what he'd feared was true. Time now seemed all the more awful, because it was working against him. He'd managed to get them off the island and moving, but this—

"*MAX?!*"

Max nodded, then sat abruptly and vomited bile, vomited, and vomited, until the whole enclosure reeked of it. This wasn't good, either. But maybe the problem was a concussion?

Max tried to get to his feet, confused, almost hysterical, but David got on his knees and held him down.

"Stop moving!" he shouted. "It's low in here, don't stand up. You'll knock your head."

He got Max to sit, then swung the Duluth pack around and behind Max's back, so he was propped up.

Max tried to focus on him, seemed to know what had happened. But then he began to talk crazy again, something about his business partner, and some patient, and he was giving orders and flung his arm out, and looked down at it, and seeing David, said, "What are you doing here?"

At that moment, Janie was back with the pot. David gave her a stern look, and taking the pot, told her to follow his tracks up the island and bring back more wood. She'd see it there, all cut.

He didn't want to ask her to do it, but he had to. He had to get her outside and away.

"Go," he said.

"All right," she said, a frightened tone in her voice, and she was gone again.

"She cut me off," Max said. "Won't listen to a thing, and then she says it's *my* problem," Max said, and then his face bunched up, and he was ranting, and crying, and David struggled to hold him down, Max's arms smacking powerfully into the rock overhead, and David both trying not to be struck by Max and trying to keep him from hurting himself, Max kicking in the sleeping bag, David not letting him climb from it, until Max had exhausted himself, and he finally stopped that, and David coaxed him to lie down again, and then Janie was back.

He told Janie to feed the fire and went out and gathered handfuls of snow in what was left of the overfly, and brought it back inside, and told Janie she was going to have to hold the snow against the side of Max's head, where the swelling was. Could she do that?

She was going to have to do it with her bare hands, and she did that, and David scrounged through the supply bag and saw, with a crushing dismay, that the seam sealer he'd used to make the patches on the canoe had been stepped on and the contents squeezed out, gluing the sides of the supply bag together.

David could almost be sure he'd done it himself, he'd been the only one moving things here, and he cursed himself for not putting the sealer in his pocket.

Now what?! he thought. How was he going to repair the canoe?

"What?" Janie said. "What's wrong?"

"Nothing," he said, but he scooted outside, didn't want her to see him freaking out.

Outside he turned his face up into the ashy-smelling wet snow and pine scent. And the rush of the wind in the pines was telling him something, and he knew what he needed was right in front of him.

But *fuck all*! What was it? He told himself he didn't have time for this.

His mind raced, trying to think what he could use to repair the canoe. Just more ripstop? No, wasn't safe—he'd seen that already. Pack canvas? No. Leather, from the tops of his boots? But even if he did, how to seal the goddamn mess?

And the most frustrating thing was, even as he was standing there, he just knew it was right in front of him. And he glanced up at the trees—what was he seeing there, in those pines?—then turned to the west.

If they were coming, they'd be coming from that direction.

He walked a circle in the wet snow. Looked up the spine of

the island. Wet greenstone, snow, on either side of the path tall pines, speaking *something* he couldn't get.

He lay his hand on the bow of the canoe, the smooth varnished wood under his hand, cool.

And then it struck him what it was. Pitch!

He'd never used a wooden canoe like they had here, so hadn't thought of it right off, but all canoes had been wooden, or birch bark, at one time, and the seams sealed with pitch.

Pitch. Pine pitch—that was it!

He felt a spring in his step, and he went into the pines off the path up the ridge, the limbs heavy with snow, and the ground crunching underfoot, and the smell of resin strong, and he got out his knife, and with excitement, went from tree to tree, cutting off the sap balls that collected where the bark had been chewed by hungry deer, or porcupine, or where the wind had broken branches, the same sap balls he'd chewed when he was younger, and spit out, because they were so strong tasting.

Bobby's guide had shown him that, had grinned when David spit his out.

He put one in his mouth now and chewed, and found he was, just then, grinning.

How could anyone in his circumstances be happy?

But here he was, just for this moment, happy, until his memory included Max, and he remembered how Max had liked to tell jokes back then, and had laughed with the other men, and had clowned around. All of which seemed cleanly, simply, and so painfully . . . what was the word?

What he'd *loved* about Max. When he was silly like that, himself. Sometimes, in his grandfather's voice, he'd made droll comments that'd had his friends laughing almost hysterically, comments David hadn't understood until later. *Things are going well for me, like a saint in this world,* he'd said one night. And on another, *If you can't bite, don't show your teeth.*

Now, perched low in a pine, he thought about that last thing. Well, he *hadn't* just shown his teeth. But against the three remaining men?

He had one pocket full of the pitch balls, and he began to fill the other pocket, for a second thinking he was ruining his jacket, and then thinking it mattered not at all, and he went at it, focused, and free, just for now certain of what he was doing, running, but then, digging at one of the pitch balls, noticed, in the light, the red tone to his bare hand, and the rim of red under his nails, blood, and he tried not to look at it, but that ruined it.

He'd torn all the blisters in his right hand, and his left wasn't much better.

————

He'd been out . . . thirty minutes at most, but when he came in, Max lifted his arm.

David braced himself for the worst of it, but all Max said was, "I'm thirsty," and David dipped into the water Janie'd brought in, then held the cup to his mouth.

He drank, and did not vomit. David had cleaned that up with dried pine needles and tossed it all in the snow outside, and it smelled, now in the sink, only of must, and damp, and cold stone.

He blew on the coals. Janie had stoked the fire, and it was just right. He set the pot on the three rocks the other campers had used for the same purpose. When the water was warm, he told Janie, "Go into the corner, over there, and wash yourself." She wouldn't look at him, so he added, "Janie, this is one of those things."

"All right," she said.

He caught her arm as she was turning. "Don't be embarrassed to ask for help . . . if—if you need it, okay?"

And like that he handed her the remainder of the chambray shirt—David had cut the entire back away from the body—and she tugged her arm free, and David scuttled outside and into the damp, snowy air.

He filled the other pot with snow again, then ducked back in, pressed a handful to Max's head, making sure Max was near enough to the fire so that his body temperature didn't drop too far.

Moments later, Janie was at his side, but he was surprised to see she still had the sling around her hips, under her pants; she was very matter-of-fact-seeming now.

"You're all right?" he said.

And for the first time Janie looked at him in a way he couldn't read, and said, "A girl's gotta have some privacy now and then."

This amused David. And he was, selfishly, relieved, only he was wrong to be relieved, but then the moment was gone.

"I think this might just do it," David said, "if you could keep the snow here."

Janie scooted in. She took the ground pad, folded it under her, and held the packed snow to Max's head while David dropped the pitch balls into the pot, just a remnant of water in it boiling.

"I've got to go out again," he said. "Don't let what's in here get too hot. And if it starts on fire—because it could, see? *Don't throw the pot out.* What's in here'd go up like gasoline. Just cover it, so no air can get in. Okay?"

David set the lid by her. "Understand?" Janie said she did. "When it's all melted, set the pot beside the coals, okay?"

"Where are you going?"

"There's some birches on the west end. I'm gonna get a few feet of bark. It'll take thirty, forty minutes."

He did not say what she should do if something happened to him out there, but it was clear enough, anyway.

"See ya, Sport."

"See ya, Flash," she said as he was going out, and he was, again, amazed at her. She hadn't called him Flash in years.

48

PENRY WAS THE FIRST TO THE TOP OF THE BUTTE, STOOPING to put his palms on his knees and breathing raggedly. They'd seen the butte from five miles west or so, and had canoed for it, draining themselves to save daylight, but the climb up it had been more difficult than either had thought it would be, and they'd lost another hour.

They'd taken the west side, the side they'd come to first, against Munson's better judgment, and had run into a headwall, nearly thirty feet high, and had had to skirt the island through brush to the south, and there try climbing again, only to meet with a hogback, a few hundred feet up, which couldn't be seen from the lake, the escarpment there broken stone that was impossible to navigate, and they'd had to turn once again, and they'd climbed from the east, finally reaching the mass of stone that had begun the hogback, but scalable, and went up a stone- and poplar-filled runnel, and now Munson clattered up the last of it, scree shooting from under his feet, to stand beside Penry, and they both turned east, the wind blowing stiffly, and the snow, while not coming down as heavily as it had, driving near horizontal at their backs, and the temperature hovering around freezing.

The problem with the wind was that it blew the smoke away. What smoke they'd be looking for.

That's why they'd climbed, to look for smoke.

"Fuck it all," Penry said.

But he was calm in the assurance that the doctor and his boy would stay put. The water had gone choppy, and the only way to travel from lake to lake would be to hug west-facing shores. Now, at this height, they could see for miles to the east.

And, if it really snowed, even dumped overnight, the doctor would have to stay put all that much longer, and, what without a tent, and he'd seen all the canned food they'd left on the island, they'd need a fire.

Munson held his hand over his eyes, a visor. He was reminded of deer hunting, and he put himself in mind of it, and was falsely reassured for a moment, but always what they'd done came back to him.

Now it seemed the only way to put it out of his mind was to think they could erase it all, and he felt a sharpening in him, considering this, and how he would use Penry to get this done. But there was no lying to himself; whether it went badly or not now, he already felt ruined, and that feeling made what he did later possible.

He turned east, southeast, so that the snow struck the right side of his face, the end of his nose almost numb, and his chin not much better, and he tucked up his shoulders, the wind at his back.

It was early afternoon now and they had not that many hours of daylight, and the islands, tens of them, pine-backed and spread out before them like battleships, all hull deep in the whitecapped, gunmetal-blue water, the doctor and his girl on one of them, and here was Penry behind him, who'd held things up, insisted they take the west side to the top, holding them up even then, insisting he, Munson, wait, and Penry going back down to the canoe, and hiking up again with a shiny black camera slung over his shoulder, which he'd said was his when Munson asked, Penry passing him on the scree.

Penry got the camera out of the case now, one like he would never own, and Munson couldn't let it go.

"What the hell are you draggin' that around for?" he said.

When Penry didn't answer, just put the big camera and lens to his face, Munson knocked the camera from him. But it was on a strap, and swung around his back, Penry reaching for it again.

"I said," Munson said, leaning into Penry, "*Why are you draggin' that doctor's camera around?*"

Penry took a swing at Munson's head and missed, and Munson caught his arm and kicked him in the side so he went down on both knees.

"You listen when I'm talkin' to you, asshole!"

Penry was trying to get his breath back. "You shouldn'ta done that," he said, a world of threat in his voice.

"You know what would happen if someone found us with that?"

"I knew it'd come in handy," Penry lied. He'd had no idea why he'd snatched it up, but he knew now, and Munson would forgive him for it.

Munson could barely control himself, he was going to give Penry another kick, but his boots were slick on the stone under them.

Penry, on his knees, was deciding, should he jump up, use the knife he had in his pocket, or should he try to work this out yet? His chances were infinitely better with Munson, if he could keep him worked up, keep him moving.

"What the hell did you think you were doing, taking his camera like that?"

"You want out of this or not?" Penry demanded.

"Jesus! Are you *crazy* or what?!" Munson shouted.

"Do you or not?"

"You *can't* do things like— I mean, *what* if a ranger had stopped us out here? Huh? What then? What are you gonna say? Oh, this camera? I don't know, isn't it yours, Munson? I mean, just *what* the fuck did you think you were gonna say?"

Penry looked up at Munson with that heavy-lidded look he got. "This thing's got a telephoto lens."

"What the fuck should I care?" Munson shouted. "You only look through the fuckin' little viewfinder and—"

"Doesn't work that way," Penry said.

He wanted to be careful not to make himself seem more clever than Munson, he had to make Munson think he, Munson, was moving this along, and had him, Penry, along for help.

Exactly the way he'd gotten to Jack, through Stacey, and through Carol.

And, anyway, Jack, he'd seen, had done the same thing with them, had done it for years, and Penry'd taken note of it, learned from him.

Only, at Dysart, it had been Jack working things so they could keep their shitty jobs.

"I oughta fuckin'—" But there Munson stopped himself.

"You oughta *what*?" Penry said, and when Munson motioned for him to hand over the camera, Penry shook his head. He held the camera, cold, so cold it made him shudder, to his face and scanned the horizon to the east.

Munson was going to step over and take it from him, and he swung the camera away.

"So help me, don't you dare," Penry said. "I mean it this time."

His heart was ticking over, because he needed something and now. He dialed the telephoto up, and when Munson tried again, Penry turned and jumped at him, and Munson jumped back, but had his fists up, only Penry saw that his attention was divided. He was looking for a stone, or something he could use as a weapon.

"Don't fuck with me," Penry said, and he lifted the camera again.

He could see, with the lens, as if through layer after layer, snow like lace, or like gauze, cascading down whitely, and he watched Munson out of the corner of his eye, while he scanned the islands to the east, and his heart kicked up when he saw a line of bare stone on an island miles distant.

He thought no, it *couldn't* be, and changed the focus, scanning the island yet again, and his heart leapt up. *Yes!* There *was* something there. Red. Triangle shaped. But obscured by pine boughs, and he lunged at Munson, who'd gotten too close again, and Munson stood now with his hands on his hips, and Penry had to start all over, he'd lost it, and then found the dark, open stone, slightly snow covered, but darker than the area around it, stone without ground cover, without lichen, or moss, wouldn't hold snow, it'd be too warm for days yet, and he was about to give up when he found the triangle of reddish brown again, left facing, and something registered in his head, something wrong about it, and when he carefully scanned opposite, there was another, dark triangular shape, right facing, and he had to make himself frown when he felt himself already moving, rushing, rushing for all he was worth, and he said, with a kind of resignation, and disgust, "All right, asshole, you try it, since you're such a big fucking deer hunter."

Munson went up the bluff from Penry with the camera and Penry waited, the time passing like eternity itself. How long would it take the idiot to see it? he wondered. He was cold, chilled, and wanted to be moving.

"Hey," Munson shouted, coming back. He had the camera, and he forced it on Penry.

"Right . . . *there*. Do you see it?"

Penry had to feign incomprehension at first. Held the camera to his eye.

"What? What are you talking about?"

He played stupid until Munson was almost unable to contain it. Penry bent forward, running the big telephoto lens out.

"Wait a minute—"

"It's the *canoe*," Munson said. "Goddammit. That *wooden canoe!*"

Munson went by Penry, knocking his shoulder as he did. Penry lowered the camera. He reached into his pocket, felt the knife there.

He lifted his wrist and glanced at his watch. Three. They'd just have time, he thought, and the two charged down the scree slope, so that neither of them saw the boy come out, moments later, or that he had a pot in his hand, which steamed in the cold.

If they had, it would have all turned out differently.

49

DAVID SLID OUT FROM THE SINK AGAIN TO COVER THE canoe with the tamarack branches. Every time he'd jostled the canoe from inside, scraping the canoe clean around the holes with the flat of his knife, the branches had fallen, and he'd had to dodge back outside, but he wouldn't bother with the branches now. He stooped and worked the green ripstop from the hull, his back prickling, holding the knife with two hands, cutting the cement from the thickly varnished hull.

He could smell the pitch inside, Janie stirring it.

"Janie," he said.

She handed out the pot, the pitch in it liquefied, the smell overpowering, and he set it carefully off to the side to cool while he fit the rectangle of birch bark he'd cut from the trees on the end of the island over the two holes in the hull.

He was chewing a massive wad of gum, something Janie'd brought along, and when the pitch cooled, and was just the consistency of thick, sticky taffy—like he'd made with his mother, Rachel, and Max so long ago, even before Janie—he worked it out of the pot with a stick in a thick glob.

He applied the hot pitch to the sheet of bark, which was held down over the cold stone with two pumpkin-sized stones, the sheet half the width of the hull, and three or so feet long, and worked the pine gum over the bark in a circle, sure to make the circle thick, and when it was tacky, he rolled the stone off the right end of the bark, pinning it with his right heel so it wouldn't curl up on itself, and rolled the stone from the left side, and lifted the bark up, which threatened to snap back into the diameter of the tree he'd taken it from, and pressed it to the wooden canoe bottom, holding his breath that the pitch was still hot and tacky enough, would adhere to the varnished wooden hull, and it did.

He pressed both hands flat against the bark and had Janie come over, for a moment, inside, and press the snow she'd been holding against Max's head against the bark, to fix it there.

He felt the pitch harden, but he held the bark longer, minutes, which seemed like forever, because he had decided not to wait.

They were going to go again, and now, not wait a minute longer than they had to.

When it seemed safe, David pulled his hands away and passed the pot around the canoe to Janie, and she set it on the coals, and when it was liquid again, he took the pot outside and sealed the perimeter of the patch.

The bark patch was so good, fit so flat, he was astounded, but still he worked the tip of his knife through the bark patch and the hull, made two holes in the corner, an inch apart, then did the other three corners in the same way, and he took the ripstop nylon from the dining fly and tore four pencil-wide strips, and he worked each strip through the two holes in each corner, running inside each time to cinch the strips tight with a square knot.

Back inside, he tilted the canoe out slightly, then poured the liquid pitch on each hole, the pitch steaming, and stinking, and when the pitch was truly tacky again, he took the bubble gum from his mouth, pinching off four wads, and jammed them into the holes, sealing them, and had Janie outside to tell him when the gum came through, and he had her flatten them.

"Not too much," he shouted.

She pushed from the outside, and the gum pressed in, and he flattened it inside, and called out, "Stop," and she did.

He scooted back on his rear and looked at the work he'd

done, then went out to check the hull, and Janie was gone, which surprised him. But the patch was flat, anchored—it couldn't tear loose now, which had been his fear, and why he'd cut into the hull the way he had to secure it.

Janie came running up from the lake. Her eyes were wide, and she was skittering from side to side.

"Someone's coming," she said.

"Where?"

"Up there," she said. She pointed up and behind her.

"You're sure?"

Janie nodded. David sat for a second on his heels, his heart racing.

He felt frenzied, but that would not do. He burst around the rock ledge, running to the ridge, and climbed it, and saw coming up the lake from the west, a mile or so distant, one of the men in a canoe.

But he wasn't paddling toward them. He was turning around, and David assumed he was going to go for the two others, they'd split up, searching, and David could almost feel them out there, or maybe they were on the island already? And he tore back down to the sink, threw things together.

50

MUNSON HADN'T SEEN THEIR CANOE YET. IT WAS BACK OF A wooded ridge, but he recognized the island all right. He slowed in the water, then thought to go around the island, and come in with Penry from the east end.

But they had hours of daylight, and the doctor and his girl wouldn't be moving, and they weren't going to mess up now.

Now they would take their time.

Munson steered the canoe up the lake, a bit closer, and waited. There was a long, second island north of him, separating him from Penry, and Penry glided out past the far shore of it, a half mile distant.

A precaution, Penry'd said. He'd be waiting if anybody tried to run.

His paddle set across his knees, he sat sniffing the air, then doing nothing, what seemed an eternity going by, and Munson wondered what he was waiting for.

Now, here, was the time. Why didn't Penry come in?

They were both to the north of the island the doctor was on, could move in when they wanted to, the ridge up the back of the island blocking the doctor's line of sight and protecting them.

Maybe, as Munson had thought before, there were things Penry wasn't telling him. Reasons to wait he couldn't even guess at. Out on the cold water, it was a thin thread that kept them together.

And Penry kept breaking it, as he had with taking the camera along, but then Munson, surprised at himself, got roped in again.

Which Penry was doing again. Working Munson. He could see Munson was wondering what he was up to. But he had to make him wait.

There was the problem of the girl. He was almost sure Munson wasn't capable, with her, so he'd have to do it first, before Munson could get to her, because the girl was the thing that could ruin them.

Not the boy—if he came at Munson, Munson wouldn't hold back. Surprised or not. But the girl. If she screamed, or ran crying? And what if Munson found out what he, Penry, had done? It could all come apart, this hope he'd planted in Munson's head, that they could still get their lives back. So he was set to take the girl when she bolted, which was what the father and brother would have her do. Send her off as a last resort.

But still, even with the boy surprising Munson, they'd pull this off. Here, on this end of the lake, in snow, these inexperienced canoeists just not making it. Drowning, it happened all the time.

And to the east, a drunken accident. Jack and Stacey going in, and the owner of the Big Lake Lodge having seen them, proof enough they hadn't been this far east.

And there Penry, still waiting, still holding Munson off, saw how it would all still work out, even his management spot on the floor Throgmorton had promised if he fixed the mess with Jack—Jack was going soft on the aliens, Throgmorton'd said, especially with this Martinez, who'd been a Communist down in Mexico—and Penry hardened at the thought of it.

He'd get what was coming to him, what was his.

He waited a moment longer, the light seeming to turn a shade darker, and he cut toward the island between him and Munson and, blocks offshore, raised his paddle in the sign they'd agreed on.

Go.

51

DAVID SLID UNDER THE LEDGE WITH JANIE, SWUNG THE BIG Duluth pack around, the canvas scraping on the rough stone floor.

"Pack the gear!" he said, and she did that, the pot clattering on the stone, Janie grunting, kicking the bags into the Duluth sack, and she went out.

He slid on his left haunch over to Max, who was still in the sleeping bag, and shook him.

"We're going to another site," David said, but Max was wise to it all.

"Leave me," he said. "Send somebody when you get back."

"Don't waste your breath."

Max reached for David's arm and bore down on it, as he had all those years ago.

"*Listen* to me," Max said.

Janie ducked back in under the ledge, grabbed David's day pack, and began to jam things into it, whimpering and shaking her head.

"You're *upsetting* her," David hissed, then bending over Max, said, "*Don't fuck with me—I'm taking you out, so shut up.*"

"Got it?" he said to Janie.

Janie nodded, and David checked to make sure they hadn't left anything, chucked the sodden, old wood on the coals, the wood smoking something awful—he hoped the men would take it to mean they were staying put, weren't moving—and he nodded to Janie, and he went out with her, carrying Max. He propped Max against a pine and dragged the canoe toward him, mounted it on his shoulders and ran with it to the south-facing shore of the island.

He passed Janie on a steep section. Yet even bungled up with her odd diapers under her pants, and all the pots and the gear hanging off her, and dragging what she couldn't carry, she slid and climbed down to shore, and David tossed the gear in the canoe, and they went back up, and when Max was going to have at it again, how they should leave him, David glared, setting him on the travois.

In the light he could see Max's left eye had gone dark as a plum; he was blind in that eye, and he hadn't said a thing.

It did something to David, and he nearly ran, pumping his legs like pistons, the travois rattling and jumping on the stone behind him, until, pulling Max down the bushy granite slope to the canoe, the travois caught, and he had to yank back on it quickly to prevent Max from tipping out, and he tore the skin from his hand, and there pulled on one of the gloves he'd brought, the right, and then he nearly bodily carried the travois on the small of his back, going down the steepest of it, the footing sandy and uneven, and his feet threatening to kick out from under him, until he had Max onshore, and Janie in the bow, and standing in the water, he drew the canoe alongside, lifted Max from the travois and set him with a thump into the canoe, and bending low and grasping the gunnels, set the travois lengthwise in the canoe beside him.

He braced his left foot in the stern and gave a big kick off-shore with his right leg, and just as he was in, he stopped, struck by something, and he reached for shore with the paddle, and got out, pulled the canoe up, just enough so it wouldn't float away, and Janie looked at him, terrified.

"*Don't go,*" she said.

"Remember what I said," David asked.

She was crying, floating there in the bow, her hands grasping the gunnels. "No, David," she said. *"Don't. Don't, please. Please!"*

And he said, his voice so cold it silenced her, "You promised."

And then he was off, charging up the slope, pumping his arms at his sides.

52

PENRY SCUDDED THROUGH THE BULRUSHES ON THE NORTH shore and beached his canoe, three hundred fifty, four hundred yards up from Munson. He climbed the slope of broken granite scree, not paying any attention to the noise it made, a rough clattering, the girl, the girl, he just had to get to her first. Everything depended on that, and he had his knife out, in his fist, rushing now, and mounted the rise of the granite ridge and, coming over it, all those old instincts from football working, he looked for the smoke, there was plenty of it, the idiots, they deserved what they got, he thought, and he powerfully moved toward the ledge and the sink, in the red willow and pines, his knife out, and coming around the front, he was ready for them, and he saw with some shock the canoe was gone, a jagged line torn in the lichen, the line rising along the spine of the island into the pines. They'd seen them coming, he and Munson, and must have run to the west end, dragging the canoe, he thought, and he spun around, Munson coming on behind him and passing him, having walked in from the east, as Penry'd told him to, but the doctor gone, west, so that Penry knocked by Munson, desperate. He could only think they were still on the island but had portaged the canoe up the steep slope of the spine, had left the fire going to bring them around to the east, all the while, going up the spine and away, and Penry ran, following the hull sign, this jagged cut in the lichen, until it was just footprints he followed, block after block after block of pine, and stone, and the rise of it killing, and now the footprints pressed in the snow angled off to a great ledge, sure, sure, they were hiding here, Penry thought, and he felt in himself this great pleasure, could see them cowering, behind the ridge, and he swelled with the thought of it, jacked up, blood pumping, but when he came around the ledge and saw the cedar stumps, he shouted, "Goddammit!," understood in an instant they were gone, and he burst back to the path, almost colliding with Munson, Munson confused for a second, Penry smacking right into him, but going by again. He had to get to the girl first, had to stay ahead of Munson, now dashing east again, and Munson behind him.

Munson, following, felt this dark something rise up in him. It was all going wrong again, and he forced himself after Penry, whose squat, powerful figure crashed through the sumac ahead, a short-cut, and then they were both charging down the steep slope, nearly a quarter mile of it, brush and willow tearing at his face and hands, and at the bottom, here was the rock ledge and the fire again, still smoking tremendously.

Penry circled there, and as Munson came up behind, Penry lifted his fists over his head and shouted, "Dammit!"

And Munson saw then what Penry saw. To the south side of the island, just yards away and over the ridge, were another set of tracks, and he went down to them, and he counted out the distance between the footprints, each paces apart.

The son of a bitch had gone right by them, on the south side of the ridge, running east as they were going west up the spine.

The son of a bitch could run—God, but could this guy run. He wouldn't have thought it possible unless he'd seen it himself in the tracks.

He'd passed them, all right. And there he began to wonder. The *doctor'd* done that?

"Dammit!" Penry said, and he strode to the slope back of the spine, but halfway, slowed, setting his hands on his knees, Munson behind him, both breathing hard and their lungs burning.

"Ran right up this hill," Munson said, "doubled around by us on the south side."

Penry didn't answer. He knew they couldn't be far. If he could just *see* them. He needed some elevation, they couldn't be far, but, again, they could have gone in any direction, and the ridge worked against them, he and Munson, now.

He got to the top of the ridge and turned a full circle, Munson coming up slowly behind him. They could see to the west, and south, but the east way out of the lake was blocked by an island, a channel behind it.

Penry thought, *There,* but didn't say it. The doctor had, what—twenty minutes on them? Thirty?

But now he'd seen this enervating fatalism in Munson, and he'd have to change that. Throgmorton had told him, You've gotta get Munson and Lawton in it with you if this is going to work. I don't know if Munson's got it in him. Motivation's going to be a problem, and, surprised, Penry'd said, You think so?

But now he wondered. Munson was going down already, he could see it in the set of Munson's shoulders, stooped, but Penry wasn't about to let him quit. He needed Munson now, and he'd need him later.

Penry cursed. Here were the prints again, out from the cedars they'd cut. The boy had dragged something, to make it look like they were moving in this direction with the canoe. He didn't want to say it, that he'd been fooled, especially since Munson would think it was the doctor who had done it.

You couldn't understand the sole of my fucking shoe.

Penry saw Munson's brows gather, and he stooped to examine the prints.

Penry didn't want that—he didn't want Munson, who was seeing something already, to get wise to there being somebody else with them, the doctor and the girl.

But the kid had big shoes, Penry saw.

"Let's go," Penry said.

"I don't want to take them on the water," Munson shot back. It was the first time he'd said anything against it all, really, had crossed what Penry was thinking.

"Why not?"

"We capsize without a fire nearby, we're as good as dead."

"No need to," Penry said. But he didn't like the way Munson was thinking. He'd just said it—what Penry'd seen in him earlier. *We're as good as dead.*

"Come on, you fuckin' pussy," Penry told him, "the only direction they could have gone now is east," and he went down to the canoes, and he got in his, and moved away across the water, and Munson, sheathing his knife, followed.

53

THEY HAD MADE GOOD DISTANCE, AND ALMOST ALL OF IT moving south. They'd caught one long, deep stretch of water, where the surface of the lake was not so rough, and David had thought to rig the dining fly to the travois, and set it upright in the hull, a yellow sail, and dangerous, but they'd made tremendous distance, carried, at first, east by the wind, and David giving Janie one of the last Snickers bars, and he chewed on the jerky, and cupped up water, and when gusts of wind threatened to capsize them, pressing too much on the sail, he let the ripstop flap, and when the same, steady breeze blew again, down the length of the canoe, fixed the end of the ripstop to the rails of the travois, its legs jammed between the rear thwarts and the ribs of the canoe, David having stood to arrange them so, which was dangerous, but the sail worked beautifully, only that it was yellow was bad luck.

But it couldn't be seen from any distance, not like red in this light, and they cut time, and again turned south, David using his paddle like a rudder, the jogs south a labor, and dangerous, and he was tempted to let the wind just carry them, always east, but the highway was south, and it was where he meant to take them, even now, struggling to keep the canoe moving south—a canoe was no sailboat, had no deep keel, and the canoe tended to scuff sideways, if he wasn't careful—and while he set his foot against the hull, and steered with the paddle, which wanted, always, to turn out of his hands, he was beginning to dream, again, while he was at it, in one short dream, the canoe capsizing, and he bolted awake, panicked, and set himself to steering again, and the next moment, even with his eyes open, he was having a terrible argument with Max, and he shook himself awake, Max talking loudly to himself, and Janie, screaming, her voice high, and sharp, *"David!"* Janie nearly having climbed over Max to hold him down, and David lurched over the middle thwart, wrenching Max's hands from the gunnels and, making a fist, striking him, and then again, until he slumped over.

Then Janie turned away and David was alone again, using the sail, which made a constant, low thrum, and he tried to change positions—his left foot was numb—but couldn't, having to brace himself against the hull there to hold the canoe on course.

Janie, in front, sitting with her paddle ready, shook herself, and after a time her head sunk lower, and lower, until it rested against her chest, and he didn't wake her, and he held the paddle fast against the hull, steering, and an early-evening light suffused the lake, and the wind toyed with the sail, the canoe moving steadily, and David, even while he clutched the paddle, slept, too, a light blue sleep, carried down this now miles-long lake, and the lake gone calm, the water heavy at the east end, until he felt the canoe lurching, quickly and over onto the right, water roiling in, and the travois sail catching the wind, so that David had to kick it up from the bottom, and away from the canoe, so it didn't turn them over, and the wind snatched it up, the sail, lifted it right out of the canoe and onto the rocky shore just yards distant, and, as if on legs, it tumbled end over end, as if striding, over one rock outcropping after another, until it was caught in the shoreline trees, David thinking to go in for it, to take it down, stow the ripstop, but he let it go, and they moved quickly now, caught in this south shore current, and blown from behind, and a vast sound rising, and David stirring, looking around him, and the lake, he saw in a second, emptied here, and he bolted up, braking with the paddle, but even as he did, they were carried around the last of the island into a fast-moving section of water, eddies, risers, haystacks, everywhere, and no course through it.

He desperately paddled, trying to make shore, Janie waking, and David shouting, "Get down! Get down and stay down!"

The canoe scraped badly, on an erratic in the rough water, and there was a long, tearing sound, or so he thought, the huge, pointed granite stone scraping up the length of the canoe and then they were by it, but there were more, and Janie didn't listen, but braced herself in the bow, and poked at the rocks, until the paddle jacked back and struck her in the face, and she went down, hugging the hull, so as not to fall out, the canoe rocking wildly on froth, and then dropping sharply again, and taking in bitter-cold water, so that they gasped, and they were under again, under a white froth of moving water, coursing water, and Max, sopped, in the middle, woke, and looked around him, and tried to stand, and David, using his paddle, jabbed his knees from behind, so he fell into the canoe again, banging his head on the center-seat stay, and still they were descending, the water boiling now around them, and still the rapids carried them lower, and finally into a still area, but short, and at the end of it was a glassy, thick lip of water, and they went over it, hanging there for seconds it seemed over nothing, and David rearing back, and the canoe nosed down suddenly, and was falling, in all that rushing water, down, and down, twenty, thirty feet, into this chasm, rock rimmed and trees on all sides, and Janie screamed, and the canoe, as if in slow motion, reared up behind them, still falling, David, in the stern, pitched over Janie, the length of the canoe upended, and at the bottom, the bow struck the water first, and David, holding his paddle and jamming his knees under the thwart in front of him, felt the canoe, in that second, flexing, midlength, and the hull cutting the froth, and the shock of the bitter-cold water taking his breath away, and under the water then, blinded, and his legs still jammed under the thwart and holding him, until like a cork the canoe violently leapt to the surface, driven from behind by the waterfall, and Janie, in the bow, was silent a moment, and then taking an enormous, ragged breath, and crying, and Max coughing and spitting, and the canoe drifted sideways, but broken somehow, and like that, they were carried by the current, out onto a lake only blocks across, but beautiful by evening light, in that way of postcards, the lake protected from the wind by towering red pine and tamarack, the water was almost glassy smooth, and David, shuddering with the cold already, drove them across the width of it, to the far shore, there a white blaze on a tree, marking a path, the water such a roar, Janie couldn't hear him shout for joy.

"Look! Look!" he shouted. He drove the canoe up on the sand, and climbing from it, stumbled.

He wanted to see the blaze—he was afraid it was just a broken branch, and the blue-green pitch that formed after, but no.

A marked trail, and here, a portage, but it would all lead south, and to the highway. All paths like this would. It was nothing short of a miracle, though one that had been inevitable—if they'd been able to look long enough. If they had some luck.

"The canoe holding?" he said.

Janie, soaked, stepped out onto the shore. "It floats," she said.

He embraced her, both of them, their clothing soaked, and their teeth chattering. They were shaking as if palsied, and they laughed, in a pitiful sort of way, and David thought for a second, his hand on his forehead.

Janie stood behind him, waiting. Even turned away from her, he could hear her teeth clattering. Janie had had pneumonia, twice, and had been hospitalized for it, one one-week stay, and one two-week, and David was reminded of it now.

"We can't stay here," he said, turning to her.

"But I'm freezing."

They were both freezing, and hypothermia was a certainty if they didn't find shelter and get their wet clothes off.

"Can't we stay here?"

She said it with a whine in her voice, and David knew she was exhausted, much worse than he was, and it scared him. Even all that time in the hospital, she'd never whined, not once, even when she'd shown him her thighs, which were black and blue from penicillin shots, her rear so bad they couldn't inject it in her there anymore.

It was back then that she'd saved him from Max, but had gotten sick, and he'd been over at the hospital afternoons, at first as much to escape Max as anything, and then to laugh at Janie's jokes, and that was where he'd started reading to her. Really wanting to read, and whole books and the two of them together.

All that he shook off.

He said nothing, only reached into the canoe and bodily lifted Max over his shoulder, but trying to stand, found he couldn't. He was stuck there, too tired, too cold, and just when he was thinking it was impossible, he'd reached the end of it, he rose, unsteadily, shuffling from the canoe, and the pain was something new, something he was unprepared for, carrying Max like this, but there were no small trees and no small branches to make a travois, and they were on this unprotected site, and they couldn't stay here.

He made it a distance, in his head counting his steps, ten at a time, and stopping, one, two, three, four—and then again, his feet dragging in the shallow, dipped path, and when he couldn't bear it, Max's weight making his legs tremble so badly he feared they would collapse, he leaned against a pine, his heart seeming to be right in his mouth, and he moved five, ten more feet, and thought he couldn't do it, not another foot, but he moved three more, and then five more, the path rough with sand over stone, and here and there more pine needles blown down, and slippery, and he tried to move the weight of Max forward, to take it on his hips, lifting Max up so high, he almost went over, but caught himself—again.

He stood there, his breath coming short, his lungs burning, and Max ranting again.

"You don't listen," he said, and David got him up and was moving again.

Counted—one, two, three . . .

Max ranting on, David told himself he wasn't listening, but he was hearing all of it, anyway, and it hurt him. Max jabbering about what a willful boy he'd been, how difficult, how impossible it had been to get him to do anything, but when that stopped, David felt a sudden fright, and lifted his right hand up to feel the side of Max's neck, but there was a pulse there, and a strong one.

And then Max was talking to who David had no idea, and he listened instead to the clanking of the pots Janie was dragging behind her, she was dragging the whole Duluth pack, but the wind would only carry the sound southeast, and David assumed, rightly, that the men had not made it down this far, so it was nothing, but he made note of it, and wondered why she was doing it, but then came over the last of the portage, in the coming dark, and here was another expanse of water, but across it, deep in a stand of trees, a yellow light, a warm yellow light, like a lamp or candle might make, and he fixed it in his mind, where the light was, off to the left of a rock spire like a high, ochre finger, and a broken pine alongside it, an eagle's nest near the top, and just then, the light went out.

Had he really seen it at all?

Or was he just imagining it, out of need, or a desire to see it? A cabin!

He thought, The sun—it was just reflection, but then, the sun had not been out all day. And anyway, the sun was below the horizon now, darkness settling over everything like an ink that washed the world here cobalt-black, a chill in the air coming with it, and it was not just their wet clothes that made it seem so.

Janie bumped into him from behind. They were on a guarded shore, on the backside of the portage, where he had promised he would make a fire, but he was not going to do that now, he was going to pack them up and take them across the lake.

"Look, see the cabin?"

He was not going to tell her what he thought he'd seen there. About the light, maybe someone inside. David lay Max down and turned to go back up the portage, to get the canoe.

"Wait for me," was all he said.

———

"Get in," he told Janie.

He expected her to say, But you said—though she only got in the bow, and he swung the pack in, now only wet clothing, and the pots on the elastic lanyard hanging out, making yet another hollow banging on the hull.

Now they were ready to go, but when he went to lift Max, he found he could not do it. He got all choked up, huffing, and furious with himself, and freezing, right there, the cabin in sight, and a path leading south, but he couldn't, no matter how he tried, lift

Max, and just when he was going to sit down and give in to it, Janie came from behind him and lifted Max's legs, and David, his eyes so glassy he could barely see, cursed, and got Max up over his thigh, alongside the canoe, and Janie went into the water with David, and they set Max in the hull, the hull looking like a coffin, and she nodded to David, and they got in and moved off, the lake an infinite stretch of water, dark, and cold, and falsely calm.

———

From shore, and dragging the gear from the canoe, David made out the square of green roof through the pines and high, surrounding granite erratics.

The cabin was hidden from all directions but from across the lake and down shore of the portage where David had been standing. He'd seen the yellow light, but he would deal with someone in the cabin if someone was there, and he shouldered the pack, and dragged the canoe into the reeds and tied the bow to the stump that had served that purpose before.

He bundled Max, in the bow, in one of the sleeping bags, soaked through, but he did it, anyway. Max was breathing but didn't stir.

"I'll be back," David said.

He'd intended to do something, but he could not think clearly, though, and it didn't come to him, so he took Janie's hand, and she scuffed along beside him as if some somnambulant, both of them, and when David turned up the small path to the cabin, the trees impossibly high here, and red willow and sumac brushing their legs with a wet rasping, both of them hesitated.

The cabin was like a black hole in the gloaming.

They moved toward it, as if toward some magnet, the cabin rough log, and the door askew, the glass in the windows strange, at the bottom the glass thicker, so what reflection there was was bowed, and their reflections in that glass were grotesque.

They could see themselves there, dark with dirt, and their clothes torn, and across David's chest, a broad swath of dark something that had soaked through his jacket, blood.

"Wait," David said.

He had his knife out, and he approached the door, and with the toe of his boot, eased it open. Whoever had been in the cabin, he knew, must have heard them, and for whatever reason, left, or—he was out there, watching them, but he couldn't think about that.

He stepped inside, shaking so badly again his teeth rattled in his head.

He stood over the threshold, listening, and then moved into the dark, and stooped, and could see no one was in the cabin, unless in one of the corners, or under something. He dug into his pocket, his cigarettes sodden, and got out his Marbles match container.

Never go out without it, Bobby had told him. Promise me you won't. Well, he hadn't.

He got the cap off, and in the flare of the match looked around the cabin, a bed in the corner of a second room in back, in the main room, here, a fireplace, and a counter with a sink, on the far end a lantern.

He went to it and felt not the bell but the base.

It was warm. That had been what he'd seen, the light from this lantern.

He got the bell off and pumped the base and lit the fine silk mesh over the gas aperture, and then spun the valve open, and when the lamp began to hiss, he touched the match to the mesh nearest him, and a ball of blue flame came alive with a dull *pfffut!* there, a plume of beautiful fire, and he lit the other, then turned the big valve, and the hissing loudened, and the light went from that lovely blue to yellow, then yellow-white, amid the powerful smell of white gas, and he dodged out through the door and took Janie by the hand, she was just staring, beyond the shakes, and swept her up, and carried her in, and shucked off her wet jacket, which dripped dark spots on the dry wood floor.

There was a kerosene heater, and he got that started, too, and went through the cupboard, cans of tinned stew, and spaghetti, yanking the cans down so they thunked and clattered onto the countertop, and he couldn't think, but grasped a can of spaghetti and jammed his knife through the side, and cut all the way around, cutting the can in half and scooping the cold spaghetti into his mouth, flipping the can over and knocking it on the countertop, so it all came out, thick and cold, and he forced it into his mouth, scooped it in with his hands, in such a way that he nearly choked, and was breathing through his nose, great wheezings, while Janie sank to the floor behind him, but not in front of the heater, and he dragged her to it, and in a trunk by the bed, found an old pair of pants, all things old, army surplus blankets, and khakis of a kind no one had worn, not that he'd seen anyway, ever.

He toweled Janie's hair off with the pants, and went back to the counter, and forced more food into his mouth, and took down another can, and this time, cut through the lid with his knife, working it around in a circle, jabbing and jabbing again until he had it off, and he turned to set it on the kerosene heater—there was a gas stove, too, and he pumped the red tank on the right of it, and turned the valves and touched a match to each of the four burners, and let them run high.

There were crackers in the cupboard, stale, but he crushed them in his hands and shoved them into his mouth until he was choking, couldn't swallow them and had to snatch down some fruit cocktail, and jabbed through the side and held the gash in the can over his mouth, and let the watery syrup run into his mouth, working his teeth powerfully, turning the crackers into mush, breathing through his nose and swallowing.

When he'd eaten, he wrapped Janie in one of the army blankets, which smelled of mothballs and must, and were scratchy, and she said nothing when he covered her with another, just lay beside the heater.

David wrapped one of the blankets around himself, tying it at his middle and cutting a hole for his head with his knife, and jamming the end in back down his pants so it would not trip him. A serape of sorts, he thought.

Then he went outside. He was weak with exhaustion, but his mind was clear again.

He got down to the canoe and saw Max had tried to climb out of it, his head in the water, and he felt something he'd never thought he'd feel, this awful hot sob in his throat, but when he got alongside the canoe, he saw Max's knee had caught on the center thwart, and it was his shoulder and right arm in the water, and he stooped, alongside the canoe and in the lake, to get Max's armpit over his shoulder, and he dragged Max out, was rough for fear he'd get stuck, this time there'd be no Janie to help him, Max's feet splashing down, and dragging, moments later on the sandy path, and when David could carry him no longer, he tossed off the blanket, wrapped Max in it, and dragged Max roughly over the dirt path and needles to the cabin, cursing and praying, he couldn't tell the difference anymore.

———

The cabin was almost suffocatingly hot, and he'd gotten Max into the bed, and he was talking nonsense again. David, just out from him, was trying to get Janie to take off her pants so he could dry them—he was drying his own clothes, and was in his shorts him-self—but she only stared into the heater and shook her head.

She ate what he gave her, but for some reason, she refused to so much as move, only stared into the leaping flames of the heater grid.

His hands on his hips, David stood, looking around the room.

All of it seemed to crowd in. He was warm, his clothes were drying, and he'd eaten. But someone was out there, they'd driven him off with all their noise, or, better, he thought, whoever it was had run. But why? A man, he could tell from what was in the room. The khaki pants, shirts, shoes, oiled and well kept.

But enormous, all of it.

He tried to keep his mind there, still moving, still going for-ward, because he found when he stopped and let his mind wander, it all came back to him, what had happened at the campsite, and he felt almost as if his mind were breaking off then, and he got caught in it, and he assumed Janie was in it, like that, staring now, but he was afraid to touch her.

He'd put a blanket under her, and she'd stretched out in front of the heater, and he was waiting for her to sleep, and then he would remove her wet things and dry them.

And he was going to have to leave the cabin again, climb the rock spire and see where they were if he could, which direction to move tomorrow. A spoon clenched in his fist, he dug into another can of stew he'd opened, swallowing and not tasting anything.

He crossed the room to Max again and stood over the bed, studying Max's gray face, his left eye blind, and shot through with blood.

Concussion, David told himself. People who had—what was it, swelling of the brain?—went into comas and lived, but standing at the bed, he wasn't sure, and he drew up a chair, and he thought to touch Max, but couldn't bring himself to do it, put his hand on Max's shoulder, or something like that, because they'd never been like that, and then David thought he was feeling sorry for himself, and tried to stop it, and when he couldn't, he let the feelings come, what had started with his being unable to say something, like people did in movies, all those things they said, to those in comas, or dying—but he couldn't do any of it, because

I'd do things differently, Max had said.

Had he not said he was sorry, for the reason David could not touch him, his shoulder even? And even here now, part of David was ready for Max to hit him, just open his eyes and begin hitting him and saying the things he had those nights, years ago.

You're no good. You'll never amount to anything. What a worthless goldbricker you are.

His *night* father, the one *only* he knew, but then what did he know of what had been going on then? More now than he wanted to know, and he had wanted to know for years. Had his mother been having an affair? But what did that have to do with him, David? And he was struck by the strange things that he found he clung to, that made his throat swell, to even think of them, the memory of Max's tortoiseshell hairbrush, always by the sink, and the fine shoes he wore, always the best, Wrights, and wingtips, arranged in rows in the front closet where the warm morning light came in, and he felt as if he owned these things now, though they were only memories, but at the thought of losing Max, he felt indescribably to cherish them, these pieces of his father, those things that made him up, for he would have no other father.

Even bad times, he clung to now. Always repairing the apartments Max owned, and the stink of latex paint, and earlier, much earlier, he recalled riding on his father's back on a sled, down a hill, and David had used his father's goggles from flying in the big war, and they'd been outside, and his father's laughter, always, had seemed not for him, because he'd hardened against him already, he couldn't even think when all that had started, so that when Max set his hand on his shoulder, he did not feel loved, or large, but small, though always there were things he loved, like visiting the sites of new homes—Max had gotten into construction—and he loved the smell of pine, in the framing, and the feel of mud-smelling fresh cement foundations, and there was this rush of motion, building things, every last thing new, and at a restaurant, he'd always order the hot roast beef sandwich, and apple pie and ice cream. He did it so often Max would laugh when he did it, and there, just then, Max would ruffle his hair, and it was the real thing.

Just that.

And there were other moments, like when, skiing once, Max tried to pass David, and David had taken him on, tucked low, Max not realizing David would hold it all the way to the bottom, where, because he was skiing too fast, he would fly off a snowbank and go head over heels down to a frozen lake, where he'd slide across.

Max had come down, and when he'd seen David there, caught up in his gear, and knew he was all in one piece, he'd laughed.

And David had laughed.

Max stirred now, but still David did not touch him, though he wanted to.

And he recalled Max had had a ferocious sweet tooth. Loved doughnuts, and pastries, but didn't fatten on them. Told jokes awkwardly, but mostly got the punch lines right, his off-timing somehow amusing Rachel.

If Rachel weren't dressing him, he'd end up in combinations of stripes and plaid, with a white belt, and brown shoes. A man oblivious to much of what was around him, or how he looked in it.

All this, now David cherished, even felt in some deep way he wanted back.

He wanted to see his father jab his ice-cream cone into popcorn, and eat it in such a way that Rachel rolled her eyes, yet hooked her arm through his.

Felt, again, from the back of the car, on those rides up north to the cabin, so long ago, the heavy, sultry, summer breeze, blowing in through the window, in it lake, and warm earth, and this green smell, passing fields of corn, or stands of pine, or marshy areas of orange-flowered touch-me-nots, and at a little place, the Wren, they'd stop and have a root beer, in mugs so cold that the root beer froze to the sides, and his father, who knew how, amusing the girls inside, who twittered at him, this oddball doctor father with the boy's face, and his oddly guileless way about him, which wasn't the real Max at all, but someone he'd created. Because, even then, as often as not he was angry and sullen. Even hostile, at home.

So who was this man, anyway?

And sitting beside Max, David studied his face, his slow breathing, and he thought he would never know, he'd only have these things, these signs, because, even when they'd been out alone, they'd always had this distance between them, this silence, there being no real fathers in the world perhaps, but constructions of fathers, in the same way he was muddling through his years now, and there being only this one certain thing, this hunger in him, visible to him as never before, here, especially here, to live.

For them to live.

He felt a kind of yearning for it, studying Max's face, and knew he would get him, and Janie, out.

David stood and went to the counter. He watched Janie, but when he went to her and tried to remove her wet pants, she kicked him.

He bent beside her and lightly lay the back of his hand along her cheek.

For Janie he felt something he could not so much as name, it wasn't just love, but something deeper, was bound up in gratitude. They were bound together by it, had been these last few years. So much of her joking around, and looking silly, had been for him—when Max had been living with them, to get Max out of his black moods, and later, after he'd left, to lift David's.

"Janie," he said, nearly whispering. And she nodded. "I've got to go out for a bit. Will you be all right? Just for a little?"

Janie nodded, and David took his now-nearly-dry jacket from the chair to the side of the heater, shucked his arms up the sleeves and zipped it to his chin, then went outside.

54

THE BOY PASSED THE BIG MAN IN THE DUCK BLIND, AND after he'd gone up the path, the man came out to watch, silently, and on sure feet, and the boy went on, and he thought he was probably going to the spire. He thought the boy did not know he was on the mainland, but he would know it soon, and he would try to move tomorrow, though the big man knew, too, from the feeling in his right arm, that the damp now would not bring snow, that the movement of the loons, erratic, and panicked, meant rain, but with the temperature holding just above freezing, it would glaze.

Getting out would be almost impossible, and he'd have to think what to do.

Which is what he'd been trying to decide from the time he'd heard them across the lake, and had watched them come in. He'd wanted to go down and help the boy carry his father to the cabin, but he was in trouble of his own, and the threat of imprisonment was a very heavy incentive against lending a casual hand.

But he could see now that that wasn't what had kept him away. Something awful had happened to these three.

They'd stumbled into the cabin, and he saw, soon enough, that it wasn't that they'd just capsized, and were cold, and slow-witted as a result. No, from the way the boy had attacked the cans of spaghetti, had eaten with his hands, it was clear this was something else.

The girl was hurt somehow, but her brother— He was her brother, but they didn't look alike at all. Were they related? The boy looked like his father. So the girl was adopted. He was worried most about the girl. She was hiding something, but she was too tired to go on with it.

And the father, he had not stirred.

From back in the woods, he'd watched it all, the boy coming to the window at first every minute or so, and then sitting by his father, and the girl curling up by the heater. The boy knew he was out here, but he wasn't saying anything to the others.

No, it wasn't him the boy was afraid of, it was somebody else.

He was running, and had carried them here, through sheer will, but he was fading, and whoever it was who was behind them had—he was sure from the birch-bark patch on the bottom of the canoe—tried to do them serious harm.

No, already had.

The duck blind was cold, and he kicked the dried reeds under his felt boots, the fresh air cool and lovely.

Helping them might mean the end of his freedom, and he wasn't sure he could stomach that again. If he could survive it.

They'd held him almost three months in Leavenworth, and he thought now he'd almost died there. Outside the one tiny window of his cell—more like a hole, the wall feet thick—had been the dreariness of Kansas, and his state-appointed attorney had come, once a month, to reassure him that he was not being tried for the murders of the FBI agents, but for contempt of court.

The FBI was certain he knew who had done it, she told him, and they were going to keep him in his cell until he gave them up.

They can wait until forever, then, he'd told her.

It had seemed the right thing to say at the time. But what he hadn't known about himself was that he would come apart when locked between those walls.

His hair began to gray. He couldn't eat. He heard voices, and things went around and around in his head and he couldn't stop them, until all he could do was hold himself together, the cell so small he could nearly span it standing and stretching his arms out.

His cell, he read in the paper he got on Sunday, was one of the better ones. Most had no window. But when he looked out on Kansas, he felt he would weep, for the sheer ugliness of the place, the drabness, the flatness, no water, and no trees to speak of, and this line, day after day, of gray cloud on the horizon like an epitaph, his.

Finally, someone raised bail. And he was out of that place less than an hour when he ran. Ran not for his life, but for his soul.

He would not mind dying out here, if it came to that. He would die in the pines, and in the islands, and with the water. He would die, and his *injchaag*, his soul, would be free, he'd thought. But already, he did not feel free. Everything in him told him he was called to this, and he felt torn because, were he to be apprehended again, it would mean certain incarceration, and that was a death he could not bear.

He believed, were he to die there, in Leavenworth, his soul would be trapped in those concrete walls, and so, here, now—if he helped the boy and his sister and their father and it went wrong— he would not allow himself to be taken back.

And that thought stilled his mind. He would do what he could for them (and he was almost sure what had happened to the girl), and if it went wrong? Here, outside in the pines, he would scale one of the spires and cast himself to the wind, and be free. Again.

But for now? He would wait—he would see, he thought.

And like that, breathing deeply of the pine- and lake-scented air, he knew he had decided already. He knew what he would do now, in both situations, with the boy and his sister and their father, how he would protect them, and what he would do if he was apprehended.

It only remained for fate, or circumstance, or life itself, for the most simple thing, perhaps a sound, or look in one direction or another, to write its part in what would come to pass for him.

55

It rankled Munson that he could not think of a better solution to things than the one Penry was stuck on. They'd tethered at the far end of the lake, the canoes bobbing listlessly, and the one long body of water to the south of them seemed the sure bet, but this wasn't good enough for Penry.

His face was dark with beard, and he looked exhausted, but his eyes had this glassiness in them Munson didn't like. Not tired glassy, crazy glassy.

"So," Munson said, "he's going to see you pass, maybe. But you keep going."

"That's what I'll do," Penry replied. He had this habit of wiping his mouth now. He did that, then spit into the water. They'd only stopped to eat once, and Munson felt his stomach stirring, but thought not to pay it any attention, certain Penry was feeling worse.

Penry had always eaten what two of them would.

"You build a fire, a big one," Penry said. "The doctor can't miss it, on high ground. He'll think it's both of us behind him, and he'll make for the highway and I'll get him there, out in the open where there's nowhere to go."

Penry turned his face into the night. It was drizzling already.

"It's gonna be hell moving tomorrow, you can bet on it, but that's the mainland up ahead, and he'll think he's lucky—if he sees your fire. If he's stupid, he'll start a fire, and he's yours." Penry cocked his head to one side, his neck cracking, and when he righted himself, glanced at Munson. "Otherwise, it's me. Can't go wrong. He'll be looking for *any*thing behind him. You'll be behind, all right, driving him to me. I'll carry my canoe in, leave it just back of the highway, you do the same with yours, and we'll get back to that resort. The rest of it'll go just like we planned before."

He didn't say what would come between their meeting; not saying it seemed to make it beyond argument, beyond consideration.

It bothered Munson, this not naming the thing they were about to do, as if they were somehow incapable of doing otherwise, were incapable of giving what they were about to do some consideration. And that Penry was doing the thinking for him didn't sit well, but he was cold, bone chilled, and wasn't up for much of an argument.

And Penry was right.

You hunted deer like this, sent someone in by them, then drove the deer to the hunter downwind, from behind. It was the oldest hunting trick around.

It was foolproof, even safe. The doctor didn't have anything, a pistol or shotgun, or he'd have waited for them earlier and let loose.

"You got the cords?" Penry asked.

Munson nodded. They were in the bottom of his canoe, the nylon cords they'd cut from the tent, which they'd use to sink the bodies, and even Penry's mention of them was a reminder of where this would all end, the thought of which made Munson sick at himself, but at the same time got him all wired, just wanting to be done with it.

"It's perfect," Penry said.

"What about if you're down there on the highway and somebody sees you?"

Penry glared at Munson, almost a sneer there. "Who's going to be out in weather like this? If it rains *and* freezes?"

There was something final in that, and Munson tried to think of anything else they needed to consider, but there wasn't anything. And the mist had collected on his hat, and spilled off the brim and down his neck, and the chill water, running the length of his spine, did something to him.

"We're clear on this," Penry said.

"Nice guys," Munson said, his voice positively dark.

Penry smiled at that, Munson's bringing up the old days, playing football, and Penry nodded, just a sharp dip of his chin, then swung off down the long, broad body of water headed south.

Munson did as they'd agreed, held off moving until the gloaming was on him, but shoving off from the island, he set on a plan of his own.

Instead of hugging the north shore, like they'd agreed he would, he let the wind carry him across the lake to the south shore, now and again cutting back into the lake, to use the north-westerly, because he assumed the doctor had used the wind, making it down the lake in the time it appeared he had.

If he had.

It was the last big body of water before the mainland, this lake, and Munson thought there was still some chance the doctor had taken one of the tributaries off the lake, behind him, and was bundled up, and waiting for daylight to move.

And Munson was having no luck. The mist had gotten heavier, was a drizzle now, and it was going to get much, much worse. On some of the trees was the white hoarfrost that would either bloom altogether or be washed away in rain that would freeze thick. And there was some distant drone he couldn't make out. A thrumming.

Either way, it was hell traveling, and his knees ached in the bottom of the canoe and he wanted nothing more than to get out of it, and he was thinking about stopping, the rise he and Penry'd agreed on across the lake a good mile distant yet, he'd build the fire there, and he wanted to make it in the last of the light, when he saw something yellow, something that very nearly glowed.

It couldn't be anything, he thought, but when he got closer, he was sure it was something stretched on poles, carried by the wind up into the trees, which even now, in the breeze, swayed as if alive, and as he got closer, he saw with a start that it was tenting material. Yellow nylon ripstop.

He swung the canoe in, so he had his back to the wind. It made no sense at first, but then he understood.

The poles were part of a travois, and he knew that he could catch them. One of them was injured, it had to be—who? The girl who was injured? he thought.

But then the doctor had to be really injured himself—otherwise, why not just carry the girl on his back, as he had all this time before?

But if the doctor had the girl on the travois . . . And again, Munson got this very sick feeling in the pit of his stomach. (What, after all, had Penry and Stacey done over there?)

Still, they were holed up somewhere now, and nearby. And, too, the travois meant they'd be getting out tomorrow, they had to know they were on or near the mainland, and the doctor'd make another travois if he had to, and he could see how they could, just maybe, make it out, elude them after all.

They had just hours, he and Penry, and if they failed at this . . .

What they'd done to Jack seemed now like something they'd done in another lifetime, that someone else had done, but he felt, all the same, as though there were some spot on his very self, one visible and damning, one that seemed all he was now, so drawn was his attention to it.

(What had Penry and Stacey done over there?)

He didn't let himself think it, concretely, but he knew it anyway.

(And what was that sound, now louder?)

But Penry was gone. Stacey was dead. He could run. But, no. Penry'd get to him with Jack. Get to him with Jack maybe the way he'd planned all along. After all, it was Idiot Penry who'd first put the idea of the trip in Stacey's head. Got him thinking he could run if the Mexican died. And was it just Penry? Or did someone put Penry up to all this?

Fuck Penry, Munson thought. He'd use him. They'd use each other, but that would be the end of it.

He grit his teeth and paddled ahead, still hugging the shore, the water cool, and black, and still, unusually so, and a block or so later, he saw the narrow channel, sluicing south, and the white water.

The water positively boiled in the channel, wind chop at the mouth of it, and Munson, for the first time in days, felt his spirits lift, if only briefly, for the rapids ahead were such that it was possible the doctor and his girl had capsized, even drowned. He wouldn't have to do it, after all. You'd have to be lucky, or very, very skilled, to make it the length of this white water without capsizing, and if they had, in this cold water? And thinking this, he backpaddled powerfully, bringing the stern of the canoe into shore, where he got hold of cattails, the stems thick in his hand, and sighted down the rapids, almost a happy doom in him.

They were dead all right, but he just had to find them now. Take the rapids down.

He could see if he capsized here, he'd be crushed on the rocks below, and there had to be a spillway, though he couldn't see it this far back.

The rapids ran straight south, then hundreds of feet along jogged abruptly to the right.

Down the middle of the turbulent water were haystacks— white, frothing boils of water. But these were not the most dangerous things here.

One standing wave, a heavy, leaden-colored rise, feet thick, lay just up and to the right from the haystacks. Under that cool, glossy water of the standing wave was a rock ledge, or bar, and he could scully his keel on it and go over sideways into the chop.

But to the left was no better. There lay one long eddy wall, where the water from the haystacks sluiced into the slower water flowing in from the lake, on the left.

This is where the doctor no doubt had gone, and it occurred to him now, maybe not.

Maybe the doctor had set him up to take these rapids? Maybe this channel was impassable? He could still turn around, but if he did, he'd have a hell of a portage in the dark, if there was one around the channel at all. In fact, maybe the shores behind him were impassable, he hadn't seen a blaze anywhere, and if he did try to portage, he'd have to wait until morning to find them. Which he couldn't do.

Turn back?

Munson sighted along the shoreline of the channel, looking for anything. In the failing light, he had to squint, and the mist formed as droplets on his lashes and he wiped them away time and again.

But then Munson saw, farther up, just before the sharp turn, where a birch grew out over the water, a number of finger-thick branches were broken, the yellow leaves tossing in the swift water.

The water was calm down from the tree, an eddy there, but something thickish about it. Something was on the other side, off to the right, and the doctor had tried to slow the canoe by the birches.

Munson read the entire rapids. Sharp dipped chutes, the water pouring like molten metal over them, and Vs, with the rocks that caused them six or so feet back from them, the rocks the dangers, not the Vs. He'd steer around them upstream, and was looking for a route through, when he saw, on the backside of an especially large V, an eddy not much more than canoe-sized, where he could stop and get another look.

Take a new line if he had to. If the water wasn't moving too fast.

He hung along the bank, steeling himself to navigate the rapids. If the doctor and the girl had capsized here and gone under, he'd be free, he could even leave Penry.

Only, he recalled then, there was Jack, always Jack to think about. He had to cover for what they'd done to Jack. He'd never be free.

But even so, now he would finish this.

He would navigate the Vs, he thought, anticipating the rocks that caused them. Miss both the rock shelf or bar, and whatever it was in the middle there, and shoot the haystacks. He'd get a little wet, but he could use his momentum to make it to the shore on the right, see what had caused the doctor to stop. Or maybe the doctor'd done just what he, Munson, was doing now, looking for a way to bypass the rapids, and had found it—the thought of which caused his spirits to fall.

He'd be long gone if that was the case.

Munson took one more look, standing in the canoe, sighting up the water, pine bordered, the water roaring so loudly it was a kind of white noise, voices in it, which he'd heard before, but not like this. Standing, he saw now that the land seemed to drop off where the rapids hooked right, or was it that the trees were stunted, the ground rocky on the far side of the island?

Munson sat abruptly. He took a deep breath and cast off, stroking into the middle where the current caught him, and he dropped as if kicked into space, falling with the water, the canoe jetting toward the standing water, and he grit his teeth, pulling right for all he was worth, but hit the first rock, and nearly went sideways and shifted left, then ruddered hard, missing the second rock, but hitting what he hadn't seen, a cellar, on the backside of a ledge further downstream, and he went up on his side, taking in water, and using his paddle, this panic kicking up in him, he knocked the stern over violently, the paddle bending, and he jammed his knee under the back thwart, lifting the bow, and pulling with all he had in him, so that he cleared the cellar but rode the stern now, so he almost went over again, and he was frantic, when he regained control, to find the eddy, and he saw now he had completely misread the water, and overshot the eddy, and he hit the haystacks sideways, and took in more water, so that now the water sloshed side to side, making the canoe hard to maneuver, and, a half-second too late, he hit the second row of haystacks, and he was battling for his life now, he saw that, he had been too tired, too slow-thinking, too preoccupied, and the canoe now shot sideways over the haystacks, the water full aboil, and Munson drove the paddle in time and again, trying to bring the canoe around, but the white water had no mass, was a froth of air, and boil, and he felt in his head this lightness, he'd failed, but the haystacks shot him out and he hit the body of thickish water at a rough angle, though the keel cut the glassy water straightening him, and he jabbed the paddle down, and striking a rock, in a panic, raked the water in a flat draw, and spun the canoe right, and he shot across the rapids up from the broken birch, and scull-pivoted so powerfully he felt the paddle bend, but the canoe veering into shore, the rapids thrumming violently under the hull, Munson gasping, and wet, and shocked at himself, hanging on to the birches, and the breaks in the branches, he saw now, weeks old.

He turned from shore and saw, ahead where the water guided

right, the granite base dropped fifteen or twenty feet, the water there heavy as molten glass, but the current under it powerful and fast.

And here, alongside him, was a rock ledge, dark basalt, seventy or so feet high. From the mouth of the rapids, he hadn't been able to see behind the birch trees, but there was no space here, in the rock face, no path, and columnar basalt, he knew, was unscalable, at least without climbing gear.

Munson tugged the canoe in against the rushing water. The undercurrent pitched and turned the hull, inviting him to test it, already, in the near dark he could barely see to maneuver. So he waited.

And then it struck him what to do.

He clambered awkwardly out of the canoe and, crouched there on the narrow rock ledge, tied the cords in his jacket pocket together, fifty or so feet, and secured one end to the bow of the canoe, and with his legs quivering under him, he skirted the shore, climbing north again, slipping, and catching himself, playing the canoe out, and leading it back up the rapids.

He'd gone maybe two hundred feet, he thought, when he struck another ledge.

He just had the afterglow to go on now. The gloaming.

He sighted from the bank there, then got in the canoe, holding to the birch onshore. There was another standing wave just out from him, one he hadn't been able to see for the haystacks above it, but if he had *any* chance at all—and he *had* to move now, he had no time—he had to jet out into the current, run up along the standing wave, and paddle on his left side, digging into the water to prevent the canoe from overturning, to reach the far bank, where he could see a blaze, and a path leading from it.

It might work, it *had* to work, and before he could lose his grit, and terrified of going over the waterfall, he shot out into the rapids, very nearly missed the end of the standing wave but got around it, stroked heavily on his right and switched left, going across, and the suck there turning the canoe on its side, and Munson hanging so far off the left and the stern, to spin the canoe back around, that he nearly capsized, coming around and striking a haystack that shot icy spray into his face, blinding him, so that he could only keep the canoe up and hope he was moving in the right direction, all the while, closer, the roar of the waterfall becoming a kind of thunder, and his canoe alight with it, as if the whole world were alive and trembling heavily, and like that he shot across the last of it, into the far shore, colliding with a stone there, and the current humping up over the side of the canoe so that Munson leapt into the bow, and taking the bowline, sprawled onto shore, wet with spray, but without his weight in the canoe, the canoe rose, banged roughly over the rock there, and glided into the small pebbled and sandy shore in the lee of it all.

He was bitter cold, wet, and shaking, but he was in another frame of mind. He lifted his fist to his mouth, bit his knuckles.

Now. Now, he thought. While he felt like this.

He went down a small path, thrilled at his having beaten the water, felt powerful, and chilled, and machinelike.

Get it done, he thought. They're dead, or they're not far.

He humped the canoe over a rock rise, and there was another body of water, and he skidded with the canoe on his back the thirty or so feet down the switchbacked trail to shore.

There were no prints on the sand, but since it had rained earlier, there shouldn't have been. He stood, collecting his wits and shuddering with cold.

He wanted, desperately, to have his life back, and at any cost.

A light came on in a window across the lake, its reflection, in all that darkness, a yellow star on the blue-black water. A cabin.

In minutes he'd crossed the water and, cold, and sharp, and feeling nothing, he looked through the window facing west, into a bedroom, and there saw the doctor.

For one fleeting moment, their eyes met.

And Munson was gone.

56

DAVID WAS STANDING AT THE BED, TRYING TO SPOON SOME soup he'd warmed into Max's mouth. He could tell Max was disgusted with himself, down like this, but couldn't bring himself to tell Max not to be.

He'd dreaded coming into the room, for fear of what he might find, Max seeming earlier very near death, but here Max was awake now, pursing his mouth in an attempt to say something. But what?

David drew the chair over to the bed and sat. Max regarded David with his good eye, the other, the left eye, darker, the white, most of it, almost red-black, the pupil normal again, but David could tell he wasn't seeing out of it, and when David tried to spoon more of the soup into Max's mouth, he overturned the bowl, making a strange choking noise, huffing, blinking with his good eye, slapping his left hand against the bed, and his right hand curled into a fist. He lifted out of the bed, staring with his one good eye, his face twisted into a paroxysm of what David couldn't tell, and let out an exhalation, a burst of air from his pocked mouth, and what soup David had managed to get into him sprayed across the bed, Max twisting violently, so that David grabbed the front of his shirt and held him so his head didn't hit the steel bed frame, Max sputtering, and spitting, and whacking his hand on the bed, saying what David thought was, Go! Go! but David only shook his head, he would not go, he told him, which made Max shake his head and toss all the more violently, until, exhausted, and thinking what David couldn't tell, he lay flat on his back, but staring into the ceiling, furious with himself, the room quiet, and David's heart slowing.

It was warm in the cabin, but things had worsened, Max like this. And Janie was still curled back of the heater, and wouldn't move, which left him to keep watch, and try to get something into Max again, who shuddered now, as if crying.

And then that stopped, too. And there was just the hiss of the kerosene heater in the other room, and the occasional tick in the roof when the wind blew, but Max still awake, still staring, the room silent.

It was exactly this silence David feared most. Because in the silence his father's death seemed close, possible, and because this was it, his last chance. His opportunity to say what he wanted to, after all this time, and he feared it, because what could he say?

He wanted to say so many things, *all* those years he remembered now, here, like this, remembered all the good things, but that, always, Max had been too hard, had criticized too sharply, and there were the beatings those years when, now, David thought, his mother had been unfaithful, and whatever else it was had been going on. But that wasn't an excuse. Any of it. And when he couldn't stand the silence, he lifted the can and tried with the spoon again, and Max shook his head and David set the can on the floor.

He'd covered the windows, but he was sure the light bled through anyway. So he felt nervous, sitting alongside Max. Still, he couldn't leave, would not leave, not even to stand back of the door, as he had for hours.

So sit he did, though he could not get himself to say anything. Even here, like this.

What was it about boys and their fathers? This hardness between them?

And hadn't it been for Max to say he was sorry, for all that darkness? Though hadn't he, David, played into it? But could he have done otherwise? And his mother, Rachel, making excuses. *He works so hard.* And Max did back then. But even here, it wasn't for David to say it, that he was sorry for it all, and unable to say it, he sat beside his father, struck dumb. Surely, they'd provoked each other. But Max had never given up his end.

And who was harder? he wondered now, sitting on the edge of the bed.

So David waited, it was the best he could do, sit quiet, and his face turned to Max's, and Max gave him this hardened look of, this look of . . . *what,* David couldn't tell, fury, or frustration at his sitting, saying nothing, and Max licked his cracked lips, bleeding now, and his left eye blind, and staring at nothing, and something in David said, his throat swelling so he could hardly breathe:

Come on, just say it, say you were wrong, say you did the wrong thing, say you made a mistake, say you were stupid about something, say you were a man, not some goddamn doctor, some righteous goddamn doctor, say you were just like everybody else, somebody who made mistakes, hurt people without trying to, or

*say that you didn't know what you were doing, not then, or even
that you did, that you knew all the harm you were doing, but
couldn't stop yourself, didn't have a clue how to.*

Just look *like you mean to say it. Just—*

Max lifted his hand, David thought to grasp his forearm, and
he did then, only gripped it harder than David imagined possible,
painful, his fingers digging into the flesh of his arm. Hurting him.

"Guhhhh," Max managed to say, his voice a whisper, and
David said, "No. I won't go. Won't leave you."

———

A short while later, he went into the other room and knelt beside
Janie and felt her forehead.

She was hot, but then she was by the heater, he thought. She'd
thrown off the sleeping bag, and her legs were scissored awkwardly. David went to the counter where whoever it was who'd
been in the cabin had left jugs of water, now yellow with iodine,
lake water.

He poured a cup and drank it, then poured another and
brought it to Janie, and woke her to drink. He hadn't seen her
drink anything, and she drank the water in gulps, her head cocked
up awkwardly, then settled on the floor again and he sat beside
her, his legs out, arms propping himself up from behind, just
watching her breathe, and he reached out, his fingers trembling,
and gently brushed the hair off her forehead, and found, suddenly,
he was choking, and got up, and went outside.

Outside, through the tall pines, a slice of moon hung low on
the horizon, rainbow ringed, and in the air was drizzle, and the
forest hush, and he thought he could feel some mass, more land
not broken by water to the south, but told himself he was just
imagining it.

He took up the hatchet and thought to go into the woods and
find legs for another travois, but reasoned that it would be easier
in the morning, and far less likely that he would cut himself. A
wound now could end things, and he had to be careful, and anyway, he was exhausted.

Yet, even then, he needed to walk. There was a path leading

west from the cabin, but when he went up it, he found that it divided, then again, so that he had to tag the directions on the fingers of his hand, and there realized he would have to rise to it in the morning, getting them out, and he trudged back toward the cabin, for a moment convinced, his heart hammering in his chest, that he'd gotten lost, and this drizzle coming down harder, and a chill on, but then saw the squarish bulk of the cabin, and the gloss of water through the trees beyond it.

There was the crack of something in the woods, almost imperceptible, which set his heart to racing, and he stood motionless for what seemed an eternity, here the true dark around him, not city dark, but this primordial dark, thick, and living, a breathing dark, which was terrifying.

He waited. Was it twenty minutes, or was it an hour, listening at the dark around him, and in him, and the water lapping on the shore, and the drizzle coming down, and the trees glossy with it, and the moon there a sickle of silver in blackest green.

And when he was sure it had been deer, he ducked back into the cabin and set the heavy five-gallon water containers back of the door, and sat in the one chair, just out from the counter, with the hatchet in his hand, and only knew it as something in his dreams when it fell, clunking, to the floor.

57

MUNSON PASSED THE MAN IN THE DUCK BLIND, AND SAW neither. He parted the brush a distance from the cabin and came at the west side again, then shouldered along the rough-hewn logs until he was at the window, no screen on it, and the glass very old, bubbled and thicker at the bottom, and he carefully peered inside and saw a kerosene heater, the girl lying beside it, and he was sickened at himself, and why he was here, the light in the room very dim, and bluish, which meant they had a gaslight, which meant gas, and it occurred to Munson to set the cabin on fire, after.

That was what held him up now, he lied to himself. He was

making plans, no screw-ups this time. He wanted to leave no sign of himself, after.

He squatted in the dark, thought, for a moment, he heard footsteps coming from behind the cabin, someone moving.

But when he turned to go around the side, there was nothing there, and he contemplated what would be most effective.

He could go through the bedroom window, and the girl would wake, and getting to her first, he wouldn't have to listen to it, how she would—

But that was dangerous. What if the doctor put up a fight? But if he took down the doctor first, he could see in his mind now the girl running from the cabin, screaming, and his legs felt leaden at the thought of it, having to chase her, and there was the possibility she'd hide, and that he wouldn't be able to find her, and then what?

And there he cursed Penry again, this was all Penry's doing, and he tried to think.

Of course, he had the rope. And the lake behind the cabin was deep, and if he weighted the bodies with rocks, there would be nothing left behind, nothing to draw anyone's attention.

So, not fire, he wouldn't burn the cabin, and he realized he'd only thought of it because he didn't want to touch them, after, didn't want to have to be left with that to remember.

But he would have to.

He would be quiet, and maybe he'd have to jimmy the door, and if that didn't work, he'd try the lake-facing window in the kitchen. There was some moonlight now, and he could see by it. And the room was lit, too, though only by a feather of blue flame, by what had to be a gas lantern, and it had run low, and they'd let it. Asleep. They wouldn't even know before it was over.

They wouldn't even know it.

So that was it, he'd come in through the kitchen window, he could see now the clasp at the top was open, no screen, and he'd come down and do the girl, and the doctor would be nothing after that.

It was the doctor's fault, anyway. Talking to Penry the way he had.

And after, after he and Penry got out, and fixed all that over to the east with Jack, he'd lay low in Austin, and later he'd quit at Dysart, quietly, without a fuss, and move, move the whole family, he didn't know where, it would all work out, he told himself, but even as he stepped toward the window, something in him cursed his every step, damned him, every moment, and he knew even now, his every breath was a lie.

Even an abomination.

The big man in the duck blind slid off his jacket. It bound him around the shoulders and he needed to be able to move, and move quickly. And he found that the cold sharpened his senses.

He stooped, watching Munson go by, and breathed deeply, preparing himself.

He was not afraid of what he was about to do, even felt it settle on him, as if some holy chore. He'd prayed, and fasted here, for five days, for a sign, and this had come and he now accepted it.

What he had not anticipated, though, was this man's size.

Or his desperation. He smelled of desperation, a coldish, sour smell, and he was filthy, as were those in the cabin, but this man, thick around the middle, and with broad, heavy shoulders, was tall, and walked pigeon-toed, had been some kind of athlete, though he'd gone to fat. He guessed Munson to be around two-forty, two-fifty.

He knew, after the fast, and the time he'd been held at Leavenworth, he was barely two hundred—which he hadn't weighed since he was seventeen and was rawboned and growing still.

But there was no time to consider any of it now, and he stepped out of the blind.

David *felt* someone in the room before he saw him, knew in that instant he'd dropped the hatchet. A cold draft came over his head. Whoever it was, he'd tried the door, found it blocked, and using the window to his right, had climbed down into the cabin, over the counter.

He was standing over Janie, waiting for something, enormous, broad-shouldered, tall.

David, his heart pounding in his neck, reached for the hatchet, his fingertips touching the rough wooden floor, something like a cry bursting through his head. *Nothing!* He could feel *nothing* there now!

Goddammit! How had he fallen asleep?!

He bent slightly and the chair creaked, and at that moment, he made a broad, desperate sweep of the floor, and—it was the one they'd called Munson, who turned, but this wide-eyed look on his face, surprise there, and shock, and David swept up the hatchet, Munson tossing his jacket over the heater, the room going pitch dark, and David lunged from the chair, swung for all he was worth, caught something, with a meaty, cutting smack! There was a grunt, and he lunged out into the room, swung again, and again, but struck nothing.

Munson knocked over the heater and a pool of fire shot up, the room lit blue and heavy with the smell of kerosene. Janie leapt to her feet, screaming, and running, and Munson reached for her and caught her hair in his fist and wrenched her head around, so that when David lunged, yet again, swung the hatchet around for all he was worth, Munson held Janie at his waist, a shield, Janie shrieking, this electrical something jolting up David's spine, so that he pulled his swing, barely missing Janie, and there was a heavy thump at the door.

Munson turned to it, a flat, dumbfounded look on his face, which gave him away, there was no one with him, or he hadn't thought there was, and David swung high at Munson's head, Munson ducking and sweeping one of the blankets off the floor, and when David lunged again, swung, Munson caught the hatchet in the blanket, and with a powerful, twisting motion, bound the hatchet up in the blanket, and with a jerk, tore it from David's hands, the hatchet clattering to the floor so that David dodged out for it, but stopped short when Munson wrenched Janie's head back, then farther back, Janie screaming, Munson forcing David into the corner, he'd break her neck, he really would, David could see that, if he didn't back off, and he scrabbled at his calf for his knife, but it was on the counter, where he'd used it to open the cans, and the light from the burning kerosene fading, the room only shadows and darkness now.

Max bellowed something incomprehensible, stumbling out of the bedroom toward them.

The front door shook again, more violently, knocking back the water containers. Here, David thought, would be the end, if the short, stocky one got in, or the one they'd called Jack.

But the door held, and Munson turned, David thought to look again, but it was a feint. He swept up the hatchet and, Janie screaming at his waist, lunged at David, fast now, driving, hard-eyed, certain, and just when he'd gotten close enough, set himself to swing around hard and low, across David's middle, David kicked up his day pack, the hatchet striking the pack, the cans he'd put in it clattering heavily on the floor, and David dodging under and around him.

The front door kicked back, even harder, Janie making a ulu-lating cry.

Max leapt from the dark, struck Munson on the back of his knees, and Munson pitched over, Janie on her hands and knees scrambling away, David bolting across the room to the counter, where he swept up his knife.

He turned with it, even as Munson loomed out of the dark, swinging the hatchet wide, backhanded, missing him, but striking Max behind him with his elbow, Max falling heavily, the floor shaking.

Munson changed his grip, brought the hatchet around left-handed, surprising David, so that David had to arch his back so as not to be caught by the blade at his waist. Low over his feet, he backed into the darkness of the bedroom, the knife held in front of him, Munson glaring, and there this moment of quiet.

In the cabin now only this deep, ragged breathing, and the kerosene all but gone out, and then it did, the cabin suddenly pitch dark again, and David, his back to the bedroom window, didn't know he was lit in moonlight.

Backlit.

But he saw, in the dark, the glossy sheen of Munson's eyes come on suddenly, and dipped down with the knife, then drove from his feet, just missing Munson's chest, Munson feinting left, and cutting down with the hatchet, the shank striking David's fingers and knocking the knife away, and Munson swinging so powerfully, the hatchet blade struck the log wall, and stuck there, so that David had a second to go by him, to the counter and under it.

He could run for the door, and if he got the water containers out of the way . . . If he could slide them away and swing out, with Janie . . .

But he *wouldn't* go out—run. Not without Max.

He stooped to pick up one of the cans that had tumbled from his day pack. He'd nearly fallen on it. Munson came out of the dark of the bedroom. He had Janie's head held hard at his side again.

David, squatting just out from the counter, readied himself, Munson coming on.

But Munson stopped, feet from David.

In that second David knew Munson could see him, Munson lifting the hatchet to strike when—

The window in the bedroom broke with a crash, a man tumbling over the sill, then standing, and standing, impossibly tall.

Munson backed away with Janie, and David thought it was the man he'd seen on the porch, but it wasn't that man, Jack, and he kicked by Munson to the counter, caught David's arm and swung him around behind him, and when Munson brought the hatchet down, the big man, almost as if in a trick of the eyes, doubled over his feet, dipped under it.

Standing, he struck Munson, and Munson went over backwards, letting go of Janie, who pattered crazily across the floor, screaming.

58

DAVID CAUGHT JANIE BY THE WAIST, AND CLAPPING HIS hand over her mouth, lifted her, and low over his feet, got to the counter and, under it, drew her tightly into the corner, Janie clinging to him.

"*Shh*," he said, into her ear, pressing her tightly against his chest.

He could hear the two men breathing, but in the total dark could not place them.

They moved, circled, the floor creaking. One of them lunged, and David could feel the air moving in the room with him, still too dark to see anything, and the other countered, dropping low, and David, pressing his hand to Janie's mouth, harder now, for her whimpering, stopped breathing himself, could feel whoever it was there, the shift in the floor under him.

When David turned his head, he could make out a bar of blue to his left, Max on the floor just in back of it. The front door was open, and he now saw Munson squatting just feet from him, and the other, nowhere he could hear, or see.

But Munson's back was to them, and he was looking at the door, too.

He was breathing deeply, and Janie stirred, and David cupped his hand over her nose, too, she was shifting in his arms, and he tightened himself around her.

And like that, Munson hurled himself at the door, tossing the water containers aside, and there came an airy whoosh, and as Munson went through, the big man who'd come in the window split the door frame with the hatchet, but Munson was going around the door and outside, and he could hear the *hush-hush-hush* of them running, and branches breaking, and then nothing.

In the dark, the cold rushing in, David held Janie by her small, bony shoulders, and when they'd waited what seemed long enough, David slowly came out from under the counter, lifting Janie by the hand behind him.

He moved toward the door and was about to go through it—they would just run, he thought, his heart beating wildly—when there came a voice:

"*Don't—*"

David froze on the threshold, Janie behind him. He heard now a vague clattering in the trees, the wind blowing and a wet mist on his face.

"Go back in," whoever it was on the stoop said. "Go on back in now."

———

The man, nearly a head taller than David, got the lantern going, lifting it to hang it from a hook jutting from the cupboard.

The room was a wreck, the heater overturned, which the big man set rightside and got lit again, and he motioned David over with Janie, spread the blanket down again, and David lay Janie there. He went to the window where Munson had come in and closed it.

In the bedroom, where he'd broken the window, coming through, he lifted the door off its hinges and stood it under the curtain rod, then packed the open sides with two of the army blankets.

They got Max back into the bed and covered him. The cabin warmed, and the heater hissing, the big man went to the cupboard and drew out three more cans of stew, opened them with David's knife, and dumped the contents in a pot and heated them.

"Here," the big man said, and handed David a mug of stew, a spoon set in it.

David put the spoon in his mouth but began to shake so badly, the spoon rattled on his teeth and he thought he would gag.

At the window, his back to him, the man said, "Whatever got you through so far, you have to think of that."

David couldn't do it. He was shaking, and hiccuping, and couldn't catch his breath, embarrassed at himself. He tried to eat, and choked, and held the mug on his lap.

Something in him said, It's too much, but another voice said, Never.

"You did good," the man said, which, for no reason David could think, made his throat swell, and he dropped the mug and it shattered on the floor, and the sound of the breaking mug stopped that.

He drove the heel of his boot into the mug, crushing it, then again.

After a time, David said, "There're more."

"More what?"

"Two others."

The big man stood, his hands braced against the counter, his head hanging, considering this. He lifted his head, glanced over at David.

"You're wondering why I waited," he said. "Why I didn't just stop him outside, something like that."

"You're not supposed to be here," David said, then added, "Somebody's after you. Aren't they? That's why you waited."

"Don't get wrong ideas in your head."

David turned his hands over, bent to examine his palms, blistered, and bleeding, as if he could read the answer there, then glanced up, the big, dark-skinned man studying him with his pupil-less eyes.

"Don't ask," he said. "It's better you don't know. And you'll hear all the wrong stories later, anyway. Maybe. Or maybe not—only, that'd be for worse reasons."

He got up then and went outside, and when he came back in he was wearing an army jacket that fit too tightly across his broad shoulders. His hair, almost blue-black, was slicked over his skull, which made his face seem even sharper, a face like something you'd imagine, or that was in David already, something out of time, as if known but forgotten, but there all the same, the beaked nose, and large, dark eyes, and strong jaw, and, just now, this unutterable melancholy in him.

When he handed David another mug of the stew, and quietly sat to eat his, David said, "I've got to get them out."

The big man nodded, said, "We'll go when it's time to," and

turned to look over his shoulder, glancing down at Janie, and David felt himself want to turn him away, because he knew, after a fashion, what he was going to say. That he'd failed her. Or was it something else? Yes, it was what David hadn't been able to deal with himself.

The big man sniffed at the room, which had a putrescent smell in it now that it was sealed up again, as if to be certain of something.

"Finish that. Then I'm going to look at your sister, where she's been hurt, but I don't want you coming near."

"Why?"

"You know why," he said.

David gulped the stew, nearly choking on it, and set the mug on the counter behind him, that red Formica on top, old and worn yellow around the rim.

"Boil some water," the man said. "Get the wood outside from under the tarp. We'll need all the kerosene we've got left for the heater."

When David came back inside, the smell was almost overpowering, urine, and fecal matter, but that awful putrescence in it.

"Get away," the man said, and David glanced over his shoulder, and saw Janie's abdomen, and he knelt there, anyway, and she moved into his arms, even twisted, up her abdomen blue streaks.

"I think she's as tough as you," the man said.

David bent into her hair, he couldn't stand to look. He'd failed Janie, completely. And he talked to her, while the big man was busy, cleaning, and then he smelled alcohol, and a powerful antiseptic smell, and he worked there, and David hummed into Janie's ear, and she shuddered, and shuddered, and the big man at one point said, "Sons of bitches, would've killed them myself I'd been there." He had stopped working just then, and David was afraid.

"What's wrong?"

"I've done my best," he said, "but this is bad. First light, tomorrow morning, no matter what, we're out. There's a station twelve miles off."

"How bad is it?"

"I'm not sure we'll make it in tomorrow."

His inclusive "we" sent a shudder up David's back.

"I could help her better if you'd let me," he said. "It might make a difference."

"Difference?"

The big man only nodded, his eyes calm and sad. What he wasn't saying struck David so forcefully he felt his eyes glass up.

"Do it," David said.

Later, Janie was shuddering again, when the big man was ready, had been at the stove, the burners going, and he knelt again beside David, David holding Janie down, David looking away, gritting his teeth, and then there was a hissing of something hot, and Janie breathed hard through her teeth, huffing with the pain of it, David pressing her shoulders down into the floor, Janie shuddering and shifting under David's hands, and there was the smell of seared flesh, and her eyes came open, looking right up into David's face, something awful there, and then she fainted, and the big man busily wrapped her up again, deftly tying things, but the blue streaks still there, on her abdomen, and he stood, letting David take Janie in his arms, and he rocked her like that, slid back to the wall with her, rocking her, and the big man covered them with the wool blanket, and David slept, cradling Janie in his arms, until he sensed something light, a flame, and woke.

Outside, in the window, the big man was smoking.

But the window looked all wrong, the image there distorted, and he saw it was ice, ice on the glass outside, and a layer of frost inside, and he lay Janie by the heater and covered her, and rubbing his arms, went outside, and nearly fell, skidding on his heels and catching himself, so that he nearly had to double over, taking small, hesitant steps to reach him there.

He slapped his arms, suddenly this sharp fear in him that this man with no name would leave them. That he would disappear as he had come, in an instant gone, and the ice now seemingly impassable, and he knew he had to get not just Max out, it had always been Max, and he'd known carrying him out on a travois would have been nearly impossible, but was truly so here, for the problem of getting purchase on the ice-slickened ground.

But now it was Janie, too, this poison creeping into her, and there already he'd seen, in that joint between abdomen and leg, swelling—*pelvic inflammation*, flashed in his mind—and the infection sending its killing blue fingers up her body, and he wanted to just stop it, stop it however he could, prayed it would stop, but that was all in his head, and his only chance, *their* chance now, this man beside him, who had come unasked into their lives, this man with his sad eyes and impassive, old face.

A man maybe not more than forty but with a look that was older than any he could remember.

And he shrank from the morning, from what was ahead, but waited, wrapping his arms around himself and chilled, not saying anything, and the cobalt dawn coming on, a fan of lighter blue in the trees to the east over the gloss of ice on the water, and a breeze in the trees, and the trees making a noise not unlike dampened wind chimes, all a-clatter, but some arrhythmic rhythm in it, lovely, but saturnine in its potential, deadly.

And Munson was out there, and the two others.

And just when David began to feel anger, or was it disappointment, or resentment, at the man's ignoring him, the man turned his big head, his eyes just dark hollows, and he held out cigarettes, and David took one and lit it on the match he offered.

And in that moment David saw he'd gathered lengths of wood, conifer of some sort, branches there, and not like you'd use to make a travois, but for something else. And strips of varnished, milled wood in the snow alongside them. Some short, some long. Behind him a length of the canoe, the bow—maybe five feet of it.

He'd taken the canoe apart, cut it in half with the hatchet. David didn't ask what it was all for, only stood smoking, and the faintest light coming on. Beside him, the big man expertly tossed the hatchet so it spun up over his head, and when it came down again, he caught the handle, perfectly. He fixed his eyes on a tree some twenty, twenty-five feet from them, a tree with a white blaze on it.

David knew he had something to say that would be . . . *difficult.*

"Your father," the big man said, "was he a little . . . *louder* than usual maybe, a little tougher? He make any kind of *threats* when you came in—what, down there in Ely?"

David didn't know what to make of this. Louder than usual? Threats? What was he asking?

And he thought, He couldn't know about the argument there at the motel. Or what Max had said: *I see you coming off the lake into our camp, I won't warn you first.* And recalling it, David had cause to wonder: Had Max meant more by it than he, David, thought he had? But then, Max was always blowing off steam.

With a sudden, downward jerk of his arm, the big man sent the hatchet spinning toward the tree, burying the blade in the white blaze.

"Maybe," David said, distracted by the hatchet, and then recalling how Max had been, said, "Yes, he was. Louder," and after a moment added, "How did you do that? Can you do that again?"

The big man retrieved the hatchet, then stood beside David and tossed it again, with identical results, burying the blade in the blaze.

"It's nothing," he said. "Something you learn to do if you're a kid in the woods and have a lot of time on your hands."

The big man bent, sighing, recalling something that saddened him, and balancing on one knee, swept up the two longest branches.

"Get the hatchet," he said, and David did that and followed him back inside.

59

BACK INSIDE THE CABIN, THEY DID NOT MENTION WHY Munson would have had cord with him, which he'd dropped, only set it along the largest two spruce branches, and though the man's hands were enormous, his fingers moved with surprising swiftness, and he stripped one of the branches up one side using David's knife, then did likewise with the other, and set the two branches, stripped sides down, on the cabin floor. While David held everything steady, he tied to the branches perpendicular cross pieces, and David saw then he was making a sled, the long, up-curved branches they'd started with, runners.

"Why not just use the bow as it is?" David asked.

"You don't have runners, the sled will hunt," the big man said, and when he saw David didn't understand, he said, "The bow of the canoe, it'll shift, side to side, and the keel will carry it off to the left and right. It'd be useless."

After he'd gotten the cross pieces tied, and the bow of the canoe fitted to them, his whole body shuddering at the effort to make the knots tight, only then did he tell David to let go, and he heated the last of the canned goods in the cabin, and David fed Max, who was trembling for pain, and then Janie, fearfully, and even then, the cabin smelled, for there was something that had been boiling on the stove, sweet-sour smelling, and the big man told him to make Janie drink it, whether she wanted to or not.

"What is it?" David asked. He at least wanted to know.

"Rose hips and sumac berries."

"Why?"

"It'll slow down the infection."

David raised Janie up so she wouldn't choke, her blond hair now gray, and pasted to her head with sweat. He was angry with her for not telling him, he would have headed south, first, but amazed at her (she'd saved them by *not* telling him—he just knew it), but that she wouldn't look at him upset him deeply, even though he told himself she was doing it because she'd been found out, and was ashamed.

But, still, her seeming condemnation, her refusing to look at him, made David almost furious at all of it, and he warmed to what he was going to do.

Get her out. He'd make up for it, for each and every last awful thing.

Then the sled was done, and David marveled at it, and the big man turned it over so the runners were up, strips of the canoe's cedar skin tied to them, and taking two red candles from the cupboard, he lit both, holding them together so they burned hot, melting the wax, and he dripped it on the runners, passing a bent lid from one of the cans over and over the runners until the wax had filled the hollows where he'd attached the spruce frame, the candle wax staining the wood bloodred, and he buffed the runners shiny with the elbow of his ill-fitting jacket.

He stood and put his hands on his hips, thinking, then ducked down and whispered something to Janie, curled beside the kerosene heater, and she straightened her legs, and he doubled the blanket around her, and using a wire hanger, made an ersatz hood over her head, fixing it there so it would not fall back, Janie cocooned in green army wool. He reached for the Duluth pack and cut two holes in the bottom, and David saw then what he was doing, and in minutes he had shucked Janie's feet through the holes, had her in the pack, then cut a second blanket in half and fixed it to the bottom of the pack, with the cords, and wrapped the blanket around Janie's legs, and he sat back on his haunches, looking over his shoulder at David.

He nodded to the door, and David had the sled out, it weighed very little, and the big man came through the door with Max in his arms, bundled in one of the sleeping bags, and he set him on his side in the sled.

Back in the cabin they said nothing, only pulled on gloves and fixed the remains of the blanket the big man had cut for Janie around their heads and shoulders. It was cold out and they were not dressed for it.

"Sit," the big man said.

David sat in the chair and the big man had him lift his boots, first one and then the other while he drove pieces of nails he'd cut with a pliers into David's heels and toes with the hammer end of the hatchet. He drew on his own boots, which he'd done the same with, and they clattered across the floor over to Janie, and like that, the big man lifted her in the pack, and David turned and put his arms through the thick leather straps, the weight pulling at him so he had to lean forward to compensate, about sixty pounds, that's what Janie weighed, and the big man went around him and cinched the straps, fitting two fingers between the straps and loosening them a bit.

They went outside, a boil of orange light coming up in the trees to the east.

David waited while the big man fixed a tumpline to the sled; then the big man took up the slack, pulling the sled with two shorter ropes, one in each hand, the sled creaking along the ice fifteen or so feet behind him, and when David began to move with him, he said, "Stay a ways back. Have your knife where you can get at it, at your waist. If I break loose, you have to stop things. Stop us falling. Drop on all fours, use your knife if you have to, but stop us."

David nodded, touching the knife on his belt, ready not just for the ice, but for Munson, or whoever was still out there, and in the near dark, they moved out, the path where it was stone so icy the going was nearly impossible, but blood spoor there, Munson's, and they strode over it, one foot or the other shooting out from under, and David landing on one knee, and then the other, and then the injured knee again, until he could feel both swelling, but he moved on.

———

Some time later, they cleared a rise and guided right, into a valley, and where the land broke open and swept away and down, to the east of them, the sun poured in, golden, and the trees, shrouded in ice, lit up from inside, skeletal, elemental tree essence lit bright with ice, like some light at the heart of the world shining through, and it was beautiful, even here, even now, this light, just here seeming inextinguishable, and that same light in him, and in the enormous man, who, pulling the sled a distance up the path, paused, and turned to see if David saw it, and when he did, when he saw David knew, he nodded, something like a blessing in it, and they moved ahead, something magic in this light, or holy, the valley burning with it, ablaze, and he and the big man bundled, and saying nothing, stopped for a moment, transfixed, and off to the side of the path the big man broke a cigarette, and made a circle of it on the icy snow and, his hand dipping, he dotted the periphery of the circle, in four directions, and stood, and breathed deeply with gratitude.

This, David would recall later, the only time they stopped, other than at blood spoor, Munson's, and the light coming on an almost blinding gold. And they crossed through the valley, their shadows cast on the bordering hillside, wraiths on the glossy ice, insubstantial, and when they moved on, under a ridge, and into dark, and cold, that light was still in him, he would never forget it, and it must have been in the big man, too, he thought, because they moved more quickly, though still stumbling, the ice under the ridge thicker for the ground having been protected from the wind, and the only sounds their hollow breathing, the crunch of their boots on the ice, the creak of the sled, and Janie's sometimes raggedy gurglings on his back, Janie trying not to cry, which propelled him, now, up a steep slope.

It was the regularity of their breathing that hypnotized him, on a steep slope, that and the fever he was unaware of, so hot was he in the blanket.

And watching for Munson—always scanning the hillsides, and where the path turned sharply, blindly, he felt for his knife at his side, he could get at it if he had to. And the big man ahead of him, he didn't even know his name, lifting his head, the hatchet in his right hand, and the tumpline and rope now tied in a carry across his chest, traces, which he leaned into, pulling the mass of Max up yet another steep slope, slick with heavy ice.

And like that, his breathing even, and labored, David came to study the side of the path, relying on the big man's figure just ahead to direct him, studied it for ground fall, which made for easier climbing, his breath coming regular now, and deep, his concentration on his feet, on not falling, on moving, on not banging his swollen knees.

On and on, he followed. He wouldn't have even known how dazed he'd become had it not been for the sled coming skittering at him, and the bellow of the big man:

"COMING DOWN!"

But there in his mind what the big man had said, and he threw himself on the path, Janie on his back knocking the wind out of him, and the sled hit him, and hard, something tearing in his chest, or shoulder, he didn't know what, but for the sudden burning, and he drove his knife through the ice and into the hard ground under it, spinning around with the sled, and catching it by one of the runners, but the big man still falling, taking great whacks at the path with the hatchet, and getting no purchase, here the path not appearing to be steep, but still deceptively so, solid ice, and there not a branch, a bit of brush to either side, only humped and ice-glazed stone, the big man spinning down, pulling in his legs to miss David and the sled, and getting the tumpline off his head and over his shoulder, there a rock face and drop-off below, David bracing himself to break the big man's fall, he must have been sliding thirty feet now, gathering momentum, so that when the last of the tumpline caught up, violently jerking the sled around, David felt as if he would be torn in two, lying facedown on the ice, gripping the knife in his right hand, the runner of the sled caught in the crook of his left arm.

But the knife held, even though he'd been jerked around to face downhill, the tumpline fixed to the sled coming up short and breaking the big man's fall.

They lay facedown on the frozen path breathing hard, and the big man crawled to the side where there was rough snow. Hand over hand, he came up the slope to the sled, then tugged the sled, with Max in it, over to himself.

They sat for no more than a minute, and then the big man got up again.

He tossed David the last of Munson's cord, had him tie it to the side of the sled so if the big man broke loose again, the sled would slide only five or so feet before David's line caught it up, and both of them walked the sled up the steep slope, David keeping the sled on the icy path, but walking, also, on the snow crust off to the side, and like that they scaled the hill, which became almost impassable, but then they were over it, and there was a long, flat stretch through a glen of alder and birch and poplar.

The sun was arcing low over the trees now, and David could hear water.

He moved forward, behind the sled, and he felt some resistance at the sound of the water, and resentment of the big man in front of him for not having told him there would be this, and hated himself for it.

Twelve miles, he'd said. Just that.

And they'd seen more of Munson's blood spoor, but the blood now was only in a footprint, and flattened, not drops at all.

The big man had studied the last prints, paced them, measuring, stooped to regard the angle of the footprints. Had pursed his mouth. Just that.

For a moment the big man slowed, hearing the water, too, but then he trudged on ahead, and David had Max to watch out for, the sled sweeping heavily from side to side just in front of him, threatening to break free again and strike him, but he opened his jacket and got moving again before the safety line played out, climbed faster, but afraid at the trembling in his legs, afraid it would get worse, and at the flush he felt in his face, and the high, distant feeling he had, as if nothing around him were real, and he carefully trod in the broken spot where the big man had put his feet down, and he realized the big man was taking shorter strides for him, was moving more slowly than he would have alone, and he felt himself moving again, this gratitude in him, and something he was not ashamed to call love.

But of a kind before unknown to him.

And this, too, moved him, and so, when they came to the falls, and the water all around, and the water rushing, a river cutting the path in two, fifty or so feet wide, and no visible way across, when he pulled up behind, feverish, there no denying it now, they were cut off here, he only settled Janie on his back, waiting, the water coursing and gushing over greenstone and ice, and when he saw what the big man was looking at, blood spoor, leading upriver, he stood, a hand on his hip, waiting.

The big man nodded then climbed alongside the rushing water, up the hillside, and was gone.

Off to David's right, from a cedar heavy with ice and snow, a pine marten chucked at him. Janie shifted in the pack, David talking nothing to her, anything, and at some point she nodded, and stopped moving.

On the sled, the blanket slowly rose and fell, rose and fell, and David thought to sit, but didn't. The shaking in his legs had gotten worse, and he was afraid if he sat, he wouldn't be able to stand again. So he waited, holding a thin poplar in his left hand, and listening, and when too much time had passed, and he heard a crashing in the brush, his heart seemed to stop beating altogether, and he saw a short man now come rushing at him, and he had his hand on his knife, drew it, moving into it, when he saw it was only the big man, foreshortened by David's looking up the slope, and the pines there dwarfing him in the light gone gray.

60

THEY TOOK TURNS LIFTING. THE HILLSIDE HERE WAS SO steep, they fixed themselves to trees, and hand over hand brought the sled up with the rope.

Then they would fix the sled there, and climb, and begin all over again.

When they got to the top, the water was rushing even more ferociously, deafening, but there was a log crossing the river, one frequently used, and the big man had been over it, breaking the ice from it.

The log was a good three feet in diameter, but the stretch over the river had to be a good sixty feet here. And there were the roots, mangled and clumped with frozen dirt and stones caught in the log's maw, here on this side, a space just wide enough for one man to pass through.

Now that they had the sled back of it, the big man paused, setting his hands on his hips.

It was unsettling that he seemed not to know what to do this time, or was undecided, and he turned to look at David, David with Janie on his back, shaking his head, and then glanced down at the sled, and Max there, just the side of Max's face showing through the hooded blanket.

He turned to look at the sun through the trees. Only he knew how far they had yet to go, and David got a sinking feeling at the look on his face, one now of dark concern.

He was talking to himself, but in a way David couldn't understand, walking from one side of the upraised roots to the other, the string of rounded vowels issuing from his mouth like some dark music, and then he turned and said, "Give me the cord."

David did, and the big man doubled the nylon tumpline, then fixed the ends to the front runners, left and right, making a loop, and with David's section of rope, did the same at the rear, using David's knife to cut holes in the thin cedar, and lifting the sled there, to test if the line would hold.

He turned to look at the fallen log.

It was the roots on this end that were the problem, and lifting the sled over them. And how to balance the sled on the log, at the least still slick, if not in places covered with ice.

The big man came around David and lifted Janie off his back, ran his arms through the pack straps and jerked the straps tight, so the pack rode high.

They stood looking at each other.

"Come on," the big man said.

David still had no idea what they were going to do. But then the man stooped, put his head through one of the doubled lines, so it set over his neck, then forced the piece of blanket he'd been using for a hood down under it so the line wouldn't cut him, and facing David, he motioned David to do the same with the other, opposite end.

David had felt, just for a moment, with Janie off his back, lighter, but that burning still in his side, so that he was afraid to lean over for the pain.

He got the rope over his neck, taking up the rear, but now, though, when he lifted Max in the sled, the big man moving too fast for him, climbing, he was afraid he would fall, from slipping, or his legs would give out.

He wobbled badly, going up after him, using the whitened, icy roots for handholds, his legs shuddering, lifting the sled with Max in it from the back of his neck, the weight there unbelievable, and the rope, even with the blanket between it and his skin, cutting badly, but the big man gave him not a second to stop, or think, and hand over hand, and up, and over the roots and the clotted dirt and stones he climbed, and he was doing it, never would have believed he could do it, but he had the line around his neck, and coming to the opening, hesitated, a fall of twenty feet to the water, the water roaring below, white froth, dampening him even here, his pants legs wet, and he knew if he went over, slipped on the log, they would all drown, all four of them, and when the big man straddled the log, then moved off across it, facing David, David faced him in return, the sled suspended between them, the big man's eyes fixed on David's, staring, something there absolutely unforgiving, and David came on.

But as he was stooping to straddle the log, his feet shot out from under him, and he came down on his thighs, doubled over, to balance there, shaking so badly he couldn't control himself, high over the water, boiling and rushing under him.

He was in the quiet place, though, his heart hammering off somewhere distant, in the place of all time, and no time, and he knew he would either die, right here, right now, or—and when he moved to take the rope from his neck, the big man slowly shook his head, no, he would not have David go in, even though David, perched there, over the water, threatened to take them all with him, dipped, and lurched, catching himself.

"Stop," the big man said, this dead calm in his voice, and David did.

He was balanced there, over the water, but how could he get onto the log? Straddle it?

"You can do it," the big man said, just that.

David nodded, and breathed slowly; when he turned his head slightly, looked to his left and down, he could see a branch, jutting off the log toward the water.

Getting to it would be a stretch.

Still, he was already sliding off the log, backwards, and in one swift motion, he heaved up on the sled, swinging his left leg out, and down, reaching, on his back, staring at the gray sky hemmed in by ragged green pines, this laughter coming at him as he began to slide from the log, and he wanted to laugh, and laugh, the branch *wasn't* there, it *wasn't* there, it *wasn't*—

And he hooked his foot under the branch sharply, the branch slippery, caught himself there by his ankle, even as he was falling, using it to lever his right leg over the log, catching the icy log in a cold embrace, his heart galloping in his chest, and he gripped the log now with both legs, the whole horizon tilting with him as he sat up, his back to the big man, and the big man said, only, "Good. Now, carefully, turn around."

Only that, and when he had, and when the big man drew the sled toward him, across the log, David helped steady it, and inch by inch, facing each other, they went across, the water splashing up and wetting their pants legs so that they were crusted with ice by the time they pulled the sled off the other side.

It was only then the big man smiled, and David did in return. But then the big man was on his knee, had found more blood spoor.

He shrugged, glanced up at David, and David only nodded, and like that they were moving again.

————

Now the big man was carrying Janie and pulling the sled, both, here, less wind and the ice crust thicker.

They moved on, and David wondered how much farther it could be. The land rolled now, and the path wound through one stand of pine after another, all of it passing as if in a dream, the fever on him, and nothing much mattering, and an exhaustion settling in him, but his body moving anyway, and the light going gray and then grayer, and no contrast in the woods, and just breathing and silence and snow and the path, always winding out ahead, and then he thought he smelled wood smoke, and he stopped, thinking to ask how much farther it was, but didn't dare, and they crossed an open field, ringed by larch trees, a crow there cawing and picking at something dead, five crows, and the man paused, only to look, and shaking his head, went up the path again, yanking the sled, and Janie visible in the pack, her legs wrapped in the green blanket, thumping against the big man's back, and in that failing light David fell again, and for some reason, maybe just that he dared to, lifted his hands, and removing his gloves, saw that he'd torn the remains of the blistered skin from his palms. When that had happened he didn't know, but he was bleeding from his hands, and the gloves crusty with it, and cold, and his fingernails, he could even see in the failing light, bluish, and he stumbled on, but the icy path here rough with pine needles, so that the footing wasn't so difficult, and the path wound through yet another stand of cedars, and pines rising over them, and then the ground broke away before he even knew what he was looking at, and below them was the highway, flat-topped but frozen slick, the ditches slick, everything thick with ice, the worst of it here, and as they stood, high above it, only a bank to be descended, David dropped to his knees, and the big man reached under his arm and lifted him, and he stumbled more than walked down, behind him, and they paralleled the road in the heavy pines, to avoid the ice, David taking up one of the lines on the sled and pulling, and when the road rose, and they could see over the rise, and there remained a mile at most to go, to a brick building set off to the right, and the road angling sharply just beyond it, David stopped, something unutterable in him.

He turned to the big man and just looked. Looked right into his eyes. Those pupil-less eyes, his sad, young-ancient face.

He got so choked up he couldn't speak.

The big man looked off into the woods behind them, calculating.

"It's not right I don't so much as know your name," David said.

"It doesn't matter," he said. "And anyway, either you'll understand, later, or you won't." And then he stepped closer. "I'm not coming in, I told you that."

David looked down the length of road. He had all kinds of thoughts, but most that maybe Munson, or the others, were waiting out there, and how long it would take him to get to the building, and who'd be in it. And he was trying not to feel, almost, this sting of betrayal—all this, and this man, silent beside him, wouldn't walk this distance.

Before David could move, the big man had gotten Janie in the pack on him and adjusted the straps, and now zipped his jacket open.

"This was my father's," he said, standing over David, and he had in his hand a pearl-handled .38, a revolver. Smith & Wesson. It was right out of the box, and David knew at a glance it had never belonged to this man, or his father. "Safety's on. You—"

"I know how to use it," David said.

"Do you?" But then, by the look on David's face, the big man understood. The boy knew whether or not he had it in him to do it—he'd found out. *Here.* And the answer was *yes,* he did. The big man looked off into the woods, then up the length of road to the small brick building.

"Listen now," he said. "It comes up they want to know where you got this, you *listen first*. Let them do all the talking, you'll understand."

David nodded.

"Okay then," he said. He slid the gun into David's jacket pocket. David didn't know what to say. "I doubt you'll need it. But—"

He didn't finish his thought, only glanced down at the sled, at Janie on David's back, her face in some unconscious repose, then at David, and after a moment that seemed—how could a second seem like a lifetime? Or anyone's eyes be that dark, but have such light in them?—forever, zipped up his jacket to go.

"What should I call you?" David said.

The man hesitated a second. "Gaiwin," he said. He nodded, and was turning toward the woods, his broad back to David, when David said, "What should I tell them?"

The big man paused, back of the trees along the road, then craned his head around, looked at David over his shoulder.

"Tell them the truth," he said. "You got them out, didn't you?"

61

HE WATCHED THE BIG MAN MOVING THROUGH THE TREES, could only make him out for his green jacket being lighter, and then he was gone, somewhere, in the pines, and David saw him no longer and turned to stare down the length of highway, here a short but steep section, and then a mile or two of flat white ice, and with the light fading he got the sled on the highway, just a graveled road really, letting the sled down in front of him, and nearly panicked when it began to drag him, and Janie trying to curl up in the pack.

The road widened, and a light snow began to fall, and on the flats he pulled against the tumpline, and began to feel this darkness about how they'd come to be here, but when that got to be too awful, he forced himself to stop it and only concentrate on finishing, and he could deal with the rest of it later.

He felt bone tired, soul tired, and he thought back to the light this morning, and it helped him move, but he could just as easily have sat, sat and slept, but he knew he couldn't, and the wet snow stuck to the ice and made pulling the sled more difficult, the runners sticking, but there remained now only this distance, and he saw up ahead, where the road turned, that building, a gas station, a sign on the roof he couldn't yet read, and back of the station another rise of land, majestic in its scale, and pine covered, and he smelled pine and wood smoke, it had come from the station, and he tugged at the tumpline, the sled jerking up to bump into his heels, behind him again, and Janie turning in the Duluth pack, the straps digging into his shoulders as if with the weight of the world, and his right shoulder burned where he'd torn it, or broken it, when the sled had struck him, or was it his side? and he felt it all at a great distance, each step smaller, and slower, so that it seemed he was walking toward the station but never getting there, all the while sensing some shadow in the trees moving with him, and knew it was his . . . *friend,* but that word did no justice to him—the big man had not just left as he'd wanted David to think—and knowing this, or was he just . . . *imagining* it, that he was there? David turned to cross a large, open area around the station, cut out of the trees, and headed onto a flattened, graveled area, still hundreds of yards from the station, but the ice here very bad, so that his feet threatened to scoot from under him, and then one did, so that he went down on one knee, the weight on his back crushing, and the tumpline around his forehead cutting him, stinging, and he rested there a moment, a hand on the ground, and the other lifting at the pack strap, which was cutting off the circulation, so that his left arm was numb clear down to his fingertips.

But he stood again, legs leaden, and the light gone, the station some few blocks across this expanse of ice-glazed snow.

He wanted to think it would just be warmth, and an end to all this . . . what he could not even think to call it, at the station, but there would be the telephone calls, and then the troopers, and an ambulance for Janie and Max, and the questions, and he had to think. He wouldn't tell about . . . *Gaiwin.* He was already thinking of him that way and he patted the gun in his pocket. He hadn't needed it after all. Just as his . . . what *was* he?

Just as *Gaiwin* had said he most likely wouldn't.

He could say he'd found it in the cabin, or that it had been Max's—

And his thoughts caught here, this sudden confusion in him.

Your father, Gaiwin had said, was he a little . . . *louder* than usual maybe? When you came in—what, down there in Ely?

And it occurred to him, he would tell very little of what happened, and none of how he'd been helped at the cabin. Because he was bound *not* to, as . . . whoever he was had felt bound to help him. And thinking so, he slipped his hand in his pocket, touched the revolver, to reassure himself it was there.

And Janie? What would she say? Could he ask her not to say they'd been helped? And David recalled his promise to her, all that time ago back at the house, before they'd left, and felt sickened at himself, how badly he'd done, and he knew he couldn't, he couldn't ask her not to, and he forced himself to move out from behind the cedars that separated him from the station, the ice here the worst, and the tumpline burning, and the pack nearly unbearable, and he thought of a joke his uncle Bobby had made at hard times, when the food had burned when they were camping, or something broke, or there was some bad news of some sort, but that he'd made it, too, this joke, when good things happened had confused him. It had the power of some benediction, David moving out across the ice and his legs threatening to collapse under him, this odd thing speaking to him, why, now, just when the station was in sight, he had no idea, but this thing his uncle, the veteran, had said, *Isn't that the way it goes,* and in it now, not a voice, but a knowing, so he didn't so much hear it as feel it, the nails in his boots just sharp enough to make a difference on the ice, but to skitter, too, on the hardest of it, and he set his eyes on the building, and looked in no other direction, because he had to, had to cover just six hundred feet, or was it a thousand?

What a thing it would be, were the man who'd attacked them at the cabin to come out of the woods now. Or the short one, with the glasses.

He put his hand in his pocket and felt the revolver yet again— heavy, cold.

And moving up the road, he got that telescoping feeling again, as though, already, he were falling into himself, and he were looking out of a cave, the world darker because it had suddenly gotten darker, but, too, because he was between everything that was behind him and this uncertain light he was moving toward.

He slipped and fell again, struck his knee, but he ignored it.

He ignored the night birds that were calling, the skritch of the nails in his right boot, which he was dragging more than lifting now.

He wanted to lie down, to sleep, to rest.

He wanted not to think, or to struggle, to be wrapped in the arms of some love that was not tainted, or demanding, but sang to him in his sleep forever. He wanted to lift up, light, free, a bird, gliding on invisible currents, lifted above all that was heavy, and dark, and difficult, like his leaden legs, quivering, his heart, beating dully and hot in his neck, and all the weight on his back, and what was behind him and gone, but not. He wanted, just now, moving across the ice, to be—

Weightless, a spirit, a nothing.

Just nothing: pure, beautiful, nothing. And light, light, more light.

62

ON HIS THIRD TIME UP AND DOWN THE HIGHWAY, HIS SNOW chains rattling, Penry decided to play it safe. There was a yellow-brick station, a Standard, which most of the year he was sure took in terrific business, canoeists coming out of the backcountry and wanting to just head down to the Twin Cities and avoid the mess in Grand Marais or Ely, filling up here, whole tanks, and all the campers buying postcards, and maybe an ice cream sandwich, but now at the end of the season, and on a day like today, they could as well have shut the place down. But there was a woman inside, and she'd lifted her head a time or two and given the station wagon with the Alumacraft on it a hard look, and that's what settled it. Her giving him that hard-eyed going-over.

He had to take care of himself, and it was just her bad luck to be out here alone, only he was wrong in thinking that, because she wasn't alone, not exactly.

Her husband had driven their snowmobile on the short path back to Vernon, a cluster of seven mobile homes where people in resort work here lived, where he could get another tank of LP to replace the one that had gone empty just hours before. There was nobody stopping by, and they'd need it, and so, bored, he'd fired up the Polaris, the old, empty tank bungeed to the back.

So Penry only saw the rusted Chrysler New Yorker, one of those ugly, heavy, concave-sided things from the mid-sixties, there with studded tires. Gray. Chrome rack on the roof peeling, but the car free of ice, the windshield anyway, which meant, in Penry's thinking, that she'd driven in. Today.

And, parked up in the trees now, on the fire road to the west, just a stone's throw from where the woman's husband had passed with the snowmobile earlier, Penry would have seen the tracks if he'd looked, Penry waiting there, certain Munson would drive the doctor, the girl, and the boy on past the station—or Munson would just arrive himself, having taken care of it and looking to meet up with Penry and to get the rest of it done.

It would take some doing, getting through the day, but if they played it just right . . .

Penry, the camera pressed to his face, scanned the woods and the road east of him for some sign of Munson. They had hours, and it would work out, all of it, even picking up Munson's canoe, and he'd make sure the woman inside wasn't going to be able to identify the car—they'd take her with them, and leave her where they'd left Jack—and she'd just be one more missing person, a casualty of the ice storm and early snow.

Maybe they'd even crack up her car—but no, that was too complicated.

Keep it simple. Know what you're after. Hit hard. Take no prisoners. Waiting is for losers. Take what's yours, boys.

But an hour passed. And then another.

Penry had to get into the car and warm himself, finally just staying put in the car and running the engine every twenty minutes or so.

———

Down the path behind Penry, the woman's husband trudged along where the snow had drifted, falling time and again on the ice and cursing the Polaris, which had eaten yet another track, the track suddenly rattling, and then slapping violently under the machine, and the engine whining, so that he had to shut the works down. When he got off the machine in his suit, he turned in the direction of the station but decided against going back. They'd lost power, but not the phone, and so he trudged on in the snow, working up a sweat, and his heart pounding away in his chest, thinking what he'd say when he got to Vernon. It was only five miles, but with this ice? And like that he pushed on, the LP tank slung over his shoulder, and clonging like a bell on the ice when he came down, time and again, until he was so exhausted by it that when he got to Vernon, he took the mug of coffee offered him, called to ask his wife if things were all right, was business running her over? Ha-ha. She told him not to rush back, she had the fort held down and didn't see any natives on the horizon. They kept that banter up for a time, and the woman's husband said he'd be back in an hour, tops.

See you then, loverboy, the wife teased.

———

Penry, in the car, was growing more agitated by the minute. He knew this situation called for patience, but he didn't have it. He'd gotten here with lots of daylight remaining, and everything would have worked out—it *still* would, he told himself—but now Munson was fucking up again. He'd almost screwed things up with the Mexican, not wanting to put it to the policeman who had been called out what they'd do to him if he didn't go along, or to Munson's brother, Lester, who was in on their stealing, Lester going hard on his piece of the pie. But Penry'd pushed for it, and things had gone down just the way he wanted—the cop had kept his mouth shut; Munson's brother hadn't made any more demands for a bigger cut, even though he'd been the one to talk to the cop; and the wetback, who never should have gotten a look at Stacey, who'd only kicked the shit out of him when he'd thought he was way past comatose, was dead.

Penry had sidestepped it all, just as Throgmorton had said he could, and this mess with the wetbacks taken care of, they wouldn't have to worry about them organizing anymore, or Jack kissing up to the likes of Martinez, talking strikes and shit that would shut down Dysart.

Just this to finish.

It would all fall into place, Penry told himself. Perfect.

But waiting now for Munson, he hit the steering wheel. He was working himself into one of his black moods, he could feel it coming on.

63

Munson, coming around the deer path alongshore, dazed, and his right arm hanging useless at his side, saw now that he had overshot the highway.

He stood with his back braced against a tree and tried to think what to do.

He'd lost a great deal of blood, but the tourniquet put him in another frame of mind. His hand, and the arm from the elbow down, would most likely have to be amputated now, and there was a certain vanity in him that whispered, *He didn't want that.* And, too, it would be proof of what had happened out here.

It would damage their story, his and Penry's, about what had happened with Jack.

He knew if he cut down to the road, Penry would be on it in seconds. On him. But he wasn't sure what he thought of Penry now, anyway.

That the boy had been in the cabin and had come at him like that, that he'd been there at all, that Penry hadn't said the doctor had his son with him, shed a whole new light on what had happened there on the island, with the girl, and on how Stacey had died.

He didn't like to think that someone like Penry had so easily used him, or that Penry had had the presence of mind to put something like this together himself. But thinking about it, he wondered if it had been just Penry. Or if there'd been someone else. But who?

And it occurred to him that he didn't know anything about Penry—not really. Or what was behind what they'd done to Jack.

So, standing with his back to the tree, and catching his breath, he thought how he might get to the highway and to a hospital, but there would be no way, once he was admitted, to avoid the police. And were he to survive, he would have to, sooner or later, have his day in court, and how could he face Lena, and John Jr., whom he'd taught to throw a pass, or the girls, whom he'd taken for ice cream, Jack's girls, the same age as his own, Marcy and Dierdre?

And he saw everything he'd done, since Penry'd told him to just pass the meat along, and slipped him the five crisp hundred-dollar bills, as a mistake. His whole life, from that moment, when he should have gone to Jack, an abyss. But Jack had just put Martinez on as floor manager, and he'd been devastated.

He'd thought then that what remained of his pride he'd salvage through screwing the company.

Screwing Jack. But he saw now he'd been mistaken, and had taken some long and awful road that had led him right to this moment. Bleeding to death—the boy had caught him just above the elbow with the hatchet—and alone, and no one to make a decision for him. No one here to blame but himself.

And something perverse in him said, If you get to Penry, you could still make it.

He lifted his head, smelled wood smoke. Was Penry nearby? Was that Penry? Had he started a fire?

There was a rise just ahead, and he forced himself along the deer path and up it, and into the pines that grew so closely together he caught his shoulders on the rough bark on the backside, where the rain had not coated them in ice.

He'd had to stop in the night, under a rock ledge, and that had cost him hours, and he'd bled badly, until he'd torn the cloth from his jacket and made a tourniquet. He'd waited as long as he could, hoping the cut was not so deep that he would have to do it, because once he did, he knew he had only an hour or so to get in, and that the tighter he made the tourniquet, the less blood would get to his forearm and hand, and he'd waited, bleeding, and when the rain had abated, crept out from under the ridge, hoping against hope that the walk in would only be a few miles, but it had been ten, at least, and over rough terrain, and he'd begun to feel dizzy from blood loss, and so had cinched the tourniquet down, finally, after he crossed the river, using the log upstream, but it had been hours, and here he was, and he'd lost his goddamn forearm and hand.

Now it hung against his side, dead weight.

———

A short while later he stood high on a wooded hillside and saw to the east, first, the station, yellow brick, and smoke rising from the chimney, and just below him, the gray aluminum of Penry's canoe, and the rim of red around the gunnel, and the car under it, and he lifted his head and stood motionless, and faint, his breathing labored, and there not much of anything left in his legs, at a great distance, a mile or so to the east, the big man and the boy coming in, and the boy's father in some kind of makeshift sled, the girl on the big man's back, the man who'd burst into the cabin, the boy, barely able to lift his feet behind the big man, and Munson breathed deeply.

He breathed for what was left of himself, and what he would do.

He would get to Penry, and they'd end it.

———

Penry glanced at his watch. It was just five after three, they had a little over an hour of real daylight to work with. He realized he'd stopped breathing, he was so tense, and he made himself breathe, but he felt as if his chest were being crushed.

It was cold in the car, but he didn't start it, because the muffler leaked, and then he had to open the windows, and that made things all the colder, and so he cursed the car, thought about getting out of it, and hitting something, anything.

But he forced himself to stay put behind the wheel. He drummed on it, played "Wipeout," and as he hammered at the wheel, his mind played over what he would do when he saw them coming in.

The doctor and the boy and the girl with them, if Munson hadn't already gotten to them.

Which he must have. That's what was taking so long, he told himself.

But then he was angry all over again.

Waiting made Penry crazy. It always had, but back when there was football, he could always hurt someone. He could hate them all, and he could pick out who it was he wanted to hurt, and sometimes, he and another boy, Dietz, had singled boys out, and they'd hit them hard, Coach thrilled at it, and there'd been those years after, brawling in bars in farm towns, the farm boys who hadn't played ball, big as bulls some of them, but slow moving, and always surprised when things went crazy, a table hit them in the face, a chair, a heavy glass beer pitcher, when Penry came on.

Sure, he was funny, all right. Funny looking.

Idjit. Stupid Penry. And the girls who gave him a consolation fuck? Or that's what Munson'd said. Who else would fuck a toad like you? he'd said, throwing his arm over Penry's shoulders in a show of drunken sentiment.

And waiting for him now, he had to laugh. Munson, who'd always joked, but in such a way that Penry'd known all along he meant every word.

If brains were dynamite, Penry, you couldn't blow your fuckin' nose! But we love you, Pen. Just as you are, Idjit!

Well, he hadn't waited, Penry thought, even after all of Jack's earnest protestations: It'll get better, Just hang in there, We'll work some angle with higher management, okay? And then Jack fucking them over with the Mexicans like that . . . No, he had not waited, not now, and not then, and his eyes on the station, and the highway running east from it, ready to get moving again, he grinned, recalling that time so long ago, when he'd pulled up to Stu's Town Tap, on that night of nights.

Who'd looked foolish then?

In their front booth, Stacey, Munson, and Jack had been overlooking the lot, where the cars they'd bought sat. Munson's that ruined Ford Falcon with the Cleveland 350 shoehorned into it, and the lime-green doodle balls around the windows, as if that made it look better. Stacey with his father's shit-brown Olds 88, with big meats on back and glass packs, but the car just a heavy, noisy turd of a car, an old man's car. And Jack with that hand-me-down Honda, tired, tomato-soup orange and rusting badly, Jack telling them he was saving to go away to Dunwoody or even the university, saving every dime, so he didn't mess with the car, not even so much as a flair to it, a fob hanging from the rearview mirror. And the others' cars, Dusters with torn vinyl tops, with big tires and Thrush decals, and a contingent of Monte Carlos, all jacked up, but no real poop. And Gremlins and Pintos, lime green and yellow.

But he'd shown them, Penry thought, had he ever!

Not a car worth looking at in the lot that night, but then, there never was, and in the window that night, he'd seen them talking, Jack, and Munson, and a guy nicknamed Doodles, because he liked to draw, sitting in Penry's place, there in the corner, and by their raised hands, and Jack's pointing his finger at Doodles, he knew it was that same old conversation. Did Doodles know there was something called BEOG? Your family didn't make enough to send you to school, all you had to do was ask. You could go to drawing school, Doodles. Really, you could.

Jack had said it for years, and about himself, until it seemed even he, Jack, believed it. There was all this money out there for people like them.

Penry, waiting in the cold, grunted, remembering.

Like they'd ever leave Austin, or their shit lives there, and this dream in Stu's, talk of other places, those too stupid to think of Dunwoody talking, maybe, the army, or the marines, but all of them living on nothing, and saving, and taking the worst jobs, Jack doing grounds work at the golf course, and working weekends at the nursing home, cleaning bed pans and tending to bed sores, and Stacey at his father's failing part-time insurance agency, and Munson at the liquor store, Penry hitting him up for free cases of Buckhorn, which was shit beer, but the only thing he could figure to hit Munson up for, Munson such a coward that Penry was sure Munson had been paying for the cases he walked out into the lot with and handed to Penry.

And none of them, not a one of them, taking a job at Dysart.

Except for Penry. Who they pretended was still one of them, but who they'd come to despise.

And Penry driving the worst car, a red AMC Matador, with a brown plastic top, the car rusted, holes in the fenders so bad Penry'd had to screw sheets of yellow plastic over them so that when it rained, the tires didn't throw mud on the windshield. The springs on the rear nearly shot, and even with a jack-up kit, the car, Munson'd said, still looked like it was six months late taking a shit, all heavy in the rear like that.

Munson had dubbed it the Mattawhore, and the name stuck, going through a number of humiliating variations. Boy I'm Pore. Shit and Snore. The name finally reduced to a final Sore, from, Gee, I'm Sore, but the name spinning off variants he hadn't even understood, Jack getting into it, when he'd had too much to drink, always Jack calling the car things that made the others laugh, but that he, Penry, had to have explained.

Chancre Mobile?

Here he comes, Jack had said one night, in the Excellent Excrescence.

So, not only was *he* a target of their humor, his car became a joke, and there being no football, since he'd dropped out of school to take the job at Dysart, he had trouble finding places to vent this pressure that built up in him, over all that he did not say, over all the slights he suffered.

But there was a time when he'd turned things around, when he'd really shocked them. That night—oh, that night had been *something*.

He grinned, thinking of it even now—waiting over the highway, waiting for Munson, or for the doctor and the boy and his sister—that one bright moment. And here, now, would be another, he'd make it that, he thought, when this was over and done, and everything in place, and he was floor manager, as Throgmorton had promised. He'd recall sitting here in this cold car, and how he'd turned it all around, had outsmarted the last of them. Idjit Penry.

There'd only be Munson to see it happen, but that would be enough, and he checked his watch again, twenty minutes had gone by, and they had that much less daylight to work with. But it could still all work out, he thought, it *would* work out, as it had worked out before, setting up all that with the meat, who would move it, and how, and setting up payments, and getting the right policemen in it, through Throgmorton, and he went back over how he'd pulled all that off, and the other management had never once suspected him, Stupid Penry, Throgmorton even saying he was the *last* one they'd suspect, which got him all riled up again, sitting in the car, but he thought then of that one night.

To calm himself, to show himself it would all still work out. That pivotal night. A diamond of a night, in a life of lumps of coal.

Because that was how he saw it, even now, and with no small pleasure.

He'd taken the job at the packing plant and had been working there night shifts, even before quitting school, and hadn't told any of them, had lied that he had a girl who was keeping him out, and they'd teased him about that. Who'd fuck you, Penry? Pencil dick. Short and thick.

And then had come the pokes, the roughing him up that they always did. Tousling his hair, playing grab-ass at his dick, knocking him around.

Just like his father had.

Teasing.

But all the while he'd been working hard at Dysart, took the worst jobs, shooting the nails through the backs of the skulls of the cattle that came baying and kicking and shitting through the chute, and then on the gutting floor he'd waded up to his ankles in blood, had disemboweled cattle until he was doing it in his near sleep, because, at first, he was still at school, still on the football team, still working out, and he drank gallon after gallon of coffee, and killed with a fury, and the nights he was off he went out with Stacey, and Munson, and Jack, and them teasing him that his girlfriend had to be a heifer, the way he smelled, for Christ's sake, and how his skin was always wrinkled, and he had to put cream on his hands to keep them from chapping, and he worked like that, fueled by rage at the world, but making money, and he'd gotten into the smaller cuts, the fine work, and the management saw that he had stick-to-itiveness, or so his supervisor said, and when he requested full time, he got it, and when he got that, he quit school, and Stacey, and Munson, and Jack looked at him like he was living shit-stink, and he'd worked the long weeks until June, possessed by this plan, saying no to the nights at the reservoir, and drinking, and the word got out that he was over at Dysart, and they barely tolerated him coming around the Town Tap, as if he were some contagious disease, and he grit his teeth through it all, taking all the overtime he could, until the weekend of the Fourth, when, instead of going out to the lake to drink with the others, to sit on the hoods of cars and talk shit about going to college, or going to one of the trade schools up in the Cities, he, Penry, had gone up to Minneapolis, and after two days of talking to dealers, at Win Stevens on 494, and Wally McCarthy, and Tousley Ford up on 61, had been reduced to nearly begging, it had turned out, because being hired full time wasn't like being full time a year or two, and did he own a home as collateral? Another car? Property?

It turned out the best he could do was a twenty-one percent loan from a place in Hopkins, a suburb west of Minneapolis, but still, after the man in the green polyester suit went over the papers with him in the moldy-smelling office, and after there was all the somber talk of payments, and vaguely made threats of what would happen if he didn't make them, only then did the man in the green suit stand and smile the biggest shit-eating smile Penry'd ever seen, and hand him the keys to a *brand-new car, near about zero miles, read 'em, two hundred miles on the odometer,* the dealer said, *just enough to get the car to the dealership.*

But the car had not just been any car. The car was a cherry-red Pontiac Firebird, even with the screaming eagle decal on the hood, and fancy aftermarket flow-through exhaust, and factory racing wheels and factory pin-striping and fancy racing seats.

Penry had spent every dime he had on the down payment, with the exception of just enough money to get him to his next Dysart check.

And money for gas. The thing ate gas like flushing it down a damn toilet.

But boy, oh boy, did it ever go.

Penry spent the day driving up and down Minneapolis streets, slouching, looking tough, even bought himself some Ray-Bans. Laid rubber a hundred times.

He drove for hours, by pools, and beaches, and sat on the hood back of what he found out was Lake Harriet, in the middle of town, just sat on the hood, and girls walked by, and looked at the car.

Girls in halter tops, and with short shorts, and girls on roller skates.

And even girls with guys turned, and Penry felt some satisfaction so deep, he didn't want to go back, not to the slop of Austin, to the killing floor, or the disemboweled animals, to the bellowing, and the lots, and the trains rolling in, unloading the cattle.

He wanted to stay here, as his new self, forever.

Even though the girls gave him wary looks, looked through him to the car, their tits high and tight and nipples showing through, and in those short shorts, and after a couple hours in the sun he felt baked, and spacey, and tried to get a beer at a bar, and they carded him, and wouldn't serve, and he went back out to the lake, circling nearly an hour just to get a parking space, and sat on the hood again, and when he heard someone spit, he turned and saw a black kid there, and he was on him in a second, hitting the kid, and hard, and this laughter, coming from behind, and a cop there, smacking him across the back of the neck, which took him out of it, and the black kid shouting, What the fuck's your problem, man? What's your fucking problem?! and the big, broad-shouldered boys who'd passed just before, the ones who'd spit, turning to look over their shoulders, grinning at the joke they'd played on Penry, and the cop looking after them, and frowning, and Penry forced to say he was sorry, which he wasn't, he was having problems with the coloreds at Dysart, too, and he went back to the car and tried to sit again, but couldn't, so drove again around the lakes, and when he saw a girl on a bicycle, he drove up right beside her, moving carefully and slowly, and reached out and cupped her right breast in his left hand, and she didn't scream, only looked utterly panicked, turning sharply away, and Penry, laughing, drove off, turning up the radio.

Coach had told them, You want something, you have to take it. That's the way it is in this life, he'd said. Winning isn't the first thing, it's the only thing.

That's what I'm here to teach you, boys. How to take what's yours.

And driving up Lake Street toward Highway 35, which would direct him back south, he thought to stop by one of the massage parlors, Donna Lee's, Beautiful Girls, Girls, Girls. He couldn't drink legally, but the whorehouses let him in. But he didn't stop. He was enjoying the car again, and enjoying the look the girl had had on her face, and the feel of her large breast in his hand.

And, he told himself, he couldn't leave the car on the street. Especially not Lake Street. Not ever. Which he wouldn't admit to himself felt like a kind of bondage, all over again, and so he got on the highway and drove south, and he cranked up the radio, and when the traffic thinned down around Burnsville to the south, he hit the gas, something almost like sex in it, the big 455 bellowing and pushing him deep into his seat, and even his eyes feeling heavy with it, and he didn't let off until he saw a car coming up, and he nearly hit it, doing well over one hundred thirty, and the big motor still pulling, when the car had swung on from the ramp, and he just missed it.

And his heart in his throat, he whooped, punching the headliner and easing back to a crawling fifty-five, which felt good, all that fucking power, and just blubbering along, the duals making this low thunder back there, almost hypnotizing him, which he jolted himself out of every few miles, hitting the gas and the car lurching forward, hungry, powerful, potent.

He felt like that in the station wagon now, all jacked up again, and ready to do it. The doctor would have to come along now, he had the tire iron under the seat. He'd snuff out all three of them.

Penry lifted his watch. Twenty minutes to four, they were cutting it very close. But he could feel it coming, it was all coming now. Just like he'd planned it, and drumming his fingers on the dash, so hard his fingertips ached, but a good ache, he thought back to that night again.

His night.

That night, back in Austin, he must have waited an hour for the shit heap that was Terry Faber's, a Beetle with some advertising on it, to pull out from in front of the Town Tap. Then, with a foot heavy on the gas, and the car roaring from both open duals, he pulled up, lights on, the music blasting from the big speakers in the car, revved the car, did a brake stand, the rear wheels spinning and smoking, but the car only inching toward the Town Tap, Munson, and Stacey, and Jack, and all the others inside looking up with great irritation. They saw the low, sleek, powerful car, and Stacey, when Penry sitting so low he could just see over the dashboard, blipped the throttle, even Stacey gave him the finger, all of them glaring, and discussing among themselves who this asshole with the aviators in the lot was, and with narrowed eyes, decided if they should go out and tell him to get fucked, get out, take his rich ass somewhere else, shove his rich daddy's car up his ass, he could see it all, even saw the word *rich* come out of Munson's mouth, and when he'd let it go on long enough, but not so long that they turned away—no, he got that exactly right—he cut the lights, and the engine, sat up and gave them a smile, but left the music on, and they looked, all of them perplexed. Is that fuckin' Penry? one of them said, and then they stood, moving out from the window, taking their glasses of beer with them, and still, Penry did not get out of the car. He left the music just the way it was, a tune they'd all liked, playing loudly, "Rocky Mountain Way," and they'd come out into the parking lot, almost gingerly, and he expected there to be insults, and the usual jokes, but there was none of that.

Not a word.

The car gleamed under the parking-lot lights like an emblem of a hundred different things, but mostly slick sex, wet sex, power, and money, and freedom, all of which they believed in, in part, if not in total, at least Stacey and Munson did. Jack Carpenter told himself he didn't, Penry knew, but it ate at him, anyway.

"Let's see the engine," Jack said.

Penry popped the hood.

The engine was spotless, shiny, smelled of hot oil and drying paint. The engine had aftermarket valve covers, polished chrome that gleamed, hoses that snaked here and there, two massive four-barrel carburetors on top of all that machinery, with throats, bronzed, open like mouths.

"Three hundred ninety horsepower," Penry said.

Neither Stacey, Penry's sidekick, who was feeling, just then, sick with jealousy, nor Munson, who was hating Penry more than he ever had, nor even Jack, who was thinking, Penry'd gotten himself into some real trouble here, said a word.

But a few moments later Jack did the kind thing:

"It looks just plain beautiful, Penry. You must've wanted one of these for a million years."

Penry, just then, he would never forget, had very nearly cried.

He never could think why, after, either, but it was that same thing, that feeling, that had made him do to Jack what he did this weekend, after Jack had betrayed them.

Because Jack had been *different,* Jack had *known better*. He'd known all kinds of things.

Jack, Penry had thought, even then in the lot, get out, go away, Jack, while you can.

But he hadn't said that, because it would have given him away, what he was really feeling, which was a kind of terror at what he'd done, sold his life to Dysart for this goddamn car, and that year, one after the other, they'd all found their way to Dysart, and the jobs there, only Jack had risen right away, showing a flair for numbers, and Penry sometimes thought with a certain meanness that he—and the car—had brought them all down, he who they'd teased so mercilessly, and needed around to feel better about themselves.

Penry the clown. Idjit Penry.

Only the car, he thought, grimly drumming on the steering wheel of the station wagon, the car, he'd found out, when he needed a repair and went to an authorized dealer, hadn't been covered under warranty because of the modifications the first owner had made to it, some wealthy guy from Indian Hills, who'd had the stuff put on before he'd even driven it, and had turned around and dumped it.

Penry'd been so furious, at his first opportunity he'd driven up to the Twin Cities lot where he'd bought the car, and had waited for the man in the green suit to finish for the day, and when he had locked up, and walked to his Cadillac in back, Penry had met him there and beaten him within an inch of his life with the car's tire iron, just like he had under the seat now.

And after, after threats, and talk about what it would take to get the car fixed, he'd left the man there, and he'd driven down Lake Street, and had bought a girl at Donna Lee's, and there had begun his habit of truly rough sex, and they'd told him never to come back, a big pimp threatening to cut him up, and he'd been so jacked, he looked for it again, and got it, at whorehouses, but he had to move around to get it, because that thing inside him had already begun to get away from him, as if it were something apart from him altogether, this hungry, vicious animal, only he'd come to use it, like he had this weekend, and now here he was, in Jack's goddamn car, waiting.

Either for the doctor to stumble out of the woods with the girl and the boy, or for Munson.

But here Munson came now, nodding, and walking stiffly, something wrong there, his face ashen, but not just with cold, and he motioned for Penry not to get out of the car, only went around the hood, and tossing the door open, swung inside, and caught the door with his left hand, pulling it shut.

Penry noticed that—*strange,* since Munson was right-handed.

"Hey!" Penry said. "I didn't think you'd ever get here."

"I didn't think I would, either."

In the car, Munson set himself against the passenger door, looking off over his shoulder to the east, this odd something still there.

"So," Penry said.

Munson's eyes were all over the car now, and he was breathing deeply. It was spooking Penry out, Munson in the car, but not saying anything.

"Well?"

"Well, *what do you think?*"

"I don't *know* what to think." Penry paused there. "I mean, *what the fuck am I supposed to—*"

"They're dead."

"They are."

"In a hundred feet of water, if it's that shallow." Munson pointed to his pants.

Penry saw there was blood on Munson's pants, his pants were caked in it. But something, brush of some sort, had drawn the blood in sharp horizontal stripes back from his thighs. Why? Had Munson been cut, and bled coming back?

"Let's go," Munson said.

"You leave any sign?"

Munson shook his head. He kept glancing over his shoulder, to the road, and up it, the direction from which he'd come. He was blinking strangely, and nodding, and catching himself.

"Where's the canoe?"

"Overshot the car, didn't see you here in the trees," he said, and it had the force of truth, because it was true. "The canoe's off to the west, at the end of the lake. I came up the path there."

Munson only stared into the windshield, still doing that strange blinking thing.

"What are we waiting for?" Munson said.

"We're gonna have to get some other clothes on you," Penry said. They'd all brought things they'd left in the station wagon. "Sink those somewhere. Blood test'd fuck us over but good."

"We'll do it when we get the canoe," Munson said. "Let's go, we only have so much light."

Penry, who'd been all nerves, waiting to go, saw that Munson was holding back on him. He was mumbling to himself, doing that blinking thing, and his head nodding yet again. Nodding to himself. And then it struck Penry what Munson wasn't saying, hadn't said:

If he'd gotten to them, he'd know about the boy. He hadn't mentioned the boy.

Penry started the car, but he didn't put it in gear.

"It's too cold in here," he said, messing with the heater controls.

Penry wasn't sure what to think, but he didn't like any of it. And he sure as hell wasn't going to ask. Was Munson all right with things, now that he'd seen the boy? Munson shifted his feet, then was mumbling again, and when Penry looked over at Munson, he couldn't stand it, not knowing, and he grinned, just to feel Munson out on this, test him a little, and Munson swung around with his elbow, knocking Penry's head back, and he came down on Penry, crushing his head against the headrest, rolling over and kicking the wind out of him with his big knee, wedging himself between Penry and the steering wheel, his left forearm across Penry's throat, choking Penry, Munson applying so much force Penry felt his neck cracking, his windpipe crushed, and this black something swimming up in his eyes, and just when he thought his neck would break, he knocked the tire iron across the floor with his left hand, swept it up with his right, and brought it around squarely on the back of Munson's head, with everything he had left in him, a spray of blood shooting across the tan headliner, and again, and again, and again, until all he could see in the car was blood.

His hands were slick with it, and Munson there, a dead weight in his arms.

64

HE COULDN'T MAKE THEM OUT AT FIRST, THE LIGHT HAD gone gray, and the windshield fogged. But he thought it was the doctor, and rolled down the window and put the camera to his face, ran out the lens.

No, it was the boy, pulling a sled made out of their canoe behind him.

He could hardly believe it. Had the kid done that? Built that thing? And a pack on his back, the straps cutting deep into his green jacket, the pack heavy enough so that he leaned so far forward to compensate, he was nearly looking right into the icy road.

The doctor had to be in the sled, the girl in the pack.

There was nearly a mile to go, and the kid was making slow progress.

For a second he admired the kid, but then he took another look through the camera. He had bruises on his face, and his eyes seemed sunken, and he was moving with great, great effort, jets of steam coming out his mouth, the tumpline biting into his forehead, the pack with the girl in it almost bending him double, and his hand, holding the tumpline, nearly black with dried blood.

Stacey's. Had to be—or was it Munson's?

The boy lifted his head, turned from side to side, looking, cautious, and Penry watched, watched him come on, the woman in the station hadn't caught sight of the boy yet, Penry could see her through the back window, she was reading a magazine, tossing the pages back as if irritated, even as the boy was coming in, like some mendicant, bloodstained and crippled.

Penry could hear, now, the wooden skritch of the sled's runners on the ice. Upwind, and the sound carrying over the ice-glazed road.

And still Penry waited. He had time. There was no going back, no going for Jack now. But here, only this to finish; he couldn't leave witnesses, and the thoughts he'd entertained for so many years, as all of them who'd been in on the stealing at Dysart had, thoughts of running off to Canada, or moving to Montana, or getting a job on a boat in Seattle, but with all that jack in your pocket, came to him, and he saw them now for what they really were, no more than phantasms, which shocked him. So much so, in the car he could think of only one sure thing that would secure a place for him in the world now:

He would wipe out any trace of his ever having been here, which struck him as . . . odd.

Erasing himself, so he could go on.

And so he watched the boy come nearer, let him, because the woman in the station would have to be dealt with, only he couldn't have her calling out on the phone, and, anxious to get moving, he studied the boy through the big lens, holding his breath again, as if that would slow time.

The boy was up the road a mile or so, and had yet to come around the curve there to be in line of sight of the car.

Penry only had minutes, and he thought he could go by the station, to get to the boy, but what if the woman got suspicious? Seeing him pass, even around back? What would she think if she saw him there?

And holding the camera, he knew he could fix all that, simply by going down and cutting her phone line. And he decided he would do that, only he wanted to get a good look at the boy, closer, because he was seeing something, but wasn't sure just what it was yet.

Penry lifted the camera to his face and ran out the lens. Looked. Pants pockets. His calf. The knife there on his belt, tied outside his jacket, hanging at his waist in the leather sheath. Was it just that? The kid's knife? But then, he'd surprised Stacey with it, all right.

Penry now studied the boy's boots, he was doing all right, considering he was walking on nearly sheer ice. Then took in the jacket again.

What was it? And then, *there*—the boy, lifting his head, and looking behind him, then off into the trees, patted his jacket, on the right.

Outlined in the nylon of the boy's jacket was something angular. It was the draw of the material over the boy's shoulder that he'd been seeing, evidence of something heavy in his pocket. Penry's breath caught at it, his heart leaping, running razzle-dazzle.

What the hell—the kid had a gun, one heavy enough to pull the jacket down like that.

———

Penry shut the car door quietly and went down the hill, his feet tinkling on the ice-coated grass. He swung himself off the path, bracing himself on the trees, and when he came to the bottom, and the expanse of the graveled lot, he crouched low, and circled around to the back of the station, moving like a wolf, or shadow, among shadows.

65

LATER, WHEN THE POLICE CAME, AND THERE WAS ALL THAT with the investigation, Cliff Hoffarber would recount what he'd seen, though it was weeks before he could make himself believe it.

Wrong place, wrong time, for his wife.

And as much as he tried to find fault in himself, and he did, a great deal: *If* he'd only gotten rid of that goddamn Polaris, bought his cousin's Arctic Cat. *If* he'd just gone along with what his wife had been pushing, Let's just warm each other up, heh? NSP'll have the electricity back on in no time. Who needs gas? Ha-ha. *If* they just *hadn't* hung on through the month so as to buy that place in Fort Lauderdale . . .

But he couldn't, in the end, blame himself, not really, for what befell him, and his wife, as some fate.

What control had he had of any of it?

That the temperature would drop and they'd use that much LP. That the ice would prevent a truck from just driving in. That he'd left when he had, even leaving the door unbolted. How could he have known, prepared for it after so many years of campers, and hikers, most of them folks just wanting to get away from it all, and those who loved the lakes and the woods, scores of people over the years who'd been cheerful, thrilled to be up north, so much so that he'd enjoyed welding the broken tow tongue on the bumper—free. Enjoyed bolting together the loose canoe rack— free, no charge. And while he worked in the garage, Lorena had poured cups of coffee, which they refused to be paid for, but when they weren't looking, people slipped fives into their mailbox, sometimes tens or twenties, no note, though some even sent post- cards and, once, someone seeing how his socks were worn sent a box of brand-new socks, three kinds, blue, black, and argyle.

All these years they'd kept a gun under the counter, but they'd only used it to scare off the squirrels in their bird feeder winters, since, in the end, neither of them could bear to kill them, and so it was the squirrels that always got to the sunflower seeds before the cardinals and jays and nuthatches, and they'd have to buy all that much more seed.

And winter was quiet, and Cliff worked in the shed, repaired snowmobiles, since gas wasn't a big seller, and they played bridge Thursdays over to Vernon, kept up with their son, who, every year, angrily informed them that, no, he wouldn't be home for Christmas, he'd gotten his fill of the boonies, and was in New

York now, and gay, he'd told them in no uncertain terms, proud and gay, and they'd finally got up the nerve to tell him, last year, Come on back with your pal, then.

Pal, Jeff had said.

Well, you know, Cliff had said, unable to say, lover? Sweetheart? Friend? It was beyond him, but he didn't care, not really, and anyway, he and Lorena weren't as tame and silly as Jeff thought. They'd both strayed, years back, but they'd gotten through it, and that was why, now, all of this came as a shock to Cliff, losing Lorena.

But worst of all, most shocking, was what he'd seen, and the odd fact that none of it felt real.

He had gone for the gas, after the Polaris had broken down, and had called Lorena from the Jorgensons', left there in short order, a new, full tank of LP on his back, Art Jorgenson's tools in his pocket, and he'd got the track back on the Polaris, even in the snow, a real trick, and had run the path at slow speed, even stopping to look out over the lake north of them, the ice in the trees beautiful, if you weren't caught out in it, but had felt nothing, no intimation of something wrong or amiss, saw nothing, but had turned slightly south and, taking another route, had come upon the car, the station wagon with the canoe on the roof, Alumacraft, red band around the gunnels, and the sun, the very last of it, had cut through a layer of cloud piled heavy on heavy cloud, just a shot of light that made him lift his hand to shield his eyes.

He'd felt a rush of blood to his head, fear. He killed the snow machine, turning to look at the ugly brown station wagon.

An Olds Vista Cruiser, rusted, and the big canoe on the rack, but a rack for two, and one man wouldn't use a seventeen-footer. But it was a junk car, and the seats taped together, and why off the road, in the trees? Why not down below, alongside the road?

He began to think of reasons, but couldn't find any he liked. Or that he believed. And he looked up the road to the west, and then opposite, and there he saw, when the sun had settled under the clouds again, what looked to be someone hauling a sled through the last of the trees, and a large canvas pack on his back, his clothes filthy, and a swatch of red across his jacket, and his feet skittering on the ice, and he thought it had to be some kid in trouble, and he came down through the trees, something in his head telling him it was all wrong, everything was wrong, but the sun was out again, shining like some beacon on the boy, and then the door to the station opened, the back door, and here was Lorena in her pink snowmobile suit, moving almost sideways, to the New Yorker, but somebody in it already, in a blue jacket, the hood up, this someone hiding there in the passenger seat, he could see him, because he was back and still above the car, or was he making that part up now, all this time later, that he'd seen that, coming around from the lake and above, or that there was something wrong with the way Lorena was moving, her steps too short, or that she'd seemed too short, and suddenly, his heart was up in his throat, and he was running, and falling, and running down the hillside.

66

DAVID SAW THE WOMAN IN HER PINK SNOWMOBILE SUIT and hood up come out of the station and wave, almost daintily. And so, apparently, did Janie, who reared in the pack so suddenly David almost went over backward, Janie then tucking into herself. She was imagining things, had reared like this a number of times, each time almost sending him over backward, and like the other times, she was still, after, but her knees jabbing him in the kidneys, yet in his head was a hot, raw buzz, even as the woman waved, and she was moving out to help him, and he felt himself softening in the cold, his whole body nearly falling into it, this soon-to-be rescue, someone else would finish it, other people would lift Janie off his back, would see to Max, and he was feverish with the thought, and the woman got into the car there alongside the station, one of those ugly Chryslers with the concave sides, an Imperial, or a New Yorker, silver-blue, and the woman held the wheel in both her hands—odd, the woman gripping the wheel like that, and the rear tires spinning frenetically on the ice, making an icy grating, and the car moved away from the station on the ice, and David came on, exhausted, moving toward the side road, a distance in from the highway now, his jacket open, and the sun burst through a cloud, and he saw on the hillside back and above the gas station a line of red, and then silver, the red line was on a silver background, in the trees, and something in his head told him *Canoe*, and he didn't know why that should be important, the whole hillside lit up suddenly, and a man in a black snowmobile suit skittering down, like a spider, deadly.

He was squat, and heavy, but something in David's mind stuck on it, and he watched the man coming down through the trees opposite, and the man fell, and picked himself up again, then was shouting over the whining of the Chrysler's tires, he was trying to get to the woman in the car, and when David came out on the ice of the service road, he fell again, the ice thick and glazed here, but got up on his knees, to face the car, the last light out of the west blinding, and the car arcing right at them and in a way David did not trust, this, too, was wrong somehow, and he quickly yanked the sled into the trees off the service road, and the car slowed, the man in the trees behind the station waving his hands, at what David couldn't tell, and shouting something, and when the car got closer, a man in a hooded blue jacket shot up beside the woman in her pink snowmobile suit, and David knew him instantly from the jacket, his heart kicking, and the car now moving with a kind of terrible mass, looming up, dented grill and an enormous length of hood, the man who'd attacked Janie there, in the passenger seat, using the woman to get to him, and David reached into his jacket pocket, and as if in a dream, lifted out the gun, and the woman in the pink snowmobile suit, a hostage he was sure, ducked, and he felt the safety under his thumb and snicked it off, and swung to track the face in the passenger seat behind the windshield, and, sure now, he squeezed off a shot, and the gun kicked in his hand and the windshield pocked, the car hugely near, but coming on anyway, still coming on, Penry dodging in his seat, even though he was sure he must have hit him, and he squeezed again, and the gun kicked, the glass shattering in a diamond spray, and a splash of blood on the windshield now, and he pulled again, and again, and again, until he was pulling on nothing, dry-firing, and he stood there in the trees, and Penry's head slumped into that space between the dashboard and windshield, and the woman in the pink suit hunched down, so he could only see her eyes through the steering wheel, the pink peak of the suit there, and the car came on still, looming up through the trees onto the side road, the windows pocked with holes and stained red, splashes of blood everywhere, and the car's tires locking on the ice, just short of David, the car swinging around, rusted chrome bumper, deadly, missing David by nothing, the passing of it making him blink, the car going around yet again, and a hundred feet beyond him, hitting a stump with a loud metal rending, and David, holding the heavy gun, his heart in his throat, and teeth clenched, waited.

And there was nothing. And this inky gloom filled him with an awful weight.

Had he shot the woman somehow? In her pink suit? Shouldn't she be screaming, or running to him?

He was afraid to look. Couldn't move.

This terrible stillness in the car, nothing but the man in the black snowmobile suit, distant, trying to get across the ice to him—he burst out from the station now, running toward him, shouting.

Was he one of them he hadn't seen?

And David, even with Janie on his back, as if underwater, his own breathing seeming loud to him, left the sled and Max on it behind him, moved toward the car, the car having spun to face the station, Penry slumped against the passenger window, so that David went to the driver's side and, looking in, saw what remained of a face, and long hair with barrettes in it, bloodied in the hooded dark jacket.

And beside it—

The pink-suited . . . *whoever* it was spun up, and into the glass. A face in the window, eyes wide, glaring.

Penry.

David tried to hold the door shut, but when he did, Penry scrambled across the seat, climbing over the body there, the body just now blocking the handle, and David, with Janie recoiling in the pack, bolted down the slope to their right and into the trees, in knee-deep snow catching the trees and spinning himself off and down the steep slope to the lake, but only gaining distance, nothing more, a little time, seconds, because the lake was down there, and Penry was cursing behind him, and it was then he felt it, or did he see it?

This shadow, paralleling them in the trees, moving quietly, and hugely there, he couldn't believe it, or was it the man he hadn't seen all this time, who'd given him the look from the porch that morning, was it *that* man in the trees? Jack? And a cry in his throat, he kept moving, but it was all for nothing, the lake coming up, more knee-deep snow here and ice, and still, he just sensed it, or was he just wishing it, that this was Gaiwin in the trees, or was that just the way you died, imagining things were other than they were, even to the last second, wishing, and hoping, and moving? And as he came through the last stand of pines, Penry bore down on them, was on top of them suddenly, reaching for the pack, catching Janie in it, Janie, just then, *alone,* facing Penry, and she let go a shrill cry, a caterwauling that cut the air, and went silent, and David kicked hard and spun to his right, throwing Penry off, Penry falling hard and cursing, and David making distance from him, Janie a leaden weight in the pack, her body bouncing with him as he leapt down the hillside, ran.

How could he be running, after what he'd felt coming in, barely able to lift his feet? But for Janie, gone again, maybe forever, but he would save her, he would, he thought, and the thought of it propelled him down the remainder of the hillside, and when he stopped, just back of shore, his feet shot out to both sides, the ice here, on the stone-lipped shoreline, the worst, and he moved along it, his lungs burning something awful, and when he came to an abutment of granite, blocking the shoreline, glazed and shining in this last burst of sun, he turned.

Penry walked slowly toward him, had a tire iron in his hand, and even as Penry moved toward them, the man in the black snowmobile suit, blocks back up shore, shouted, "Stop, for God's sake! Stop, or I'll goddamn shoot you!"

But he couldn't shoot. Penry, in the pink suit, was in the way.

Just out from the abutment, there was a snow-covered hummock, trees growing around to the side and over it, and David tried to go over it, and slid back down. It was only eight, ten feet high, and not that steep, but the ice made climbing it impossible.

Penry came on, this dull look in his eyes.

David glanced up into the trees. He could try to climb back up the slope, but it would be too slow. And so he turned, and he lifted the gun.

But Penry came on anyway, he knew about guns, and this one a revolver, he had heard the dry-firing, or had counted the shots, had planned it all, even with whoever he'd had in the car, Penry stepping closer, this solemn look on his face, they were all done fooling around, Penry was done fooling around, and when he was nearly on top of David, in that pink suit, but the suit bloody, spattered with blood, David dropped the gun, reached for the knife on his belt, but his hand trembling so badly he couldn't get the snap off the sheath, get the knife out, even as Penry moved closer yet, brandishing the tire iron, smeared red.

Penry held it by the angled end, had reach on David, nearly two feet.

He feinted right, whipped the iron around, nicked David's cheek, then brought the iron around again, closer, and David swung the knife at his middle so Penry reared back, David nearly losing his balance on the ice, Janie's dead weight in the pack throwing him off, David ducking when Penry sent the tire iron whiffing by his head again, and, too low on his feet now, David thought, in that bubble of no time, and all time—

He would have to do it. Spring from the ice, stab Penry, not cut him, and if he was quick, and put all he had into it, Janie would survive, he could do that much, he would do it.

But as he was preparing to spring at Penry, Penry whipped the tire iron down, so that David checked his jab, the tire iron barely missing the knife in his fisted hand, and his feet skidded out from under him, Penry bolting in to stand over him.

He raised the tire iron over his head to strike, and just then, David heard an airy whirring—something flying at them from the trees—and there was a hollow, fleshy crack, Penry, the tire iron lifted above his head, the hatchet buried in his mouth, and in that stunned moment, David yanked Penry to himself by the pink suit, even as Penry let go a howl, struck David across the neck with the tire iron, the blow knocking David sideways, but David plunging the knife into Penry's middle.

Penry's shocked face in his, staring, he rent Penry from his stomach to his ribs, drove the knife up and through Penry, Penry falling on him, and David's head over Penry's shoulder, he saw the long silver blade of the knife slick with blood jutting from Penry's back, the black-suited man up shore bellowing, "My God! WHAT HAVE YOU DONE?!"

David fell to his knees, his lungs burning. He turned Penry's body off him, Penry in the pink snowmobile suit in front of him, on his stomach, and only a shadow in the trees above him, a sound, a crack, a broken branch to make him believe anyone had been there at all.

But for the hatchet.

And then, even as the man in the black snowmobile suit slowed, nearing David, his brows furrowing, and this look of confusion on his face, from a distance seeing the cork-soled boots jutting from the pink fabric of the snowmobile suit, no—*not his wife's boots*—David had the knife free, brandished it in his direction.

The man in the black snowmobile suit stood an arm's length back of David, his pistol hanging forlornly from his hand, Penry between them on the ice. Janie in the pack lay inert against David's spine. A jay called raucously in the trees.

And only when he saw the man meant them no harm did David set the knife on the ice.

———

Later, Cliff Hoffarber would say someone had been there with David. He'd swear it. No, not Penry, he'd tell the police. *Some*one had been in the trees. Or some*thing,* he'd say.

But both the knife and the hatchet, David would protest, had been his. And all had been confusion just then, anyway, and who could say what the man had seen?

After all, Cliff Hoffarber had mistaken Penry, in the pink snowmobile suit, for his wife, hadn't he? He'd dropped to his knees beside David, rolled the body over, and the hood fell back. Here Penry's face, the hatchet having nearly split his jaw in half, and one eye opaque from having been in contact with the ice, Penry rent up his belly, and in that instant, he realized who it had been in the car, who David had shot in the car, and what this man here, lying on his back, staring at nothing, had done.

Not only to his wife, but to this boy and, he assumed, his sister, on his back.

And he asked, "Who is it up there on the sled?"

And David told him, and the man scrambled back up the hillside and returned moments later, bent low over David, and in a near whisper, said, "I'm sorry, son. Your father didn't make it. He's dead." And David, this some*thing* torn from him, a wail rising shrill and long in him, but not a note of it issuing from his mouth, sat heavily on the ice, in the blood that ran from Penry, sat right in the blood, a pool of it, turning the ice pink in the late-afternoon light, and in his pain, he lowered his gloved hand to the pearl-handled gun in the water, thinking to lift it, reload it, have done with things, having failed so badly, but he had no more shells, so instead pressed his finger into the blood, then raised the finger of the glove to his mouth and tasted it, as he did, the man saying something about the police coming, he'd fixed the phone line, and his wife dead, and he asked where they'd been, and who it was here, and he went to the pack behind David, and after a time, kneeling, a quiet, and a tenderness in him, the man kneeling in the blood, too, the blood staining his pants, he got Janie out of the pack, and he didn't have to say it, David already knew, the man cradling Janie, who heard and saw nothing, in his arms.

"He hurt the little girl here?"

"Yes," David said.

The man lifted the hood away from Janie's head. He gritted his teeth and nodded, Janie's pallor and unconscious weight making it clear just how sick she was.

"You did all right, son," the man said.

David let his mouth drop open, and out of him came something like a sigh.

Bloodrock

67

At the university hospital in Duluth, the doctors attending David held him the better part of two weeks for observation. He was badly dehydrated and three of his ribs had been fractured, which they only taped, while measures were taken to save Janie, who was battling an infection that had spread to her kidneys and liver. She'd bloated, the infection having traveled to her lymph glands, too, and she was feverish, her skin having a waxy pallor, and turned from side to side, called for David, but when he tried to reassure her, talk to her, she was not there, only pumped her legs, running in the bed in her catatonia, whimpering, and shuddering, and the police had nearly to threaten David to get him away from her side, and even then, he was uncommunicative and unwilling to be of much help.

And Rachel was not making matters easier, either. She had driven up to Duluth the afternoon they'd come in, and was staying at the Radisson, and when David saw her, in the hospital, she was in her most severe blue skirt and jacket, always a scarf tied around her neck, businesslike, no nonsense.

At first this put David off, but, studying his own face in the mirror of his hospital bathroom cabinet, after she'd left for the evening, his eyes flat, and showing nothing, he'd understood, and as the two weeks went by, he came to fear what would happen when they left the hospital, when they were alone and in the house in Edina.

But, until then, there was the police, and all their questions, to think about.

The police wasted no time, and as soon as David had gotten a clean bill of health, and Rachel had an attorney up to guide David, and to deal with the suits that had been filed against them, against Max's estate, David had gone off to the station downtown, riding in the back of the patrol car, the car smelling of cigarettes, and sweat, and the attorney Rachel had hired sitting beside him, in somber blue, Morrie. Morrie he'd spoken with at length in the hospital, until Morrie had ascertained that there was no reason David shouldn't talk to the police, and they paralleled Lake Superior, and where the avenues intersected, David looked off onto it, the lake so large, and broad, and endless, it seemed more a cold gray ocean than a lake.

At the station, in a smallish room, fluorescent lights buzzing overhead, and the walls down to the baseboards white, perforated, so the room was especially quiet, David sat, Rachel on his left, Morrie on his right, two officers and a court reporter taking seats across from them at the table. But they did not begin, and the officer in charge glanced up at the large, bland clock on the far wall—the kind used in schools, a Waltham, with arms like black needles—and made notes, and at precisely ten, another man, tall, and with dark eyes, and lines on either side of his mouth, stepped into the room, pulling the door shut behind him and sitting, far end left.

"Walter Meyer," he said, "representative for—" and he named an insurance company.

The policeman across from David, who had a habit of pulling at the sideburn on the left side of his face, glanced up and began it.

There was all that with where he, David, had first seen the men, and how many there had been, and would he describe them, and did he get their names.

"And *why* were they arguing, your father and the men?" the officer asked.

David, surprised at this turn in the questioning, told them he hadn't known, since he was off at the outfitter's and had only returned to find them in the middle of it.

"Would you say your father provoked them?"

"Provoked them?"

Morrie, the attorney Rachel had brought in, nodded, and David said, "He was responding to something. I don't know what it was, but they were all pretty hot about it."

"But it must have been enough so that your father'd change

his plans, give one itinerary at the headwaters office, and then go off elsewhere."

"I didn't argue with him about things like that. Nobody did."

"You didn't say *anything* to him?"

David shook his head. "I was happy to be out of there myself."

"But it wasn't enough for your father to get out the gun he'd put in the stern ballast compartment of the canoe. He didn't do that—earlier, I mean?"

David felt a rush of blood to his face. His eyes felt hot, and thick, and that dull feeling he'd had for days was lost in a rush, and he couldn't breathe.

The gun he'd put in the stern ballast compartment?

"Did he?" the officer said, pushing now, his voice noticeably edgy.

David struggled not to shudder, a chill running up his back. Was *that* why Max had gotten so out of control, arguing with those men? Got wound up the way he was on the trip, and David giving him trouble, and all that there between them?

Your father, Gaiwin had said, *was he a little . . . louder than usual maybe, a little tougher? He make any kind of threats when you came in—what, down there in Ely?*

"Did he?"

"Did he what?"

"Did he get the gun out earlier?" the officer said again, now the subtle edge in his voice cutting. The officer slid a gun in a plastic bag across the table. "This is the gun, isn't it? Your father's gun that you fired through the windshield of the Hoffarbers' Chrysler?"

David said he thought it was. He'd dropped it there on the ice, assumed Cliff Hoffarber had picked it up.

"You *think* it is?"

"Well, I can't be sure."

"You can't?"

"Thirty-eight Specials like that are all pretty much the same," David said.

"It's registered to your father."

David was going to answer that, yes, then it had to be the gun, but Morrie touched his arm.

"I'd like a word with my client," he said.

They went out of the room, into the hall, and Morrie bent over him.

"They're trying to show that the attack was motivated by threat, one your father supplied. Or that your father acted first. They're going to go after your father now, and have him waving that gun around in their faces. Did he? Did he do that? Make threats, or even—did he fire the gun?"

"I already told you he *didn't*," David said.

David had told Morrie all of it, how the two men, Penry and Stacey Lawton, had attacked them on the island. How Munson had appeared at the cabin and he'd cut him, so that he'd run off. How Penry'd come at him in the pink suit at the gas station.

And he'd made it clear to Morrie that he hadn't known Cliff Hoffarber'd been coming at them to defend his wife, maybe even to help. He'd thought Cliff might be Munson, or this other man he'd seen earlier, Jack Carpenter.

Clearly, all his actions had been taken in self-defense, Morrie'd told him. "It's a *great* defense, David," he'd said, "the best. Self-defense. Nothing ambiguous about it. You got nothing to worry about, that is, *if* you're telling me the truth." David had assured Morrie that he was, and Morrie filed countersuits against Penry's, Lawton's, and Munson's estates.

Civil suits that included damages, for attack and rape. "With civil suits," Morrie told David, "you don't have to prove beyond a reasonable doubt."

Still, the tangle of it, especially the allegations raised against him, stung.

"It's no blot on your character these son of bitches came after you. You did what you had to do," Morrie'd told him. "Don't you *ever* forget that."

But now he was giving David that X-ray look again.

"He didn't—"

"No," David said.

He could barely feel his legs under him, here, in this hallway, and all its congestion, a policewoman in full gear, blue uniform and Sam Browne belt and nightstick, going by so that he had to turn slightly, Morrie sidling in behind him, and a man glancing up at him from the water fountain midway, this look in his eye, sizing David up, Here was the kid who'd done it, he must have been thinking, nearly taken Penry's head off with the hatchet, and then gutted him, belly to breastbone, and Morrie at his ear again, with his elbow pinched in his hand, and David was thinking, he was marveling, at what his . . . *friend* had done, the cabin he'd burned—the police had written that off to David having just incompetently left the kerosene heater going, which had started the fire, and burned everything around it, but not past the sand down to the shore where the two canoes sat, Munson's, and their cedar canoe, cannibalized for the sled, and the compartment left for them to find, and make their assumptions over.

Max had had the gun in the stern flotation compartment. And how would they have known that with such clarity, unless Max had hidden a box of shells there, too?

The big man—Gaiwin—had left all that for the police.

And thinking it, David realized, his head as if in some fever, *the gun had been there all along.* From the first. And if he, David, had known . . .

Was that what Max had been trying to say in the cabin that night?

Gun?

"You're sure now," Morrie said. "Munson's and Lawson's wives are claiming your father attacked them out there, that they just passed the island you were on and your father opened fire."

"What would they know about any of it?" David blurted, furious. "They weren't there!"

"Stacey Lawton's widow is claiming one of the men missing, Jack Carpenter, called her. Jack was her brother. She's saying Jack called her from Ely and told her if he didn't come back, to look into it. That he'd been threatened—there was somebody who might try to kill him."

"I don't get it," David said.

"Listen," Morrie said. "If your father got out of hand with that gun, so that you had to—"

David glared.

"If they win, you won't have anything left," Morrie said. "So if Max *did something,* you have to let me know. And *now.* You *can't* protect him. Or you'll be tied up in court so long, you'll spend every dime you've got just trying to hang on to the house and what Max left you."

It was this last thing Morrie said that made David look into his face.

"So, I'm asking you," Morrie said. "Is there something about this gun, or how it all happened out there, that you're not telling me? Because something tells me you're lying.

"It just doesn't all add up, David. And those policemen in there know it, too. Are you understanding me?"

David turned his head away. Down the hallway, a woman was at a desk typing, the staccato rhythm echoing up the tiled hallway.

He wanted to say, What things? What things don't add up? Had they found something? Or was it just that it seemed implausible he'd survived? He and Janie had? And he saw now, even as they'd waited for the police to arrive at the gas station, the big man had headed back to the cabin, to make an end of it.

"Well," Morrie said, "this is it, David, for all time, right now. Right here."

He thought back to everything he'd told Morrie earlier, right down to how he'd cut Munson with the hatchet, which he had. And this Jack Carpenter's whereabouts? He had no idea.

It was a good lie, his story, as it was very nearly the truth. And he had no idea why Penry'd killed Munson in back of the gas station, if it weren't just that Munson'd figured out what Penry'd done.

Why should he know? And this man, Jack Carpenter, David had only seen on the porch that morning. So why were they assuming Max had had anything to do with him disappearing the way he had?

Glancing up at him, Morrie said now, "It's going to get very,

very complicated if you're not telling me all that went on out there."

"And I'm telling you," David said, "I *didn't* know the gun was there, *never so much as saw it* until I took the canoe apart. Had to have been there the whole time."

"It was just you then, at the cabin, and before—you and Janie and Max. Not anyone else. There wasn't anyone else, right?"

David shook his head, his eyes on the yellow tiles in the wall opposite them.

So—

This had been the first question he'd been asked in the patrol car on the way down from the station, too, only this . . . Cliff Hoffarber had told the officer what he'd seen, blathering one moment that he was sure he'd seen *some*one in the trees, or some-*thing*? and the next, contradicted himself, as if he couldn't catch his breath, said, "I don't know, I mean, I thought the kid was killing my wife down there, for Christ's sake, that she was driving the car—I mean, it turned out she *was* in the car—"

And David, all the while, sitting in back in the wire cage, and watching the trees, and stone, and water go by, and the rain coming on, heavy, and the windshield wipers squeaking, said nothing.

"It was just you?" the officer had asked, craning his head around to look at David. Square face and hard eyes. "Right?" He seemed to want something from him. There was something sneaky about it, which made David all the more determined to say nothing.

"You're sure what you've told me is the truth," Morrie said.

David nodded. "I'm sure."

And back in the conference room, or interrogation room, or whatever it was, he sat at the table with Morrie again, and told, all over again how Lawton and Penry had attacked them on the island, and then this Munson, at the cabin, and finally Penry, in the car, using the body of the station owner's wife to get him to unload the .38, a trick, and they asked questions until it was lunchtime, about the shells.

How many had he fired? And David had to ask himself, Why were they asking? Had Max brought only part of a box of shells?

And were they thinking those shells missing from the case had gone into Jack Carpenter, wherever he was?

And even that the police would be thinking these things made David furious, which was strange, given he felt almost nothing now—

But for Janie. Why wasn't anyone saying anything about Janie, except Morrie? About what had been done to her?

And when they took a break, he sat in the hallway with Rachel on a bench and tried to eat a tuna sandwich he was given wrapped in wax paper, and he got halfway through it, and stood, going up the hallway to an officer who was smoking, the officer looking him up and down, but with a certain respect, then saw he wanted a cigarette, and seeing Rachel knew what this was all about, and seeing how she did not move her eyes from the wall in front of her, the officer smacked his pack on his palm and offered David a cigarette, clanking his Service lighter open and holding out the flame.

"Thanks," David said, and he started up the hallway, and the officer watched him sit, and followed him, offering the pack to Rachel, and the lighter, and then went on down the hallway to an office and shut the door.

His back against the cold wall, David smoked, Rachel beside him, not moving, and his ash collecting on the floor so that David swept it under the bench, and it settled in him that this life started out there in the woods was not going to be easy.

68

HE WAS QUESTIONED ALL THAT MORNING AND AFTERNOON, AND the day after, and the day after that. It had been raining, and hard, three inches in as many days, and this southern wind blowing, melting the tracks in the snow and ice in the boundary waters, and obscuring what had been there before the inclement weather, which had made it hard to search the islands.

The police found Max's car, and what had been the campsite where they'd first been assaulted, in David's telling.

But there were no bodies yet. Not Stacey Lawton's, which the attorneys for Lawton's widow claimed would prove assault. Lawton's body, were it found, they contended, would be bullet-riddled, his cause of death gunshot, from the doctor's pistol. It turned out, unluckily for David, that the case of Federal .38s Max had bought before leaving the Twin Cities had been found empty in the flotation compartment, all twelve bullets gone, the case having been purchased the day they'd left Minneapolis, from a sports shop off Excelsior Avenue.

David claimed he had shot six of them, and the police accounted for each, in Lorena Hoffarber, and in the car, but what about the other six?

"The other six? I wasn't exactly in a frame of mind to care just then," David told them, "how many shells were in that box. You can understand that, I hope," he said.

And now there were phone calls, at all odd hours. From journalists. Since David was a minor, his name had not been released from the Duluth Station, but nonetheless, it had been leaked somehow.

David talked to none of them.

Still, there were articles in the *Tribune* about the case, and it became more tangled, the attorneys for Dysart then involved, when it looked as though the assault line against Max would be renewed, and Lawton's and Penry's initial actions attributed to retaliation, and what had been done to Janie downplayed, or written off as retaliatory fury, by a number of criminologists hired by Dysart to prove it had been Max's provocation, not Dysart's temporary suspension and threat of termination of Penry and Lawton both, that ultimately brought on what had happened, the figure the attorneys asked for in settlement astronomical, and Morrie's countersuit blocking them at every turn, and the case now about money, and celebrity, each investigating officer taking his turn before the KSTP 9 or WTCN 11 cameras, and through it all, there was, still, no sign of Jack Carpenter, but an unknown source phoned the police, saying Jack had revealed a theft ring within the company, involving the Cirricionis in Kansas City, and the police were following the informant's tip that Penry, Lawton, and Munson could have killed Carpenter, for what he knew about the theft, and then gone after the boy, his father, and the girl they'd run into, about the same time. Maybe the boy or girl, or the father, had witnessed the murder? one journalist speculated.

Through it all, David stuck to his story. But by then he'd said so many times there hadn't been anybody else with him, other than Max and Janie, that he almost believed it himself. Though, truly, in his quietest moments, he never forgot that his life had been spared by this stranger. Or that he had failed Janie.

Failed himself.

———

At the funeral for Max, the week he'd come in, David had talked to Bobby, his uncle. They were walking to the cars, to the black sedans, from the grave site, and he was dry-eyed, and feeling nothing, and it seemed Rachel was, too, feeling nothing, and Bobby surprised him, gently setting his hand on David's shoulder, then lifting it.

"Call me anytime, day or night," he said.

David had stopped walking, the grass underfoot lumpy and uneven, and the smell of wet earth, and damp in the air, and Bobby had continued on to his car, his aunt Katheryn, in it, smiling stiffly through the window at him, and Rachel went by, and to the limousine, a man holding the back door open for her, then waiting for him, but he couldn't move—if he did he was afraid he just might shatter, he was suddenly gritting his teeth so hard against all he felt.

Which was why he talked to no one about it after.

———

But now there were strange thoughts that came to him, at home and waiting for Janie to join them again. Because it was too quiet in the house. And at school, people avoided him; everyone had read about what had happened to him, and his father and sister, in the *Tribune*. But since David had been somewhat of an enigma at Morningside, had been a kind but sometimes painfully shy boy, and not many had really known him, they took license in embellishing on what they knew, were motivated to speculate. And so the rumors grew, and they were, in that adolescent way, dark, some almost as dark as the truth, but all of them, in the end, only entertainments.

And because of his fractured ribs, David was not allowed to run.

He got on the bus mornings, stayed all day at Morningside, even playing uninspired games of chess with the High Q Club, the members of which he now felt he had nothing in common with, Jerry Ziegler and his fears about not getting into the Ivies, and Tom Stratton and his model airplanes, and Judy Bingham, and Alice Lief, and their grades, and student council, and forensics, and pep rallies, and school colors, and all the small things they were caught up in at Morningside, which he'd been indifferent to before, anyway, had stood at a great distance from, all of it flotsam, something old, like a barely remembered melody, one he'd never keened to anyway, there in him this thought that he had died, after all, in that moment, sitting in Penry's blood, and lifting his gloved finger to his mouth, the blood, coppery tasting, and salty, making all of what had happened real.

Just then.

Nothing would ever be the same, and there was no use waiting for it to be, he knew, waiting was useless, the only thing to do was to move on, and know that things changed, inevitably—and one day he simply left Morningside after lunch, skipped all of his afternoon classes, and walked to a bus stop, and took the bus to Fairview.

He'd never visited Janie during the day, or alone, and hadn't gone inside her room for some time, and didn't now, but he was surprised to see that with this yellow light streaming through the window opposite her bed, she only stared blankly at the ceiling, still.

She looked . . . *fragile,* he thought, as if she might evaporate if he so much as breathed heavily near her. And he feared that if he went inside, he might just break down weeping.

So he stood at the window in the hallway, looking in, his hand pressed to the cool glass.

For some time he'd had been too afraid to ask Rachel what the doctors were saying, what Janie's prognosis might be; up until now, that'd she'd recover from the blood poisoning was enough, and she'd done that.

No. There was nothing physically wrong with her now, but her cheeks were sunken in, and her skin ashen, her hair greasy, and straight, and in a dark, dishwater-blond spray on the pillow.

Still, here she lay on her back, staring at nothing, as she had that night.

Under Penry.

David set his forehead against the glass, closed his eyes. He understood his mother's silences at the house now—she spent most of her time here days, had seen this over and again—and told himself to go in. Do it, he told himself, but all he could bring himself to do was loiter there in the hallway, around him the hospital smells, isopropyl alcohol, and disinfectant, and starch from the linens, and this unceasing chatter from the intercom.

Get in there, goddamn you, he told himself, but couldn't, and he alternately felt nothing, and then a guilt so deep his throat swelled at it.

He should have done something, there in the parking lot, listening to Max arguing with Lawton, and Munson, and Penry, he thought.

But that moment, like his life, was gone.

69

JUST AFTER THE HOLIDAYS, RACHEL BROUGHT JANIE HOME. He'd gotten though them, the holidays—the dinners, and the conversation, much of it couched in whispers just out of his hearing, and the pies, and food he had little interest in, and the gifts, from both sides of the family, which he dutifully thanked people for— like a sleepwalker.

"David," Rachel said, "could you—" and he did, clean, wrap presents, scrub the bathroom. He made dinner when she was out, because she was out often again, working extra shifts, since, as Morrie'd warned, the claims against Max, and then against David, wrongful-death suits, all of which Morrie would show to be frivolous—a legal term Morrie seemed to relish—needed rebuttal, needed to be addressed in court.

And David had met with a review board, and they'd gone over his case.

Somehow, they always came to that moment when David, thinking he was shooting at Penry, had put six bullets through Lorena Hoffarber's head, and had then run from Penry, intentionally, to a place where Penry would have no purchase on the ice, and David, with the nails in his boots, had stabbed Penry, when he came on, stone dead, when Cliff Hoffarber was even then behind them, would have caught Penry up, stopped Penry, as Cliff was armed then.

David had done Penry unnecessary harm, the men on the board claimed. It was possible that some kind of rehabilitation might be warranted. Rehabilitation? David had asked. Somebody's blowing smoke, Morrie said. Somebody wants this story to disappear. Or to discredit you, to cut this insurance mess short. "The best defense is a strong offense," he said. "Believe me, sooner or later, they'll drop this nonsense."

Still, at the end of that week they'd even dragged his English teacher in, the awful Mrs. Schwartz, who, with obvious peevishness, incorrectly recounted what David had said in class discussing Hamlet's motivations, that he could see being *angry enough* with someone to kill.

David hadn't explained. Not about Max, or those nights years ago. Or that what he'd really said was, Anyone terribly wronged could feel angry enough to *entertain thoughts* of killing.

And now, even when the radiologist who was monitoring the progress of his recuperation expressed surprise that there were signs of earlier breaks on David's ribs, David held silent.

Fell, David told him, bike wreck, and I didn't want Mom to keep me in.

But David knew: That had been the night Rachel had not come home, though Max had.

Yes, Max had.

And even threatened with the review board's continued attention, their digging into the trouble he'd been in with his friends, Vern and Cleve, he said nothing, his winter, January, and February, and March, a gray waste of days, simply put one foot in front of the other, but in his days these moments that terrified him, as, when very late, Rachel would come in from Janie's room, where she lay on a cot beside her bed nights, and she'd find David at the kitchen table, his head in his hands, and as often as not, he'd be remembering what had happened out there, remembering for all he was worth.

Because he believed he had to know it, had to own it, make peace with it, as though it were some black diamond, one that—once he had turned it in his hands and seen it in all its sharpness and awfulness—he would be able to toss in a pool, in deep water, an abyss, and walk from.

But he couldn't.

And so, one night, failing that again, he thought back to that last good time, the birthday, and the cake, and the laughter, and how they'd wrenched themselves out of a bad moment, smearing the cake on their faces, and laughing, this the last time they'd been themselves.

When they'd had one another, for better or for worse. This the last moment.

And so it was while he was remembering this, and holding it, this true gem, that Rachel came up the hallway in her blue robe with the gold monogram, Max's robe, and sat at the table, this night now in April.

"Can't sleep?" she said.

No, I'm a somnambulist, and I'm just honing my craft, David thought.

It was a Janie thought, Janie, always joking, playing silly, the clown. He understood her now, in a way he'd never dared to before, saw how brilliant she'd been, how invisible in her efforts, and his loss was all the greater for it.

Rachel glanced at the clock. It was a little after three.

"How are you doing in school?" she said.

David shrugged. It really wasn't a question about school, but about . . . something else now. After his time of skipping classes, Rachel knew, he'd applied himself—so much so his calculus teacher had called to suggest David consider early entrance at a local university, the teacher's alma mater. He'd help get David in. The teacher had also sent away for catalogs from a number of small, well-known colleges, most of them on the East Coast, but the thought of going away hadn't sat right with David.

In fact, he knew he *couldn't* go. He *wouldn't*. Even though he'd dreamed of going to such places. He would try to leave Morningside early, as his teacher had suggested he might. Stay in town. He was sure of it.

For Janie.

And, too, he was sure now Rachel would probably ask him what she needed to know, after all these months, and he wouldn't tell her, he didn't have the heart for it.

"Coffee?" she said.

David nodded, then took the cigarettes from his pocket, knocked one out and lit it.

The microwave dinged, and Rachel swung back to the table with two mugs, both steaming, and David sipped at the rim of his, wary.

"Your coach called."

"Did he?"

"He wants to know when you can start practice over at the university. There's an indoor track there."

With a shrug, David took a deep, angry drag on his cigarette.

"So?"

"I think you should. It'd get you out of the house and . . . you know."

"What?"

Rachel set her elbows on the table, turning to look out the window. What had been snow now came down as rain, pelting the window.

"Sitting there beside her isn't helping, just sitting and reading like that," she said.

David had taken to reading trash books by her bedside, cheap thrillers, and espionage books, and science fiction adventures, spent whole afternoons there, not saying a word, and getting through one and starting another, and smoking sometimes, which Rachel thought was bad for Janie.

"She knows I'm there."

Rachel wasn't brave enough, or was it that she was just too despairing, David wondered, to argue with him?

Even after all these months, Janie'd shown almost no sign of so much as knowing either he or Rachel was there. And it was Rachel who insisted she clean the sheets, move Janie so she didn't get bedsores.

Tonight, though, it wasn't going to be about Janie. David just felt it.

"David," Rachel said, not turning from the window, "I've wanted to ask you something."

Cupping his hand, he flicked the ash off his cigarette, sat wondering what to do with it, then stood and went to the sink. He dropped the ash and ran the tap, the ash, caught in the water, gone.

He needed to think, but there wasn't anywhere to go with it, so he stood with his back to Rachel.

"When you were on the trip with Max," she said, this hook in her voice.

How was it? David thought. What should he say? What could he say?

He wasn't about to tell her that the last thing he'd said to Max, when Max was in his right mind, was for him to fuck himself, and many times over. It turned his stomach to think of it, and he felt that weeping-boy thing all over again, how impossible it had been, all that whatever-it-was between them.

When Rachel didn't go on, David turned from the sink. Rachel's hand was shaking, and he offered her a cigarette and she took it.

She glanced over at him, her eyes glassy, and she looked girlish, and embarrassed, and hurt, very badly, in a way that frightened him.

And so he struck on what he thought was the truth, and what he could live with.

"You know, he was really trying. Really, really trying. He was still . . ." But he wasn't going to say it, though he wasn't going to lie, either. "He was still Max, you know, but I think . . ." He shrugged, glanced up at her. "I think it could've worked out."

Rachel let out a sob, but in it relief, and David felt something like grace in that moment. There, he'd said it, and all it meant that went with it:

That she hadn't made the wrong decision, for nothing, letting Max back into their lives.

That there had been something there, some reason, to send them out in the first place.

That the man she'd loved had, after all, loved them enough to really do something with himself, the part of him that was trouble.

And all of it was true.

But out there on the water, it hadn't seemed like that, or had David just been expecting too much? Had he been too hard, too set against him? Or had it been that, for whatever reason, it hadn't been in him to forgive Max, that in him, always, would be this hard place, as there was, even now, this hard thing in him that made him grit his teeth, while Rachel cried, that made him feel nothing? Or was it just that he wouldn't *let* himself feel it?

Lifting her head, and turning to David, Rachel said, "Thank you," and she reached for his hand and squeezed it, and David smiled.

"Wasn't me," he said.

"Oh," she said, "but, David, you were always a wonderful boy. Did you know that?"

And David, so torn up by this, couldn't speak, or bring himself to move away from the table.

70

HE WAS RUNNING POORLY, HIS STRONG SUIT DISTANCE AND uneven ground and hills, but here at the university in the center of town was just an indoor cinder track, in an immense, high-ceilinged brick building, really only four walls and a roof to keep out the elements, which seemed to amplify his sense of pointless-ness, this going around and around for nothing, in an echo-filled, empty space, and it being far too muddy to run outside yet, and he paced himself to Simonson now, neither distinguishing himself nor embarrassing himself, but only orbiting the field like something caught, like an injured bird, and so Coach decided to put David in the middle of a relay, so that others would depend on him, and see if David could have at it that way, get his old nerve back.

A relay of university students, all on track scholarships. Redshirts. Freshmen.

Eight-eighty.

And so it was on a rainy day in late April that David doffed his warmup suit, intending to run with Simonson, and today Pretorius, when two runners he'd watched, and admired, with a kind of beaten-down, tired kind of admiration—this wasn't his game anymore, but then, nothing was—sauntered over, for what reason he couldn't think.

But it recalled all that with Rick Buddy, so he was looking for something he could use to defend himself with, something on the track, or near him, anything, when the taller of the two said, "We got a runner out today. We need somebody for relay. It's just prac-tice."

David shot a look over his shoulder. Simonson and Pretorius were off the track, stretching. David had already gotten his in.

Coach was farther back, pushing some sophomore wanna-bes, blowing his whistle in short jabs, and shouting, "Push it! Push it!"

Which made David feel like doing anything but.

"Ask them over there," he said, pointing to Simonson and Pretorius.

"Can't hack it?" the shorter said now. He had legs that were heavily muscled, a sprinter's legs.

David felt the excuses heavy in his mouth. All the excuses. All of which made him feel even more leaden, caught in himself. Coach didn't care, and he thought, with just this bit of spark, Why not? The sprinter would take him in the first fifty, and after that? He'd blow his stupid doors off.

"All right," he said.

––––––––––

He had his hands on the track, the cinders sharp, and there this surprise now: He smelled things, as if for the first time since . . . since *back then*—a dusty smell, and a sour body odor, and the tang of new running shoes—and he heard the clap of the starting gun, and he bolted away, the others pulling ahead, but this . . . something surging out of him, and he fixed his eyes on the back of the tallest, the strongest, and passed three others, including the sprinter, who shot him a hostile look, all breathing heavily, and he came up behind the front runner, and he paced himself there, the others behind, around the track once, and not seeing, not feeling, not hearing anything, but this clock in himself, this elastic something, this bubble, and he ran into it, and only if he pushed hard, very hard, could he stay in it, and the pain there was something almost unbelievable, he'd almost forgotten that part of it, lungs burning, but this elastic power in his legs, and his body alight, light, something burning bright, and he was on top of the runner in front of him, and he came up on the second man in the relay, his teammate, waiting there, poised for the handoff, and was so focused on passing the runner ahead of him, he was just feet behind him and closing, that he overran his teammate, who charged by him, taking the baton, and there were angry shouts from his ersatz teammates, but they were as much startled as angry, because David had nearly run down Eric Joiner, a favorite for the coming AAU tournaments. But David knew none of that, though Coach did, and because of it, he did not go over, did not congratulate him, the others would tell him, and the possible future was written right there—possible, Coach thought, as he knew potential was only that, possibility.

He'd seen dozens of runners with potential. But it took more. That was the real mystery of running. It took something—something he could not, even after twenty years of coaching, define. But he called it heart.

It was a disturbing thing to discover in a boy, because this same heart had caused one of his runners to kill himself—after he'd lost an NCAA conference, he'd hung himself from a rod in a clothes closet at home. Another had driven insanely and had met his end that way, crashing his souped-up Mustang, the State Hi-Po had said he'd been doing over one twenty when he went off the road. And still another had taken a nosedive into alcohol, which, when he saw this once-runner around town, a man in his thirties, he could see what had once made him unbeatable now was killing him.

So it was not so much a gift, sometimes, as it was . . . what?

And now this kid. David.

You don't wish demons on people, he thought, watching David run, but he knew them when he saw them, and this kid had them in spades.

But even more, he had heart. This kid would give the sons of bitches a fight.

And here, with the university boys, those he'd goaded into running with David, he could see now tremendous resentment, they didn't congratulate him, either, or have a kind word, the kid was just sixteen, but there was that other thing there, too—admiration. In the way they whistled among themselves, and glanced over their shoulders at him, David there, alone, kicking his shoes in the cinder track, wondering what to do with himself.

David, just in that moment, alive again.

Coach blew his whistle, three short, for all in.

71

BUT AT HOME THAT EVENING, THE DAY HE'D RUN THE
relay, it was more of the same. Rachel was going to be late, and he
put together a hotdish from a box and the things Rachel had left in
the refrigerator, set it in the oven, and went down the hallway, and
there said hello to the nurse Rachel had hired, a silver-haired woman
who like to darn, or read *Redbook,* or *Woman's World,* or clip
recipes from newspapers on her shift.

"Hello, Doris," David said.

Doris looked up cheerfully from her magazine. Sometimes her
cheerfulness made David want to hit her, he felt so irritated by it,
yet today he felt—

He wasn't sure. Different.

"All right, then," Doris said, and standing, she passed David,
nodding, smelling of the awful ointments they put on Janie, and
spearmint gum, which she chewed by the pack, and she got her
things in the hallway, and she said she'd be back at the usual time,
just as she'd done now for the last two months, and Everything
all right? And David answered that it was, and with a curt nod
she went out the door, pulling it shut with a click of the lock
behind her.

Doris had already fed Janie (it was a job David couldn't bring
himself to help with) and David went into the kitchen and got an
orange, and then it struck him what he wanted to do.

He went into his room—he'd been studying in Janie's, so hard
at it he had moved his desk there, after Rachel had taken out the
cot and hired Doris—and rummaged through his books, boxes
and boxes of books, none of it organized, his room a mess. He
hadn't really *seen* his room in months, he'd slept here every night,
sure, but he hadn't seen it, and it looked awful, the sheet on the
bed thrown back, and the dresser cluttered with letters and
brochures from universities, crumpled exams, pens and pencils, a

worn three-ring notebook, magazines, a tape player, the last thing he'd thrown there a speeding ticket.

He hadn't had his license a week when he'd gotten it, and then a second, and then a warning.

The room seemed suddenly suffocating, the clutter, and the mess of it, and he saw it now as if he were someone else.

And seeing it, he felt a kind of temporary panic, digging through the books, now in the closet, then under the bed—dust bunnies galore, and a sock, suspiciously dirty, which embarrassed him somehow—and he stood, setting his hands on either side of his head, surprised at how angry he felt, so angry he couldn't think.

Where *was* it? What Janie had loved him to read to her, and what he'd hidden, at least put out of sight, because it had hurt him to remember anything. Before. Because he'd come to think he *had* died out there, and thought of the date, even, as that, his death, and the resurrection he'd been waiting for—to come out of this void he was in, so far inside himself he was surprised his very thoughts didn't echo—hadn't come, but he felt something of it in him now, and he had to act on it.

Not later. Today. Now.

He began to dig through things, a box of old Heathkit radios, a shortwave kit, car models, a box of Junior Great Books, and he began to throw things from a box, the contents strewn across the floor, as if there lay his very childhood, model airplanes, and grotesque creatures he recalled as having been named Weirdos, and he tossed out the contents of one box after another, until there were no more boxes.

He thought of Janie then, in the room across the hallway, and he straddled the mess, digging again, now in his dresser drawers, under the bed again, in his book cabinet, ripping a page from *Green Eggs and Ham,* and balling it in his fist, and punching a hole in the cabinet's glass doors, cutting his knuckles, but still he continued to dig, this strange whimper in him, this panic, it's not here, it's not here, so *where is it?* he thought, but still tore lids from boxes, overturned them on the floor, kicking through the junk, until he'd nearly overturned the whole room, and then remembered, and was—

almost—elated.

(He wouldn't have said it, didn't think it, but in his mind was magic, was incantation, was elixir, was potion, was magic word, was—because the neurologist had said nothing was wrong with her, with Janie, not really, that she could, just any time, pop out of it, and he warned them that when she did, she might be screaming, right in it, there was no saying with cases like this, with—but he didn't say it—catatonics.)

David left his room and went into Janie's, and at his desk yanked out the bottom right drawer, packed with junk, Estes rocket parts, discarded pens and pencils, fishing lures in crumpled packets, baseball cards, and he lifted all of it out until he had what he was looking for, the book Janie had loved, this once seeming saccharine book, but which he now saw might be some flip side of the coin they'd tossed, he and Janie, heads down.

He felt, holding the book across from Janie, both something awful—because somewhere, sometime after what had happened, he'd thought to do it, but hadn't been able to, he'd been too afraid, not for Janie but for himself—but now, just today, after running again, for the first time he also felt . . . *hopeful.*

He would try this.

And he sat by the bed, Janie turned to the wall, and he opened the book, and when his throat swelled up, he imagined himself with the tumpline around his head, and the pack on his back with Janie in it, told himself this was nothing sitting here, lied to himself, but falling inside himself again, frightened for himself at it, he turned back the pages anyway, and quietly began.

"'The mole had been working very hard all the morning, spring-cleaning his little home.'"

He had to stop at that, his throat had swollen so badly at it, and he looked at Janie, wishing for some change, this miracle, but she didn't move. He couldn't even tell if she was awake.

"'First with brooms, then with dusters; then on ladders and steps and chairs, with a brush and a pail of whitewash; till he had dust in his throat and eyes, and splashes of whitewash all over his fur . . .'"

He read to her until he smelled the hotdish burning, then went into the kitchen and scavenged what had not burned for himself, leaving a large portion for Rachel, who was out late tonight.

David knew it might be Jarvis, he'd called and asked about her, and David had hung up on him. He'd called a few times since all of it had come out in the papers, what had happened, and how the district judge had dismissed the lawsuits that had been filed against them as insubstantial, of no merit.

So deep had they been in reclaiming their lives that the judge's decision had caused not much more than a ripple in their day. A sigh of relief, soon glossed over by their concern for Janie.

David took his bowl and went back into the bedroom, where the book had fallen onto the floor. He picked up the book, trying to find the right page, the hotdish perched on his lap.

He opened the book to the first page again, and he began to read, his voice taking on the tone of a hymn, or of a cantor, or of benediction, and he knew to fill the room with that voice, and he read.

———

He read the book all that week, and part of the next. And he ran. He ran over at the university, and there was some flap about his eligibility if he did run, and David paid it little attention, because cross-country would start soon, and he would have months before fall and the football team coming out, and Buddy out with them, but Buddy was never far off in his thoughts.

Just his name, some dark premonition. Buddy.

And he ran. He ran into the bubble, and he was out again, himself, running, if just for those moments, and he began to think he really would leave early, leave Morningside, there was nothing in it for him, it was long over, he'd toss it as he had everything in his room—he'd taken his models, and radios, and junk out in bags, knowing, maybe, someday, when he was not so hard on himself, he would regret this, but he did it anyway, threw away his childhood, threw away everything, but for a baseball Max had given him, autographed by Harmon Killebrew, and in this destruction was a dark joy.

But his greatest joy was Janie.

Now when he read, if he stopped, she would shift in the bed. Now when he paused, she stiffened, waiting. And it was this he was doing, testing her.

He said nothing about it to Rachel, who sat, evenings, in her grief, so silent he wanted to tell her if anything she was hurting Janie, just hovering there, and all this dread and loss in her quiet.

All these months.

And David said nothing, because he hoped—a kind of hope against hope—that what he saw was real, the twitch of Janie's fingers, how her legs stiffened, how she tilted her head to better hear.

And he hoped she could feel what he brought into the room, almost as if he cupped this light in his hands, carried it from his heart, and set it there, for her, in his voice, in his footsteps. In his setting his hand on her shoulder while he read, turning the pages with his thumb, sometimes hating her for her messing herself, and the rubber sheets under the linen, and the horror of feeding her, which he couldn't bear, but did anyway now, and feeling weak and terrible for not being able to do it more often, and so he all the more brought this calm to her in reading, and he was true to his promise, though today had been an awful day, Buddy showing up at the field house, a soon-to-be redshirt for the university football team it turned out, lifting weights on the far end of the fieldhouse, and Buddy eyeing him, and there in David this terrible sinking feeling, and he was feeling it so powerfully, he almost turned from Janie's room, but decided to go in, anyway.

Read to her.

She'd saved his life, earlier, in that bad time. How could he not?

"Okay, Sport," he said.

He hadn't used her nickname since . . . back then. And it surprised him that it just came out.

He balanced his hotdish on his lap; he could never get himself to use a TV tray, because that would be too permanent, and the book fell, and he picked it up, and suddenly he could barely breathe, for the pain he felt, but he opened the book—he'd been in the middle somewhere—at the first page, and began again, and Janie said, "You were at that part where it goes, 'The mole subsided forlornly on a tree-stump and tried to control himself, for he felt it surely coming.' That's where you stopped," she said.

David sat in his chair, stunned.

Janie turned slowly to look at him, her eyes still gray-rimmed, and sunken in, and he couldn't control himself; he bent around her, and gathering her up in his arms, wept.

After a time, she said, "Put me on the throne, I need to go."

"Okay, Sport," he said.

And he did that.

72

RACHEL WAS HYSTERICAL. SHE WAS ONE MOMENT IN TEARS, beside herself with something beyond joy, and the next cried out of relief. She could not sit, but went on a whirlwind cleaning, threw out clothes that were worn, threw out magazines and papers and books that had risen on anything she'd been able to set them on in the house; and the rubber sheets were gone, and Janie's spindly legs were the issue, spindly like when she'd first come to them, and Janie's diet was the issue, and she'd grown, almost two inches, lying there, and when she was on her feet, it was odd to see how there was this change in her, and they went for walks outside, always in well-populated parks, to Como Park, in St. Paul, or Hiawatha, and the grass was coming up, and there this smell of wet earth, and the tulips came up, and in the lilacs, everywhere, there were buds, millions of buds, and the air softened, and the snow smell, that ashy dry snow smell, was replaced with the smell of warm earth, and pavement.

Now came evenings of billowy cumulus clouds, warm sunshine, the windows open. And to children, bicycles, and kites, and for boys, toy gliders, and to some, silly model rockets, and baseball tryouts, and cleated shoes, and the end of school not far off, and track in full swing, and passing fields, the bright yellow sounds of whistles, coaches shouting, and the dirt of the winter washed down sewer gratings, and robins, red breasted and so common, familiar, but each a sign, a portent, of abundance, of life, of light.

This was the world David and Janie returned to.

Which was itself a miracle—and that Janie was with them, at the table evenings, eating, emaciated but putting on weight, and joking, she was always joking, and Rachel cut her hours back, and was let go, but she hired on elsewhere and seemed happy, and David ran afternoons, taking seconds off his time, and David and Janie and Rachel laughed there, over dinner evenings, what seemed for the first time ever.

All of which David held close to his heart because he took nothing for granted now.

His very life was a miracle, a blade of grass a miracle, the nuthatch that came to the feeder, and sang, no small thing.

But he could not make himself work at school. Something, something almost perverse, closed his mind to it, kept him in a state of agitated distraction. He'd been warned his admission to the university in town the following year wouldn't work out if he didn't change things. Apply himself. Do the required extra work.

He didn't.

He ran.

———

In physics, he listened to Mr. Kepling, then perfunctorily carried out experiments. He wasn't rude about it, though his lab partners were frustrated with him; he'd take part in lab, even carefully do his portion, exactly, as in the wave generation experiment, but just that, and nothing else. Not the extra work. And the same in History, and German (his relatives still asked him why he would study, of all things, German, and he'd joked, to know the enemy better). And in English, they were doing *Lear,* and not a one of them in the room understanding any of it, or why David stood abruptly and left the room at Lear's speech, David almost flying out the door at the second "never."

And outside of his classes?

Polished floors, the ruffle of corduroy, and Tabu, a perfume that was popular, cliques, girls in huddles in front of lockers, and charm bracelets, and the guys, in leather, or letter jackets, or burn-out gear, jeans torn through the knees, and cannabis leaves embroidered here or there, all yakkety yakkety, and he knew he was long gone, and there was no coming back, but what he couldn't say to himself was this: He'd *never* been there, anyway.

————

But on the track, at the university field house, he caught his stride. The gun would go off, and he'd bolt, and push himself, and push, and push, and push, sometimes almost in a panic, until he found his sweet spot, his bubble, his rhythm, which he expanded and pushed at, further, always closing the distance between himself and the fastest runners, and he stopped smoking, just as Coach had known he would, and he ate voraciously, the kid would down three Whoppers at one sitting when they were on the road, in Madison, Wisconsin, or up in Duluth, after a meet, paying no attention to anything, or anyone, only a jab, from Simonson, or Pretorius, whom he shared a word with, though David was no longer a boy.

Coach saw that, but Rachel didn't.

And Coach saw this bigger kid, still in high school, but a red-shirt for the university for the following year, this Buddy—he'd asked about him, and what he'd heard was not good—hanging around, running sprints, Buddy a lineman, and huge, and Buddy and David avoiding each other, or was it David avoiding Buddy, so that he knew there was some history there, but knew not to ask David about it.

In his years, he'd seen his fair share of Buddys, this big goober, this lout, this asshole.

There were kids who played tough, got mean, even hurt other kids, but most of them were just boys, hurt at home somehow, and venting.

Not Buddy—no, he was the real deal.

And so one afternoon, after relays, he'd waited until the two were watching each other, Buddy on the free weights at the end of the field house, doing sets of military presses, and squats, and David with a towel around his neck walking off an 880. He'd quietly come up behind David and stood beside him, Buddy glaring at them both, and Coach putting this look on his face David had never seen. Was reminded—for a second—of Penry.

Coach meant for it to be a warning, but David knew it for how Buddy took it.

A challenge.

73

DAVID DID NOT SEE BUDDY, THOUGH, THE WEEK FOLLOWing, the second week of May. At the field house, or at his meets. Or even at school. And not seeing him around, he worried he was waiting just out of sight. At the water fountain when he got a drink in the hallway at Morningside. Or in the parking lot when he walked to his wreck of a car, a tan Buick Skylark. On the path around Lake Cornelia when David ran, now, perhaps faster than he'd ever run, or ever would again.

Heart ticking like a racing engine, and his legs pulling hard.

By the trees, willows, and enormous elms and oaks, and by the lake itself, by bulrushes, and cattails greening and swaying in the spring breezes, and by lilac now burst into purple resurrection and the air thick with it, sweet, lovely lilac, and he felt his legs, sinewy, carrying him up the steep hill, and he sprinted then, uphill, and into the now-green yard.

But even then, the moment was marred by thoughts of Buddy. He was out there.

One night, after a late run, David waited until Rachel and Janie were asleep, then went into the garage. He brought with him a baton and a roll of cloth athletic tape he'd taken from practice. There was a large vise on a tool bench, and he lay the baton and tape alongside the vise, and rummaged through the boxes of old plumbing under the bench. Max had been a thumb-fingered do-it-yourselfer, but he'd also been one never to throw things away. In the boxes were old sinks, rusted traps, and here, what David had been looking for, lengths of inch-and-three-quarter lead waterpipe. He found one that was long enough, nearly two feet, and setting the baton over it, marked it, and then, thinking again, rummaged through the box of old plumbing supplies until he found two lead end caps, both nearly the thickness of the cloth tape wrapped at either ends of the baton. This would make for more work, but David was good with his hands, and he went through Max's tools, and was suddenly stricken with grief, recalling Max, how he'd laughed with them at the lake that evening. It surprised him like that, nearly blinded him, his eyes glassy, but then he had it, Max's tape and threading tools—Max had had all the tools you needed, and, in typical Max fashion, had used them, maybe, once.

David measured the depth of the threads in the caps, then measured the length of pipe against the baton again, and marked the shaft a second time.

He clamped the lead pipe in the vise, and using a hack saw, he cut the pipe to the length of the baton, minus the end caps. He fixed the threader to the right side and lay in the threads, then did the same opposite.

He screwed the caps on and measured the length of what he had against the baton.

Same.

The baton was silver, the lead pipe dark gray, and David fixed that, with a can of silver paint. Set the pipe upright on one of the end caps and sprayed it, until it looked to be aluminum. He went outside while it dried, and lit a cigarette, there nothing boyish in him now, and his mind made up.

If Buddy came after him, in the field house, he would kill him.

No kid stuff. No warning.

He'd promised to injure David, and publicly, and David wouldn't have it.

He sat there on the stoop in the dark, a hundred voices in his head, telling him, Don't do this, go to Doctor Parker, he'd listen, or tell Coach, tell Rachel, but there was something in him that refused to do any of it, any of this *telling* anyone anything, even in that word some awful humiliation, *telling,* and he would not be bent to it, or anything else. It was between him and Buddy, he thought, sitting calmly.

He had failed up north because he'd been surprised, and unprepared.

Not this time.

———

He went back into the garage, the paint fumes all the more noxious for drying off the pipe. But the paint was glossy now, hard. He opened the windows, and a shaft of moonlight fell on the bench.

He removed the stripe of green tape from the baton and wrapped it around the lead pipe, wrapped the ends in the white athletic tape.

He lifted the new baton, four and a half pounds of lead. He swung it. The caps were a good idea after all. There was heft in the baton.

Now he was ready.

———

The following morning, he left the house with the baton in his book bag. At the field house that afternoon, he had the baton in his track bag.

When they took a break, and Simonson and Pretorius were at the east end of the field house, David hid the lead pipe baton behind the water fountain, opposite, in a broken cinderblock full of crumpled candy wrappers.

When he left the field house, no one noticed his bag hung lightly on his shoulder, or that there was a hardness in his eyes.

Or was it just determination?

———

On Thursday of that week, after dinner, and watching some inane show on television, the three of them laughing, and after Janie was in bed and sleeping, Rachel asked David to come out, sit on the steps as they used to do. It was a cool evening, and along with the scent of lilac, now there was also rose, and crab apple. They'd blossomed up and down the road in from Sixty-sixth, the roses in well-tended gardens, and the crab apples heavy with blossoms, enormous pink or white trees just in from the street, but like phantom shapes in the dark, and the breeze blew the scent by the house, and neither David nor Rachel spoke.

David got out his pack of cigarettes.

"I thought you cut that out," Rachel said.

"I did."

There was a contradictoriness to his behavior at times, and Rachel thought not to mention it. So when he offered her a cigarette, she took it.

They smoked there, all they'd lived between them buoyed up in the dark, with the smoke, and, just sitting, there really wasn't anything to say. And when he got to thinking about Max, and remembered an evening like this, when they'd played catch on the lawn, he told Rachel about the meet.

Rachel told him Coach had already called about it. David was a minor, after all, she said, and chuckled, this in itself a joke.

"I think it's wonderful," she told him.

She'd wanted to tell him that he shouldn't pin all his hopes on this track meet the following afternoon, or the athletic scholarship to the university in town he might win at it. That there would be other meets, other opportunities. That, maybe, he shouldn't cut his last year at Morningside, that he could make things easier on himself. She'd wanted to tell him that, if he could just . . . *wait*, the money would come, and they'd be able to afford one of those schools he'd wanted to attend, out east, but it was all wishful thinking with Max gone, and it was too late for her to do what she'd wanted to do, and because she'd let what David feared happen to her, her life thrown off, because she, herself, had helped put Max through school, had held things off, she was not going to do it with David.

Especially not given what they'd been through.

Which made her feel, in the dark, as if she were in some

strange dream, her life, so unlike what she'd imagined for herself, the girl in drama class, meeting the doctor-to-be taking the class for distribution, and so awkward, but sure of himself anyway, this thumb-fingered boy she'd taken on.

And here she was. Max gone, and her own son leaving, already. Max had left home early, too.

But David was nothing like Max. This boy-man beside her.

Oh, the things she wanted to say to him, her hands crossed over her knees, the cigarette smoke curling up in the dark and gone. Everything gone, but this, her children, really. And David, her first.

All she loved in him, just the way he was, so much the very things Max had so *dis*liked in him—that David could seem impossible, once he made his mind up, which was like Max, only David *knew* people. Like he'd known Janie, when they'd brought her home.

At a glance even. Understood them.

Max had always called him willful. But Rachel had known it from the first as something else. And other people saw it, too—David had not been popular, or silly, and he'd come home hurt, one day, because someone told him he had an "old face, like someone from a long time ago." Not boyish, or cute.

And he stared at people, or, really, into them. Didn't turn away.

Exactly unlike Max.

All this she thought in a second, in the graceful lift of her hand, and the tap of the cigarette, the ash falling, and she wished for her son some happiness, but she knew his life would have other satisfactions, perhaps very difficult ones.

And in the darkness, and knowing, maybe, this would be the last time they would sit on the stoop like this, she did what she knew she should.

She said only this: "I'll be there tomorrow with Janie to cheer you on." And she allowed herself this one small thing.

She rumpled his hair and he smiled, not pulling away, not shrugging her off as he'd done for some time, though he didn't say the words she wanted to hear.

He said, "Thanks," and nodded. And crushing out her cigarette, she went inside.

74

BABEL. THAT'S WHAT IT SOUNDED LIKE TO DAVID, IN THE field house, a thousand or more people in the bleachers set up on the south wall, twenty feet high, and bristling with spectators, color like confetti there, and on the field house floor—windbreakers and bright flags with *Andover* and *USC* and *BU* printed on them in enormous white or red letters—and on the track competitors from as far away as San Francisco and New York and Chicago in striped warm-ups, blue and red and yellow and green, and this constant din, the brick walls echoing, so that all the noise was like some ever-present background roar, and there would be the crack of a starter's gun, and runners taking off from the line, and the ground shaking under their feet at it, and there, too, this dirt smell, and damp—there was wet dirt back and to the right of the bleachers, where coaches dumped the ice and water from their coolers—and David's legs alternately heavy under him, but not with inertia, but this longing to bolt, but being unable to, the aluminum baton clenched in his right hand, and the crowd larger by the moment, people still coming in, and the qualifying heats winding down, he'd already finished his, and paced, now, as Coach told him to, the length of the bleachers, as other runners did.

Trying to stay in the bubble.

But it was hard, the other runners jabbing him with their elbows when he went by, and frowning at him, all of them looking off, at anything, and he was working at staying in the bubble, it didn't matter that Rachel hadn't gotten off work, and hadn't come with Janie, it really didn't, he told himself, but the thought messed with his legs, anyway, with the light in him, and so he shut the thought out, and tried to stay in the bubble, tried to imagine himself on the line, the last man in the relay, and Roble, coming around behind him and passing him the baton, and even thinking it made David want to bolt, press to it, but there was time.

And that time passed, now, in a wash, and he sprinted to the right of the bleachers, a short run of a hundred feet or so, to the far wall, and turned again, headed back, walking light on his feet, on the new shoes Coach had gotten for him, proud in his outfit, and worried.

They could disqualify him for not being a registered student, but then, what of it?

He needed only to get the scholarship, and if he didn't fuck up, he was pretty much assured of it.

And if he didn't? If he didn't place? Or if he fell?

The starting gun went off and he turned to watch the sprinters, all heavily muscled, and low over their shoes off the starting blocks. And at the end of the track, seconds later, a storm of flash-bulbs lit the field house, now a roar of sound, cheers, and shouting, and a PA system running over it, an announcer with one of those typically adenoidal voices droning on: "And Stevens wins by a narrow margin for BU—boy, can that kid run. Don't doubt we'll see more of Washington, though. He's just a redshirt and he was coming on strong . . ."

It was on his way back from the far wall that David saw Buddy. Buddy now larger than ever, pumped up, hulking in his black windbreaker with the word *CREW* across the chest, Buddy with his small, inset eyes and his big hands, there in the crowd back of the tape that kept the spectators off the field. Buddy half a head taller than the largest of them there, and neckless, a red towel wrapped around his shoulders, David only making him out when Coach waved him over, it was time, they'd run in minutes, and Coach a good seventy feet down the line from Buddy, and there a narrow space he'd have to walk to get by Buddy, and he saw now that Buddy had planned this, Buddy, who, when he passed, would step out from the crowd and give him the charley horse of his life, or—*no*, it would be something worse, much worse.

He could see it, how Buddy would plant one of his feet on

David's, fixing it there, and falling heavily—as if by accident—on him, tearing his Achilles tendon. Something like that. He was heavy enough, big enough, but Buddy'd have to get right on top of him.

"What?! What is it?!" Coach shouted.

David waved the baton over his head, and Coach nodded. Sure, he was coming. But just then David fell back into himself, the world grotesque and impossible and ugly, recalled—

that day in September, on the field, throwing the baseball, and it going over the fence into the creek, after Buddy had so abused Greg Becker, and he thought of all that his throwing the ball that day had brought him. All this in a second, thought what these things had brought on, could bring on even now, given what he was planning to do, and he thought, he'd help Becker, do it all over again, even though it had led to this, here.

Coach waved him over, now a certain irritation in it. "What are you waiting for?" he shouted in all that din. "Get moving!"

David stood out from the crowded bleachers as if rooted there, immobile, Coach glaring, and Buddy waiting for him back of the yellow strip. Coach wanted to talk to him, but David couldn't move. He could climb under and through the bleachers, he thought, and come out the side opposite, and go out the door, onto the street. But he couldn't bring himself to do it. Or he could cut in front of all the spectators and coaches on the track. And he'd have to explain himself. What are you doin', kid? Get off the goddamn track!

The crowd sounds dimmed, in his head this dark hum, Coach pointing to his watch. David lifted his head, steel beams, and the roof broken by skylights. Glanced again, into the bleachers, and saw them—

Here was Rachel, packed in with the others, ten or so rows up, holding Janie around her waist so she could stand on the seat and wave, which she was doing, and he felt this burst of—what? Clarity, like light? Or was it something larger?

And he bent for a second, hefting the baton, the baton weighing only ounces, aluminum, useless, and he doubled back to the west wall of the field house, and stooping low at the water fountain, tossed the baton he was carrying behind the plywood partition there, and, stretching, as he feigned drinking, swept up the baton he'd made nights before from the hole in the cinder block, weighty, dense, and he slowly rose and turned, set his eyes on Coach, who saw something on his face, and was confused by it, and he watched Buddy out of the corner of his eye, Buddy who was already moving out from the others, but was still behind a man in a blue coat, hidden from Coach.

David felt his body moving out and carrying him, all that he'd felt before in him, crossing the ice that afternoon, the gun heavy in his pocket, and the car coming at him, but this time, sure of what he meant to do, and Buddy, as he approached, larger, stepping out from all the men crowded along the tape. Buddy turned and looked at him, huge, head like a melon, and only he and Buddy here, and this quiet in him, and Rachel and Janie up above watching, and this thing in him, calling him to run, to turn, so that he was divided, but there was this light in him, carrying him forward, deeper than love, because it was life itself, and because Janie and Rachel had seen Buddy there, and Janie *knew*, because Janie *knew*, having seen the bruises, because she *knew*, and because he'd been given his life back once already, and it was his now, not to run, not to run this time, no friend in the trees this time, and Simonson was not here, or Pretorius, just David, moving light on his feet, and Coach shouting, distant, what he couldn't hear, and Janie, almost hysterical, seeing Buddy, and tugging at Rachel's arm, and Rachel standing, and shouting to Coach, and Buddy a step away, David coming on, and Coach, seeing it, open mouthed, cursing, even as David brought his right foot down, and Buddy stepped out from between two men in dark coats, forcing them aside, his heavy foot coming down on David's, a crushing weight, David's whole body alight—

This the real moment, this the moment he had come to, this the true end of it all, he would yield nothing, hold back nothing, he would kill Buddy, the baton heavy in his hand, leaden, this white-hot fury in him, Buddy, pretending to be pushed from behind and falling, his thick-fingered hand on David's neck, to bring him down, to cripple him, already David's leg pulled long, and burning, and in that moment, that less-than-a-breath moment, David swung up with the baton, clasping it with both hands, his whole body with it, catching Buddy with the baton, not on the side of the head, as he'd meant to, wanted to, felt compelled to, but alongside his face, something in him sparing Buddy, sparing himself, yet driving up, lifting, and he felt the baton break bone, break teeth, break flesh, Buddy's head driven back and his hand leaving David's neck, Buddy going over backwards, David going over with him, but Buddy grasping the big man he'd waited behind, and bringing them all down in a tumble, and David landing on his back, and jumping to his feet, the baton, low, alongside his left leg, bloodied, and heavy, and Buddy, trying to get back up, his hot eyes on David, blinking, trying to get up, and not sure what had happened.

"DAVID!" Coach called, striding to him.

David stood waiting, the baton in his hand, and Coach caught his hand, down low, wrested the baton from him, knew what it was immediately, and did not show it, and taking the back of David's jacket, and nearly lifting him, swept him away, though he turned to see Buddy stand, and even injured like that, he began to come on, and David yanked free of Coach, and strode back toward Buddy.

They were nearly at each other when they were pulled apart, Coach yanking at David, and David only leaning into it, toward Buddy, who rose to point his finger at David, who said, in all that noise, something only Buddy must have heard, from the way he froze.

I will— and he didn't have to say the remainder.

"Call an ambulance," one of the men Buddy'd pulled down said.

Buddy put his hand to his broken jaw, spit blood; a med-tech walked him from the bleachers.

In moments, Buddy was gone, and there was some commotion, around Coach, about whether they'd allow David to run now, and where was the baton, an aluminum baton couldn't do that, break bone like that, and Coach handed them a baton, and David could see, even from where he stood with the others on the relay, that it was not the baton he'd held earlier, the baton he'd made in the garage, Coach there arguing, and throwing up his hands, saying, "He hit the big son of a bitch, he was gunning for him, you saw that. So don't tell me he shouldn't defend himself! I don't care what you fucking have to say!"

Then coming out to stand behind David and the other runners, as if nothing had happened but a ruckus, and he was shouting, "Focus! Quiet mind. Push it!"

"Got it!" they shouted in unison.

David stood back of the starters.

His heart was racing so it seemed it might burst. He glanced up in the bleachers, Janie there, standing, and Rachel beside her, staring, right into him—she *knew*, had seen it in this thing with Buddy, and Janie wide-eyed, afraid, and David, smiling for her, smiling for life, threw them a kiss, and he took his place.

The gun went off, and the front men ran, and he waited in his lane, pumping his legs, this almost weightlessness in him, in the bubble, and his whole life there waiting to come, the crowd deafening, the third group coming around now, and everyone in the bleachers rising, and David in that moment, feeling lighter than he had felt, maybe ever, just then, and crouching, breathing deeply.

Waiting, as if he'd been waiting for this moment his entire life.

And when he felt the baton in his hand, he flew.

Epilogue

75

IT WASN'T UNTIL THE END OF AUGUST OF THAT YEAR, WHILE David was painting the house in Edina, and the heat almost unbearable, nearly a hundred every day, and humid, and the heat holding for a record twenty-one days, that the body of Jack Carpenter was found.

The unusual heat had ruined the fishing up north, and a boat of bored fishermen had set jig lines with treble hooks, trying the deep water, and had gotten their lines caught on what they thought was a log.

Due to the placement of the body, and the stones holding it down, the case was reopened, and David received a call from the police, and in the heat, in Saint Paul, in a room not air-conditioned, and intentionally so, he went over the whole thing again.

How they'd planned to canoe the area where the fishermen found Jack Carpenter, but because of running into the men, and what his father had said to them, had moved to the east, never submitting a new travel plan to the area ranger—in fact, feeling safer for having not done it.

There was some conjecture that maybe the three others had killed Jack in some premeditated way, and about that time, a man who had worked with Jack Carpenter came forward with a story that became a media sensation overnight. About the three men, Penry, Lawton, and Munson, stealing meat, and all those involved, even in management, and the call Jack had made to this Mr. Martinez, just two days before the attack on Max, and Janie, and David.

There followed, in the *Tribune,* an exposé on the living conditions of the Mexicans working for the company, a spread in the paper that included color shots of the ramshackle trailers the illegal aliens inhabited, with outdoor privies and mangy dogs and the like, and in the paper, beside those photos, were ones of mansions on Lake Minnetonka, where Dysart's owners lived and played, collectors' speedboats tethered at docks and smiling children water-skiing. And there were photos of the killing floor at Dysart that so infuriated the owners, and the meatpacking council, that a suit was filed against the *Tribune,* and another followed, from the National Council of Beef Producers.

The paper made it clear, in later articles, that what the lawsuits concerned were not the photographs the *Tribune* had published of the broken-down trailers the Mexicans lived in, the photographers having had to trespass on Dysart property to get them; or the *Tribune*'s allegations that the owners had used illegals to drive the wages down; or even the *Tribune*'s discovery and exposure of Dysart's dumping massive quantities of untreated effluent in a nearby river. No, none of that.

The lawsuits concerned the pictures the paper had published of the workers on the killing floor.

The cattle forced through a chute, and the men and women below, decapitating, disemboweling, and dismembering the cattle, all in color.

And those working on the killing floor, missing fingers. Photos of saw scars, surrounded by what looked like white pimples, remnants from the stitches that had been sewn around them. At home.

A man in black gum boots standing inches deep in blood.

A blood-spattered cinder-block wall.

Animals shitting themselves as they came through the galvanized-tin killing chute.

The dazed eyes of a man ten years on the floor as he ran an electrical saw through a cow's skull, a sharp spray of blood running from his chest to the peak of his hairline, on his forehead, the blood crimson on putty-colored skin.

Pictures of third shift on the killing floor, denim shirts and rounded shoulders, tattoos on forearms slathered in blood.

All of it, on the killing floor, bad for business. But not even the complaint Dysart's attorneys filed with the State Commission addressed the obvious: Beef sales had fallen because consumers didn't want to eat meat handled by these people on the killing floor, these untouchables.

These castoffs.

One article in the series had ended with a photo of one of the owners of Dysart on Lake Minnetonka, a highball in his hand, leaning out of a deck chair, big-gutted, bald, glaring. Under it ran what he'd said about the controversy at the packing plant.

"We bear no responsibility for the presence of illegals. All of them had papers when they were hired. For all I care, send the whole lot of them back."

David read each of the articles devoted to the story, the story running nearly a month, some deep sadness in him, especially about Jack Carpenter's friend, who, by coming forward, had received death threats, and had had to move away.

Joseph Martinez. A musical name, and his face one David liked. His dark eyes, and this wistfulness there, and not one bit of shock in it. Because this Joseph Martinez *knew*—had known—what it would come to, his coming forward. And even then, though he was not caught up in any of the stealing, he did not fault the men for it.

"A family can't live on the wage," he was quoted as having said. "What are you gonna do?"

And there was this about the whole story, for David:

Mr. Martinez claimed that he and Mr. Carpenter had been working out some joint arrangement on the floor, to force the management to improve working conditions and wages. This was unheard of. Usually, Mr. Martinez explained, the management encouraged hostility between the Mexicans and Americans, using the illegals, whose very lives were threatened, to keep the wages down and working conditions as they were.

It was company policy, he said. But Mr. Carpenter had been trying to change that, and he'd been killed for it, Mr. Martinez claimed. Probably by one of the Cirricionis, who ran the operation from Kansas City.

There appeared a column the following day, a rebuttal by the company, outlining its policies, a picture of one of the trustees at the bottom, this Tom Throgmorton quoted as saying:

"Mr. Martinez's claims about management conspiring to remove Jack Carpenter from his duties as floor manager, by whatever means, are preposterous. They're just allegations, nothing more. There's no proof whatsoever to substantiate any of it, much less that the Cirricionis are involved."

When asked about the possibility of *his* being involved, Throgmorton had laughed, and replied, "Me? I don't have anything to do with lower management."

David, reading the column, broke out in a cold sweat.

It was the name: Throgmorton.

He went into the garage and rummaged through his old camping things. The police had returned what remained of it to him some time ago. The Duluth pack, he knew, had been sent back to Herter's, where he'd rented it, but he was desperate to find one thing that might not have gone with the pack. So he tore into the box with the sleeping bags in it, the bags smelling stale and smoky, then into the box with his day pack in it, and the remains of the tent, which he knew he would throw out now—he hadn't been able to so much as open the boxes their things had been returned in—dug to the bottom, there just aluminum tent stakes, tent line, mosquito netting, and rushing now, he lifted a third box out from under the workbench and tore the yellow police tape off the flaps.

Dug into the box, here the cook kit, frying pan, spatula, and reflector oven, and under that, a square of green vinyl, a yellowed plastic window in the center of it, rimmed in black.

He got the map bag out and zipped it open, and his hands shaking, reached under the map, and slid the piece of paper he'd taken from the phone booth that night out, and looked down the length of it.

At the bottom was the name, *Throgmorton,* and a phone number.

But it would prove nothing, he thought. Or would it? That he'd run into Penry that night he made the phone call to Rachel? Penry was dead. And in the silence in the garage was the answer.

He sat on the cold cement floor, listening.

It was right—*there*—in front of him, the answer. But he couldn't get it.

76

HE TOOK TO SITTING IN THE LIVING ROOM, BY THE SLIDING glass doors, where he could watch the birds, jays and finches and cardinals, in the trees, his books open—he was taking an advanced calculus class in the fall, even though he'd never gotten through his integration—but was getting nothing done, until he drove his car, the old, battered Skylark, to pick up Janie, who, seeing David more quiet and tired by the day, joked with him, and told silly stories, which he made himself laugh at, but felt he shouldn't burden her in this way.

He knew now, from her not having told him about the infection, the distance she'd go for him.

And he didn't want her to go an inch of it for him.

Not because he wasn't worth it, but because he refused to bring the least bit of what had happened up on the border back to her.

It was as if whatever light he'd loved in the world had disappeared again, or seemed never to have existed. The whole world this immense killing floor. Throgmorton, so cavalierly skirting his responsibility for what had happened, the Cirricionis behind him, silent.

Had he, David, inadvertently given Penry a reason to do what he, David, thought he had now? Come after them, because he couldn't have anyone knowing he'd been working with Throgmorton?

And were he, David, to come forward with what he knew, what would happen? And what proof, other than this sheet of paper, did he have that any of what he was thinking was true?

And what if he didn't follow up with what he knew, didn't do anything?

(He didn't want to endanger Janie, or Rachel, and were he connected to what he knew, publicly, he feared what the Cirricionis might do.)

But he would do *some*thing, he promised himself, but waiting, for what, he couldn't think, he shamed himself now: Cutting something in the kitchen, the thought occurred to him to . . . just *run* the knife through his chest. But why would he think it, when he'd gotten through all that up north? And when he'd been helped like that, by a stranger? And he knew he'd done what he'd done in the field house, at the meet, at great risk to himself. And he hadn't killed Buddy, when he could have. Even when it had been in him to do it.

And Rachel saw it all now.

The doctor who had observed David, in November, told Rachel, when she called him, what David was going through was not uncommon.

Survivors, he said, especially in cases like David's, where individuals seemed to bear up uncommonly well, sometimes they suffered . . . symptoms.

Symptoms? Rachel asked.

They discussed what David was doing, his starting at the university early, and how his friends Vern and Cleve had moved away.

Keep an eye on him, and call me if you need to, the doctor'd said, just that.

So she'd watched, and seen this darkness in him, kept after him weekends to go out, or see a movie, call this Simonson he admired, go run with him then, she'd urged, and he had, and they had struck up a friendship, after all, and she tried to do his laundry, and all the cooking now, but he wouldn't let her.

And then, one Saturday evening, when Janie was away at a sleepover, Janie dressed in spring green and in her red shoes, and excited, sent off, and Rachel, giving David a kiss on the forehead and going out, on a date, her first date, with this Joel, who, at the door, had shaken David's hand, this self-possessed quiet in him that David liked, she'd seen something . . . *decisive* in David.

David disassembling the grill that had shorted out, and repairing it, so he could make pancakes for Janie the following morning. A ritual of theirs now. Late every Sunday morning, David made pancakes for Janie, in all kinds of animal shapes. Brunch, really.

"You okay?" Rachel said, at the door.

David, smiling, said he was fine, but walking to Joel's car, Rachel wondered.

When they were gone, and the house was quiet, and this yellow light came through the sliding glass doors, David went out into the yard, which he'd mowed that afternoon, fresh green grass smell, and looked to the west, where thunderheads were rolling in, high, enormous clouds, and a green quiet settling over everything, storm quiet, and he locked the house and got in his car and he drove west until he reached a field on elevated ground, and out of the car, he strode through a stand of oaks. Coming out the opposite side, he stood in a field of corn, the rows reeling out in lazy, gentle lines, on a sloping hillside, the corn nearly shoulder high, here, in this light, possessed of some final internal greenness. He hesitated, and as the lightning began to come down, brilliant blue bolts, David calmly walked out into the middle of the field, the leaves clattering about him like a million green voices, the lightning outpacing the rain, and now, over him, and striking the field, jagged bolts of blue-white and an electrical smell, ozone, the thunder so loud it shook the ground, shook his chest, and the wall of rain, glassine, the drops big as marbles, and cool, wet, struck his upturned face, and he raised his arms.

And in that green and blue light, there was something wonderful.

No, beautiful. The lightning coming down all around him, his arms raised.

Bright.

White.

Light.

And when he was wet, his clothes heavy on him, and the lightning had passed, and he was shaking with cold, he walked back to the car, and starting it, laughed.

He knew what it was that he'd forgotten, or hadn't understood. Why he'd waited all this time with what he had in that sheet of paper.

And there was always Janie. And Rachel. Thinking how this might affect their safety.

77

HE WANTED SOMEONE TO BE WITH HIM WHEN HE WENT down to the police station. Rachel he didn't want to drag into the darkness of it all over again. And he didn't want Bobby along, Bobby, who, as much as David loved him, was a dubious witness. And not Morrie, who, David was almost certain, would advise him against what he intended to do.

So he went to Dr. Parker, who, all that time ago, had brought him ice for his face when Buddy had attacked him, had understood what David was up against, without David having to elaborate.

"I'm a little anxious," David told him, in his office.

David had stopped by at the end of the day, just before the office closed.

"It's about that mess at Dysart, and what happened . . . you know, up north."

Dr. Parker, he'd been surprised to see, had come to Max's funeral, had sat in the back.

Just that.

David explained about the telephone call he'd overheard and the sheet of paper he'd taken. He explained about all of it. Dr. Parker set his elbows on the white Formica of his desktop, cradled his dark head in his hands, his skin nearly blue-black, a whorl of gray in his otherwise ebony hair.

"You don't think I should go," David said.

Dr. Parker stood, took his coat off the coatrack, set his hat on his head, as if infinitely weary.

He put his wide hand on David's back and directed him toward the door, shutting off the lights, and as they both passed through the door, he said, "No, I didn't say that at all," and with a certain tenderness, pressed David's shoulder.

"But this is nothing," the officer said, holding the sheet of paper up. "You have a name here, a phone number, and you claim it was Penry in the booth, making the call, but what proof is there the call was made? That there's any real connection?"

Dr. Parker studied David from across the table, a shadow of a smile there.

"He called Throgmorton *collect*. It'll be on his phone bill. Throgmorton *accepted* the call, he had to have, or Penry wouldn't have been talking to him."

At this the officer craned his head around, glanced at the detective across the table. The room was suddenly hot, and the light in it sharp. Still, when the officer glanced back over at David, there was this confusion in his face, but excitement.

"*Why* do you think that? That it was a *collect* call?"

"I got into the booth after Penry did," David said. "He didn't close the door because the light would come on, and I didn't do that, either. You felt too . . . vulnerable, too . . . exposed, all lit up in the dark like that."

The officer leaned into the table. "But *why* do you think he placed a collect—"

"When I got into the booth, I was worried Penry was still around with Munson. It had to have been Munson who started roughing Penry up when I was waiting, so . . ." David glanced down at his hands, then over at Dr. Parker, who just nodded, and David said, glancing back across the table at the officer, "It made me nervous, see? And when I put my coins in, to call, the machine made *so much noise* you couldn't miss it. I mean, that racket nearly sent me running from that booth, it was *that* noisy. *That's* what I *didn't* hear when Penry got into the booth, and why Throgmorton on the other end—"

"You don't know that it was Throgmorton—"

"He said 'Throgmorton,' when he was on."

"Right, you already told me that," the officer said. "But that doesn't mean it *was* Throgmorton."

David kicked back in his chair.

"But you can check that, see what calls came collect to Throgmorton's house," Dr. Parker said.

"Sure," the officer replied. "We can do that if the call was collect."

"But see," David said, "that's why *whoever it was* on the phone was furious. But Penry called collect because he didn't want anyone to see he was there making that call. I mean, he couldn't be walking around with all that change in his pocket, could he? And he'd already called from that phone, and knew it was noisy. And if Munson, or Stacey Lawton had found him out—"

The officer across the table stood, then nodded to the detective.

"We'll try not to involve you," the detective said. He'd been silent throughout the whole hour. He ran his left thumbnail around the nail on the ring finger of his right hand, then, his eyes narrowed, looked up at David.

"You'll testify, if it comes to that?"

David had his hand set over the piece of paper on the table, the one Penry'd written on. He slid it in the direction of the detective.

"You get your evidence first," he said.

78

DAVID DID NOT HEAR FROM THE POLICE AGAIN. BUT HE read in the paper when Throgmorton was arrested. He was offered a plea bargain, giving up the others involved, including the Cirricionis who were indicted on racketeering and extortion and first-degree manslaughter charges.

Throgmorton moved to Detroit, at the end of August of that summer, and a week later, on a Sunday afternoon, was found shot in a Kmart parking lot, a talking doll for his daughter on the seat beside him.

It had been her birthday, and he'd gone to buy the doll, which had been on sale there.

———————

And David? For a time, David ran. He ran in the bubble, and he ran for the love of it, and he ran in Georgia, and Massachusetts, and Delaware, and upstate New York. He ran cross-country, and relays.

But the concerns of the team were not his, though he still had no idea what to do with himself.

So he ran for Janie, when she came to his meets, and ran for Rachel.

And at the house in Edina, he repaired the bad plumbing, mowed the lawn, cooked, even reshingled the roof one cool week in May. Summers he took Janie swimming to the lakes in town, the children shouting and splashing, and jumping, and playing, and evenings he ate dinner with Janie and Rachel, who was seeing more of Joel.

Jarvis was gone, finally, and so was the old Rachel, and she'd taken up painting, and had a show that did well, and he loved her work, landscapes done in heavy paint, sometimes applied with a palette knife, so that the paintings were a study of something essential.

Something of what he'd seen in the field that night of the lightning.

And he wanted to give this living thing to Janie, tried, by watching over her, until she felt safe, to walk down the street herself, or be outside after dark, or ride her bicycle over to her friend's house, just three blocks down the street.

Which took years.

He read to her nights, until she no longer listened. Helped her with her math, which she hated.

And then Janie was no longer a girl, and she didn't tell David much, or seem to need him, though he watched out for her, and when he was accepted at graduate schools, elsewhere, again he stayed in town, finally moving out, he thought he shouldn't hover over Janie, but he visited weekly, often to mow the lawn, and still made the pancakes most Sunday mornings.

And every spring, he traveled up north, and asked Janie to go with him, and she said, at first, *never*, and then, *not yet*, and finally, *sometime*, and all those years, alone, he searched when he was up on the border lakes, slowly, not even aware at first that he was doing it.

Always he went by himself, or with Bobby, his uncle, who said little, though he taught David to read what was there, in the spring, moccasin flower, and red teaberries, and bunchberries with their white blossoms. And coral root, with its tiny orchidlike flowers, and Indian Pipe, and he came to enter again that world that he'd lost, it blossoming, each thing he learned an invitation, and what was nothing to others was his home, the very names there something beautiful, a world not so tainted, and glowing with some asymmetrical symmetry, perfect, and the image of the thing he sought in it, so he felt it there more than anywhere, this light, not just in wild strawberries, and Indian paintbrush, and the flowers, in spring, embedded in verdure itself, caribou moss, this eternal green, springing from loamy hollows set in granite and basalt, what the area natives called bloodrock.

But here he could see it, he could feel it, could trust it. Life.

And every autumn, there were the softwoods, poplar, and cottonwood, and elder, ablaze, a million leaves of gold, fluttering in the cool breezes that blew in from the northwest, and the hardwoods, oak and elm, red, red-brown, and the evergreen, all the ranges of green you could imagine, tamarack, and white pine, red pine, yellow-green, blue-green, red-green, and autumn, after a rain, mushrooms would carpet the forest floor with rust red, and chrome yellow, and bone white, and they'd fry the edible, like chanterelle, in butter, and if they had Lukas Fisher, his uncle Bobby's friend and drinking pal, along, they would have the mushrooms with walleye, and if Bobby wasn't along, with duck, Lukas able to hunt on the reserve out of season.

But it was Lukas, who'd been his uncle's friend, Bobby's friend, who finally knew when David asked. Or, maybe, it was just that Lukas knew David well enough to understand.

About Gaiwin.

All these years gone by after what had happened that fall with Max and Janie, yet somehow, no time at all, and this thing David was looking for not found, so that when he finished medical school, he began to look for a place to do his residency on the border, in the north lakes area—only, which place he might be assigned depended on government programs that would forgive his debt.

For David, by this time, was deeply in it. Max, David had not been surprised to find, had left them almost nothing, his life insurance barely covering his debt, which had been substantial.

"Luke," David said, one opening weekend when he'd come up without Bobby.

A quiet had settled on the water, and David just then felt at peace. Or was it just the night, the boat bobbing slowly in the breeze that blew in offshore where the pines whooshed and tossed?

He reeled in, then set his rod against the hull and put his feet up on the gunnel. Lukas tossed his lure, the line in the evening light gossamer, the lure splashing seconds later, like music.

"Luke?"

Lukas turned to him, the whites of his eyes darkish, and his irises so brown as to seem almost black, so that oftentimes he seemed to be studying David from some world not his.

Here, where life grew out of greenstone. Precambrian. Ancient, but scoured fresh, and new, even the marks of the glaciers still in it.

Like Lukas, whom he'd known nearly twenty years now.

"What?" he said.

David took a deep breath, but thought not to say it after all—since he'd gotten such strange reactions from others in the area over the years—but then surprised himself.

"You ever meet somebody named Gaiwin?" he asked.

Lukas glanced over his shoulder at David, grinning, his teeth white in the dark, and laughed.

"What's so funny?" David said. "Is it just a common name, like John or Jim or—"

Lukas cast out again, that same gossamer thread, and musical, watery *plunk*.

"Who told you that was his name?"

David didn't answer. It occurred to him that he'd been wrong to ask in the first place. And anyway, he couldn't explain, doing that would bring it all back, make it real again, which he didn't want. And then, too, he'd never told anyone—not even Janie, when she'd asked about it later; "No, there wasn't anyone else there," he'd told her—and wasn't about to now.

"You owe this man something?"

David said it was nothing, stretched over the bow plate, his back cold with it, overhead high, billowy clouds scudding by, big as his boyhood dreams.

Lukas reeled in and set his gear down.

"It means 'Nobody.'"

David slid from the bow plate, eyed Lukas to see if he was kidding him again. Lukas often did that, pulled his leg and then some.

"You're kidding, right?"

Lukas shook his head.

"Nobody?"

"But, see," Lukas said, "it's something you usually say when . . ." He scratched the back of his neck, pushed his red-and-blue cap back, glanced up at David, not sure how to put it. "You say it when . . . when you help somebody out, but it's a kindness, see? You say it so the person who's helped isn't indebted. Because otherwise you would be."

"Indebted?"

"No," Luke said. He reached out and gave David's shoulder an avuncular poke. "That's just the point. You're *not*. You only say it when you know there's no fucking way on this green earth the person can pay you back."

Luke lifted his head, motioned around them. He spread his arms.

"You're only indebted to life then, see? It's just . . . *life*, and it's yours to give back *somehow*. That's what it means."

Lukas tried to catch David's eyes, David looking away, and set a hand on his forearm.

"You all right?" he said.

"Shit, I just got something in my eye is all," David said. "Is that a crime or something?"

———

That autumn David put in requests for placement.

There was a waiting list for the placements, some in inner cities, Detroit, Chicago, Los Angeles, some east, D.C., Richmond, Miami, but the one he wanted was just south of where it had all happened that week, so long ago. Thirty others wanted the clinic at Fond du Lac, because it was a short drive from Duluth, a real plum, and only three hours down to the Twin Cities and doctors in the program connected to the Rochester/Mayo clinic, which would be a great leap, if you could make it. But that was not why David wanted Fond du Lac, along with the others—some of those candidates more qualified, and from better schools.

He didn't have much of a chance, he was told, of a placement in his home state. David told them that wasn't it, his wanting to stay in Minnesota, but he couldn't explain. Still, out all those who had applied, he got the position.

"Just luck," he told Bobby, the night after he got his acceptance letter, and Bobby laughed at him.

"You believe what you want," Bobby said, "but you won't need to tell Lukas you're coming up. In fact, you won't have to tell anybody up there."

79

His first autumn in Duluth, he rented a cabin deep in the woods of Fond du Lac, near the clinic, so he could sleep in it the nights he was on rotation. He told himself he'd spend his free time there, too, what free time he had, fishing, or duck hunting, or later deer hunting, after his rotations, but he did none of it.

He was restless, when the work at the clinic was over, and instead of going back down to Duluth, and his house on the north shore, he visited shut-ins around Fond du Lac, those too abashed to come into the clinic, battered women, especially, and tended to children with injuries no one would account for, contusions, and abrasions, broken bones, and burns, and because he knew no one would come to him, would bring their children to him if he contacted the local authorities, he did not, but worked out something with Lukas, once Bobby's friend, and now his, and he learned not to ask, at least directly, about this someone he'd met years ago, very tall, rawboned, spoke the old language, had a tattoo of an eagle on his forearm, and eyes that seemed to have no iris—

Because, when he asked, the woman with the black eye, one of the American Horses, or a young man, a La Fleur, with a knife wound, or one of the old ones, a Stronghold, with tachycardia that needed attention, would shake his or her head, eyes blank.

But he got it. Finally. They knew exactly who he meant.

————

Into his second year of rotation, autumn come again, at the home of Norvil and Louise LaChapelle, a trailer off a pristine lake, David delivered a baby boy, his first. Norvil was so beside himself that when David handed him the baby, he kept blinking, Norvil not more than eighteen, and pacing back and forth, cradling the baby, and then looking at the baby, and he was saying names out loud, Angus, and Able, and Elija, and Louise, propped up, said no, or maybe, and then they started in on how they were going to repay David, but David knew they couldn't, it was obvious, from the trailer, the tin dishes in the sink and the chintz curtains, and the knickknacks, made of birch bark on the windowsills, and when David couldn't take it, he prepared to leave, calling to Lukas, who, like Bobby, his uncle, he called Luke now, and this Norvil talking in the other language to Luke, and Louise with the baby, who was crying, and Norvil said, tugging on David's shirt, "No, seriously. Where should I send this, okay?"

David shook his hand and went for the door.

Someday you'll understand, and if you don't?

"All right, I'll send it to somebody else," Norvil said.

David nodded.

"All right? So who do I send it to?"

David headed out to the car, and he and Luke got in. Norvil followed them. Setting his hands on the roof, he leaned into the passenger window.

That early-evening quiet had descended, and a breeze whooshed in the trees.

David sat, the passenger window open, not sure how he should say it, or if he dared.

"No, seriously, man," Norvil said. "Let's really do this thing. Who should I send it to?"

And David told him: "Gaiwin."

And Luke, smiling, pulled away and down the drive.

———

The week he delivered the baby, he was called out to Grand Portage, early Saturday morning. A woman there had been in labor some seventeen hours, but it was feared now that the birth would be breech, if at all without cesarean, and he swung by Luke's place, and with Luke sleeping, his copper-skinned face pressed against the passenger window, David ran the old Buick up to one hundred and held it there, in a cold sweat, the narrow two-lane road dipping and rising, and the horizon rolling out under him, the sun just coming up now, and in the early-morning light he was reminded, once again, of that trip he, and Janie, and Max had taken, and pressed on, and when he got to Grand Portage, a small, ramshackle reservation, he was directed up a sandy dirt road by a man who spoke almost no English but seemed to know, somehow, who David was, and Luke sat up, wise to something the man had said, and twisting the cap off the thermos, he handed David a cup of coffee, and Luke was grinning now, and told David to slow down.

"Take your time, boss," he joked.

But David insisted, even when Luke said, "It's no rush, you'll find your giants to go after somewhere else," which struck David as cruel, and when he asked Luke to pay attention, was about to tell him to look for a rock spire, Luke said, "Take a right there, go about three miles, then follow the shore around to the left. Nobody's having a baby out there, all right?" Luke said.

David brought the car to a skidding stop.

"Just go, you'll see," Luke said.

The road narrowed, now in tall, first-growth pines, and the air, warming in the September light, was thick with pine scent, and lake, and the road now was not much more than a path, hip-high weeds growing up the center between the ruts, and then it became that. Ruts.

They got out and walked a distance and came to a lone, weather-beaten cedar.

The cedar had grown out of a cleft in the shoreline granite. A warm late-September breeze blew across Superior here, and David turned his face to the sun, angry, and a little confused, but certain all the same he was going to meet him, after all these years.

David did not have to ask about the tree. It was a shrine of some sort, rawhide-wrapped bundles under it, tobacco, small pieces of bone, coins.

Luke got out his cigarettes, and David was about to reach for one when Luke broke the cigarettes in his palm, and under the twisted cedar, made a circle.

David had only seen that done once before, when . . . Gaiwin had done it beside the path.

Luke stood back, brushed his hands on his pants, and glancing at David, shrugged.

And like that they waited, in the soft morning sunlight, birds calling in the pines, and after a time, David saw someone coming up the path, and his heart quickened, but then he saw it was not him, it was a man in his sixties, round shouldered, and dark, in a red-and-black wool shirt, green pants, and cordovan boots.

He said nothing approaching them, and David stepped aside, letting Luke deal with it, he was still an outsider, and always would be, however much this place was a part of him, its true life mysterious.

The man, David saw when he glanced up, was nearly blinded

by cataracts—or was it some advanced glaucoma? It was so common here.

He looked David over, what he could see of him, then reached into his pocket and handed him a matchbox, the kind farmer's matches came in, with something heavy in it that rattled. David slid the box open, six .38 caliber shells there.

It was almost as if, even now, here, he'd been saved again, but this time from himself. Sitting in Penry's blood that afternoon, he'd thought to put the gun to the side of his head, end it, so badly had he failed, but he'd had no more bullets.

It had occurred to him, coming up the road to the gas station that day, Gaiwin—or *whoever* he was—should have given him more bullets, and like that he'd assumed there hadn't been any, so that business the police had brought up, later, about Max buying a case of twelve, had always bothered David, a mystery.

But that afternoon, the gun in his hand, spent, and nothing in the world to be done, he'd reached down with his gloved hand, tasted Penry's blood. Instead.

Even now, he couldn't think why he'd done it, but he had.

The old man was reaching for him, tugging at his sleeve. He pressed into David's hand a grayed, much-handled square of paper, and having done that, he turned, and David was about to say something when Luke shook his head.

"He doesn't know where it came from, he was just asked to give it to you."

"Miigwech!" David called after him, Thanks! and the old man lifted his hand over his head, and was gone.

David bent over the paper, his heart swelling, and this fear in him, this expectation.

He unfolded the grayed paper, once, twice, four times.

On the paper, in a fine, looping cursive, pencil, was this:

Call an end to your looking for me. I am everywhere, and nowhere. As is what brought you to us.

Where he would have signed his name, he'd written, simply, *Gaiwin.*

David, shaking his head, laughed, a burning in his throat.

80

BUT THERE WAS STILL THIS NAGGING, UNRESOLVED SOME-thing in him, something he could not name, something that gnawed at him and made him restless, and so he continued to work at Fond du Lac, and Grand Portage, and Deer Lake, and in Duluth, where he ran a clinic with another doctor. He was driven, but spent his weekends at the cabin, did not hunt, other than to photograph deer, and moose, and the eagles that nested in his pines alongshore, but more often he could be found at the clinic, working—again.

Bobby came up often, and sometimes Rachel, but never Janie, whom he worried about, and drove to Minneapolis to take to lunch. Janie with this crooked but beautiful smile, a tall girl now, almost five-eleven, and always funny, but this skittishness still about her, as if her skin were too sensitive—she jumped if you touched her from behind, just her shoulder, though schoolboys wanted to touch her, very much, because she had beautiful eyes, and this mysteriousness that boys were attracted to. This was so much the case that, shopping at Dayton's, a photographer there asked her to model for their catalogs, but she'd declined, not wanting to feel exposed, she'd said. And even given how difficult she was rumored to be, the boys called her, and took her to movies and to dinner. Yet, over their lunches, David could always sense this deep loneliness in her, and he asked her up to the cabin, time and again, until he saw it embarrassed her, that she always said yes, she'd come up with Rachel, or with one of the boys she was seeing, but never did. Until he stopped asking, and only asked, instead, when she'd like a freebie lunch again, huh, Sport?

So it came as a surprise to him when, almost ten years after all that with Max, and that awful year, on Friday of Memorial Day Weekend, Rachel came up with Joel to the cabin, and a little later,

Janie arrived with her boyfriend, Andrew, who parked back of the cabin, where the lawn stretched like green carpet to the lake.

David and Rachel and Joel were sitting on the dock, drinking from tall glasses of lemonade.

"What are they waiting for?" Joel said, when neither Janie nor Andrew, this boy Janie'd told David she really cared for, got out of the car, and David and Rachel said nothing.

It was as if, here, they were holding their breath, Rachel for her reasons, David for his, but both for fear of failure, that they'd failed Janie.

That's what David realized, standing and waving them down.

It was this, he realized, *this* was the weight in his chest.

Andrew got out of the car, came down the green lawn that stretched to the lake, his hand over his eyes, a visor, and stopped halfway, there in the shade of the ironwoods, until, with visible embarrassment, he'd waved David over, whom he'd never met.

"Hello," David said, and they shook hands.

David liked how Andrew faced the lake, smiling, and said, in a low, concerned voice, "Wouldn't get out of the car the whole way here. Not even to use the loo at the Texaco in Ely. Won't get out of the car now. Says she wants to talk to you. Is there something I should know here?" he said. "Some way I can help?"

David just grinned and pointed to the dock where Rachel and Joel were sitting on a lime-green towel.

"You go on down and we'll be with you in a minute. All right?"

"You sure?" Andrew said.

"Sure I am."

David walked over to the car, without thinking, jingling the coins in his pocket.

"All that filthy lucre, Dr. Geist, have you been corrupted?" Janie said.

They both chuckled. David was doing well at the clinic, but his real love was here.

"Chump change," he said, and set his hip against the car door, and bent down.

"How are you doing?" he said.

Janie cleared her throat. "A little rough."

David was not going to push it. He did not have to ask if she'd told Andrew, and, anyway, that almost amused look on Andrew's face told David he hadn't seen the scars, and it made David sad.

"I'm sorry," he said.

Janie put her hand on his. "Hey, Davey, I'm here, aren't I? Aren't I?" she said, and she was crying, and David was, too.

"Shit," he said.

Janie got a Kleenex out of her purse. "Boy, you aren't kidding." Which made them both laugh, or was it cry, again?

"Listen," David said. "If you open the door, and come out of there, I promise, I promise, old Sportnik, I won't let you down."

And he added, almost in a whisper, this desperate thing in it that, just then, shocked him:

"I didn't before, did I?" he said. "Did I, Janie? I mean, I—"

He felt the door opening before he even knew she was getting out.

"Here," she said, threading her arm through his.

She was seventeen, and long-legged, and coltish, and they headed down the grass, moving slowly, and as if they were both just walking down, all the time in the world, and for just that moment, David felt he was ushering a daughter down some aisle. Rachel on the dock there, in her black suit, laughing with Joel, and Andrew with his hands in his khakis, shucking off his shoes, and sitting to put his bare feet in the lake, looking, for a second, like Max, which frightened David, but then he realized Janie had known another Max, and when they got halfway up the grass to the dock, Janie stepped away and kept moving, lovely, doelike, until she'd got to the others at the end of the dock, where there was a diving platform, and she turned to smile at David, and for a second posed, elbows out, her hand cast across her forehead, some silly ingenue, so that they all laughed, something triumphant in it, after her having had such trouble getting out of the car, *this* the old Janie, joking even now, though only Rachel, and Janie, and David understood.

"It's beautiful out here," she said, swinging her arm around, a hook, light as love itself. "Come on!" she shouted.

And like that, David did.

ABOUT THE AUTHOR

Wayne Johnson is the author of the critically acclaimed novels *Don't Think Twice and Six Crooked Highways*. He was a Teaching-Writing Fellow of the Iowa Writers' Workshop and is the recipient of the prestigious Wallace Stegner Fellowship from Stanford University. His short fiction has been published in The *Atlantic Monthly, Ploughshares,* and *Story,* among others, and has been featured in collections including *Prize Stories, The O. Henry Awards,* and *The Norton Anthology of Literature.* He lives in Lawrence, Kansas.

The Devil You Know

About the book

In Edina, Minnesota, a well-to-do suburb of Minneapolis, nice people don't talk about dirty things like domestic abuse. And so David Geist, fifteen years old and an up-and-coming track star, keeps his secrets to himself. No good can come of anyone knowing about the late-night beatings he has suffered at the hands of his now-absent father, Max, and the psychological humiliation that went along with them. Besides, David is too busy keeping his bereft mother calm and his troubled little sister happy to focus on his own problems; he knows he's the linchpin holding his precarious family together. But as David's parents attempt a reconciliation, David is forced to confront his own deep anger at the man who made his childhood a living hell. When Max proposes a ten-day canoe trip in the wilderness of the Boundary Waters—an outing designed to win his children's trust—David and his sister agree to go, gingerly hopeful, but braced for the worst.

The events that unfold in the gorgeous waterways separating Canada and Minnesota, however, transcend even David's nightmares. When Max's foolish bravado snags the attention of a gang of four down-and-out friends on a dark journey of their own, the Geists become the victims of a savage cat-and-mouse game that will forever alter the lives of everyone involved. In the wake of a vicious attack, David must rely on intuition, logic, and brute strength to single-handedly transport his fallen father and sister to safety before their enemies find them and finish them off.

Author Wayne Johnson underscores the dazzling life-or-death action of his story with a brilliant counterplay between David's interior monologue and the spiraling desperation of his pursuers. The resulting cacophony explores in pure, honed language the complexity of forgiveness, the nature of kindness, and the ability of the human spirit to survive.

Questions for discussion

1. David is a creature of moral absolutes. He vows never to forget Max's violence toward him, never to utter one word that might hurt his mother; never to let Janie down in any way. How does this rigidity limit him? Does it affect your ability to like him as a character? Does it change over the course of the novel?

2. On page two of the novel, as David strides toward Buddy on the school field, the author writes, "What happens now will eventually culminate in the death of one of David's family; and, in his thinking when it is all over, perhaps worse. What happens now will change David's life forever . . . " It's an unusual stylistic choice. Why does Johnson prepare us in this way for all that is to come? Why not leave the approaching threat vague?

3. David first becomes aware of the men on his way to the phone booth. How does the author make this scene particularly nerveracking? Discuss the devices he uses to create tension as the

two parties approach their deadly run-in. Why does the hum of the Coke machine by the phone booth become a significant detail at the end of the novel? Why doesn't David mention the incident to his father?

4. As Jack begins to understand the depth of his sister's complicity in the meat-stealing scheme, he thinks, "Scratch the surface and don't be surprised what's under . . . but he was always surprised anyway. Always, he wanted to believe people were better than they were, himself included." Is Jack a victim of his own naiveté? Could he have avoided this whole mess if he'd "scratched the surface" sooner? In a situation as nefarious as this one, at what point do you think family responsibility falls away? Is Jack right to try to help his sister?

5. Five pages into the novel, David envisions himself divested of all human burdens: "He empties his mind of one thing after another, as if casting off physical baggage . . . all that he jettisons . . . running lighter . . . until the time he is only breath, and motion, free, in his dream of life nothing sticking to him, even himself—no, especially himself." Nearly three hundred pages later, trudging toward help, David has the same fantasy: "He wanted to lift up, light, free, a bird, gliding on invisible currents . . . weightless, a spirit, a nothing . . . pure, beautiful, nothing." Can it be argued that every character in the novel is motivated by a desire to divest of the self? If so, describe this desire and how it plays out in Penry, Max, Jack, Rachel, Janie, Munson, and perhaps even Buddy.

6. David receives moments of attention that are fatherlike from various men in the novel. Jack Carpenter offers him badly needed advice by gesturing him away from the argument between Max and the men. Gaiwin offers him unconditional solidarity and companionship. Cliff Hoffarber offers him validation ("You did all right, son") at perhaps his most desperate moment. His track coach offers him unspoken protection when he does not let on about the lead baton. Does David grasp the significance of these

deeds? What point do you think the author is making about the nature of fatherhood?

7. Throughout the novel, we are offered glimmers of Munson's potential as a good guy, which is invariably crushed by his herd mentality. His ultimate excuse for going forward with Penry's scheme is that "he already felt ruined." To what extent is this novel a study in despair? Does the author suggest that Munson could have made different choices if he'd tried harder?

8. David's discovery of the cabin, complete with its lamps and fuel, food, and dry clothing, is timed perfectly in the narrative to correspond with reader fatigue. In other words, we almost can't take another moment of tension and upset at this point in the story—thus we get maximum satisfaction out of the cabin episode. Where else do you see the author's skillful use of rhythm and timing? Do you think *The Devil You Know* is suited to screen adaptation, or is the work too word-driven to make an effective film?

9. Much is made of the survival gear involved in the canoe trip—both the gear that David provides, and that which Max fails to provide. What emotional survival gear do David, Janie, and Max bring to this journey? When does it fail them, and when does it actually enable them to survive? Discuss David's improvisational skills, both tactical and emotional.

10. Why does Gaiwin provide David with only six of the bullets?

11. David's overdeveloped sense of responsibility and self-determination cause him to blame himself unfairly for almost everything—"so that If I had onlys stemmed and blossomed and multiplied tenfold from actions he could only guess the outcome of, some of them seeming inconsequential at the time." By delving deeply into David's if I had onlys throughout the narrative, what point is the author making? That every minute action in life has a

ripple effect? Or that fate happens regardless of our actions—and by being overly scrupulous, we torment ourselves?

12. *The Devil You Know* is a cautionary tale about the dehumanizing effects of underpaying labor in general, and the meatpacking industry specifically. According to the Bureau of Labor Statistics, meatpacking is the most dangerous occupation in the United States, with a serious injury rate five times the national average. And according to a spate of recent media investigations, it is an industry notorious for substandard pay, unionization conflicts, illegal immigrant labor pitted against local labor, and the falsification of injury records. During the writing of this discussion guide, a worker in a Kansas City meatpacking plant went berserk and killed five fellow employees before committing suicide. Discuss how Dysart, the plant in the novel, contributes to the feeling of disenfranchisement that leads Penry, Munson, and Stacey to commit their crimes. In the author's estimation, what would bring about the reforms necessary to this industry?

13. David's decision to prepare to kill Buddy is uncharacteristically calculating and merciless. Do you read this as a trauma-induced glitch in David's mind? Or is it an understandable logic, given his realization that "He had failed up north because he'd been surprised, and unprepared"? After he attacks Buddy, does his urge to kill simply dissipate or do you think it is a permanent feature of David's now? Why do you think the author chooses not to tell us what happens with Buddy after this incident?

14. "In the quietest moments . . . we tell our stories," writes Johnson. "All we have are our stories, and embedded in them are ourselves, what bits or pieces remain, that we carry, or are carried in us, what of ourselves we can grasp, even as we, too, are passing away." Yet, David "talked to no one about it after," and as the novel closes, Janie's boyfriend has heard nothing of her ordeal. Discuss this irony. Are there ways we tell our stories without verbalizing them?

15. Stacey is described as following "in his drunken father's footsteps"; Munson "had no father, had been looking for one all his life without knowing it"; Penry despises the guys for knocking him around "just like his father did"; and David is aware both that his quickness to anger is "a gift from his father," and that Max's gruffness is a result of his having had no father. How does this theme of the paternal imprint contribute to the novel? What do you make of David's musing that there are "no real fathers in the world perhaps, but constructions of fathers"?

16. Johnson describes Penry as the group's scapegoat: "Fool, idiot, clown, dumbshit, failure—and much worse—he had become the physical personification of all that his so-called friends feared in themselves, and because he brought it out, where they could see it, and make light of it, he was precious to them." To what extent does Max use David as a scapegoat?

17. David is fatigued from having to "manufacture a personality to show to the world"; Janie is worn out from clowning to please the family—"she was so tired from it, it was killing her"; and David guesses that Max's "entrapment in himself . . . had to be exhausting." At what point do these characters allow their true selves to show? Are they ever released from their self-imposed exhaustion?

18. *The Devil You Know* explores in exquisitely painful detail the subtle and not-so-subtle humiliations teenagers suffer at the hands of their parents and classmates. Why is this theme significant to the story? Do you think that David overreacts to Max's jibes?

19. When and how do moments of grace punctuate the misery of the canoe trip?

"This is a well-written book and offers insights into wondrous possibilities for the future of humankind. Please read this book and apply these principles to your life."

   —Dannion Brinkley, author of *Saved by the Light* and *Secrets of the Light*

"*A Manual for Developing Humans* is PMH Atwater's great work. It takes the reader on a deeply useful and inspiring journey into the true relationship between mind, body, and soul with a clarity that I have rarely seen elsewhere. Practical, useful and magically powerful."

   —Whitley Strieber, author of *Communion* (the series)
   and *Super Natural: A New Vision of the Unexplained*

"The passionate pursuer of meaningful mystical realities was catapulted from seeker to experiencer when PMH Atwater underwent three physical deaths in 1977. In 1978, she was guided to focus her research on the mystery of the near-death experience. The present book, *A Manual for Developing Humans*, is the volume that her higher consciousness told her to write immediately after surviving her third experience. The sincere reader will gain true spiritual growth from an appreciation of her wisdom and knowledge."

   —Sherry Hansen Steiger and Brad Steiger, author of
   Real Visitors, *Voices from Beyond*, and *Parallel Dimensions*

"I have read many thousands of books in my lifetime, and interviewed hundreds of authors. However, *A Manual for Developing Humans* is one of the most absorbing and important books I have ever read. I was informed, fascinated, and uplifted by its huge range of topics. When I finished reading this wonderful book I just wanted to go back and read it again. Brilliant!"

   —Barry Eaton, broadcaster and author of *Afterlife* and *No Goodbyes*

"Who else would be bold enough to write a book titled, *A Manual for Developing Humans*, but PMH Atwater? This book inspired me big time! She of course deals with near death but also how to eat and breath and live, with common sense reminders for how to bring meaning and joy to everyone's life. Her next to last chapter title sums up her many books so well: We are all 'Gods in the Making.' I have known PMH Atwater for many years and her books just keep getting better."

—Michael Peter Langevin, author of *The Secrets of the Ancient Incas*, *The Secrets of the Amazon Shamans*, and *Spiritual Business*

"*A Manual for Developing Humans* is another practical creation by PMH Atwater. After my NDEs, life in my body was very difficult. PMH Atwater's manual looks at living in the body from various angles that create a life of alignment. Once again, she has written a book that experiencers and non-experiencers can take to a higher level of life enhancement, singularly, as well as with others for planetary cohesiveness."

—Jan Hunt Dawson, Ph.D. author of *Love Only: Lessons from My Near-Death Experiences*, *Past Life Reviews*, and *Aftereffects*

"PMH Atwater has done an excellent down-to-earth advice manual on the many stages of life from raising children to aging. A theme in her life has been an exploration for knowledge due to having had and surviving three Near Death Experiences (NDEs). Due to these experiences, she is a prophetess also giving us the patterns of existence for humans. As with the work of William James, the father of American psychology, delightful explanations and exercises are shown which teach us that as humans we exist in partnership with the worlds of the seen and the unseen. Also, coinciding with the work of Carl Jung, a Swiss psychologist, she touches upon the realm of nuclear psychics and the conception of the space-time continuum. The call of a prophetess is to teach people with their animals to live well on their soul frequency. She does that and much more!"

—Karen E. Herrick, Ph.D., author of *Grandma, What is a Soul?*

"There are so many wonderful books on the market about spirituality, humanity, and bridging the gap between them. There are equally as many endorsements touting them as 'must reads' or 'the most informative works of our time.' Never have I been so excited to become a cliche. With every fiber of my being, I can tell you that the vibrations and frequencies of the incredibly genuine text in A *Manual for Developing Humans*, come straight from the Source of All That Is. As someone who has lived to tell the tale of what happens when we die, I welcomed the tears of joy while reading this work of love, because it resonated so deeply with everything that I learned about my soul's time and intention while here on Earth. Finally, someone has written the manual! In my opinion, this manuscript will go down in posterity amongst the inspired words of love found in some of the world's most ancient scriptures. It was an honor and a great adventure to read this book and I envy those who are reading it for the first time."

—Dr. Mary Helen Hensley, author of *Promised By Heaven*

"PMH Atwater has been researching near-death experiences since 1978, the year she had three NDE's in three months. Since then she has had contact with nearly 4,000 children and adult NDER's. She has written 15 books on the subject and this book is the masterful compilation of many years of research and studying NDE's and related topics. This unusual book is a virtual encyclopedia of topics that will fill your soul, inspire your inner child and creativity, provide a path to greater understanding of consciousness and give you hundreds of ways of developing different attribute's and knowledge that will lead you to a better you." Congratulations PMH, you have another amazing book that I am sure will benefit many people.

—Diane Corcoran, RN, BSN, MA, Ph.D., president of International Association for Near-Death Studies (IANDS)

"From tips for the garden to tips for the soul, PMH Atwater's *A Manual for Developing Humans* is a delight to read! It is rich with philosophical insights, interesting stories, and practical suggestions for improving your life that will educate and stimulate you on all levels—mental, emotional, physical, and spiritual. This is one manual you'll want to read from cover to cover!"

—Nancy H. McMoneagle, president & executive director, The Monroe Institute

In *A Manual for Developing Humans*, PMH takes us on a 'spiritual safari' to track down and observe the most evolved yet elusive species on Earth—the New Human. The *Manual* also assists us in awakening our highest potentials so that we may become New Humans ourselves! How? By including the latest scientific research and her own mystical perspective on such topics as nutrition, the nature of consciousness, justice, economics, even child rearing, PMH provides a celestial view of the Great Shift, our entry into the Fifth World, and our unique role within it. She also opines on the New Human paradox – our ability to create a utopian or dystopian, fixed or flexible future, with the outcome dependent on our ability to quickly integrate Universal Laws of the cosmos. I loved this book and benefited immeasurably from its transformative power, which elevated my soul and prepared me for the next stage of my mission. Thank you, PMH!"

—Laura M. George, founder of The Oracle Institute, builder of the Peace Pentagon, and author of the Oracle Trilogy: *The Truth: About the Five Primary Religions; The Love: Of the Fifth Spiritual Paradigm;* and *The Light: And the New Human*

Occasionally provocative, always pragmatic, PMH Atwater has written the definitive manual needed for humans at this time. Packed with juicy morsels of insight and wisdom, you'll be stimulated, entertained, and you'll read it to the end.

—Virginia P. Collier, Ph.D., Professor Emeritas of Bilingual/Multicultural/ ESL Education, George Mason University

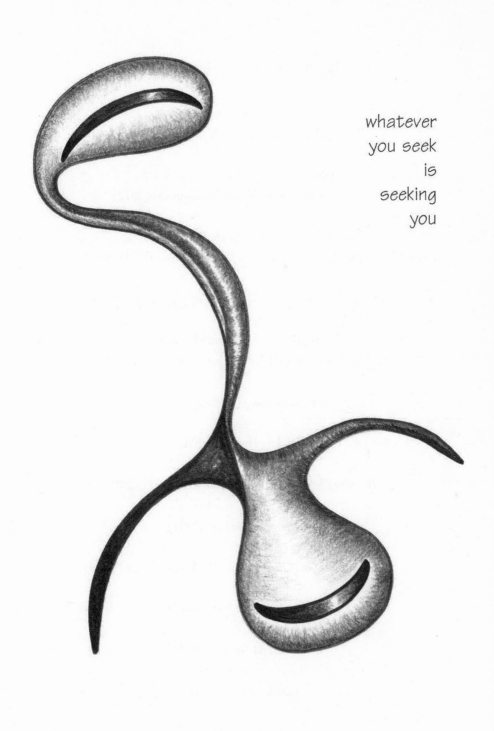

whatever
you seek
is
seeking
you

Books by P. M. H. Atwater

Dying to Know You:
Proof of God in the Near-Death Experience (2014)

Children of the Fifth World: A Guide to the
Coming Changes in Human Consciousness (2012)

Near-Death Experiences, The Rest of the Story:
What They Teach Us about Living and Dying and Our True Purpose (2011)

I Died Three Times in 1977—The Complete Story (2010)

The Big Book of Near Death Experiences:
The Ultimate Guide to What Happens When We Die (2007)

Beyond the Indigo Children (2005)

We Live Forever (2004)

The New Children and Near-Death Experiences (2003)

Coming Back to Life (2001)

The Complete Idiot's Guide to Near-Death Experiences (1999)

Children of the New Millennium (1999)

Future Memory (1999)

Goddess Runes (1996)

Beyond the Light (1994)

A
Manual
for
Developing
Humans

P.M.H. Atwater

RAINBOW RIDGE
BOOKS

Cover and interior design by Frame25 Productions
Cover photograph © Yuriy Seleznev c/o Shutterstock.com

Published by:
Rainbow Ridge Books, LLC
140 Rainbow Ridge Road
Faber. Virginia 22938
www.rainbowridgebooks.com
434-361-1723

If you are unable to order this book from your local
bookseller, you may order directly from the distributor.

Square One Publishers, Inc.
115 Herricks Road
Garden City Park, NY 11040
Phone: (516) 535-2010
Fax: (516) 535-2014
Toll-free: 877-900-BOOK

Visit the author at:
www.pmhatwater.com

Library of Congress Cataloging-in-Publication Data applied for.

ISBN 978-1-937907-47-1

10 9 8 7 6 5 4 3 2

Printed in the United States of America through
The P.A. Hutchison Company, Mayfield, PA

Table of Contents

REDEFINING HUMAN

We have things backward.

We think being a human is having a body with a name and the potential to grow up in a world filled with lots of people, who compete or cooperate to ensure continuing opportunity for health, advancement, relationships, and the fulfillment of our desires.

Wrong.

We wear these physical bodies and lead animated lives thanks to them because we are here to either test ourselves or be tested. This happens the way it does so we can integrate throughout every level of our being what was already known "at the beginning." Thanks to this process, the little self (our personality) has a way to unify with the greater self (our soul). What results can make us stronger, more confident and intelligent, more compassionate . . . whole.

We are not here to be spiritual. Does that surprise you? Nor are we here to be bully prophets or wealthy tyrants, or, to save the world. Such are examples of backward thinking that gets us nowhere.

As humans, we exist in partnership between the seen and the unseen. Our breath is the potential we volley between the Great Breath and the Great Breathing, connecting life with Life. We enter this world on an in-breath, we leave on an out-breath. Back and forth, motion and rest. Our job during our many journeys: *remember who we are and act accordingly*. Making the world a better place depends on this.

WHAT THIS MANUAL IS

Consider this manual an invitation for you . . . to think for yourself . . . take control of your life, both its unfoldment and the responsibility that comes with that unfoldment . . . and align yourself with the directive of your soul.

The underlying premise throughout is simple: If you can't use what you know to be true, it isn't worth knowing.

Each section is crammed with as many "how-tos," suggestions, and ideas as possible covering the six major areas of anyone's life: brain/mind, bodies, environments, relationships, life exercises, and guidance. And, each section is viewed three ways—initial (conscious), intimate (subconscious), and multiple (superconscious).

All material is an amalgam from what I've learned in the 80 years I have spent tearing up my environment, challenging then pushing every limit that stood in my way—exploring the corners of business, community service, relationships, mystical and alternate realities— then creating Inner Forum, Idaho's first non-profit metaphysical corporation devoted to separating truth from fiction. Well over 3,000 people took part in its programs. When I died, three times in three months in 1977, and each time had a near-death experience, the world I thought I knew ended. Another began when I was faced with relearning the basics from the bottom up: everything from crawling to walking, recognizing the difference between left and right, seeing and hearing properly, and rebuilding all my belief systems. The following year I initiated research on near-death states because I was told to during my third near-death experience. This investigation encompassed four decades, involved nearly 4,000 adult and child experiencers, and filled fifteen books—at least at this writing (not to mention blogs, articles, and papers).

No explanation exists for the incessant drive I have always and still have, or my need to test everything. Yes, I was born with dyslexia and synesthesia, but even that does not explain the levels I have taken since childhood to refuse limitation. Early-on I discovered that no one is interested in your questions—they just want your answers. So, this time, with this manual, you will not find the usual footnotes, referrals, or appendices. I'm giving you what you said you wanted . . . a manual about what works.

A Manual for Developing Humans is the "missing book," that third of the trilogy I was told to write when I died the third time. Actually, it was written first. Peer review at the time advised that I put the manuscript in a box and forget it. I did. In a very big box. That was the early eighties—never to be touched again until Robert Van de Castle died in 2014. Bob was a world authority on dreams and a dear friend. At his memorial, he manifested first in my car saying he knew I would come, and then again during the eulogy when he winked at me and said, "It is time." I knew what he meant. I drove straight home afterward and opened the box. You are reading the result.

You know, all of us are subjected to "tests" before we realize there is a "curriculum." That's why life is so puzzling. What seems beyond our control often shifts once we change our attitude and responses—and many times for the better. We make a difference, you and I. To prove it, *use* this manual . . . Don't just read words and glance at the pictures.

Achieving success, status, and wealth is not a measure of life. Nor is becoming a religious or spiritual paragon of things holy. Undergoing an intense transformation of consciousness—through something akin to a near-death experience, baptism of the Holy Spirit, kundalini breakthrough, shamanic vision quest, numinous episode, being bathed in "light," deathbed visions, any of these—constitutes a single step . . . an awakening. *However,* we can accomplish the same thing, reach that step, without all the drama such intense transformational events cause. Move past name and number, race and roots, and you automatically begin to enter realms of mind and memory that reveal a larger consciousness of truth. We recognize ourselves as co-creators with the Creator once that occurs. Years ago, people used to chant "hu" as a way to invoke this revelation, our identity as hu-mans . . . gods in the making.

A feature in awakening to who we really are is the enhancement and alteration of faculties normal to us, plus, the very real possibility that thought-forms can become visible. Thought-forms are simply an issuance of energy that "out-pictures" an idea stream from a person's brain. To say it another way, when one thinks a thought, energy is released . . . and that energy can be seen.

Twenty-eight thought-form drawings "popped" in for inclusion in the original version of this manual. I kept them intact to use as breaks between the various parts and sections. Each was an attempt at that time for me to depict a particular stage in the life of a thought when it moved from the energy that initiated it to form the shape words would eventually take. The phrasing on each drawing identifies the energy of the idea stream that produced it.

DEDICATION

I dedicate this manual to those who, without their presence in my life, I would never have survived childhood. They are:

Amanda Washburn Sogn, the woman I called "Momma" until I learned differently. She filled my soul with love so unconditional, so pure, that I became convinced she was one of heaven's angels.

George S. H. Sogn, the man I called "Daddy" until I learned differently. If ever there was a perfect soul, a model of grace and forgiveness, kindness and compassion, it was he.

Irene Kuder, my paternal grandmother, guardian, and best friend. Under her protective wing, she proved to me that joy and faith can heal any heartbreak and any tragedy.

Kenneth L. Johnston, my adopted father. A paragon of patience, he taught me to look beyond the limits of sight to find the depths of heart and mind. His gifts of discernment and clarity were unequaled.

Ann Marie DeKeyser Johnston, my birth mother, a woman I have both hated and admired. Time—the great healer—revealed to me the depths of her courage and strength.

Spirit Keepers of Southern Idaho's deserts and canyons. These bright ones from the energy world came to me during my darkest hours. They introduced me to the many levels of Creation's story and the truth hidden in mystery.

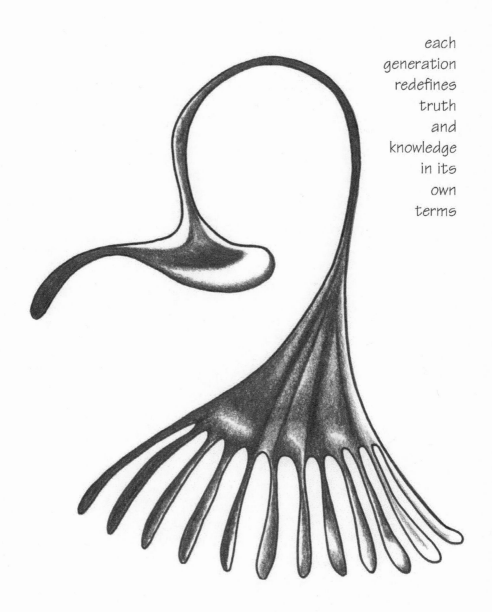

each
generation
redefines
truth
and
knowledge
in its
own
terms

PART I

OUR TRIUNE BRAIN/MIND

Intellect—Conscious Aspect

Intuition—Subconscious Aspect

Knowing—Superconscious Aspect

A new or original idea, if exciting and intense enough, can rearrange the brain in as little as fifteen minutes. Yet brain is not the same as mind. So, let's refer to the whole of this as the "brain/mind assembly."

In the brain/mind assembly, conscious and subconscious states of awareness are commonly associated with specific brain hemispheres: these hemispheres can be trained to learn language and engage in thought processing. The language of the right-hemisphere (related to the subconscious) is symbolic imagery, and it follows abstractions of intuitive knowing. The language of the left-hemisphere (conscious state) is detailed glyphs, like letters and numbers, and it follows sequential ordering and deductive reasoning. Each brain hemisphere performs on par with the other.

There is a third major area in the brain/mind assembly and it includes temporal lobes (our libraries of shape/sound/relationships) and neocortex (the higher brain). Both are directed by the limbic system. The limbic is a conglomerate of various parts and sections located in a semicircle in the middle of the brain and capping off the top-most extension of the brainstem. It wraps around our primitive reptilian brain, translating our basic instincts for sex, hunger, sleep, fear, and survival into more flexible and social forms of behavior. Often referred to as our emotional or feeling center (gut brain), the limbic is also the seat of our immune system and the body's ability to heal itself. Smell is the only faculty that accesses the limbic instantly. All other stimuli take longer to register, hence, the importance of odors.

Few realize that the limbic operates as an "executive office" in deciding what information is stored in memory, what is forgotten, and what will be further elaborated upon and refined in the two main hemispheres and throughout the brain/mind assembly. And, *it has a direct neural connection with the heart*. This small, but extremely efficient system, has been around for hundreds of thousands of years of brain evolution. Many scientists suspect that if the limbic does not originate mind, it certainly is the gateway within the brain to higher realms of mind and more diverse types of consciousness.

To simplify:

Left-Brain Hemisphere: conscious, objective aspect of awareness. Mainly analyzes, clarifies, categorizes, separates. Intellect and reason are its regions of expertise; science and education its preference.

Right-Brain Hemisphere: subconscious, subjective aspect of awareness. Mainly collects, absorbs, enhances, abstracts, connects. Imagination and intuition are its regions of expertise; creativity and fantasy its preference.

Limbic System: gateway and guide to superconscious, synergistic aspects of awareness (utilizes temporal lobes and neocortex). Mainly senses, embraces, and knows that it knows (gut response). Relationships, memory, and the collective whole are its regions of expertise; mystical knowing (gnosis) and convergence within realms beyond self (unification with a greater stream of intelligence) its preference.

The mind is not necessarily divided into parts or sections doing only what has been ascribed to them. By recognizing the various states of awareness our mind has *in context* with brain support structures, we can better appreciate the inner workings of our intellect and how our awareness of what seems real naturally alters as consciousness shifts.

Pictures say it best, so here are four drawings I've made to illustrate how the triune aspects of mind can differ while still comprising the same whole.

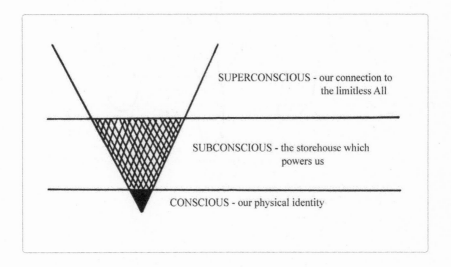

SUPERCONSCIOUS - our connection to the limitless All

SUBCONSCIOUS - the storehouse which powers us

CONSCIOUS - our physical identity

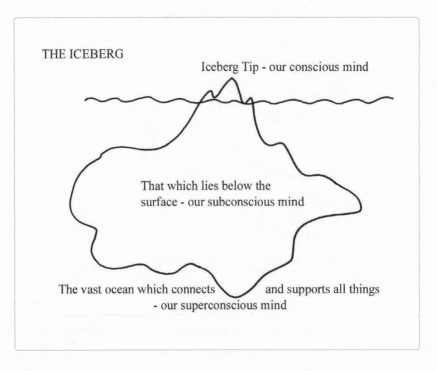

THE ICEBERG

Iceberg Tip - our conscious mind

That which lies below the surface - our subconscious mind

The vast ocean which connects and supports all things - our superconscious mind

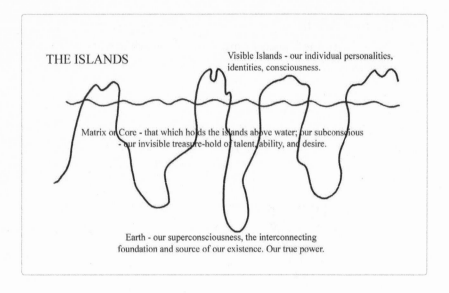

THE ISLANDS

Visible Islands - our individual personalities, identities, consciousness.

Matrix or Core - that which holds the islands above water; our subconscious - our invisible treasure-hold of talent, ability, and desire.

Earth - our superconsciousness, the interconnecting foundation and source of our existence. Our true power.

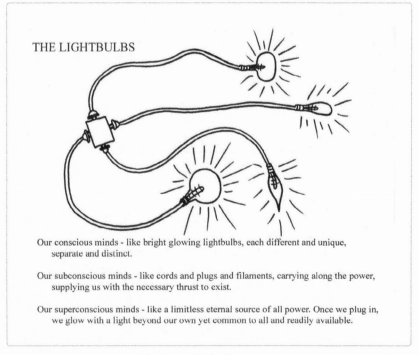

THE LIGHTBULBS

Our conscious minds - like bright glowing lightbulbs, each different and unique, separate and distinct.

Our subconscious minds - like cords and plugs and filaments, carrying along the power, supplying us with the necessary thrust to exist.

Our superconscious minds - like a limitless eternal source of all power. Once we plug in, we glow with a light beyond our own yet common to all and readily available.

Let's not forget that the brain itself operates at varying speeds. These brain-wave speeds are both rhythmic and non-rhythmic and are classified by the frequency of cycles per second. Electroencephalographs and biofeedback machines are among the equipment used to measure brain-waves, each wave is associated with certain basic functions and activities. They are:

Gamma Waves (30-60+ Hertz): modulate perception and consciousness, relate to simultaneous processing of information from different brain areas, e.g., involve memory, learning abilities, integrated thoughts, information-rich task processing.

Beta Waves (12-30 Hertz): dominate during normal waking state of consciousness, present when we are alert or even anxious or engaged in problem solving, judgment, decision making, information processing, mental activities.

Alpha Waves (8-12 Hertz): present when dreaming and light meditation (eyes closed), access to a wealth of creativity below conscious awareness, gateway to deeper states, aids overall mental coordination and learning, calmness, inner awareness, mind/body integration.

Theta Waves (4-8 Hertz): dominant in sleep state and meditation (body asleep/mind awake), gateway to learning and memory, associated with mystery, an elusive and extraordinary realm we can explore (like a waking dream), focused on mindscape.

Delta Waves (0-4 Hertz): slowest rhythm but highest amplitude, generated in deepest meditation and dreamless sleep, profound feelings of peace, can release a growth hormone at certain frequencies that is beneficial for healing and regeneration.

Note: Dowsers can register both Gamma and Delta Waves simultaneously while in the "dowsing mode." Many children born since around 1982 do the same thing, making it difficult to measure their intelligence using standard IQ tests.

A host of health and emotional complaints can be controlled, creativity and solution finding greatly enhanced, once you learn how to increase or decrease brain-wave speeds at will. Biofeedback training is helpful but not necessary, as a good book or smartphone app can be just as helpful in giving you exercises that apply.

As a brief aside, you don't need much of a brain to have a mind. Scientists have discovered that people who had lost at least 95 percent of their brain gray matter to fluid (hydrocephalics), still had IQs greater than 100 and were able to switch around right- and left-brain hemisphere functions as needed. Also discovered was that damaged nerve cells, supposedly unable to ever repair themselves, could return to normal if the fluid pressure in the brain was released.

Did you realize that 90 to 99 percent of what goes on in the universe is either infra (below) or ultra (beyond) our faculties of perception? Because of this, at any given moment, we are only aware of a small fraction of what is happening within or around us.

Our perceptual range expands during "awakening" experiences, or because of sensitivity/creativity training, or with the shift a transformation of consciousness can cause. Once our brain shifts, our perceptual range expands automatically. We see more because we are more.

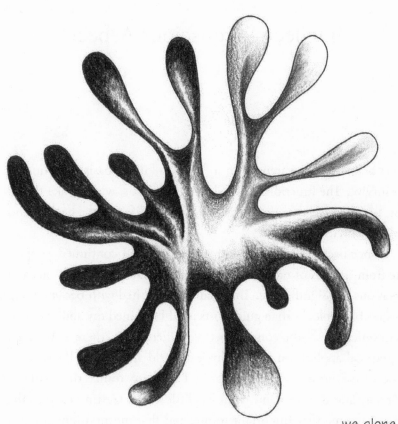

we alone
are
responsible
for what
we have
become

1

Intellect—Conscious Aspect

Our brain filters awareness on a "need-to-know" basis, enabling us to survive. The functions of left-brain, conscious, wide-awake thinking and skeptical questioning are necessary if life is to be healthy and worth its living.

Once back after my encounters with death, I continued to operate from "realms of radiance" to the extent that every day events and decisions lost significance. The wisdom I returned with became more as stumbling blocks than guideposts until I regained my ability to discern differences—the contrast between "here" and "there"—between a practical application in the physical world and what I knew to be true in the greater worlds of spirit. I came to realize that without contrast and discernment, truth has little value. Getting back to the basics became very important to me, and that meant asking a lot of questions and conducting countless experiments. Let me share some things I learned with you.

The average person has about 60,000 thoughts per day. The brain can only absorb so much before it takes an interlude, a short break, so it can integrate and organize input. Even so, *we recognize only what we are prepared in advance to see.* Why? Perceptual preferences—the thought models we have built up over time because of the natural bias we were born with that tends to block out details that seem unnecessary. This filtering system (shut-off valve) protects us from being overwhelmed by what constantly bombards us. The catch is, we need to re-examine our attitudes and opinions from time to time (our filters) to make certain they still operate in our best interests . . . discarding those that no longer serve us. People who go through a brain shift of some kind have their filters "cleansed" so quickly they appear as if "spacey" afterward. Relearning discernment skills can be a struggle.

Discover the Major Way You Take in Data

Have a friend watch your eyes when you think about a violet, then have them give you feedback about what your eyes did while you were thinking. Illustrations below show the primary access modes—how eye movements reveal whether you respond better to images, sounds, or feelings. Which one applies to you?

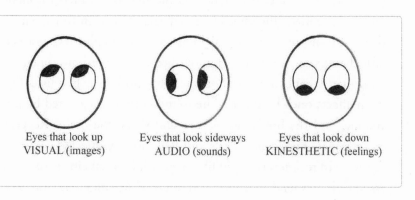

Eyes that look up
VISUAL (images)

Eyes that look sideways
AUDIO (sounds)

Eyes that look down
KINESTHETIC (feelings)

Different ways of taking in information show that there are varied types of thinking abilities. Seven exist—an individual may possess all of them to some degree, but one tends to dominate:

- linguistic (words/speech)
- logical-mathematical (reason/analysis)
- spatial (space relationships)
- bodily-kinesthetic (feelings/movement)
- musical (sound/harmony)

11

 ♦ interpersonal (social skills)

 ♦ intrapersonal (introspection/reflection)

Western societies as a whole, and school systems, in particular, emphasize linguistic and logical-mathematical styles. People who show abilities in the arts, social interactions, intuition, and other areas of self-expression are often overlooked or devalued. Yet all forms of processing thought are purposeful and need to be developed and refined to the greatest degree possible.

Did you realize that sounds made when language is spoken have a direct effect on the shape of the brain and how it functions? In working with hearing-disadvantaged children, researchers discovered that the language learned in infancy influences the way right- and left-brain hemispheres develop. Native healers and religious leaders throughout history have made the same claim, especially those in India. Sanskrit, they say, transports one into higher states of consciousness, not necessarily because of word meanings but because of word pronunciations. Gregorian Chants are based on the same principle. Just listening to them affects one's brain. It is the sound currents, regulated by pitch, volume, and rhythm, that massage and shape the brain. Repetition ensures that intelligence levels and behavior are affected. As regards music: hard rock tends to "dumb down" while enhancing sexual prowess; the classics tend to inspire and uplift while enhancing intellect.

Engaging the Hemispheres of Your Brain

The nostril that passes air more freely controls what brain hemisphere you are using at that moment. If you notice more air passing through your left nostril, then your right hemisphere is engaged; conversely, if the right nostril passes more air, the left is in charge. To switch dominance—let's say you want to be creative for a while—gently close the right nostril with your finger and breathe slowly through the left side of your nose for about ten minutes. That should activate right-brain activity. If you want to analyze a report or study for a test, gently close the left nostril using the same procedure. Presto, your left-brain should now be at work.

Get this: Ninety-five percent of all learning occurs below the verbal level. This age-old fact creates unexpected stress today. Blame the demands and pressures of the 21ˢᵗ century for most of this, as few can know or even prepare for the rapid accelerations now occurring. The brain, as an ongoing "construction site," is being reshaped by the digital world and by a barrage of chemicals few need. Like it or not, we are evolving—the human race is undergoing a makeover.

In brief:

> Two key gene mutations to "build a better brain" (around for thousands of years) are suddenly "on the move." Our scientific community estimates that 70 percent of the world's population now evidences one of them; one-third have both. What is happening because of these two mutations lies beyond prediction.

> In countries using standard IQ tests, there has been a sudden unexpected rise of around 27 points on test scores. One-third of the kids now score between 150 to 160—genius level. All explanations given—permissive parenting, better nutrition, rise in gene pool capacity, kids exciting other kids, more stimulating environments—fall short of explaining why isolated kids without any extras or recognizable advantages score the same.

> Two types of tests are used to measure intelligence: Wechsler, which measures "crystalized intelligence" (what you've learned); and Raven, which measures "fluid intelligence" (what you can learn). Not a single autistic child taking the Wechsler test ever scored in the high range. Yet with the Raven test, one-third scored between 150 to 160.

Consider the after-effects experienced by children who undergo near-death states include marked changes in brain structure and function; the younger the child, the greater the shift. I found that enhancements in music (85 percent) were almost as high as those in math (93 percent). This is important because the centers for math and music are next to each other in the brain. When one accelerates, the other tends to as well, *as if they were a single unit*. (Good mathematicians are usually music lovers, many are musicians themselves.)

Music, math, brain, mind, language... inseparable.

So what does all this signify?

Children today know more than the majority of their parents and educators. Children *and* adults who have revived from undergoing an intense, transformative state/near-death experience "awaken" to who they really are, their true self. Both fronts have necessitated that genius be redefined. Intelligence means to "select among" and describes someone with detail recognition. But genius "shakes" everything together or "clusters" information (dumps everything into the "same pot"), almost like a small child would, so data can be rearranged to form different or larger wholes.

So where is this rise in genius throughout the world taking us?

A woman by the name of Soleira Green in England put together what she saw happening today as per the jump with intelligence across the human family. I agree with her vision, for this is what I have seen as well. Her vision:

Intelligence Equals Expanded Conscious Awareness

IQ: Mental Intelligence Thought—Individual

EQ: Emotional Intelligence Emotional Intuition—
Opening to others

SQ: Spiritual Intelligence Wisdom—Connecting
with higher self and higher purpose

WQ: Wholistic Intelligence Knowing, Innate Telepathy—
Connecting profoundly with others and with potential

QQ: Quantum Intelligence Hyperspeed Bandwith,
Super Creativity—Connecting to Allness

A significant number of our new children (those born since around 1982) fit SQ through QQ. This is why parents and teachers are in such a quandary. Intelligence beyond what can be measured with standard IQ tests is considered fiction.

Counterpoint: the huge jump in brain disorders and learning disabilities exploding worldwide. Most of this can be traced to the excessive use of digital devices/installations/towers, manganese in drinking water, pesticides, flame retardants on toys and furniture, dry cleaning solvents, iron in paints, weed poison cloned into food seeds (specifically wheat and corn), plus high dosages of chemicals/medication given to children and teens without long-term studies to know impact.

The smarter we get, the dumber we are becoming. No question—our fast track is littered with mine fields.

Priority number one: Cut-back on as much over-exposure as possible to digital devices and electronic fields, chemical coatings and substances, toxic metals, drugs, and processed foods. All directly alter or weaken the brain.

Number two: Practice common sense, like what follows:

Drink lots of water. Once a day squeeze a slice of fresh lemon or lime into your glass of water, then dunk the whole slice in and drink it down. Don't tarry because lemons and limes are acidic. (You can use bottled juice if fruit is not available.)

Protein is a must, but that protein doesn't all have to come from meat. Learn how to prepare a meal that combines foods to produce a full protein (all eight amino acids).

B-Vitamins, especially B-12 for adults, are known to aid in nerve sprouting for better and more efficient "highways" between brain cells.

Be as drug-free as possible. Addictive drugs either dull or hot-wire the brain in ways that interfere with intelligence. Alcohol does not destroy brain cells as much as it disconnects them from cellular "highways"—impeding healthy brain function.

Get outside or open a window. Breathe fresh air. Fill your lungs with it and often, to further oxygenate your bloodstream. This directly and instantaneously affects your brain.

Do exercise routines that stretch arms and legs, such as: hanging from monkey bars, climbing ropes, swinging arms in unison with legs when walking, calisthenics such as "jumping jacks," dance routines, hiking, yoga, etc.

Do activities that stretch the mind, such as: rope courses, mountain climbs, educational travel opportunities; participate in music fests or sports events (even walk-a- thons); "hands-on" artistic endeavors; puzzles, books, classes and workshops that challenge or excite.

Engage in "flow states" where the mind blanks out into nothing and seems to float free for a while. No thoughts, no day- dreams. Just a brief interlude of nothingness (known to enhance intellect).

We are the only one who has to live with our thoughts, and we are the only one who can change them.

Thoughts move in circles. Whatever goes out, comes back—at least to some degree. Thoughts that are concentrated (focused/directed) have a stronger effect than confused thoughts (unfocused/undirected). Add emotion to concentrated thought, and you get results. Reinforce a thought over time, and you have the power of belief, a power that leads to manifestation.

The idea that belief determines result is backed up by clinical evidence. Scientists familiar with the placebo effect—where clinical trials of individuals told that a placebo (sugar pill) would cure their cold and it did—decided to try the reverse strategy. They told a test group that the new drug each had been given (again a placebo) would make them sick. Sure enough, everyone became ill. Whether suggestions were positive or negative, the individual's health *consistently matched* what they were told it would be.

Buddha put it succinctly: "All that we are is the result of what we have thought."

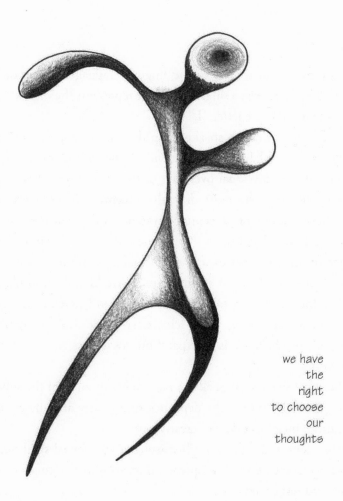

we have
the
right
to choose
our
thoughts

2

Intuition—Subconscious Mind

There are forty-four sounds in the English language . . . yet only in English does there exist a single letter that represents the individuated, independent self—the letter "I."

Significantly, English speakers top the list of people most noted for vigorously emphasizing and defending the rights, privileges, and freedoms of the individual over that of the group. And it is English speakers who have the most difficulty accepting or even honoring the subtle variations of perceptual awareness other cultures take for granted. Life usually turns around issues of ego for such achievers: the forward thrust of daring and risk, challenge, and the accomplishments of intellect. Ideas of an inner, reflective life, of mind play, are not only foreign but threatening—intuitive and psychic realms are hardly worth mentioning. Since science has made clear, "there's more out there," the challenge is to expand our awareness and our perceptual faculties.

The expansiveness we seek is a natural component of the subconscious—the right brain—the depositor of memory and the engineer of intuition, imagination, and creativity.

When left- and right-brain hemispheres are viewed symbolically, we tend to arrange how they operate in terms of male/female characteristics and responses:

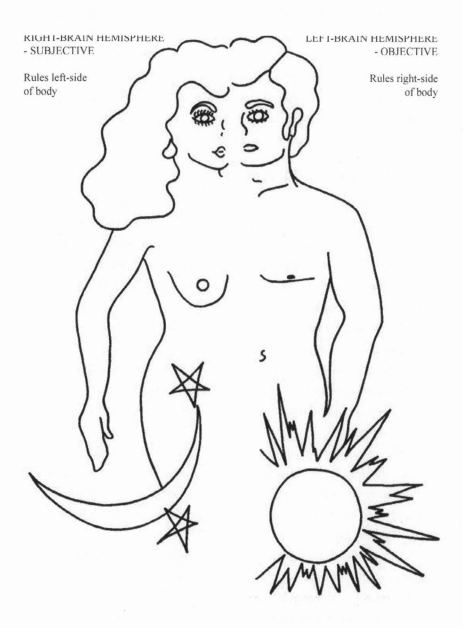

RIGHT-BRAIN HEMISPHERE
- SUBJECTIVE

Rules left-side
of body

LEFT-BRAIN HEMISPHERE
- OBJECTIVE

Rules right-side
of body

Some symbolic traits of the left-brain hemisphere: things like sun, day, gold, teaches, reasons, schedules, academic, direct, proceeds, judges, fights, manipulates, aggressive. Some symbolic traits of the right-brain hemisphere: the moon, darkness, silver, learns, cycles, psychic, subtle, withdraws, understands, pleases, cooperates, passive. Symbolic characteristics such as these are ancient and found in every culture. New research, though, makes plain that differences between the hemispheres are based more on how one responds to life promptings than on what sex an individual is. Oddly enough, this new research also shows the subconscious cannot tell the difference between fact and fiction, as both register the same in memory.

Let's Explore Our Memory

Our brain readily remembers all manner of data, storing it biochemically throughout the body—not just in the gray matter between our ears. Even so, only symbols are integrated. Integration, as a deeper process of memory, forms larger, more usable patterns by combining and connecting the subtle impressions and feelings that underlie images and actions (symbols).

As we age, we tend to reassemble our memories, taking accurate bits and pieces and inaccurately reconnecting them. If a given memory is never cross-checked or questioned, "false memory" can result. I have noticed that hypnosis is no guarantor of truth either, for the fine line between real and unreal is easily violated by careless or clever cues from the hypnotist.

The video-like quality we can retrieve from our memory storage banks can be so fully developed and so detailed that it can appear as if a current event, not something "past." The subconscious is noted for its ability to store, access, even recreate veritable mountains of material. The best super-computer pales by comparison.

The power of the subconscious is boundless. As our "right brain," it exists as a goldmine of resources we can use to our advantage once we learn how to develop and direct the capacity it has.

The importance of right-brain development, especially for being able to visualize three-dimensional objects—a talent required by architects, doctors, engineers, to name a few—is crucial in our quickly changing world. Problem-solving hinges on "3-D" skills, so does the core of creativity itself.

Observation/Memory Experiments

1. Get a piece of fruit, maybe an apple, and place it in front of you. Stare at the apple, then close your eyes. Can you see the apple in your mind? Open your eyes. Now, with your eyes still open, relax and allow the tension in your body to slip away while you envelop the apple with your eyes. Follow in your mind as your vision curves around the smooth skin of the fruit, looping to the depression at the top to ponder how the stem must have once looked, then snaking along the bottom until you can snuggle up to where the last remnants of the bud remain—a circled fringe of fuzz. Shut your eyes. Is the apple in your mind clearer this time? Open your eyes. Compare both tries at visualizing. I'll bet the latter worked best. That's because, to engage the power of the subconscious, we must first engage our various senses and *play* with them.

2. Do more. Light a candle in a candle holder and treat it as you did the apple. Experiment with other objects, too. It's as if our eyes are an object beam, our senses a reference beam. Where the two meet, visualization results. Three-dimensional images easily surface from the interference patterns created once the two beams of "light" come together.

3. To extend the ability further, find images printed on a flat surface of paper (like those of cubes or pyramids) that await scissors and glue and nimble fingers to assemble into fully dimensional objects that can be held in hand. Gaze at the paper. Imagine what the image will look like once assembled. Turn the image around in your mind and spin it. Note contours and how the material seems to respond when touched. Continue playing until the act of visualization becomes effortless. Construct the item and compare what it really looks like with what you saw in your mind. Make this an ongoing project until your mental imagery matches actual objects.

Mindplay

Test how far you can extend the reach of your mind by taking a trip without your body—a visitation.

- Decide on a place you want to visit, perhaps your favorite Aunt's living room. Know that your mind will reach this destination without effort and return to its present focus whenever you wish. *Never invade someone's privacy.* Check first for permission before "going" anywhere.

- Relax in a quiet place or continue whatever you are currently doing. It doesn't matter which, as the subconscious can handle simultaneous tasks with ease. Should you be interrupted or distracted, just affirm that everything is under control and you are fine. Know this is so.

- Direct your mind to the location of choice. View it in exact detail in your "mind's eye." Be open to receiving first impressions, rather than resorting to memory. Fully experience everything encountered.

- Return to body awareness by affirming you are doing just that. Blink your eyes several times or massage your hands to make certain "you are back." Drink cool water or breathe fresh air should you have any problem refocusing.

- Record what happened, plus time and date. Check in with your Aunt later on and compare what you saw, felt, and smelled during your "visitation," with any feedback she might give you. Note discrepancies, and there may be many until you feel more confident about doing this. Once you are relaxed and willing to experience *whatever you find* the more likely you are to be accurate.

A mind that wanders is part of being a human with a brain. This exercise enables you to guide and direct those wanderings until you learn how to extend the range of your faculties and the accuracy of your perceptions.

When I "visit" using this method, I see and feel my physical vision alter as it switches first to double vision, then clears for detail recognition. My head feels slightly larger, my face puffy, and sounds distort somewhat when my mind "disengages" from one location to "travel" to another. People watching me when I do this have said that I appear as if "not all there;" pupils dilated, skin waxy. Normal configurations return once my mind re-engages with body awareness. I used this technique when my oldest daughter was being operated on in Portland, Oregon, while I was living in Harrisonburg, Virginia. I was able to see more, do more, and help more doing this than I ever could have had I flown there physically.

Visualizations

The "here and now," what we have been playing with to improve our 3-D skills, can be used simply to create fantasy daydreams or to create and attain future goals. We can even co-participate with whatever energetic force is primary in the creative process. *We, of ourselves, do not make anything happen . . . we provide instead a channel within us through which things may happen.*

Each and every one of us has the power to realize what we visualize, in the sense that we can choose the direction our subconscious will take to attract to us what we desire.

The practice of visualization makes full use of our subconscious mind. Doing it enables us to hone our creativity, imagination, and problem-solving abilities in useful and wonderful ways.

The basic steps for any visualization:

- Choose a particular goal (one per visualization exercise).

- Find a quiet place where you can be alone for a while. Relax.

- Close your physical eyes. Visualize your goal in your mind's eye.

- Be clear about your goal. Embrace all its aspects. See, feel, sense, smell, hear whatever is required to achieve your goal, then follow through. Experience every detail, every emotion. Rehearse as if you were an athlete preparing for the big game (most athletes, by the way, use visualizations as part of their training). Involve all your sensory faculties as you savor your success in reaching your goal.

- Do not set limits, only direction.

- Adopt an attitude of gratitude. Be thankful.

- Relax more, then open your eyes. Stretch your limbs. Drink some water.

Make strong, positive statements as part of your visualization. Acknowledge others who have aided you and be willing to pass along the favor.

A word of caution: your goal may be inappropriate for you.

Visualizations, if done properly, are powerful. More often than not, you get what you want. The question is: *do you really want what you think you do?* You could be mistaken or deluded in your desires. Because this is true, I have learned to be careful of what I choose as the subject of my visualizations. I have also learned to keep God central to my goals by invoking Divine Order in the exercise and affirming that whatever happens, happens for my highest good and the highest good of all concerned. This extra step helps me to elevate my perspective beyond self-centered wish fulfillment and whatever else might be motivating me at that moment.

Mind Manipulation

The subconscious aspect of mind absorbs whatever it is exposed to like a giant sponge, including subliminal signals that bypass the scrutiny of choice. Usually, our beliefs and attitudes automatically filter out such extraneous data, but not always. We can suddenly find ourselves responding to cues we have no conscious knowledge of. The brain can be programmed or manipulated this way. (Advertisers often use subliminal messages to create new markets for products or promote certain ideas. Governments use them to spread "disinformation" or "double speak," so the population can be influenced or controlled by leadership.)

A way to combat mind manipulation is to inventory your filters from time to time, clean out old attitudes and opinions that may no longer serve your best interests, and be more discriminating about who or what you expose yourself to—a big deal on the internet, with blogs and social sites—as honest requests and reports are hard to verify. A healthy individual is one who is open and receptive to new and different ideas. Your thoughts, though, are always *your* responsibility. It is up to you to be alert, cross-check your sources, and educate yourself as broadly as possible.

The buffer of time prevents every thought we think from manifesting… thank goodness! It's those we think about repetitively that tend to actually occur.

Realize that the subconscious expands and enlarges whatever it absorbs. It is literally a performer/producer that never sleeps, never takes a coffee break, in a continuous search for creative ways to connect material or form new avenues of linking thoughts and feelings.

Dreams

You can learn in your sleep because of this, and enjoy a richly rewarding dream life. Although dreams may seem little more than a mishmash of fantasy gone wild, or merely the aftermath of late night snacking, train yourself to both remember your dreams and interpret them. You will have harnessed an invaluable ally if you do.

Dream Journaling

Keeping a dream journal will help you remember your dreams. There's something about making the commitment to record and date each one that automatically prompts recall. Have pen and paper next to your bed. Since dreams occur in predictable cycles throughout any sleep period, you might want to tell yourself to remember the last one on waking. Trying to remember all of them can be tiring.

Pay attention to how you *feel* about your dream immediately upon waking. Make a note of this. Typically, everything in your dream represents some aspect of yourself and is seldom literal. As you describe it on paper, highlight what *feels* important. Consider different levels of interpretation as you seek for meaning—include any worries or concerns. Even though dream symbols are personal to the dreamer, dream dictionaries can be helpful in the way they jumpstart ideas and give you perspective. Other suggestions:

1. Draw what you can of your dream, maybe a particular scene. Name what you've drawn, give it a label. Doing this can identify the major theme of your dream and help you isolate any overall message.

2. Act out each dream symbol. Let's say you dreamed about toddling along a highway in your car. No message there, or is there? Get two chairs. Set them facing each other. Sit in one and be the road in your dream. Reflect out loud what it was like for your road to have a car traveling on it. Get up, turn, and sit in the second chair. Be the car in your dream. Reflect out loud what it was like for your car to travel along the road with you at the wheel. Get back up, turn, and sit down again in the first chair. Be the scenery next to the road. Give each portion of scenery a voice that is able to speak out loud about the sight of you driving your car along your road. Get up once more, turn, and sit in the second chair. Be you, the driver. State out loud what you felt, what you saw, and any thoughts you were thinking as you drove along. It's good to have others in attendance when you do this or have your tape recorder on so that feedback can be objective. The result

may surprise you. For instance, the message may be to slow down, that you're missing too much in life.

Dream language is symbolic. It can also be literal or prophetic or instructive. You can even become aware you are dreaming *while you are still dreaming*. This is called a lucid dream, and it can be cultivated as a handy way to change dream content to what you really want addressed.

Intuitive/Psychic

Intuition is the direct perception of truth independent of any reasoning process. Three characteristics distinguish it from impulses or emotional promptings: (1) you can think about it, (2) it comes back if ignored, and (3) you can dwell on it without changing content. Intuitive abilities peak during periods of low-intensity magnetic fields and during minimal sun spot activity. Some physical locations are known to increase one's intuitive capacity (like being near water or a sacred site).

You cannot make intuition happen, but you can court it by creating an atmosphere through which it may happen.

Keys for becoming more receptive to intuition are relaxation and openness, plus paying attention to body cues that accompany intuitive episodes (i.e., a sudden twitch, chill, itch, uplift, or "high"). Physical sensations such as these signal the release of endorphins (brain hormones) that are integral to the validity and value of what is occurring.

Do not invite intuition by concentrating on problems. Start with a desire for solutions or guidance: a positive approach. Clearly "see" the situation at hand in your mind's eye, as with any visualization. Then release it, all of it, and change your environment: take a walk outside, soak in a tub, nap, bake muffins, daydream, paint, listen to music, or simply go on with your life. Usually, when you least expect it, the solution or guidance you seek just pops in your mind. You know it's real because of the sensation in your body that tells you so. Test what you receive if it feels appropriate to do so.

Every question contains its own answer, at the next highest level.

Psychic abilities are similar to intuitive abilities. Quite frankly, if you are alive, you are psychic.

The label "psychic" scares some people because of its long association with secret societies, dark deeds, and strange powers. "It is the work of the devil," the intimidated claim. Yet, nothing could be further from the truth. Psychic abilities are merely extensions of sensory faculties normal to us. Developing them enables us to enhance our perceptual range while increasing our sensitivity to "the energy of the moment"—what the heart knows—instead of what the head thinks. Using them is an exercise in intimacy, an opportunity to experience what exists beyond what seems to be our limitations. Rather than anything spooky, psychic abilities are a natural adjunct to spiritual development. They are "gifts of the spirit."

Nothing in life is paranormal, only misunderstood or misused.

Projecting Questions

There are many ways to project questions, like "waving a flag" for the subconscious to notice. Two are described here, using story form to present "the how" of what can be done.

Arthur Yensen, a long-time friend, built his home utilizing the intuitive guidance he received. He had a basic knowledge of carpentry and possessed a few rudimentary tools. With each puzzle he encountered, he would sit in a comfortable chair, close his eyes, and clearly visualize the situation, knowing that the solution he needed would be revealed. Then, he would blank his mind and relax more fully, drifting off into a flow state (suspension of thought). In a few minutes, he would return to conscious awareness and apply the first thing that came to his mind. The result? An innovative house made of pumice (volcanic "sponge" he and his sons cut from nearby deposits). Townspeople thought he was nuts, as nothing like that had ever been done before. Yet, his amazing creation was cool in the summer, warm in the winter, weathered storms, and required little maintenance.

The aftermath of my near-death experiences left me in a state of confusion. Facing new challenges and re-identifying my place in the world was almost more than I could bear. Juggling choices required that I find a way to investigate the answers to my questions *before* they occurred. To do this, I clarified the choices I had to make in my mind, then I fully relaxed—similar to doing a visualization. In my mind's eye, I formed a giant fan, opened wide by energetic spokes. Each spoke contained one of my questions, what I might do. One at a time I projected a spoke or energy line (containing one of my questions) out from the base of the fan. Carefully I watched to see if that spoke fully developed, stopped short, or evaporated of its own accord. Of the spokes that projected/extended the farthest, I spread them open to see what was going on inside. I did this by deciding to, then seeing it actually occur. In short order, I was able to discern probable results from each question and decide what route would be best for me to take.

There's very little difference between what Arthur and I did. We both needed answers to specific questions. We both projected our questions into the vastness of our subconscious mind, knowing we would get good answers, then we waited for that answer to come. Where Arthur went into a flow state to passively wait for his, I actively directed a form of mind play to see in advance how things might turn out for me. Both methods worked, and with the same success.

The Art of Dowsing

Dowsing, in the physical sense, is the act of observing the movements of simple tools (pendulums, forked twigs, dowsing rods) to interpret answers to questions asked. Dowsing is perhaps best known as a way to find underground water for the purpose of digging or drilling a well. The classic scenario is of a man or woman walking through a field or wooded area holding a forked stick in hand. When the forked stick tugs downward of its own accord, the dowser identifies this as a location to dig or drill for water. The depth, amount of water, and other characteristics can also be determined, usually by holding a pendulum over a standard list or scale of options and watching what it does by itself, how it moves.

Dowsing is based on the fact that everything is energy and we can connect energetically with any landscape, situation, or question to find out what's there. Dowsers are the "doers of psi" in the sense that they actively utilize the expansive skills they have. The art form can be used in any manner, like searching for lost persons or answering questions. *Note:* A good dowser will first ask three questions before any project is undertaken—Can I? Should I? May I? This acknowledgment of a higher power and a greater will ensures that integrity is an integral part of any dowsing project. Children are natural dowsers, and they are good at it.

An advancement of the dowsing technique is deviceless dowsing. This literally means the full energetics of the human mind coupled with the human body create an open source of information. I prefer this method and find that whenever I use it, my body becomes as if a rod, rotating and swaying while the needed information "feels" its way through to me to reveal the answer I seek.

All Uses of the Subconscious are an Act of Creativity

Creativity is a point of focus in the subconscious mind. Using it keeps us young and active, healthier, smarter, and forever at play. We are changed by what we create, as creativity reveals whatever is hidden . . . in the process of Light finding more Light.

The main reason most religions, political groups, criminals, and governmental concerns are threatened by transformational episodes like the near-death experience and warn restraint in both research and acceptance of them, is because such states open wide the door to ever deeper, richer aspects of the creative mind. No one can control this. The creative mind, once activated, mines the uncharted territories of higher consciousness, higher intelligence, and the limitless realms of wisdom and knowing.

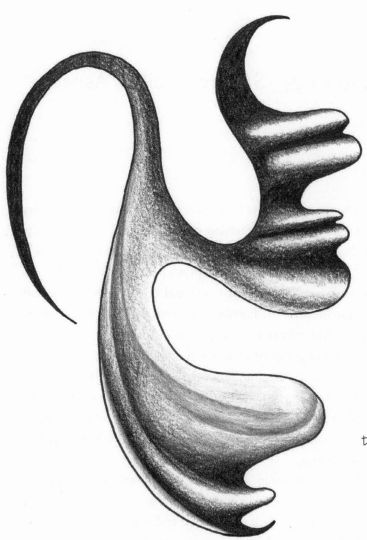

thoughts
are
reality
birthing

3

Knowing—Superconscious Aspect

Evolution has assembled the brain to depend intimately on emotions and sensations to guide its decision-making process. You can be conscious without thinking anything, but you cannot be conscious without feeling. This is just the opposite of what we have been told.

Emotions are primary. Our emotional intelligence matters more than our intellectual intelligence. What we can feel and sense and know affects our successes in life quicker and more directly than any clever orchestration of reason and logic. And it is emotion that strengthens memory. Yes, the neocortex is the higher brain. Yet, it is the limbic system, not the neocortex, that appears to control higher brain enhancements and greater reaches of consciousness, as it decides what information goes to left or right hemispheres for further elaboration and processing.

The limbic is targeted during transformational events, catching the full brunt of any shift that occurs. This may account for why intellect soars afterward, as well as intuitive and psychic skills, creativity, plus multiples in what becomes a sensory-dynamic world. Sensory multiples are referred to as synesthesia (conjoined senses).

This is one of the biggies in why people who see more of the electromagnetic spectrum begin to think they are going crazy. Sensory multiples can seem just plain weird until you learn they are actually a fortunate "extra." Others who have exhibited synesthesia: Einstein spoke of how he *saw* a light ray in his mind and *knew* he was right; French composer Olivier Messiaen *saw* the color of tones; Picasso *saw* numbers as patterns of contour. These people *knew* to trust what their mind and heart gave them. They trusted because it *felt* right to do so.

The ability to see what others cannot typifies the shaking together and clustering of data common to geniuses. This "extra" is one of the aftereffects of having had a near-death experience or something akin to that. Such experiencers, for instance, are apt to buy a painting for how it sounds, not just how it looks. They may also be able to *smell* sound or *taste* vision, or respond to any type of stimuli in a unique manner (like in school when I was the only kid in the first grade who could see music, hear numbers, and smell color). Synesthesia gives one a multisensory awareness of the world that is consistent in its pattern of uniqueness. Experts believe that everyone already has the capacity for this trait but don't know it. We can awaken this ability within us by desiring to, through visualizations, testing ourselves, perhaps with instruction.

We humans are knowing by nature. We know things, and we know that we know. That knowingness is a strong sensation, above and beyond intuitive or psychic impressions.

Sessions with a Paper Bag

Let's play with this by conducting an experiment about our ability to know things, and how that ability might function.

Gather together a diverse group of people, preferably picked at random, so they don't know each other. Have a large paper bag handy. Sit in a circle and pass around the paper bag, requesting that each person remove some article (like a watch or piece of jewelry or pocket item) and place it in the bag. Introduce yourself while the bag is being passed and explain that after a brief session of relaxation, the bag will be passed around again.

That brief session of relaxation could be something like inviting people to sit comfortably, feet flat on the floor. In their mind's eye, ask them to visualize every part of their body, one area at a time, relaxed, safe, healthy, and secure, going from feet to head. Give a pep talk about how easy it will be for them to "know" something about the item they will soon take from the bag, or about its owner. At the count of three, assure everyone they are wide-awake and feeling energized.

During that second pass of the paper bag, each person with eyes closed is to take something new to them out of the bag and just hold it, fondle it, while being open to whatever "pops" into their mind. No peeking. Keep the atmosphere playful and fun. All eyes open, then each person, in turn, shares a response to whatever they "picked up" about that item. The only time I've seen people fail to obtain meaningful results doing this exercise was when they made up their mind in advance that either the whole idea was bogus or they couldn't possibly do such a thing. Keeping an open mind encourages success—for belief determines value. That keen receptivity we can all have to what surfaces from deep within is a sense of knowing.

Our Perceptual Tool Kit

Both the heart and the limbic system communicate with each other continuously . . . and with the immune system. And there is a direct link between the limbic and the heart.

This is important for us to know.

The intensity of electrical currents surrounding heart activity creates a field 1,000 times more powerful than that of the brain; 5,000 times more magnetically powerful. The infinite harmonics the heart creates moves throughout all bodily systems and reacts to *future* events 4 to 7 seconds before anything occurs, sometimes even a minute or two before. Literally, our heart is our first responder; its electromagnetic field is identical to that of Earth. And, 60 to 65 percent of heart cells are the same type of neural cells that are located in the brain, making our heart our fifth brain (the other four are reptilian, limbic, neocortex, and pre-frontal lobes). What you "think" in your heart is how you feel in your life.

Emotions are perceptual tools. They are the logic of internal reality.

Of the forty-nine different ways we humans can perceive information, three comprise the perceptual "tool-kit" we rely on the most:

Feeling: intuitive survival/pleasure responses (involves heart and limbic plus body fluids, the circulation system).

Sensing: intuitive search and data recognition (involves the "antenna" supplied by the nervous system).

Knowing: intuitive cognition and understanding (involves hormonal triggers in the brain/mind complex).

Our five faculties of sight, hearing, touch, taste, and smell can be extended and broadened to encompass psychic dimensions (beyond reliance on physical forms) and collective/spiritual realms (grander realities, the larger view). Such extensions increase our perceptual range considerably, enriching our lives while enabling us to circumvent whatever factors may seem to limit the knowledge and wisdom we can access. I consider faculty extensions/expansions to be practical and easily learned or refined via classes, how-to books, or as the result of the desire to do so and the will to try.

Faculty extensions are defined as follows (notice what happens to intuition and perception once our faculties expand and broaden):

Physical Faculty	Psychic Extension	Collective/ Spiritual Version
See/sight	See without use of eyes; research term—"clairvoyance"	Vision
Hear/sound	Hear without the presence of sound; research term—"clairaudience"	Music
Feel/touch	Feel, or have an effect on an object, without touching; research term—"psychokinesis"	Art

Taste/flavor	Flavor without the use of tastebuds; research term— "clairgustation"	Discrimination
Smell/scent	Odor, without the use of the nose; research term— "clairolfaction"	Integrity
Sense/ intuition	Aware without or in advance of recognition; research term— "clairsentience"	Grace
Perceive/ perception	Apprehend without or in advance of physical stimuli; research term— "precognition"	Knowing

The ability to smell is our most important faculty in that odors reach the limbic system instantaneously and with immediate results. Incredibly, even the average nose can recognize over 4,000 different smells. (This explains why aromatherapy is so effective in facilitating mood alterations and responsiveness to healing, and why just a few whiffs of cigarette smoke, drug, and chemical odors, heavy perfume, can be so disturbing.)

The Dot Test

What we perceive has a lot to do with how we perceive, which in turn is colored by our preferences and biases—the emotional overlays from our feeling nature. To test this, take a large sheet of white paper, put a black dot in the middle, and then step back. Look at the paper. What do you see first, the large sheet of white paper or the black dot?

If the paper was your initial preference, you respond best to large, expansive imagery that can be seen with a quick glance (often characteristic of gregarious people who are outgoing and expressive). If the black dot first caught your eye, you respond best to details you can belabor, investigate, or analyze (usually characteristic of cautious, quiet types, or those who are reflective). This exercise reveals whether our natural viewing range tends to spread out or focus inward once stimulated, and it indicates how certain personality traits can emerge from the way emotional overlays are allowed to control perception.

A little secret: 95 percent of what goes on around us occurs below the conscious level. Literally, we see only what we are prepared to see.

The intellect is practically revered in Western cultures, yet in the East *knowing that you know* is still celebrated as the highest form of wisdom one can attain. The idea, then, is of a "gut" brain or that which instinctively connects to the fullness of being.

Electric/Magnetic

Experience has demonstrated to me that thought is electric in how it feels and responds within the body/mind complex, while knowing is magnetic. This same distinction has emerged from the "new sciences"—those connected with the study of subtle energies, vibrational medicine, and consciousness. Electric responses and magnetic ones register differently because *thought* requires personal participation to give it form and character (the electrical charge that comes from stimulation produces mental activity), whereas *knowing* operates independent of personal participation, more like a gut response (the magnetic appeal of receptivity invites as it attracts).

What we sense really has more to do with magnetite crystals in our brain tissue and sinus bones (especially around the nose and brow). Like bar magnets, these microscopic crystals are strongly magnetic, existing in long chains, and responding like a compass needle to magnetic fields. This explains why some people have a better sense of direction than others, and it may also explain the art of dowsing.

Life itself is electric. Bioelectricity as a life force results from the interaction between positive and negative charges generated by the movement of ions within cell structures. Experimenting with the brains of rats, biophysical chemists discovered electrical fields as strong as 15 million volts. Applied to humans, the experiments indicated an average adult possesses the electrical power of a lightning bolt! But get this: the electrical power in our brain *changes* with our state of consciousness; the brain itself makes at least *a million new connections per second*. All of this cradles the consciousness we possess.

Consciousness has quantum field properties. Because of that, at the most primal level, we are all connected. We are part of, live in, and respond to the same or similar vibrational fields. This opens up ideas of mass mind (we're all part of the same mind), changing trends and fashions (how quickly we "match" or "follow" whatever leads), behavior patterns (especially those that correspond to the vibrational and magnetic levels of any given place/environment/location).

Examples of quantum field effects are flow states and synchronicity. I know we have discussed flow states before, yet to me, they seem more like periods when consciousness rests for a while in, or encircles around, its own electromagnetic center. We are at peace in such "zones" because we are at "home." There's more to say, though, about synchronicity.

Synchronicity

The Swiss psychologist Carl Gustav Jung coined the term "synchronicity" to describe the phenomenon of seemingly unrelated events occurring in unexpected relation to each other, not connected by cause and effect but by simultaneity and meaning. Defined as "meaningful coincidence" by others, Jung himself corrected that statement by saying: "There is no such thing as a coincidence."

Synchronicity is so commonplace with those who have undergone a transformation of consciousness and with those who choose a spiritual life, that it becomes almost routine. When the phenomenon occurs, you feel as if you are caught in a flow state: things connect, somehow everything just flows together—on cue—without decision or effort on your part. This is how I would compare flow states with synchronicity.

ASPECTS OF FLOW

Internal to Self	External to Self
Subjective environment	Objective environment
Without a focus	More in focus
Release of thoughts	Release of goals or vested interests
Stimuli fade away	Stimuli increases in clarity
Blank out into nothing	Perk up to new possibilities
Consciousness expands	Experience expands
The mind flows	The life flows
You know more	You do more
Connect with a source of wisdom greater than self	Connect with a source of guidance beyond self
Gain information	Gain harmony and an orderly rhythm to life experiences
Unify in consciousness	Unify with the world at large
A state of mind	A state of being

Synchronicity is a signal that movement in the brain/mind assembly has "switched gears"—for however long.

The superconscious aspect of our brain/mind assembly encompasses the many stages and steps we take on "a journey without distance" to the deeper more expansive realms of our consciousness. Displays of knowingness, or the ability to suddenly know things without "rhyme or reason," are typical. So is the "sparkling" spread of psychic skills and talents, like "frosting on a cake."

Psychism, when pursued for its own means, seldom brings about any sense of balance in one's life. Such skills and talents can all too easily turn superficial (like that frosting), feeding the ego instead of the soul. If one chooses instead to develop spiritually in life, pursue higher states of conscious awareness, psychic abilities just seem to "pop up" by themselves, enriching one's life in a healthy, balanced way that assists others as well as self. A clue as to why this might be so lies in the original meaning of the word "psychic." Coming from the Greek word "psyche" (soul), the term infers by its very existence that our faculties can indeed expand into realms of collective and spiritual realities . . . the treasured "gifts of the spirit": wisdom, knowledge, faith, healing, prophecy, peace, joy, patience, kindness, and goodness.

According to the natural order of how life tends to unfold, psychic power by itself builds the ego—spiritual power, on the other hand, dissolves the ego. The difference is desire.

When we choose to live in a spiritual manner (taking on a personal relationship with God/Source/The Inner Journey), we begin to raise our consciousness to levels that transcend personality (the little self), so we can align with that part of us more whole and balanced (the greater self). Doing this enables us to reach grander vistas of collective wisdom and knowledge, mass mind, universal or cosmic awareness. We rejoin with our soul so we can reunify with Source.

If all of this seems too lofty, bear with me as I share with you the modern allegory of "the manufacturing plant and the shipping clerk."

The Manufacturing Plant and the Shipping Clerk

This allegory is offered as a word-picture game. Once you catch on, you'll find that it portrays the stark reality of your life as nothing else can. Not only does it clarify and simplify the various processes of the brain/mind assembly, but it also enables you to turn around past misuse and abuse so you can reprogram your mind and your life. Six steps are involved.

Step 1: Relax. Consciously create a mental picture or clear awareness in your subconscious of a giant manufacturing plant. Takes up a whole city block. Your manufacturing plant can create or build anything you can possibly imagine. There are no limits to its abilities. And it is all yours, to serve you, and to help you on command.

Step 2: Create a mental picture or clear awareness that your manufacturing plant is run and operated by a shipping clerk. This shipping clerk is absolutely the best. He or she never makes a mistake, is totally efficient, is always on the job day and night, and has absolutely no sense of humor. Your shipping clerk is perfect for the job and never misses or mislays an order.

Step 3: Your conscious mind is the front office where all orders to the shipping clerk come from. The front office is where the sales people, staff, management, bookkeeping, and personnel work. Your conscious mind is literally the eyes and ears, the director of all orders made. It performs necessary sales jobs and unnecessary ones (like talking you into something). It has the necessary management and staff to study, argue, investigate, evaluate, report, defend or reject, and finally decide what course of action should be taken. The comptroller or bookkeeping section does the final calculations before the actual order is complete and ready to be sent to the shipping clerk. Once the order is sent, input ceases. The front office has done all it can; its "signature" is on the bottom line. As the order moves, it sets in motion a chain of events committing the order for delivery.

Step 4: See in your mind's eye this picture and realize fully the processes taking place. The conscious mind utilizing all its many objective and progressive parts decides and directs all orders. When the shipping clerk receives the orders, they exist in precise detail. No questions are asked because that's not the shipping clerk's job. The only job he or she knows is to fill orders as received. The shipping clerk functions as a gatekeeper to the vast manufacturing area inside the plant (the subconscious mind). The source of all substance and all materials used by the manufacturing plant (subconscious) in creating what was ordered, comes from the superconscious (God, The Universal All, Unlimited Good, Source). The superconscious or limitless universe continuously and non-judgmentally supplies every manufacturing plant connected to its route. No one is left out, all deliveries guaranteed . . . *as long as* the back doors of the shipping dock are left open and unlocked. Lock up or block those huge doors (biases, prejudices, and plain 'ole laziness do this), and deliveries will pile up outside, waiting to be discovered later on and brought in.

Step 5: Know this entire allegory, what seems like a super-slick arrangement, operates like any other facet of life. Glitches can occur. The front office could be asleep on the job (after a night on the town). It could be disinterested or sloppy in making out orders. They could be unable to make clear decisions because of conflicting arguments, not realizing that no decision is still a decision. There is no such thing as maybe, if, someday, perhaps, in a minute, or any other such excuse. An order is an order, whether you meant to give it or not. Yes, there is a buffer zone in the sense that not everything you say or think manifests. Yet, if enough energy or repetition is involved, that manufacturing plant of yours (subconscious mind) will indeed churn out something that either complies or seems to . . . sooner or later.

Step 6: Now that you have a clearer picture or analogy of how the brain/mind assembly and its various operations function, and how a decision tends to work its way in and through the mind, let's take another look at what constitutes an order. An order is any statement of fact, belief, or intent we think or say. Once we have formed in thought or physically spoken a statement, our order (that statement we just made) is committed to our shipping clerk. Our order then shifts from conscious mode to that of the subconscious. There the actual creation or construction begins. Unknown to most is that all of this activity, every bit of it, is directly or indirectly influenced by the superconscious, depending on how open and receptive we are to such an influence.

Variables

There are times when we think or say something we did not intend. We make a mistake, and we wish to correct it. Orders can be stopped. To do this, think or say: CANCEL REJECT. You can also imagine the front office or the shipping clerk grabbing a huge red stamp that says CANCEL REJECT, and using it to cancel the order. The catch here is speed. The quicker you do this or something like it, the better. You could also think or say something like "I didn't mean that, or let's start over, or that's not what I meant." Orders sent repeatedly, or often, or given with a strength of commitment are those that are the most likely to manifest.

Comments

Understanding the brain/mind assembly should be easier once you can grasp how thought and speech tend to gather, flow, and manifest. The Manufacturing Plant and The Shipping Clerk is a game of visuals. The embarrassing and startling part comes when you "wake up" and realize this process isn't really a game. It's an image of daily life, illustrating how much of our discomfort, confusion, disappointment, and misery is our own fault. We program ourselves without recognizing that we are doing so.

Examples

1. A woman selects an item to buy in a local drugstore and picks a cashier's line to stand in, hoping to hurry and pay for the item so she can leave the store. The line turns out to be slower than the others she could have picked. Irritated and impatient, she either thinks or verbally says: "I knew it. I always pick the slowest line to stand in." Did you hear the powerful order this woman sent to her shipping clerk? Guess what's going to happen to her every single time she steps into a store to buy something?

2. A man comes home from work dog tired and disillusioned with his job. "That job of mine is killing me. I can't stand it anymore. Something's got to happen to change things." Sure enough, either an accident will occur, the man might become ill, or something will manifest to end the way things are—especially if he keeps making such statements over and over, day after day. It's like he's "praying" for disaster to strike and end things *for him*, instead of the man taking charge of his life and looking for alternatives he could implement.

3. After a long day, a woman complains how tired she is. "I am so tired I cannot go another step." Almost immediately she becomes more tired than she was when she first made the statement. Her shipping clerk filled her order accurately. By affirming how tired she was, she actually ordered her shipping clerk to make her more tired than she was before.

4. A child says, "No one will play with me. None of the kids around here like me." Age or intelligence offer no exception. The process works regardless. That little child will go through a lonely time until he or she changes the order for a better one.

5. "My husband is incompetent. He doesn't know how to do anything right. He's just a bungling idiot." Whether or not the woman's husband actually heard her or not, he will fulfill her image of him as if directed to. She will cease being receptive or supportive. His front office gets the message. He isn't appreciated. He isn't good enough. So why try?

6. Perhaps you've heard many a parent say, "That kid. He's nothing but a worthless bum. He never minds anything I tell him. I yell and scream 'til I'm hoarse. No matter what I do he ignores me." This mother or father has just locked the doors on any meaningful relationship he or she could have had with the son. The order sent was explicit.

7. "I cry every time I peel or chop onions." For most people, most of the time, preparing an onion means watery eyes and a runny nose, depending on the strength of its odor. By stating that an onion makes your eyes water all the time, they will. Should you give the opposite order and really believe it, your shipping clerk will fill your order as stated. You can override natural, physiological responses if you really want to. Yogis, students of mind control, and athletes have been demonstrating this for centuries. Some can stop their hearts or start them on command. They can stop the function of their lungs or control what lobe they breathe from. The mind is more powerful than we think.

8. One very successful businesswoman was so busy going here and there, phone calls, appointments, business meetings, rush, rush, rush. Almost under her breath she said, as if a curse, "I wish I had more time. I never have enough time to sit back, relax, read, think, or listen to music. I'd like to just watch the birds in my garden and enjoy the sunset. Oh, how I'd love to have more time." She knew about the idea of a "shipping clerk" and how the process of mind worked. Still she kept on wishing. Within a month, she was involved in a serious automobile crash and injured her back. She wound up strapped to a board for six months, unable to move anything but her head. While lying there feeling sorry for herself, she flashed on the words she had so often muttered to herself. "Good grief," she shouted, "I did this to myself. I asked for this and I got just what I ordered. I never specified *how* the change I wanted could happen. I just wanted more time." When she realized who was responsible for her plight, she recovered rapidly, amazing all her doctors while creating the better life she wanted.

Language

Remember, it makes no difference if you think an order or say one. Both have the same impact on the shipping clerk. Thoughts are just as real as words. Thoughts are powerful energies which once created, go out and have a life of their own. Everything that exists was once a thought. Everything begins in thought. Talking is just moving air, perhaps for notice or to release pent-up feelings, until real energy and interest emerge. This sets up a chain of events in the body/mind assembly that leads to action of some sort. Statements can result, things happen.

Changing the way you think and talk is an incredible feat, yet it can be done. We set ourselves up so easily or fall into traps of our own making as if half-asleep. Suggestions follow of how you can alter what you say while still maintaining your own integrity, for better results.

Old Way: I'm always so forgetful. I never seem to remember anything.

New: *I had problems in the past remembering things, but I have an excellent memory now.*

Old Way: I am so tired I just can't keep going.

New: *I temporarily feel a little tired but it won't last. Soon I'll be ready to go.*

Old Way: My children have been a nightmare to raise. They've caused me so many problems.

New: *Yes, I've had a lot of challenges in the past with my kids, but no more. They're really good kids and every day our relationship is better than the day before.*

Old Way: My job is terrible. You can't trust anybody. It doesn't matter how hard I work. I can't get anywhere.

New: *Up to this point, things at work have really been rotten. But me and everyone else are really pitching in to make things better. It's a good job I have and I'm going to make it even better.*

Notice in these examples I did not cover up or pretend away reality. I acknowledged what existed, but no power was given to the negatives, nor did I dwell on self-perpetuating statements I did not want to take place. Listen to what you feel and think, then choose—that's the secret. Make it a habit.

Can you ever have full control of everything you feed your mind? It is possible, but few are able to maintain the discipline it requires. You can, however, make tremendous changes in your life once you have a deeper understanding of the brain/mind assembly, its many parts, and how it tends to operate. (*Love that shipping clerk!*)

Glitches

Our life tends to follow our dominant thought. Yet, the capacity to learn and grow is always with us. Should we cut off the creative flow that emerges naturally from imagination, we become fodder for mind control; whatever is dominant takes over. To think is to create. A thinker is a creator. *To change your world, change your thoughts.*

The power is yours. Don't give it away.

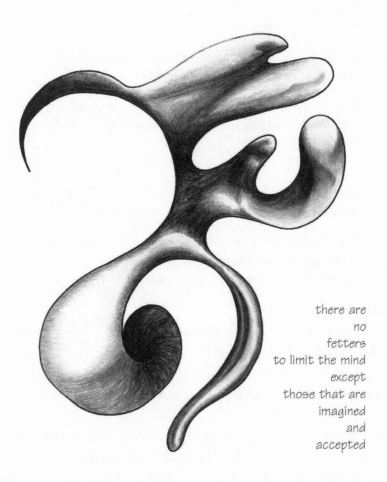

there are
no
fetters
to limit the mind
except
those that are
imagined
and
accepted

PART II

OUR TRIUNE BODIES

Physical Body—Visible/Overt

Energy Body—Invisible/Subtle

Spirit Body—In-Between/Soul

After dying three times in three months in 1977, I could no longer relate to me as myself. My former habits, personality, clothing, possessions, and lifestyle, were foreign—an irritant. Yet, when I looked into a mirror, there "she" would always be, looking back, all five-feet-seven inches, two-hundred pounds of her. "She" was shaped like a pudgy balloon with a deep sadness in her eyes and a washed-out face rimmed with short wavy hair. There was ample proof in her belongings that she had once been a bouncy, spontaneous woman with a love of song and a lust for adventure, be it exploring caves or ghost towns, and she loved rocks. Everywhere I turned, there were rocks, even in her purse. Rocks in her head too, I mused. It took me a long time to figure out the whats and wherefores of my own existence, and I went through many stages in what later became a program of self-discovery. The very nature of "self," though, became primary. This is what I was finally able to clarify:

> *I truly am an immortal soul, an extension of the Divine,*
> *who temporarily resides within a carbon-based form of*
> *electromagnetic pulsations that produces a solid-appearing,*
> *visual overleaf of behavior patterns more commonly referred*
> *to as a "personality." The name I had was given to my*
> *personality, my temporal self, but the real me is I AM. And*
> *what I AM everyone else is, for all of us are cells in*
> *The Greater Body—an expression of The One God.*

This clarification of my true identity flooded me with so much joy I could hardly contain myself. Yet, almost immediately, I ran afoul of a simple question—since I am an immortal soul, why do I need a body? The human body and my presence in one had to be faced if life on the Earth-plane was ever again going to make any sense to me. Now that I knew my greater identity, maybe my body had a greater identity, too. To find out, I took another look.

Examining my body more closely, I beheld a dense, slow-moving conglomerate composed of layers and levels of multitudinous life-forms arrayed in various sizes, shapes, colors, and designs. Each minute particle was quite alive, active and noisy, intelligent, a being unto itself. I was in charge of this collection in the sense that I, as a soul, provided the force field necessary to hold everything and everyone together and in place, similar to how God's Presence holds together and in place all of creation. Yet we coexist, my body collective and I, as teammates, a miniature version of the universe at large, a microcosm of the macrocosm.

This meant to me that I am the guardian of my part of the universe because my mind is the major power source the others within me are plugged into. Should I leave, my teammates would eventually wither and die. As long as I stay, we can all then accomplish our given tasks, learn and experience whatever we need to, grow-change-recycle, grow-change-recycle, until we are free to disconnect our vibratory alignment and go our separate ways—die, if you will, to the physical.

There is choice, mutual choice, theirs to be where they are, mine to be where I am. It is no accident we are together sharing the same journey, but it is mainly up to me to provide the direction we travel for I, as a soul, have a larger energy surge, am more highly developed, and can see farther ahead. As I am the source of power for the membership within my body, God is The Greater Source wherein my help comes. God, then, is the central current, that all-encompassing power source everything ultimately plugs into for the kind of sustenance that enables existence to exist.

In coming to grips with this understanding, life—mine and everyone else's—began to make sense. I could acknowledge my body as the living temple of The Living God, filled with beings cycling through births and deaths and rebirths as they, too, grew and evolved—all the myriad forms of intelligence, all the promise and the potential, all that was inside me—this my body, the incredible collective I wear.

What a privilege. What a remarkable privilege to be here, to be me, to be a soul sojourning through the Earth-plane with a whole conclave of intelligence accompanying me, a conclave that shares my challenges and opportunities unselfishly, dependably, lovingly. All of us evolving. All of us changing. All of us in the state of becoming more of ourselves.

How could I possibly ever abuse or misuse my body?

How could I reject it?

When I, at last, accepted my body, I also accepted the responsibility that came with wearing it. In recognizing that I was once again back inside its protective folds, I could then, comfortably, claim my body as mine.

A New Way to Look at Old Stuff

In rediscovering bodies and blood streams, bones and energy fields, I recognized that we really have two bodies—one that's visible and one that's invisible. Each works with and reflects the other. The energetic or invisible body can readily be felt, also seen if a person recognizes auras (energy colors) or picks up on vibratory deviations in the energy field surrounding any given being or thing.

Correlations follow:

Physical Body—Visible	Energetic Body—invisible
Endocrine glands	Chakras (spinning vortexes)
Spinal column	Kundalini (can rise up spine)

Nervous system	Meridians (energetic component)
Digestive system	Absorptions (sensing overlay)
Procreative system	Co-creative system (overall shift)
Brain	Mind

I plugged back into ancient wisdom, no matter the culture, and saw additional correlations—those of Earth, Air, Fire, and Water—were there as well, helping us to better understand living forms and what constitutes health. In a nutshell:

Earth (solids): skeletal system, muscles, organs, tissues

Air (gasses): respiratory system, various micro gasses within body

Fire (plasma): brain/mind assembly, central nervous system

Water (liquids): circulatory, digestive, and endocrine system

Reminders are everywhere throughout complementary and alternative schools of healing about *body maps*, places in our body where each gland and organ and major body part are "pictured" and can be accessed via the prick of a needle or the pressure of a finger or tool. We were born with this primal information system firmly in place. Acupuncture and reflexology are so based. Our ancestors regarded body maps in the same vein as we today identify a hologram—that which connects and reflects each part with the whole. Practitioners who have studied the various body maps are able to treat an individual based on the signals and signs they find in whatever map they access.

Locations for these maps are: the soles of both feet, the palms of both hands, both ears and lobes, the iris of both eyes, and inside the mouth. Each location contains a "hologram" of the body's systems. Connective tissue is piezoelectric, generating electrical fields when compressed, pinched, or stretched. These piezoelectric collagen fibers facilitate the continuous flow of information and energy throughout our body . . . as if a single holographic fabric . . . enabling the practitioner to study the scope of any problem, sometimes fixing it within the map itself, before going to the actual body part for further diagnosis (an excellent "step ahead" in the healing process).

Body Talk

You can talk to your body, listen to it as it talks back to you, even converse back and forth. You do this by desiring to. Set your intent. Know that this will happen.

We intuitively know about this type of "body talk." We've done it since we were kids. We just choose to ignore such signals and feelings as if, now that we're grown, we've moved past the need to do anything so childish, so over-imaginative.

To do this, relax as if you were preparing to do nothing else but contemplate the moment. Put your mind at whatever area you wish to contact. See that area clearly. Imagination is fine—like "seeing" cells running around or tiny beings "at the ready." Project your thought or question. Relax again. Wait, with no expectations. Whatever pops into your mind, go with it. If it makes sense, if the contact seems real, pretend that it is. Dialogue. See and feel what that part of your body wants you to know. You might make an agreement to be more alert from now on, to listen better to promptings, to be more aware that all of your body, every single inch and speck of it, is intelligent and more than willing to let you know (signal) if something is amiss, or there is need to "talk things out."

One of the first things you learn once you decide to become human again, is that the creative function of mind is the place of power. Tell yourself you're going to be well, heal whatever problem plagues you, and chances are you'll do just that—or at least you'll begin a regimen that leads to a successful outcome of some kind. The reverse is true. If you accept failure or affirm that only one type of procedure and one type of advice will work, the future that results may not be what it could be.

Science has discovered the same thing by experimenting with the placebo effect. Divide up volunteers, give them all sugar pills instead of medication. Tell one group they were chosen to receive a miracle drug that is amazing everyone with its ability to heal. Tell the other group the drug they have is chancy, maybe it will help and maybe not. Percentages say it all. Encourage people—they tend to get better, feel better, do more, have faith, even "move mountains." Discourage people or play pity-parties with them, and not much follows—they either remain where they are, as if suspended in time, or they get worse.

You can communicate with your body or at least learn its signals when it's trying to talk to you. If you're a doctor, parent, employer, school teacher, spouse, friend, or a stranger who wants to make a difference, remember this: talking, touching, and listening are enrichment tools. Magic makers.

I said we had two bodies. Actually, we have three. The third is our spirit body, the realm of the soul.

Life is consciousness expressing itself in form.

All is alive.

All is intelligent.

Communication is constant throughout all of creation.

Any idea that there are limits to the range of our consciousness, we were taught. No such limits exist.

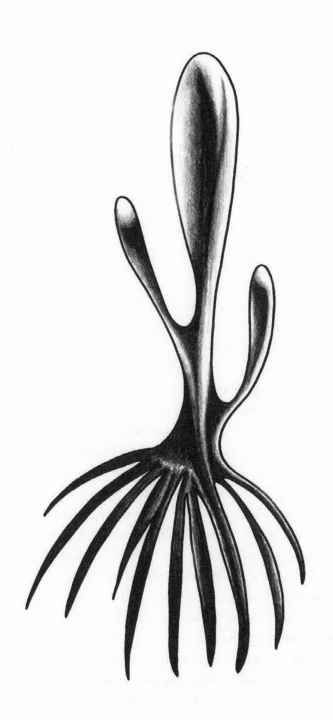

true
healing
is
waking up
from
the sleep
of
ignorance

4

Physical Body—Visible/Overt

Think you know all you need to know about breathing just by taking a breath? Let me challenge you on that one.

Mouth or nose? Unbelievable but true, most people breathe through their mouth. Yet it is the nose that filters, cleans, and adjusts air temperature when we breathe. If we use our mouth instead of our nose to breathe, we shock our lungs with air not properly prepared for their use. Our lungs must work harder and under a handicap.

How about when hurt, shocked, or surprised? I know this sounds silly, but, just when your body needs more oxygen than usual, you tend to stop breathing. Force yourself. Breathe.

Go a little further. Monitor yourself. How many times each day do you forget to breathe and under what conditions? You may be surprised to find that your breathing rhythms alter depending on what you're doing or feeling or thinking. Same with kids.

Take advantage of your breath. Objects will tend to weigh less if you lift on an in-breath, release on an out-breath. When climbing stairs, step up on in-breaths, put your foot down on out-breaths. When relaxing, see or feel yourself breathe in positive, supportive thoughts, as you breathe out worries and limiting self-beliefs. If you pace the living of your life with the natural cycles of breath, you'll feel better, stronger.

Breath can cease for periods of time, however, and without reason or warning. This happened to me and many others after our near-death experience; similar for anyone else who also underwent an in-depth, transformational shift. And, such stoppage isn't missed, not even the slightest. Life goes on. Periods can last minutes, for some over an hour. No lung action. No breath. No problem with the brain/mind assembly. Speaking for myself, this strange stoppage continued off and on for a year—the longest "time out," about eight minutes. After a year, normal breath patterns returned. Others noted similar occurrences.

Masters of breath control are yogis. Many have broken medical records with their feats of body/breath manipulations. In Hatha Yoga, every student learns that how you hold your fingers controls where in your lungs air goes as you breathe. There are three basic positions: upper-chest or shallow breathing (basically folding the hand into a fist over the thumb); mid-chest or normal breathing (fingers still somewhat folded in but thumb out and free); and low-chest or deep breathing (with index finger barely touching the thumb—making a circle—fingers out in an easy fashion and free).

I'm dwelling on this for a reason: virtually no yoga instructor tells you "the rest of the story" about low-chest or deep breathing. I am, and here it is. Drawing first.

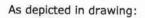

As depicted in drawing:

tips of index finger and thumb touch lightly to create a circle – other fingers hang loose and open.

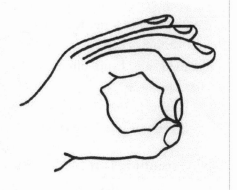

Placing the fingers of both hands in this position automatically enables the air we breathe to fill all five lungs lobes—while grounding and stabilizing the fullness of breath over our diaphragm and solar plexus (mid-section of our body). Doing this as often as you can (while watching a movie or television show, while taking a walk, while meditating, etc.), for at least six months, and once in a while thereafter, *retrains your breath flow as it increases lung capacity*. No special gimmicks, no counting breaths or sports exercises. Just get in the habit of holding your fingers in the low-chest position from time to time. When you do, you automatically tend to become:

- calmer, steadier, more comfortable and at ease with your body

- desirous of telling the truth, and being recognized as trustworthy

- more interested in and motivated by spiritual practices

- able to sing easier and hold musical notes longer and fuller

- stronger and more prepared for physical activities

All of this simply because of how you position your fingers.

Modern society demands fisting or semi-fisting. How else are you going to use the phone, grab a pen, use utensils, a shovel, handles and switches, gesture, or make a point? How many times each day do we tense up, tighten up, fear, or feel trapped or uncertain? How about your clothes? High heels force high-chest or shallow breathing. Belts and tight waist bands often restrict the diaphragm and further weaken the solar plexus.

Use your fingers to repower and rebalance yourself.

If you learn nothing else from this manual, learn to do this.

Movement is Life

Everything translates into muscular tension, whether you're being physical, mental, emotional, or spiritual. Simple everyday acts such as walking, lifting, bending, sitting, standing, climbing stairs—all have a direct effect on blood pressure, breathing, excreting waste, sleep, mental alertness, cheerfulness, even coping with stress and change.

You are the center of your universe.

Like it or not, posture counts.

In order to move, not only gracefully but in harmony with life and the universe in which we live, we must center our bodies within our own field of gravity. When your body is centered, you'll automatically walk straight but relaxed, climb stairs erect yet with grace, sit with a sense of pride yet enjoyment, stand from a sitting position in a flowing easy way, bend without stress, lift from the knees and legs (not the back). When your body is balanced, good posture comes naturally. Lazy or harmful posture is learned. Our inner world influences our outer world; our outer world reflects our inner world. Our body is the monitor of balance in-between.

The healing power of a brisk walk is the best exercise you can do. Also great are Hatha Yoga and T'ai Chi, gym workouts, water exercises, jogging, trampoline bounces, dance steps. In case you didn't know, the postures you do in Hatha Yoga are designed for body centering. For instance, every posture done to the right is followed by one done to the left. A forward posture is balanced with a backward one. The slow, continuous, flowing movements of T'ai Chi are patterned after birds, animals, streams, clouds, wind, to increase circulation and vigor while freeing the mind to rejoin with the Life Force. Other exercises may stretch you, toughen or limber you, but Hatha Yoga and T'ai Chi re-center and re-balance your body/mind/spirit as part of their design.

Psychic/Intuitive Dancing

This is where, as the music plays, you become each note and sound. You allow your body total freedom to fit and form itself into whatever is heard at whatever rhythm or pace the musical notes take. This is not free-form dancing. It is more than that. You actually *become* the music itself. Forget that you're human for a while, and become, instead, a physical expression of the music. Tips:

- Stand completely and totally relaxed, in a state of abundant expectancy. Place no limits on what happens next. Know that you can let yourself go and become the music without harm. You are centered. The exercise will be one of joy and adventure—a chance to experience the sacred beauty of form and sound.

- Have someone start a musical recording. Classics are the best to begin with. You can experiment with other types later.

- Once the music begins, release your reasoning mind and become one with the music. Allow no divisions or separations to occur between you and the music. Affirm no harm, no danger.

- Typically, your body will begin to move, jerky at first. Don't be embarrassed. You see, hear, feel, think about nothing else but the music. Give your body freedom to do this.

- When the music is over, relax in a standing position with your eyes closed. Give yourself time to sense and probe your body. How do you feel? Did the experience affect you? What emotions, feelings, or images surfaced for you? Did you learn anything? Did you experience anything? Bless yourself and know that you are you—fully conscious, aware, and awake. Open eyes.

- Try different types and styles of music. You may be surprised at how much you can learn and grow from doing this. Free-form and modern dancing enable you to feel and then express that feeling. With psychic/intuitive dancing you actually become the musical notes themselves. Musical notes do not move. They seem to because of how our brain connects things. When you actually become music, you tend to jerk or snap or roll from one note to another. This is unfamiliar territory. A real adventure.

Exercise Your Face

Two ways to do this are toning vowels and acupressure facelifts.

Toning Vowels

- All sounds must be verbal. All actions involve straining muscles.

- Say in turn each vowel—a, e, i, o, and u (uuoo).

- As you say each vowel, tone it slowly and loudly on an out-breath.

- Exaggerate facial muscles in toning each vowel. Strain. Strain more. Look weird. Protrude neck, chin, and lower lip out as far as you can. Pretend you're a clown.

- Go through the whole series ten times. Relax.

- Be aware of how much better your face feels. Muscles tingle. Good to do daily, or maybe once a week.

Facelifts without Surgery

When pressing certain points on your face, you literally activate a major stream of energy in your body. Called "acupressure points," these areas are well-defined in acupuncture and throughout holistic methods of healing. You do not need a needle to activate these points. Finger pressure is sufficient—firm but not too hard. Judge this for yourself.

Follow positions 1-18 in the drawing. Most positions require you to press skin/muscles with index fingers in a circular manner—always toward the outer edges of the face (never inward toward nose or mouth). With some positions, an upward lift is better than circular. While you do this exercise, do your inner work too, thanking your body for doing what it does in a healthy way and your face for projecting the peace you feel. Notice how the various positions follow "lines of energy" that naturally cross the face.

Position 1: at hairline, in line with middle of forehead and pupil of eye

Position 2: at middle of forehead

Position 3: at temples on hairline; if area is super-sensitive, don't do

Position 4: lower corners of each eye

Position 5: under eye pupil, on bone ridge—gentle, upward circling

Position 6: outer reaches of upper area of cheek

Position 7: in line with lower part of nostrils, easier to do if you smile

Position 8: corners of mouth—use finger pad, not tip; be gentle

Position 9: near upper lip but lined up with eye pupil

Position 10: below corners of mouth

Position 11: at jaw hinge, don't do if jaw hinge incomplete/TMJoint—but use palms of both hands to sweep face upward from jaw line to cheek ridge, about three or four times or so

Position 12: thumbs underneath brow ridge next to nose, lift in and up

Position 13: under nose cleft, swirl circle to the left using one finger

Position 14: directly under lower lip, swirl to the left using one finger

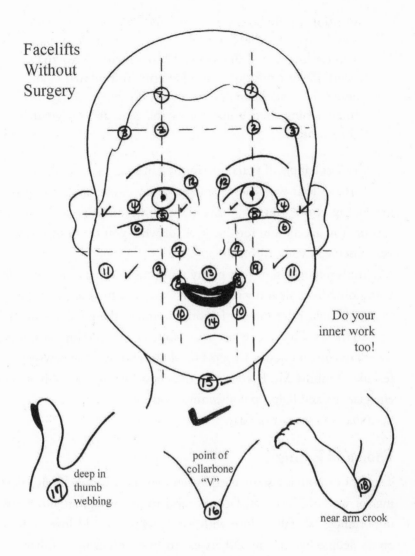

Facelifts
Without
Surgery

Do your
inner work
too!

deep in
thumb
webbing

point of
collarbone
"V"

near arm crook

Position 15: slap full range of upper neck under jaw line many times. At the Check Mark—press slightly in, then up at middle of throat, brief hold

Position 16: at point of collar bone, swirl to the left

Position 17: deep within thumb webbing swirl/press in several times

Position 18: do both sides—put one arm across chest to shoulder; with other hand, place finger on crook of that arm circling several times about 2 to 3 inches above the bend. Reverse positions for other arm. To find that "spot" above the inner bend of the arm . . . if it hurts, you're there. Doing circular massage on that spot also invigorates the sex organs.

The first couple of years I performed this exercise, I did it daily.

Three to four years later I skipped a day. Now I might skip two, depending. Until you memorize the routine, practice in front of a mirror. You are aiming for the "feel" of what you do to match what you observe in your mirror.

This exercise is now part of my morning routine: clean up in the bathroom, dress, sit at my meditation altar, read from a spiritual magazine or book, offer prayers for others, affirm the goodness of each day, do the facelift exercise, neck exercises, leg lifts and hip rolls, negotiate stairs up and down, then eat breakfast and read the newspaper. I feel like climbing Mt. Everest after these routines because of how they energize me and light up body, mind, and soul.

Nice way to start the day.

Food and Eating

The act of eating is a sensual explosion. For most people, it gives feelings of warmth, love, satisfaction, tenderness, caring, attention, and importance. We fall in love with eating as if it could love us back. Some people live to eat. Others eat to live. Somewhere in-between those two extremes is an enjoyable middle, where the fixation of being in love with food morphs into a simple sense of well-being.

We should enjoy what we eat, but not get swept away by the gratification of eating. Food used as a substitute for love/sex/touching will lead to weight problems and loss of self-esteem. There's an art to eating and a science, too. Not only does it matter what we eat, but in what combinations, and at what time of day. Foods are really packages of chemicals, and, like all chemicals—natural or processed—it is wise to know what best combines with what, when, and how.

Example: a carrot isn't always a carrot. Forget looks, it matters more where it was raised for good enzyme ratios. Without enough enzymes, food doesn't "sing" in your mouth or have the kind of flavor your taste buds light up to. Food in the eastern U.S. tasted "flat" to me once I moved from southern Idaho to the northern suburbs of Virginia. After a lot of checking, I found out that farmers throughout North Carolina and Virginia (where the food was coming from), did not fertilize properly for a good enzyme/vitamin base for their crops. I learned to seek out food stuff from organic/sustainable gardens/farms.

A few pointers:

- Sweet and sour fruits should not be mixed together at the same meal

- Bread and red meat should not be eaten together

- Oranges and apples are best consumed separately from other foods

- Corn is best fresh, never canned; if frozen, heat up with milk in pan

- Bread, butter, beans, squash, tomatoes were made for each other

- Do not combine fruits and vegetables in the same dish

- Pie cherries and milk do not mix

- Fruits can be combined with lighter meats like fish and fowl

- Smoked meat and cheese appease a hunger for sugar

- Lemon and/or lime juice and vinegar are all salt substitutes

- Eat a handful of fresh lettuce before bed—a natural sedative

There's a whole science to eating and lots of good books to read that will help you to better understand what might be best for you. The question of eating red meat together with bread challenges the tradition of sandwiches—what we put in them and whether bread should be consumed at all. Today's grains, especially wheat, are a product of genetic modification. Although claimed safe, such grains are increasingly discovered to be at the core of serious health problems. European and Asiatic methods of serving small, single courses spread out over several hours harmonizes with our digestive system. Stuffing everything into a single meal does not.

The time of day we eat matters. If you are active during daylight hours, then you should eat during daylight hours. If you have a night job, eat at night. Split-shift workers would be wise to eat their heaviest meal in daylight, smaller meals at night. Actually, the biggest meal should be lunch, not dinner, with sweet things/desserts for breakfast.

Color is a big thing with foods. There's a whole psychology of food colors and food appearance. Get this: red, brown, orange, and yellow are the colors of "hurry up and eat me." Thus, fast-food restaurants and drive-throughs use those colors in their signage and décor. These so-called family eateries are where a lot of people are stacked, charged less, eat quickly, and get out the door faster. The colors of green, blue, ivory, gold, silver, pewter, delicate tonal shades, encourage slow, careful, discerning eating habits and more intimate conversation. Hence, you get less and pay more for the privilege of "gourmet dining."

At home, have a burning candle at your table when you eat or at least a centerpiece of natural, colorful beauty. The lovelier the table setting, the more cooperative and happy are those who eat there. Say grace or hold your hands over your food to bless it before you eat. Soft music is nice but not necessary. Just the colors of the food, good smells, and an attractive centerpiece are enough to invite better digestion and good conversation if others are present.

Sugar

Notice I have yet to mention sugar. There is no drug on Earth more addictive or more debilitating, in my opinion, than refined sugar, and, no "safe" sugar substitute. Throughout history we've celebrated, equated with love, the sweetness sugar has, and we've over-piled our meals with it. True, sugar is necessary for health. Our brain cannot live without some of it. The catch is, our brains are not as greedy as our eyes, taste buds, and psychological makeup. When we overload with the stuff, damage results. I cook with a little honey for sweetening, or mashed fruit. That's it. No more is needed. Read your labels. Certain brands of meat now have sugar added to them, as well as most canned vegetables and beans. "Turbinado" or unrefined sugar (sometimes called raw sugar) isn't the problem white sugar is, but you still don't want to overuse it. Cane and corn sugars can be handled in small amounts, same with molasses. Moderation applies.

Changing Weight

Forget diets, scales, counting calories—instead:

- Listen and pay attention to your body-mind. The deeper wisdom within you knows your best weight. Avoid scales and measurements. Trust your body's knowledge.

- Bless your body just as it is. Caress it without shame or regret or guilt. View yourself in a full-length mirror. Appreciate yourself.

- Vow never again to punish your body, mind, emotions, or soul with diets, denials, damnations, criticism, or doubt. Know that you need not follow others. You are okay as you are. Respect yourself.

- Promise yourself that you will eat whatever you *really* want to eat, whenever you *really* want to eat it. And that the food you eat will be nutritious, healthy and tasty.

- ◆ Agree with yourself that weight is a state of mind, not a measurement of calories.

- ◆ Photographs of slim people posted to your refrigerator, theories, methods, suggestions are just crutches. Know that you are doing what you are doing because you love yourself and respect yourself.

- ◆ Each morning, affirm how lovely and perfect you are. See yourself as beautiful/handsome. Say with firmness: "Every day, and in every way, I am getting better and better. I am becoming more and more of who I really am." Wear whatever clothes appeal to you. Meditate some time during the day and evening, affirming and knowing the perfection you are. Take self-development classes if available and whenever you can.

Challenges and Changes That Occur and How to Handle Them

Eat only what you want when you want it.

This is literal. If you're the chief-cook-and-bottle-washer for your family or group, this edict still applies. Cook what you need to for others, but eat only what you truly want for yourself. If you want snacks, so be it. The catch here is *what you truly want*. If you don't truly, really want a morsel, don't eat it—regardless of what others are doing. What I found when I did this is, I wanted less food more often throughout the day, and, I wanted to do more as I ate less. Amazing! When all rules and druthers were tossed, my own natural inclinations took over. My body didn't want a lot of food at a single meal. Thus, I began to eat differently because it felt right.

Vow never again to punish yourself or follow others.

Example: You're in line at a potluck. Tables of food are spread out before you. There's a person to your right and another to your left. In meal lines like this they usually put desserts first, so you have to pass by favorites or heart-stopping yummies before you get to the real food. The person to your left says something like, "Oh, that pecan pie looks so delicious. But I know I'll gain 10 pounds with one bite." Then the person to your right chimes in, "Yes, pie like that has so many calories in it. I don't dare have any." Silence follows. Both are waiting for you to say something. Alert. Alert.

This moment is part of the social contract.

Yup, simply by being human, we have all agreed on some level to participate in the social drama around us. This applies to being at a dance, dinner, argument, fight, disagreement, social engagement, party, family outing, whatever. "The Group" expects you to be a participant. They expect you to be engaged. The person to your left and right, in this situation, are waiting for you to say something. If you don't, they will wonder about you, whether you're anti-social, or not feeling well, or if there's something wrong. Out of respect for others, while still remaining respectful to myself, I learned *The Power of Praise*. What did I do in that food lineup? Out loud, I stated how beautiful that pie was and how much I admired the handiwork of whoever had cooked it. I praised the pie and the cook who made it. That satisfied the person to the left and the one to the right. The line moved. Had I really wanted a slice of that pie, I would have taken it. But I didn't, so I passed it by, *in an attitude of praise which I had verbalized*. Everyone was happy. So was I, for I had upheld my part in the social contract.

Even when alone, pay attention to how thoughts combine with emotions to produce results.

Example: Just before noon I'm waiting in my doctor's office for an appointment. I picked up a large, colorful magazine and flipped through the pages. One particular page stopped me. It was a full page photograph of a chocolate torte. I mean this torte was so beautiful, the photo so luscious, I noticed that saliva was beginning to curl back and forth between my teeth and my stomach began to growl. Instantly, I recognized what was happening . . . I had made a focus.

A focus is where all your senses, mind, memory, desires come together at one point—a single point of utter, complete clarity. With such a focus, you suddenly become the most powerful you can ever be. It is a moment of pure unadulterated power. Whatever you think or project into that moment, happens. I recognized this moment, the focus, the clarity of power, and I acted. Into that focus, *I lavished all the praise I could* to the photographer who took the picture, to the cook who baked the torte, to the publisher who printed the page, and to the editor of the magazine who made the final decision to use that photo. I so filled my mind, my life, with praise that I became utterly full. No hunger. No desire. No regrets. I was full— of praise—then I turned the page.

A Surprise about Eyes

Did you know that in the development of color in our eyes, all of the early languages acknowledged only black and white? Later on in history, people described red and yellow as we see them today, also green. *But no blue.* The only exception were the Egyptians who both saw and spoke of blue. Blue did not exist as a color in Biblical times either, nor with any "original peoples" (tribal groups). Even today those with color blindness have the most difficulty telling the difference between blue and green. The ability to see blue and shades of blue (even of the sky) is considered a modern refinement of vision . . . and not everyone is so gifted.

Hint

We now know that the DNA molecule has an energy body. That which we used to call "96 percent junk DNA" is actually the energetic field that controls, manages, and directs the molecule. DNA speaks two languages—that of its physical properties and that of its energetics. Without its energy body, DNA could not exist. A major function of DNA is to inform, connect, manage, and direct all life in its operation—it's the universal internet. This same counterpart, DNA energetics, is within us. If this were not so, we could not be who or what we are, nor could we participate in life itself. We would be nothing. We would not even exist.

As we moderns have learned and are still learning to see the color blue as a refinement of vision, we are also advancing in our ability to see and respond to energy itself and the field it creates—in us, and in everyone else.

when you
change
your weight
you
change
your life

5

Energy Body—Invisible/Subtle

Everything that exists in the visible world has its exact complement, a template of sorts, existent in the invisible world. The visible, then, is an outworking of the invisible. Without an energy template (a "circuit-board" of power), nothing in physicality could survive, grow, or flourish. Our energy body is as real as our physical body. Both generate, expel, receive, and maneuver varied pulsations of life force.

The carbon-based, electromagnetic life form we wear (otherwise known as a physical body) is:

	Physical Body Visible	Energy Body Invisible
WIRED BY	Nervous System	Meridian System
POWERED BY	Endocrine Glands	Chakras
GUIDED BY	Brain	Mind

Our head is a beacon, thanks to the magnetite crystals in our brain cells and the mineral deposits around the ridge of our nose and brow. *Our hands* are sensors, because of the incredible number of nerve endings that interweave the skin-cover of both palms. *Our feet* are grounds, enabling us to stabilize and balance power flows internal to us with that of earth.

We are natural transmitters/receivers of signals from throughout the entire electromagnetic spectrum by virtue of the simple fact that we drink water and breathe air. And, as a "living antenna," our energy is capable of boosting the electrical charge to items like light bulbs and remote controls. Any alarm installer knows this, that human beings can jumpstart electrical signals in much the same manner that holding onto television "rabbit ears" corrected blurry signals (during the days when people had antenna atop their sets).

Upward motions recharge us (getting up, raising our arms, massage strokes toward the heart). Downward motions relax us (sitting down, lowering our arms, massage strokes away from the heart).

Connect with Your Energy Field

To feel the energy that fills you, bring both hands almost together but not quite. In that "not-quite-touching" pose, take a deep breath and relax. Gently gaze at that space between your hands. Do you see anything? Sense anything? Feel anything? No??? Rub your hands together vigorously to create static electricity. Now, try the same not-quite-touching pose again. Is there a presence of "something" between your hands now? Creating the static electricity enables you to feel what most people can readily sense—the body's energy field—more commonly called an "aura."

Most people, when they speak of an aura, refer to that thin band of white or semi-transparent light that outlines things. With humans, the band alters in color and size relative to the ever-changing moods and attitudes of each person, especially if he or she is ill. Yet those who claim to see auras, and dowsers who measure them, agree that what is visible is merely a couple of inches of concentrated energy near the skin. The aura itself is an energy field extending about twelve feet around most individuals. Fields in close proximity overlap. That overlap makes it possible for one person to "pick up" impressions from those nearby and from the immediate environment.

Seeing Auric Fields—Hearing Sounds

Invite a group of people over. Explain that the goal is being able to see auric fields, then lead them through a brief relaxation exercise. Erect a large screen or use a plain white wall as background. Dim lights. Each guest takes a turn standing in front of the screen facing the group. The rest simply gaze at whoever that person is, allowing their vision to double slightly as it slides past body contours. Auric light is easier to see around head and shoulders (clothes make no difference). Vary the experience by asking the person in front of the screen to move his or her aura around (by thinking it so). Does what is seen match what the individual actually did? Have the person in front pretend he or she is angry. What affect does that have on the aura? Request that he or she bring to mind thoughts and feelings of love. Anything change? In what manner?

Experiment with sound, too. Where is it that we hear? With our ears? Have everyone close their eyes and relax in preparation for sensing where in their body they might react to sound. Use a metal tuning fork and a wooden stick. Strike the metal with the wood several times, allowing the sound to fade after each strike. With eyes open, each, in turn, describes whatever body sensations were felt and any perception arrived at about the sound's affect. Notice how often people claim that high-pitched or metallic sounds "play out" most in the upper body, while low-pitched or wooden sounds vibrate best throughout the lower body. Even though all of the body seems able to "hear," subtleties are specific to each person.

We resonate to whatever sound is in our environment whether we realize it or not. Our behavior and moods are influenced by the pitch, tone, and rhythm of that sound. Here's how this generally works:

FAST MUSIC	SLOW MUSIC
Eat faster	Eat slower
Hurry with activities	Relax with activities
Buy less/do more	Buy more/do less
Speeds up	Slows down
Tightens	Loosens
Accelerates	Decelerates
Tension	Comfort
Fast-food restaurants (strive for quick turnover, quantity, indigestion common)	Gourmet restaurants (strive for the pleasure of "atmosphere," quality, ease of digestion)

HARD ROCK / PUNK MUSIC	MELODIOUS / NATURE
Entrains the brain	Entrains the heart
Stimulates endocrine glands, nervous system	Stimulates chakras/meridian system
Tends to dull hearing/senses	Tends to accentuate hearing/senses
Promotes separation	Promotes unity
Leads to alienation and defiance	Leads to cooperation and compassion

Stimulates passion	Stimulates healing
Stunts plant and animal growth	Nourishes plant and animal growth (except for marijuana)

Note: Birds and most land animals migrate according to the pitch and tone of sound, while whales and most sea animals (fish) follow vibratory sound-waves and sonar.

Secrets about Sound

Plants not only grow higher, healthier, and more beautiful with melodious music, cows give more milk, children concentrate better, and families contend with less tension or stress. Raise the pitch and add the pounding heartbeat of rock—and everything and everyone reacts . . . usually by shrinking, withholding, withering, irritating, yelling, fighting. Sound sells according to pitch and rhythm. When you play music, you "play" people.

Formulas: to sell sex, imitate the sounds and movements of sexual intercourse. To sell drugs, imitate the heightened sensations of heart and brain waves in repetitive beats. To sell productivity, imitate the sound of fast stepping marches, Polka or Latin music. If you want people to buy more goods, give them romantic swells of music with feel-good themes.

Pounding, rhythmic chants or decrees that quickly, loudly, continuously repeat can control and manipulate masses of people before they have a chance to think for themselves. The secret behind this is hyper-breathing, word alliteration, and incessant rhythm. Keep this up for more than 21 minutes and you'll own the crowd. Add flashing strobe lights and they'll do whatever you tell them to and won't know why (the quickest way to hypnotize crowds). Get people to raise and lower arms and legs in rhythm to the sound, and the hypnotic effect will lead to brain washing. Hitler used this method to buy the soul of Germany and sell its people a nightmare.

Why do we flock to the harbingers of hate and greed, always begging for more? Because that loud, low pounding beat, rhythmic rhetoric, and screaming sound mimics the primal energies of hunger and sex, lust and greed, danger and survival. We all have that in us. It's part of being human. It harkens back to our beginnings before we decided to settle down and civilize. No virtues here—only pleasures, stimulation, and satisfaction. Addictive, like taking a drug, we get hooked and grab for more without realizing there's always a price to pay. We cannot enjoy this type of stimulation for long, without giving to get. That's the hook. So, we give up our ability to hear with clarity, our right to think independently, our natural creative drive, the freedom to say no. We give up our dignity. Beware of the hook.

Chants, decrees, and repetitious alliteration can be just as helpful and healthy as detrimental. For instance, from the depths of Eastern philosophy, we come to know and tone the sound of the Universe or OM, or "roll out" the yogic AUM (the precursor to the Christian AMEN).

Chanting sacred sounds is one of the safest, best ways I know to get a high you can keep. Sanskrit words are meant for chanting and so are many prayers and hymns from all the world's great religions. The high we are gifted with from them hurts no one . . . everybody benefits.

When we use sound to enhance our life, we are cradled in givingness. Sounds in nature, melodies, harmonic voices in swells of highs and lows, chants of the most beautiful words we know, laughter, bells, giggles of joy . . . these sounds, and others like them, lift and inspire us, filling us with confidence and strength. Our mind sharpens and we think clearer. We expand beyond where we are.

More on Faculty Extensions

Transcendence of physical limitations leads to an awareness that we exist simultaneously on multiple levels, not just one. (You may want to refer here to "Faculty Extensions" in the KNOWING section.)

These levels are layered like onion skin and appear to extend outward from our visible form in a manner that is both interactive and interpenetrating. Eastern mysticism teaches that the physical body is enveloped by an *etheric layer* (where the body's "blueprints" reside as energy templates), an *astral layer* (for emotions), a *mental layer* (for the mind), a *buddhic layer* (for true intuition), an *atmic layer* (the spiritual planes), and several *layers of adi* (higher spiritual planes) . . . for a total of seven levels. Western tradition teaches four levels: physical, emotional, mental, and spiritual. Still others, twelve levels.

Although the identification of levels varies from culture to culture, one tenet holds: the physical exists as an outworking of energetic and spiritual realities—each having its own anatomy (body of information).

The life force itself is dual in nature, described best by the Chinese and Vedic understandings of "yin" and "yang." The yang aspect of the life force is considered positive by energy charge in the way it stimulates and contracts (depicted by male symbol). The yin represents the negative pole of the life force in how it relaxes and expands (depicted by female symbol.) These two aspects of the life force underlie all basic polarities: hot/cold, day/night, black/white, right/wrong, love/fear, bitter/sweet, life/death, and so forth. Health depends on the balance of yin and yang, otherwise "dis-ease" results (not at ease/lack of harmony). A system of "meridians" (energetic "power lines") distribute life force throughout our energy body, similar to how our physical blood stream, nerves, and lymphatic circuits operate. Blocks in the flow of energy along the meridians are what practitioners of acupuncture look for and seek to correct by manipulating precisely placed needles. ("Acupressure," or finger stimulation of meridian points, is the basis of the facial exercise you learned in the last section.)

Central to the healthful flows of life are "chakras" (which means "spinning wheels" in Sanskrit). Chakras are the energetic complement to our endocrine glands. They function as generators that pump, spin, take in, or throw off energy. They are active centers of power—seven in number. Schools of thought differ on the full relationship of chakras to the endocrine system (and hormones); still, a brief rendering of the two main versions is worth considering.

The two different charts that follow illustrate what I've been talking about—one comes from the psychic discourses of the great seer Edgar Cayce, and the other from a comparison made by Dr. Swami Gitananda in an attempt to reconcile Eastern mystical traditions with Western science.

BASIC LOCATIONS OF CHAKRA/GLAND CENTERS:

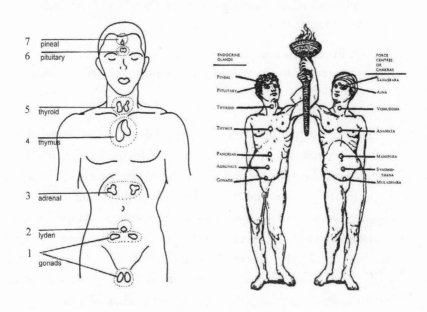

SYMBOLIC CORRESPONDENCES OF CHAKRA/GLAND CENTERS:

1. Gonads (*reproduction*): security issues, Earth-oriented; relates to red/white, planet Saturn, sound scale "D." Key: patience/desire.

2. Lyden-Leydig/Adrenals (*creativity*): pleasure, water oriented; relates to orange/black, Neptune, "Re." Key: fair-play/temptation.

3. Adrenals/Pancreas/Spleen (*energy*): activity levels, fire oriented; relates to yellow/red, Mars, "Mi." Key: courage/fear.

4. Thymus (*emotions*): affection and beauty, air oriented; relates to green/pale shades, Venus, "Fa." Key: love/attachment.

5. Thyroid (*will*): decision making, voice/Lesser Mind oriented; relates to blue/neutral, Mercury, "So." Key: communication/confusion.

6. Pituitary (*ideals*): intuitive awareness, belief/service oriented; relates to indigo/silver, Jupiter, "La." Key: dedication/dogmatism.

7. Pineal (*mastery*): soul awareness, vision/Greater Mind oriented; relates to purple/gold, Uranus, "Ti." Key: spirituality/domination.

First through third are the lower chakras—self-oriented. Fifth through seventh are the higher chakras—oriented more to others. The mediator between self and others (life's balance or fulcrum point) is the fourth . . . love/heart. Primary colors depict the rainbow of life energies; secondary colors indicate how energy changes once an individual matures and begins to develop spiritually. Keys highlight positive and negative aspects. *Note: White is aligned with the first chakra, not the seventh. That's because white, as the unification of color, represents the successful completion of a given growth cycle and our "graduation" to the next phase (energetic octave) of our learning.*

I have noticed that the chakra system operates through twelve major and twelve minor energy centers. The majors are the seven already discussed. The minor chakras are "energy gates," places where energy can enter or exit easily—like through the open doorway our joints provide. The most active energy gates are located at the bottom arch of each foot, both knees, anus, both sides of the hip, both shoulders, middle palms of each hand, and that "knob" at the base of the neck in the back. (Gateways that are blocked to whatever degree from the free flow of energy are more vulnerable to injury or being crippled by dis-ease.)

Our energy body is a vital arrangement of blueprints, templates, circuitry, and generators—an anatomy of power empowered by floods of pulsations in the physical body, along with an amazing variety of hormones and chemical switching agents.

Emotions Determine Results

We have electromagnetic fields. We also have emotional fields. Emotions are energy in movement, specific in effect because of how the energy body works and because of the strength we give them. Positive energy lifts and frees. Negative energy holds and binds. This range of feeling is what "paints" the atmosphere of our mind with ever-changing hues of mood. We *feel* before we think—which then releases a chain of reactions that will respond to the amount of energy we gave the feeling. A few examples of how this tends to work follow.

Anger arouses the sympathetic nervous system (triggering chest expanse, spinal cord, and the larger muscles of the back), while gratitude touches off the parasympathetic (stimulating head and pelvis, heartbeat, and pupil dilation). Translation: the sensation of anger activates the chemical that prepares us to take a stance, to challenge or fight (in whatever manner). The sensation of gratitude, though, excites another type of chemical, one that engenders a posture of willingness and cooperation.

The two instinctual feelings we least understand are anger and fear. Looking at them as directional movements of energy may help.

The energy pattern of anger is a straight line, pushing out away from us in the trajectory of an unleashed arrow seeking its mark. It knots up into a fist wherever it lands for the purpose of hindering, hurting, or exploding for all to see. By its nature, anger is external yang energy that pushes us, moves us. Because it has so much power and force it can be distorted into violence and crime. If held in and not expressed, anger can disfigure a person, armoring the larger muscles of arms, legs, back and neck, and/or twisting the face as it bunches or knots tissues.

The energy pattern of fear curves out and returns just like a boomerang does. Its trajectory, based on a curving arc, picks up on anything hurtful, warning if danger is found. Fear is subtle, sneaky, quiet—it's what you take in and mull over, sometimes to the point of being weakened, drained. By its nature, fear is internal yin energy that holds back. If kept inside too long, fear can erode like acid, leeching away your energy, weakening as it drains, paralyzing any type of forward motion or progress, even to the point of mental illness.

Natural Anger

* True anger seldom lasts longer than 30 to 60 seconds. Anything longer than that is left over from something else.

* Anger is pure, innocent displeasure—a brief moment of clarity, illogical in its spontaneity, but never vindictive or hateful. Extremes of anger come from suppressing or repressing it. When held in, it can twist into something else (like rage).

* Anger in its natural state is like a breath of fresh air, pushing for new perspectives, a change. Anger cleans up and clears out. It only drains and debilitates when you don't know how to use it.

* Anger is a necessary "tool," a release valve for our inner "pressure cooker." Only so much stress, tension, and strain can be handled before health issues arise (like cancer). Change often heals.

* You express anger by self-assertion (like screaming in your car where no one can hear you, or beating a log with a rubber hose, or jumping up and down on a trampoline, or running around the block, or house cleaning, or mowing the lawn or pulling weeds).

◆ You cannot talk yourself out of anger. It is a physical force. To release it, *be physical*, but in a constructive manner as suggested. Lack of self-assertion is incredibly exhausting, like the bone-weary avoidance of starting or stopping something that needs to be done.

Natural Fear

◆ Fear is the intuitive awareness that something isn't right; danger. It is positive as a signal to be alert, ready, cautious, careful.

◆ Fear gives us the time and space needed to react or respond. It helps us to know about things ahead of time, setting the stage and motion for us to handle unknown threats or cautions.

◆ We need fear. It is our friend, but like anger, fear does not last on its own, nor does it linger. The only time fear can be troublesome or turn on us like some poisonous dart is when we refuse to let it go. Fear rises suddenly to the occasion, then recedes. It is us who alter things—through selfishness, weakness, confusion, or choice. Fear, if left to its own natural rhythm, will leave of its own accord when no longer needed.

◆ Unnatural, abnormal fear is learned.

A Litany of Fear

When I was faced with the enormous task of rebuilding my body after I died, I had to confront fears I didn't even know I had—constant fears, in-your-face kinds of fears, paralyzing waves of fear. A friend suggested I read *Dune* by Frank Herbert. Early-on in the book is a "Litany of Fear." Why I changed what was there, I do not know, but my version of that Litany became a lifesaver. It enabled me to see and know and feel exactly what fear really is and how I can handle and overcome it. I pass this on to you. Chant as needed. Feel each word. Taste it.

Litany of Fear
(Atwater version)

Fear is the mind killer.
It is the little death.
I will face my fear.
It will pass over me, around me, and through me.
And when it is gone,
I will remain.

Flip the Switch

Laugh. Often.

Laughter is a powerful antidote to stress. It builds trust and rapport between people, stimulates problem-solving, and can even stop hostility and anger. There's nothing like a good laugh. It has been said that humor adds years to our life and life to our years. So true. How it helps us physically reads like a wish-book of shortcuts for better health. Laughter even helps diabetics control their blood sugar, and reduces the risk of stroke and heart attacks. Need I say more?

To handle yourself, use your head. To handle others, use your heart . . . for love as an intention flows from the heart with a vibrational frequency of 528 hertz. *As light is sound you can see, love is light you can feel.*

We now know that DNA is nothing, can't even exist, without the energetics that manage, control, and direct its existence. The same is true of the universe and of creation itself. That which is invisible to us, the energetics of existence, "speaks" two languages—that of the physical and that of the spirit.

And everything is energy.

emotions
are the
wings
thoughts
ride

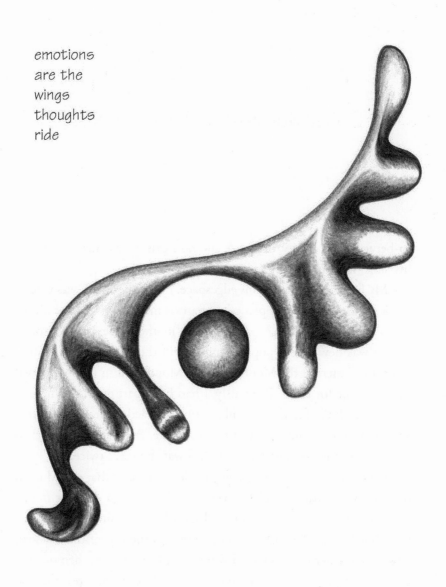

6

Spirit Body—In-Between/Soul

In-between all polarity, existence and non-existence, what is visible or invisible, is a gap . . . the "edgespace" to power.

My first experience of this edgespace, this in-between, was when I stuck my head over the open core of an atomic energy reactor offline but a few hours. This happened back in the sixties when atomic energy was new to the popular mind, and the Arco Testing Station (past the Craters of the Moon National Monument in Idaho) opened to the public for tours. Previously, I had been part of a tour there of the hanger built for the first plane to be fueled entirely by atomic energy; a project later scrapped as impossible. But when they opened the doors to the Testing Station itself, I was there . . . twice.

Everyone had to wear a badge inside the facility that would warn of excessive exposure whenever we walked through a detector frame. I always ditched mine as soon as I could, so nothing would hamper what I might feel. Once you climbed to the top of the reactors, white-coated personnel greeted you with a little speech, then quickly guided you past the open core—where you could glimpse the real thing: atomic power. I always broke ranks and stuck my head in as far as I could before I was jerked back. I'd wait around on the main floor until that official was gone and another took his place; then I'd climb back up to the core and do the same thing again, and again. I could taste it, feel it, smell it, see it, and I couldn't get enough of that power. I'd stand over pools of irradiated rods glowing blue in the water. They say our senses cannot register that power. I could. When time to leave, I'd find that "tucked-away" badge, slap it back on, and walk through the detector as if nothing happened. Nothing did.

I can make a comparison. The love that flooded my being on the other side of life, when I died three times in 1977, felt just like the power I absorbed when exposed to the open core of a supposedly "cool" reactor taken offline a few hours before.

Because of this I can say . . . the love we find on the other side of life is not an emotion. It is power beyond what we can name as power. It is a state of "is-ness" impossible to describe. We don't *move* there. We *become* there. We *are* there—already—as a soul.

"Edgerunners" mimic this space because they take you to that "edge" in consciousness, that in-between-ness, located at the edge of where the gap resides. Drugs like ayahuasca, ketamine, and DMT are one type of edgerunner; the experience they give is rapid, followed by dramatic aftereffects that seldom stabilize, uplift, or heal. Meditation, deep contemplation, prayer, the stillness of entering into The Silence are another type of edgerunner; slower to attain, but with aftereffects that stabilize quicker, are long-lasting, and lead to satisfying lives of service and meaning. Whether you take the fast or slow route to the edgespace of the in-between, the only guarantee that serves the goal is your willingness to surrender to a power greater than you, to The God of Your Being.

Tricks of Perception

Meditation, and other practices similar to it, train your perception to see both motion and rest *simultaneously* and *separately* at the same time. This simultaneous-everywhere type of consciousness preexists and can be accessed from any point in the universe at any moment by anyone—as if it were a hologram, where each piece reveals the whole.

Quantum physicists tell us that everything that exists actually flashes in and out of existence about a billion times per second. First you see it, then you don't. During an "on flash," existence is illuminated, and everything is visible; during an "off flash," there is only the darkness of invisibility, and nothing can be seen. On and off. Back and forth. Motion and rest. Our built-in perceptual prejudice (what we are taught or choose to believe) is what enables us to determine if anything is continuous (as if a wave) or solid (as if stationary/a particle). This natural prejudice shields us from the fact that motion and rest are separate sequences. We see solid objects and we see continuous movement and we think we are seeing both at the same time, when, actually, we are not. The world around us exists as perceived because of how perceived. Creation, as we think it exists, is a physical illusion. You encounter this as a truth on the other side of life. Suddenly you have 360-degree vision and can observe time and space as what they really are . . . simultaneous. You don't return from edgespace with the same consciousness you had before.

The Soul Has Its Own Will

During my experience in death, I saw the souls God created as showers of sparks, nuclei of holy fire that spread out and expanded in waves, thought-waves, similar in movement to what happens to the wake caused by a speedboat zooming across a placid lake. The farther afield each wave projected (in a plasma-like "ocean" of etheric substance or spirit), the more the individual sparks separated from their wave, spinning off into positive and negative poles of energy charge, mimicking what causes the central pulse-beat to oscillate. I observed that the nucleus of holy fire, once divided and freed from its wave, is able to take on any manner or type of existence, shape, or form. Yet no matter what experiences it takes on, the nucleus spark carries within it the urge to attract unto itself that which will unify its charge (the rejoining of its positive and negative poles back into the full nuclei it once was) and fulfill its ultimate purpose (reunion with the original source). *The many ever seek to rejoin with The One.*

I experienced, fully and completely, that each and every one of us, all of us, are holy sparks of fire at our core. Our core-self or soul appeared to me as a matrix or mass of pulsing intelligence, sometimes undulating as if wavelike, sometimes flashing or sparkling as if a power grid or circuit board of energetic particles of light. Physically, souls are infinitesimally small, hardly more than a "wink" in size; yet each contains a power mass so intense, a consciousness so unlimited in function and potential, that it is beyond our ability as humans to fathom either its makeup or design. I saw that what resides within our earthly frame, what we think defines us as human beings, is but a "finger" of what or who we are—a projection from our soul's mass.

Then I realized that what all of us call our "mission" or special role in life, our part in the grander Reality, is that contribution that is possible for us to make once we merge into, or are cooperative with, our soul. The will of every soul is to "outpicture" (project) the Greater Will, and in so doing carry out God's Plan for creation. We are separate from our Source only for as long as we think we are separate. In truth, our connection to a higher order never ceased and it never will. We are indeed created in the image and likeness of God as souls, and, as souls, we are charged with the ability to co-create. This gives us the power to experience the result of our own evolving thought. *Although feelings are the primary stimulus in Earth-plane living, consciousness is the only geography.*

I also discovered that the soul sets and experiences growth or learning cycles. These cycles evolve around an overall theme and are planned according to whatever is necessary to carry out and fulfill the theme of the cycle. For instance, if the soul wanted to explore the nature of courage, it would plan various incidents and opportunities that would enable it, once individualized in flesh and bone, to embark upon such explorations. Time would not matter, since time has a different meaning to a soul than it does to a human personality.

These thematic soul cycles can be fulfilled in one lifetime, cover a series of lifetimes, or happen in different or multiple forms of existence on other levels besides that of the Earth-plane. Results depend on how the soul develops along the way, what it learns. Souls can unite in groups for the initiation and carry-thru of a common purpose, mission, or goal. Tremendous amounts of focused energy are produced and released when souls do this, enough to influence sweeping changes in society or cause major alterations in the world at large.

Commitments like this often involve souls who choose to be born into bodies in the Earth-plane during the same time. This enables them to either be part of each other's lives or interact with each other in significant ways that will affect the larger human condition. Examples: the signers of the Declaration of Independence, all men in their twenties and thirties, whose courage and intelligence fashioned a nation out of a conflict in loyalties; and families like the Kennedys, who, aside from being a tightly knit bunch prone to personal foibles, sponsored service-oriented projects that benefited millions. Another example is the period from the late 1800s to the early 1900s when the synergy of inventors across the globe brought forth the industrial revolution and achieved phenomenal changes in everyone's life. This exact same pattern (groupings or clusters of talent) played out in other fields of interest as well, making those years in history forever remembered as "earth-shaking."

Holy Spirit

Our "higher self" responds to spirit (the life breath) *as a soul* (that which breathes the life breath) *that comes from deity* (originator of the life breath). The root word of "spirit" means "breath" and is equated with "the life force." There are over seven-hundred names from across the world for this mysterious force. Some of them are: prana, ki, chi, Odic Force, mana, noetic, energy, tachyon, elan vital, bioplasma, baraka, yesod, orenda, mebe, Holy Spirit. At its core, "Holy Spirit" means *The Breath of God Breathing*.

Wilhelm Reich, a medical doctor and Freudian psychoanalyst, attempted to identify this energy as the fifth force in nature. Terming it "orgone," he described it as all-pervasive, primordial, without mass, pre-atomic . . . the force from which all other forms of energy derive. As a fifth force, this spirit breath enlivens and quickens all that it touches and is often equated with "mystery" (a word that means "keep silent"). References to "the mysteries" illuminate those core or mystical teachings that undergird religious thought; and to the "mystery schools," those secret groups or arcane societies that teach "the mysteries."

Our faculties automatically heighten and expand whenever we enter into "the silence of mystery." As with mystics of old, this meditative process can lead us from sight to vision, sound to music, touch to art, flavor to discrimination, scent to integrity, intuition to grace, perception to that sense of knowing which transcends rationale. "Gifts of the spirit" begin to flower when this occurs, and we encounter our true self—our soul.

Kundalini

Looking back a few pages to the charts I gave to illustrate the chakra system within our energy body, imagine a flow of spiritual power that runs straight up the body from our tailbone to our head, next to and accompanying the channel provided by our spine. This spiritual power is called Kundalini ("coiled serpent") and is said to reside at the base of our spine until activated. We activate or uncoil it through spiritual and energetic practices that help us develop each of the chakra centers. Once awakened, it will flow up as if part of the spine, igniting each of the chakra centers until it bursts out through the top of our head.

If we're not ready for something like this—if one or more chakra centers are plugged or undeveloped—Kundalini energy will either not rise or partially so. The gift of its transformational power that takes us from self-centered interests to spiritual and collective ones, falls short or is delayed until we are ready. Conversely, if Kundalini energy rises too fast—zooms up the spinal passage before an individual has matured in thinking and in deed—mental illness could result, even physical disabilities.

You don't fool around with Kundalini.

Spiritual power is fueled by hormones and the varied aspects of character development. If you're not ready—if you haven't been honest about what motivates you and what you see as the purpose of your life—don't concentrate your energy on spiritual power. Leave it alone until you are willing to bring balance back into your life; until you are able to embrace what is called "Christ Consciousness," or "The State of an Awakened Soul," as a reality in your life.

Spiritually awakened energy can routinely:

- produce orbs of light around a person

- fill a room with snake-like streamers of light

- produce colorful light shows

- activate in the individual a sensitivity to anything electrical—physically affecting computers, light bulbs, television sets, car batteries, cell phones, digital gadgets, medical equipment, electrical cords, and anything else that plugs into an electrical socket, including the flow of electricity itself.

Once the individual learns how to control the enhancements of their energy, life settles down to a new normal. Sensitivities to light, sound, electricity, magnetics, taste, touch, texture, and temperature become daily enrichments, not debilities.

Night Symbols

Dream life changes, too, after your energy has shifted from "you," as an ego concerned mostly with daily life issues and personal needs, to a more expanded, enhanced version of "you" that is more in touch with others and things spiritual—the reality of soul. Entertaining images that once filled our life, usually cease to be that entertaining afterward. That's because our symbol-loving-mind tends to switch around what it is exposed to. "Teaching tools" or "guides" or "revelations" emerge to give new meaning to life, along with a way to access higher modes of wisdom and knowledge.

Why is this so? Simple. Our brain integrates symbols, *not facts*. Thus, awake or asleep, the power of the "dream" is always at work.

There is no argument that the dreamlife of sleep can and does become more colorful and vivid afterward. Visions abound, often predictive. And, lucid dreaming can occur. Never heard of it? Well, let me surprise you.

Lucid dreaming is where you become consciously aware of the dream state while you are dreaming it. You feel as if you are wide awake when you are not. You are still very much asleep. Yes, during lucid dreaming, you can engage with or change dream characters, stage outcomes, experiment, do all of this and more . . . but not as a controller. The secret here, what makes lucid dreaming so unique, is the direct awareness you can attain when speaking to, participating with, and questioning the actual characters of your own dream . . . *as if they were teaching you something you needed to learn or to know.*

Scientific experiments have shown that lucid dreaming is *the only form of dreaming* that lights up the frontal cortex of the brain. Normal dream states do not do this. That makes lucid dreaming *a hybrid state of consciousness.*

Just in case you didn't catch the full import of what I said, allow me to explain. *Lucid dreaming is a hybrid state of consciousness that actively engages with the core self as plans, rehearsals, and experiments are laid out in the mind to assist the personality self in the development of its experiences.*

How do you cause a lucid dream? By deciding to have one. By knowing you can. By making this a priority. How do you remember any of your dreams to begin with? Same way. Set paper and pen on your nightstand next to your bed. First thing when you wake up, write down everything you can recall. Even if you're just going to the bathroom to relieve your bladder, grab that pen and start writing immediately upon returning to bed. As many times a night as you can. Do this. Be amazed.

Day Symbols

Awake or asleep, the symbol-making process is contiguous with the life you live. Actually, there are two streams of time/space awareness, not just one. They are:

WAKE TIME	DREAM TIME
Visible: true experience; reality.	Invisible: true learning; preview or review of waking reality
Our central focus is here.	Blueprint level where our focus runs slightly ahead of clock time.
Informs, alerts, warns.	Integrates.

Both flows mirror each other and are sense-oriented/physically experienced. Even when we are asleep, our body is actively involved in whatever we are dreaming but responds internally. Children naturally flip back and forth between these two streams of awareness; night or day makes no difference. Adults consider this "silly kid's stuff," too much imagination. Yet for the child, it's a trial and error process in figuring out which time/space continua is the most advantageous at whatever time. Anyone on drugs, alcohol, medication, or dealing with the stress of trauma or loss, or is exposed to excessively strong odors like incense, can get lost between these two realities and not know where they are. Meditation and prayer, various spiritual practices, and mystical traditions, educate us about this. So do classes in developing and managing psychic/intuitive skills as the enhancement of faculties normal to us.

When in dream time, wake time is the dream. When in wake time, dream time is the dream. Because of this paradox, you can interpret the symbols of each *the same way*.

Before we go much further, a little education about symbols might help. Symbols are subconscious statements we make about the status or condition of our lives. They are what language seeks to convey. Everything we think, say, feel, or do bases itself on whatever was previous. The "statement" we make to ourselves about that creates a symbol. Your symbols will always match whatever you currently believe.

Our brain processes the symbol we created about what happened, rather than the fact of what happened. Feelings matter more than words. Here's the clincher: *The process of symbol making is the <u>same</u> <u>process</u> we use to create our own mythology—the theme or message of our life.*

Day Symbol Exercise—One

Did I lose you? Time for a quiz. Get together a group of people. Each one takes a sheet of paper and draws two columns down the front. On the left, give names to what is listed below, using a separate line for each. On the right, opposite each name, write the first thing that pops into your mind about that person. You don't have to know anything about them. Just record what comes to you simply looking at them. Be *very* brief. Do this *very* fast!!!

LEFT SIDE	RIGHT SIDE
First name of each person in room (if more than one, use lines to match)	
Name of your spouse or lover	
Name of your boss or employer	
Your occupation	
House or wherever you live	
Car, vehicle, of method of transportation	
Your mother's first name	
Your father's first name	

List first names of siblings	
List first name of children	
List common names of pets	

Each person reads aloud what he or she wrote. Discuss. If you do this super fast, you will cross over into that other stream of awareness that never misses a thing—subliminal or exposed—and records some kind of statement about it, as a symbol.

A day symbol is anything that catches your attention . . . as if life were a waking dream. Pay attention to what catches your attention.

This world and everything in it is always in communication with you. Stop long enough to look and listen. Treat a day symbol as you would a night symbol.

Day Symbol Exercise—Two

On the way to our wedding, the car radiator overheated. Had to cool down. *Message*: There will be a sudden outburst at the wedding that has to do with out-of-control emotions. *What happened*: My husband's mother got so upset during the service she stomped out of the church, creating a scene. Because we knew in advance that something like this was going to happen, we were prepared to soften the "blow" and continue on with the service.

Day Symbol Exercise—Three

I stayed in Washington, D.C. for four days on a training assignment for business. In the hotel room, I encountered three strange bugs (later told they were water bugs). The first was as large as a dollar bill. The second one was small. The third was fairly large. Each was returned to "divine substance" when the place was dusted. No more problems. *Message*: Day One—there will be astronomical problems, difficult to handle. Day Two—little will interfere, goes fairly well. Day Three—will have large problems but they can be handled. Day Four—much success, no problems. *What happened*: Each of the four days exactly matched the encounter with bugs and what was done about it. Knowing in advance made a huge difference in how events were handled and in how enthusiasm could be used to replace stress.

Day Symbol Exercise—Four

I drove to Seattle to take a special class, took a wrong turn, and got hopelessly lost. While driving, I passed through beautiful country never seen before. Nobody in the car panicked. Felt right. Completed all homework studies in the car in preparation for the class. Route turned out to be a little-known shortcut. Took almost two hours off drive-time. Arrived in Seattle early by taking the off-the-beaten-track. *Message*: The class would not be what we expected or wanted. We would cover ground we had never heard of before, and learn helpful, useful techniques that would make life easier. *What happened*: We were prepared in advance to be both disappointed and surprised. By listening with an open mind, we learned easier, quicker ways to handle life's problems.

Wrap-up

With day symbols, pay special attention to:

- Anything that happens to your car—what side, front or back, dashboard (choice of controls), brakes (what slows you down), windshield (your view), engine (your energy, power).

- Anything that happens to your home—basement or roof, water issues, broken windows, appliances, curtains, carpets, fireplace, furniture, upstairs/downstairs, closets, doors, color and design.

◆ Any seemingly minor event that occurs just before a
major one will presage or foreshadow the event to come.

Create a "Stage" for Day Symbols

Have a question front and center in your mind. Pick a park or a special
place that has numerous paths, objects, or environments you can use
as a "stage" (or setting) where day symbols can appear. Be open and
receptive. Say a prayer for guidance, knowing that the answer you need
is there. Start off with no idea of where to go, simply explore. Replace
thinking with feeling. Observe. Note any and everything that catches
your attention. Right it down in a small notebook. Meander. Be curious. See what really catches your attention. Allow that to "speak" to
you in the sense of any meaning it may have. Pause there, then go
on. When through, you will have connected with many things. Rest.
Either the answer to your question will pop in your mind, or advice
will emerge that will be useful.

Forget Going to a Psychic

You can find the advice you need, or have your questions answered,
by allowing the world around you to speak through the symbols that
present themselves to your eyes and heart.

Another quiz. Right down your answers on paper.

1. Describe your favorite vase.

2. You see a lake. What do you do?

3. Describe your house.

4. Describe inside your house.

5. You see a bear. What's it like?

6. In back of your house is a fence. Describe your fence.

7. What is beyond your fence?

What your answers unveil in symbolic form . . .

1. Your true love.

2. How you handle risk.

3. Describes your dream house.

4. How you would furnish your dream home.

5. Your problems and how you handle them.

6. How you feel about death.

7. What is beyond death.

To view something—to look at or give your attention to something (even if it is a mental thought or psychic impression)—is to give it power and become a participant with it. We become a part of that which we see, regardless of how, when, or where we see it. To view is to influence; but to really see and recognize something, we merge with it.

The Mirroring Process

There are two separate but parallel time/space continua. Because of this, we humans have been given the power to have experiences that are like our own evolving thought. Every one of us creates our own environment. The environment we create is an *exact mirror* of our inner self at that moment. This is the process of mirroring. It is how the soul awakens to itself in human form.

health
is
the balance
between
our
inner
and
outer
worlds

PART III

OUR TRIUNE ENVIRONMENTS

Physical World—Animate

Energy World—Hyper-Animate

Spirit World—Super Animate

New tools, new scientists are turning upside-down what was once known about planet Earth, the universe, and the very environments all of us take for granted. Found is another Earth (about 1,400 light years from us); a baby Jupiter (a mere 490 light years away); and a whole raft of dwarf planets, each large enough to be of significance in the galaxy we call home. Plus, an estimated 50-billion other galaxies exist "out there"—many like ours. This proves, at least to me, that questions of "life in outer space" and "aliens amongst us" are moot.

Water is everywhere, with comets but a sperm bank of oxygen, alcohol, and sugar. This guarantees that the universe has the ability to function as if a cosmic sea of energy, a vast ocean of possibility and potential . . . where "God can play." No question: *The universe is a vast chemical laboratory devoted to the creation of life.*

People such as myself who have undergone a transformation of consciousness, irrespective of how or when, come back convinced that the universe must be the creation of a Great Mind . . . because . . . it operates like a Great Thought . . . continuously creating, shifting, experimenting, changing. Science tells us that the push-pull of gravity and huge currents of electrically conducting gas called "plasma" shape the universe. Gas. Plasma. Cosmic breath. "The universe breathes," says adult near-death experiencers. Child experiencers echo: "Yes, but not as the nose does."

Planets hum, some have bell tones. In fact, sound fills the "everywhere" of universal vastness. *And sound is the carrier wave of consciousness.*

Did you realize that:

- There is intelligence in every speck of matter, even dark matter.

- There is intelligence in every energetic and non-energetic wave form.

- There is intelligence in the breath that breathes throughout creation—and that breath is what fashions life.

All matter, all that exists, is actually condensed light, and that light is conscious.
Nobody ever told us (except the mystics of old) that there really are two suns in our solar system. We can't see the other one because it's dim. Called the Blue Sun, or Scholz's Star (in honor of its discoverer, Ralf-Dieter Scholz), this companion was once equal to the big bright ball we are used to—peg that about 70,000 years ago. A binary star (meaning two stars together), our second sun actually consisted of a red dwarf and a brown dwarf . . . meaning . . . we once had three stars that did the job of warming our planet, not just one.

Our solar system passes through a region in space that radiates intense electromagnetic radiation twice in every 24,000 to 26,000 years. Shaped more like a band or belt (some call it a "photon" belt), this invisible cloud of high-frequency particles takes around 1,400 to 2,000 years to negotiate. These intense energies permeate whatever passes through, and in a way that tends to "shake things up." We're once again beginning to pass through that band. If you don't believe me, check in with your local news source and read the headlines.

Hang with that number of 26,000 for a moment, because, interestingly enough, it shows up often as a "coincidental number." Coincidental numbers are intriguing in what they signify and in how they "fit" important aspects of creation so perfectly that it's as if someone or something uses them "as part of a larger plan." Examples:

- Distance between Earth and the galactic center is approximately 26,000 light years.

- Circumference of the Earth is approximately 26,000 miles.

- Current human life span is approximately 71.2 years or 26,000 days.

- Human gestation period is 260 days.

- Physical development into adulthood is complete in 26 years.

- Mass extinctions on Earth happen approximately every 26 million years.

Other coincidental numbers exist, such as:

- The Vesica Pisces (shape of a woman's vulva) is a pattern held sacred in every religious and spiritual tradition throughout history. To reveal the pattern, draw two circles, each touching the other at its midpoint. The Vesica Pisces, two 360 degree pathways, unfolds in three dimensions or 720 degrees.

- 720 degrees is necessary for structural integrity.

- 720 degrees creates the torus "doughnut" (its shape). Ring-like, it is the only self-organizing wave form in creation. Its shape contains the basic movements of up/down, in/out, across. The tilt of its doughnut curve, as viewed from various angles, reflects every essential color and image known, as well as the letter shape of all ancient languages.

Get this: matter always travels in rings.

The torus is what maintains matter—as matter travels in rings. The movement the torus makes while doing this, provides the respiration necessary for creation to maintain its place in the "breathing" universe.

I could stuff this book with streamers of "coincidental" numbers, each one playing a special part in Creation's Story. Angles, shapes, and symbols found at sacred sites and within the construction of all the world's great cathedrals, temples, pyramids, and holy places contain numbering such as this (sacred geometry). Every culture has known the importance of this, and of the power of thirds (the universal baseline of order, beauty, and strength).

Take that key again of 26,000. It's the same number in astrology for the Great Cosmic Year (the precession of the equinoxes—actually 25,920 years, rounded off to 26,000). The last 13,000 years (just passed) is considered to be a time when humankind has been "sleeping"—dark times. The next 13,000 years (just entered), is a time when humankind awakens to the light-filled consciousness of galactic light. Same number for Earth's duo-passages through that band of highly-charged electromagnetic radiation I mentioned earlier.

Are you catching this?

Based on ice core data from Greenland, the infamous Ice Age began about 12,900 years ago, when, it is theorized, a giant heavenly body like a meteor/comet/asteroid hit Earth. A sudden catastrophic warming between 1,200 and 1,800 years later jerked the planet out of that Ice Age. The resulting meltdown caused a rapid rise in sea levels, submerging many civilizations: according to Plato, Atlantis. It is also the same timeframe when Gobekli Tepe in southern Turkey was suddenly covered over and hidden by its mysterious residents—as if they knew what was coming and were trying to save the place.

Whether the cooling of the Younger Dryas, the Holocene era, the Cambrian period, periods of major evolutionary shifts, or climate change . . . all fall within this same basic timetable, same rhythm. Artifacts, remnants left behind, pop up yet today *that prove advanced societies existed BEFORE 11,500 years ago; even knowledge of the Atomic Bomb, how to build it, and how to use it.*

You don't believe me? Compare large tracks of land in today's India that show signs of vitrification (sudden melt from extreme heat) with descriptions found in the ancient epic poem "Mahabharata"— same area of land involved then as now, same descriptions given then after the "rods of Brahmin" were dropped . . . *as were eye-witness accounts from survivors of Nagasaki and Hiroshima (Japanese cities incinerated when the Atomic Bomb was dropped there during World War II).*

There's more . . . like . . . how about the petrified footprints found in the mudflats of the Palaxcy River in Texas (called the Happisburgh Footprints) that *prove humans and dinosaurs existed side-by-side during the SAME timeframe in history.*

Darwin was wrong.

Proof continues to stack up that catastrophes and what exists in the historical record about them, best describe how life evolved on the Earth-plane. Yes, there is ample evidence for uniformitarianism or the gradual formation of beaks and bodies. Yet, all the major swings between advancement and decline *exactly dovetail* the occurrence of terrifying events that physically altered the planet, its weather, the appearance or disappearance of water—in hours or days—and in the collective amnesia we all possess that comes to the surface in our dreams, the telling of tales, and the "fictional" stories we still write.

J. R. R. Tolkien, language and folklore expert, when asked about his stories of Middle Earth and hobbits, replied:

Yet always I had the sense of recording what was already 'there' . . . that I was not inventing but reporting . . . For when Faramir speaks of his private vision of the Great Wave, he speaks for me. That vision and dream has been ever with me . . . What I might call my Atlantis-haunting.

Plato told us: "All knowledge is recollection." Deeply within our heart of hearts we know, *without knowing we know,* there is another history, another version of what science insists is true.

The great prophets, loremasters, and wise ones of old gave us other scenarios to the advancement of human form on Earth. The scientific explanation says we evolved from apes out of Africa who discovered they could stand and walk. Mystical versions, however, spin tales another way: that we evolved through the comings and goings of Root Races (core DNA groupings) that first began billions of years ago, with the first form being that of etheric shape-shifters—hardly more than a whiff of air—beings who could pass between dimensions at will. Then, about 12 million years ago, these etheric whiffs began to take on mass and became more physically endowed as they sought to experience whatever fascinated them. It is said that the downfall of these early projections was animal sex and plant life—the reproductive act/process. When they "entered" the body-forms they were curious about, they became stuck and could not withdraw. Relief and release took time, lots of it. Symbolic drawings of such mix-ups—man-beast and man-plant—can be found throughout every culture known to have existed.

If you look at *all* the evidence that exists, clearly, hominids did not develop as the history books claim.

Enter "polygenism" . . . evidence that humans rose independently and in different parts of the world at different times. For instance, early types of hominids were all over the Americas, not just via the landbridge at the Bering Straits of Alaska. Long-headed people and round-headed people, along with older types of Neanderthals and giants (really big ones), left their skeletons, skulls, and tools behind to forever puzzle us. Relics such as these are regularly sold off by university libraries, denied by scientists, or destroyed (when no one is looking). Problem is, artifacts are now being unearthed faster than science can deny or destroy them . . . including evidence that an ancient race of Little People, sized like hobbits or squat gods, were in fact a spiritually advanced civilization once present worldwide.

Face it. We live in a self-organizing planetary system of rhythmic advancements and declines, best described by the chaos theory—order out of disorder. Considered a curious truth when first discovered, this "order" is governed by previously unknown natural laws that spin out "strange attractors"—patterns that push, nudge, and shove existing shapes into new forms—similar to what a choreographer does with dancers as they seek to perform what has not existed before. These graceful, flowing patterns are "fractals" . . . random phenomena that spread out into new forms of what previously existed. Chaos and fractal patterning apply to activities as well—in business, education, healing modalities, computer technology, storms, earthquakes. Never end points . . . just new beginnings.

We are benefitting right now from the longest interglacial period in the last several hundred thousand years. During warming phases, there is more food, higher cultures. During cooling phases, there is less food and darker times. By 2030, it has been predicted that our Sun may enter a period of "sleep" where there is less solar activity, less solar flares. Climate change, although affected by human excess, is in league with cyclic changes of timetables already noted.

Currents on Earth manufactured by nature's own powerhouse (charged particles from the Sun) set off oscillations in the Earth's magnetic field at the edges of the atmosphere to produce electricity. These currents follow fault lines, ley/energy lines, water flows, any presence of water, the "feel" we pick up that signals "aliveness." If you notice how humans, animals, and energy lines have intersected over time, where they form or congregate, you can pinpoint what later became cultural centers. Draw lines from here to there and the patterning of a soccer ball is revealed. Where each pentagram connects is a sacred or holy place, a house of worship, or a spiritual setting of some sort. How have people throughout the ages known the best place to live, sleep, evolve? By sensing this energetic patterning.

Earth is a giant crystal of exact "faces"—geometric shapes, lines, designs— that can be sensed, measured, and used advantageously.

And, Earth has a heartbeat. Its liquid crystal core usually beats at about 7.8 hertz (cycles per second). What appears throughout Earth as solid matter is actually the interweaving of frequencies held in balance and order by the Earth's heartbeat. Called the Schumann Resonance, this core "sound" is like the beating of an immense drum.

Suddenly, in 2015, the Schumann Resonance doubled to 16.5 hertz. This is harmonic to the Solfeggio tone of 528. (Solfeggio frequencies make up the 6-tone scale that has been used throughout the ages in sacred music, like with the beautiful Gregorian Chants.) Why is this important? Because 528 is the exact frequency used by genetic biochemists to repair broken DNA—life's genetic blueprint.

Earth is speeding up. And . . . it is repairing itself.

Nature self-organizes. When it appears to fall apart, it begins to reconstruct . . . at another level, another frequency.

Shift time has returned.

Walked out your door recently? There is a new design to what you see and feel, smell, taste, and touch . . . an intelligent one.

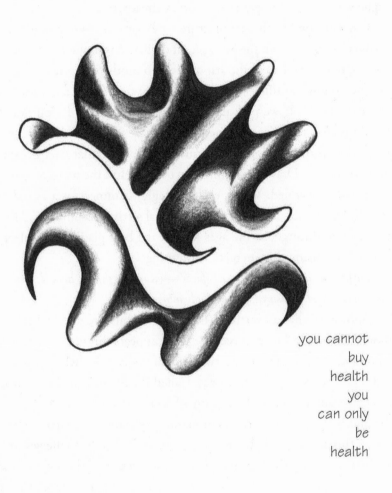

you cannot
buy
health
you
can only
be
health

7

Physical World—Animate

The Arctic is an ocean surrounded by continents. The Antarctic is a continent surrounded by oceans. This is why Earth's top and bottom are subject to different sea-ice forming and sea-ice melting processes. Although sea levels around the world have been rising for years, the Antarctic has contributed little to that rise, a situation that will dramatically alter if levels of carbon dioxide from burning oil, coal, and natural gas continue to spike. Yes, there's enough fossil fuels to supply all of us with the energy we need for centuries. Granted. Yet the speed at which our climate is changing is a surprise. It's been said that if we burn it all, we melt it all. Forget polar bears. That break-off rate from the southern ice shelf is what will remake our planet. It's happened before. Cycle extremes come and go. This time, though, billions of folks are milling around wondering what, if anything, they can do to make a difference. Truth is, even the smallest of acts can render big dividends. So, let's begin there, with ourselves and where we live.

A few starters:

◆ Protect water sources, including reservoirs—cover somehow, maybe with plastic balls. Employ water dowsers for new wells.

◆ Better restrictions need to be applied to fracking for underground shale oil and stretching out pipelines across large expanses of land. An emphasis on renewable energy must take center stage.

◆ Homes should be self-reliant with electricity from solar panels and windmills, rainwater collectors, gardens— even if in window boxes, roof tops, sides of buildings and slopes, community plots.

◆ Geodesic domes and round houses protect from high winds and ground tremors. Use curves and arches in construction instead of 90-degree corners, even in traditional house designs. Use an earth berm outside for insulation whenever possible, with sod roofs.

◆ Architecture is art we live in. Remember that in designing all types of structures.

◆ Consider shared housing, agri-hoods (housing around the edges of nearby farm fields), eco-villages, and common-space (where microunit apartments share in space with a chef's kitchen, game room, TV room, social activities, and parking for bicycles). Be careful of living spaces near high-tension wires as they can cause abnormal cell growth.

◆ Convert from microwave ovens to mostly slow cooking. Cut down exposure to electromagnetic fields (EMF) and digital devices such as smart meters, broad coverage WiFi, routers, and too much reliance on "screens" such as smart-phones, tablets, computers, etc. Never allow screen devices of any kind in bedrooms or near where you sleep, rest, or eat. The "electromagnetic hash" created from excessive EMF exposure is negatively affecting our brain and nervous system, especially in school rooms where kids sit.

◆ Our polluted air, which is losing its ozone layer, holds negative thought forms longer. This provides the perfect breeding ground for them to multiply and become more powerful (aided by 24/7 news coverage and social media).

The Environment We Create Recreates Us

Your home, apartment, wherever you live speaks volumes about you, constantly mirroring back who you think you are *and* want to be. How you position things, choose colors and shapes, create a "feel" to how energy flows or gets stuck. There are lots of how-to books about "Feng Shui," the ancient Chinese method of directing the flow of energy inside/outside buildings and across landscapes. Yet the real key to success in redirecting energy comes when you trust your own common sense and intuition. You are always the final judge. Simply follow the "feel" of energy. Can it move like air does, or, does it feel stagnant or dull? You want a sense of aliveness throughout where you live, and you get that by altering placement, shape, color, light.

Deeper levels of the mirroring process address the symbols that abound in our physical environments. Remember, symbols are subconscious statements we make about the status and condition of our lives. They outpicture what language seeks to convey.

So, right now, walk with me through where you live:

- *Whatever you see first when you open your door* is an affirmation of whatever is true in your life.

- *Whatever you display at eye level throughout each room* is what you are praying for. Pay special attention to what is on your walls and in which room.

- *Large, overstuffed, crowded furniture* tend to reflect over-eating habits and lack of exercise. If piled high with papers, magazines, and "stuff," it can indicate a lack of self-discipline and willingness to honor self.

- *Closets and drawers* are where you hide what you do not want to see. They can also represent what we would rather forget. When clutter builds up, so does dust, bugs, and unpleasant smells. Cleaning them out occasionally trains you to face what you don't want to see and rearrange priorities. Open closets are best, with easy stackables, colors, and art pieces splashed around.

• *Electronic devices such as a computer* should be in a separate room, well-ventilated, with plenty of light and houseplants. The electromagnetic fields the equipment produces can easily become toxic if used too often or left on for long periods.

• *Bedrooms are the most important room* in any home or domicile, and should be the loveliest. Your bed is your protector for sex and sleep, intimacy, and sacredness, as all our chakras open wide once we are asleep. Have an altar in the room if you can—for prayers and meditation. Change sheets regularly; get a new mattress if it sags. The last thing you see before falling asleep at night and the first thing you see upon awakening should be spiritually uplifting, soft, pleasing. Abstracts are fine in other rooms but not the bedroom. No electronic or digital devices in the room—except for a clock and radio. This is especially important in children's bedrooms. No cell phones in bed.

• *Bathrooms are where we go to eliminate and cleanse.* Sparkling surfaces help to reflect the power of soap and water and what we can release once we let go and get our ego out of the way. Here is also where acts to reveal or conceal are created and carried out. Once the room is empty, leave door ajar or partially open so bathroom space is never cut off and air freely circulates.

• *Living rooms* are where we connect to the other worlds outside.

• *Family rooms* are where we connect to the tribal worlds within.

• *Kitchens are where we go to form and shape the body we wear* and the way we want to feel from what we obtain from outside sources. This is where the love you feel in your heart directs how you express that love to self and others. Anything negative passes into whatever is touched, and can drain needed vitamins from food. This is why saying grace before you eat is so important.

◆ *Be careful of microwave ovens.* Test for yourself. Have two cups. Put the same type of plant in both. Water one from faucet water. Set on a window sill in good light. Water the other from water previously heated in a microwave oven, then cooled. Place on the same window sill. In experiments I've conducted, the plant watered from microwave water withered quickly, while the other flourished for days. This raises questions not only about the food and drink we consume after it is heated or cooked in a microwave oven, but what to any degree might this affect our blood. Restricted use is okay. Common use is questionable, regardless of "guarantees."

Did you know we *consume/absorb* the designs, shapes, colors, sounds, and frequencies we surround ourselves with? All is energy, including us. We cannot divorce ourselves from the world we live in. We can, however, make better choices about what we expose ourselves to and how we can alter or change results.

Exercise about objects

Take a deep breath. Let it out slowly. Swallow. (Swallowing, as the last step in this exercise, clears out synaptic [nerve] intersections in your brain so thoughts can flow better). You are now ready: ask your furniture where it wants to go (out loud or in your mind). Do the same with objects. You will feel, hear or sense their answer. With design and construction, always ask the materials what they want to be before you build. Recognize and honor the life in all things ... for everything is part of the same overall consciousness and can respond.

What seems obvious is only obvious to you. Always check again—at another level—for a larger view.

Deeper Mirrors

When we consciously accept responsibility for ourselves, our lives, and what we have become, we start to recognize a larger scope to "the big picture." That larger field of vision shows us that whatever we have in our life we either put there, accepted, chose, agreed to, made, found, brought, bought, invited, or somehow said "yes" to. We may not have consciously agreed to anything. Still, we made the initial choice that headed us in the direction we went. It is easy to misinterpret choices or place blame. Trick: *Not deciding anything is still a decision.* Choices are either yes or no. There are no maybes, ifs, perhaps, or variables. If we put something off, in essence we are saying, "No, not now." Yes, there are accidents and alternatives, but even those have a strange way of "fitting in."

The "YOU" You Symbolize

At some time, at some level, remembered or not, we have chosen the basic "script" of our life. Ask yourself the following questions, then quickly, without thinking, jot down whatever pops into your mind.

> *What kind of spouse or partner do you have?*
>
> *What are your children like?*
>
> *What kind of friends do you have?*
>
> *What is your home like? Its rooms? Any yard?*
>
> *What kind of neighborhood do you live in?*
>
> *What kind of job do you have, and what is it like to work there?*
>
> *What kind of town, city, or area do you live in?*
>
> *What is your state and country like?*
>
> *What kind of church do you attend? Or spiritual group?*
>
> *What kind of social, political, business groups do you frequent?*

What are your hobbies, recreations, sports, creative activities?

Where do you shop?

What do you dream? How often?

Now, take a good look at your answers. What might each one symbolize *about you*? Are there common or repeating patterns? How do you feel about any discovery you notice?

On some level, everything you see, or sense, or respond to represents a part of your personality and lifestyle. And that "everything" has a special tension, feel, and character of its own—as if a mirror—reflecting back to you whatever you are sending out. *Don't like what you receive? Change what you send.* We outgrow people, places, and things. Change is healthy. Just remember, you can't run away from your mirrors. Your world will always reflect back to you, where you are and who you are at that moment in time. Mirrors help us keep our head "screwed" on straight, because, there's no phony stuff or deception with mirrors. We are who and what we have built or allowed ourselves to be. We all are participants in a greater story.

Physical First-Aid

Illness tends to manifest on the etheric (energetic) level at least three days before surfacing in the physical. This implies that we have time, always, to alter or change what we think about, what we feel, and what we're doing.

Timing is everything. Detox four times a year, at each change of season, as that's when we're the most vulnerable to colds, flu, and varied upsets. Smart doctors heed these rhythms, daily and monthly cycles, life pressures, and tension. There is such a thing as "chrono-therapy," where you pay attention to time of day (asthma grips mainly at night, heart attacks hit mostly in mornings); time of month (female surgeries tend to be more successful if performed midway through menstrual cycle); time of year (heavy foods/fats/lack of exercise compound during winter months). Humans have an internal clock. So do plants and animals. That's because certain genes switch on or off in 24-hour cycles. The master clock is a tiny clump of cells located in the hypothalamus of the brain, over the optic nerve. This clock is reset daily, even with the blind, controlling biological events that unfold in sequence. Match treatment with timing for better results.

Healers have always known this. Modern doctors are just catching on and, to, the real power of meditation, visualization, and prayer. You can't use the brain to change the brain. Mental conviction is not enough. You must move over to *soft power*, the power of the heart, our feeling nature, pure consciousness . . . and that has a *feel* to it, a sense of wholeness. Negative thinking can creep in from time to time, but seldom is it the true core of illness. More often than not, it is the soul that is troubled. That's why placebos and nocebos are so effective.

The psychology behind healing suggestions, of expectation, addresses powers of healing that confound medical science—yet have been proven again and again in clinical trials:

> **Placebo:** tell a patient the pill is a wonder drug and convince them of its healing power, and they will either completely heal or nearly so (regardless of "item" used).

> **Nocebo:** tell a patient the pill does nothing, is a waste of time to take, convince them of this, and they will either get worse or remain unchanged (regardless of "item" used).

Results in medicine and healing have little to do with actual drugs. It is the expectation of the patient, based on reinforcement from the medical staff or healer that makes the crucial difference.

Healing is a pulse phenomenon

This amazing discovery was made by Stephan A. Schwartz when studying healers of various types. He discovered that healing sessions operated more like the swings of a hammer. Each phase had a period of buildup (information exchanged, patient readied, pulse of energy increased), a moment of discharge (healer releases full pulse of healing power, prayer said), followed by a period of relaxation (taking in what happened, feelings, gratitude).

That pulse, that moment of sensed power building up then being released, is based more on warmth, the desire to help, and the willingness to change, than a guarantee of wellness or recovery. The pulse phenomenon does not guarantee anything. Sometimes the patient dies. Yet the pulse itself is real; it is an energy that has a feel to it. You know when it builds up within you, passes from you, then enters someone else. Can some healers produce a greater pulse than others? Of course. Still, the pulse itself in some strange way explains placebos and nocebos, and why some things work and some do not.

Modern medicine was originally based on electromagnetism as the foundation of life. The regeneration of bone and tissue possible through biomagnetism amazed everyone. Then a major outbreak of flu hit, followed by the discovery of penicillin. Medicine changed utterly, switching to a biochemical model and the technology of a "quick fix." Anything counter was labeled fraud. Today, with the new discoveries that cell membranes are liquid crystal structures, brain cells magnetic, every cell a miniature antenna, electromagnetism is being reconsidered. The fact that one's electromagnetic field changes after a near-death experience (as well as following any other intense transformation of consciousness), and that more and more children and adults are being shifted in this manner, necessitates a balanced approach to healing.

To help you wade through changes in healthcare, learn everything you can about the seven schools of natural healing. They are Ayurveda, Chinese Acupuncture, Chiropractic, Holistic Medicine, Homeopathy, Naturopathy, and Osteopathy. Allopathic medicine is the name given to the Western-style based solely on the chemical model.

A shamanic healer will ask you four questions if you have a problem: When did you stop dancing? When did you stop singing? When did you stop being enchanted by stories? When did you stop finding comfort in the sweet territory of silence?

Take a deep breath, then, turn the page.

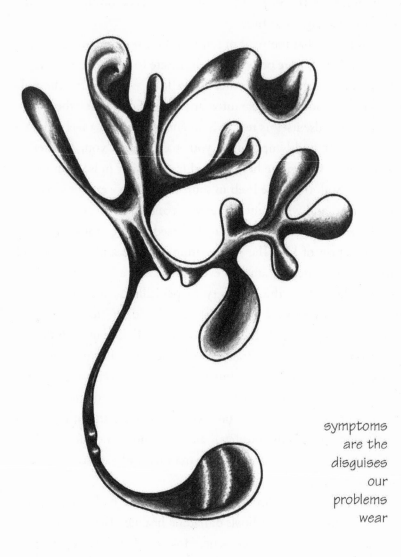

symptoms
are the
disguises
our
problems
wear

8

Energy World—Hyper-Animate

Orgone, the primordial pulsation throughout the energy world, is usually blue in color, maybe a blue-gray. I see it as the more active, visible extension of the ether and the vortex energy that spins creation.

Energy lines carry voltage loads such as these throughout the cosmos, detectable on Earth via planetary meridian lines. Thirty degrees north latitude is the principal meridian. The Great Pyramid and the mouth of the Nile sit on that meridian as does the mouth of other great rivers, plus sites of many ancient civilizations. Another major energy band is 19.5 degrees north latitude; this, a meridian that strings active volcanos in Mexico and Hawaii, marks hurricane storm lines in the Caribbean that slam Florida and help to feed the Bermuda Triangle. If you look at the physics involved, along with spherical geometry, then map in platonic shapes and the energy paths they manifest, you wind up with some fabulous facts: East/West energy is electric, North/South energy is magnetic, major convergence spots are hyperdimensional gateways (like "doors" to other worlds, other planes of energy, other timeframes).

Ever been with a group of dowsers hunting for high energy spots and active entry/exit portals? Try it sometime. It's a lot of fun.

While playing around with the big questions of life, consider this one: *How did solid matter come to be?* We know that matter is actually dense light. So? Well, if you experiment with the sound/wave theory

(Cymatics), you discover how bits of virtually nothing come together, combine, form solid layers and dimensional shapes . . . from just the continuous vibration of sound. The result? Solid objects/solid patterns.

We're talking sound waves here. Everything in nature, in the cosmos, makes them. Everything. All languages developed out of these primordial sounds. And all sounds carry their opposite at the same pitch. Our body, all bodies, all forms, contain the DNA energetics that comprises nature's script. We are immersed in this sea of energy . . . *a quiet so loud its very silence mesmerizes, transforms, creates.* The power of waveforms exists far beyond the aliveness we think it has, for it supplies the hyper-drive the energy world uses to fuel itself.

Plant Rumbles

Cleve Backster started it all back in the sixties when he hooked up potted plants to a polygraph lie-detector. He asked a question, got an answer through pulsed response. This happened when he threatened to burn a plant's leaf. The plant instantly pulsed out a fear response like a human would. Even if one person in a group of people passing through his lab thought about knocking a plant over, that individual could be identified days later—by the plant. Plants expressed loneliness if Backster left for the day (like any pet would), perking up the moment he headed for his car on return. No matter the question or concern, the plants were always right. His experiments, although pooh-poohed at the time, resulted in several books and opened up the scientific field of plant communication.

New findings: *all plants have intelligence, are able to learn and remember what they learn, have the same senses as humans, can hear and taste, sense gravity and water, avoid obstacles, and . . . they can actually eavesdrop on each other, talk to their allies, call in insect mercenaries, and nurture their young.*

The plant world oozes with activity. No kidding. Plants are fully capable of communication, cooperation, and, waging all-out war. A PBS television special, "What Plants Talk About" (now a DVD), used time-lapse photography to show how plants compete with each other and interact with the soil to structure natural communities. The way this happens—interactions with soil, insects, disease—forms the basis of what today is called "behavioral ecology."

Strange how we need a science like behavioral ecology to validate what humans have known for millennia. Ask a tree or plant or bush where it wants to live and how, honor that request, and it will reward you. How do you ask? Relax, move your mind into that easy alpha rhythm of your brain (kids call it "being in the zone"), ask your question—answers simply "come."

Example: *You have a tree or bush you have to move. Explain this to your plant, how necessary it is that the move be done, thank the plant for all that it has been, that you have enjoyed it, but times have changed. Pray with, and for, the plant . . . assuring it that if it lets go, there will be little or no pain, the experience will be quick and easy.* Whenever I have done this, plants did indeed cooperate and were easily moved; their life form energetics altered as they did to accommodate new forms, be they ashes or wood chips.

Another Example: *A move north of town put us at the edge of a forest so thick with growth, vines hung like green drapes, cutting out light. I walked out a ways, stood still, and intuitively tuned into the area. I introduced myself, my faculties on high alert, so I could hear and feel at subtle energy levels. A full range of "voices" replied. I explained that I was from Idaho and was used to forests one could see in and walk through, then I asked permission to pull vines, remove this and that, to create more open space. I staked out the area I wanted to clear and waited for a response. Wish was granted by a cacophony of support. In nothing flat, the job was done. You could actually see and appreciate the trees afterward. The following year a lawn expert noticed the area I had cleared and asked how I did it and if I wore gloves. "No gloves," I replied. "Just asked the forest for permission to change things, got it, then did the job without effort." He looked at me kinda funny. "Lady, that's poison oak you pulled out. The forest is full of it." I smiled.*
Honor plants and they will honor you.

More Surprises about Plants

There exists a "Doctrine of Signatures"—the idea that God/Allah/
Deity marked plants (gave them a "signature" or sign) as to how
they could be used and for what purpose. Plants with red flowers, for
instance, were deemed good for blood. Yellow flowers for digestion
because liver bile is yellow. Walnuts are excellent for mind and memory because of their shape—like the brain. Same with Liverwort, helps
the liver because it is shaped like the liver. Same with herbs. Herbs and
herbal concoctions are often better than pharmaceuticals—they are
nature's first aid, the original healers. Plants that have managed to
survive in places where they shouldn't can also carry unusual healing
abilities—for any illness or condition that matches what they went
through in order to live.

Raise lots of calendula flowers, echium, and borage. Why? Bees
love them, and we need bees for pollination. Many of our food sources
will disappear without the help of bees. Plus, honey by itself is almost
magical in its ability to nourish, heal, uplift, and remain viable for
extraordinary lengths of time. Honey and limited amounts of fruit are
now my only sources of sweetener. After I died, and for who knows
why, I could no longer tolerate refined or even unprocessed sugars.
We know that sugar in excess is toxic. A word to the wise—don't use
the stuff.

Gardening Tips:

- Surround your garden with rows of marigolds and nas-
  turtiums. They are perfect for pest/disease control.

- Always leave a portion of your plants for bugs to eat.
  Bugs, in turn, will usually leave most of the rest of the
  plants for you.

- Be gentle pulling weeds. Let them know they are not
  welcome where they are; you are simply releasing them
  to divine order.

+ Have plants inside your house too, especially spider plants and ficus. They remove the build-up of gasses in the house, turning it to oxygen—plus—they are especially good for removing radiation around computers, routers, and digital equipment.

+ It is the condition of the soil that determines what seeds will germinate. Weeds cannot grow in rich soil. Make it mineral rich.

+ Open-frame, pyramid-style shapes built over a garden enrich it to unbelievable degrees. Round towers constructed of paramagnetic stone (that which has a weak attraction or repulsion from a magnet) are also desirable. Lush growth/harvest can result.

+ Raised beds for vegetables are great, but even better/easier are hay bales. Arrange the hay bales in your yard, add some nitrogen (maybe half a cup) to feed the bacteria and fungi, spray with water until inside temps drop from hot to warm, plant directly into the hay bales, water once a day. Bales are high enough to keep out predators. No weeds. No fertilizers. Little water. Great crops.

Interspecies Communication

You've heard about elephants. They are sentient beings just like us, with a range of emotions and social interactions that mimic human behavior. They are empathetic, have morals, grieve for their dead, treasure children and families, possess legendary memories, and can be taught the fine art of painting. They communicate best at sub-levels that spread out for miles around, which means they hear earthquakes, storms, and rampages long before anyone else does.

Dogs have a level of sentience the same as that of a human child and respond best to the images we send them and the sounds they hear when we think of them. Yes, they hear thought as sound, and are tuned to higher frequencies. There is a striking similarity between dogs and humans in both structure and function of a key brain region rich in dopamine receptors. Positive actions net positive response. Their sense of smell is utterly amazing, so is their loyalty and intuitive knowing.

Bees make wonderful pets. Besides being very industrious, bees seem to know who will help them and who won't, and that they are the protectors of ecological diversity. Their dances and their hives comprise higher dimensional aspects of sacred geometry. Hive collapse is linked to dangerous pesticides ("neonics") which chemical companies refuse to stop making. Any crisis with bees could be avoided if more farmers practiced biological/organic farming.

Cats, dogs, elephants, monkeys, whales, dolphins, parrots (and many other birds) are some of those who represent higher orders of intelligent life in the animal kingdom. Stories are legendary about all of them in their ability to show self-awareness, compassion, higher intelligence, emotions, empathy, creativity, even "tool making," and the ability to perform and enjoy music (for instance, whales rhyme and fashion poems so as to remember time). Yet most of the inhabitants of nature's wondrous world are thrown off by disturbances in the magnetic field of their environments. (Did you know that birds can actually see these fields and the energy lines that run through them?) Throw off the field, and you could strand, confuse, or kill untold numbers. This is a major issue whenever the military alters air/water magnetics.

Climate's Tricks

All life begins in darkness—seeds, embryos, you name it—with sunlight supplying the energy necessary for life forms to grow, blossom, expand, procreate, whither. That which emerges from darkness eventually returns to the darkness from whence it came. Its energetics, however, merge into and expand light. Thus, the life cycle. The trickster in this scenario is weather and the specter of climate change.

Low pressure, low spirits. Why? Link it to how the body takes up water from the intestinal tract. Swelling, depression, or irritability can occur if this internal "plumbing" is out of whack. Some scientists think weather can induce crime—more riots and abnormal behavior when temps and humidity are high. So says science. Any good observer, however, can readily match climate and topography with variations in human and animal behavior. Docs and cops decry full moons and how crazy things can get.

Many times traveling in the United States and around the world, I witnessed amazing relationships between climate/terrain and behavior. Examples: (a) closed-in vegetation, plant life like "walls" = more conservative, hesitant people; (b) wide open terrains where all is visible = wide open people; (c) warmer climes with average vegetation = industrious, emphasis on education, farming; (d) really cold = people avoid who they do not know, more rigid behavior; (e) hot and wet = sexual, laid-back, willing to let others take charge; (f) hot and dry = tend toward sexual aberrations, unreasonable traditions and politics.

Besides detailed studies of how people's general behavior tends to correspond with the basic environments they live in, what fascinates me is the reverse . . . the effect of human thoughts and emotions on climate conditions. Weather, Earth movements, or temperature anomalies tend to move in tandem with the predominant thoughts/passions of the people in that area. Consider these reports:

- Former head of Ku Klux Klan elected to Louisiana State Legislature, two days later a tornado hits the area

- Turks attack their Kurdish population, soon after the bloodshed escalated, a major earthquake hit the area and killed over a thousand people

- After the strange and sudden death of Pope John Paul I, it rained for seven straight days in Rome

Coincidence? Nope. Happens too often for that, but neither is superstition involved. Look for correspondences. You'll find them if a real connection exists. The Earth plane and all that exists within, no matter at what level, whether animate or inanimate, hyper or super energetic, are interconnected, intertwined, and interdependent. We are part of each other, like it or not.

Psychic First-Aid

There are meridian lines throughout your body. They are the energetic component of the nervous system (just like the chakras are the energetic component of the endocrine glands). *Within the meridian system are major "cables" or power lines (invisible to see).* The one in front of your body extends out about an inch (into the air) from the lower lip, down your front, to the top of the pubic bone.

> **"Run that line."** You "run" your line by holding both hands out in front of you, finger tips touching, palms open towards you. Move up your line: energizes and uplifts. Move down your line: relaxes or weakens. Such maneuvers literally zip or unzip your energy flow.

> **Surprise!** *This major energy cable is wide-open and is easily and often affected by common gestures. Upward arm motions in front of another person, lifts energy. Downward motions in front weaken or slow their energy. Important to know when interacting with children. Typical gestures for "come here," upward arm/hand motions. Typical gestures for "go away," downward arm/hand motions. They will feel what you mean, even if you say nothing. Do not abuse this. The "blowback" is usually about 10 percent (a portion of what you give comes back).*

Problems with negative or toxic energy affecting where you live? Use color and sunlight. Colors that cleanse and clear energy are cobalt blue, purple, lavender, green. Get glassware in these colors—not painted on—but the color of the glass itself. The most powerful cleanser is cobalt blue. Get drinking glasses that color, maybe plates, bowls, whatever. Put them in full sunlight or where light will often shine through them coloring your rooms. You might get curtains one of these colors and hang them over a window. That way whenever the light shines through, that color will permeate everything. It is possible to purchase lengths of ribbon in any of these colors. Tack the ribbon around the inside of windows. That alone can make a difference. The goal here is to infuse rooms with any or all of these colors, decorate with them. They help to cleanse what is toxic, including negative behaviors.

Surprise! *You can "drink" color. Fill a green glass with water, put it in the sun for a while to solarize it, then drink the water. The color green, if a pure true green, is a great healer. You can do this with other colors too. Study what colors go with what ailment or problems.*

The color magenta is different from the others. If stressed, afraid, depressed, or in grief, you can't pick a better color to help you. Wear it. Surround yourself with it. Magenta's uniqueness is because it is the pivot color, that energy you move through when "graduating" from one phase of chakra development to the next one. You cannot integrate into progressively faster/finer levels of energy without the balance magenta provides.

Surprise! *Magenta is the color of natural lithium. Do not confuse natural lithium with the pharmaceutical variety (it is bonded to sodium carbonate). Natural lithium is a nonmetallic mineral, the 13th cell salt. The job of natural lithium is to bond spirit in matter. Animals, plants, soil, humans, must have this lithium to maintain their infusion of light or spirit. It is commonly found and easily replaced if depleted. The richest sources in the plant kingdom are lemons and limes (their chemical compounds are similar enough that they function like lithium). Even the scent of lemon on the job reduces errors around 50 percent. The richest source in the mineral kingdom is lepidolite, followed by kunzite and rosy tourmaline. If negative, angry, or fearful, the lithium in one's body tends to transmute into potassium. Potassium has an odor. The adage that "Dogs smell fear" is literal. If positive, joyful, or meditating, lithium tends to accelerate beryllium levels (the "fuel" of higher* *consciousness and higher brain development). Lithium levels in your body fluctuate as you do. This is natural and happens automatically.*

Handy Tips

First aid for computer use. Place lots of amber (polished or pieces or plain chunks) between your keyboard and your monitor, or, all around your laptop when stationary. Amber transmutes the radiation (blue light effect) from computers. Don't wear it. Use it. Have lepidolite and carnelian near where you are sitting; a glass of water about 2 to 3 feet away. Drink often. Be sure there are plants close by and a window. In an alpha (meditative) state, talk to your computer. Introduce yourself and assure your "technological friend" you appreciate its help and cooperation in tasks the two of you perform. Establish a relationship based on respect. Fewer glitches occur when this happens.

Energy patterns in your bed duplicate the Tree of Life in the Jewish Torah. It's eerie but true. That's one of the reasons why it's so important to have a beautiful, clean bedroom. Your bed is literally the altar that protects your body's energy during sex and when chakras open while you sleep. Energy patterns that result can be revelatory.

Earth energies constantly shift. That means geopathic stress, underground streams, negative/positive grid lines and how they change, can affect your health and sense of well-being. Certainly, your attitude and spiritual practices make a difference. You can communicate with rivers, mountains, trees, and rocks simply by deciding to, then doing it. Help them help you. Hear their stories. Tell them yours.

Communicating with Nature

Lean against a tree and feel what it is like to be the tree leaning against you. When you walk across the floor, feel what it is like to be the floor supporting the weight of the steps you take. As you press the wall with your fingers, feel what it is like to be the wall pressing back. As the wind blows your hair, feel what it is like to stand in the way of the wind, blocking its free passage. Such simple exercises flip your cognitive abilities into another mode of perception. You slip into the energetics *inside* form.

Living Water

Water exists in *four* phases: solid, liquid, vapor, and structured. A new finding: water can move from H20 to H302. We all know that water is the carrier of the most important molecules of life—like proteins and DNA. Yet, water in our cells is not like water in a glass. Cellular water is ordered or structured like a crystal, like ice. It is not actually a liquid . . . *because the water molecules inside cells line up in an orderly fashion, in arrays and strata.* These formations stay put thanks to the way water is absorbed into protein surfaces.

Hang with me on this . . . . Structured water forms honeycomb-style hexagonal sheets very similar to ice because this water (liquid crystalline) is H302, the fourth phase of water. In the ultraviolet range, just shy of that which is visible, structured water actually absorbs light. *The more light it absorbs the more stable it becomes.* This means it can hold the structure it has even if you leave it sitting around.

Everything is energy. That energy is alive, conscious, awake. What we call "spirit" is *the breath inside* of what gives energy life.

death
is the window
to
dimensions
beyond the unfathomed
and
unrecognized

9

Spirit World—Super Animate

To understand the spirit world *on its own terms*, we need to have a sense of what and how that might be. A little science may help here.

"Mind" creates time, continuity, and space as it responds to what appears to be the curvature of gravity. Yet gravity behaves more as if a cohesiveness that keeps the cosmos ordered and organized: similar to the ether, that immaterial, omnipresent, omnipotent "vault of memory" that ever coordinates and arranges what can never be forgotten.

Gravity's counterpoint is biogravity (what Russian scientists call "torsion waves" or "orgone")—an information carrier that transmits order within a system to prevent decay or loss, and is associated with psychic phenomena, sacred sites, crop circles, and dark energy/dark matter (that which is transparent). Think waves with biogravity as it can propagate in the future, as well as in the past and present.

Measurements of gravity and matter give us the speed of light. *Displace gravity/weight, and you automatically alter light and the speed and focus of consciousness.* Such a switch to biogravity enables you to suspend, bypass, or transcend the gravity-bound world of everyday life, thus proving that ripples in the time/space continuum are real!

The gap this creates reveals the in-between, spirit's realm.

To help you understand what can happen once gravity/weight is displaced by the in-between, here's an example from history . . .

Indian runners in America's Southwest who competed with the Pony Express. The runners reliably delivered messages hours, sometimes days in advance of man and horse. To answer the question of "how," trackers followed them. What they found is that runner footsteps got lighter and lighter in the sand, until vanishing altogether. Once footsteps vanished, the runner would suddenly appear onsite... *arriving literally BEFORE they left.* Asked how they could bend time and space the way they did, each claimed that as they physically ran, *the real run was done in their mind—the more intently they focused, the faster they went, until engulfed by the light they became.*

Once again: To transcend time and space, switch to the ripples and waveforms of biogravity. This is done in the "light" of your own mind. Sometimes by decision. Sometimes entirely by accident. The latter is what happened to me while canning a batch of fifteen-day sweet pickles as a young mother.

The Pickle Syrup Story

I was adding the last increment of sugar when the huge kettle I used to prepare the pickle syrup, a kettle nearly filled with thick bubbly-hot liquid, boiled over. I mean all over. Imagine the scene that followed, for that thick sugary goo not only spread out to cover the entire stove top but it quickly coated the inside surfaces of all burners, drip pans, inner framework of the whole appliance, the large drawer beneath the oven, all pans in that drawer, the sides of nearby cupboards, until finally puddling underneath and to one side of the stove.

The mess was unbelievable. What happened next was even more unbelievable.

I was at the kitchen table readying jars when the syrup boiled over. Instead of screaming in horror, which would have been normal for me, I calmly stepped forward into what seemed as if a resplendent, gauzelike, misty netting. As I did this, time and space overlapped, folded, then converged into each other, while my movements slowed tremendously. The integrity of my kitchen as it existed, even the very fabric of the air, shifted. Dimensions switched, waves altered course.

When I reached for the kettle, my arm seemed to glide through the bright gauze, which I experienced as threaded strands of tiny, sparkling bubbles—microscopic but clearly visible. My face, my entire body, registered sensations of touching and being touched by this stringy fabric netting. There was a smell present similar to that of ozone with a slight hint of ammonia, not pungent but "flat."

Without thought or effort, I slowly, gently, and ever so easily removed the kettle and put it in one section of my divided sink, turned off the stove, filled the other section of the sink with hot sudsy water, and proceeded to wash every single inch of every single thing. Then I unplugged the stove from the wall and pulled it out to the middle of the kitchen, mopped the floor, pushed the stove back, and re-plugged it. Not just once did I scrub and mop, but three times. Sugar syrup is quite sticky, you know.

When the job was completed I looked at the clock. Six minutes had elapsed. *Only six minutes!* At least forty minutes should have passed, possibly an hour, for the amount of cleaning I had engaged in was extensive.

The surprise of seeing the clock snapped me out of the state I was in. Dimensions readjusted, while time, space, and motion resumed their regular speed and proportions. There was enough syrup left that, with additional sugar and water, I went ahead and completed the project. After finishing, I sat down for a while, my mind racing with questions.

When I had first stepped forward, it truly seemed as if I had stepped from one waveform or dimension of existence into another. Even the composition of the air had changed to that of a buoyantly touchable, completely visible substance of a string-like netting. Colors, sounds, sights, sensations, even smells, had somehow been altered and enhanced.

When time and space had ceased to exist as the states they once were (what I was accustomed to), unlimited versions of both had instantly filled my kitchen, enveloping me as they did. This peculiar paradox had enabled me to access infinite amounts of pure energy while gliding through what seemed as if the webbing of a ripple in time. I had become a human dynamo because of this, accomplishing the impossible without the slightest effort or tension and in less time than imaginable, yet my awareness of what was happening as it was happening, and my actions and activities throughout, had been that of *total slow motion*. As I had gone about the task of cleaning up the mess, everything, including me, had felt weightless, bouncy, peaceful, and harmonious. And I had felt unified with everything, as if I and all the objects in my kitchen were connected to each other, similar in essence yet one in spirit.

There is no difference between what happened to me and those Indian runners. Edgar Cayce once said there are three dimensions: time, space, and patience. Without trying, I discovered what he meant—*PATIENCE: an effortless in-between state that establishes flow as a dimensional constant*. Our consciousness, once gravity and weight are displaced, flows naturally into in-between states . . . super stratas that extend the range of what we can perceive and participate in. The claim that 96 to 98 percent of space is empty is nonsense. What seems empty or dark is simply transparent . . . a dimensional constant of flow.

A Hidden Order

We are guaranteed worlds within worlds because of how flow can function (internal to us, external to us, or throughout the in-between worlds of spirit). Hyper and super stratas—dimensions of activity, of life, of an existence every bit as real as what we see around us in the physical—are capable of co-participation, not only within the wide-awake world of now, but with each other.

Because this is true, numerous options existed during our earliest beginnings when we entered the Earth-plane and eventually took on human bodies, or thought-forms that would later become human bodies. Some of us chose to enter through mineral orders, some chose soil, some roots of growing things or as rocks and landscapes, others as the very elements that enable our planet to support the rest of us. Those who remained as angels or "devas" (another name for angels) developed a full range of nature/spirit lineages to aid and assist them, plus the many characters and denizens of the invisible worlds throughout what exists today as "A Hidden Order." Many of these formed cultures hardly a skip from our own, vibrationally. In scientific terms, you could explain all of this as "nonlocal information fields that guide the development of biological, energetic, and spiritual systems."

I bring this to your attention because folklore from every culture and religion known to have existed have similar stories about A Greater Plan and about the mysterious "Third Order of Creation"— not angels, not demons, not humans—but a hidden peoples who appear and disappear at will, passing through physical matter, and violating the laws of physics. Forget ideas about aliens. This, an elder race, is engaged in a symbiotic relationship with us, their "first cousins," and in a common ancestry we share. The rods and cones in the human eye restrict us to a small range of ultraviolet and infrared ends of the spectrum. This keeps us from accessing common memories and from validating what people claim who stumble into the pre-existent worlds we all share.

Imagination Versus Imaginal

The difference between these two is important for us to know. *Imagination is intentional fabrication*, where we make it up from our own minds, feelings, and preferences. *Imaginal is what is presented to us*, intact, from and within a world that is as real as what we see, touch, hear, feel, smell, and know intellectually.

Imaginal realms exist beyond the three-dimensional world, where things are real in the sense that they are not being imagined for our own liking or benefit. Imaginal imagery has integrity yet exists apart from what we create or control.

Let me reframe what I just said. *Something imaginary is created by and comes from us. Something imaginal comes to us from another realm beyond our own.* When an imaginal image or being presents itself to us, we may be awed, afraid, surprised, puzzled, confused, or emotionally moved. Such an event stirs something deep within us, awakening us to a feeling or emotion. The imaginal realm carries within it "thoughts of the heart" that can awaken universal archetypes, as well as deeper processes of creativity. Archetypes are defined as "symbols with meaning" that can take on a life of their own and exist outside of individual consciousness, thus bridging the gap between objective reality and what is imagined or imaginal.

Our intellect can grasp this, whether or not we fully understand. Kids get it instantly. They know if they've conjured up something via their own effort, or if what came to them did so of its own will and volition. "Night School" is a case in point. So many children today attend "school" instead of dreaming at night. These "schools" are real, how real I discovered quite by accident when strolling through a shopping mall. A young boy to my right, walking with his mother, suddenly bolted from her and ran toward another boy further down the walkway, yelling his name. The other boy did the same. Both embraced and very excitedly discussed an assignment they were given in class the night before. These boys obviously knew each other and by name, had attended the same school, received the same assignment. The catch is, the boy and mother beside me were local. The other boy and parents were tourists and had never been in the area before. There is no way these boys could have known each other or attended the same school. Even shared dreams don't explain this. Imaginal realms do.

The places and planes shamans visit are imaginal. Same with artists and musicians and inventors, including Einstein. Imaginal realms are pre-existent. They appear to us or invite us in when the time is right, and, when we're ready.

Those Worlds Within Worlds

The in-between reveals itself once gravity/weight is displaced. What is revealed when this happens is the place-space of spirit, a consciousness so vast only utterness can describe it. Still, there is a dignity to all of this, as if the very core of spirit's nature was somehow "guided."

What many call the "etheric level" of spirit is a reference to energy blueprints that support physical life while alive and fade when physical bodies do. The "astral level" of spirit holds the soul in place during sojourns in the physical and when traveling to other planes and dimensions (often associated with "fey" or fairy enchantments). Yet references to "spirit" embrace not only imaginal and spirit beings, but entire stratas, ripples, folds ("bandwidths" of consciousness) that spread from slower vibratory frequencies to faster ones and beyond.

Think spirit, think super-animate—an utterness that encompasses while existing apart from energy, form, and dimension.

How fast or slow our journey is in life or how many journeys we take, who or what we encounter along the way, how often we encounter them and at what level, depends for the most part on us and the daily choices we make. It's our call. Still, ever present is spirit, overlighting creation and every created thing—no matter what we think, say, or do.

Over time I have come to recognize a triune arrangement, a sense of order, to all of this. My description of what I have seen follows:

INTRADIMENSIONAL (within levels/folds)

A. *Astral planes.* Middle earth, the muses, fairy folk and wee people, energy beings, ghosts, disincarnates, demons and devils, the hag, emotional discards, passion forms, psychic reside, imprints, futuristic manifestations, most abduction accounts (alien or otherwise), psychic creations, enchant-ments, animal and nature spirits, guides and guardians, orbs, shape shifters, phantoms, lost souls, watchers.

. . . lower kingdoms of ensoulment.

B. *Inner planes.* Higher beings, ascended masters, spiritual hierarchies, angels, the elders, matrix stewards, spirit keep-ers, the untarnished soul, access to the Great Plan.

. . . higher kingdoms of ensoulment.

INTERDIMENSIONAL (between levels/folds)

Immigrants from other worlds, visitors, and travelers from other planes of existence, some aliens, parallels, wind walk-ers, light workers, soul surfers.

OMNIDIMENSIONAL (beyond
dimensional folds and vibratory frequencies)

Abstractions of luminescence: that which is omnipresent, omniscient, omnipotent—The Godhead.

Spirit First-Aid

Want to see little people or fairy folk? Look out the corner of your eyes when busy doing something else or even when turning your head. Quick moments like this of *"seeing sideways"* can catch energy forms and the otherworldly unawares. No, it doesn't work every time, but enough to give you a tickle of a good smile when you actually see one.

Just because someone from another dimension drops in on you, does not mean they are wise or wonderful or even worth your time. Far too many people get suckered into thinking they're now in contact with some holy entity who turns out to be nothing more than a "trickster." Always affirm that you are a child of God/Allah/Deity, an extension of The Greater Reality, and nothing and no one has the right to interfere with you or your life without your permission. Mean what you say.

Think you are a "walk-in"? The claim is that one soul can replace another one in a given body (walk-in) if the original suddenly leaves. This short-cut to adulthood supposedly carries with it a stipulation that both souls must agree to the deal with all its ramifications. I've studied this phenomenon for decades, interviewed those who claim to be walk-ins, and have only found three that I think could actually be one. The rest? Every one of them had undergone an intense transformational shift like a near-death experience, baptism of the Holy Spirit, kundalini breakthrough, and/or sudden luminosity—plus—the full range of aftereffects typical for such an illumination. *They had become a changed soul—not a new one.* Those who claimed to be walk-ins took the same amount of time to integrate their aftereffects as did those who experienced a shift in consciousness through natural means. A short-cut to adulthood or starting a special "mission" of some kind? Hardly.

Be careful with this one. Evidence does not match the vast majority of walk-in claims.

The truth about orbs

They're balls of plasma, every one of them, and can appear in a wide-range of forms—everything from tubes, lights, cloud-like shapes, cylinders, rods, or even as "alien" ships. Commonly visible are those resulting from piezoelectric effects deep underground, usually caused by rifts/rocks/fractures/fissures rubbing together and "sparking" visible displays of moving, waving, or bouncing light. Those developing psychic ability, opening up the kundalini channel, in prayer, meditating, going through a transformational episode like a near-death experience . . . spew out orbs as if they were an uncontrolled result of freeing one's spiritual nature. Sometimes visible, sometimes not, the *best "witness" is a photograph.* Orb displays can also happen with people who are overly stressed, emotionally disturbed, or angry—the idea of emotions out of control or in excess (typical for children going through puberty). Understand that orbs are a natural phenomenon (those that are not traceable to a faulty camera lens). They follow or hold consciousness and because of that can tag along, go where you want them to go, or change forms to match or challenge your state of consciousness. Since *plasma is the perfect "container" for spirit energies,* the deceased can be seen *inside* orbs, so can guides, guardians, "visitors," or even the face and energy of a loved one. Enthusiastic, happy emotions can stretch out plasma forms into long snaking light-tubes, frequently seen in photographs taken at parties, and in nature where doorways/portals between the many worlds of spirit appear.

Let's not forget ecto-plasma

Just as gravity and biogravity are complementary opposites of each other, so is plasma and ecto-plasma. Plasma can be scientifically understood, but ecto-plasma stretches us past our comfort zone. "Back in the day," mediums while in trance could produce a plasma-like material that flowed out of their body orifices. Photographs were taken;

many proved to be fraudulent yet just as many escaped explanation and remain today as evidence that a form of spirit, maybe that of the soul, is indeed real and manifests as a type of plasma. *Filmy fragments of the sheerest fabric*, released into the air as a corpse burns (clings to rocks, trees, bushes—even far from the funeral site), is a well-known phenomenon in India where dead bodies are cremated outside on wooden biers. This filmy "fabric" is said to be that part of spirit cast aside by the soul once freed from form.

Crop Circles

Real crop circles, the ones that evidence impossible twisting of plant stalks and other such anomalies, present more of a puzzle than extra-terrestrial authorship. I don't deny alien involvement, but I do wonder about other links. Consider this, most crop circles in the world form between 3 to 4:00 a.m. That's the same time that melatonin levels peak in the pineal gland of the brain and when deeper functions of the pineal in the production of DMT (the spirit molecule) also peak. Same with the Schumann Waves (the base frequency of earth's heart-beat); and "The Hour of the Wolf" (medically when more deaths are reported, especially from congestive heart failure). "The Hour of the Muse" also has the same timing, when states of heightened creativity, inspiration, uplifting ideas, innovative art, angel contacts open up. The first prayer of the day for Muslims is 4:00 a.m. *There is an energetic rhythm to our universe, a mass consciousness that is in tune with urges greater than that of cavorting aliens or clever humans.*

Visitors from other realms prefer "left."

Hospital nurses and hospice personnel have shared with me that 80 percent or higher of patients who are ill or about to die, say that their "visitors" (deceased loved ones, disincarnates, and/or otherworldly beings) appear to their left. Most near-death experiencers leave their body "to the left." The majority of healers, specifically hands-on body workers, claim that their best guidance/intuitive knowing comes from the left (left hand, left eye, left side, sensing upper left). Sculptors, wood workers, artists often infer the same. Perhaps why is because the amino acids of all living things twist to the left. In space, most spiral galaxies rotate to the left. Nature prefers this—for the exotic, the sublime, and for spirit portals.

The Time Fan

We have created a measurement of time thanks to gadgets like clocks and observatories tracking planetary movements. Biogravity shows us something very different about time: it can warp, go backward or forward, travel in circles, wrap around vortexes, spread out in torsion waves, be circular, even ripple.

Makes you dizzy just thinking about it, doesn't it?

Time can be inconsistent because you can shift it with your own consciousness. Anomalous shifts have occurred throughout history and still do. You've already read about runners who arrived before they left. How about that Minuteman ICBM missile, launched from Vandenburg Air Force Base in 1973, that suddenly vanished from radar screens . . . *only to reappear three days later in the same place.* Scary.

You know the pickle syrup story, about when I moved into another dimension/realm/state quite by accident, and what happened when I did. Well, I've got another story to tell you—about The Time Fan.

I was desperate after surviving death three times in three months in 1977. There was so much that needed to be done: exercises, classes, new therapies to try, a body to reform and rebuild, plus a deep desire to learn more about the power of prayer. This meant I had to restructure my ability to think and reason. All the energy I could give to the focus of creating time, I did, and then some.

Within a few days of that intense focus, a flood of hot adrenalin coursed through me. My whole body got hot, accompanied by an abundance of prickly sensations and the feeling of electrical currents charging my frame. After the physical sensations had slowed, I relaxed completely and formed very carefully in my mind all the things I wanted to do and think about and pursue. I asked God for guidance and direction. The next thing I knew my body, my soul, my mind instantly divided out into numerous directions at the same moment. Another part of me became like an objective observer, a traffic cop, whose job was to keep all the many parts under control, separate and distinct, yet on track. Thirteen divisions of myself spread out like a fan, a time fan. My visualization was detailed and complete, including the assurance that when I was ready, all parts of me would reunite and I would be one again. I was at work when this happened.

I got what I wanted but not in the manner I thought it would occur. *Everything around me switched into slow motion. Me and my divided parts lived, worked, and existed at the regular speed I was used to but all around me—everywhere—sounds, voices, movements, even how I moved—visibly, audibly slowed. The physical world around me became so slow, I could actually see expelled air and energy pass from a person's mouth after a word was spoken, and arc across the room, touching and passing through me, stroking my brain as it left. I could also see and hear my own words, air, and energy leave my mouth, take flight and reach their destination across the room, passing through the person waiting for a reply. It was spooky! I discovered that I could not change the rate of speed of anything around me or the response of my brain to them. Nor could I change the slow speed of my own physical movements, like lifting a hand or walking. I had prayed, focused deeply, for more time and now I had it.* **Time accelerated by slowing down.**

My awareness and all my divided parts worked incredibly fast, accomplishing the tasks I had lined up. I remained in this state, day and night, for two weeks.

On the second day, my boss called me into her office and asked what was wrong. She said I looked like a 45-record going 33 1/3. I told her everything. The fact that my physical world and me in it was reduced to turtle-slow created a myriad of problems. I had to be extra careful walking, talking, driving, cooking, preparing food—especially with a knife. The other employees in the office also asked what was wrong, why was I so different? I requested patience, explaining that I was trying out a new healing regimen. Two of my children still living at home commented numerous times about why my motions and speech were so slow.

Those two weeks I felt feather-light and experienced many subtle tingling sensations and feelings of floating. I adjusted to the new speed, even came to enjoy it, but I could not cope with the outside world being so much faster.

To break "the spell" I consciously gathered all my scattered parts and demanded that they return to normal. I remember clenching my fists, tensing up and exerting all the energy I had in making that demand. Slowly I seemed to gain weight, get heavier, fuller, cooler. Physical sounds became louder, faster. People moved quicker. I could talk and move faster, too, but I "caught" myself before the process completed itself. I had come to enjoy the slower rhythms. The slower speeds gave me more time to savor food and drink in colors, sounds, places, people. I could notice more, hear more, feel more, relate deeper and more intensely. Me and my divided parts had learned and experienced years of material in just two short weeks. So, I called on God and asked not to return completely. I wanted to fit back into society while still retaining the special world I had discovered. I got my wish.

I now alter time a different way.

Whenever in a hurry or traveling some distance, I affirm the presence of Holy Spirit as I sit at the wheel of my car. I relax totally, focusing on where I'm going and how best to get there. While driving, I become the car, the road, the stoplights, the other cars. This is done by focusing deeply while my breath becomes shallow, my head lighter, my awareness of myself gone. Everything merges. Everything becomes one: in fact, in purpose, in motion, in reality. Safety is assured because every possible thing becomes highlighted, known, and acknowledged. I am no longer me when I do this. All is me. All in one. In that oneness is joy and thankfulness, respect and total awareness. Whenever I drive like this, time is cut by half. I merge like this only when necessary. I have no need to push time, just enjoy it.

What I learned from this that will help you, too, is: *focusing on time slows it down; focusing away from time speeds it up.*

Everything exists together in an instant, because an instant is all there is . . . the instant of perception. The spirit world is not what the "commercial marketplace" claims. Please don't make it into something it is not.

we use our
words
to hide
our
thoughts

PART IV

OUR TRIUNE RELATIONSHIPS

Self—Initial Focus

Others—Intimate Focus

Groups—Multiple Focus

A group of prospectors near Casper, Wyoming, noticing an odd color pattern in a vein of solid granite, started digging. That was in 1932. What they found was a mummy 14 inches tall, weighing 10 pounds, with a full set of teeth including wisdom teeth, estimated age at death: 65 years. One of the biologists who examined the find theorized the being might have been a member of some unknown race who could have roamed North America during the Pliocene Age.

Tiny people?

During the last 150 years skeletons have been found in such countries as Ireland, France, Mexico, and the United States, that measured 8- to 9-feet tall, some 12, one 25-feet-6-inches from skull to heel ball, others around 19-feet or so. The Smithsonian Institute was called in to verify some of these finds. After quickly stamping "fraud," each giant-sized artifact mysteriously disappeared. Cries of "cover-up" against the Smithsonian continue to this day. More such skeletons have been found, proving that: "Yes, there were giants who once roamed Earth."

Big people?

Get your nose out of history books and channeled revelations for a second and hear this: *human bones have been found in layers of rock millions of years old.* That's "M" for millions. If you want to consider psychic material, refer to the readings of Edgar Cayce. He was told humans began 4.5 billion years ago. That's "B" for billions.

When did we really birth? How big? What were we like?

Various schools of thought refer to the Bible where it talks about times when the "Morning Stars" (cherished souls of God) came forth to populate the Earth. New versions of that tradition, however, state that the "souls of God" were actually extraterrestrials.

Before you comment, consider these two scientific findings:

. . . Studying the Y-chromosome and DNA mitochondria, the earliest female traces back 150,000 to 250,000 years ago; the earliest male 60,000 to 100,000 years ago. How did we reproduce for eons of time without males? Some animals can, notably sharks (best guess as to how: sperm can come from female bone marrow). Obviously, males are "the new kids on the block." *Note:* Births of hermaphrodites (both sexes in one body) are now on the rise globally. Why? No one knows.

. . . Tracing haplotypes (blood types), the X-haplotype cannot be linked to our ancestral beginnings in Africa. Too soon yet for any final confirmation, still, current evidence traces the X-haplotype to Berbers, Basque, Mound Builders (of the Great Lakes), Royal Iroquois, Picts, Brazilians, Egyptians (especially those who settled in Northern Ireland)—all said to be the survivors of Atlantis when it sank. And where did Atlanteans get that "X"? Current thinking says . . . off-planet.

By the way, haplotype research is turning upside down what our history tells us about migrations, who settled where, and who is related to whom. For instance, many Blacks are finding they are European, not African; same thing with Eskimos; Chinese pop up all over Aztec-lands and throughout South America; some Arabic people come from northern Japan. How do we reckon what our new sciences are telling us?

Perhaps the esoteric teachings of "root races" (core DNA groups) might at least give us a hint about the comings and goings of evolutionary cycles. Please know that all early cultures and indigenous groups told stories and had prophecies about sweeping timeframes of radical Earth changes accompanied by evolving cycles of upliftment or digression in the human family. These cycles (sometimes referred to as life streams, rays, suns) built on each other in such a manner that they seemed as if an "illustration" of movements we have taken throughout time and space . . . following "guidance" from a grander plan.

The two best versions of root-race progressions that I have found come from the traditions of Theosophy and Cayce. Seven are described in Theosophy, five throughout the readings of Cayce. Here's a brief sketch of each version:

Theosophy:

First Root Race: etheric, began about 18 million years ago as the entry of spirit into matter.

Second Root Race: Hyperborean, began about 8 million years ago, with early physical forms and gender differences, centered in what is today the Arctic and northern climes.

Third Root Race: Lemurian and Mu, began about 1 million years ago; full flowering of genders and racial groupings with the introduction of darker skins, movement to southern regions and the Indian and Pacific oceans.

Fourth Root Race: Atlantean, began about 85,000 BCE in the Azores and the lands now lying beneath the Atlantic Ocean; progenitor of modern body types (including what supposedly became the first Adam).

Fifth Root Race: Aryan, began 10,000 BCE to 3000 BCE with right-brained megalithic cultures, and from 3000 BCE to 2400 CE with left-brained modern cultures (*consciousness separated into two hemispheres—East and West—now fusing back together; a global leap in species refinement*).

Sixth Root Race: originally unnamed but now called Aurorean, begins around 2400 to 3000 CE, centered in North America and Europe (fuses all global patterns into one planetary consciousness).

Seventh Root Race: unnamed, begins 7000 to 8000 CE and centered in South America; graduated from any necessity for Earth-plane schools; perhaps etheric in nature, with a different means of reproduction and growth.

Cayce:

- *First Root Race (initial creation of humans)* about 4.5 billion years ago, began as spiritual, free-will companions of God who were curious about the dense world of matter and how things worked.

- *Second Root Race (fluid, ethereal beings)* about 12 million years ago; androgynous, could move in and out of form. Pacific Ocean.

- *Third Root Race (retained some spiritual power)* began 200,000 years ago. Lived long lives. Created hybrid beings—half animal /half human, part plant/part human. Became the Atlanteans. About 108,000 BCE genders developed and a new physical body. Hybrids disappeared. Communities became common.

- *Fourth Root Race (the origin of the five races/five senses)* began between 90,000 and 12,000 BCE. Red race developed in Atlantis (sensitivity—feeling/touch); white race around Ararat, the Carpathians, Iran (vision/sight); yellow race in the Gobi area of China (sound/hearing); black race in African Sudan and Egypt (emotions/taste); brown race in the Andes area of South America (earthy/smell). Progenitor of the history and culture known today.

- *Fifth Root Race (lighter bodies, cosmic-conscious minds)* began during the closing years of the Mayan calendar, between 1998 and 2015 CE. Described in the Book of Revelation as a time when "Satan will be bound for a thousand years." The indication here is that the human species will flower as never before and achieve great heights of knowledge, invention, and spiritual growth.

Basic Color and Awareness Mode for Each Root Race:

First: red, physical world.

Second: orange, astral world

Third: yellow, mental reasoning

Fourth: green, mental abstract

Fifth: blue, higher intuition

Sixth: indigo, inspiration

Seventh: violet, spiritual

Prophets of old say that in each of the Great Ages, new models of human behavior emerge. Basic archetypes remain the same—those of Adam, Noah, Messiah—yet new people move forward to take on those roles, people of a rare genius who weld a type of strength that transforms notions of personal glory, wealth, desire, or identity into strengths all can profit from. As the Fifth World continues to ascend, several "way-showers" have already emerged. Those I have recognized:

ADAM . . . Gandhi, he showed us what the force of democracy, independence, nonviolence, and peaceful protest really is.

NOAH . . . Nelson Mandela, he showed us the power of forgiveness and reconciliation—both needed to free us from the tyranny of our own actions and deceit.

MESSIAH . . . Contrary to many claims, I have yet to recognize anyone who could model our next Messiah. Current Jesus/Buddha archetype remains until such time.

We are moving from the Great Age of Pisces to the Aquarian Age. That means progressive energies are steadily moving us away from superstition and the blind faith religion has demanded of its adherents in the past, to the importance of scientific discovery and the personal knowing that can only come from direct spiritual experience. Although this movement is already broadly seen and felt, and has been since the '60s, the fuller affects won't begin to take hold until the years 2132/2133 with the 33rd passage of Halley's Comet.

As this occurs, our physical bodies will change. You'll see a bonding of male/female energies as sexual differences either fade or become less relevant; 12 chakras extend the seven we already have; bodies are lighter of weight; we operate more from spiritual essence and with a tolerance for novelty.

A perfect world ahead of us? Depends. The digital world and the rapid exchange of tools and techniques are pushing evolutionary models faster than anyone predicted. As the human race evolves, so too does our brain, nervous system, digestive system, and cellular structure, not to mention how this impacts relationships. We cannot avoid this. What constitutes a human is being overhauled.

Remind yourself of this from time to time: *everything that lives emerged from the same cells.* We have more in common than different.

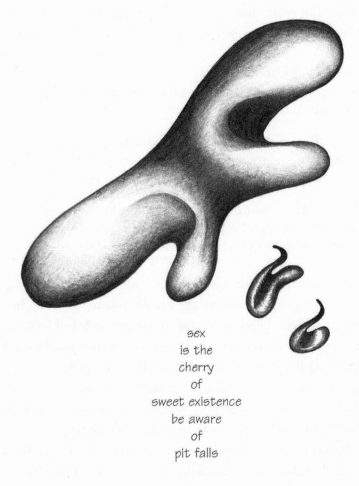

sex
is the
cherry
of
sweet existence
be aware
of
pit falls

10

Self—Initial Focus

So, here we are . . . human beings . . . needing to be heard and touched and wanted and loved. We seek out all types of relationships in skin games devoted to these needs until it finally dawns on us we forgot something—the "me" in we.

Pick where you entered into this modern version of the March of Generations:

1901—1924, G. I. Joes (builders)
Signature: perseverance / stubbornness

1925—1942, Silents (care-givers)
Signature: compassion / disillusionment

1943—1960, Boomers (rebels)
Signature: enthusiasm / selfishness

1961—1981, Generation X (survivors)
Signature: resourcefulness / suicide
and depression (self-condemnation)

1982—2001, Millennials (fixers)
Signature: tolerance / anger (a peculiar impatience)

2002—2024, 9-11s (adapters)
Signature: adaptability / fear (insecurity)

2025—2043, Aquarians (universalists)
Signature: humanitarian / instability (crisis)

Note: The Millennial Generation is the "shift" generation in the age of shift. (Pluto, the generational planet, moves through *three* signs during their birthing years, giving them uniquely different characteristics. We passed through the Mayan "Gateway" into the Fifth World under their aegis.) The Aquarian Generation brings with them new ways of thinking and living. (Pluto remains in this sign throughout the entire span of birthing years, giving us our first opportunity to witness a fuller development of Aquarian energy within the population at large.) The "signature" . . . (found within each generation) refers to the *underlying energy that both supports and challenges generational patterning.*

This brief glance will tell you something about yourself and the pressures you have faced or fought, and to some extent still do, because of when you were born. Your habits, your likes and dislikes, even your dreams of the future, were influenced by the fashions, expectations, and preferences of your generational group. This does not "fix you in time," but it does help you recognize traits and values you may wish to alter, change, or update rather than just repeat as you go along life's way.

Ego

There's nothing wrong with having a good sense of self, your ego. We wouldn't be here, even exist in this dimension, if we didn't have one. Ego is our tool for identity, expression, and individuality. It enables us to negotiate and navigate our life experience. It is our servant and our friend.

Only when we allow our ego to overwhelm us and expand out of proportion to our true nature, does it become a problem. We can forget who we really are once caught up on the slippery slide of narcissistic, self-serving-self-admiring behavior. Myriad types of "self-worship" are hard to recognize at first. Volunteer at food banks or senior-citizen centers for a crash course in what really matters. You'll quickly "wake up." Honest feedback keeps our ego balanced.

Some Basic Basics

1. Medical science tells us we naturally fall into the rhythms of a 25-hour day, not 24. Trying to "force 24" is one of the main reasons we never seem to "catch up" in our sleep cycles.

2. There is a general pattern of how your biorhythms tend to fluctuate, based on your birth date:

Six weeks before your birthday . . . a time of weakness and tiredness.

Six weeks after your birthday . . . a time of strength and ready-to-go energy.

Six months from your birthday . . . times of unexpected challenges that can confuse or mess up your plans.

Six weeks after that date . . . your energy can pick up with a rise in creativity and solution finding.

3. Every 28 years (count several years before and after that 28th year as well), your *Saturn Return* occurs. In astrology, that means transiting Saturn returns to the place where it was when you were born. Saturn, symbolically, is known as "the disciplinarian"—its "return," a time of major life changes. Upheavals and unexpected shifts are commonplace during such times—along with things like reassessments, changes of venue, divorce/marriage, new decisions, hospital stays, the house burns down, an accident "happens," or you just feel like more stuff is going on in your life than you can handle. General patterning:

Ages 26-32: A time of self-discovery, when what you believed was true and how you were raised/trained loses its value. The challenge: what do you want to do with your life? You become your own person, a true adult, during this phase.

Ages 56-62: A time of reassessment, of looking back on your life with either contentment or regret, adding up choices. Can you retire? What do you need to do to make things better or turn things around? Life is often seen as a gamble; did you choose the right cards?

Ages 86-92: A time of joy or nightmares. More people are living to these years and beyond. The contrast is great: handicapped or in pain, angry about poverty/losses; or bright with new ideas/making a difference in the world. Either way, the big issue is God/Allah/Deity and the lasting value of things sacred, of forgiveness and love.

4. We express ourselves daily through four vocabularies, not just one. They are:

Verbal: *I versus you* (biases are pre-programmed by how we were raised and our preferences);

Body: *physical postures* (how we move and why);

Emotional: *feelings* (value of touch and being touched, feelings, sensory input);

Perceptual: *prejudicial barriers* (exposure or lack of it to other types of existing/being in the world).

5. If you examine the patterns of your thought and the demands you have made in life, this truism will pop up like a neon sign: *You received exactly what you asked for.*

The mistake we make in living is not recognizing the power of our thoughts or the fact that ten percent of whatever we put out comes back to us. Mistakes are learning lessons. Do better next time, or, do differently. Science tells us that we have 90 seconds to act on an idea before our brain shifts its attention to something else. Test that.

Finding/Entering Your Center

There is within all of us a special place. A place of power. Our core center. I once thought this idea was a silly play on words until, in my determination in 1977 to be healed, I discovered: *Our center is both a location and a feeling—a place where extremes cannot exist and only honest clarity and understanding reign—a place that has a special feel to it that can be forever helpful to recognize and know.*

Personality does not govern our center, nor does race memory, religion, philosophy, thoughts, desires, or needs. We cease to be what we see in the mirror. Once we enter our center, we are engulfed by a gentle sense of radiance. We stop living our life as who we think we are and start becoming our higher and greater self. Here we experience true balance and wholeness, true power. Without doing this, we miss the "all-there-is-ness" of humanhood.

Yes, there are many ways to ease into our center. But, for me, physically finding "the place" and going "there" proves the better route. Try this:

> **Identify**: The "place-apart" within you operates like a "horizon" on a compass or the level-bubble on a carpenter's tool. It holds and maintains the equilibrium of your existence.
>
> **Enter**: Stop! Turn off your world. In your mind, enter into silence. Be quiet, relaxed, breathe deeply and slowly, with your focus of attention inside your deepest sense of self.
>
> **Feel**: You'll never forget the feel of your center. Some say it is a tingling feeling, like fresh dew. For others, it is warm

and snuggly, or a dreamy peacefulness, floating, weightless, or a sense of "allness."

Expand: Mental clarity increases noticeably while in your center, so does a wisdom of knowing and understanding. Confidence, compassion, love, blend into a detached objectivity that has a sense of the sacred.

Discipline: This simple "place-apart" within offers a way to tap into a form of guidance and peace that often transcends any need for answers. Recognizing the power of finding your center and going there has nothing to do with developing psychic awareness. Rather, it is a handy and quick way to keep yourself grounded and clear. If you asked for assistance while in your center (as if a prayer request), know that what you need will manifest upon your return to the consciousness of the busy, noisy world around you—*when the time is right.*

Visualization: If you prefer imagery to find your center, try this:

- Stand straight and tall, arms at your side, feet a little apart.

- Close your eyes and relax.

- Feel roots growing downward from the bottom of your feet. Really feel them—roots—your roots growing through the floor, dirt, and rock, far below. As they do, feel a thick warm golden liqueur from the depths of Earth now rising up the length of your roots, all the way up to your feet, up your legs, and swirling around in your chest area.

- Feel now branches growing upward from your shoulders and head, moving ever upward into the vastness of space. A cool misty water-like vapor begins to flow downward from the sky, down and down until it reaches your branches, and continues its flow down your head and shoulders until it swirls around in your chest area, dancing with the thick golden liqueur already there. The two flows become as if one—heaven and Earth joined. In this state of oneness where the two aspects of your nature become as if one, you stand in the power of your own center. Pure. Refreshed. Fulfilled.

◆ When you are ready, feel your branches disappear into the vastness of the sky. Feel your roots vanish into and past your feet as they seek deeper depths. Both liqueur and vapor within your chest area blend into heartbeat and breathing. As everything returns to normal, the *power* of who you are remains.

Remember the feel of this, your center. Go there whenever needed.

Inner Dialogue

Self-talk for the average person is 75 percent negative. We tend to be self-critical and non-supportive of ourselves and what we're capable of. Since our brain learns faster from bad experiences than it does from good ones, the key to turning this around in the brain lies with the sensory input from experiences that are rewarding. Good feelings bump us up; encouragement keeps us going; suggestions of better ways to accomplish something gives us the courage to try again.

Brain neurons that fire together wire together.

By turning your self-talk around, by engaging in direct-willed mental activity . . . *physical force is generated.*

Did you get that? We have the ability and the right to choose our own thoughts, and what we choose carries with it actual physical power.

Turn Your Inner Dialogue Around

Whenever you become aware of aimless chatter bouncing around in your brain, maybe worry thoughts or a parade of voices that seem over-powering or in conflict . . . Go into your mind, blank out what offends, and insert whatever enables you to pursue what you want. You do this by deciding to. How? *Bring into* **focus** *what you don't want,* **forgive** *it for being there, then* **release** *it. Nature abhors a vacuum, so . . . immediately* **put something back** *to fill the space,* such as positive images, interesting voices, maybe some affirmations or ideas that are creative and helpful. You may need to do this often at first, like every few minutes, then every half hour, then several times a day, weekly, until the new inner dialogue feels natural. The formula again: Focus . . . Forgive . . . Release . . . Replace.

We face advertising, 24-hour news coverage, radio and television, movies and instant streaming, all designed by experts to hook your attention so advertisers can create markets, politicians can mold con-stituencies, and governments can control you. Social media and the myriad platforms they offer inform, bring people together, save lives and ruin them, while erasing forever the quaint idea of privacy—all of this in the name of conversation and sharing.

Fact: *Whatever you think about the most, you become.* This fact should guide whatever you expose yourself to and for how long.

No matter your source or information stream, YOU are always in charge. So, take charge.

Changing a Habit

Habits are a form of security. They're time savers so we don't have to labor too much with thought. We need them, but not too many of them. Know this: *You never break a habit—you alter or change it—repro-gram.* (Should you try to "break" one, it will bounce right back.)

Life is made up of habits. Some serve us; some don't. Problems come when we live too much of our life wrapped up in habitual responses. We get "stuck in a rut" when we cut off the stimulus of new and different. In order to alter or change a habit, you *must* also be involved in actively replacing it. Same notion as before: nature abhors a vacuum.

Habit Inventory

Take a piece of paper and write down your habits. Examples: What shoe do you always put on first? When you take a step, what foot leads? When you eat a piece of pie, do you leave the crust, eat it first, or last? When you enter your home, what door do you come in? What is the first thing you see? Do you always make your bed in the morning? How do you clean your dishes, wash your clothes, take a bath or shower? How do you greet a stranger or a loved one? Where do you put the fork when you set the table? What hand reaches for a glass to drink? What do you put in your mouth? What kind of books do you read? What route do you take to work? When do you cough? When do you snack? How do you kiss or touch, or do you? Do you hang up your clothes? How many pills do you pop and what for? Do you always buy the same brands at the grocery store? How do you sign your name? How do you handle money?

Get the drift? Write down as many habits as you can, then look at what you wrote. How many are automatic versus how many require thought/decision? Are you in control of your life, or, basically "sleep walking"?

Note which habits feed off each other. *Examples*: Do you head for the refrigerator whenever worried? Scream more at employees if you've had a fight at home? Have a beer when you can't think straight? Also, notice that habits are sometimes cyclic or temporary. Changing moods can alter them. You can be one way at home and another way at work, one way in springtime and another when winter comes. There can be all kinds of psychological reasons behind habits. Yet, the vast majority of them can be shifted around without having to see a therapist (do go to one if you feel the need).

Basic Formula For Changing A Habit

Most nerve cells replace themselves (complete their cycle) every 21 days. This timing is important, for it is the nerve cells that are involved more directly with habits. The quickest way to work with nerve cells is by using your fingers and hands (because they're loaded with nerve endings).

Focus on your ideals and goals, then list them. Use your fingers and hands to do this by taking pen/pencil to paper and writing things out. Shortcuts provided by using computers and phone apps do not have the same effect.

Pick a particular habit you want changed, like eating whenever you are worried. Decide when you will eat each day and eat then. If tempted to do otherwise, devise a physical behavior to remind you to stop. What I did whenever tempted to cheat was train my right hand to grab my left and pull it in toward my solar plexus. That "behavior signal" took a few days to become a habit, but it worked wonders. Keep doing it for 21 days.

To turn-around a deeper, more established habit. Use a pen and lots of paper. Create an affirmation like, "Every day and in every way I am getting better and better; I am becoming more and more." Write this affirmation, or something like it, 100 times every day for 21 days (no cheating). *Underscore each sentence after you write it.* After 21 days, rest for three days, then start up again, writing your affirmation 100 times each day for 21 days. Take that second three-day rest, then do the 21-day exercise one more time. That's it. Do not do it again for at least a year, if then (you can overload your nervous system). The formula: 21 days on, three off; 21 days on, three off; another 21 days on, then stop. This is the timing of nerve cell die-offs and regeneration and directly involves fingers and hands as well as your mind. Expect miracles of self-discovery and self-love.

Who Are You?

The image we have of ourselves—who we think we are—seldom matches what others see. A way to touch those deeper depths of our psyche and learn some things about ourselves we normally would not recognize is through the powerful exercise of "Day and Night Letters."

The span of time, same as before: 69 days (21 days on, 3-day rest; 21 days on, 3-day rest; 21 days on, stop), then evaluate. Yup, you need a pen, have lots of paper handy, plus five shallow boxes and three colored marking pens. Label one box: IDEALS AND GOALS. The second: NIGHT LETTERS. Third: DAY LETTERS. Fourth: FOLLOW-THROUGH. And fifth: THE REAL ME. Although we're using the same formula as before, the exercise is far more intense.

On the first day: take a page and state the reason you are doing this exercise. What do you hope to gain? What is your purpose? Then create and write down four ideals, one each for physical, emotional, mental, and spiritual. An ideal is long-term, like an overview of what you want to accomplish.

At the start of each 21-day period, do a separate sheet for short-term goals—as many as you want—that you'd like to do during those 21 days. Put your ideals, and the goal sheets (as you do them for each period) face down in IDEALS AND GOALS box. Do not read them until the 69th day.

Also on the first day: create a picture (maybe several of them) of what you want to be. Look through magazines and newspapers to find images that "feel right" and cut them out (or draw them). Paste to a blank sheet, along with whatever large bold words you can find that say what you want to say. Consider this a "wish" page(s) of the qualities you want to have, the way you want to look, who you want to be with, the job you want to have, where you want to live. Then, boldly print something like this on the sheet(s): THIS WILL HAPPEN IN ACCORDANCE WITH MY HIGHEST GOOD AND THAT OF OTHERS. Put your creations face down in THE REAL ME box.

Every night for 21 days: just before you go to bed, write a letter to your Higher Self (or God/Allah/Deity). Start like, "Dear Higher Self," or "Dear God." Pour out your heart in this letter. Talk about the day, your thoughts, feelings, whatever you want to say. Be honest. Hold nothing back. Sign your name when finished. Put this letter face down in the NIGHT LETTERS box.

Every morning for the same period: just as you rise for the day, write a letter from your Higher Self to you. Start it, "Dear (your name)." Whatever pops into your mind, write it down. Don't think. Don't read what you wrote. Even if all that comes out is one word, record it. Sign the letter, "Your Higher Self." Put it face down in the box marked MORNING LETTERS. Never read these letters until the 69th day.

At the end of 21 days: go to the NIGHT LETTERS box, turn them over, and have two different colored pens (maybe red and green). Carefully study each letter. How many times did you use the letter "I"? A lot, or hardly ever? Circle the verb closest to the "I" with red (there may be several). Now, take the green pen and circle the noun *after* each circled verb. Do this with every Night Letter.

Take a separate sheet of paper and draw a line down the middle. On the left, title the column, "Action" (in red). On the right, title the column, "Reward" (in green). Down the left, list all your verbs (red circles) and down the right, list all your nouns (green circles). With another color (like violet) go down the right column only and change any nouns you don't like to something you do. Examples: "weakness" to "strength"; "overtime" to "vacation." Leave entries on the left column as is. Once done, put this sheet face down in the box marked FOLLOW-THROUGH.

Give yourself three days off, then start again for a second 21 days: do the exact same thing: Morning Letters, Night Letters, Follow-Through. Put sheets face down when finished, then place each in its proper box.

Give yourself three days off, then start the final round of 21 days: Morning Letters, Night Letters, Follow-Through. When finished, stop.

On the 69th day: read for the first time all your Morning Letters. I think you will be surprised, even astounded when you do this. Next, read over your Ideals and Goals. How many were realized during those 69 days, or, at least started?

Now you are ready to really tackle what your Night Letters revealed. You do that by turning over the three Follow-Through pages and reviewing the left "Action" column. *Verbs show how you act in life.* Are you using your energy from a weakened position of always dealing "out there," thereby pulling your energy away from you? Or, are you using your energy from an inner position of self-awareness and self-confidence? Do not judge any of this. Seek clarity instead. *Nouns in the right column show what you are asking to happen to you* (what you are really praying for). What are you programming into your life? What are you drawing to you? How many are negative or undesirable? How many are positive or closer to what you want? How did you change any of them, and why?

Go back to your Night Letters. Take a good, long look at any time you wrote: "I am." Whatever followed that phrase is literally a command. Not just a verb or noun . . . a command. "I am" is the most powerful phrase you can utter. What are you commanding?

If you followed instructions exactly, this exercise will strip you bare. How you act, what you want or don't want, and what you're doing about you—unmasked.

Your picture(s) of The Real Me re-centers you in your heart of hearts. Be there, in your center, then read again your Morning Letters. Who you are becomes "what I am"—an awakening. This exercise works well with a group. If you start and finish together, and can trust each other, discussions can be revelatory.

Sex and Sex and More Sex
Redefining Gender
More and more people are taking their private struggles into the public arena, demanding their deep inner sense of what gender they believe they are, versus the body they were born with, be seriously reconsidered . . . not as mental hallucination or trickery, but as a state of valid human existence deserving of public acceptance. Some cases are a simple fad, some experimental, some reincarnational memories of previous lives, others a cop-out in disgust for a life they must now lead versus what they would prefer. Not all are genuine mix-ups, even with small children (who quite naturally seek to continue living as "they had been before"). Is gender switching the best route for kids? Only time and prayer can answer that (in consideration of the soul's will being respected over that of law or religious tradition).

In native societies the world over, "two-spirit" people (lesbians and homosexuals) have been revered and turned to for guidance and for healing. In conventional societies, they are punished or ignored for being "queer," irrespective of the monumental achievements many have made in art, music, and innovation. Our new children (the Fifth Root Race) are taking on the gender issue full throttle; the last statistic I read pegs them at 46 percent bi-sexual—they tend to swing both ways.

At this writing, fifteen countries have legalized three sexes: "F" for female, "M" for male, and "X" for indeterminate (your choice). That third choice reflects a cultural change to what is now called "Intersex."

Intersex recognizes: male, female, masculine female, feminine male, hermaphrodites (born with both genitalia), androgynous (no preference for sexual identity), and transgender (gender by decree, not body parts).

The upshot of this is the growing realization that some men make better mothers than women, and some women repair cars better than men. Admit it, gender roles do not necessarily reflect cultural, sexual, or religious tradition, nor should they. Still, *nature demands gender roles, irrespective of who fills that role.*

Sexual Attractions

We humans are "herd" animals by nature, needing the challenge and comfort of companionship, friends, and enemies, something to remember and look forward to or rally against, as we deal with differences between survival and "arousal," power and competition, freedom and commitment. Sex in all its many forms drives us. There is no religious book ever written that offers teachings or examples about fulfilling sexual relationships. All you get from them is how to claim and control. So, let's toss a few myths.

Abuse Issues

Most convicted felons for sex crimes were either acting out what they learned from pornography or from child abuse. The same is true for dictators of repressive regimes and bullies. Boys ages 12 to 17 are the biggest consumers of sex magazines and violent computer games. Education during the early years will prevent much of this, starting with pre-schoolers (keep it light, focus on pictures and what are good types of touching). By the 'tween years (9-12) be more specific with diagrams and how to handle peer pressure: say "NO" and mean it. Boys have "wet" dreams early in life and can "terrorize" their sisters. Sessions of "let's talk about this" solves most problems.

Virginity

The hymen does not completely block a girl's vagina. If it does, it has to be surgically opened. Having blood show on sheets after the husband has sex with his new wife, as blood-proof of virginity, is a cultural myth. The hymen's condition is *not* a measure of virginity.

Sexual Orgasms

Felt as an ecstatic rush of all-consuming bliss, the power of orgasmic energy seems to blow out your scull as it burns your soul. Once ignited it owns you—and takes you places beyond intercourse. It can be a brief gasp of delight, or it can propel you into the godhead of universal majesty—power—enlightenment. Yet the average orgasm lasts but ten seconds; opportunities for it occur maybe once a week. As stress relief, you can't top it. Sexual intercourse itself is a healthy feel-good exercise. Any shame or fear connected with it can be traced to either previous mistreatment or from cultural/religious biases. There is no shame in nudity or in sharing the pleasure of sensuality. Responsible sharing, however, is primary: PARTNERS MUST BE OF AGE AND MUTUALLY CONSENT. Use a condom, tell the truth about skin conditions or diseases you may have, respect each other's preferences and feelings, wash or shower after. Do not make promises you cannot deliver.

Removing the clitoris from a girl does *not* deny her the ability to achieve an orgasm or to enjoy sex. Females can achieve orgasm from multiple areas if stimulated in the right way by herself or her partner: nipples, clitoris, vaginal walls, cervix.

Intimacy and sex are not the same thing. Sex is an exercise that can lead to wild flings of enjoyment and pleasure. Bed-hopping can be fun for short periods, experimenting with different postures and techniques, but it does not foster in-depth caring and the respect that comes from valuing another person's thoughts and feelings. Intimacy is a loving way to caress and protect the pulse of life, the uniqueness of two people in a relationship who deeply care about each other.

Sexual Magic

The nourishing juice of sexuality explodes if you first prepare. Turn it on: aphrodisiacs like oysters and dates, ginseng and ginkgo biloba; the sweet perfumes of almond and rose; shimmering gowns, velvet pillows, silk brocade. Sounds like tales of the *Arabian Nights*, doesn't it? Well, why not? Your partner should feel special. There are books galore on time-tested rituals, such as sacred gestures of the hands and body to raise vitality and improve endurance; positions to ensure the best sex for each sex. Professional coaches can teach you how to please your partner while unleashing the inner you. If this sounds a little "over-the-top," try something simple—oils.

A *simple mixture you prepare yourself*

My favorite mix of one-half refined peanut oil, one-half refined castor oil, and a teaspoon of liquid lanoline is supreme—for both pleasure and healing. Add fragrance if you wish. Lay on toweling or extra sheets. Massage slowly, curving with contours, stroking away from the heart to relax, toward the heart to energize. Each one massages the other, then together as one slides into the other's embrace and sexual union. Even dancing can be a wonderful tease or taking a shower together.

Guys hold off, give women a chance

Male ejaculation can be held back through a conscious desire to allow more time to engage females in foreplay. This is an enormous plus for both partners. Females are quite capable of extreme orgasmic highs. I've been able to maintain an unbelievable, virtually explosive orgasm by stimulation of both clitoris and cervix simultaneously and with altering rhythms for nearly 10 minutes. Wound up at the doctor's the next day to repair my cervix; still, I have no regrets. I did learn from this, though, to respect bodily limits. Good advice, as many are those who prefer the orgasms they can achieve through violence and pain. Not recommended.

Celibate sex

Intercourse is not necessary for sexual fulfillment, intimacy is. The romance of touching, massage, flowing gestures, and real caring can and often does lead to a type of union that transcends sex. Love prevails. Sharing and companionship become more valuable.

Sexual Pitfalls

Sex can be the trapdoor to deviance and betrayal. Lonely, unhappy people, or those with hormonal imbalances, can use sex as an excuse to prove how neglected or misused they are. Alcoholics and heavy smokers often play the same blame game. Those who wish to blaze a trail of conquests have easy pickings with the unwary, thinking themselves winners when in actuality there was never a contest to begin with. Initially, you attract the opposite of what you really want. Online dating, thanks to the new computer world, is a mixed blessing—variety is assured, safety isn't. This "back door" to endless opportunity can result in pregnancy, identity theft, depression, or disease.

Medical studies are in about Internet porn: Heavy adolescent viewing by males of pornography on the Internet results in sexual dysfunction. Brain learning patterns are switched around via the constant arousal online porn gives, resulting in habits that can become psychologically harmful. The "movie" replaces the real thing. Girls are hurt, too, by the demand that they look and act like starlets. Nothing online can compare with the real thing and the utter enjoyment of true intimacy.

Aka Threads

In the philosophy of Huna, the secret teachings of spiritual truth from the Hawaiian Islands and the South Pacific, Aka translates "life"—the idea being that life threads, tiny filaments of our energy much too small to be seen or felt, attach to whatever we touch or touches us. Normally these threads break off easily or evaporate. But, if touching continues overtime, Aka threads may thicken, eventually becoming like connecting cables or rubber bands returning whatever seemed lost. Think of them in terms of pulsating networks of light, of vital force, that apply to both the living and the inanimate. This shows us why multiple sex partners can "bounce" back or eventually drain us of vital force—and—why that old pair of jeans always feels so good.

Lovemaking

Sex is not lovemaking. This level of intimacy and passion morphs into depths of interest and gratitude and promises kept that can flower into lasting commitment. Beauty is never created—contrary to the fun of *Arabian Nights*. *Real beauty reveals itself through hearts that are open and responsive to all that love is*. Sex can lead us to the sensual, the creative, the procreative, the recreative.

Who Are You, Really?

The full expression of the human mind requires the full span of the human experience, directly or indirectly felt. Our vision of who we are changes as we change. Life is too short for dwelling on loss, so laugh often and smile more.

In truth, love—and love only—defines who we are.

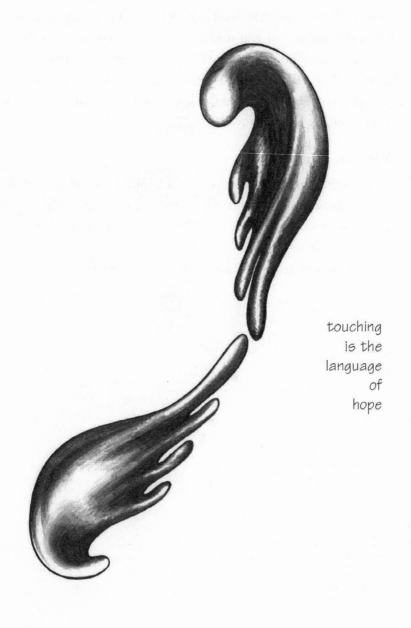

touching
is the
language
of
hope

11

Others—Broader Focus

A friend of mine once confidently declared there are only three types of people in the world: those who love people, those who love things, and those who love ideas. I agree.

Most of us blame our parents for who we are and society for what we do. Karma says we are responsible. Karma is an ancient but loaded term that flatly states: one's balance scale of life is out of balance. This infers that whatever is negative (deeds/behaviors) is way out of line and needs to be corrected. And, whatever is positive (deeds/behaviors) is, at last, getting deserved recognition and reward. Or, as my mother used to say, "You make your own bed, and then you lie in it." Both the term karma and the musings of my mother say the same thing: some-how, in this life or another, we made a decision that led us to where we are now, and that decision either helped us or hindered.

Yet it's not events that cause us stress. It's our opinion of them that does, how we feel. Our beliefs actually direct our genes and those beliefs are based mostly on emotions.

Time to reclaim conversation and language
Conversation enables us to recognize the emotion behind actions and points of view. We are able to feel our way through whatever confronts us while becoming sensitive to the ideas and thoughts of others. It's

a matter of language, of ensuring that all participants involved construe the same or similar reality from the various notions given. The breath we use to speak unites us. When we share conversation, we share the breath of life. The same with elephants, whales, dolphins, crows, ravens, and parrots. Believe it or not, each communicates in a language similar to our own. Whales even rhyme and have a cadence in their poetry. I include pets here, especially dogs, for they quickly "tune in"—almost more to your thoughts and feelings than what you say. And they psychically know things, often before we do.

Time to reclaim the importance of touching

We crave this, even those who shy away or claim they were "violated" when touched without permission. Babies can die or suffer brain damage if they don't get enough. Children tend to whither or distort in some manner if they aren't touched in protective, loving ways. Adults develop extremes in thought and mannerisms without it. Touching literally is matter nourishing matter. When we are not touched enough, cravings and frustrations develop, such as chain-smoking, alcoholism, becoming workaholics, obesity problems, compulsive gambling, overspending, and so forth. Body rubs and constant fondling can be offensive, yet we must have some. Touching, both the ritual and the sensation, is the most critical and ancient of languages. When you touch you leave a thread of yourself behind . . . Aka Threads.

Time to reclaim the power of emotions

Our mind thinks a thought and produces an idea—yet it is our emotions that give us the power to manifest that thought, to make it real. Emotion is accelerated, heightened energy that enables us to move dense matter around, to mold and form, to build and create, to destroy, and start all over again. Emotions only become a problem when we allow them to run away with us. If that happens, imagine riding a horse. You need to give the animal some rein or you won't go anywhere, but if you give too much, the horse will run away with you. You'll feel as if a victim when in fact the horse was just being true to its own nature. Translation: hard-nosed, imposed limits tend to backfire . . . establish common-sense boundaries that help you bend or shift with the energy of the moment while honoring mutual agreements.

Dating and Marriage

Men and women speak different languages. Most women enjoy a good conversation and the opportunity to explore creative ideas and possible solutions. Men often regard "talking things through" as a waste of time; speech, an extension of fighting or the need to win. The old idea that says, "men are from Mars, women from Venus" has a lot of truth to it. Attraction, that special feel or interest or opportunity to make a new acquaintance, draws people together. Friendship can result—you've found a good buddy. If arousal occurs, sex can follow.

A little caution here—women mature sexually usually between 18 to 22; men, not until around 30. Since the human brain is not mature for either sex until age 26, dating for the young is more of a game than anything serious. Should it be otherwise, you can almost bet past lives are involved. Either you've known that person "before," or your souls needed to touch on some level for whatever reason—like to help others, launch a project, or work out past karmas together for good or ill.

Marriage (the new term for this is "conscious coupling") is a union of two people who have agreed to change and grow together in a loving, bonded way that accords with whatever is lawful. Sounds good, but the truth is . . . *we tend to marry whatever "parent" we had the most trouble with growing up and could not forgive*. I did that. In my first marriage I literally "married my mother." The man was exactly like her, even spoke like her—the two became good friends. At that point in my life, I could neither talk with my mother without crying or forgive her for the way I was raised. Right on schedule, I got the exact relationship I needed to face all the issues we had together and find solutions. It took me twenty years. Then I woke up. *What we resist, persists: you have to let go to grow.* Once I did, I eventually met and married my twin soul.

Oh, before I forget, divorce today is called "conscious uncoupling." The idea behind this switch is to rid the anger and divisiveness that all too often accompanies court decrees, and to make it easier for parents to continue as mom and dad—even though they now live apart and have separate lives.

Soul Mates, Companion Souls, and Twin Souls

Soul mates

Soul mates connect to and reflect past lives where two people as a couple formed lasting bonds with each other. Such pairings are more than physical attractions. They are the union of complements, of loving and deeply committed people who know each other and help each other grow in the togetherness of spirit and love. Said to be the most desirous of unions, finding your soul mate feels as if a reward, that somehow this union was fated. It is possible to have parent/child soul-mate bonds. With these, the parent must be very careful of any urge to commit incest. The idea of bonded helpmates does not necessarily involve or need sex to be effective or loving.

Companion souls

Companion souls reflect more of a spiritual connection, a devotion to aid and uplift each other, and "be there" when someone special is needed. Companion souls take friendship deeper than simply the idea of trust. They are confidants of the highest order possible—almost like spiritual mentors who truly enjoy being in your life and having you in theirs. There is a feeling of "richness" to their presence, a comfort. You may have several or even dozens in your lifetime, coming and going as mutually needed or wanted.

Twin souls

Twin souls are vastly different from the other types and may or may not have anything to do with loving relationships. Twin souls are each other's *opposite*. Typically, the attraction between them is so great they come together quickly, then blow each other apart. Seldom do twin soul couples stay together for very long. The power between them is too strong. What you usually find is that one remains in spirit while the other manifests in the physical. They can more easily help each other that way without having to deal with any conflicts that could arise. You can have enemies who are twin souls—each committed to a different way to achieve the same goal for the largest number. You can have leaders who are twin souls—always with the sense that two together can accomplish more than one. Parent/child missions can occur (such as with Mother Mary and Jesus). The point here is that the full charge of directed soul power (two opposites in unity), will somehow change things. Twin souls can marry. Look for extremes if they do, and usually a deep and lasting love bond, as if the two were one.

Think of it this way: Soul mates are like love mates; companion souls are like the best of buddies; twin souls merge together when something difficult or important needs to be accomplished.

Abortions and Births

The woman's right to choose is *not* primary with abortions. What is primary is the soul's will. What does the soul want? No law, no religion, no woman's choice is more important than this. The near-death research I have done turned around any thoughts I had before about abortions . . . because . . . the aborted can come back to face issues and often do during near-death scenarios. Energy which envelops a fertilized egg is conscious, aware, intelligent, knows its purpose and can communicate. The term "fetus" does not apply.

About half the child experiencers I spoke to could remember their birth (never found an error when I checked with parents), and 1/3 had pre-birth memory beginning at around seven months in utero. The unborn can hear their mother's thoughts as well as her words, sometimes their father's too, and talk about this once born and old enough to speak plainly. Anything tinged with fear or anger—picked up from either parent—is what the unborn are the most apt to remember. *What can be seen outside the womb while still inside* is so surprising, even shocking, that it challenges how we define the bodies we wear, the souls we are.

What I recommend with unwanted pregnancies is this: check in with the soul and find out what it wants. You can do this through prayer, in meditation, or via dreams and visions. If you really want to make a connection, you will. "Announcing dreams," where the soul contacts the mother ahead of time, can occur even a year or so before pregnancy occurs. Usually the mother, maybe the father, sees a globe of light in the air hovering around, maybe hears a tone, or is somehow contacted in a way that says, "I'm coming."

During such contact, the soul may agree to leave. A miscarriage could follow, or an abortion could be performed without difficulty. Still, contrary to any and everyone's wishes, the soul can insist on staying. Even if unwanted, conditions terrible, poverty or abuse rampant, the soul knows what is best for its growth and the growth of others. I've learned to respect the soul's voice as an emanation from spirit.

A new birthing trend involves choosing the best day/best time for a baby's birth with astrology, or selecting the date and time according to the doctor's convenience or the family's wishes. The resulting Cesarean delivery can cause fetal distress and birth defects. It also messes with both karma and the soul's will. Planned births negate heredity markers and risk, removing the child from the family's karmic line. Admitted or not, family groupings are no accident. Slanting life trajectories according to astrology or personal convenience could backfire and wind up affecting society in ways we cannot fathom. Sometimes C-sections are necessary to save lives. But to plan them based solely on preference runs counter to wisdom. Natural is better. The soul knows best when it's time to be born.

Fetal abuse occurs in ways we prefer to ignore. Examples: infertility treatments with older mothers, either parent hooked on drugs, mothers who smoke or drink alcoholic beverages, infectious diseases that have a direct bearing on a baby's intelligence, religious sects that make little or no provision to feed, educate, or employ their increasingly large populations.

A bright spot: the majority of people born since around 1982 have a strong sense of social responsibility. They couple easily but are far less likely to rush having children of their own. Many expect to be childless. They are more inclined than previous generations to form extended families in the sense of supportive community. Even if they had a typical birth in a typical family, they still tend to view their family's lineage in a unique way, as if it has little meaning for them or is somehow objectionable, or simply does not apply.

Children and Parenting

The more you think you know about being a good parent, the less you actually do. Each child is so different that what works for one will not with the other. The fact is, you are not raising a child; you are raising an adult. Many children not only remember their birth but even time spent in the womb. Some, though, recall the previous worlds they come from. These could be alien or reincarnational; stunning memories that reveal a murderous streak, or unusual compassion and a desire to heal others. You never really know "who" you have. All you know is that in your arms is an innocent bundle you have taken unto your heart to love, protect, guide, teach. Don't feel guilty if your child for no reason you can detect is upset with you. Failures are as important as successes. Language is crucial. If everyone talks out issues together, giving equal time for listening, fair solutions can be found. Be in the *present moment* with kids. That's where they live, and that's where you can find them.

By age three, 85 percent of the brain's neural networking is complete. By age seven, basic personality traits have formed. *That spread of time between three to seven is when spirituality is the most real, present, and powerful in children's lives. (From three to five, however, kids can actually spend more time in the future than the present, interacting regularly with otherworldly beings.)* This is *not* imagination. Children enter the world knowing God/Allah/Deity. Most can see and converse with spirit entities and bright ones: like the "red man" who comes when they're ill (fever); the "white lady" who appears when they struggle to heal (recovery); "shadow beings" and "monsters" when they need to face their fears and take a stand (confidence).

Teaching children to pray opens the door to trust, and shows them that faith is purposeful and meaningful. Find a church home that feels right to the family. If you can't, create one of your own where weekly everyone gathers to read and study sacred teachings, to sing and share. Take up a collection to donate either to church or those less fortunate. Share in leadership duties. Encourage each one to create a personal altar at home. Children love this and know exactly what an altar is for.

Opening up to the spiritual world automatically elevates intuition. Teaching them to listen to their intuition, their smart hearts, gives them the power of discernment—when to trust, who to trust, what to do next and how. Our resilience, our ability to handle anxiety, traces back to this period in our lives. Never deny the world of a child. Chances are what they see, hear, and do has real integrity, real value.

Any collapse of parenting occurs when discipline is forgotten or avoided. Children do not engage in behaviors without a payoff, but that payoff can be how good it feels to participate in rule making, in having your point known, defending your position, accepting and carrying out your punishment, and profiting from the results in the sense of what you learned and how better prepared you are now for the future.

My son once asked me, "How do I recognize truth?" My reply: "When everyone agrees with each other, and there is no dissent, run for the nearest door and get out. All you have found is illusion. But when you find the paradox of unity in opposition, stay as long as you can and learn as much as you can. You have found truth."

Remember elephants? What they teach us about socializing readily applies. Matriarchs and adult females show calves and teenagers how to act, how to respect each other, how to do their part to help the herd. Patriarchs and mature bulls, just by their presence, simmer down teen tempers, correct errant male behavior, thus ensuring the herd's protection and future success. No different with humans. Adult males are needed in families. Just by their presence, they calm, protect, and lead. If you think females can do it all, read newspaper headlines. We're losing our teenage boys faster than we're saving them.

What Makes Parenting So Tough

Glitches starting out:

- Children as young as 12 months emulate behavior they see on television. (*Never put either a television set or a computer in a child's bedroom. Nix to cell phones and such, too. Radios are fine.*)

- Television as a "background noise" in the home retards the mental development of toddlers. They do not engage the mental muscles they need to concentrate and solve problems.

- Chronic depression is now found in children as young as three. Even in grade school, depression and lack of sleep are major factors in learning.

- Obesity in three-year-olds, particularly a problem in Hispanic and Black populations, is beginning to spike in other racial and ethnic groups as well. A good nutritional diet is a must.

- Toddlers should *never* walk around with a cup of juice in their hands. When they do, they drink way too much. Too much juice can physically change their taste buds to prefer excessive sweets.

- Language skills are established by age three. Read to your kids!

- Baby DVDs created for infants between eight and sixteen months, to enhance their cognitive abilities, actually lower intelligence and the ability to understand words. This is the boomerang effect of too much too soon.

- *Never* allow your child to be implanted with an under-the-skin identity microchip. This can subject them to unwanted microwave frequencies with unknown consequences.

- Make changes in the home or try natural remedies before you allow drugs like psychotropics, anti-depressants, or stimulants to be given to your kids.

- You can legally avoid unwanted immunizations you and your doctor do not believe are necessary. If your school doesn't listen, go to the Attorney General of your state.

- Many toys today are X-rated, teaching sexiness to the very young. Images and behaviors like these increase the risk for a child to be a victim of a pedophile. Children do not know the difference between the signals they are encouraged to exhibit and the danger this exposes them to.

- Preschool curricula for two- and three-year-olds are not as important as helping the child to feel safe and well cared for. Preschool should teach how to engage with teachers and other kids and little else.

The Quicksand of Technology

The industry behind movies, television, DVD's, and streaming videos is flooding our screens with nonstop entertainment of every type imaginable that seems as real as the real thing.

But what seems good has glitches. The way the brain reacts to radiant light (from television and computer monitors) is one of them. After a few minutes of exposure, the brain nods off. The industry counters this with the use of startle effects (unexpected sounds and actions) to trick the brain into paying attention. Eventually, the brain zones past false alarms into a hypnotic state. This means bigger and bigger startles are necessary. Today, even children's cartoons and family fare average sixteen startles per half hour of viewing time. The most common startle used is violence, which throws the heart and emotions into overdrive and releases the stress hormone cortisol into the body. Most kids have watched between five to six thousand hours of TV by the age of five or six. This massive, no-letup, over-stimulus is causing maladaptation of the brain (losing the ability to detect shadings of color, a reduction in awareness of the natural environment, a tendency toward anxiety/boredom/violence when deprived of high-density stimulus).

As if this isn't enough, family movies feature one female character to every three males, and those females are often scantily clad or wear sexy, tight, alluring attire. The upshot: the more television a girl watches, the fewer options she believes she has in life; the more a boy watches, the more his views become sexist. And while TV teaches girls to become onlookers, it teaches boys to go out and do interesting things.

The quicksand of technology (how it really works and how we respond to it) is rewiring our brains and our hearts. Too much, too soon, too often, results in shorter attention spans, less exercise, superficial relationships, loss of self-control and sustained thought, hearing loss, fried brain cells from cell phones held too close to the head, isolation, sleep disorders, shallowness, plagiarism, disrupted hormones, obesity, language loss, a fear of silence. High-density stimulation emboldens hurtful speech and abusive behavior while decreasing empathy and the ability to recognize emotional facial expressions and voice tones.

Whatever you accept, you teach. Anybody listening?

Schools/Education

None of the geniuses of the digital world who revolutionized society educate their children in public schools. You may be surprised to know why . . . *to protect their children from computers and digital screens until they are old enough to handle them without harm to brain development.* Yup, the very people who design, build, and sell computer programs for the young keep their young away from them.

You may scream now.

To protect the brains of the innocent: *no screens of any kind before age two.* After that, limited exposure can occur, increasing as the child ages, up to the 'tween years (9-12). By then, and certainly by puberty, a child's brain is finally ready to be stretched, toggled, turned upside down, and fried by computer use. Public schools start kids way too soon on computers, while doing away with cursive writing—*the very skill that enables the personality to flow through the hand in an act of emotional connection to forms/shapes/lines/curves.* Computers are utilitarian. Handwriting is an art form. An antidote: calligraphy.

That abundance of nerve endings in the human hand can also be used to teach the value of money. If you're in a store to buy something, give the money to your child so he/she can give it to the clerk and pay for the item. The clerk gives change back to your child, then she/he returns it to you. Money is not just digits on a page, nor is it a plastic card. It is real tender that enables society to serve people in multiple ways. If you show your child that it has heft, a weight, and a feel, you take the idea of value and make it genuine. Establish a savings account early-on for each child (if possible): the passbook in their care. Money distribution: 10 percent off the top given to church or charity, another 10 percent toward college or retirement, 40 percent regular savings, 40 percent to spend for whatever is needed or wanted. With adults, give yourself a tip from your paycheck—*money in your hand*—that you can feel. As long as your hands physically connect from time to time with actual money (even just a dollar), you will tend to balance and respect its worth and value.

The word "education" actually means to *remember what is already known*. You don't just pound facts into children's heads. You help them discover what they already possess. A way to do this is through total-immersion language training. Start as early as possible, in most areas that's kindergarten: half day in one language (let's say Spanish), the other half in another (perhaps English). Only Spanish can be spoken during its part of the day, only English the other. Keep up this style of teaching for as many years as possible. The result: children grow up with TWO native tongues and a brain capable of executive functions— reasoning, multitasking, spatial awareness, the ability to reconcile conflict. Such children work faster and expend less energy doing so, while developing an understanding of multiple cultures. This can occur *before birth* if the mother is proficient in several languages.

Teaching for tests defeats the whole purpose of education and denigrates teachers to mere repeaters of information. Socrates warned, "I cannot teach anybody anything; I can only make them think." How to turn around schools lies in the nature of philosophy (which should, by the way, be taught from the third grade on up). And that is: how to think, question, contemplate, investigate, test, and evaluate. Have class courts, so if anyone misbehaves they must appear before "the court of their peers" and plead their case. Always with a teacher present, the court reaches a decision and metes out punishment. The kids themselves ensure fairness as lessons are learned.

Great ideas

Have classrooms built so the children themselves can rearrange room shapes from time to time. Recess is a must along with music classes. (*Note:* You cannot have good mathematicians and physicists without opportunities for music/band. That's because the sections in the brain for music and math are next to each other, as if integral to each other.) Routine screens for hearing and sight must also be alert for signs of mental illness and depression. Kids that need extra help should get extra help, and that includes those with problems of obesity. Allow students to design their own curriculums, sports and movement exercises, and participate in "real-life" problem solving—especially with standup board games that require a team effort to study/evaluate/activate. Less homework, better lunches, and more sleep will almost guarantee alertness.

And get this: *Instituting 15 minutes of silence in the morning and 15 minutes of silence in the afternoon*—applying to everyone including the teachers, principals, workers, visitors, students—*can turn around attention levels, discipline problems, and learning achievements by nearly 80 percent* (as reported by those schools that did it). The student can dream, pray, meditate, practice mindfulness, or just sit there. Silence heals as it enriches! Just silence.

In troubled classrooms, have the kids write a memoir of their life. Doesn't matter, short or long. Once finished, students read what they wrote out loud. The result always rattles both teacher and students—because once everyone knows each other's stories, differences fade and compassion begins.

The language systems of old had breadth, scope, and depth, which enabled them to honor both masculine and feminine principles of polarity. Each alphabet symbol incorporated sensation and feeling. (Sanskrit, for instance, had 96 words to describe the various nuances of feeling and thought that comprise "love," thus recognizing both male and female perspectives.) Modern English has a single approach which is masculine in its efficiency. Yet once you recapture the feeling behind and within words, you reconnect the feminine element of that word's origin—the other half of its soul. This reclaims the spirit of thought and the inner dynamics of energy, returning language to a richness of textured meaning. All language systems, all alphabets, are rooted in the heart's desire to nurture the mind as it continuously seeks its own source.

Recapture the fullness of language with poetry, memoirs, plays, vignettes, or just letting your mind wander as you watch clouds drift by.

Recapture the fullness of education with dance, music, singing, calligraphy, art, invention, creativity, rhythmic marching, cooking, gardening, sewing, building, celebrating, laughter, sharing, exploring, having pets, climbing, acting, storytelling, cleaning. All of these activities activate the limbic system in the brain. Without the limbic directly involved, education is superficial and incomplete.

What We Forget In Relationships with Others
When beauty is acknowledged, everyone benefits.

pain
is the
sentinel
of our
growth
guiding or
crushing
according
to our
choice

12

Groups—Multiple Focus

We are facing today something we have no precedent for in modern history . . . an aging population. We have more seniors now than juniors (way more), and they are healthy, active, and not about to retire. This is exciting, even wonderful on one hand, this collective of ready wisdom and real know-how; yet, on the other hand, the situation spells diminished quality of life for juniors who are expected to support this top-heavy, what-has-become-a-burden, with a sweat equity that doesn't match expectations. The disparity is forcing all of us to rethink and reimagine just about everything.

New ideas are already taking us new places, and not a moment too soon.

Go back 29 generations. That's all it takes to find we are all related. We are literally one family . . . with a core DNA pattern that is currently undergoing a makeover. Evolution in our time.

This started with those born around 1982, although many of our middle-aged and senior citizens display the same pattern. Figures used here come from my published study in *Children of the Fifth World*:

- ⅓ have both gene mutations that build a better brain.

- ⅔ have one of them (some exceptions globally, but not many).

- ⅓ of autistic kids who take the Ravens IQ test score genius.

- 70 percent of kids with autism are male (fluctuates at around ⅔), about ⅓ are female.

- ⅔ of kids with dyslexia are female (fluctuates at around that figure), with about ⅓ male.

- ⅓ have no sense of living a full life and are okay with that.

- ⅔ have no intention of ever marrying, going to college, or becoming parents.

- ⅓ are profoundly gifted.

- ⅓ are quite intelligent, intuitive, creative, inventive.

- ⅓ are amoral or too violent to handle.

These percentages have held in the same general bracket for the last 15 years. I am the first to admit this is impossible. It simply can't be true, but it is. And there are more . . . *thirds* . . . lots more.

Note: *Thirds are the baseline of universal order. Divisions of thirds (and triangles) strengthen construction, materials, and design. We have The Holy Trinity to help us understand sacred relationships. We have Karma, the third spiritual law (cause and effect); and the Golden Rule, the third spiritual tradition (do unto others as you would have them do unto you). Thirds are rhythmic proportions in the Golden Mean (sacred geometry). Thirds are nature's preference for harmony, balance, and beauty.*

Think for a minute. Thirds ensure balance. Wouldn't all these percentages make sense if a Universal or Divine Plan were in place for order and growth? Our newest generations are showing us this, how human energetics are altering the rhythms at play in today's world:

- ⅓ uplifting (positive, light-filled)

- ⅓ challenging (negative, shadowy)

* ⅓ in-between (tuned to that very edgespace where collective truth resides, and the guidance that designed this manual in a continuous loop of thirds)

Our Shadow Side

It has been said; all evil must now surface so we can see for ourselves what it really is and deal with it. Truism: evil always serves the good. Facing this truth requires a confrontation with the shadows that haunt us, that part of our nature which seems separate from who and what we really are. Because souls usually travel in groups, we cannot run away from anything. Sooner or later we will face what we'd rather avoid.

Charles Darwin once said: "It is not the strongest species that survives, nor the most intelligent, but the one most responsive to change."

The vast majority of those who commit suicide are male, the young, the old. Especially at risk are those who have lost their jobs, their homes, their families. With the young, it is usually because of confusion over sex roles and what seems to be expected of them no matter where they are or who they're with. Deviation (with girls too) means facing criticism on the order of harassment. Depression is wide spread for both sexes. No matter who you are, the raw emotion of never feeling quite good enough hides behind many a smile. People snap in anger for the slightest reason, turning to alcohol or drugs or both for solace.

Are we destroying ourselves? Our children?

Time for bedrock honesty.

Everything in life moves toward its opposite

It is not the strengths of any given business or relationship that draws us . . . it is their flaws. Whatever problem or flaw that exists within ourselves that we are working on or need to work on, will draw us to a situation that exhibits the same flaw. Our outer life matches our inner life: whatever exists within us will manifest outside of us. It is our flaws, our states of imbalance, that draw us together. We humans are ever seeking wholeness and unity. Because of that driver, our subconscious desire *always* is to heal and grow . . . to mend our flaws.

All life proceeds in a spiral. Always there is a dip before the next advance. Those dips can be dark, shadowy, painful. We can easily be misled when feeling vulnerable, especially to cults or groups like them.

Know the alarm signs for any gathering of the "like-minded" that follow a central authority or a central teaching that has an answer for everything. Do they also . . .

- Emphasize low-protein diets?

- Insist on rigid schedules you must follow?

- Practice repetitive movements and sounds?

- Prevent questioning or thinking independently?

- Consider you and any income you earn as theirs?

Although repetitive movements and sounds can be central to various types of healing and the process of spiritual development, when combined with the rest of the alarm signs listed, benefits reverse.

This warning applies to any yoga center, ashram, spiritual retreat, shamanic or Wiccan circles, church/seminary, or school that is excessively strict. Leave any place or any group that does not honor free will and the right to question. *The quickest way to control the masses is via low-protein diets that are coupled with chanting.* Tyrants maintain their dictatorships using this same formula (protein is necessary for strong bones and a healthy mind).

How to move energy to uplift or control a crowd

The average human energy field extends out 12 feet in every direction. Certainly, you want to project your voice to the person farthest away—but—have children or young people gather close to you, ideally to fill in that first 12 feet. Win them over, excite them, and their energy field will quickly bounce to those behind them, who will expand and enlarge that initial wave and keep it going. By aiming for the back while loading the front, you are more apt to be successful.

We are told that a speaker who engages an audience has great charisma. Charisma is simple math, how one can move energy. Same thing in churches. If the front pews are empty, the minister has to work two to three times as hard to deliver a message. Load the front.

We all have shadows—tendencies to give in, allow ourselves to be led, take advantage of others, bottom-out on our own selfishness, anger snaps. Courage is every day. Darkness, though, is really our friend. That's because all births, all growth, everything that's fresh and new, begins in darkness. Darkness enables us to say goodbye . . . and hello.

Our Precious Thorn—Pain

We are time capsules. Life layers itself in us through emotions and memories. Most of the time we have no idea what we have stored away within ourselves, our muscles, our mind. We keep tucking stuff, building up layers, until pain takes over—pain—the thorn in our side.

Pain always has a message to deliver.

Carl Jung put it straight out: "There is no birth of consciousness without pain." To suffer pain is to ask questions: What needs changing? What do I need to learn? What is the message my body is trying to deliver? What is my opportunity in this? Who else is learning with me? What is it that I've been trying to avoid? Pain brings us back to NOW . . . right here, this instant. On the wings of pain, we either wake up or suffer more.

If you're willing to face what seems indefinable, try this:

◆ Stop whatever you may be engaged in, or thinking about.

◆ Focus on whatever pain you may have—become your pain.

◆ Fully experience the pain.

- Ask the pain what it wants—open yourself to any thought, image, feeling, or memory; accept whatever comes without question.

- Are you willing to let go of the pain and any excuse you have for it?

- Bless your body and your mind as you explore the gift your pain has for you—allow this to unfold.

Some examples from people who confronted their pain to find out why it was there:

- *Sudden loss of voice and pain in throat*—individual did not want to go on the radio to talk about newly published work. There had been embarrassing and painful repercussions in the past when the individual was misunderstood and misquoted. Trust was violated.

- *Growing pain in stomach with all the symptoms of flu*—individual did not want to attend a group picnic. He/she was tired and just wanted to stay home and rest.

- *Continuous pain in big toe for no apparent reason*—individual tired of mowing large lawn alone. Had avoided asking others for help.

- *Continuous pain in middle of chest near bottom of breast bone, plus trouble breathing*—individual nervous and apprehensive about being alone in life and making a go of it. Afraid of not making enough money and not having good friends.

- *Vomiting, shaking, high temperature*—usually a sign of avoidance or the need for extended rest (unconsciously manifested when needed).

Be aware of your language. "She gives me a pain in my neck" (you develop a stiff neck). "You're going to be the death of me" (you develop a serious illness). "I can't live without you" (you develop something like leukemia or a deep depression).

Sometimes it's who's the matter with me, not what.

Over the years I have learned that any pain or hurt or difficulty in life is really a gift. By "unwrapping" your own gifts, allowing pain to speak for itself, you create an opportunity for in-depth honesty and wisdom to emerge in a way that reveals what you need to know.

Betrayal

During the first decade I spent researching the near-death phenomenon, I discovered things that made a huge difference in the field. But because I used police investigative techniques as my protocol instead of the scientific method of inquiry, I ran into a "buzz-saw" of opposition that included being cursed, slapped, renounced, made fun of, scorned, even threatened with lawsuits. Several audiences walked out on me mid-sentence in protest. The very people I trusted the most and admired greatly betrayed me again and again, accusing me of things I never did or had no control over. I was labeled a fraud and a phony; attacks continued weekly for seven years. On top of that, I was swept up in publishing "buy outs" by corporate raiders who nearly wiped out the books I had written. Bankruptcy threatened several times. My accusers were *both* fellow researchers *and* experiencers. I was shaken to my core and sunk into a deep depression lasting one winter.

What did I learn from this?

- I learned that facing my attackers and talking with them solved most of the problems between us—plus it saved everyone a lot of time and money and grief.

- I learned that what my attackers did was done out of fear, *their fear* that I would not credit their work and honor their sacrifices.

♦ I learned that any new idea or unique protocol is an automatic flag for attack. No one wants some brash newcomer messing up their theories.

♦ I learned that a long walk on "the dark side" is good for you. It keeps you humble and helps you to find different ways to accomplish what you want to do.

♦ I learned that your attackers are the best teachers you could ever hope for, as they keep you honest and enable you to explore what you need to know . . . about yourself.

♦ I learned to bless what hurts. That's just your soul trying to catch your attention. Negativity only has the power we give it, so what about you? How do you handle your accusers, your attackers, your enemies?

Racism and Planting Justice

The presence of "other" has bothered we humans for millennia. Never have issues really been the color of anyone's skin, or point of origin, religious beliefs, dress, hair style, or the shape of body parts. Prejudice has always arisen when the majority reacts to difference. That sense of other ignites our instinct for survival. Can we trust the newcomer, the odd one? Rather than stepping forward to find out, the average person hesitates, then scurries for the shelter of sameness. There is power in collective preference—the idea of exceptionalism, of absolutes, of majority rule. Yet differences enrich relationships, not divide them.

Case in point, the year 1980, when my husband and I were dating in southern Virginia. Terry is black. Actually he's a golden brown. I'm white, with speckles and freckles. Whenever we entered a restaurant, people would drop their silverware, turn toward us, frown, and stiffen. I'd always connect eye-to-eye, smile, and give a little wave. Invariably, whenever I did this, they'd smile back, pick up their silverware, and go back to eating. One day, in great concern for my safety, Terry pulled me aside and cautioned, "Don't you know what those people are doing in there?" "Yes," I replied, "I know exactly what they're doing. They are giving me their power, and I happen to think that's a precious gift. So, I said thank you."

Wherever you put your attention is where you put your power.
Remove the glare, tension dissolves. No exceptions.

This is why people stage riots. Media, cameras, reporters, police. A point is made, but change doesn't actually occur until the various sides agree to hear each other and cooperate. How do you avoid the lure of crowd violence with riots? The minute people start moving and yelling in rhythmic swells, leave. If you stay, you will be pulled into doing things you'd never do in "your right mind." Crowd violence is based on the same ratios you've already learned in how to use energy to uplift or control a crowd. The main difference between the energetics of charisma, seduction, and manipulation . . . is intention.

Living with Terry taught me a lot about racism, including reverse racism, when Terry's beloved grandmother threw bricks at white people who dared to walk on the sidewalk in front of her home. And when he'd go to a nearby store and the black cashiers would loudly complain that he spoke and dressed like a whitey. A Greek restaurant owner kicked him off his property once because he feared Terry's presence would scare away customers.

Where did this take us? To gratitude and courtesy and the joy of knowing that cooperation and respect get you further than complaints.

There's no justice in revenge

Remember that when you think in terms of punishment and imprisonment.

Along this line, a nationwide movement to convert prison yards into gardens is gathering a great deal of support. Prisoners raise what they eat while learning valuable skills. Called "Planting Justice," the idea also emphasizes flowers, cooperation, design, and the construction skills that will enable convicts to erect whatever is needed to support and encourage the growing of crops and marketing of flowers.

Planting Justice spawned from a global movement to teach, not just isolate, prisoners. In those countries where social skills, cooking, cleaning, and educational opportunities are emphasized in the prison system, less than 17 percent of the offenders ever return to a life of crime.

Conflict is human. Creative responses to conflict work in amazing ways, like with this technique:

- Remove item of contention or call time out.

- Each person verbally expresses his/her side to the issue—others must listen without interrupting.

- Acknowledge pain, anger, any feelings present—each person is acknowledged.

- Ask each person to find five solutions to problem.

- Collect responses then negotiate to find one everyone will agree to.

- Carry out solution.

This technique should be taught in every school. It builds community because people learn how to be affirmative with each other.

There is a wisdom built into life, a rhythm that flows throughout all forms, all climates, everything that breathes. Life doesn't just happen. It moves with our vision of it.

Webs

There are active, energetic loops—looking more like webs—that connect us. That's because we live three-dimensionally within a world that consists of threaded web-works—millions, billions, trillions of them—interacting within and past consciousness itself, defying time and place. Not everyone can actually see them, though they're often felt or sensed. James Burke, a film maker, discovered these loops and he called them "learning webs." Ideas spark along the threading of these webs, linking any part of life to anywhere else, be that in this century or another, in this realm or somewhere else. Similar to how mass mind works, the threading formed around an idea, desire, or goal can link seemingly unrelated people, events, and ideas together in a conscious webbing that will seek out whatever idea or knowledge matches, or could match. We're talking linkages here. An example Burke gave was about a reporter's tape recorder and how that connected to malaria.

"The ferrite recording tape was made by Germany's BASF, the Aniline and Soda Factory of Bavaria," said Burke, "a company that came into existence because an Englishman named Perkins, looking for a malaria cure in 1857, dumped an experiment in the sink and saw what it did to the water. He became a millionaire overnight because he invented the world's first aniline dye. And, in true British fashion, he makes his money by selling the idea to a German . . . The people he sold it to became BASF."

Synchronicity? Not exactly. What happened here is that the spark of an idea ignited another spark and another, until that energy, those threads, looped in, around, and through space and time. Richly interwoven webs like this can connect various aspects of consciousness with various stratas of existence. We're talking globe, universe, the in-between. Moments of inspiration/desire/need activate them. No one plans this. Connections happen when a web "lights up." Burke called them learning webs. I recognize them as another example of how consciousness can seek out what will help it connect possibility with potential.

The Magic of Community

People interacting with other people in a mutually shared environment that is supportive, respectful and congenial leads to a longer, happier, healthier life for all those involved. This fact defies medical studies, lifestyle choices, financial and emotional issues, religious preferences. Supportive contact with other people is the single best barometer for successful living.

Human beings have a magical effect on each other.

Generations of families are starting to live together as they once did in times past. From birth to death, they are sharing the same house or remodeling or redesigning the place so they can. This divides up expenses and chores, enables the elderly to stay home as long as possible, guarantees child care, and spreads out chores in an equitable fashion that enables more leisure time and makes vacations possible. In families where meals are shared, children tend to grow up happier and better adjusted. Conversations at the dinner table bond the family and can teach self-worth.

For those who can't stand the thought of staying with their parents one more night, there's cohousing. This is where several people, maybe a group of folks, sign their name on a dotted line to either rent space or co-purchase space, with each person having his/her own room or section and arrangements made for sharing common areas, chores, and household bills. Such agreements must be kept legal and always have an "out clause," as just shaking someone's hand doesn't cut it. Cohousing is popular between siblings, a child and a parent, relatives, or between friends. Divorced women with young children are finding that cohousing solves an infinite number of problems while maintaining a sense of home and security. An added benefit: kids are more apt to learn "whole thinking" when encouraged in family-like settings to converse in whole sentences.

Immigrants keep populations lively. Community embraces the gamut of skin colors and body types—not as a swing toward multiculturalism, *at least not if we're smart*, but rather in recognition that strength comes from diversity. The different skills we have and the unique stories we tell are much too valuable to dilute or absorb or forget or blend or legislate. What can develop is *a community of minds*, people more interested in sharing their gifts and ideas and talents than in hiding behind curtains and front doors.

Popular living spaces are now rentals, maybe a flat, or an efficiency (room pared down to basics). Some apartment complexes, though, are going all out to attract the "green crowd" with every type of holistic, sustainable feature imaginable (such as lighting systems designed to sync with your circadian rhythms and electromagnetic-free-zones). Common space "dorms" are similar, except the small rooms folks rent or buy actually encircle the type of common space that includes food, games, and television. Most employ "social directors" who plan activities while keeping an eye out for any problems or needs residents may have. It's amazing how quickly these alternatives to owning a home develop into full-fledged communities.

Agri-hoods, as mentioned in a previous section, are homes and rentals built around community farms. They are planned developments that support farm life, crops, kids, and sustainable living. People who yearn to get back to nature and get their hands dirty from pitching in and helping out, are flocking to these places, as well as to "Earth Ships"—homes off the electrical grid that either have a self-sustaining ecosphere or a hacienda (central garden around which rooms are built).

The idea of church as a place of common worship is radically altering to fit the views and needs of new generations of people. "Spirit-led" assemblies shake and yell; house churches operate from individual homes or bars; "techno-mass" is turning sanctuaries into raves with techno sounds and ultraviolet light; meditation groups, pilgrimage travelers, metaphysical study groups, orb and crop-circle investigators, intuition camps, Earth-energy seekers, participants in sacred service via computer, global prayers and chants and joyful voices singing praise, even atheist churches—are part of the new way to worship in the new communities. Gurus of the past, charismatic leaders and teachers, are falling by the wayside. They are being replaced by smiling folk who already know they are okay—who know we can do this, we can be better, we can help each other.

The Third Way

The Third Way illustrates how people, when faced with life issues, tend to react in one of three ways: (1) we play ostrich and pretend we don't see it; (2) we label it an enemy or a devil and attack; or (3) we confront the situation squarely and honestly, search for the truth behind the appearance, and take decisive steps to initiate a constructive solution. The first way creates victims, the second victors, and the third responsive and responsible participants in life, committed to growth and learning. This Third Way of dealing with life issues is in-between dualities: between victors and victims, good and evil, darkness and light. The Third Way requires mediation and diplomacy skills, mindfulness, and a willingness to consider *what is appropriate* as a greater priority than self-centered interests. It takes time and patience to learn, and it necessitates cooperation and compromise, but it is the only way of living that shows any promise for a future that is worthwhile. The Third Way upholds dignity and value and wholeness—and *wholeness is spirituality made manifest.*

The issue is not good/evil, right/wrong, but appropriateness.

Holons

A holon is a situation where opposing sides come together to accomplish a given task or project that is of mutual benefit for the greater good. Opposing forces are not going to change ideology, so forget that angle. Still, solutions are needed to make improvements, so create a holon and here's how:

- Get all sides together.
- Figure out what needs to be done and how to pay for it.
- Empower the people in the group to make work assignments.
- Figure out details.
- Do the work.
- Finish the job.

By working together to accomplish a task at hand, progress becomes an organic mix of discovery—that opposing forces are really the same at their core. The greater good wins. No one changed, yet everyone changed. A holon was created . . . *the strength of a whole comes from the diversity of its many parts working together.*

Problems in your community or on the job?

Invite all sides to come together to work together.

If a holon is in place, the very act of "doing the job" allows the mind to open . . . by itself . . . in its own way.

within
every
question
lies
its own
answer

PART V

OUR TRIUNE EXERCISES

Education—Invention/Science

Economics—Investment/Service

Government—Law/Justice

Let's put a few things in perspective.

As our focus shifts in this manual to broad topics like science, business, and government (the exercises we humans engage in), we need to first explore the greater implications of "territory" and "timing."

Territory

Think about this: we live in a four-percent world. Everything else in existence, in the world, in the universe—the other 96 percent—cannot be seen or measured or touched, by anyone, still, we know it's there.

With DNA, same deal. We can see, measure, and experiment with four-percent of it. The other 96 percent—what scientists used to call "Junk DNA"—cannot be seen or measured or touched.

Same identical conundrum.

Four percent of everything that exists registers on, through, or with our faculties of perception, or, via whatever we can create to perceive, respond to, and register this for us. The other 96 percent *of everything that exists … is a complete and total blank.*

We have a habit of naming anything we can't see or register as "dark"—dark energy, dark matter, dark DNA. Just because we can't register any of this doesn't make it dark. We name things this way out of ignorance.

The massive bulk of our world, our universe, our DNA—the other 96 percent of every single thing—*is the energetics, the subtle energy, that invisible pulse-presence that shimmers the vacuum and informs the ethers, enabling what we call "creation" to exist as Creation.*

By detecting ripples in the fabric of space-time (the gravitational waves), we are at last privy to the motion, the jiggle, "the music that sings," whenever something celestial shifts or blows up or trades places or moves, whether we actually see any of this happen or not.

Territory: a four to 96 percent split.

Existence: what ripples reveal.

What's it all about? Life.

What's behind it? An intelligence that spreads the consciousness of its knowing—everywhere—via "tracks" in the silence of its breath.

Timing

We have studied, wondered, recorded, and measured what we can of this world, this universe of ours, since the first beginnings of our beginnings. Our earliest "textbooks" were the stars and planets, rocks, rivers, and mountain peaks, nature's rhythms, plants, animals, disincarnates, wisdom keepers, the gods and goddesses of our imaginal worlds/dreams, the many orders of lifeforms (human or not).

We know from this wealth of knowledge that our Sun takes 25,920 years to complete a full rotation around its parent star, creating what is called a Cosmic Year (modern parlance says this circuit is caused by Earth's axial wobble). We also know that every 2,160 years we pass into another Age (referred to as a Cosmic Month). Each Age brings to the forefront its own unique story of changing temperament, energy, and style, defined by the astrological sign or archetype associated with that Age. Every gathering of humans known to have existed has practiced some form of astrology so that life's cycles could be used for fullest advantage and benefit. It was a survival issue.

Today, good astrologers are trained and excel in recognizing cycles—many have professional degrees in the skill and a track record that can be verified. Anything that reeks of "fortune telling," avoid.

Hear me when I say, the Cosmic Year is completing a full rotation. That means we are now caught in a 25,920-year flip of the dial. This is major big . . . not just biblical . . . massive! That's why our exercises under the headings of science, business, and government—globally—are so unwieldy, extreme, unpredictable, frightening, and ever so wonder-filled. Metaphorically, "the cap is off the bottle, the genie is free."

There is not a single country, leader, religion, corporation, school, industry, utility, or business, not a single farmer or household, that is prepared for the unstable energy/weather/climate/Earth changes now upon us. Far from any doom or gloom, this range of unpredictability is *exactly* what sparks new ideas and new ways of doing things.

To gain a better sense of this Great Shifting, let's revisit catastrophism (as a primary agent of change), the Fifth World (now ascending), the changeover of Ages (as we move closer to the full span of the Aquarian Age), plus a host of other helpful-to-know timelines.

Catastrophism

The late Immanuel Velikovsky, a Russian-American scientist, came up with the idea that catastrophes had more to do with what happened on planet Earth and the changes that have occurred over the ages, than evolution. His research led him to believe that Earth and Venus once collided, resulting in a type of chaotic aftermath that may explain the history on our planet of a type of collective "amnesia" (a global sense of depression, anxiety, and nightmares), as if we were suffering from some type of "post-traumatic stress syndrome." Velikovsky was struck down by his peers, his research maligned; yet professionals like Sigmund Freud and Carl Jung upheld his ideas about a collective "amnesia" as a way to explain what they kept finding with their clients. Modern-day scientists are reconsidering and re-examining his research about Venus and Earth and the possibility of a collision.

Catastrophes throughout time actually do tell us more about our planetary cycles of ascent and cataclysmic downfalls than any other way to regard history. The theory of "uniformitarianism," that life forms and planetary changes follow a uniform and predictable path, doesn't explain our planet's tilt, the deep gouges in our ocean bottoms, or even the Cambrian Period when the oceans were suddenly oxygenated, major animal groups appeared, flowers bloomed, and crystals emerged.

Nothing began on our planet quite like science insists, nor has Earth evolved in a manner logic would suggest. Do we have more cataclysms in our future? You bet we do. And always will. This is how life, our planet, us, and the entire universe, self-corrects, remodels and begins anew. The growth and maturity of a human life is no different.

The Fifth World

Wisdom keepers of the various traditions have in their memories records of "worlds" or "suns" humankind has gone through. Invariably, no matter the tribe or culture, five worlds were counted: five ascending in energy (increasing intelligence and light), and five descending in energy (decreasing intelligence and light). The Great Cosmic Wheel of Life turns again and again as we develop our potential as co-creators with the Creator. Choice is ever the key to triumph or tragedy.

We are told by these wise ones that we are emerging from a long period of darkness into the light of the Fifth World. Others say we've been in the Fifth World for some time and are now ascending higher in energy as that pattern completes itself . . . as the Great Wheel begins its turn toward the Sixth. What I have observed leads me to believe that the latter is true. The energies of the Fifth World have been around for a while. Yet, with the coming of the new kids (around 1982), Fifth World characteristics skyrocketed—to the point of ascension (moving into higher orders of the energy that propels it). I offer the following "fives" to illustrate the qualities and conditions now in ascension.

> **Fifth World:** A time when polarities shift on every level, and that includes gender issues, genetics, the two brain hemispheres, religious factions, wealth, relationships, governments, business/politics. A time of fusion, merging.

> **Fifth Root Race:** Children as volunteers, here to establish a new Earth and possessing the attributes, skills, weaknesses, and

strengths necessary to do the job. Coming in waves. To them, the universe is alive and intelligent and stuffed full of potential.

Fifth Element: Ether (also spelled *aether*) as the substance of space, an invisible, interconnecting, threaded fabric or webbing that constitutes the matrix time/space collapse into when energy expands. Ether is not an element; rather, it is a sea of patterns and causality. All manifests from here. The Akashic records (the record of all things, all people, all life), written upon the skeins of time, are found here.

Fifth Dimension: 1st through 3rd concern the laws of time and space; 4th includes the astral/etheric planes. The 5th dimension frees us from time/space dynamics, while enabling us to weave our intentions directly into the fabric of what we want to manifest. Nothing is hidden in the 5th dimension; all is revealed. Intention directs movement and manifestation. Consciousness exists here as a resonance pattern.

Fifth Chakra: The job of each root race is to fully develop the power of its corresponding chakra throughout the populace, thus energizing those particular qualities, activities, and challenges within the social structures of the time. The 5th chakra (willpower) is associated with the throat, thyroid, neck, mouth, and nervous system, and has to do with the world of ideas. Fifth chakra energy wraps around issues of will and domination—power "over" or power "to."

Fifth Brain: Scientifically we know that 60 to 65 percent of heart cells are the same as the neural cells in the brain. Because of this, the heart is considered our 5th brain. It produces a field 1,000 times more electrically powerful than the brain and 5,000 times more magnetically powerful. This field is the shape of a torus (the only self-organizing wave form), enabling it to convert energy into infinite numbers of wave harmonics . . . *that react to conditions four to five seconds, sometimes minutes, before occurrence.* Literally, our heart is our first responder.

Fifth Basic Force: Add to electromagnetism, gravity, strong nuclear force, and weak nuclear force, one more basic . . . torsion waves. Existing in two forms: one spins to the left, the other to the right; one slows time, the other speeds it up; one increases order in a system, the other decreases order. Torsion waves are the information carriers of the universe. They ensure that nothing is ever lost. They transmit order and preserve information within a system to prevent the increase of entropy. They warp and modify time/space, and are associated with psychic phenomena. Torsion waves travel through space at tremendous speeds, propagating in the future and past, as well as the present.

Fifth Brain Wave Frequency: A fifth brain wave has been verified as gamma waves. Operating at 25 to 60 (plus) hertz, it modulates perception and consciousness, and relates to simultaneous processing of information from different brain areas. A dowser, when in the dowsing "mode," can register both gamma and delta waves simultaneously (a sign of being wide awake while fast asleep). Our new kids do this often.

Fifth Communication Wave: 1st was sign language; 2nd a stelae to inscribe markers, stones, flat surfaces; 3rd concerned the invention of papyrus as a paper-like material for scrolls and documents; 4th heralded the printing press and movable type. The 5th is the personal computer which came online in 1982—the very year the new kids began to surge in births globally, each bearing "the mark" or the energy frequency of the computers' entry into the world at large.

Fifth Discipline: The development of organizations, corporations, and businesses as learning centers—able to go beyond adversarial approaches and endless debates. This marks a new synthesis for combining the desire for profit with the dedication of seeking a higher road to the future and better ways of operating. It is the discipline to overcome obstacles using a structured framework of personal mastery, mental models, shared vision, and team learning.

Fifth Agreement: To live a healthy good life, shaman Don Miguel Ruiz recommends making five agreements with yourself: 1st agreement—be impeccable with your word; 2nd—don't take things personally; 3rd—don't make assumptions; 4th—always do your best; and the 5th, be skeptical, learn to listen. Another way to regard that 5th agreement, he says, is to simply "show up, tell the truth, and don't be attached to the outcome."

Fifth Intelligence Type: IQ measures processes of thought and rational analysis; EQ measures intuitive, emotional understandings of the heart; SQ measures wisdom in connecting with higher self; WQ measures profound connections to potential and knowing; QQ measures super-speed creativity and connections to Allness. Many of today's kids operate at QQ—a range considered fiction by scientists and educators.

Fifth Destiny Ray: Certain light rays are said to function as beacons that overspread evolutionary movements (not to be confused with personal rays or aura colors). The 5th Destiny Ray is symbolically connected to the planet Venus and the qualities of mercy, compassion, and unconditional love.

It signals the return of the Divine Feminine, the power of women, the joy of consensual sex, and the healing possible when we honor and care about each other.

The Millennial generation is America's 14th (1 + 4 = 5). They are the shift generation in the age of shift. Born during that null space when the Great Shifting moved into place, there's never been a generation like them before, nor will there be again. You will find this to be true regardless of country or hemisphere—because—the birthing year of 1982 marks a pivot point in *global* evolutionary history.

The Changeover of Ages

On February 4/5, 1962, Sun, Moon, Mercury, Venus, Mars, Jupiter, and Saturn were all in the sign of Aquarius. Immediately, many declared that the Age of Aquarius had begun. It is true that such a celestial lineup is rare, not to occur again for thousands of years. Yet what I see is something else: *a signal that both the Age of Pisces and the Age of Aquarius have fully moved into an overlap state . . . each no longer biting at the heels of the other, but now interspersed* within *each other.* Overlaps usually last around 500 or so years. They are times when energy doubles, intense dichotomies become the norm, and law and order, plus a sense of balance and peace, seem somehow "quaint." This is why stress is the number one health problem in the world today.

I believe that we finally move more fully into the true Age of Aquarius by 2132-2133, with the thirty-third passage of Halley's Comet. Astronomers disagree, pointing to star charts that show several thousand more years needing to pass before Aquarius will be in full swing. None of them, however, recognize that the future always signals the present with what is about to come. Events of import foreshadow themselves.

These are the energies presently overlapping each other.

AGE OF PISCES	AGE OF AQUARIUS
traditional	non-traditional
strong beliefs and belief systems	open-ended, experimental
religious, church doctrines	non-religious, spiritual vision
strong leaders, domination	flexible leaders, group consensus
toil, suffering, war as solution	entrepreneurs, variable solutions
women as servants or mates	women as equal partners
lifelong devotion to convention	life as creative opportunity
God as disciplinarian, destroyer	God as life-giving creator
"other" as enemy	"other" as potential friend
worship as an act of submission	worship as surrender to joy
world based on ownership	world based on collaboration
hidden truths, secrets	revealed truths, open knowledge
illusion, escapism, fantasy	new maturity, fresh approaches
masters and servants	leaders and collaborators

How are you handling this overlap of Ages in your own life?

A Host of Other Timelines

To keep track of social structures, moods, and how the "eye" of public focus alters, you need only watch the orbit of planet Uranus. Its passages rotate in seven-year cycles through the Zodiac. Symbolically, Uranus is known as the awakener, the reformer, that "heavenly flashlight" that illuminates whatever needs changing. And it means change for the sake of change—fast, like a lightning bolt—reasons can be debated. Here's some of what occurred in the past, a few to come:

1975—*Uranus entered Scorpio*: sexual revolution, rise of the counter-culture, psychotherapies, drug use more common than realized, misdirected wars, secrets/crimes revealed.

1981—*Uranus entered Sagittarius:* New Age Movement, "Jesus Saves," merger mania, foreign exchanges, unparalleled desire for higher knowledge/global travel, an all-time high in sports money and gambling.

1988—*Uranus entered Capricorn*: political revolutions, death of Communism, earthquakes on all levels (whether physical, cultural, or personal), "greed is good" mentality, excesses, business takeovers, middle-class pain.

1995—*Uranus entered Aquarius*: information explosion, global Internet, high technology, the quick fix, U.S. jobs shipped overseas, nervous breakdowns, media rule, new hope, a flood of inventions.

2003—*Uranus entered Pisces*: rise of the need for meaning-making, spiritual technologies, clash of religions, explosions of imagination, innovative usages of entertainment/fantasy and drugs, alternatives in medical treatments.

2010—*Uranus entered Aries*: digital rant, bullying, worldviews clash, pioneering discoveries, global freedom cry, overthrows/revolutions, warriors/fighters, courage, weather extremes/quakes, male power versus female, widespread anger.

2018—*Uranus enters Taurus*: security/safety issues, fortunes alter, power changes hands, fertility problems, Earth changes, farming/sustainability revolution, rebuilding infrastructure, differing usages of plant/animal intelligence, banking issues.

2025—*Uranus enters Gemini*: (Same timing for Pluto's entry into Aquarius, the sign ruled by Uranus.) Lightning bolts of change and transformation on every level, new forms of global and outer-space communication/travel/exchange, new innovations, national and business barriers broken.

A Few Other Timelines

2009-2023—*Pluto in Capricorn*: corrupt politicians, corporate imperialism, the great global contraction, shifting of wealth, rethinking growth, the rise of the three R's (reduce, reuse, recycle), practicality/responsibility emphasized, a return to fundamentals, wealth excesses, possible class war, food and water scarce.

2010—*Uranus and Pluto* square each other on seven occasions.

2018/19—*Times of great pressure and stress*, meltdowns, collapse of major institutions (like the European Union), energy at play comparable to what started the American Revolution (1754-1758). Triggers in place for a major depression or rebirth.

2011-2025—*Neptune moves into own sign—Pisces*: Lifting of the veil, hidden truths revealed, borders dissolve, consciousness of true self emerges, dreams important, compassion (only 5 percent of the earth's people are ready for higher states of consciousness). Our nation almost bankrupt, drastic changes in Middle East, Russia, and throughout Europe.

2013-2122—*The foundation years*: preparation for the Sixth World and Sixth Root Race due to begin a century or two later.

2019—*The year when Saturn ("the disciplinarian) "sits atop"* Pluto in Capricorn, could experience serious climate and cultural changes/die-offs, caution.

2020s—*Asia's middle class is slated to double* during this decade and will dwarf all other markets and account for 40 percent of global consumer spending. Leads up to China in the 2030s reaching its greatest growth.

2022—*Transiting Pluto returns to birth placement in U.S. chart.* People don't have Pluto returns but countries can—a 248-year event. "Corporate America" (what we have become) could implode. Unprecedented challenge/massive change on all levels, good or ill. A time of extremes. Will actually cover the years of 2020 through 2024 (not just 2022).

2025-2033—*Pluto in Aquarius; Uranus in Gemini*: healing of opposing views possible. New ways to communicate, travel, and entertain. Outer space issues, struggle for liberty and social justice, determined/independent/revolutionary. Exceptional growth possible, depends on move towards modernization.

2034*—*Timeframe for potential World War III* is the strongest, or, possible aftermath of a meteor strike; critical stressors worldwide, especially in food, water, and ecology.

2035—*China is projected* to use 4/5th of the world's paper, 70 percent of the world's grain, and have more cars than all the other countries combined.

2036-2040*—*Russian scientists warn of asteroid/meteor hitting Earth.* NASA disagrees. (Note risk in years from 2034 to 2036.) *Half the U.S. population will be brown and black.* Educators must prepare children of differing backgrounds how to do better in school and improve language skills.

2040-2050—*Battles with Muslim extremists* at its peak globally.

2043-2067—*Pluto in Pisces:* illusions/delusions of the past disappear, as do religious persecutions, regrets faced, acceptance of Christ as a state of consciousness possible to attain by anyone (the true "Second Coming"). Messiah figures emerge, female and child abuse and denying women equal status a major global issue, alternative/complementary healing procedures now standard.

2045—*Uranus opposite Pluto in the U.S. chart:* sweeping changes for the working class that effects the global collective. Tied to climate/planetary reversals.

2048—*100th anniversary of Universal Declaration of Human Rights:* a set of fundamental human rights for all people adopted in 1948 by all countries in the United Nations. Its five basic freedoms: speech, environment, religion, from want, from fear. *2048: Humanity's Agreement to Live Together* by

Kirk Boyd (San Francisco: Berrett-Koehler, 2010) dispels the myth that peace and prosperity are unattainable.

2050—*World population is expected to peak:* 300-year population boom ends. Empty buildings, fallow fields, extremely low births (some countries already below replacement rate). Power will reside with nations able to attract immigrants.

2060—*Isaac Newton predicted* this year would end the world as we know it. Interestingly, this year the turbulent stressors of 2023 that could have led to World War III, end.

2076—*U.S. energy back to full potential.* The nation could become the "wounded healer," a true humanitarian for the world.

2132-2133—*Age of Aquarius energies now measurable* with the 33rd passage of Halley's Comet. Energy of planet alters, consciousness accelerates.

2375-4335—*Age of Aquarius according to star charts.* Pisces energy continues during earliest years, then fades. Christ spirit heightens, rise of the Seventh World and the Seventh Root Race in latter years.

2948—*Predicated beginning of the Thousand Years of Peace.* Solar energy wave forms are in descent afterward.

The timelines just shown highlight dazzling and dramatic changes that lie ahead of us. Although painful contractions continue, we are reminded during each major period to clean up our messes as we go along. The future can be fickle, anything can change, including the timelines just given . . . and in the twinkling of an eye.

Note the years 2034-2036 are thought to be "trigger years," when significant asteroid/meteor strikes could plunge into the Earth, leading to global die-offs of around 70 percent. None of the Armageddon predictions made by religious leaders, psychics, near-death, or visionary experiencers about such "final days" have ever come true. That is because there was no "trigger" significant enough to start things. Without something to trigger it, prophecy, at least on a grand scale, is usually impotent. Remember always that "final days" signal the end of life as we know it—*not* the real end of life or of a continuing future.

sharing
heals
the
scars
of
prejudice

13

Education—Invention/Science

Complaints are stacking up about the genetic alteration of our food, our trees, our plants, and what this is doing to the world's health. Chemical companies, however, cry foul, saying that everything they do is safe and everyone else is nuts.

Here's what is really happening: the *Second Homogenocene since the time of the dinosaurs is now in full swing*. (A "homogenocene" is the mixing of unlike substances to create a uniform blend.)

Why this is important: Geological forces split continents apart more than two-hundred-million years ago. Each of the two halves created by the split developed totally different plants and animals, and cultures. This separation ended five centuries ago with one footprint— that of Christopher Columbus . . . and his crew . . . and what came with them: earthworms, mosquitoes, cockroaches, honeybees, dandelions, African grasses, bacteria and fungi, viruses, rats of every description, malaria, various diseases, not to mention habits and ideas (like that of slavery)—all foreign to anyone and anything native. The modern age was birthed in this single event. Any goal of finding a quick route to China was tossed in a mad scramble for profits.

What came next . . . a worldwide network of ecological and economic exchange that fostered the rise of Europe, devastated imperial China, disrupted Africa, and for two centuries made Mexico City the center of Asian and European interactions with the Americas. Within 100 years of this single event, one in five people across the world died because of the Columbus homogenocene (from diseases, multiple types of slavery, brutal working conditions, industrialization, hunger, environmental destruction, etc.) The modern world as we know it today began with a trade route miscalculation. What followed the extremes of convolution and change, produced enormous and profound benefit.

Five centuries later, the same thing is happening again.

Large biotech firms like Monsanto, DuPont, BASF, and Syngenta, are in a rush to take full advantage of another miscalculation, a law that allows "improvements" in seed stock to be patented. Billed as a move to alleviate the world's hunger and raise better crops, these biotech giants are investing vast sums in genetically modified organisms, or GMOs. The result of their genetic manipulation has already created nightmare convolutions—super weeds, pesticides engineered into grain heads, genetically altered nutraceuticals in "organic" baby food, and unfair trading and economic policies that place an undue burden on farmers. There's more, and the list is long.

Genetic modification is the specific goal—a goal that affects the chemical codes of every living thing. Christopher Columbus never meant to cause a homogenocene. Nor has Monsanto, or any of the other companies trying to climb aboard the genetic gravy train. What they seem to have forgotten, though, is how what they do affects us all, their children, our children, and the "drippy" chem-line of cells and genes. The revolution in genetics now occurring is huge. Add to that the die-off of bees and butterflies, which threatens the very existence of popular fruits and vegetables. After convolution extremes have spread far and wide . . . unimaginable benefits could follow.

The first homogenocene resulted in the birth of the modern world.
This, our second one, will result in the birth of a unified world.

First Steps

You cannot stop a homogenocene once begun. You can alter its dynamics and results . . . and you do that by strengthening diversity within the whole as you rebalance relationships within systems.

Example: climate change helped to fuel the Syrian conflict. Farm land dried up, farmers moved to the cities, food became scarce . . . a perfect scenario for long-simmering political and religious conflict to escalate. Make no mistake about this: our thoughts and our emotions feed into mass mind. Yes, all is cyclic, but those cycles can be re-imagined and redirected by the very people involved. The Earth will respond *if the pressure from mass mind is great enough.* (Think of group prayer, world prayer, dedicated individuals who buck "the system" by proving that anyone can make a difference.)

Pressure that is great enough comes from initiating innumerable points of change—sometimes surprising ones.

How about redesigning cities?

Urban centers create their own weather because of where and how they're built. Limiting auto exhaust, for instance, cools and cleans city air; using light-colored roofing and paving materials (instead of black tar) reduces the need for air-conditioning. Better designs and lower building heights cut storm damage and injuries, *and,* improve the health of city residents. But, if skyscrapers are really needed, engineered timber (like laminated veneer lumber), can be used. It has the same strength as concrete and steel yet without heavy weight and high costs. You can do something similar with mud bricks. Yemeni City of Shibam is an example. Their brick skyscrapers have survived the erosion of time without steel or concrete support.

How about tiny houses, mobile tent homes?

Even those used to luxury are downsizing. The idea of an 84 by 170 square foot living space is no longer associated with poverty; many prefer it. Waterless, odorless toilets, clever usage of space and built-ins makes this possible, giving residents much more time for outside activities, travel, and a social life. For migrants, those on the move, even folks who love adventure, "Weaving a Home" tent is ideal. These unusual tents are based on traditional basket-weaving techniques that mimic the movements of snakes and worms, which move by expanding and contracting their ribs, muscles, and skin. The tent structure can fold up for easy transport, then expand to become a shelter against rain and sun. An added plus, the tent is made from a waterproof fabric that has its own water collection system and uses the channels formed by the tent skin to direct water to a storage reservoir.

How about geobiology and soil?

For thousands of years, geobiology has been used to determine the relationship between Earth and life on Earth. Those who practice the techniques use the latest in electronic equipment to locate underground water, stream cavities, ground radiations, electromagnetic fields, anything harmful that needs rebalancing. Similar to dowsing, the goal is a healthy environment, and their focus is energy. Sustainability begins with the soil. The results of yearly tiling plus the use of inorganic chemicals: dried out fields and the destruction of microbial life. If you keep soil nutrients in, you not only have healthier foods but entire ecosystems that reconnect with each other. Nature's interconnectedness can balance the effects of climate change, absorb and transmute most carbons, and cleanse the air. Plants talk to each other, as do all living things. Be a part of the conversation.

How about water and flow forms?

Water will be the currency of the next century. That's why good water dowsers and river wizards are so valuable. Rivers self-organize and energetically recharge themselves through the spins and twists of their meandering curves. DO NOT straighten out rivers and streams. It's their swirling motion that cools, sucks motion without friction (a centripetal inward motion) to increase order and harmony. Remember, living water has a unique structure and clusters its molecules in organized relationships; it has memory, stores and transmits information rhythmically. The short-sighted engineering of clear-cut forests, mega dams, and irrigation canals brings on floods and tampers with the circulatory system of our planet. To add more surface tension to water (which gives it more life and increases its healing properties), build flow-forms—like a cascade of small pools that mimic waterfalls—in garden areas, near homes, down ridges. We don't just drink water . . . we are protected and healed by its living presence.

How about the "bioneer" approach to innovation?

Bioneers are those who practice "whole systems" approaches and networking. They include scientists, innovators, even ordinary citizens who celebrate and share nature-honoring solutions for restoring health to people and planet. Biomimicry is their specialty, studying how nature does it so we can redesign things to fit what living models show us. Example: "bacteria blocks." You *grow* them by using a formula of water, nitrogen, calcium, and organic waste. As byproducts of environmental cleanups, these "bacteria" blocks are as strong as construction blocks. Another example: the algae miracle. Algae eats up nitrates, phosphates, and ammonia. Some types of algae can be used for food and clean fuel, others to produce fabrics, medicine, and clean up the environment. Algae is so valuable, in fact, that vertical algae gardens are being built as if walls in buildings. Whatever the environmental problem, a solution exists. The problem is not "can the Earth sustain us." Rather, how do we reach people "who refuse to, or cannot, be educated."

Education

Education never ends. College is great, but by no means can it compare with, or take the place of, self-education. We can, and we must attend seminars, keep up with news (at least in general), travel when possible, experiment with ideas, take classes in whatever skill or talent catches our fancy. None of this takes as much money as you might think, but it does take a commitment for self-betterment—plus—the willingness to meet others, engage in conversation, and share stories.

Conversation and storytelling are how we convey our humanness. It's how we care for each other.

Irrespective of when your child begins school, *by the first grade or before, dual-language training should be well under way*, and by that, I mean "total emersion." This will ensure more than one "native tongue," plus the opening up and refining of the executive functions of the brain. Among advantages, this will give the child a broader understanding of how people in other cultures think. Soon after, or certainly *by the third grade*, philosophy should be part of the curriculum. *Philosophy enables the young to prepare themselves for what they see on television and in the world around them—so they don't become numb to violence.* By the *fourth grade*, board games and team efforts should be used to role-play the process of decision-making, and the ramifications of what might result from those decisions. This lays the groundwork for our children to be prepared for the new business models now forming.

Encourage "making things" and hanging/climbing exercises to increase dexterity and hand/eye coordination. *Some form of music—either music appreciation, singing, playing an instrument, or marching in a band—is a necessity to make higher mathematics/physics easier to learn. Enrolling in some form of art, be it painting, pottery, or carving, helps a student to develop sensitivity and the givingness of spirit.*

High school should last another two years, which will eliminate the excessive need we have now for university/college degrees. Follow that with a gap year (serving as a volunteer helping out with social programs), then perhaps apprenticeship, vocational school, or STEM schools (which train heavily in science, technology, engineering, and math, and guarantee a good-paying job upon completion).

"Stackable credits" are the best way for the average person to obtain higher degrees. The system works like this: individuals obtain certificates/credits in certain skills or talents when they have the time and money to do so (online courses count); each credit is stacked atop others, until sometime later, maybe years later, the individual has enough credits for a degree. Need necessitates that this system be nationwide and apply across institutional verities.

Don't forget inmates. Many prisons already have large gardens "behind the walls" where inmates not only learn how to eat well, they also learn valuable business skills and new ways of thinking.

The world is finally waking up to this important fact: Life experience (what you did with what life taught you) trumps any degree. True innovators cannot be taught—give them a few tools and get out of their way.

Science

Isaac Newton, the inventor of calculus, discoverer of gravity, and devoted alchemist, had the largest metaphysical/occult library around. Most of our early scientists were either Christians or Muslims, many were Freemasons, some were Rosicrucians. Over the centuries, science has devolved into "scientism:" the worship of science as a dogmatism that rejects what cannot be proved via standard theory.

Fact: you cannot separate reason from non-reason, mathematics from emotions, science from religion, because they're all saying the same thing—consciousness undergirds reality.

Science just observed: gravitational waves in space. This strongly suggests a Big Bang occurred so rapidly, with speeds exceeding that of light, that a fabric formed capable of warping and jiggling to accommodate ongoing inflation.

Science recently observed: a zero-point field that interacts with the fabric of space. This field is organized and informed as if a data bank of information.

Science has acknowledged that: information's carrier is DNA. It's coiled antenna follows all the rules of language and possibly that of music as well, making it readily available biologically, universally, and on all levels of memory.

Science finally admitted that: 96 percent of once-classified-as-junk-DNA actually regulates gene function and the non-verbal, non-local flow of information. This enables every part and particle of existence to communicate with each other.

Science recently illustrated that: DNA properties are fractal in nature. DNA, dubbed the "universal Internet" through its quantum functions, is capable of infinite expression.

Science recently understands that: fractals are infinite possibility made manifest. They form never-ending patterns of self-similar shapes that emerge from chaotic endings to rearrange themselves as new beginnings.

Science now knows that: fractal geometry renders science as incomplete. Fractals free what we think exists to reveal what really exists.

Science, in order to keep up with advancing knowledge, must recognize and utilize non-verbal, non-linear, non-local approaches.

The brilliant physicist, Max Planck, once said: "I regard consciousness as fundamental. I regard matter as derivative from consciousness."

Abstractions/Valid Science
Life Flash/Death Flash

There is a bright flash of light at the moment of conception. When sperm meets egg, an explosion of fireworks occurs. Some eggs burn brighter than others, showing they are more likely to produce a healthy offspring. This life flash has been photographed many times and has been verified scientifically. Same thing at death. There is a sudden flash of light just before the living die. This establishes that light is the major component of life.

Intention as Science

An electron is not a precise entity, but exists as a potential, a probability, until observed or measured. Then the electron freezes into a particular state. Once we stop looking for it, responding to it, the electron dissolves back into the ether of possibility. The observer brings the observed into being. The field of energy connected to everything in creation is a pulsating energy field—the engine of consciousness. What we intend, what we think about most, directs this engine, creating our world or helping others create it for us.

Psychotronics

An interdisciplinary science that tackles the interactions between consciousness, energy fields, and matter, *with a type of instrumentation that needs only the human energy field and the thoughts we think to run it*. Once referred to as "voodoo," an arsenal of verifiable evidence now proves otherwise with healing people and farm land. Modalities used include radionic "black boxes" (need a piece of hair, nail, blood sample, or photo to "tune in"); others are magnetism, bioelectronics, color, light, sound, gemstones, crystals, homeopathy, flower essences. Trained practitioners detect and balance multi-dimensional energy patterns/distortions in living systems. Dr. William G. Reimer, the man who treated me after I died, used radionics/ psychotronics in my treatment. I am alive today because he did.

Wilhelm Reich and Orgone Energy

Reich was a student of Sigmund Freud (psychoanalysis) at the same time as Carl Gustav Jung. Jung became a pioneer in the new field of human behavior at the same time that his classmate pursued energy itself, including the human sex drive. Reich's discoveries about illness and treatment were so advanced he was shut down by Federal agents charging him with practicing medicine without a license. He was imprisoned and died in jail. Claims used against him were culled from imitators who lied about results. His discoveries of life energy (orgone) and how to accumulate it for use in healing (orgone accumulators) are legendary. His inventions and books, supposedly destroyed, were resurrected by people like James DeMeo who continues Reich's work at the Orgone Biophysical Lab in Ashland, Oregon. In-depth explorations of life energy, the disease process, human sexuality, desertification, and the effect of weather on living systems, are done here; classes offered. Yes, I once participated in building an orgone accumulator, and today have an orgone blanket accumulator which adorns my rocking chair—a wondrous blessing.

Alternative Energy Sources

Huge solar grid installations are popping up faster than you might imagine, supplying needed energy for cities and towns. Residential solar panels enable individuals to cut power bills while selling "excesses" to local power companies. Once you factor in Tesla's inventions, cold fusion, antigravity, and zero-point energy experiments, you discover that we are well on our way toward inexpensive, readily-available energy sources. The U. S. Patent Office has a large backlog of applications for "over-unity" machines (devices that produce more energy than they use) *that they refuse to patent, because, they say, such a device is impossible and cannot exist.* Well, it does exist. I've seen some of them. Slamming atoms across a special crystal using a powerful electric field creates cold fusion, repeatedly. We have no lack of ways to produce alternative energy sources. What we have are governmental bureaucracies and utility companies that refuse to recognize what has already been proved.

Medicine Gets Real

Today's medical systems value surgeries, scans, and other procedures more than checkups from trusted doctors who encourage and help to achieve wellness. Blame this on insurance companies that pay mainly for treating disease, not preventing it. This system exhausts medical personnel and burns out doctors. To turn the equation around, pay frontline doctors a fixed monthly fee, which keeps the patient as the central focus. The result: better health care, less money. Opioids currently prescribed by physicians for arthritis, migraine headaches, and lower back injuries, are dangerously addictive and ruin lives. Most patients can be taught how to handle pain mentally and through visualization. Most of our diseases are the end-product of lifestyle: type 2 diabetes, heart disease, high blood pressure, some cancers, osteoarthritis (affects joints), nonalcoholic fatty liver disease, obesity. Treatment means lifestyles and attitudes must change. Always . . . a doctor should look at a patient's nutrition before prescribing any medication. With gene editing a global practice, medical ethics is now more important than ever before.

Quantum Energy Medicine

Besides psychotronics, there are other effective methods of energy healing that work on the quantum level (non-local, consciousness based). Reiki, a method of directing life-force energy with certain gestures/mental symbols, is effective with pain and injury. SCIO Quantum Biofeedback is a non-invasive scanning device (like a computer program with "eyes") that can, in a fraction of a second, do a complete analysis of a person's physical, emotional, mental, and spiritual health, and zero-in on best treatment—while optimizing organ function, pain management, blood pressure, and heart stabilization. Trinfinity-8 crystal wands are also good (you hold onto the crystal handles, in essence directing energy to work where needed). It is possible to send small objects through the ethers, using only the minds of those involved, plus instrumentation to achieve a single focus. This type of teleportation has been accomplished successfully. Integral medicine, which uses the best of chemical and electrical approaches to health, must now accommodate quantum realities. Just as science must now accept and work with entanglements, subtle energies, and non-local existence, so, too, must medicine. We are moving from three-dimensional polarities to five-dimensional, and beyond—with the help of research venues like near-death states, kundalini breakthroughs, and spiritual transformations.

Electromagnetic Fields (EMFs) and Fatigue

We are hit daily by field effects from television, cell phones, digital devices including clocks, WiFi, airport/wireless functions, radar, modems, cell towers, microwave ovens, smart meters, electrical wiring, sensors, computers, electronic devices, and so forth. We work harder, deal with more stress and less job security, then face "hash" from ELF or extremely low-frequency exposure. Price paid: immune system breakdown and fatigue plagues. The new virtual realities are whimsical, otherworldly pleasures, beyond wonderful to the wearer of a headset, yet beyond horrible to brain/body with overuse. The Internet can be like digital cocaine, putting at risk creativity, memory recall, language, attention span, and empathy. To help balance the overload, switch your life around to 20 percent digital, 80 percent analog (human skills). Spiritual practices, spending time in nature, being with kids and pets, cooking from scratch, sports, recreational fun—all of this balances the wizardry upon us and helps to protect from "dark stuff" (like possessing entities, psychic parasites, mind control, and inter-dimensional beings). "Viewer beware" applies as much to the digital world as anywhere else.

The Miracle of Lithium

Everyone needs lithium, absolutely everyone. Most of us obtain enough from our food and environment to give this trace mineral nary a thought. But with extensive use of computers and digital devices, overly stressed lives, pollution, and sudden spiritual transformations that confuse as well as enlighten, knowing more about lithium can be a godsend. Most medical professionals prescribe the pharmaceutical version, which is bonded to sodium carbonate. Necessary for many; a problem for others.

Natural lithium is a nonmetallic mineral, a cell salt. Twelve cell salts are used in homeopathy; lithium is the 13th. It has tremendous energy and helps to grow new dendrite connections in the brain. The main task of lithium, though, is to bond spirit in matter. Without sufficient lithium, this cannot be done properly. Animals, plants, soil, humans—all must have lithium to maintain their infusion of light (spirit).

Should lithium levels deplete, they are easy to replace. For instance, in the plant kingdom, lemons and limes are the richest sources of a substance virtually identical to lithium. Squeeze a little fresh lemon or lime into your drinking water from time to time—once a day should be plenty—or use these juices in cooking as they make a perfect salt substitute. In the mineral kingdom, lepidolite is a rich source, as well as rosy tourmaline and kunzite. Wear lepidolite as you would jewelry or put it in your pocket and use it as a "worry stone" to fondle whenever troubled or stressed. I have mine on the desk in back of my chair where I sit at my computer.

Experiments have been done at large architectural, engineering, and construction firms to test certain scents on workers. When lemon was pumped in, human errors reduced 50 percent. Even in small amounts, I have observed that natural lithium perks up the brain as it centers the human energy system and emotional levels. It is subtle but effective.

During experiments I have participated in, it was found that with individuals who were negative, angry, or fearful, the lithium in his or her body appeared to have transmuted into potassium. Potassium has an odor. The old adage, "Dogs smell fear," is literal. What they smell is the potassium. If an individual was positive, in a joyful mood or meditating, the lithium in his/her body accelerated the use of the mineral beryllium—recognized by many as the "fuel" of higher consciousness and higher brain development. (There is a type of crystal available, called phenacite, that is supposedly the stone to use for developing higher states as it is a rich source of beryllium. The problem is, expanding higher states without the bridge of grounding and balance that lithium supplies, can be more delusional than constructive.)

Lithium truly is the key; the "bridge" spirit uses to bond spirit with matter. Magenta is its color. Symbolically, magenta represents the phase shift that separates one advancement through the various stages of spiritual development and chakra centers to the next highest level. Magenta balances (coheres) that shift. Wearing clothes accented with magenta, or using the color as an accent in room design, also helps. Knowing this about lithium can be a "life saver" for you.

True Science

Sometimes the truest science is natural science, knowing how to use what is available to make things better. Nicola Tesla once said: "The day science begins to study non-physical phenomena, it will make more progress in one decade than in all the previous centuries of its existence."

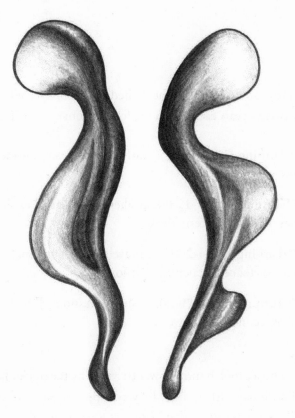

fear
creates strangers
who
should be
friends

14

Economics—Investment/Service

A repeating economic cycle in the United States consists of four turnings of about twenty years each. With the fourth, comes crisis. Take a look:

1ˢᵗ **Turning** (1946-1964): confident expansion, leadership, new world order.

2ⁿᵈ **Turning** (1964-1984): awakening, spiritual exploration, rebellion, alternatives.

3ʳᵈ **Turning** (1984-2005): unraveling, growing malaise, incompetence, deepening divisions.

4ᵗʰ **Turning** (2005-2025): crisis, depression, climate of chaos, economic disasters.

The previous fourth turning was triggered by the stock market crash. Civilizations don't decline; they collapse. What has helped most of the Western nations to skate along at a pretty good clip compared with other countries are these powerful advantages: competition, scientific breakthroughs, rule of law, modern medicine, consumer-based society, and a work ethic that enabled wealth accumulation—which created the middle class. This formula is now up for grabs, and not because Republicans and Democrats hate each other. There are extreme forces at work, both here and across the world—new ones we haven't faced before—like the tragedy of 40 to 50 percent of young adults unemployed (included in that figure newly minted college graduates who carry individual debt loads of around $30,000 in student loans).

The free enterprise system has brought more people out of poverty than any other economic system the world has ever known. As the world's people divest themselves or are pulled away from excessively lenient/fiscally undisciplined governments, or, restrictive/religiously controlled governments, the free enterprise system continues but in ways no one expects. As power moves away from New York City and Washington, D.C., seemingly to China, glitches pop up—among them what to do about populations versus land and natural resources.

Our planet cannot supply the additions of a burgeoning middle class in both India and China, for instance, without adjustments. Knowing this, China seeks construction, farm, and natural resources bids in Africa and South America, not only for profits, but so it can move in their own people to work and settle there, rather than hiring and training locals to handle things. This smacks of colonization. Their claim to tiny islands around them, followed by land-grabs, worries neighboring countries that cannot protect themselves. Yet, China is not the only country trying to resettle people or enlarge borders.

Excessive regulations stifle trade and throttle entrepreneurs—like the demand that apprentices be paid and given benefits, when, traditionally, opportunities like this were freely given. Over-regulating stopped European growth. While some regulation is necessary, too much backfires. Muslim nations that use terrorism as a foreign policy and source of their gross national product, are blinding themselves to the price they pay for human trauma plus the destruction of their own environment and natural resources—the ultimate in "over-regulation."

So many glitches. So much noise. Yet, below the radar of notice, something else is occurring. The world is being swallowed up in a new industrial revolution on a scale beyond belief. Everything is changing! Some history to give you perspective:

- *First Industrial Revolution*, begun in 1784, was facilitated by the use of mechanical production and steam power.

- *Second Industrial Revolution*, starting in 1870, featured mass scale production and electrical power.

- *Third Industrial Revolution* began about 1969 when the forerunner to the Internet opened up a whole new way of communicating, doing business, manufacturing. Smart networks set up side-to-side movements that enabled top to bottom, all around restructuring of human relationships, with profound implications for the future of society and governance.

- *Fourth Industrial Revolution* started about 2015 when the growing capability of artificial intelligence, 3-D printers, electric cars, and data on a massive scale was finally recognized.

Third/Fourth Industrial Revolutions

Notice what has just happened: *In less than fifty years everything in the job-money-business-manufacturing-distribution-sales-lifestyles-communication-entertainment world has turned upside down. In another five to ten years, every traditional way of making a living will be disrupted. The economy has turned friction-free.*

Friction-free means, with virtually no capital, anyone can start a business that can compete with capital-heavy, brick-and-mortar, store-front competitors. Examples: Alibaba, the world's most value-laden retailer, carries no inventory; Airbnb, the world's largest provider of accommodations, has no real estate; Uber, the world's largest car service, owns no cars; Upwork, the world's largest provider of people who can do anything, has no employees; HourlyNerd, the world's largest placement of business-school graduates capable of high-level assignments, has no mandate and recognizes no boundaries.

Friction-free means a world where labor, information, and money moves easily, cheaply, and almost instantaneously. It means companies form fluid relationships with customers/workers/owners—while rethinking the role of capital—and finding that less of it is needed.

Business thrives in ways where performance is measured by the new metrics of free agency. What used to be employees (with guaranteed retirement) are now freelancers, who can pick and choose jobs, projects, locations, and lifestyles. Instead of being on a static track, movement flows, creating a peer-to-peer or sharing economy.

Want a sample of where this is going? Hang on.

Who needs lawyers? Because of the IBM Watson computer program, legal advice can be obtained in seconds with 90 percent accuracy. Who needs a doctor to diagnose illness? The same program can do it four times more accurately than medical personnel and far quicker. Need a car? Phone in your order. A self-driving car shows up at your location; you catch up on workload or take a nap en route; arrive fresh, pay only for distance driven. Self-driving cars reduce accident rates significantly, which reduces the need for insurance, hospitals, medical staff, road repairs, morticians. Traditional car companies either go bankrupt or adjust to high-tech construction methods, electricity as fuel, and Tesla-style designs. The problem of storage batteries with solar production is solved, enabling the desalination of water to supply abundant water needs everywhere. Lower costs for 3-D printers makes the machine more readily available. Need new shoes? Print yourself a pair with your 3-D printer, or perhaps a new tool or a new piece of furniture or a dish or almost anything you can imagine. By 2020, 70 percent of all humankind will own a smartphone, which means that everyone will have access to a world-class education online. Worried about war? New plasma energy weapons, robotics, and artificial intelligence means new armies need fewer people and are run by remote control.

Who needs a meteor or an asteroid to tear up our world? End-of-the-world drama is here, now, with growing suicide rates to prove it.

What's Getting in the Way

Our current, outrageous financial system is the true villain of progress, fairness, distribution, sustainability, and investments. Exploitation is built into the system—excessive credit costs force borrowers to exploit both people and natural resources—which has institutionalized the goals of ambition and greed.

No bank, anywhere, is too big to fail. Spotlight Iceland. They let it happen. Instead of resorting to austerity, they upped social spending and certain state programs, implemented some 100 new taxes, and took steps to enable their people to witness justice being done. This created an enormous hardship . . . followed by remarkable recovery.

Rana Foroohar, in her book, *Makers and Takers*, came up with five ways to redo monopoly capitalism: make finance more transparent, stop rewarding debt over equity, rethink who companies are run for, build a national growth strategy, and redefine who's "making and taking." She shows that *the biggest reason for long-term slowed growth is that the financial system itself has stopped serving the real economy and now serves mainly itself.* Only a fraction of money washing around the financial markets actually makes it to Main Street, cutting back on research and development. Other countries deal with the same "disease" . . . state-directed capitalism is as faulty as market-driven. What's the solution? *Making the financial system a servant of business, rather than its master.*

Rethinking Money

Bristol, England, was the first in modern times to create and use their own money. It's called the "Bristol pound." Katie Taylor of Bristol said: "Big corporations control everything. You just don't have anything to say anymore. We want to have a voice in the community and to support our own local businesses." Today, it is one of the world's biggest and most successful complementary currencies . . . making the community stronger and more socially minded. The Bristol pound is supported by "Cyclos," a software program created by the Social Trade Organization (STRO). So far it is the best software around for local-currency initiatives.

The idea of a circular economy that is light and fast, cashless, and gives the unbanked the same chance for growth and profit as the banked, is the Bitcoin. A digital, cryptocurrency, Bitcoin can secure financial transactions without the need of a central authority—no banks, no government regulators. It is free money based on the I.O.U. system (I owe you). You express and add value in terms of what you will do and when. This value remains "online" until the action/product is completed. Your contribution as a producer is the source of your money. There is a "block chain" (an encrypted shared public ledger) that records all transactions. A software protocol (containing the rules) enables computers to talk to each other so that they can send out Bitcoins once earned and paid. No interest is charged. Bitcoin promises global democratization and the decentralization of money—no need for savings accounts or credit cards.

The Internet is the backbone of the sharing economy, one that looks at money in a whole new way.

Also, peer-to-peer lenders create or join Lending Club Accounts and through bank transfers invest in projects of their choice. Lenders shoulder the bulk of risk with this method, but peer groups tend to trust peer groups. They profit from helping someone else.

All of this, the Bristol pound, Bitcoins, peer-to-peer loans, the drama and crisis of the Third and Fourth Industrial Revolutions, can take us all to the same place . . . a shared, collaborative, altruistic world.

A Values-Driven Economy

The discovery: price and value are linked to natural and mutual resources. *Price* creates choice. *Price* is the mediator of cooperation. *Price* forces change. *Price* expresses humankind's opinion of itself.

+ Already Sweden and Norway have switched to six-hour work days because tests showed employees were less stressed with the new arrangement, did more work better, and enjoyed more time with family.

+ More and more business owners are giving full-time employees an ownership in the stake of the company.

+ One CEO by the name of Dan Price established $70,000 as the minimum wage for all employees.

+ Semco employees (Brazilian) set their own work hours, parking space, whether or not they attend meetings, and how they do what they do. No one has a secretary. Rules are considered obstacles to creativity.

◆ Whole Foods Markets proved that a company can prosper based on love. And with that goal in mind, a Conscious Leadership Academy was formed to help employees gain the emotional and spiritual intelligence needed to make the impossible possible.

The quickly spreading Altruism movement has already proved that business can be values driven, not profit driven, and still succeed. Not free trade, but fair trade—where everyone benefits. This new way of conducting business is redefining philanthropy and the meaning of profit—how to do well when you're doing good.

Business is the most powerful man-made force on the planet, re-directing it for good makes a powerful statement.

The New Kid's Business Model

Skills of the young wrap around collaboration, teaming up with oth-ers to create a renaissance of self-direction and meaning. They do not see themselves as either an employee or a resource. They're partners who direct their own lives in and through the creative space of a hub . . . not an office, but a "docking station" where they can plug in, dis-cuss ideas and do their best work.

Hub space is defined as "a center everywhere and a circumference nowhere." These spaces operate on chaos theory: out of disorder comes new order; divergence from random data can spin out wild, new pat-terns and exotic pathways to better solutions. Hubs buzz with activity and endless curiosity and odd environments where creative thinking is not only allowed but encouraged. The goal: build, invent, create what is useful. In a partnership position, the new kids are able to self-govern, act with choice, and work interdependently with others.

Young adults of today and tomorrow are optimistic, value diverse, and civic-minded multitaskers who want to be recognized for their achievements. Although they communicate well electronically, they flounder with personal skills and need a lot of hand-holding and encouragement. They require a certain amount of supervision and structure, have short attention spans, and lack patience for menial chores—yet they are absolutely brilliant, clever, and innovative.

No doubt about it, the new kids are the most high-maintenance generation in history, while simultaneously operating as the highest-performing.

What's their business model? One told me: "My purpose in life is to be amazed. To join with friends and strangers to enjoy, help, uplift, and protect each other and our world. Money serves me; I do not serve it." Translation: meaning trumps promotions. They truly want to make a difference in this world. They are the perfect group to handle lateral power, network broadly, and utilize intuitive/psychic guidance. Businesses, if smart, will encourage "swarm intelligence." That's where employees self-organize on the spot without a manager's okay, pool their intelligence, and creatively find the best response to rapidly changing markets. Our younger people believe that businesses bear as much responsibility as governments for driving positive social change.

They want to buy things from companies whose values they share, and work only in places they choose to work. Their belief in a shared economy also covers such things as shared adventures, renting out guest rooms and items in their home, trading errands with others, insisting that experiences be given in lieu of gifts. And, they are devoted to service—finding time to give back, trading comfort for working in soup kitchens, homeless shelters—wherever aid is needed.

New Leaders

Job recruiters worldwide are desperate for top talent. Myopic tribal leaders are just as desperate to hold back the tsunami of technologies that are flooding their countries, nullifying the effectiveness of force, rape, and slaughter. Hatred has become too expensive to control!

Some suggestions for moving beyond any lack of leadership:

- Redesign the way you think: observe, watch, experience to build confidence. Remember—no one is a victim of either their genes or hereditary traits.

- Use your intuition and psychic ability as a business advantage, tools for core creativity.

- Share products and services: emphasize experience over excess, community over commerce.

- Overcome obstacles by developing "learning organizations" structured around personal mastery, mental models, shared vision, team growth.

- Build bridges across disciplines, sectors, with a vision/systems perspective.

- Regard anger on the job as an opportunity to make something better.

- Bring your compassion as well as your intellect to work.

- Light up when you think about giving: become a "thrillionaire."

The best leadership trainers are individuals who have previously undergone either a near-death experience or a spiritual transformation of some kind. What they went through "redesigned" their mind in the sense that they returned clustered thinkers (as opposed to sequential, selective thinkers)—a sign of genius—with the ability to abstract and be comfortable with ambiguity. Thinking outside the box does not apply; boxes don't exist for them (as they see beyond limits). Most rely on the sacred silence of meditation/contemplation/mindfulness to guide their decisions and their lives. They have discovered that "to change outcomes, you must change the questions you ask."

New Anger

The doubling of two industrial revolutions at virtually the same time excites and thrills. The downside, though, can all too often be a nightmare.

The digital age concentrates wealth in fewer hands, exploits personal information, and makes possible undeclared cyberwars where hackers use malicious codes to enact physical damage. The new technology destroys job categories at the same time that it creates them. This breaks any guarantee of a social contract: no pensions, no worker-rights, no company insurance, no days off.

The two biggest complaints about the disruptive economy: too little time, too little money.

Young adults and their children are the generations hardest hit by the "new normal" of stagnant incomes, a shrinking middle-class, cheap labor from abroad, smart robots at home, rising inequality, and stalled upward mobility. The result: the highest rates of suicide ever seen, accompanied by off-the-wall surges in sex, drug, and alcohol abuse. Churches are being replaced by the type of entertainment where women wear fewer clothes and men wrap themselves in violence.

Yes, "doom and gloom" have been a part of every sweeping change the world has ever known. Still, deep inside the fearful backlash that erupts from change comes this truth: we all love to hate. We need bad guys to embody all that we want to get rid of—our greed, our anger, our fear. The self-versus-others mindset dehumanizes whoever we deem an "enemy," making it easier to defend ourselves. "Enemy formation" is a powerful emotional investment in avoidance.

It is vital that enemies talk to each other, and see each other for what each really is. The key reason countries and cultures refuse to teach debate and compromise skills, is that "right/wrong" thinking is easier to enforce and negates any need for diplomacy or "disguising" weakness.

New Traps

Corporate, business and banking executives sometimes tend to be amoral/sociopaths. Don't kid yourself. That type of personality can sometimes handle "the art of the deal" better than those committed to "caring and sharing." A few practice the trickery of occult "magic." The presence of psychic parasites, voodoo curses, and inter-dimensional beings of ill-report is more common than you might think. Perennial headlines about the "New World Order," a conglomerate of the super-rich who fear their power is declining, keeps conspiracy theorists front and center for the nightmare circuit. Folks who dabble in illusion tend to believe whatever is often repeated—true or not.

Take a breath.

Certainly, worry, depression, and a host of addictions can ripen anyone for such things as entity takeovers, possession, or strange invaders of one type or another. Negative "stuff" sucks up your energy and feeds on your fear. No fortune teller or psychic reader can get rid of these for you. A good healer can—who recognizes that core issues may have more to do with a lack of self-worth than curses or subterfuge.

Here's a clue on how to handle all of this.

Work for good, not against evil. Damning what frightens you, gives it power.

Joseph Campbell once said, "All the gods are within, within you, within the world." All the stories, all the myths, all the real and symbolic representations of good and evil are part of the human journey of self-discovery.

Understanding the demonic factor means understanding the passive-aggressive, dependent type of personality some people have. Any dictatorial "voice" achieves domination and control when conditions are not right in a person's home or because of their background as a youth. Throughout history, a pattern of possession emerged from the mistreatment and derangement that came from alcoholism and drug addiction. Anger or fear can lead us there. Some people never get enough wealth, fame, power, recognition, or attention. They convince themselves they deserve ever more. No different with governments that display a "casino mentality" of turning to lotteries and legalized gambling whenever fiscal responsibilities cannot be met.

New Truths

Businesses emerge out of the communities that surround them. All too often they grow and expand without regard to that community or what they owe to those who support them. Doing everything possible to prevent failure either breeds creative innovators or amoral "shells" who place profit ahead of humankind.

To be fair, the Native American caution of planning always to the seventh generation seems rather quaint now—as the world changes much too rapidly for that responsibility to apply. Still, consequences matter. Be it executive or entrepreneur, *"aftermath" must be part of every business decision*.

> Fact: The greatest achievements have come from small groups and individuals who were motivated by conscience.

> Fact: Consciousness separated into two hemispheres—East and West—is now fusing back together, a global leap in human refinement.

Gifted artists, psychotic killers, exceptional geniuses, enraged bullies, spirit-led cripples—these are our new kids, the people of our new world, each possessing the same overall pattern of traits. Forget categories, ages, and labels. "When the tide comes in, *all* boats rise."

A Few Hints

Give your job, your business, your company, a soul. Doing this strengthens meaning and value, as it weakens deviations toward jealousy, revenge, or victimization.

Invest at least a tenth of your money towards retirement (I wish I had started this as a kid). Give another tenth to wherever you receive the type of spiritual guidance that uplifts your heart.

I still write checks and keep a ledger, a carry-over from the days when I worked at a large bank as an analyst/tech writer. "Thank you God" headlines every ledger page. What is ever so clear to me . . . is that ALL my expenditures are my investment in life.

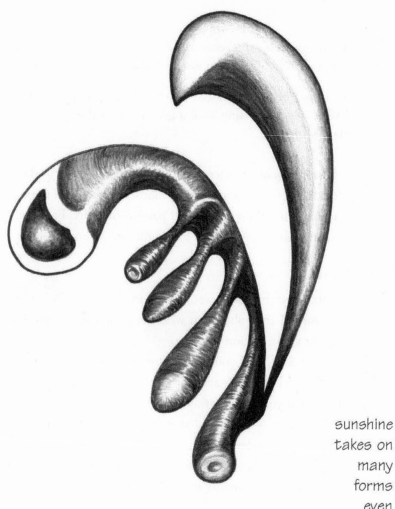

sunshine
takes on
many
forms
even
darkness

15

Government—Law/Justice

How is it possible that eight billion people who want the same thing have not been able to get it? What will it take for civilization to civilize?

Giant questions. Simple answers.

We, the people, have always known how to do better, be better. So why haven't we? Take a look at what no one wants to admit:

- Self-governance requires self-discipline and self-responsibility.

- Our global citizenry isn't interested in forms of governance, like a constitutional republic or a democracy, that require participation.

- The majority still prefer to live under a benevolent dictatorship, where they don't have to think for themselves.

- Vast numbers have no training in, or knowledge of, debate. For them, decisions are final—with no give, no understanding, no discussion, no middle ground, no compromise.

- The global citizenry has only recently been encouraged to explore the creativity of innovation, entrepreneurship, and alternatives.

◆ Because of that, there is still little difference between religious and dictatorial governance for the majority.

◆ Most folks do not adjust well to change, let alone major change.

What has consistently held civilizations back are the twin needs of "rich" and "rule"—how that is handled individually and collectively.

History's greatest thinkers were shaped by their surroundings. Classical Athens was open to foreign goods, odd people, and strange ideas, making it a source-place of creative thought. Song Dynasty in China created a culture of generalists and poets, leading to a flood of inventions that produced great riches. Renaissance Florence had patrons, that, to save themselves from embarrassment for "excesses," sponsored some of the most powerful and dramatic religious artwork ever done. Silicon Valley in California became a "talent magnet" for digital genius because of their open doors for the "far-out and why not," a mindset that changed the world.

Third/Fourth Industrial Revolution success keys: modernization and *innovation.* So what are way-too-many countries doing? Returning to the Old World Order of grab land, threaten conflict, declare fraud as an excuse for takeover. Corporations are today's rulers. Because of this, cities, even entire countries, are going bankrupt. No advance planning. Too much politics. High volatility. Support systems breaking down. The super-rich? Last count, there were 80 of them.

Our Country

The United States? We were never a democracy. Our founding fathers did not trust that form of government because *all true democracies throughout history failed.* Instead, they established the U.S. as a constitutional republic, based on representative engagement—the power of the vote, the power of law. This worked during our early years, even through World War I. It took the bombings of our ships at Pearl Harbor to shove us into World War II. After that, unabated progress paralleled what seemed a moral duty for us to "protect the world," which blinded our country to the aftermath of what we thought were "good deeds." Accusations of war crimes that we committed seemed unbelievable until we witnessed the consequences of our bombings in Iraq, reciprocal bombings of the Twin Towers in New York City, the bloodbath that was once Syria, followed by the march of ISIS in a breakout of terrorism on levels unseen before. If you're keeping score on body counts, we're the heavy. If you're looking at short-term profit interests of corporate and banking executives, the shipping of jobs to other countries, the slashing of our ability to manufacture, then we're the victim. The laws that have kept us safe for hundreds of years have eroded to the point where the freedoms guaranteed by our Constitution are at risk.

We hit "a brick wall" when we tried to promote our culture and beliefs in other countries. *Example:* a Middle Eastern belief that if even one strand of a woman's hair emerged from under her headscarf (hijab), "a dagger is drawn towards the heart of Islam." To us, this is utter nonsense; to believers, this is law. Our challenge is to become more realistic as we work towards balance and mutual respect. The practice of "freelancing hate for hire" is practiced by far too many nation-states—us among them. Included here is the media, well-known as an instrument that can be used to manipulate minds and passions.

Our radical crisis point as a nation comes during the Pluto Return in 2022 (covers 2020-2024). We'll soon see how wide awake we are and how willing to engage in a renaissance of community worth and value.

Other Countries

The concept of the nation-state is defusing. Smaller, stronger groups are rising and taking power into their own hands. With defusion is chaos. The digital age has also opened wide the gates for a free flow of weapons, rare metals, stolen treasures, animal body parts, and sexual slavery—altering the concept of leadership and purpose. Governments degenerate when the power is held only by leadership.

North Korea is the perfect example: a family-run dictatorship that needs enemies so their media can whip the country into a frenzy from time to time, to keep everyone in line. Anyone trying to escape or think for themselves disappears into prison camps in the north. Stalin, Mao, Marx, Lenin, Trotsky, and Engels (the "founding fathers" of Communism and Marxism) were all advocates of war, slavery, racism, ethnic hatred, genocide, mass-murder, and the deportation of men, women, and children to prisons/gulags. Often "drunk" on sex and drugs, they placated and controlled the masses through clever usages of the media. (Hitler did the same thing.)

An effort to establish viable business, banking, medical, and educational systems is now global and gaining strength. People are catching on. Everyone's weak spot, though, is still what to do about those who think that progress is best obtained via force.

Since men love battles, either of wills or of armies, let's "listen in" on the thinking of a master on the subject. *The Art of War* was written by Sun Tzu, 2,500 years ago. It is actually more about strategy and leadership than war. Here's a peek into how he thinks:

1. A leader leads by example, not by force.

2. Sometimes you win a war by avoiding a fight.

3. Make sure that all your troops share the same goal and mindset.

4. Always be prepared. Never let down your guard.

5. Keep your plans and intentions from your enemies, be mysterious.

6. Use deceit whenever you can. Trick your opponent into believing you are weak when you are not, or that you are strong when you are weak. All warfare is based on deception.

7. Always give your opponent the option of retreat. Do not press a desperate foe too hard.

Violence and civil disorder around the world are the predictable results of an attempt to force diverse cultures and peoples into a specific or consumer-based monoculture. Notice that Tsu says all warfare is based on deception. That brings us to terrorism, a barbaric contagion supported by both religious tradition and religious governance.

Terrorism

The largest purveyor of savagery on a scale not seen in modern times is ISIS, a Muslim contender trying to unite the Arab world so the "12th Imam" can appear (the counterpoint in Islam to the Christian idea of the "Second Coming of Christ"). ISIS emerged out of a leadership vacuum left when Iraq collapsed and Syria "melted." Historically, high levels of social violence are not uncommon in the Middle East, Asia, and Africa (refer to *Saharasia* by James DeMeo), but this time something different is happening—deception on a global scale . . . thanks to the Internet and clever "documentaries" designed to fool the gullible.

ISIS is Djinn. No, not the cute genie that pops up out of a lamp in Walt Disney cartoons. The subterfuge here is that ISIS has nothing to do with Islam. Nothing! The leaders of ISIS sold out to the forces of Djinn, one of the Old Orders that incarnated shortly after humans emerged from the beginnings of all beginnings. Djinn is the Middle Eastern version of Satan/Devil in Christian texts. Although some Djinn can be helpful, basically they are but etheric drifters who specialize in shape shifting to meet a moment's need, or to get their own way, or to make deals with the unwary. Like many of the Old Orders, Djinn can materialize and dematerialize at will. They prefer hilly, mountainous terrain, caves, deserts, and form family groups/societies. Their color is black or gray like smoke, and they have been referred to as The Men in Black, Shadow People, or Phantoms. Their "signature" is black flags. Djinn crave sex and pleasure, demand blood sacrifice, and are famous for abductions. They are easily upset if not obeyed . . . and paid . . . since their "evil eye" is always for sale. Djinn are masters of deception.

The new kids run after anything that is idealistic. They are high-maintenance/high-brilliance performers who want to make a difference in the world, change things. ISIS knows this, and gears all recruitment programs toward heroism and the fulfillment of prophecy (complete with music). Recruits see themselves as heroes and are willing to pay any price to fulfill the "dream" ISIS paints for them. That "dream" is a mirage coaxing any and all into an inferno of abject horror.

A new voice proclaiming the truth about terrorism is that of Sadiq Khan, Mayor of London, England: "I am a Londoner, I'm British, I'm of Islamic faith, Asian origin, Pakistani heritage, so whether it's Daesh [ISIS] or these others who want to destroy our way of life and talk about the West, they're talking about me."

The Qur'an sets the record straight about Islam: *Whoever kills a soul kills mankind; whoever saves a life saves all of mankind.*

Rhythms of Politics and War Events

People in worry, doubt, or fear, are easy to control—especially if there is not enough protein in their diet (that's why so many tyrants starve their people).

History shows us that: *concentrations of wealth in too few hands destroys democracy—the middle-class disappears. Conversely, the diffusion of wealth throughout the middle-class creates democracy.*

History also shows us that: *over time, the positive approach to governance leads to beneficial results that heal, uplift, and honor the spirit. The negative approach leads to a depletion of value, loss of choices and free will—a controlled and limited life.*

> **Political Rhythms of Global Governance:** Crisis begets reform, a boom results, profit spreads, complacency follows, reforms die out, a new crisis follows, which begets reform, and so the rhythm goes.
>
> **Twenty-Eight-Year-Cycle of War Events in the U.S.:**
> Check out your own country to see if this is true for you. It certainly is in the United States, as our war events occur

about every 28 years. Our last was September 11, 2001. The next: 2029, if the cycle continues.

Please know there is no cause that can justify terrorism; no scandal that cannot be broken by an electorate that refuses to be silent. Know also that the 80 percent of anger that escalates into violence can be rechanneled by choice into the type of energy that uplifts and energizes, rather than destroys. Victimhood exists "by consent."

Law and Justice

Law school teaches state/national/international law, not moral law. Courses are based on ruling principles, established by precedent.

Moral laws come from what we can learn via our religions, our spiritual values, and the pragmatism of what makes good sense.

In the "rule of law," three questions are asked: Is there a problem? What are the possible solutions? What would be the unintended consequences of any ruling that might be made?

The difference between governmental laws and moral laws, and how any law gets passed and becomes a valid measure, should be taught in every school by the 5th grade. Too many laws today pit church against state. The new movement toward *human rights* asks that we reconsider what the law teaches, versus what our churches and spiritual centers teach, versus what we feel within the depths of our own heart.

This human rights shift moves us closer to Third Way Principles and Holons (discussed in Section Four: Groups—Multiple Focus), Restorative Justice, and the Eco-Legal Revolution.

In sync with this, Dominic Barter, an Englishman living in Brazil, developed Restorative Circles (acknowledged by the Brazilian Court), whereby trained communicators and listeners communicate directly with the people involved. This community-based justice system works through thousands of schools in a plan of action to meet everyone's needs. This plan of action is followed up within a certain time-frame and has already cut crime significantly. Sylvia Clute, a lawyer in the United States, has initiated similar projects with similar results. Restorative Justice/Restorative Circles are based on Third Way Principles and Holons.

The Eco-Legal Revolution re-examines the very theory and philosophy of law. Based on the book, *The Ecology of Law* by Fritjof Capra and Ugo Mattei, this approach traces history and in so doing discovers that there are surprising parallels between the conceptual structure of law and natural science. The laws of nature and humans evolved together. Today, as we move from mechanistic approaches to broader ecological worldviews, current forms of law struggle against the needs of globalization. By changing how we view law, we can shift human law and justice to a fairer ecological order.

Ever heard of the "radical middle" (once a book by Mark Satin, title changed to *New Age Politics: Our Only Real Alternative*)? Mark noticed that it was "the radical middle" where real solutions lay. Not Democrats or Republicans, Greens, Socialists, Communists, Marxists, or any of the other form of governance; rather, a type of compromise that sought a middle ground. "To change society at the third level of analysis," said Mark, "we can't stay in our comfort zones—and we can't allow other people to stay in them either."

Ho'oponopono, the Hawaiian Huna method of true justice, emerges from the act of forgiveness. The aggrieved and everyone else involved face each other, admit what occurred, defend or explain, with judgment coming from the vote of the many and is carried out by them. Dr. Ihaleakala Hew Len, practitioner of a higher form of ho'oponopono, puts things this way: "If you take complete responsibility for your life, then everything you see, hear, taste, touch, or in any way experience, is your responsibility—because it is your life. This means that terrorist activity, the president, the economy or anything you experience and don't like—is up for you to heal. They don't exist, in a manner of speaking, except as projections from inside you. The problem isn't with them, it's with you, and to change them, you have to change you." Dr. Len's reputation of individual and group healings, even inside State Hospitals and prisons, proves that justice is and can be for everyone.

It's Time for Women

In 2020, we celebrate the 100th year of women's suffrage in the United States. Other countries beat us in doing this, like England and Turkey, but finally, after great sacrifice, women here obtained voting rights, legal rights, ownership rights, and so forth. The proverbial "glass ceiling," though, is still there. Women, working the same job as men, are paid less. At the top levels of business, banking, politics, and governance, women are very much the minority. For several thousand years, even more so within the world's great religions, women have been looked down on or restricted or owned—more as "slaves" than wives. Ideas of the "weaker" sex apply only to bulk, not ability.

Face it: poverty is sexist.

Any business, any board room, any governmental, banking, investment, or professional position . . . has profited from female involvement and direction. Women naturally intuit best ways to obtain consensus or solve a problem—quickly. Case in point: a woman police officer is called to break up a mob of unruly teenagers on a city street. She suggests a dance-off to the crowd; they all participate, have a great time, and disperse happily. Problem solved.

In 1980, when I married, I asked in prayer what my new name should be. A most unusual vision directed me to become "P. M. H. Atwater." At the time, I thought that was the dumbest, stupidest, most egotistical name I had ever heard of—then I caught myself cursing the very name I had been given. I shut up, went back into prayer, and asked if that name was right, had I misinterpreted it somehow, was it okay. At the end of nine days I felt as if I had been born with that name, so, I went to court and legally made it mine. Twenty years later, when wondering about my crazy name, others pointed out to me that my research on near-death experiences would never have been accepted had I had a female name. My name had to be either male or neutral. Even to this day many professionals still think I am a man, and they treat me accordingly . . . as if a man, with respect for the work I have done and the discoveries I have made.

People say the days of the "goddess" are back, when feminine energy and power will finally be accepted. I say, it's time both sexes were accepted on par with each other, as the partners they truly are.

What No One is Acknowledging

The major earth changes cycle began in October of 2004. That also includes climate change. You don't need me to remind you that our planet is going through a "mid-life" crisis; storms are now past-biblical.

Look at this: temps are rising so fast Earth seems to be losing moisture as oceans are making a comeback; the magnetic field is weakening and thinning; our moon is slowly distancing itself, while the Schumann Cavity Resonance (our Earth's heartbeat) has jumped to 16.5 hertz—proof that our planet is speeding up at the same time it's getting heavier and somewhat bulgy in the middle. Solar flares will probably peak in 2022 (putting digital advancements at risk). Soon after, about 2030 to 2040 (maybe longer) solar cycles are slated to cool, creating another "small" Ice Age (the last time this type of Ice Age occurred was in 1645—the Thames River in England froze). All of this affects the amount of oxygen in the air that we can breathe. It affects crops and plants and food sources. For the sake of oil, Oklahoma has fracked its way to over 900 earthquakes per year. Yet with less sun, what comes from the solar energy/clean energy revolution?

Both Third and Fourth Industrial Revolutions could be derailed by climate change, earth changes. Still, *we could avoid most of the trauma ahead of us if we modernized now instead of rushing for profits.*

Are you ready for an emergency, if we have one? Do you have an emergency fund set aside; do you know routes to safe shelters; are you up-to-date with methods for handling injuries, with a handy kit of bandages, basic medications, blankets, tools, flash light with batteries, candles, matches, and bottled water? Have a radio. Know neighbors. Check on the elderly.

The United States alone has been hit by one over-the-top storm after another. No governmental body can bear damage costs for citizens year after year after year. So far, we've skated along. As incidents increase, budgets won't.

What nobody is acknowledging is that no country, ours or anyone else's, no local government, church, family, or individual, is prepared for past-biblical changes to occur, let alone increase. They will.

I come from the reclaimed deserts of southern Idaho. You learned early how to survive there, how to start over again and rebuild if necessary. And, you helped your neighbors. Together we thrived, welcomed outsiders, built a Treasure Valley that grew opportunities like potatoes. People may have changed, but what was once true still is.

Margaret Meade said: "Never doubt that a small group of thoughtful, committed people can change the world. Indeed, it is the only thing that ever has."

This is my world. This is your world. Everything we do counts.

What's ahead of us is likely to be a fantastic and fun ride.

Participate!

According to the law of fluid dynamics, it only takes four people out of every hundred to make a change. This causes a ripple effect to take place. This "power of four" is actually a tipping point. Should more than four change, maybe double or triple that number, increase it even more, the initial ripple can become a tidal wave sweeping across boundaries to the point where that original change-point can no longer be stopped nor contained.

Like I said, participate!

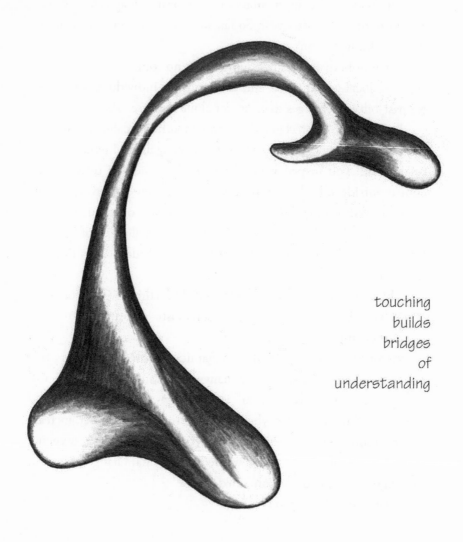

touching
builds
bridges
of
understanding

PART VI

OUR TRIUNE GUIDANCE

History—Religion/Interpretive

Vision—Spirituality/Experiential

Universal Law—Mysticism/Collective Whole

Ever since the Hubble Space Telescope started taking pictures of the deep universe, we have all been startled by what its "eye" sees: *galaxies beyond number . . . staggering amounts of planets orbiting their parent stars within a habitable distance . . . alien civilizations possibly in the trillions . . . three new Earth-like planets within viewing distance.*

Life? Beings like us? Anywhere?

Well, comets and their fragments do indeed spread life—for they contain water, oxygen, alcohol, sugar, spores, and microorganisms. And, they shoot around the universe like sperm spreading "seeds" everywhere. The idea that "comets started it all" (panspermia) has some merit. But, get this: a few comet pieces contain nano-bacteria (fossils). Shocks of heat and cold, long journeys through space, kill off anything alive . . . yet we have chunks with real fossils in them. And Mars for sure once had breathable oxygen, oceans, sea lilies, herds of animals, tree-like structures, canals, maybe pyramids and other buildings. And the sky on the red planet is blue, almost as blue as ours. Once inhabited? You bet! Probably still is.

Recent discoveries prove that water on Earth predates the Sun, AND, there is a Planet 9 . . . ten times more massive than Earth and four times larger, lurking on the outer edge of our solar system. It has a super-elongated orbit that apparently takes an unbelievable 10,000 to 20,000 years to complete. Adding to its high strangeness, Planet 9 is actually an exoplanet from a neighboring planetary system that our Sun stole from another star. Only in 2016 did we finally notice its presence!

Scientists recently took a back-step on this. Still *something big* is there. Is Planet 9 *or something else* there the missing planet Nibiru?

Enter the "Intervention Theory" of Zecharia Sitchin, a historian and linguist, who believed from his studies of Sumerian clay tablets that the human race was created by the Anunnaki, supposedly a race from Nibiru, a planet in our own solar system with an extended super-elongated orbit of 3,600 years (sound familiar?). His translation of the Sumerian inscriptions suggests that these Anunnaki took their own genes and implanted them into primitive hominids already here to attain the genesis of Homo sapiens.

Many other credible researchers have reached similar conclusions, of how human history is intertwined with that of advanced beings from here on Earth itself, from off-worlders, as well as those in and through other dimensions. Their work challenges the very beginnings of modern civilization and its religions, governments, and cultures.

Chief among these challenges are the findings of John E. Mack, Ph.D., Harvard psychiatrist and Pulitzer Prize winner. He stated that: "At least four species of alien have been visiting Earth for thousands of years. Some of the aliens hail from the Zeta Reticuli, Pleiades, Orion, Andromeda, and Altair Star Systems, and may have different agendas."

Dr. Mack was adamant in saying that alien encounters and contacts are both literally and physically happening. Mack and I knew each other and followed each other's work. He phoned me one day and said we needed to get together. A date was set. He died shortly before.

There are thousands of credible witnesses—from astronauts, scientists, pilots, to police, lawyers, and medical personnel, who have spoken about personal contact with non-human intelligences and sightings of unusual lights or anomalous flying objects and UFOs. Images of beings from other worlds and their craft have been found with giant skeletons and unusual skulls—globally. Indigenous tribes have always acknowledged "star visitors," especially the Dogon Tribe of Mali, West Africa. Consider that Haplotype-X cannot be fully traced to "earthly" origins, and that in studies of human DNA . . . there are anomalies suggestive of early manipulation in our evolutionary line, plus, of current notice . . . *new* anomalies have crept in.

Immigrants from Other Worlds

The flying saucer craze officially began in 1947. But that's not what Mack and I were anxious to discuss. Some of my findings were different, very different, and he wanted to know more. Allow me to share some of what we once discussed on the phone prior to the meeting that never happened. A little history first.

Go back in your mind to the days of the Cambrian Explosion, about 530 million years ago. We already know that humanoid projections billions of years earlier were pretty much filmy beings who came and went at will. Hundreds of millions of years passed before Earth was more hospitable to higher forms of intelligence. It was the Cambrian Explosion that set the stage for momentous shifts to occur. Toward its final days, around 55.8 to 33.9 million years ago, and before the Age of Mammals, the Eocene Period birthed. Deciduous trees (those that annually lose leaves) appeared with a host of other vegetation on the order of paradise. Eocene seas covered much of what is now the United States, especially California and into Canada. Their shales (vast quantities of organic matter and volcanic ash) became the oil shales we covet today.

To put this timeframe into perspective, Mu/Lemuria came millions of years afterward, then Atlantis (approximately 250,000 years ago). Mythic memory tells us that the First Adam inhabited the First Eden during the time of Atlantis. The separation of male and female sexes occurred then as the hermaphroditic bodies of the past disappeared.

That timeframe before mythic memory, during the Eocene and somewhat during segments of the Cambrian, our planet became shelter, later home, to uncounted immigrants from other worlds. Yes, I said other worlds. Yes, I said immigrants.

Surprise! The aliens are us.

Many came. Many died. Some merged into life forms already here to ensure survival. Others went underground, especially at the poles and through "portals" forming in rock shafts. A few were successful in being able to leave as they had come—as if they were "visitors" to begin with and never intended to stay.

One of the many groups who came was a somewhat-humanoid/ slightly reptilian type from a water star in the Sirius System that went nova. As many beings as possible fled and in ships so huge they were more akin to floating cities than to spaceships. Fourteen ships made it, each carrying around 200. They hovered above the Earth for over 700 years, waiting for better conditions; finally choosing several different spots in which to set down. The one I am more familiar with landed where Mount Palomar is today in southern California. Then, the area was mostly ocean with a few rock outcroppings. Since they were basically water beings, conditions there seemed perfect until the long-term effect of Earth water added up in ways they were not prepared for. The harshness of the water resulted in lesions and skin decay. (It reminds me somewhat of the Hollywood movie, *Arrival.*"

No one was sexed. They multiplied through a procedure called "separation" which took months to occur after they had entered open-air units powered by massive crystalline stones. Separation was a division; one becoming two, and happened every century or so. Their ships eventually evaporated, leaving no trace, no remnants to prove they were ever here. What sealed their fate was how they multiplied. Their open-air units would not work here. They learned about sex by studying animals. How to manipulate evolutionary advancements yet continue their race became important to some, but not to all. Mack knew about these beings and the Eocene timeframe as perfect for many off-worlders to immigrate here. Sorry we couldn't compare notes before he left us.

As a brief aside, *biologists today suggest that humanity may have had a more aquatic evolutionary history than previously thought.*

Plasma Tricks

Sharing some of what I discovered makes this point: stories about extraterrestrials, memories of alien abductions, channeled messages from the so-called "Ashtar Command," orbs that follow us as if spying on our every move, lineages that spread across history in a mythic memory that crisscrosses all boundaries and time itself . . . may not necessarily be what we think it is. Always there's more to the story, cues we missed. For instance, the Hudson Valley Lights in New York State are not UFOs. Contrary to photographs, books, and testimony (I was one of many witnesses), these UFOs are actually plasma balls, changing color and form to match the expectations of witnesses. Plasma balls, tubes, twinkling lights, and energy flows are usually either free-form creations or match the consciousness of observers; or they can form in concert with earth fractures, nearby power lines, and reactors. They alter shape/form if exposed to human consciousness. Any type of plasma can become the perfect receptacle/container for spirits, guides of various types, disincarnates, loved ones, the newly deceased. Floods of emotion, especially that of joy, can unleash plasma "fireworks," as can ecstatic states of kundalini breakthroughs.

UFOs are real. Extraterrestrials are real. But they're not always what we think they are. Do your work. Investigate, verify, test, cross-compare with different people, different times, different areas. There are many levels and layers to reality, not just where we dwell most of the time. And there are the imaginal worlds and Older Orders of ensoulment. In memory of Edgar D. Mitchell, Ph.D., former astronaut and founder of Noetic Sciences, a huge landmark study has begun to gather information about UFOs and the alien world of extraterrestrials, abductions, and witnesses—worldwide. It will take several years to complete. ET Support Groups have popped up because of the demand of so many who claim they were abducted or harassed or frightened by aliens. The new kids, as tiny tots, point to sky worlds far away as being where they're from.

What Children Tell Us

Mary Rodwell, Ph.D., when talking about her book, *The New Human*, explained: "In my work as a counselor, hypnotherapist, and principal for The Australian Close Encounter Resource Network (ACERN), I have researched over 3,000 cases of families and children who believe they have been experiencing extraterrestrial encounters. Their stories and understandings are profound and leave me with little doubt non-human intelligences are visiting our planet and interacting with humanity on multiple levels of human consciousness." She speaks of hybrids, children who are half alien and half human, and of beings from other worlds who are no longer capable of reproduction, hence their need to mate with or intercede with human reproduction to save their race.

Although my research numbers are not as large as Dr. Rodwell's, what I discovered in researching child experiencers of near-death states is worth considering for it invites us to rethink what we thought we knew.

With adult experiencers of near-death states (based on three thousand cases), I found that 20 percent identified as being from another planet, and 9 percent claimed to have been abducted by a UFO. Child experiencers were somewhat different. Based on 277 cases, only 9 percent identified as being from another planet, 14 percent said they had been abducted by a UFO, and 39 percent said they were from another dimension. I didn't find this sense of interdimensionality with adults.

There were two camps to interdimensionality, though. The largest centered on *an orientation to the life continuum.* Kids with this orientation were concerned with life embodiments and the progression and grouping of souls. Their memories embraced pre-birth and after-death realms as exit and entrance points to a single life stream or life continuum inhabited by the type of spirits they once were and will be again—their true home. (The majority, about three-quarters of the 39 percent, recalled this.)

The lesser numbers *were oriented to the cosmos.* Children with this orientation were concerned with the universe's inner working and the progression of Creation. They identified with formlessness: gasses, attractors, particle sparks, waves, energy pulses, plasma, and so forth, as if the substance of their being and their place of residence were one in the same—part of the mechanism and structure that holds together and maintains Creation itself. (Fewer respondents, about one-quarter of the 39 percent, claimed this orientation.)

Although of lesser number, those oriented to the cosmos challenged the very notion we have of soul and how life is identified.

They seemed possessed of almost pure intellect, and they spouted advanced concepts about things like wave forms, energy sources, and power grids in the same manner as the average child might quote football scores. And they were explicit about their origins: "Not here; not there; elsewhere." Just because these kids occasionally mentioned other planets does not mean they considered themselves from them.

Don't confuse these children with those who remember past lives (the life continuum). These kids acted as if they have never been on this or any other planet before and, frankly, considered the human body, any body, a useless, clumsy appendage. They appeared utterly unconcerned with family issues or personal relationships. Creation to them was alive and conscious; the very gasses we breathe, living intelligences. Often they referred to themselves as stewards, guardians, or keepers of that which enables cells and molecules to exist, rather than as evolving souls. True, their memories could be interpreted as awareness in the womb (plasma waves); still, they were adamant about being here for the "changes." Most stated that they were called here by a signal from the Earth itself for help.

Dates given in most near-death narratives are useless, so I asked each child to describe what he or she would look like when the changes arrived. Matching their present age against their image projections, I arrived *at the same timeframe with each one: between the years of 2013 to 2029.* No exceptions.

The majority of adult and child near-death experiencers I had sessions with spoke of the solar system as the university of the soul. They said we are each here for a reason, and that God/Allah/Deity (The Divine Supreme Intelligence) has a Grand Plan and we are part of that plan. You get the sense from them that reincarnation and those intriguing stories of "life after life" are just window dressing for something larger.

The Cygnus Mystery

Andrew Collins wrote the book. His research concerned the constellation of Cygnus, the Swan, located in the Great Rift of the Milky Way. He discovered that bird effigies found from Mississippi to

Mexico, India to Egypt, Great Britain to Turkey, and many places in-between—all the early religious centers of the world—oriented their temples and monuments toward Cygnus. Let me repeat: Collins found that every one of Earth's sacred sites is oriented north to the rising and setting stars of the Swan constellation, as if the numinous begins and ends there. Deneb, the brightest of Cygnus stars (70,000 times brighter and 25 times larger than our Sun), is symbolized at the heart of Judaism, Christianity, Hinduism, and Islam, and in the spiritual practices of shamanism.

Universally, and in all cultures, this one point in the sky was regarded as the gateway of life, death, and rebirth.

Universally, and in all cultures, the belief that the real stuff of life comes from the cosmos . . . survives still.

Universally, and in all cultures, history shows that the knowledge, even the technology we have needed as a species, has always been but a dream away. Our benefactors came from the stars.

there are
no
mistakes
in life
only
opportunities
passed
by

16

History—Religion/Interpretive

Both religion and mathematics are said to have begun during the latter part of the Paleolithic Period (50,000 years ago). Yet traditions of the elder Vedas (India) push dates back into the millions. New research into megalithic sites hint at 70,000 plus years. Even at Göbekli Tepe, the temple complex in southern Turkey (dated 11,500 BCE), there is evidence to show that *their artisans were familiar with 3-D imagery and used it in their carvings.* Stone Age research is now up for grabs: it appears as if what we consider "ancient history" is really "aftermath recoveries" from a series of manmade and earth change disasters that forced survivors to reinvent themselves and their world.

Worship of Deity, a knowing of a Greater Intelligence, a Creator God of which we are a part, is engrained within our very nature as if a "stamp on our heart." Go back through written and oral histories, back through dreamtime and mythic memory, and you confront patterning that exactly matches the revelations and aftereffects of a near-death experience and/or an intense spiritual transformation the likes of near-death episodes. Doesn't matter child or adult or previous beliefs, 90-95 percent of experiencers today return *knowing* God. Imagine what that percentage could have been during ancient times.

Enter "religion." The term itself is "modern" in the sense of its Latin roots, meaning to tie, bind, unite, re-tie, and rebind. The idea of a tie that binds later came to signify "a way" or "the way" as a path to God . . . *a path as a living transmission that leads us to our essential, genuine selves—our true identity.*

Religious Movements Over Time

Here are the major ones. Prepare yourself for a few surprises.

Hinduism began in India around 5,500 years ago.

Jewish faith was founded by Abraham some 4,000 years ago.

Buddhism, as a set of beliefs, emerged from Hindu and Taoist teachings in what is now Nepal and China. About 500 BCE, the Buddhism that exists today began with Siddhartha Gautama.

Roman Catholic Church is credited to have begun with the Christhood of Jesus in the year 33.

Islam started with the visions of Muhammad in Saudi Arabia around 600 AD (additional sources are included with this credit).

Eastern Orthodox, as a separate sect originating from Roman Catholicism around the year 1,000.

Lutheranism was founded by Martin Luther, an ex-monk of the Catholic Church, in 1517.

Church of England (Anglican) was established in 1534 by King Henry VIII because the Pope would not grant him a divorce with the right to remarry.

Presbyterian religion emerged in 1560 when John Knox brought the teachings of John Calvin to Scotland.

Unitarianism began in Europe during the Enlightenment Age of the 1500s. Known as rational, liberal "heretics," they merged in the 1800s with Universalist ideas to become the Unitarian Universalist Church.

Congregationalists branched off from what was to them the excessive demands of Puritanism during the early 1600s in England.

Baptist faith is based on the religious tenets of John Smyth who launched the faith in Amsterdam in the year 1607.

Methodist beliefs were established by John and Charles Wesley in England during 1744.

Episcopalians brought their religious beliefs with them from England when they established the American Colonies, later forming a separate faith founded by Samuel Seabury in 1789.

Mormons (Latter-Day Saints) were established by Joseph Smith in Palmyra, New York, in 1830.

New Thought Transcendentalists began as a spiritual movement based on healing and individual enlightenment in the United States and Canada during the 1800s, and especially from 1840 on.

Salvation Army (yes, they are a religion) began thanks to William Booth, London, England, in 1865.

Christian Scientists started as a religion in 1879 thanks to Mary Baker Eddy, a well-known healer who used mind/thought principles.

Jehovah's Witness was established by Charles Taze Russell in Pennsylvania during the 1800's.

Pentecostals were established in the United States in 1901.

North Korean Cult Worship of "Dear Leader" started in 1912 when Kim Il Sung declared his status using the North Korean Calendar based on "Juche."

Unity Society of Practical Christianity was incorporated in 1914 by Charles and Myrtle Fillmore, Kansas City, MO. Unity Movement, as part of sweeping New Thought ideas, actually began publishing in 1893.

Sufism, as an international peace movement, was established in 1923 by Hazrat Inayat Khan.

Science of Mind, using tenets of spiritual revelation and New Thought ideas, was established by Ernest Holmes in 1927. The Church of Religious Science became a religious order in 1949.

Interfaith Seminaries began in the 1960s training ministers and clerics about the "living transmission" possible through spiritual truths and their application found in all religious orders. New Thought based.

Peace Pentagon, built to counter the War Pentagon in northern Virginia, was dedicated to service July 3, 2016, on the banks of the New River in Independence, VA. Based on Thomas Jefferson's *Act for Religious Freedom*, the Peace Pentagon is rapidly becoming a model hub of Interfaith Worship, New Thought Spiritual Principles, and a Culture of Peace that can be duplicated by anyone, in any location, anywhere.

According to the *World Christian Encyclopedia*, there are over 10,000 distinct religions; within Christianity alone, there are 33,820 different denominations. In Islam there are at least five major sects (not to be confused with denominations); with Judaism, four major branches; Buddhism has three major denominations; in the Pagan world there are over 30 distinct types of witches. Almost all religions and religious orders count numerous extensions and divisions. China boasts of having 700 million people religiously unaffiliated. Their leaders strive to maintain what is billed as "an atheist's paradise," yet in 2015/2016, *A Course in Miracles* was a best seller among "underground outlets."

More Amazing Religious Histories

There are facts in this section that may leave you speechless.

Atheist . . . . There is no God

Agnostic . . . . Skepticism about the existence of God

Polytheism . . . . . . There are many gods

Monotheist . . . . . . There is One God

Mystic . . . . There is *only* God

Native American term for Man
who aspires to be god-like . . . . . . Yahweh

The unpronounceable name of God in
the Old Testament . . . . YHWH (Yahweh)

The "wings of the brain" (the prefrontal lobes) are directly connected to the heart and limbic system. Since the pre-frontals cannot handle more than seven items at once, all symbolic archetypes/myths are based on the ability of pre-frontals to order and remember things. Thus, seven is held as a sacred symbol throughout all religious and spiritual traditions and across time.

The founders of the three monotheistic religions received their fundamental revelations on a mountain (less oxygen on mountain tops makes it easier to have visions). With each major "round" of earth changes a new religion appeared. According to experts in Christianity, every 500 years there is a complete upheaval in religion itself and in religious views. We are on course for another such upheaval . . . now believed to herald the coming of the Age of Spirit.

During the early days when the Bible took shape, 570 books were kicked out, among them the *Seventy Books* where Michael the archangel spoke of God's Great Timing of future events. The story of Adam and Eve was not written until the 10th century BCE; the earliest writings we have about Abraham came 45 generations after his death (if he lived at all). The Sinai Bible is the oldest known. It contains the first mention of Jesus, beginning when he was 30 years old. When the New Testament of the Sinai Bible is compared with modern-day versions, 14,800 editorial alterations can be identified. Early Gospels never mentioned a virgin birth. Christ's suffering, the crucifixion, and the resurrection, did not appear in the Gospel until the 12th century—coinciding with an upsurge in Christian militarism and the beginning of the Dark Ages. "The Great Omission" is the crucifixion/resurrection story. "The Great Insertion" is the final chapters of the Book of John that detail this story. Warnings about an "Anti-Christ" were never given credence until the Reformation of 1517 when the reigning Pope was declared the Anti-Christ by Martin Luther.

I could go on and on like this. To the question of—was the Bible doctored to coincide with political needs of the Roman Catholic Church throughout its history—I would say yes. Still, the Bible, in spite of its questionable history, remains a book of inspiring and uplifting stories that speak of love and forgiveness, helpful messages for all of us even today. Just don't take everything literally. The same can be said of the Qur'an.

Credited with being a collection of divine revelations given to Muhammad during the 23 years he wandered about, there are links in the Qur'an to Hebrew scriptures and traditions, the Apocrypha, Nestorian Christianity, notions that Jesus did not die on the cross, and Arab folklore—with an extreme Wahhabist version "tacked on" that sanctions fanatical terrorism (Muhammad himself warned about what would come from the village where Wahhab was born). Written to be intoned as if poetry, the Qur'an itself is filled with beautiful passages and inspiring upliftment, and is not the sole source of edicts "invented" by the Muslim Brotherhood. Women, for instance, have full rights to their children, divorce, an education, ownership, and careers of their choice in Islam. Anything contrary to this comes from traditional views, not the actual Qur'an. Keep in mind that the Prophet Muhammad was a theologian, a preacher, a warrior, and a politician, all at once. Thus, in Islam, religion and politics are intertwined. This runs counter to the tenets of Christianity—until you take a good look at the Popes of Rome.

The Prophecies of St. Malachy

Pope Leo X was probably the biggest embarrassment to the Roman Catholic Church, not because of his obsessions with sex, as a homosexual, or his penchant for power and wealth (as this applies to many Popes before and after him), but because of the ease with which he spoke his mind and revealed the Church's best kept secrets.

His predecessor, Julius II, was known as "Pope Terror." He was another militaristic and disbelieving pope, who drank and swore heavily, fought long and bloody wars—leading his Catholic troops into combat, dressed in full armor. He had at least three children, in spite of his 'unnatural vices,' and declared a papal belief that "Christians are the unstable, unlettered and superstitious masses." He once advised his secretary to take three mistresses at one time, "in memory of the Holy Trinity." When examining the statue that Michelangelo had carved of him, he asked with a puzzled expression on his face: "What's that under my arm?" When Michelangelo replied, "A Bible, your Holiness," Julius roared "WHAT DO I KNOW OF BIBLES, I am a warlord, give me a sword!"

These are just two examples. The Popes of Rome were not always inspiring, or even honest. Many prophecies were written about them. The most famous came from St. Malachy, who recorded 112 brief descriptions—clues to the identities of Popes from medieval to the present. These end with what Malachy predicted about the last Pope, and that "he would oversee the fall of the Roman Catholic Church and bear witness to the Last Judgment." All 112 were deposited in Vatican archives and remained hidden for almost 400 years. They were rediscovered and published in 1595. This "sudden" rediscovery enabled them to be used to promote Pope Gregory IV to the throne, amidst rousing debates of falsehood that continued for centuries. Studies of the prophecies' accuracy, both before and after publication, have maintained they are "reasonably accurate"—to the extent of symbols and words given that have proved meaningful.

According to the count of St. Malachy, Francis is that fabled last Pope. Born in Argentina in 1936, he is the first non-European to be elected Pope in the last 1,300 years. St. Malachy identified him as "Peter the Roman," which made absolutely no sense to anyone until . . . Jorge Mario Bergoglio chose the name Francis I. The original name of St. Francis was Francesco di Pietro di Bernardone. Pietro translates as Peter. The allusion to being "Roman" infers having held office in the Vatican administration, which Jorge had . . . five positions in the Roman Curia. The last Pope was said to be a humble man who would focus on poverty and abuses in the Church (money, power, sex).

Yup, Pope Francis matches the prophecy.

He also matches the character, accomplishments, and promises of the famous rebel, Priest Miguel Hidalgo Y Costilla. Hidalgo was the father of the Mexican Revolution. He attained Priesthood at the age of 25 after attending college. He spoke several languages and was able to read enlightenment philosophies (ideas about the worth of each person, that the church was not everything). Thanks to Gayle Geffner, an astrologer who discovered this: "Hidalgo was a very humanistic Priest, helping the indigenous people try to gain some power through their own economy using science. He wanted everyone to have economic power, not just the conquering country. He implemented the industries of brick making, silk worms, and grape vineyards for the people. He did not believe in celibacy (actually living with a woman and having two daughters) and did not believe in the authority of the Pope. Incredibly progressive, he was taken to Spain, to the office of the Inquisition, and sent back to the New World, presumably to behave himself. He eventually became militaristic, fighting for the people, and was killed in a battle—with his head put on display for all to see."

Hidalgo left undone many promises and goals . . . that exactly match the driving force guiding the actions of Pope Francis. I do most sincerely believe that Pope Francis is the reincarnation of the rebel Priest Hidalgo.

Whether or not this is true, it is true that Pope Francis is changing the Church . . . returning Roman Catholicism to its roots, paring down properties and expenditures, insisting that the Vatican Bank be audited, and returning the central focus of the Church to the condition of the poor and needy. He is the "People's Pope" as Hidalgo was the "People's Priest."

The Roman Catholic Church, through almost 2,000 years of its history, has moved steadily in the direction of wealth and power, and away from its central mission. The end of the Church may indeed be what is happening now—a transformation of epic portions—the return to the truth of its original purpose. You might compare this to a near-death experience, where what is false is stripped away as God's Light shines through. Who better to oversee this than Hidalgo/Francis?

Death doesn't always mean "the end." Sometimes it means "transformation" and "a new beginning."

The Issue of Messiahs

I know of eleven "messiahs" with the same or similar pattern to that of the Christian version. It's as if the story of Jesus was "copied" from other texts. The list below, except the first two, consists of only basic notations.

> **Zarathustra:** 9,000 years ago he was known for his gentleness and wisdom, a "Lamb of God" with Iranian roots, whose influence spread throughout many regions and the passing of years.

> **Mithra:** Indo-Persian about 3,500 years ago. Point for point, his story is an almost *exact duplicate* of the entire Jesus story. So stunning is this duplication that it appears as if Mithra and Jesus are, or at least were on some level, the same figure.

> **Krishna:** world savior who rose from the dead.

> **Buddha:** ascended bodily to heaven.

Lao-Kiun: savior, virgin born deity, ascended bodily to Paradise.

Zoroaster: world savior, the ancient Persian God, ascended to heaven.

Aesculapius: the Son of God, the savior, after being put to death rose from the dead.

Adonis: world savior, rose from the dead.

Osiris: the Egyptian savior, after being put to death rose again.

Frey: the ancient Scandinavian world savior who was put to death, and then rose from the dead.

Quetzalcoatl: the Mexican/Central American savior was crucified, died, then rose again.

Jesus of Nazareth: count him as number 12 in this list.

There are many others. Those listed had the greatest effect on the largest number. History tells us that whenever the human family needed spiritual encouragement, assurance of the Divine, miracles of light and love to inspire and uplift, someone was there to show the way.

What later developed as Islam is no different. Muhammad is revered, not necessarily as a savior-type, but as a Prophet and Way Shower. There is no central authority in Islam, so, what continues today of the original "miracles," lies in the hands of the various clerics and Imams. There is a legend that the world is now ready for the appearance of the 12th Imam, a Messiah figure like Jesus. "Twelvers," as believers like to be called, claim that each Age has its own special Imam (similar to the esoteric/mystical belief that each Age has its own Adam/Noah/Messiah figures). Twelvers state that their 12th Imam is currently alive but hidden. In order for him to reveal himself and save the world, it must first be in a state of violent chaos. Their dedication is . . . "to make it so."

So, we have Christians looking for the Second Coming of the Christ, Jews still waiting for the appearance of their long overdue Messiah, and Muslims who are busy creating a world that will ensure their 12th Imam will come forth.

Where, in all of this, is religion itself?

Reclaiming the Subversive Way of Jesus

Question: Why do religions preach forgiveness, kindness, and peace, but are at the same time one of the principle contributors to war, division, persecution, and oppression?

Answer: Blind faith. Any form of fundamentalism tends to cripple the mind. People overly religious or set in their ways often lose their sense of wonder, their sense of praise, their sense of joy.

The story of Joseph of Cupertino, Italy, says this best. Whenever celebrating Mass, he would be so overcome by the ecstasy of what he was doing that he would scream and then levitate, sometimes to the ceiling and all around the church to the amazement of his many onlookers. The Church panicked, put him through the Inquisition several times but to no conclusion. If he saw angels in flight, he would join them, flying around tree tops. If weather worsened, he never got wet. He once said, "If God is everywhere, then we can be happy anywhere." A gifted healer, he produced healing miracles all his life . . . to the embarrassment of his church. If ever there was an unbridled follower of Jesus, it was Joseph of Cupertino. He dared to live what his heart declared.

Similar to the other Messiahs I listed, the special message of Jesus, in essence, said, "All that I have done you can do, and more also." He was a true heretic, subversive to the core. The reason for faith, for church, for religion, is a simple one: *there is a holy foolishness to the service of love.* Try it and see for yourself.

Howard Storm, a near-death experiencer, was once asked the question: What is the best religion? His answer: Whatever brings you closer to God.

Church, to my way of reckoning, is people of a like-mind who come together to worship and join with a power greater than they are. It is not a building or a temple, mosque or synagogue, pagan circle or medicine wheel. It is fellowship, caring, and support, plus a form of teachings that advance ethical behavior and gives people, especially children, direction and purpose.

Church is people. Religion is a love song to the God of our being, an oasis for the soul . . . as we spiral ever *outward* in our journey to the truth of who and what we really are.

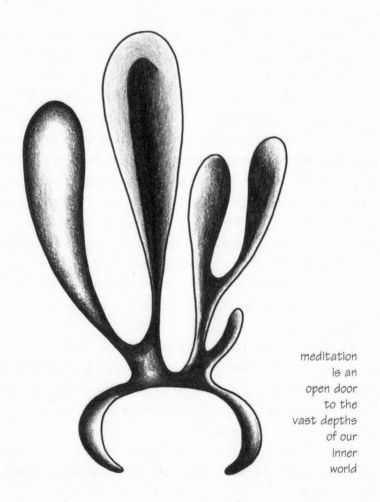

meditation
is an
open door
to the
vast depths
of our
inner
world

17

Vision—Spirituality/Experiential

Three languages are spoken on this planet—*only three*. The most predominant: the language of survival, of basic needs and desires—"self" oriented. The second most common: an outgrowth of education and circumspect, of approval and accomplishments—"other" oriented. The third: associated with the many forms of altruism, of service and sacrifice—"spirit" oriented.

The three languages are a product of the three levels of thinking.

Ever try to explain Level Three understandings to someone at Level One, or even Level Two? Didn't get anywhere, did you!

Each Level can be subdivided into three more divisions. Let's do that with Level Three: Religion, Spirituality, Mysticism. Same deal. Ever try to explain mysticism to someone who is committed to a religious orthodoxy? Ever stand up in front of a large church, as I have, and say to the congregation: "There is only one being in this room—God having a conversation with God."

Absolutely! *There is only God*. Not one God. *Only God*.

The journey from Level One thinking/speaking to the third level of Level Three can be tough going, maybe even nightmare tough. *Heart understandings at that level do not match what you see around you in your daily life or at church, with your family, your job, your country.* Suddenly you are an outsider.

An old saying goes like this: *The farther along you are on The Path, the fewer there are and the lonelier it gets.* I would add: " . . . *until you and the Path fade into the Allness of Love that's been there all along.*" Mystics have been accused of double-speak. That's only true until you awaken to what's behind the curtain thought provides.

During the time when our various avatars (saviors) walked the Earth, the term "messiah" meant *conversation.* Stop for a moment and let that sink in . . . because . . . it means EVERYONE HAS A VOICE IN THE DIGNITY AND UNIQUE EXPRESSION OF LOVE, INTELLIGENCE, BEAUTY, AND HEAVEN IN THE GLORY OF GOD.

Everyone!

What turns your life around and puts you square in the middle of that *conversation* is some type of "awakening" or "experience of the numinous" that is so real, so vivid, that you're never quite the same again. A friend sent me this list of what typically happens afterward:

The 12 Symptoms of Spiritual Awakening

1. An increased tendency to let things happen rather than make them happen.

2. Frequent attacks of smiling.

3. Feelings of being connected with others and nature.

4. Frequent overwhelming episodes of appreciation.

5. A tendency to think and act spontaneously rather than from fears based on past experience.

6. An unmistakable ability to enjoy each moment.

7. A loss of ability to worry.

8. A loss of interest in conflict.

9. A loss of interest in interpreting the actions of others.

10. A loss of interest in judging others.

11. A loss of interest in judging self.

12. Gaining the ability to love without expecting anything.

Sounds wonderful, doesn't it? Yet the idea of dark forces, demonic factors, and insanity is all too real, and I want to address that. We can become victims while feeling "saved."

Alcoholism, drug use, abuse issues, even egotistical or overly demanding priests/ministers/spiritual teachers, are all attractors. With addiction or abuse issues, what they attract are possessors like hungry ghosts, evil spirits, or negative thought-forms who prey on the disaffected. With ego-driven priests/ministers/spiritual teachers, their attraction is that type of "blind slavery" that results when those who seem higher, better, more powerful takeover the minds of adherents. Victimization and the myriad forms of "giving ourselves away" lead to the same condition . . . the loss of self-love.

Realities of Breakthrough

What if it's not just an awakening that's at hand? What if a breakthrough into higher consciousness occurs? Perhaps even a conversion event where the soul of your being is turned inside out, and instantly you're awash in sensory extras, visions, and knowings you cannot explain, and abilities you never had before?

We know from near-death experiences and other intense, transformative events, that physical changes occur afterward—things like alterations in brain structure and function, increased intelligence, changes in nervous and digestive systems, skin sensitivity, and the manifestation of electrical sensitivity—along with unusual sensitivities to sound/light/taste/touch/texture/smell, and the loss of tolerance for pharmaceuticals. The individual may, occasionally or often: hear voices, see lights, witness visitors "who are not there," heal others, attract children and wild animals/birds, surrender personal will to "A Higher Will," have a vibrant dream life, become comfortable with things future, take on a new vitality, know more, and/or affect magnetic fields. All of this plus the psychological changes of becoming less materialistic, more service oriented, joyful, psychic, intuitive, generous, patient, accepting of "differences," attuned to God/Allah/Deity and the concept of unconditional love. And, become quietly resourceful or openly child-like. Dimensional splits and time shifts take on an "almost ordinary" quality afterward, as does synchronicity.

Look again at prayer: we do not pray to God, but *in* God. Non-directed prayer is more powerful than directed prayer, because, once you remove "the obstructions of preference," the intrinsic wholeness of the universe takes over. Prayer is its own answer. Never force, allow. The people in India when showing respect, greet others with hands held in the prayer position. This is "Namaste" and it means: "*I honor the place in you of love, of light, of truth, of peace. I honor the place within you where, if you are in that place in you and I am in that place in me, there is only one of us.*"

Look again at mindfulness: it's the simple act of actively noticing things. Yet, it is almost more powerful than meditation in the sense that the world comes alive to you. You see more. You appreciate more. You connect and understand more. It is where mind and body join as one. Being mindful helps in the art of choice-making so you can respond to relationships in natural, positive ways. Movement meditations, like trance dancing, enable the mind to enter the quiet of the intuitive heart—while making deliberate, repetitive movements that enable the scaffolding of the body to open up more, to bend and stretch with grace.

Look again at forgiveness: more than words, forgiveness creates conditions where demands, pretense, and guilt are absolved. *Example*—In a matter of four days, after several Amish girls

288

were killed in a school shooting: some of the Elders visited the mother of the murderer to offer forgiveness; families of the slain girls invited the killer's widow to their own children's funerals; requests were made that all relief monies intended for Amish families be shared with the widow and her children; and, more than 30 members of the Amish community attended the funeral of the killer. Forgiveness is putting yourself in the other's shoes to see and feel who and what is really there. This is why the various factions of Islam still hate each other; they refuse to see anything differently. We are all members of one family; what hurts one, hurts all.

Look again at spiritual unfoldment: there's order to it, as if musical notes spread across the musical scale. "Do"—valuation of the path, recognizing its vital importance; "Re"—application of spiritual teachings plus honoring self-knowledge; "Mi"—resistance within ourselves, the proverbial "pushback" from stepping out from the norm; "Fa"—the shock of *remembering* one's true self, then stepping forward to actually experience the truth of unseen reality; "So"—cooperation, realizing that one's personal path is the path of all; "La"—hearing the call to move beyond what seems limiting; "Ti"—transformation, both personal and collective; then, in returning to "Do"—energy begins at the next octave of the next version of the next path. The journey continues.

That Crazy Left Hand of God

Read again the breakthrough pattern. Now be honest. Doesn't that seem more a path to psychiatric disorder and insanity than a way to God? Some folks even dub it "the surprises from God's Left Hand."

Holy Spirit informs through rituals of Appalachian snake handlers, shamans who dwell between worlds, Wiccans who prefer the powers of the natural world to the oligarchies of heaven, Holy Rollers, those who speak in "tongues," plus countless others. No one can limit what or who God's Breath touches, or how. Jesus was once considered a man possessed, as was Muhammad, and all the great prophets of history. What separates "wheat from shaft" are testers—adversaries. That means Lucifers and Satans and Djinn and Devils, and "oops-I-gotcha" kind of folk are a necessity.

Some of the clues nobody told you when you were young about what makes reality valid and really real, follow:

> *Darkness exists with light. Without this contrast, we cannot recognize anything. Without change, we cannot see differences. All life begins in darkness. The energy worlds and energetic realities that shimmer in darkness, are what balances light and enables the fulfillment of spirit. Shadow lands and what appears as vague or empty, or the stuff of tragedy, are "holy" in the sense that once an individual can see "beyond sight" ... interferences large and small are revealed as "other" states of consciousness ... part of our movement up or down evolution's grand spiral. Survival of the fittest is false thinking. Cooperation is the first rule of nature.*

Mountain-top dwellers (those awash in revelations of the most high) are seldom as helpful as those who have fallen to the valley below and are "making mud pies" with everyone else. A spiritual truism puts this in perspective: "After enlightenment, the laundry."

Myths, symbols, and stories are maps of consciousness that center around birth, sex, growing up, growing old, danger, fulfillment, and death. They help us to remember that we make anything sacred by the power we give it and how we hold it in mind. And they help us to value ancestral memories, racial memories, past lives, archetypes, mystical states, dream work, and union with all things. *They unlock memory.*

Granted, taking drugs to do all of this offers a short cut to the drama of it, and can sometimes take you deeper and farther into territories of indescribable splendor. Psychedelics are favorites for this, along with drugs like LSD (common mind bender), DMT (the spirit molecule), or Ayahuasca (mind-blowing tea concocted by Amazonian shamans)—even handfuls of "magic mushrooms"—which I once ate by accident thinking they were just overgrown puff-balls (took me 2 ½ days to "land").

Young people today like to play around with mind-benders and spiritual trippers for a quick way to explore inner realms. I've spent time with doctors who used hallucinogens in treating Post Traumatic Stress Disorder. Controlled tests like this have been "over-the-top" successful. But since such drugs are for the most part illegal, medical people have no way to explore the range of possible benefits: we only hear about dangers.

Hallucinogens in native societies were only used in a ceremony for spiritual purposes and with elders in attendance for support and aid. Never were they used for amusement or recreation. Anyone as sensitive as I am doesn't need the stuff. Music, dance, scents, spiritual rituals, chants, vision quests, breath work, mandala art—all are very effective and very much safer than psychedelics. Awakenings that occur naturally overshadow chemical versions and powerful herbs.

Face it; science has been around for 300 years. Spiritual elders have walked this Earth for hundreds of thousands of years, probably longer. The knowledge and wisdom passed down to them from previous generations and through oral histories are breathtaking in value and scope. Still, BUYER BEWARE! *Same rule on the spiritual path as in the shopping mall.* Some elders are phonies and just want to make a quick buck tricking the starry-eyed and foolish.

Chaos and Discipleship

The claim that "there are no accidents," that we alone create our reality, falls into place once we realize that because of free will we can reshape, readjust, and realign more than we think—as an individual and as a soul. Details can alter, outcomes can change, but the end result is always "on course," as all things sooner or later work together for the good of the whole—whether or not we made it happen.

Have you ever studied chaos theory in mathematics? Briefly put, it shows how new order emerges from disorder; how no matter the extent of devastation or destruction that occurs, the various systems involved automatically mutate in ways that transform and transfigure one whole into another as if "orchestrated." There is rhythm, grace, and beauty in whatever seems chaotic: a progressive orderliness that interweaves what appears to be "random" events.

I have recognized this phenomenon, this miracle, in the lives of people and businesses and nations and landscape expanses. Regardless of the situation, be it positive or negative, energy out of balance with itself will build up to where a "tipping point" is reached, to where circumstances get "top heavy" from the weight of intense pressure and stress. When this happens, the situation topples over or shifts form. The law of chaos guarantees this. It is what led to the fall of the Berlin Wall, to every tyranny that ever existed, to every paradise ever built, and to every economy that ignored the growing needs of its people.

All major progressive movements throughout the world and history were originated by small groups of people, like Quakers, who had undergone an awakening and were possessed of a new consciousness. Their change, changed countless others, and very much for the better.

What guarantees success when one awakens? What's the crucial key for enabling transformative change in the few to uplift the many?

Discipline.

The discipline of discipleship.

When you're through laughing, read the rules.

Rules of Discipleship

♦ Don't freak the natives (careful how you act).

♦ Test truth (what looks good isn't necessarily good).

♦ Listen to what you say (and how you say it).

♦ Give yourself timeout (too much intensity scares people).

♦ Cleanliness matters (if you want to accomplish anything).

♦ "No" is a complete sentence (save explanations for when needed).

♦ Attention is power (be careful where you put it).

♦ Honor life, honor yourself (a prerequisite to love).

♦ Use Third Way principles (you create holons that way).

♦ Practice grace and gratitude (the twin keys to peace)

♦ Remember the mirror effect (the inner life reflects the outer).

♦ Visioning is a skill (enables you to see beyond the view).

♦ Be aware of what you send out (it can boomerang back).

♦ Value work and play (necessary aspects of joy).

♦ Heal with love, mend with laughter (basic common sense).

♦ Recognize that free will exists for all (variation is healthy).

♦ As the many ever seek The One, The One ever seeks the many ("impossible" only exists in the closets of closed thinking).

Living Resurrection

It used to be, long ages ago, that the fine art of living was said to be incomplete without a deepening relationship with "mystery." For some, that meant becoming an "initiate"—one who walked out on conventional life and devoted his or her remaining years to "the mystery schools" (what we today would call in-depth spiritual training) for the purpose of becoming a prophet or a seer, priest/priestess, or a teacher of God. They had rituals then, usually three-day or three-week affairs (almost always in threes, the "number" of spirit), that put one in dire stress, as a simulation of death's physicality. These rituals were sometimes horrific; probationers died. If, however, the probationer lived through the tests, they returned "changed"—glowing, physically altered, and of a different mind . . . one now attuned to higher realities who could see beyond sight, hear beyond sound, feel beyond touch, smell beyond odor, sense beyond thought.

In the Gnostic Gospel of Philip (one of those kicked out of early versions of the Bible), there is a passage of note: "Those who say they will die first and then rise are in error. If they do not first receive the resurrection while they live, when they die they will receive nothing."

Philip, by the way, goes on and on about this, about how resurrection rituals were held in caves or secret chambers or a sarcophagus—a widespread practice, a self-powering experience.

Doesn't all of this sound like a near-death experience or a near-death-like experience or an intense transformation of consciousness? And how about awakenings, mountain-top experiences, baptisms of the Holy Spirit, vision quests, experiences of the numinous, visitations from spirit beings—all of them and others—constituting that first step beyond regular living?

Making room in one's life to engage the sacred in everyday things is important and magical, and revealing—for it allows:

- ◆ a new picture to emerge

- ◆ a new truth to be revealed

- ◆ a direct, personal experience of God to occur

- ◆ a new awareness to flower

- ◆ a new vision of being human to show itself

- ◆ a new pattern of evolution to take hold

We Need a New Story

The old stories are good and teach us a lot about basics. But they are not necessarily helpful when your six-figure salary drops to zero because your job was shipped to China and you have to teach your replacement how things are done . . . with a smile on your face and speaking pleasantly. Nor when on vacation your spouse and child are slaughtered by gunmen trying to prove their religion is better than yours.

The end of things spreads daily across our television sets and newspapers and the Internet, spreading fear that the whole wide world is wrapped in chaos.

Don't believe it. Every ending brings a new beginning. Always. There is more good in this world than ill. People, instead of closing up, are opening up to solutions and ways to thrive in unusual times. We have more to be grateful for than to fear.

I know what I'm talking about. I lost everything when I died in 1977, including myself. The only logical thing I could say afterward was "God is," and I chanted that by the hour. It kept me sane. I had to relearn everything, from crawling to cooking, from putting on clothes to putting on a smile when I had no idea why I was smiling or why my children called me "mother" or why my employer called me "needed at work." I reached out and took every class I could find, did every exercise recommended, learned and relearned every single thing—and more also. No stone was left unturned.

Hear me when I say this. No matter your position in life or where you are, or what you are, or what you believe or disbelieve. I have only one question for you and your answer will change everything:

What is the vision you have of your life?

Begin there.

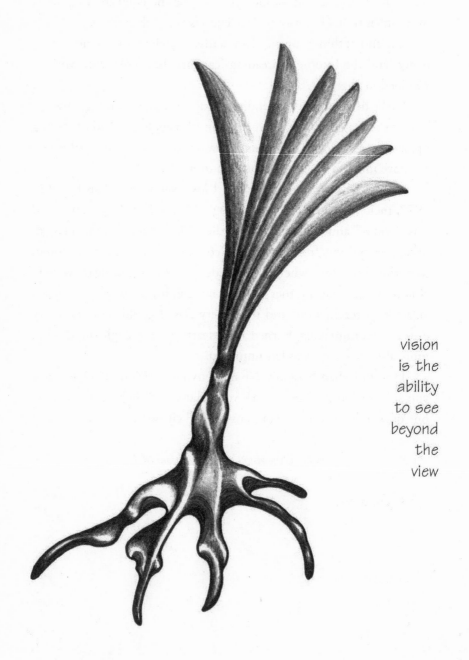

vision
is the
ability
to see
beyond
the
view

18

Universal Law—Mysticism/Collective Whole

You knew this was coming . . . the big stretch.

We dealt with *outward movements of life's spiraling energy* in the first section of Our Triune Guidance. In the second (what you've just read), we focused on *inward spirals* up or down. Here we tackle *beyond the spiral*— that deeper dive into bigger pictures of greater, more expansive realities.

That means . . . the true subject of this manual is and has always been consciousness awakening unto itself.

Fate and Free Will

Time and space are but concepts relative to how we perceive them. Each individual has his or her measure of time. Beyond what seems to be reality are realities without number. Yet the illusion of time and space and of stable matter—life as we think it is—serves an important purpose. To understand why, consider electrons. The *actual electron* is stable, like true north on a compass. But the *virtual electron* can fluctuate, like magnetic north on a compass. The former presents a model considered "true" because it is long-term and consistently dependable, while the latter offers an "approximation" based on its short-term capacity for maneuvering. The short-term version could not grow or change or alter without the long-term's stability, yet the long-term needs the short-term in order to experience itself.

Think God/Greater Intelligence as the actual electron. Think creation and all created things, including us, as virtual electrons. We can change, grow, and alter because "central intelligence" is steady. Variation is guaranteed because that which seems real, isn't!

As long as the world around us appears to be what we think it is, we have all the "elbow room" we need from time and space and matter to learn and grow and evolve (like with the virtual electron). We would be lost in a meaningless jumble if we could actually see everything that exists *as it really exists* before we are ready to (the actual electron). Both fixed and flexible futures are real and exist at the same time—*because that which has already happened, is still happening!*

What we call fate can waver. But, what we call destiny, our job in life, seems fixed in our cycles. We are each here to accomplish a given task, meet certain people at certain times—unless—by altering how we feel about the task at hand (our response to it), *we change so much* that our direction in life, our job and the reason why we are here, changes too.

Good and Evil

Personal stories handle this subject best. So, here are some to ponder.

Saturday mornings at the movie theater were special to me when I was a child (we didn't have television then). Always there was a serialized adventure thriller, cartoons, a Western featuring someone like Roy Rogers or Lash LaRue or Sunset Carson, then news. That news always zeroed in on Hitler and his "goose-steppers" (proud and loud), bombed out cities, families herded like cattle onto railroad cars, prisoners like toothpicks with hollowed-out eyes. All of it: same stage, same theatre, same popcorn, same sunshine waiting for me after I left the theater and went outside. Good? Evil? I finally arrived at a way to tell the difference: "good" felt good and "evil" felt bad.

My juvenile formula changed overtime when I became aware that there is always more involved in any situation than what meets the eye. I learned to first ask: "What is appropriate in this situation for my highest good and the highest good of all concerned?" Lashing out, getting angry, scared, or confused didn't help anyone.

This awareness was put to the test when one of our daughters was abducted from the city park by a man with rape on his mind. Police officers and I were able to track down the culprit and rescue our young daughter, scarcely in time. When the case went to trial, the judge gave me an opportunity to help decide the punishment. I said that I thought the man wanted to be caught since he had left a trail that could be followed and his actions were consistent with someone "begging for attention." Also, because of what she went through, our daughter had been jolted from years of ambivalence about school to wide-awake alertness. Her grades jumped from C's and D's to A's and B's. Although I could not and would not condone what had happened to our daughter, it was as if the man had done her "a favor," and I felt it was now time to do one for him. I recommended counseling and vocational training instead of prison. The judge agreed, and such was given.

What finally blew apart the good and evil issue for me was this incident: a man suddenly headed my way as I was walking along a highway of beach. It was dark, and he was muscular, like a dock worker. Instantly our movements froze while time and space expanded, sending a shower of sparkles everywhere. My possible attacker and I merged into one. His thoughts were mine, and mine his. Yes, he wanted my purse. Money. The eyes of my mind quickly scanned every item in my purse, searching for anything of value, wondering what decision to give him. No, the money would be of no great loss. Yes, I could replace everything, although it would be troublesome—but wait, my children's photographs— they could not be replaced. "No," I said to him, "I will not cooperate. What are my options?" "Well," he mumbled, "I just ate a heavy meal and I want an easy hit. I won't follow if you run." Just as suddenly as expansion had occurred, time and space contracted back to normal dimensions and animated behavior resumed. I ran! Like a track star, flying over a retaining wall and back to lights and people. A brief glance over my shoulder revealed that the man had tried to catch me but missed. He was too slow. At that moment I got it—how the issue of "good and evil" works.

At some level of mind, in some manner, we either are or can be in "conversation" and decide outcomes in advance.

Same thing happened on a day when my former husband, our son, and a friend went elk hunting. Groceries were sparse. We were desperate for meat. My son saw the elk first. The man shot. Missed. Instead of running to safety, the elk ran toward the men and stopped. My husband took his turn, missed, shot again, missed again. At the moment he readied for the third and fatal shot, the elk calmly looked him straight in the eye. As the elk did this, my husband felt a strange, weightless, floating sensation take over as he and the elk seemed to merge. He distinctly heard the elk say: "It's alright. Take all the time you need. I will be the meat your family needs this winter." Tender and sweet, we came to regard eating it as a Communion with Love.

More is involved in matters of good and evil, and what happens to us in life, than who's right or wrong and how we respond to outcomes. A greater mind is always present when consciousness seeks to respond to itself.

Millions of near-death experiencers return absolutely convinced there's no such thing as good and evil—at least not as we were taught.

Such "either/or" judgment misses entirely "the rest of the story" and what else may be involved—maybe on another level at a previous time.

On *www.pmhatwater.com* read, "The Challenge of September 11," to learn what I found when I went out-of-body to the site just before the second plane hit the second tower. What I discovered surprised even me. Think about other tragedies, perhaps some of your own.

The buildup of human consciousness in the ethers constitutes the realm of mass mind. All is conscious and known at that level. Here we can intervene, help, and heal. Judgment, though, lies elsewhere.

Heaven and Hell

Hell is just as real as heaven, and people go there—more than any-one wants to admit. The "other side" consists of layers/levels of varied vibrational folds, stacked like a "layer cake." Some levels are dense and slow moving, increasingly dark the deeper you go. Others are lighter, finer, faster until disappearing into light. At death, we are drawn to whatever level resonates at the same vibrational frequency we do . . . *within our heart of hearts.* This frequency is not determined by what we say about ourselves or think we believe, or our religion, or what we have done or not done with our lives. Our frequency is the "real us" at the core of our being.

Over time, the accumulation in the ethers of people's emotions, feel-ings, thoughts, dreams, and desires is what forms the worlds of heaven and hell. Because of how this accumulation clusters by rate of frequency, layered bands result. These layered bands or fields stick together and form a matrix of identifiable substance, shape, and activity, as more and more "material" is absorbed into them. That is why basically the same imag-ery shows up across the globe in myths, dreams, visions, and journeys into spirit, with details and designs altering as societies modernize and individuals gain a broader understanding of themselves and the world around them. The soul needs this arrangement to process, cleanse, heal, and unify what it learned during the physical sojourn just completed, so that it can continue its evolution back to Source; to become a fully conscious, individualized co-creator with the Creator.

Hell refers to levels of negative thought-forms that reside in close proximity to the Earth-plane. The vibration in these levels is slower, heavier, and more dense. It is where we go to work out whatever blocks us from the power of our own light: hangups, addictions, fears, guilts, anger, rage, regrets, self-pity, arrogance. We stay in hell (and there are many levels to this vibratory frequency) for however long best serves our development. There is no condemnation here, rather the outworking of our own errors in judgment (more commonly called "sin"). We do not leave the realms of hell until we have changed our attitudes and perceptions and are ready for another chance to improve/advance.

Heaven describes levels of positive thought-forms that reside in close proximity to the Earth-plane. The vibration of these levels is faster, lighter, more subtle. It is where we go to recognize or enjoy whatever reveals the power of our own light: abilities, joys, courage, generosity, caring, empathy, givingness, virtue, cheer, diligence, patience, thoughtfulness, loving-kindness. We stay in heaven (and there are many levels to this vibratory frequency) for however long best serves our development. There is a sense of benefit here, as if one has found one's true home and all is well (commonly referred to as recess or a time of reaping rewards). We do not leave the realms of heaven until we have advanced as an awakened soul, unified in the spirit and consciousness of love.

Neither heaven or hell is an endpoint, as there is no top or bottom. You no more "rot in the dungeons of hell" than you "play harps forever on some cloud." There is movement, and that movement is dependent on choice—your choice to grow and evolve, or not.

There are borderlands (shadow lands) distinct from the domains of heaven and hell, where individuals in spirit-form may tarry, or refuse for whatever reason, to merge further with its soul and remain "apart." Situations like this can be temporary or long-lasting, caused most often by the intensity of an individual's desire not to leave or perhaps from disorientation or confusion, feeling lost, or maybe because of a vow or a promise.

Those in the shadowlands have not detached from the Earth-plane or the life they once had. "Way stations" exist at this vibration, places/ beings/angels ready to help new arrivals deal with conflicting feelings or deeply held desires. Also, many religions and spiritual traditions make allowance for such "death distress" by encouraging the living to pray for the departed, so any who are lost may be found.

Death Flash/Light Flash

Verified scientifically: a bright flash of light marks the incredible moment life begins when sperm meets egg. No different with animals, bugs, nature. When life begins, there is a light flash. Same thing at death. Light flashes as the soul lets go of its "container" and fades away—a death flash.

Think about The Holy Shroud, stored at a church in Turin, Italy. It is believed to be the burial cloth to have covered Jesus after his crucifixion. It exhibits an exact imprint of the man's body it once wrapped in both positive/negative formats and containing such detailed information, that there is only one way this unusual imprint could have been made . . . with a flash photolysis (the breakdown of materials under an intense emission of radiation/light).

Think about a person just before they die. Suddenly they light up, seem to revive, and have a glow about them. Some nurses say this happens about three days, perhaps even three hours before death. Relatives and medical staff see this too.

Think about near-death experiences, many of them involve a splash of light, suddenly finding yourself bathed in a light of great brilliance. Adult experiencers describe this light as brighter than 10,000 suns— instantly you're fried, but there's no pain.

Think about intense transformations of consciousness, kundalini breakthroughs, "mountain-top" experiences, spiritual awakenings, others too. Usually, the individual suddenly finds him or herself surrounded by, filled with, or facing radiant light.

Think science, as it discovered that matter is actually frozen/dense light.

Enlightenment

Let's go further with this, because it is easier to understand the essence of spiritual awakenings and what can result from them, when the most oft reported directional path of power currents is considered.

Western Version of Directional Path: Top Down (outside in)

The Western version emphasizes descending force, originating for the most part from outside a person's body, passing down through the top of the head or through the chest area, and spreading throughout the body. It is an outward-directed process that seeks outside guidance and looks for God On High. It receives outside energy in. The most familiar teaching of this version is Christos—an early Greek term (Descent of the Logos).

Eastern Version of Directional Path: Bottom Up (inside out)

The Eastern version emphasizes ascending force, originating from within a person's body, usually from the base of the spine, rising up until it bursts through the top of a person's head. It is an inner process that seeks inner guidance and looks for the God Within. It projects energy from inside out. The most familiar teaching of this version is Kundalini or Ku— Vedic and pre-Mayan terms (Ascension into The Godhead).

> *Note:* This finding is reminiscent of a formula for exposure to strong doses of high-powered energy. It could well be that the path to God revolves around the challenge of how one handles intense power, how one deals with The Force. *The only difference between Eastern and Western versions of spiritual/ religious development, if viewed from the level of essence,* **is the directional path of energy currents.**

Awakening to spirit seems dependent on the force of energy itself, differing by degree and type of voltage, and how this energy force can be accessed and utilized. All spiritual/mystical/ religious teachings can be condensed to this same core finding.

Now, compare what happens with lightning and what happens in major transformational events such as a near-death experience:

Lightning: *an explosion in our external environment that by releasing built-up pressure through a sudden visible charge equalizes energy differences while producing nitrogen compounds essential for healthy plant growth.*

Spiritual Transformations: *an implosion within our internal environment whereby releasing built-up pressure through a sudden burst of light equalizes energy differences while stimulating the expansion of consciousness for human growth.*

And that's not all. There's more.

Convergence

I can show you how all of this works—that moment of convergence where power and spin and light make us new—and I'll do that by explaining the colloidal condition. Stay with me on this. Don't let terms scare you.

The colloidal state is a peculiar in-between condition that results when forces suddenly collapse, then converge. This in-between state creates anti-force, which is antigravity. Particles caught in this unique state between implosion and explosion transmute, and remain forever changed by that transmutation. On a molecular level, these particles show evidence of enlargement and of having taken on different and enhanced characteristics.

To better understand what a colloidal condition is, let's use water as an example. Rotate a vat of water. Spin the water. Round and round. Faster and faster. Then stop the direction of the spin. Stop it dead in the water and reverse direction. When you stopped the spin, the water collapsed into itself creating an implosion. But, just before you initiated a reverse spin, where the water could explode back out, conditions mysteriously changed and both the water and everything contained within the water were briefly held in suspension. This is called a colloidal condition and particles caught therein are referred to as colloids.

I believe a colloidal condition best describes what happens during and after a near-death/spiritually transformative state. This colloidal condition reflects the core mechanism for the shift energy makes, a shift that suspends, expands, and transmutes whatever is caught within it, either instantaneously or seemingly so.

Once again, only this time step-by-step, a colloidal condition is where:

- forces suddenly collapse, then converge

- a momentary state of suspension results

- everything caught in that suspension expands and enlarges as antigravity is created

- inherent or unlimited potential is released

- whatever is present is imprinted (becomes permanently altered by what happened)

- whatever is present then transmutes (takes on different characteristics)

- as reversal of motion is completed, forces are restored, suspension ends, but the imprinting (transmutation) remains

Remember, a colloid is any particle caught in a colloidal condition.

Once suspended in this manner, the particle will automatically enlarge and expand and remain permanently and forever altered by the experience.

The process that creates colloids correlates *exactly* with what happens to those who undergo spiritual transformations and near-death episodes. The majority who go through such a process, experience: an enlargement and expansion of consciousness; exhibit the sudden surfacing of latent abilities; face a confusing array of psychological and physiological aftereffects; and, are never quite the same again.

The reason this process of convergence and transmutation (transfiguration) is so universal and basically the same for all, is because all of us, every one of us, now and throughout the ages, are and have always been imprinted by the same creative impulse that originated us. The mark of our creation is what we display whenever our consciousness is freed to rediscover itself and the source of its being.

We are born again.

Folds and Spirals

Any discussion about the colloidal condition invariably leads to mention of "The Vertical."

Throughout all cultures, and all ages, and in all sacred teachings, there is but a single image said to signify transformation. Appearing variously as a pillar or column, hourglass, huge tree with roots and branches, ray or beam of light, upward path or road or stairway or ladder, pairs of cones or vortexes or cyclones (one inverted atop the other with spouts or points touching) . . . whatever shape taken, the resulting image is always vertical and always dominates any given scene, be that of a dream, painting, or visionary experience. And always there is a sense that this large vertical object connects Earth with heaven, and that ascending or climbing up its length will lead one away from all horizontal concerns (the law of cause and effect, duality, the stages and cycles of life) to the limitless realms of radiant grace that exist beyond what most can reach (the reverse being true if one falls downward or descends). Traditionally, The Vertical refers to the act of redemption and resurrection, and it symbolizes the spiral's edge—the energy pattern of the number thirteen.

Since legend and lore about The Vertical abound cross-culturally and are timeless in scope, I'd like to share a brief summary surrounding these teachings. Along with The Vertical, I'll also cover The Horizontal and its corresponding energy pattern of the number twelve.

The Horizontal and the Number Twelve

Twelve is easily divided by 2, 3, 4, and 6, giving it mathematical order for that which is rational and logical. Traditionally, all numbers up to and including twelve, represent the varied aspects of earthlife stages and cycles and the many levels/layers of Earth-plane existence, whether visible or invisible, embodied or not. The energy pattern of the twelve itself establishes and maintains the framework that provides a path toward completion of any given phase of life. It holds together in harmony and balance that which populates and celebrates the circle of life. Time, space, and matter take on form and shape within the horizontal folds and storied layers of this magical energy.

Key phrases: numbers up to and including twelve—"The Play of Life Upon Itself" and "Graduation." (Samples: 12 disciples of Jesus, 12 sons of Jacob, 12 tribes of Israel, 12-tribe system of culture bearers, 12 divisions of the Tree of Life, 12 signs of the Zodiac, 12 months of the year, 12 harmonics of sound, 12—the mystical number for the Sun, etc.)

The Vertical and the Number Thirteen

Thirteen cannot be divided by a number below itself, making its connections beyond what is rational or orderly. The energy pattern of thirteen itself shifts octaves of vibration at the completion of any life phase. It enables life-forms to transform and transmute in a continual process of evolution or devolution. Time, space, and matter lose form and shape within the vertical convergence and suspended animation of this mystical energy.

Key phrase: "The Breath of Life Breathing." (Samples: 13th Tarot card—death; 13th century, the Inquisition; 13th guest, the uninvited; 13th number of bad luck or unexpected gift; 13th generation of America's star-crossed "Generation X"; 13th Apollo space flight launched the 13th minute of the 13th hour, then on April 13th had an oxygen tank rupture.)

Key sign of evolution: "The In-Between." (Samples: 13—the mystical number for Jesus Christ, 13 colonies in early America, 13 stripes on the U.S. flag, 13—the predominant number throughout the Great

Seal, 13th amendment to the United States Constitution abolishing slavery, 13—the mystical number of the Moon, etc.)

Thirteen energy offers a pivot point, where we either ascend into higher realms of spirit or descend into the lower realms of ego. Thirteen energy is a guarantor of transformational change, not of the direction taken. Direction is determined by our readiness, or lack of it, to make a major shift. Stories about The Vertical are fraught with perils of unpredictability and what can be done to ensure safe passage.

When viewed from afar, especially if you're out-of-body, the layers of horizontal and vertical energy appear to spiral—more like a DNA strand than of circles and spikes. Not just expansion or contraction is involved, their energy whorls and spins and spirals in wave patterns that seem to mimic the spiraling of galaxies—the universe as a brain—imploding, exploding, breathing. All of Creation spiraling in a *Sacred Spiral of Remembrance* that flashes the very wave patterns that became alphabets, that became the many names of God, in a matrix that mirrors itself through the Greater Self.

Universal Laws

Depends on your faith-base. Those from the recorded observations and teachings of Hermes Trismegistus (Thrice Blessed) of ancient Egypt are still recognized as the universal standard today. Hermes was said to be the originator of science, mathematics, astronomy, and medicine in Egypt. His discoveries were later used as the foundation of alchemy.

> **Law of Divine Oneness**: everything is connected to everything else. What we think, say, do, and believe has a corresponding effect on others and the universe around us.
>
> **Law of Vibration**: everything in the universe moves, vibrates, and travels in circular patterns that spiral. Each sound, thing, and thought has its own vibrational frequency, unique unto itself.

Law of Action: we must engage in actions that support our thoughts, dreams, emotions, and words, in order to manifest things on earth.

Law of Correspondence: the principles or laws of physics that explain the physical world, energy, light, vibration, and motion have their corresponding principles in the etheric: "As above, so below."

Law of Cause and Effect: nothing happens by chance or outside of Universal Laws. Every action (including thought) has a reaction or consequence: "We reap what we sow."

Law of Compensation: the visible effects of our deeds are given to us in gifts, money, inheritances, friendships, and blessings. Abundance follows what we create for others, as well as ourselves.

Law of Attraction: our thoughts, feelings, words, and actions produce energies which in turn attract like energies. Negative energies attract the negative; positive energies attract the positive.

Law of Perpetual Transmutation of Energy: everyone has within them the power to change the conditions of their lives. Higher vibrations consume and transform lower ones.

Law of Relativity: everyone receives a series of problems for the purpose of strengthening the light within them, challenging their heart. No matter how bad our situation, there is always someone worse off. No matter how good, someone is always better. All is relative.

Law of Polarity: everything is part of a continuum and has an opposite. Transform undesirable thoughts by concentrating on the opposite.

Law of Rhythm: everything vibrates and moves in a rhythm. This establishes seasons, cycles, patterns, stages of growth, and reflects the regularity of God's Universe.

Law of Gender: all things manifest as masculine and feminine; in the animal kingdom as sex, in nature as male/female qualities. Both are required for life to exist.

A more modern version of Universal Laws follows:

Love: love is love, and it starts with you.

Harmony: harmony is balance, what is out of balance will rebalance.

Karma: cause and effect, both individual and collective.

Wisdom: knowledge is based on learning, wisdom on experience.

Grace: deep soul realities: can erase karma

Free Will: your choice/your life, you create every situation.

Ego: your motivator, not your director.

Resistance: what you resist the most comes to you: fear based.

Attraction: you only attract what you are; opposites are still you.

Abundance: within you is everything you need to create abundance.

Manifestation: always occurs in right timing, awareness, and trust.

Cause & Effect: in essence, are merely energetic ripples of love or fear.

Other versions name: The Law of Pure Potentiality, The Law of Giving, The Law of Karma, The Law of Least Effort, The Law of Intention and Desire, The Law of Detachment, The Law of Dharma (one's purpose in life).

Regardless of what version you honor and respect, this much is true: *Everything in Earth and throughout the heavens is ruled by law. The Universal Laws are the fundamental laws of mind and spirit. They operate as unchangeable principles.*

The One Great Paradox

Paradox illustrates parallel principles that have crossed over.
Examples: To control your body, use your mind; to control your mind, use your body. The only way you can keep love is to give it away.

Every visible manifestation has an invisible counterpart.
Examples: science/gnosis, oneness/separateness, brain/mind, nerve networks/meridian lines, endocrine glands/chakras, personality/soul.

Life is inherently paradoxical.
Example: Both/and thinking, the modern application of yin/yang

Being able to see things from opposite perspectives all at the same time gives us the ability we need to negotiate the challenges of the 21st century. Termed "integral consciousness," this type of thinking is the next step in human evolution. It develops around our desire and our willingness to understand value. Only in paradox does truth, real truth, reside. Either/or thinking no longer works, nor is it of value.

Both/and . . . the power of paradox . . . is needed now.

> *"Your task is not to seek for Love, but merely to seek and find*
> *all the barriers within yourself that you have built against it."*
> —*Rumi*

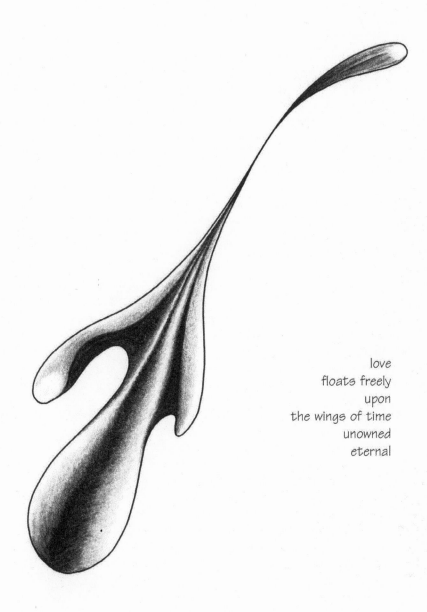

love
floats freely
upon
the wings of time
unowned
eternal

PART VII

GODS
IN THE
MAKING

Holy books and teachings throughout the ages have emphasized that we are gods in the making. From the Christian tradition, several passages in the Bible state this. Here are two:

> *Is it not written in your law, I said, Ye are gods?*
> —John 10:34

> *I have said, ye are gods; and all of you are children of the most high.*
> —Psalm 82:6

The many versions of the Christ story (not just what is covered in the Bible) give us an opportunity to learn more about the change process when one's consciousness alters, then transforms, and what can happen next. This material and its amazing wisdoms are "hidden in plain sight" when we reconsider the one called Jesus and the import of who he really was.

Yeshua/Jesus was not born Christed. "Christ" is a state of consciousness one attains. The term "Christ" variously means "the anointed one," "savior," "great teacher," "avatar." Yeshua/Jesus, from what we know of him, never claimed to be the "Son of God" (as misquoted in modern biblical translations); rather, he referred to himself as the "Son of Man." Again and again, he made it plain that anyone could attain the Christhood, that we are all "gods in the making," capable of doing what he did "and more also." He presented himself as a model for individual empowerment and the expansion of consciousness, and he never wavered from such teachings. It is only in conservative sects that he is regarded as the "great exception," instead of the "great example" he sought to convey.

An interesting thing about consciousness, once it expands it can keep on expanding. If coherent (well-ordered, balanced, guided by higher intent), it can magnify in power hundreds of thousands of times—enough to reach a state of super-fluidity where it cannot be contained. Those who expand in this manner transcend individual beliefs, cultural ideologies, and religious dictums.

Yeshua/Jesus became the Christ, and, in so doing, passed on the template of what this is, why it is a preferred state of consciousness, and where it can lead. His teachings apply to every religion, every nation, every people, every time-frame, every experiencer of a transformative state of consciousness.

Millions today are saying we need a new story. Here it is . . .

A NEW CHRISTOS
The Template

Template Basics

Characteristics that lead to expanded consciousness (whether achieved over time or suddenly in near-death or transformative states).

- Know thyself (be self-actualized and free as the soul you are).

- Open your mind (awaken to broader insights).

- Welcome change (only in change is growth possible).

- Learn from opposition (we attract what we dislike, to become better).

- Pray often and without hesitation (there is a power greater than you).

- Breathe in gratitude (that greater power loves you).

- Treat others as you wish to be treated (pass the love on).

- Acknowledge intelligence in all things (everything is interconnected).

- Communicate respectfully (service boomerangs).

- Accept tragedy as well as success (sacred intervention wears disguises).

- Bless what you achieve (a positive mind expands even more).

- Forgive all hurts (you become whatever it is you cannot forgive).

- Allow passion to be egoless (surrender to a Higher Power).

Template Activation

Linkups that operate in tandem (brain shift/spirit shift).

Bodymind level: hearing, emotions, smell, immune system, temporal lobes, prefrontal lobes, survival instinct, memory.

Spirit level: love, ecstasy, integrity of memory, upliftment, otherworldly realities, empathy, awareness that life continues, knowing.

Template Caution

Mess-ups that can jettison the creativity of a free soul.

Evil that grows as a cancer. *Cause—lack of empathy.*

Solution—put yourself in another's place. Care about that person's feelings, needs, wants. Recognize that he or she is part of you and what you do to each one, you do in some manner to yourself.

Violence begets violence. *Cause—kundalini misused.*

Solution—spiritual power can backfire without guidance. Engage in service projects, volunteerism, helping others. Learn about intention and how to redirect your mind from "me first" to "us in relationship."

Yearnings for a Golden Age. *Cause—control issues.*

Solution—wake up to the trap inherent in feeling "chosen," or following another who claims to be. Double-check your feelings and drives to see what motivates you, as the distinction between "will" and "willfulness" is a fine line.

Template Spread

As consciousness expands, it spreads through deep structures. The core of what it means to be human and alive in your own body radically shifts—to an awareness of perfection on every level—the universe, memory fields, darkness and light, DNA's biological/energetics internet.

- *Percentage of spread from the individual to the masses*—based on how the study of flow states and fluid dynamics can be applied to such things as traffic, crowd behavior, animal migrations, trends, fashions, and ideas "whose time has come."

- *Spread figure of any such shift is 4 to 5 percent.* That's all it takes to change a pattern, muck up or straighten out any activity (external or internal as relates to the greater whole), start or stop something new.

- Current percentage of population worldwide reporting near-death experiences and transformations of consciousness: *4 to 5 percent.*

Template Results

A NEW MIND . . . There is a Presence that breathes through us, feels through our heart, thinks through our mind, hears through our ears, speaks through our mouth, touches through our skin. When we are aligned with this Presence, we are healthier, more alive than we could possibly imagine or describe. This Presence is a subtle, quiet force that possesses great power and sets "afire" an ego-less passion waiting within to be set free.

A NEW REALITY . . . We live in a giant hologram that reflects back to us One God, One People, One Family, One Existence, One Law—Love, One Commandment—Service, One Solution—Forgiveness.

A NEW CHRISTOS . . . The template Yeshua/Jesus taught for expanding our consciousness is a biological imperative for the advancement of the human family. Transformative states reflect this. To whatever degree we manage to transform, it is the sum of the whole that tips the scales. *And we are there: the tipping point has been reached.* You can tell this by the degree of negativity suddenly at loose in our world. Step forward. As you do, remember: good always triumphs over evil, because at some level, eventually, evil always serves the good.

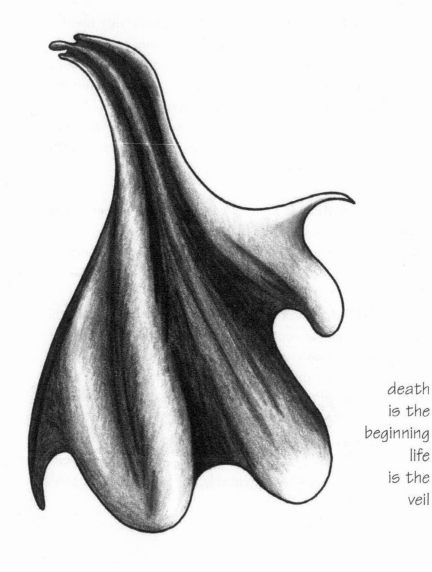

death
is the
beginning
life
is the
veil

GIVERS OF GIFTS

This simple reality holds sway. We are each givers of gifts. We give the gift of our potential at birth, what we can become. At death, we leave the gift of our achievement, what we did with what we had.

Two gifts: one we bring in with us; one we leave behind after we're gone. Whether coming or going, living or dying, we bless this world with the gifts that our existence bestows.

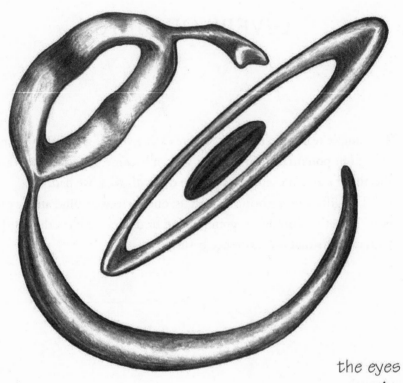

the eyes
you're
looking with
you're
looking
through

About the Author

P.M.H. ATWATER is the author of more than 15 books, including *Future Memory*, *Beyond the Indigo Children*, *We Live Forever*, and *I Died Three Times in 1977—The Complete Story*. She has been researching the near-death phenomenon since 1978, and is considered a world authority on the subject. She is a workshop leader at major spiritual/holistic gatherings, and has addressed audiences at the International Association of Near-Death Studies, as well as the United Nations, and in numerous countries. Her books have been translated in over 12 languages. She has appeared on *Larry King Live*, *Regis and Kathy Lee*, and *Geraldo*. She lives in Charlottesville, Virginia.

Related Titles

If you enjoyed *A Manual for Developing Humans,*
you may also enjoy other Rainbow Ridge titles.
Read more about them at *www.rainbowridgebooks.com.*

The Big Book of Near-Death Experiences
by P. M. H. Atwater

Dying to Know You: Proof of God in Near-Death Experience
by P.M.H. Atwater

Conversations with God, Book 4
by Neale Donald Walsch

God's Message to the World: You've Got Me All Wrong
by Neale Donald Walsch

Where God and Medicine Meet
by Neale Donald Walsh and Brit Cooper, M.D.

The Cosmic Internet: Explanations from the Other Side
by Frank DeMarco

Rita's World
by Frank DeMarco

*Consciousness: Bridging the Gap between Conventional Science
and the New Super Science of Quantum Mechanics*
by Eva Herr

Messiah's Handbook: Reminders for the Advanced Soul
by Richard Bach

Rainbow Ridge Books publishes spiritual,
metaphysical, and self-help titles, and is distributed
by Square One Publishers in Garden City Park, New York.

To contact authors and editors, peruse
our titles, and see submission guidelines, please
visit our website at *www.rainbowridgebooks.com*.